# SHADOW'S PREY

# SHADOW'S PREY

K. D. EDGE

WEATHERED TEETH PRESS

Cover Art by Syd Mills

Cover Design by Sarah Brilli (brilliantdesigns.ca)

Interior illustrations by Juniper Whitney (juniperwhitney.com)

ISBNs: 9798999628701 (paperback) , 9798999628718 (ebook)

*For my family,*
*& for those who have had to make their own.*

# ACT I

## THE PRINCE & THE HARBINGER

# A FEATHERED THING WITH TEETH

## KANNA

Kanna knew this:

When she closed her eyes, when she tilted her head back and breathed deep, she knew the night was coming. Despite the metallic tang of blood and the musty adrenaline that threatened to cling to her throat, she could feel the cool welcome of it. And she knew that when the black iron gates before her opened, someone would die.

It had been nearly five seasons she had awakened, her memories from before all empty shadows and half-formed sensations. But her body knew how to move, how to break an enemy.

It remembered longing and waiting.

It remembered death, and it knew darkness. That dark was alive inside of her, a feathered thing with teeth, constantly scratching.

Kanna was in Lifrasir, and she was in Gegenes. She was in Gegenes, which was not a part of the Empire, and she was in its Theatre.

The gate unlatched and scraped open. The body of the previous player was dragged into the wings, his feet leaving furrows in the sand. His blood was a trail leading to a cold stone in a musty room where they would place stones on his eyes and hand the shell of him over to whoever bothered to claim it.

A throat cleared, almost polite. Kanna clenched her right hand then released it, repeating the motion to ease the stiffness in her fingers as she stepped through the grates.

Her opponent entered on the other side. He was bulky like many of the Gegenii, the muscles on his ochre arms veined in relief, his blonde hair smoothed back and tied tight enough to pull at the corners of his eyes. He circled the arena, a short knife strapped to his thigh and the point of his gladius held out to the crowd to raise their fervor. It was a decent blade, simple yet effective.

Kanna brushed the palms of her hands against her own sheathed blades. On her right, the black blade was simple and almost crude to the untrained eye. Something about it told her it was a set, that it should match, but the one she carried on her left was ever so slightly longer, the handle wrapped to hide what was beneath. She knew the weight of them, what they could do and what they could reach.

The sand beneath her feet was uneven, gouged where fighters had dug in or stumbled, sticking in clumps where blood pooled from previous fights. The crowd's frenzied howls rose when she appeared, the voices driven to a mad pitch after a long day of heat and blood. The feral energy of it crept over her skin and thrummed in her bones. The darkness stirred in response, fluttering inside of her. She calmed it, pressed it down and held it tight in the caged hollow of her ribs.

Kanna checked the guards around her forearms, pulling them tighter against her skin. The man turned to her, the gladius pointed in her direction, before mockingly sliding it across his throat.

The corner of her lip curled as she finished adjusting the bracers. If she knew nothing else, she knew this place and its false soldiers couldn't kill her. The idea was almost laughable. Since arriving here, she'd stopped counting the bodies that had fallen to her blades, didn't know if there were numbers that could hold them.

The man widened his stance, held his weapon at ready, then charged in. He would have fought before, had probably known victories here or elsewhere. He was confident, sure in his step, but had sacrificed stance and balance for a show.

When he neared, she shifted one foot back and stepped aside.

The man stumbled past, and she allowed him the precious time to regain his balance. He whirled on her, surprise gleaming in his pale green eyes. The fleeting vulnerability narrowed into anger.

Closer now, her opponent swung his free fist. But he telegraphed his every movement in the readying pull of his shoulder, the shift of weight in the flat of his feet. It connected against the bone of her cheek and she moved with it, staggering to the side.

He knew how to throw a punch.

Kanna knew how to take one.

Taking a hit was necessary, sometimes, upon the stage. She let out her breath, her tongue darting out to lick the metallic taste of her own blood. The pain reminded her where she was, and what she was.

Kanna twisted and kicked straight on, her foot landing squarely in her opponent's chest. It knocked the wind from him, sending him stumbling back and throwing off his heavy footing. Then she moved in.

He swung the gladius, but she was too close now. She curled her arm around the one that wielded the blade, jabbing up at his jaw with her palm. His head flew back and her hand went to the back of his elbow, knocking the nerves there. His hand opened, and his blade dropped.

He wrenched free and grabbed at her, trying to use his size advantage to ground her, but she twisted as she fell. He couldn't hold her, her small frame shifting out of his grip.

She took the fall on her hip, using her other leg as leverage to shove off the ground and roll before his weight came down. The sand caught in her hair, scattered in the wind as she straddled him and punched down. Blood sprayed from his mouth as soft flesh splintered against teeth.

A flash of light caught the corner of her eye as she struck again.

He'd unsheathed the knife at his hip, an inelegant tarnished thing. He swung and sliced through the skin of her arm before she rolled away, the sand sticking like salt in the fresh wound, and the pain brought the darkness. She could feel the black in her eyes, the loss of control threatening as she crouched on all fours in the sand.

She could not lose control. She knew this, more than anything. She pressed her hand against the wound and it came away slick. She kept her head down, focusing on the grounding pain, the warmth of blood against her skin.

While she hesitated, her opponent took advantage.

Kanna's head snapped back and she sprang to her feet. She side-stepped again, this time catching his foot with hers as he barreled past.

His leg locked straight.

She slammed her other foot down, hard and fast.

His knee popped, his screams echoing as the ligaments tore.

Now hobbled, his hands grasped at the sand as he scrambled away from her, dragging his newly useless leg. Kanna drew her blades and stalked after, her steps even and controlled while the shadows writhed in the pit of her, grasping and hungry.

The man's hands found the discarded gladius. In a last desperate measure, he used his good leg to launch himself at her.

Kanna dodged and drove both of her blades into the back of his neck, following him down to the sand. The tips scraped through bone and muscle, stopped only by the pressure of the ground beneath them.

His body flinched, his soul flickered, and he stilled.

Kanna withdrew her blades and rose to standing, releasing the breath she held, every muscle in her body uncoiling.

The audience howled as their tension broke, but the sound was a muffled vibration in Kanna's ears as their mass blurred into a shapeless thing. Above the stands, sapphire pennants snapped against the mottled tapestry of the setting sky. The sun's last rays slanted over the Theatre, casting shadows on the walls that surrounded the stage.

Kanna tilted her head back, shut her eyes to feel the dying warmth of the sky, and the shadows calmed for the briefest of moments.

It was almost like remembering.

---

NIGHT HELD the city in its grip when Kanna left the Theatre, the stars winking in the narrow slashes of sky between cramped sepia stone buildings. She wound through the twisting back alleys of the city of Gaoler, where once straight roads narrowed and widened to make room for the circular arena that had shoved its way into the heart of the city.

When Kanna had arrived in Gaoler she'd slept in alleys and doorways. Eventually, concerned parties insisted that she get lodging in the Keeper's castoff barracks with other fighters passing through. From what she'd been told, an unspoken detente had arisen between independent regions and the Solarian Empire in recent years. With the ease in tensions the Keeper's ranks had dwindled, leaving vacant space that the Governor rented for a pittance to those willing to live without modern comforts.

Not that she'd asked.

Kanna approached the squat, nondescript building from the side alley. She rubbed her palms together, running her left hand over the aching joints of her right, and ran at the building on the opposite side of the alley. Vaulting from the wall, she grabbed the hanging escape ladder. It jolted down, the mechanism loosening before ratcheting tight once more, and she hoisted herself onto the landing.

She waited for the screech of metal to die, crouching on the landing until she was sure she hadn't been followed, before beginning her climb to the top floor on quiet feet. There, she pressed her hands flat against the cool glass of the window and pushed it up and open before ducking inside.

Sitting on the windowsill she kicked off her boots and let them drop to the floor, the thunk as the rubber hit wood breaking the silence. The room beyond was dark, as she kept it. It was small and cramped, furnished with a wash basin and a single narrow bed with barely enough room to move between them. Kanna shrugged off the grey jacket that guarded her against the desert night, wincing as the fabric pulled against the tacky blood on her arm, and dropped it across the thin pallet.

On bare feet, Kanna edged to the water basin. Above it, a mottled mirror revealed the purpling bruise on her cheek, a stark relief against pale skin. She leaned into the reflection, squinting to check the damage in the ambient light from the outside streetlamps. This close, she could almost make out the smattering of blood that blended with freckles and red hair.

Kanna turned her attention from the specter and plunged her hands into the water in the chipped metal basin. It was frigid, chilled from sitting out in the night air. She scooped it over the gash with one hand and the cold ran down to the tips of fingers, the red turning pink as it whorled in the water.

Finished with cleaning the surface, she pressed her fingers against the cut and hissed when the barely knitted skin popped and fresh blood welled from it.

She didn't have anything for it here.

Kanna unlocked the door to her room, stepping into the orange light of the hallway. Oil lamps flickered intermittently, though some had long run out their wicks and remained dark. The top floor wasn't used as much, with most of the remaining Keepers opting to bunk in the lower levels, and the difference in maintenance showed as she descended. The light was brighter at each level, the lamps' wicks properly trimmed and their oil replenished.

At the ground floor, voices drifted from the lounge and the light from it glared out into the dark hallway. Kanna followed the sound, blinking when she stepped in the uncomfortable glare of the white lights of the common room. The counters of the gathering room were cluttered with unwashed cups, the air filled with the wheaty scent of local brews. The static hum of the barrack's single generator buzzed in her ears, and the lights flickered with the unsteady current.

The assortment of Keepers and fighters inside jerked to attention at her intrusion, and the card game they were playing shifted with the movement. A few cards fluttered off the rickety table , one catching a draft before landing at her feet.

Kanna reached down and picked it up, turning it over. On the face of the card was a thin building rising through dark clouds. A storm beset it, with a single bolt of lightning captured in the moment of its strike. The precipice of the building was alight in flames, and waves curled at the base of it.

She returned the card to the table, laying it down face first. She then aimed for the disused medic box hanging on the wall past the card players. It opened with a metallic screech, and she began sweeping small bottles and rolls of gauze, as well as loose bandages and packets into the crook of her arm. The gazes of those in the room settled between her shoulder blades, their anxiety a prickling awareness along her skin. Once finished, she exited the way she had entered.

Bandages and single use foil packets of ointments drifted from her arms as she returned to the fifth floor. Kanna waited again, listening for any movement in the room, before pushing the door she had left ajar open with her foot, leaning back on it to shut it behind her.

In front of the bed, she crossed her legs beneath her and dropped to the floor, releasing her plundered medical supplies. The wound on her arm had continued its slow flow, the blood on her thumb and forefinger smearing against the foil packets as she tested their contents by touch. She knew how to do this, once, but now she often found herself muddling through until something seemed right. An opened cardboard box of bandages revealed a prize, and she hummed happily as she removed the suture patch that had been shoved inside before tossing aside the rest of the box. Holding a brown bottle to her ear, she shook it. Satisfied by the slosh of the contents, she cracked the lid then placed it nearby.

Kanna sat back, drumming her fingertips against her knees. A plastic wrapped tin drew her. She ripped through the seal with her teeth, spitting out the piece that came away. She pried open the clasp with jagged nails and a curved needle and its accompanying thread greeted her. The glint of thin metal caused her stomach to turn, and she snapped the case shut and flung it away.

While she attempted to ease her breath, she plucked a roll of gauze from the pile as she considered her array. Without thinking, she began unwinding the gauze, running it over her knuckles and under her thumb. The movement had been a reflexive thing. She hastened to untangle it, dropping it near.

No longer hesitating, she grasped the disinfectant bottle and poured it over the wound. The first contact of the liquid was a stinging jolt, sharp and alive. The pain cut through the fog as it jarred down her elbow and to her fingertips. She closed her eyes and grit her teeth, waiting for the tremors in her fingers to ease before refocusing on her task.

Using the wadded gauze, she wiped away the remaining blood and dried the skin around the gash. After peeling away the backing of the suture patch, she shifted her arm and angled her elbow to see past her shoulder. With only one hand to work with, she placed the patch over the gash as best she could. Contorting uncomfortably, she used her teeth to grip one side of the zips to hold them steady while the other hand pulled. She repeated the motion, knitting the skin closed.

After wrapping the suture patch with the remainder of the gauze roll, she sat back and surveyed the detritus strewn about the room. Stiff, overused muscles protested the movement, and she rubbed her neck to ease them.

At least she wasn't bleeding anymore.

She stood, wary of her footing, and moved to an empty space before peeling out of her jeans, the mix of dried blood and sand flaking from the denim and falling to the floor. She then removed her uninjured arm from her shirt first, easing it over the injured one and dropping it in the gathering heap.

Kanna kicked some of the loose supplies to join the pile, a reflection catching in the cracked mirror and drawing her attention. The gold veining on her skin radiated from her right side and threaded out from the scar below her ribs. If she stared long enough, it almost pulsed with the beat of her heart, but it was off rhythm. She ran her fingertips over the lines, like tracing a path on a map she once knew.

It reminded her of the smell of copper and dust. Not like the Theatre, a place soaked in it, but a fresh, sharp taint. It reminded her of blades of light raining down and screams. Flashes of white, blood blooming, the wet thunk as flesh tore. And pain, and falling. Falling, falling through the cold and the dark.

It was something like a memory, both fresh and old.

It came at night, in the day, with each breath she took. Not a thing she could understand or see, but the impression of it, something that lived inside of her. The only time it stopped was when she was fighting, when she allowed her body to take over and the shock of new pain outweighed the figment of it.

She sunk into the mattress and lay back, waiting for the sharpness of the memory to fade. She closed her eyes and pressed the heels of her palms into the back of her closed lids until she saw bright, bursting spots. When she was certain it was safe, she opened her eyes and turned her gaze to the window.

On the top floor of the building, she was never out of the light of the stars. They were a bright thing against so much dark, a constant, something that she could be sure of. She watched them as her lids drifted shut, her hand pressed against the cold glass.

## 2

# SURVIVORS

## HARU

IN THE AMPHITHEATER, Haru wound his hand wraps over his thumb, over his wrists and around, falling into the rhythm of the practiced motion. He didn't have to think about it. Didn't have to think about anything here. It was the only place his mind could be still long enough for him to let go of the cyclical thoughts that threatened to eat him alive, both chasing each other and caught.

Haru hadn't slept in days. It wasn't an uncommon occurrence for him, not anymore. In the last year he had often found himself a sentry to the dark, waiting as the black of the night faded to grey, with only the brightest stars daring to shine. But when the night was gone, this was the only place that he could feel close to it.

The amphitheater within the Palamidia's Tower was washed in white. Circular slabs of marble formed both the seats and stairs, which staggered through the rows in the four cardinal directions and narrowed as they descended, ending at the mat covered floor.

From his place at the lowest tier, Haru kept his eyes on the east entry, but the open passageway remained empty. He finished his wraps and stepped onto the mats. They had little give, but the Palamidia's design did not protect or preserve. The Palamidia broke anything it presumed weak, held nothing sacred but its own power.

There were always willing bodies that wanted to test themselves against him. Despite the fact that he remained the Legatus's Second in name, he had failed in his duty, leaving the Palamidia without a leader. And without without that leader, brutality was the most prized thing an officer could have. Haru did not have to invite confrontation. It found him in the form of an eager Prospect, a soldier new to the Tower that had yet to earn a title. The world was at his feet, and he had yet to taste the bitterness of it.

The boy approached, and Haru was comfortable considering him as such. He had been the same when he first stood here.

Haru set his stance, and nodded to him. It was all that was needed. His opponent went for a quick offense, closing the gap between them without testing the limits. The boy brazenly attempted a roundhouse. Haru caught the kick with one arm, swept out his support leg and shoved him back to the mats.

Another joined, and then another. Even a shared victory could be a victory.

It didn't matter.

Haru struck, clenched fists slamming with every taunt his mind threw at him.

She wasn't dead.

If she wasn't dead, then it was something far worse.

He went low, one fist digging into the soft belly of his opponent, the other swinging up. It collided with the jaw of the challenger, the boy's teeth snapping as his head went back and he fell to the mats.

Haru didn't want to think about what could possibly keep her away, so maybe it was better if she was dead.

She couldn't be dead.

The second tried to move into Haru's space but he kicked out low and his opponent stepped back. Haru lowered his weight in preparation.

She wasn't dead.

Haru's kick landed, sending his second opponent sprawling.

He pulled his arms in to guard against a blitz attack. He could barely feel the hits land, the pain failing to break through the numbness inside of him.

He remembered the way she had moved, the sleek shifts of weight to distract before attack, how even her shadow wouldn't betray her. And he remembered the hard drop of her heels when she walked the halls, eyes forward but distant and then how, alone, her feet would barely lift from the floor. He remembered the way her head would tilt when she concentrated, as if she was listening to something ancient that only she could understand.

Haru could never understand the same way that she could. She knew the cipher for the noise, could find the thread of a simple truth buried in the ever shifting intentions of those around her.

When his knuckles cracked the nose of the final Prospect that had challenged him, red blood spilling on the scuffed mats, Haru wondered what she would think of it.

It should matter, and it did. He pulled back his fist and struck again, twisting the Prospect's shirt in his grip to keep him where he wanted him. And again, because she wasn't here to stop him.

"Haru."

A familiar voice cut through the haze and Haru stopped to glare at Osawa, who had entered with Vahn. Osawa was a simple constant, a simple connection. Osawa was classically Icaunian in appearance, dark hair and dark, deep set eyes as calm as a wakeless lake.

Haru blinked, attempted to focus.

"Are you done?" Vahn's lips quirked into his ever present, coldy amused smirk. The Saint of Fire's violet eyes could draw more attention in a room than Haru, but it still took him a moment to recognize him. Haru was used to Vahn's long white hair contrasting sharply with his bronze skin, but Vahn had hacked it off. That was nearly a year ago, Haru reminded himself.

"I think he is," Osawa said, nodding to Haru's opponent and adjusting the glasses that rested on the bridge of his nose.

Haru looked back to the Prospect he held. His head was lolling back, his eyes soft as he neared unconsciousness. Haru shoved him back into the mat, knocking what sense remained from him, before standing.

He left the defeated behind and paced past Vahn and Osawa, unwinding the hand wraps. The blood that soaked them streaked on his skin, and beneath his knuckles were bruised from the repeated force. He traced the scarred gouge between his thumb and forefinger that trailed over the back of his right hand.

He flexed his fingers, knew there was pain.

It wasn't enough. It would never be enough.

---

THE REST of the Tower was as blinding white as the amphitheater. From the marble of the floors to the stone of the walls, each hall was a mirror of the next. Even veteran officers sometimes found themselves turned around in the labyrinthine halls, but Haru had never found the Tower's structure confusing. When he first arrived he'd searched each level, every unmarked twist, endlessly following a trail that he hadn't understood then.

That trail had grown cold, but Haru remembered the path. Haru wound his way through the halls to the Legatus's quarters, Osawa and Vahn haunting his heels. The locked door lacked a keyhole, but he didn't need one. He placed his hand against the door and called the light on the other side. It wove through the mechanism, pushing aside the pins and twisting the catch, opening his way.

Early afternoon light streamed through the floor-to-ceiling windows that took up the outside wall of the room, overlooking the eastern gardens and beyond. Though the marble floors continued here, they were heavily veined in smoky greys and black. The room was expansive, but nearly empty. The cold scene was broken by the warm wood of the Legatus's desk, a simple, dark antique. Next to it was a single armchair and side table positioned between the door and the desk and facing neither.

"So, we're having one of these days," Vahn said. He brushed past Haru and walked over to the desk, though his lean frame did little to block the light.

Behind Haru, Osawa slipped into the room, sliding off to the side and shutting the door behind them.

Vahn moved behind the desk and began to sit.

"Not there," Haru snapped.

Vahn straightened, his hands held up and empty, and stepped away from the desk. He fell instead into the single chair, tossing his leg over one of the arms.

Haru stalked past Vahn. He leaned over the desk, placing his hands on the smooth, sun warmed wood. Its surface held an assortment of unopened reports on one side, and the dates of those that had been opened and read were over a year past. Haru reached across to straighten one of the stacks, only to slide it back how it had been previously.

"There isn't anything here, Haru," Osawa said. "How long are you going to keep doing this?"

He shut his eyes when Osawa spoke. He replayed the reports he had heard, tried to piece together what he had found. Five seasons earlier, the Tribuni Velinius Catarr had returned from what was supposed to be a routine scouting mission with a tale of horror. The regiment had been attacked near the Ilazki border, slaughtered by insurgents who had set an ambush. The Legatus had fought bravely, but fallen with her command.

Velinius was the only survivor.

After, Haru had taken the Legatus's remaining guards and set out to see the devastation. Haru remembered the cold, the numbness that dug into his hands as he turned over body after body, the white of their uniforms stained and stiff with blood and death. They identified their fallen, the faces of their companions frozen in twisted masks of death. Despite Velinius's account of the conflict, however, they did not recover the body of the Legatus.

A part of Haru was still out there, still searching.

Osawa interrupted his thoughts and continued, carefully. "I know you want to believe she's alive—"

"She is." In the silence that followed, Haru heard the sound of a wooden drawer scraping open. He turned to see Vahn reach into the side table next to the chair and pull out a deck of cards. He snapped the rubber band off, discarding it onto the table's surface.

"If she's alive, why isn't she here?" Osawa prodded. "Why hasn't she come back?"

Vahn smirked and began to shuffle through the cards.

"I don't know," Haru said, his voice low. "She could be captured, or—"

"Or she's dead," Vahn reminded them, his eyes on the cards in his hands. "Or she left. People do that, you know."

"She wouldn't." The heels of Haru's boots clicked against the floor as he paced, falling silent when he treads on the edge of the rug and rising again when he hit marble once more, hissing when he reached the end of the room and turned back. "She's not dead," Haru reiterated, because he had to. If he didn't repeat it, constantly, he wouldn't move past the opposing thought, and then he wouldn't be able to move at all. "But she would've said something. Would've taken us with her. Something is wrong."

Vahn snorted. "What isn't?"

"Vahn," Osawa sighed the name. "You aren't helping."

"Was I was supposed to?" Vahn went back to focusing on the cards. He ran his fingers around the deck to align the edges and bent them at the middle, splitting it and shuffling.

Haru left the two behind him, their voices becoming indistinct as he moved through the attached hall and into the Legatu's private chambers. This room was far darker. Light filtered in from the open doorway, but there were no windows here. Rugs piled on the floor, three deep in places, covering the marble and preventing the white from reflecting the ambient light. A long bureau was on one side of the room, two spindles standing upright on each side but empty where the mirror had been removed. A chain of folded origami swans hung from one, unfinished.

Haru's steps were silenced by the rugs as he walked past the bed, its coverlet loose upon the mattress, to the bath. With a warming buzz, the electrical lights flickered and brightened, or at least the bulbs that weren't black and burned out. The room was cold and clean, and smelled of nothing.

Even her ghost was gone.

He turned the light off.

The conversation in the Legatus's office ceased when Haru re-entered, both Vahn and Osawa turning to him.

He stood straighter, his eyes narrowing. "What is it?"

Vahn looked to Osawa, but Osawa looked to the floor.

"Apparently," Vahn started, shuffling the cards again. "Velinius has been named the Legatus *ultra vires*."

Vahn didn't offer any more, and neither did Osawa.

"What?" Haru asked through gritted teeth when neither continued.

Osawa shook his head. "What did you expect, after yesterday?"

Haru clenched his hands to fists again, remembering the devastation that had followed the attack on the train lines. An unknown fire loa had synched in one of the public transit cars, and the blast had taken out the entire train, as well as the line itself and several city blocks. The Palamidia rushed to aid in emergency recovery, but there wasn't much left to recover.

"Without the Legatus, we have no recourse against attacks," Osawa continued. "Something had to be done. Someone needed to lead, and Velinius was the last person to hold the title."

Haru put his hands in the pockets of his jacket and leaned back against the Legatus's desk.

"Weird that it was a fire loa," Vahn said, though his voice was even and pointed. He leaned over and placed the cards back into the drawer and slid it shut. "Considering the regions we come from are all within the Empire."

Haru's eyes widened, and he looked up, meeting Vahn's violet gaze. Vahn's stare was steady, glinting with something dangerous, as he leaned back into the chair.

Osawa had the same knowing gleam in his eyes, but his was tempered with concern.

"That's it," Haru said, sitting up. "This was her plan all along."

"Velinius doing whatever she deems necessary for control," Vahn muttered bitterly. "Shocking."

There was nothing else to say. There were lines that were never meant to be crossed, and Haru was about to leap over one and he knew it. He stalked to the door.

"Where are you going?" Osawa asked as he pulled it open.

"I think it's time I speak with Velinius."

"What?" Osawa called behind him. "Haru, wait—"

## 3

---

# LEARN TO STAND

## KANNA

THE SUN BURNED in the early morning, warming the sands of the Theatre's stage. Kanna tilted her head back, her eyes shut against the light. It was heat, and warmth, and something dangerous. It almost reminded her of something.

Almost.

She lowered her face and opened her eyes to take in the expanse of the stage. When the plays were done, the sands transformed into a makeshift training center. Even in these off hours, it was cluttered with bodies. Breathing ones. At one end, the city's Keepers drilled in groups of swords and spears. They were accompanied by earth loas in another area who shaped and reshaped the land around them.

The Theatre's temporary fighters were relegated to a barren corner, though few bothered to work their techniques. Instead they lounged, eyeing each other, as if they would somehow better their chances.

Yassen arrived among them, his emerald eyes bleary with sleep. He stretched his arms over his head, the gesture casting a long shadow over the orange sand. He was tall, even for a Gegenii man, though he was just out of boyhood. He rubbed the sandy-blonde hair at the back of his head and it stuck in place. His attention caught on the earth loas that were practicing and stayed there.

Kanna stalked toward him.

"Hey, Kan—"

His greeting was cut short when Kanna's fist collided with his jaw, his teeth clacking together. His head tilted back and he stumbled.

Kanna bent her knees and fell to a crouch to keep her balance as a rough pillar jutted from the ground beneath her. She held onto the sides of it as it rose several feet in the moments it took Yassen to recover before stopping.

"Gods' graves, woman," he grumbled, rubbing his jaw. "I was just saying mornin'."

Kanna stood and crossed her arms at her chest, glaring down from her perch at him. "You're late," she said. This time, she pulled her foot back.

He stepped away, his hands up in surrender, and she put her foot down.

Kanna had met Yassen on her first day in the Theatre. She had been paired with him for a team match, the duo meant to serve as someone's idea of comic relief considering their difference in stature. The crowd had distracted her that day, so many people and so many lives, and Yassen had taken a knife wound that was meant for her. Since then, Kanna would take his fights when she could. She slipped whatever coins didn't go to her keep under his door.

Kanna sat on the pillar. She pulled up one knee to her chest, her other leg hanging over the side of it.

"What's this about?" he asked.

Kanna shrugged, swinging her dangling leg through the air. "You won't learn anything from them," she said, nodding to the practicing loas.

"How else am I supposed to learn?"

Kanna shifted her weight and dropped from the rock she had been resting on. She scratched her fingertip against it, and nothing came away beneath her nail. It was about her height, rough hewn but solid, and formed by Yassen in an instant, without even a thought.

"You need a proper weapon," she said as she circled the pillar.

"I can use lots of weapons," Yassen grumbled.

Kanna drew her the blade at her left and tightened the wrap around the handle, watching the sun as it danced over the clean steel. When she drew the second, it didn't gleam like the other, its spine mottled by an artist's hand.

Yassen back peddled across the sand when Kanna began her approach. He found the cache of weapons set aside for the Theatre's players and reached for the first thing his hands could grab, coming out with a spear.

As Kanna continued her advance, he thrust it towards her.

She knocked it to the ground with the black knife and jumped onto the end, snapping the wood shaft.

"Try again," she said, stopping her approach. She spun the white blade, pointing it out. "I'll give you a moment."

Yassen turned, fumbling with the hilts of the scattered weapons. He pulled out a heavy, two handed sword, grinning with self-satisfaction.

Kanna lifted her brow and spread her arms, bowing slightly to her opponent.

He charged, swinging the broadsword wide and down. Kanna danced out of the way, leaving the sword to slice through air. She stepped into his reach, under his outstretched arm, and slammed the butt of her knife into his side.

When he turned his body to the attack, the sword swung with him. With both knives, Kanna slowed the blunt attack and slid beneath it. She pulled back the white knife, once again striking with the butt of her knife. This time, it was into his elbow. He yelped and lost his grip on the broadsword.

Kanna stepped back, sheathing her blades in a single motion. She crossed her arms, studying Yassen as he rubbed his bruised elbow.

"What was that for?" he asked, not moving for the weapons pile.

Kanna walked past him to the assortment of practice weaponry. The ones in the pile were chipped, some of the blades rusted from lack of care. She kicked away a few of the simple, mid-length blades at the top of the pile and then crouched next to it. "I will not always be around."

"You going somewhere?" he asked, genuinely curious.

She turned to look at him over her shoulder. Yassen looked almost hurt, and as genuine as ever, and it twisted something inside of her. "Maybe," she said, then turned her attention back to her task. "I don't know. Either way, you need to learn."

"You didn't have to punch me."

"It is one way to learn."

Kanna found the end of a halberd and pulled it from the pile, the other weapons scraping and clanking against each other as they slid away. She walked over to Yassen and held it next to him. She shook her head and dropped it.

"What are you doing now?" he asked, finally coming out of his sulk.

She ignored him and continued rummaging through the pile.

"What do I need a weapon for if I can use the ground? Those guys don't have them." He gestured to the loas at practice.

Kanna paused in her scavenging and rocked back on her heels. She turned to the group he was referring to, watched as they struggled to get the earth to listen.

"Controlling the earth is tedious and slow. If you were ever in a real battle, those Keepers would throw the foot soldiers before their loas as sacrifices. You would be safe behind those falling bodies," she said, then turned to him. "Is that where you want to stand?"

"No." Yassen rubbed the back of his neck, frowning at the ground. "I don't think I'd want that."

She turned back to the pile. "You aren't like them, anyway."

Kanna spotted what she was looking for and realized it was what she wanted in the same moment.

"Why am I not like them?"

Kanna rose with her prize, dusting the sand off her knees. The khopesh was battered, but it would do for practice. It was wide and curved with a hooked nose, heavy enough to ground and focus Yassen's strength without heeding his movement.

"They beg." she said, waving the nicked blade in the direction of the loas before gesturing to the pillar he had formed. "The earth comes for you. Allow it only enough. Or else it will swallow you."

Kanna turned the khopesh in her hand, pointing the blade to the ground and holding it out for Yassen. He took it from her and jumped back on guard. When she didn't move to strike, he relaxed, moving the khopesh from one hand to the other.

It looked right. "A blade helps focus. It can also ground you. Something outside of yourself to remind you who you are." The words were an echo, faint and half-remembered, but not right for this. Kanna furrowed her brow. "Where you are," she corrected. "You are connected to the earth. It wants to help. But you tell it how, and when it is needed."

Yassen turned his attention from the blade to her. "How do you know all this?"

Kanna shrugged. She couldn't answer that, didn't even know herself. "I just do."

"So what kind of loa are you?" Yassen asked. "Haven't seen you moving any rocks. Fire?"

She didn't answer.

"Nah, too obvious."

She stared at him, unblinking.

"Water? No. Air, right?" He grinned, and nodded. "It's gotta be air. You could be from Panotii."

He meant well, but even trying to think of her past made her side ache. "It doesn't matter, Yassen."

His brow furrowed, and he lowered the khopesh. "I'll find out eventually."

"Sure," she said. "Maybe."

# 4

## THE POLITICIAN

### ASTAR

Just because Astar was a resident of Gaoler didn't mean she enjoyed the heat. She looked forward to the cycle's storm season, but it was a ways away and at least the winds of the arriving growing season had begun to cool the nights.

The city was packed, the main boulevard thick with bodies that choked the flow of traffic. Governor Hautman had begun advertising a Gala for the Theatre, promising an extraordinary new act unlike anything that had been seen before. Of course, it was on Astar to make sure her father's prized actress was willing to play the lead she had been cast for.

At the dress shop, she paused to eye the new gowns. The styles in Gegenes were shifting away from their traditional loose silks and towards conservative Lugosian cuts, with closer tailoring and fine embroidered designs. While Astar could admire the skill behind it, it wasn't for her.

Turning on her heel, she cut across the boulevard, dodging the mix of chariots and slow carts that clattered over the packed dirt road. At least the stone walkways on the opposite side of the boulevard were cooler on her bare feet, the buildings blocking the sun from directly bearing down on the path. Next to the grocer, Astar shoved open the solid wood door to The Dirty Trick.

She blinked when she stepped inside, her eyes adjusting to the dim light of the tavern. On one side of the room, a semi-circular dark wood bar hugged a wall with an assortment of glass bottles ranging in size, color, and what was left of the dregs inside of them. The smell of an indeterminate food being either fried or burned emanated from the back.

On the other side of the room sat Astar's quarry. Kanna sat at one of the battered tables in the corner where a game of Palamedes was well into play. Despite the heat Kanna wore a long grey jacket, though it did little to conceal the fact that she carried her ever present knives. She slouched in her chair, her expression unreadable.

Yassen was at her side, his own cards face down on the table already. He kept trying to lean to see Kanna's hand, but she shifted it back to her chest every time.

Three others sat with them. One held his arms crossed at his chest, another fold.

As Astar watched, Kanna played another hand. One of the two remaining players slammed her cards onto the table and shoved her chair away. She made a beeline for the bar, followed by the other that had folded, leaving one remaining player against Kanna.

Astar slid to the now unoccupied chair next to Kanna and sagged into it.

Kanna's shifting grey eyes left her cards long enough to acknowledge Astar. "How is my horse?" Kanna asked, sliding one of the cards in her hand to a new position.

"The horse is fine." Astar crossed her arms and leaned back into the chair, the back of the worn wood creaking in protest. "What about me? No 'you look lovely, Astar,' or 'it is so wonderful to see you, Astar'?"

Yassen sat up, his face breaking into a grin. "What's doing, Astar?"

"Thank you for asking, Yassen," Astar replied pointedly. "I am doing splendid, even after walking all this way to see my friend, who cares more about her horse."

The man that remained in the game with Kanna played a card face up on the board in front of them. Kanna's next play was quick, and her opponent went back to studying his cards.

"Why are you here?" Kanna asked.

"I can't just come to say hi?"

Kanna's brow knit in thought. "You could." Her eyes slid from her cards. "You don't."

The other player reached out to remove one of the cards from the board, replacing it with a new one.

Astar sighed, but it garnered her neither sympathy nor a reaction from Kanna. "Father is planning an event of sorts. He would like you to be the star of the play."

Kanna turned away from Astar long enough to glance at the table before sliding one of the cards out of her hand and absently putting it into play. "What makes this one different from others?"

Astar shrugged. "I don't know, but you know how he gets. He feels like he's losing favor, so he wants to put on a show to try and get some support drummed up."

Kanna's opponent played his turn.

"He's inviting some people from Adur," Astar continued. "Probably the kind of people with money, and he wants to impress them."

Kanna sat back in her chair. She eyed the board, then fanned her cards in and ran her fingers along the edges to make a neat stack. It was almost as if she was going to fold, but Astar had yet to witness Kanna lose a game of Palamedes. "The pay?"

"Honestly?" Astar crossed her arms. "A lot. Even for my standards."

Kanna placed her cards face down on the table. "It sounds like I don't have a choice," she said, her hands falling to her sides. "But leave Yassen out of it."

"What?" Yassen asked. "Why?"

When Kanna's opponent reached for the prizes at the center of the board, Kanna moved. In a flash of grey and steel, the blade of her knife came down. It pierced through the back of the man's hand and buried into the wood below, his howl of surprise and pain nearly drowning out the sound of the coins that scattered across the table.

Astar jumped back as the man flailed, pinned at the end of Kanna's blade. She kept herself from screaming along with the man. "Kanna, what are you doing?" Astar asked, forcing her voice even through her panicked breaths.

Kanna rose, drawing her other blade when the man attempted to reach for his own. She pressed the tip to his throat and he leaned his head back to avoid it, his body shaking as he met her eyes. Kanna withdrew the knife enough to slip her fingers into the sleeve of man's pinned arm. Three cards emerged from under the cuff, and she dropped them to the table. "I am not a fan of those who cheat."

Astar folded her arms at her chest, her eyes narrowing on the man. "Cheating at any game with monetary involvement is illegal in Gaoler, sir."

"So is stabbing people," the man managed to growl out.

Kanna twisted the knife in his hand and he yelped.

Heart pounding, Astar fought to keep control of the situation. "I didn't see anyone getting stabbed. Yassen? Did you see any stabbing?"

Yassen had sat back in his seat, his hands on the table and his eyes wide. He looked from the knife in the man's hand, to Kanna, to Astar. He looked back to Kanna, who's glare didn't leave the man at the table, then to Astar again.

"Uh," Yassen said. "No?"

"Kanna?"

Kanna didn't move.

Astar cleared her throat and tried again. "Kanna? Did you see anyone get stabbed?"

Kanna's eyes slid to Astar's, and she was grateful that the anger that writhed in them had never been directed at her. It wasn't even on the man, but on something buried in nightmares and half-remembered notions. She yanked her knife free.

Clutching his bleeding hand to his chest, he raced from the tavern, not looking back.

Kanna wiped the bloodied knife on the table's cloth before sheathing both. She sat back in her place and gathered the scattered cards. When she had the stack, she aligned it, her fingers running over the edges to straighten them before tucking the battered deck into the pocket of her jacket. With the back of her arm, she swept the winnings from the game to Yassen, the blood wet on the glinting gold of the coins.

"Here," she said to him. "Get a better weapon."

## 5

# PRECIPICE

## OSAWA

OSAWA AND VAHN followed Haru down the stairs of the officers' quarters. They fell behind when Haru made it to the central hub of the Palamidia's Tower, and Osawa almost lost sight of him among the white coated soldiers that clotted the cavernous room. The circular construct made it difficult for the foot traffic to move in any kind of logical way, and people wove and ducked between bodies to get through. Stairs lead up to different wings of the Tower, stopping at various floors and bypassing others, but only one rose to the Tower's precipice.

Haru disappeared up that staircase, his black hair a sharp contrast against the white of the walls.

"You've got to be kidding me," Vahn muttered behind Osawa as they shoved through the bodies that had been upset by Haru's route.

"It's where Velinius usually is," Osawa replied.

"That man is stone cold crazy." Vahn shifted to the side, avoiding a Prospect with her arms loaded down with sealed missives. The Prospect leapt in place when she recognized him, the papers falling from her grasp and sliding over the floor. Vahn stooped to retrieve them, forcing Osawa to kneel to help.

They slid the papers into a pile and Vahn offered them to the girl. She saluted, bowed, then saluted again before snatching them away and disappearing into the crowd.

"He is going to get us killed," Vahn hissed to Osawa.

"If she is alive," Osawa said. "I'm not the one who will have to tell her that Haru isn't."

Vahn didn't reply. Either he was too annoyed to, or he knew that Osawa had a point. Finally making it through the bodies, Vahn hit the stairs first. His legs ate them up two at a time, and Osawa had to move faster to keep up. The white marble twisted through the walls of the tower, moving behind and beyond the rooms nestled within, a cold and unifying reminder wherever they went. They continued through the spiral, chasing the faint echoes of Haru's footsteps.

The pair reached the top of the stairs and the hall widened. Ahead, the looming doors of the Temple whispered shut. Twice the size of any other doors in height and width, the marble was carved in a basket weave. Vertical wood handles set in the door were warm and inviting to the touch. Inside, the Temple was one of the only places not washed in white. Long, dark wood benches were lined up from the front to the rear of the temple. Fluted pillars, carved at the base, and soaring colonnades reached skyward, drawing the eye to the rib vault ceiling and the glass dome above. Three oversized chandeliers were suspended above the central aisle, their light refracting off thousands of clear crystals. Frescoes and stained glass windows spanned over the walls, the myriad colors a shock after the sameness elsewhere.

Velinius stood in the semicircular apse in front of the Temple's altar. She was looking up to the rose window, dark in the dim of twilight. Her hair was braided tightly at the nape of her neck, not even a strand out of place.

"I hope you do not intend to disturb the sanctity of this place," she said without turning.

Haru stood just below the steps to the altar, his hands clenched into fists at his side. "There is nothing sacred here."

Vahn made a low groan in the back of his throat, and Osawa raised a finger to his lips to quiet him.

Velinius turned to confront Haru, her movements unhurried. Her eyes were a honey brown, but the cold of the expression tempered any warmth. "This is a place for quiet contemplation. Not your...." She waved a hand toward Haru before clasping it behind her back once more. "Whatever this is."

It would be near suicidal to try and come between Velinius and Haru, but they didn't have much of a choice. Osawa exchanged glances with Vahn, gesturing forward with a nod. Vahn shook his head and signalled for them to wait. His violet gaze was intent on the scene playing out before them, seeking his own confirmation.

"What did you do to her?" Haru asked.

Velinius shook her head. "I am sure I do not know what you speak of," she replied, something like pity in her voice.

Haru took a step and flickered out of view, reappearing just before Velinius like a trick of the eye. He grabbed her by the coat, pushing her back into the altar.

Velinius wrapped her hands around Haru's wrists, deadening the hit, and leaned close to him. She tilted her head, her face a breath from Haru's. "I know I bear some resemblance to the departed Legatus," she said, then pulled away. She straightened back to her rigid stance. "But do not think that you can lay hands on me."

Velinius's words cut true and Haru released her, backing up a step. She righted her jacket, smoothing the folds where Haru's hands had been. "You are not thinking clearly, Haroun."

"I am the only one thinking clearly," Haru's anger rose, the crystal chandeliers shivering with it. "You wanted to control her, and when you couldn't, you tried to get rid of her."

Velinius's features froze for a moment before recovering, but even Osawa caught the slight slip of cover. Which meant that Haru would have read it like a beacon.

"I do not try," Velinius said, no longer trying to conceal her intent. "I succeed."

A blast of light erupted between the two, knocking Haru back.

Osawa shielded his eyes from the blinding flash. When he opened them and blinked away the colors that danced in his vision, he saw Haru. He had hit the marble, unmoving as Velinius stepped down from the elevated daise.

Osawa rushed forward, Vahn at his heels.

The lights flickered.

Before the two reached Haru, the candelabras danced and flashed. A wave of light scorched down the aisle, called to Haru's side.

Vahn grabbed Osawa's arm and yanked him into the nearest bench, the two collapsing as the end of it splintered behind them.

Velinius swept her hands before her and a wall of light moved at Haru. He crossed his arms in front of him, scattering the attack around his body. The force splintered with a piercing howl that shattered the stained glass windows.

Vahn pushed Osawa's head down, covering them as the shards rained into the temple.

Haru caught one of the tails of the light before it escaped and it turned blue in his hands, hissing and charged. He sent the lightning crackling at Velinius.

Velinius held her hands before her, ever calm, never flinching. When the lightning hit it split then, caught, orbited her body. But while Velinius was distracted with the lightning, Haru had closed the distance between them. Light curved along the back of his arm into a blade, and Velinius created a shield to block the attack.

"What did you think you would accomplish with this?" The lightning crackled in the air around her, but even the static feared to move a hair on her head.

Silence was Haru's answer.

Vahn made his way to the other end of the bench that he and Osawa hid behind, then signaled Osawa to move in.

Haru backed up and released the arc of light. Velinius redirected it with the shield and it streaked by Osawa, slicing through one of the marble columns. The top of the column slid to the ground and broke apart, splintering the floor beneath it.

The give in the support of the ceiling brought one of the chandeliers crashing down. Vahn jumped out of the way, rolling into a crouch as the crystals scattered across the marble.

Haru attempted to move through the light again, but Velinius caught him before he completed the transfer and yanked back. Haru was pulled out of the movement and he tripped backwards, hitting the ground. Osawa could hear the air as it left his lungs in a gasp.

Velinius stepped on Haru's chest, keeping him down.

"I am curious." Velinius leaned her weight into the heel that rested on Haru's diaphragm, stopping him from catching his breath. "How are you so convinced that Ananke is alive?"

Vahn and Osawa moved in, but before they could get close enough, Velinius's attention snapped to them. Keeping her heel in place, she lifted a hand. Ropes of light twisted up Osawa's legs and caught, yanking him to the unforgiving floor. Osawa put his hands out to catch himself, but his head knocked against the marble and his vision swam.

When he blinked it clear, Vahn was on his knees. Light was twisted at his neck and he clawed at a rope he couldn't touch.

Velinius turned her attention back to Haru. "She was quite fond of her pet."

Velinius's hand twisted, tightening the rope around Vahn's neck and he fell forward, catching himself before hitting the ground.

"You will want to be still," she said to Haru. "We do not know what will happen to him if I lose my concentration."

Haru opened his mouth to respond but Velinius reached forward with her free hand, pressing two fingers against Haru's chest, and his voice came out as a scream.

Her cool detachment shifted to anger. She pulled back. "What did you do?"

Haru still struggled to breathe, but he clenched his jaw. The blue of his eyes flashed gold when they met Velinius's, and he smirked.

Her nostrils flared, then her composure returned. "Easy enough to undo," she said, then pressed her fingers once again against Haru's heart.

Before his screams broke, the door to the Temple opened.

Velinius released her holds. Vahn fell to the marble with Osawa, gasping for breath. Velinius's hands moved to clasp behind her back as the guards swarmed the Temple, glass cracking under their steps.

"These traitors made attempt on my life," Velinius said, pressing her open hand to her chest for emphasis. "Take them, so that they may answer to all for their crime."

Osawa managed to sit up, only to be knocked down by a blow from behind. His vision swam, but this time it did not return.

# 6

## FRIEND OF THE FAMILY

### ISCO

THE TRIP to Gegenes was uneventful, even if it was a bit uncomfortable for Isco. After leaving Adur, the passenger car of the train had been moderately occupied. However, with each passing stop, more bodies filled the available space until he was clutching his bag to his chest and clenching his jaw each time someone slipped and trod on his foot. He was both glad he could sit and cursed it. The bodies that loomed above him blocked whatever flow of cool air was in the car, and for just a moment he was sure he was going to suffocate.

Isco wasn't the only one disembarking in Gaoler. When the train screeched to a halt, he was swept into the wave of passengers as they streamed out onto the dusty, wind whipped railyard startion. Isco squinted after the dim of the train interior and sneezed.

After the first several strides out of the narrow doors, the crowd began to release him. Still clutching his bag to his chest, he stumbled out of the pull of bodies and found shelter behind a wooden post to catch his breath and orient himself.

The wood planks of the platform had buckled from the heat, and the uneven lean of them didn't help to shake the sense of motion that lingered after his journey. The Cardea had told him he would be met at the platform, but they hadn't given him information beyond that.

While he knew they didn't actually want him to succeed on this mission, they didn't have to make an impossible task even more difficult.

It didn't matter. He would do this, and then he would be free of them. One way or another.

Isco released a sigh of relief when the crowd thinned. He unknotted his hands from his leather bag and slung it over his shoulder. He brushed back the hair that had loosened into along his forehead and attempted to dust the wrinkles from his waistcoat.

"Hey, handsome," a woman's voice whispered close.

Isco jumped and whirled to check behind him to make sure he wasn't blocking someone's path. The post was behind him, and he jerked back to avoid hitting it.

The same voice laughed, and Isco recovered enough to turn. Before him was a Gegenii woman, her blonde hair cropped short on the side and long and swept back at the top.

"You look lost." The woman's green eyes sparkled against her dark tan Gegenii skin. She propped a hand on her bare hip, the silk she wore shifting with her every movement.

"I'm just getting my bearings."

She squinted at him, then lowered her voice as if they were sharing a common secret. "Is that fancyman talk for lost?"

"No." Isco cleared his throat and tried to straighten to his full height, though it brought him only a few notches taller than the woman. "I am waiting for a representative from your Governor."

"Ah," the woman said, her brow raising as she leaned back. She eyed him from the top of his brown hair down to the scuffs on his leather shoes. Then, she stuck her hand out. "I'm Astar."

Isco eyed her hand before taking it. "Isco."

The grip on his hand was firm when she shook it, the gold bangles on her wrist sliding against each other. "Isco Madeiros. I'd think a representative of the Camarilla Group would have arrived in Comfort Class, at least."

"The Camaril—right," Isco said, shaking his head. The woman's appearance had thrown him, and he'd forgotten his cover. "The Camarilla Group representative. That is my. Me."

Astar winked and backed up a step before turning and weaving through the crowd. A few steps away, she stopped and looked over her shoulder. "You coming?"

"I'm supposed to be waiting for..." he stopped, realization dawning on him, and pointed at her. "You're the Governor's representative."

"Yeah," she said, then turned and continued through the crowd. "And you were late. We're going to miss it."

Isco struggled to catch up with Astar's confident strides as she stepped off the train platform and into the city streets. When he caught her, he hovered close behind. The people that clogged the roadways stepped to the side, letting the pair pass. "Miss what?"

"The exhibit," she replied, not looking his way. "A small sample of The Harbinger's work. It was arranged so that potential investors can get a sneak preview before the main event." Astar slowed her steps and raised her brow at Isco. "That is what you're here for, right? To see The Harbinger?"

"Yes," he said, and at least he didn't have to lie. The Cardea, under the guise of the Camarilla Group, had been tracking the fighters in Gegenes's Theatre. Though most that had appeared where low level earth loas, they suspected that the Theatre's new "Harbinger" character may be something more. Isco had been sent to assess the stranger and, if warranted, return with them.

"The fighters in the Theatre," Isco started. "Are they under some kind of contract?"

Astar shrugged. "Some are, some aren't. When the Palamidia backed off on expanding their empire, there were a lot of soldiers that didn't have any other skills. The Belisarins saw an opportunity, and they took it."

Isco shook his head. "Aren't the Belisarins merchants?"

Astar nodded. "Sure are, and they started trading in people."

"So they enslaved them."

Astar stopped short, whirling on Isco with narrowed eyes. "Not slaves. As far as I know, Adur is the only region that allows that kind of barbarism."

Isco held his hands up and backed away from her heated glare. "I'm just a medicus."

Astar leaned back, but her eyes stayed suspiciously narrowed. She took a few more steps before stopping, and turned on Isco again. "Why is a medicus representing a trading coalition?"

Isco opened his mouth to defend himself, but he couldn't think of a lie. Instead, he looked past Astar. He tilted his head back, trying to take in the sight of the Theatre. Walkways ran along the outside of the circular structure, starting at the third tier, with arches along the facade to allow viewers to their seats.

"Is that the Theatre?" he asked.

Astar squinted at the pennants that batted against the sky. "Shit, we gotta hurry."

Instead of moving to the main entrance, Astar darted to a smaller door at the side. Keepers on each side unlocked the gate in anticipation of her arrival, and Isco quickened his steps to meet her. Inside the darkened stairwell, Astar took the steps two at a time, and Isco hastened to keep pace. Astar ducked through an angled opening that led them back out into the Gegenii sun.

Isco found himself blinking once again in the bright light of Gaoler. By the time he opened his eyes fully, Astar had already alighted into a seat on the daise.

"Your friend's here," she said, her gaze roving over the stage below.

A Gegenii man in formal attire rose to meet Isco. Gegenes was known as the Land of Giants, and the man was a true specimen. He didn't stand so much as loom, barrel chested and dark as oak. His robes were sapphire blue, matching the pennants that waved against the orange sky. Dark flowing pants were cuffed at his ankles above flat-footed leather boots. A woven leather belt wrapped his middle, and the scarf that draped over his shoulders matched Astar's sky blue silks.

He smiled, but it was too wide. There were too many teeth in it.

"Welcome," the man said, and laughed. Isco suppressed a cringe. The sound was loud, false and echoing. He stepped forward. "Isco, it is an honor to put a face to the name." He reached out and grasped Isco's hand in both of his own. "I am the Governor here. You may call me Hautman."

"Right." Isco looked down at their hands. Hautman squeezed once more, Isco's knuckles threatening to grind together, and released him.

"You were almost late, but we held the final act. I do hope my daughter was not disagreeable. I meant to send another, but they were called to a different task."

Astar sat back in her seat and crossed her legs. She rested her elbow on the armrest, her head on her fist.

"Daughter?" Isco asked.

Astar waved over her shoulder with her free hand, but didn't turn around.

"Please," Hautman said, stepping to the side. He looked away from Isco and turned his strained smile to Astar. She rolled her eyes and stood, taking a different chair behind the one she had previously occupied. Hautman turned back to Isco, his smile never faltering. "Sit."

"I could've sat somewhere else."

"No, of course not," Hautman said while waving his hand to dismiss the idea.

"Thanks," Isco said as he slowly lowered himself to the stone chair, "I think."

Hautman sat next to Isco in a rustle of silk. Once he'd adjusted his scarf, he lifted a hand, a gold ring flashing on each finger. A horn blast followed his signal.

Isco's attention turned to the Theatre's stage. From this height, he could still see the stains of blood in the orange sands. There were tracks in the soft soil where the fighters had struggled, ghosts of previous battles.

At the sound of the horn seven black iron gates opened in the Theatre, one for every ordinal and cardinal direction save for the east gate. Fourteen fighters emerged onto the sands, chained in pairs, presenting themselves to the crowd.

When they'd finished their rounds, accompanied by the audience's polite applause, the eighth and final gate opened. A Gegenii man stepped out, and the crowd cheered. He moved into the light, holding a khopesh aloft and dragging a chain behind him.

"You chain them?"

Hautman's hungry gaze left the gate and he turned to Isco, his smile faltering. "What?"

Isco indicated the trailing chains, and Hautman laughed. It was a jarring thing, too loud and too close. "It is only to keep things interesting. People would bore if every bought were the same. Now wait, the Harbinger comes."

The chain attached to the last Gegenii man shivered against the sand. Once drawn out to its length, it began to contract. At the other end, a woman emerged from the dark tunnels into the harsh light.

Her features had settled since Isco had first seen her, whatever softness she had then chiseled away by the passing years. But her eyes were the same cold grey, sweeping over the stage and the audience, seeing everything and the nothing beyond it.

As if she could feel his stare, she turned to the daise.

Isco's nails dug into the arms of his seat, his body screaming at him to run.

# 7

## IN THE DARK

### HARU

HARU WAITED.

# 8

# THE PRINCE & THE HARBINGER

## BEFORE

FROM HIS PLACE in the doorway, Isco could only see her back. She curled into a corner, ghastly pale, half-stripped, and still bleeding against the dark stone floor. Her hands were wrapped around her body, tucked where Isco couldn't see.

He shut the door behind him.

Despite the Cardea's best efforts, she hadn't said a word. Had barely made a sound. They'd tried different drugs to keep her both malleable but conscious, needed to know what she was in order to properly test her, but she'd yet to reveal any abilities beyond an unnervingly high tolerance to pain.

Isco knelt before her and pushed the tangled mass of hair from her face. The skin on her forehead was clammy and feverish, but her eyes were open, alert. He had never seen someone with coloring like hers, but it was her eyes that gave him pause. They were the color of ash in snow, or a bright, clean metal.

"You should tell them what they want to know," he said.

Though weak, her lips quirked into a smirk and her eyes narrowed dangerously.

"They'll ease up if you say something." Isco settled on the ground next to her. "It doesn't have to be true, just interesting enough to distract them."

Her cold smirk fell, and her brow furrowed. They sat together in silence for another moment, and then she shifted. She attempted to sit up, but she kept her hands tucked and struggled with the movement. Halfway up, she slipped, and her left hand went out instinctually to stop her fall.

Isco felt his heart drop into his stomach when she tipped and he reached out, catching her before her weight landed on her mangled hand. He helped to right her, then grabbed her wrist and pulled her hand towards him.

"Dead gods," he whispered under his breath. The fingernails of her left hand had been yanked from their beds. Her pinky and ring finger were cleanly broken, and the others jutted at odd angles.

Isco grabbed her right wrist, turning her hand over. It was in far worse condition. The bones of several of her fingers weren't just broken, they were shattered, and the bone of her ring finger jutted from the skin.

There was so much damage Isco didn't know where to start, didn't know if there was any way to fix what had been done with what he had. His hand shook with hers in it, the other rummaging through his bag.

The woman pulled her right hand from him and held it against her bare, bloodstained skin. She held out her left to him instead.

"But the other one needs immediate care," he attempted to argue.

She just pushed her left towards him again.

Isco took it, the realization dawning on him. "You're left handed?"

She bit her lip, but made no other motion.

"All right," Isco said. "We'll start here."

While he attempted to focus on what was before him, tried to fix without causing more pain, her attention drifted. Her eyes moved to the opposite wall, then back to her hand. She shifted, then it happened again, but the second time, her gaze stuck.

Isco looked up, tried to follow her line of sight, but it was the same damp wall it had always been, darkened in spots where the humidity coalesced. But she was focused on something far beyond it.

When her eyes shifted back to him, they weren't human anymore. They had eclipsed, black as a starless sky. She broke her silence, her voice dry with disuse, and she said, "He's here."

The sound that followed was nothing like anything Isco had heard before. It was a high-pitched screech and a predator's roar together. It was the scream of air when lightning rent it, but it was as if existence itself was tearing, the scream quaking with anger. It rolled above and then through the compound, primal and unstoppable.

Isco pressed his hands over his ears when it came close, but just before reaching them it stopped.

It was followed by an eerie silence. Isco removed his hands from his ears, waiting.

Then, something like thunder. The earthen roof above the compound shook, rocks cracking and breaking loose from the tunnels as the buildings above them collapsed.

Isco turned back to the woman. "We have to go."

She shook her head.

Isco knelt near her, attempted to wrap his arm around her waist and lift her. She gasped from the pain, and the shrill keening tore into Isco's ears in response. He had to release her to try and cover his ears once more to block it out.

The sound stopped, only to be replaced by the screams of the Cardea. Isco stumbled to the door of the cell and opened it, only to be shoved back. The members of the Cardea were racing through the twisting corridors, knocking each other back and over as they were routed into a chaotic retreat.

A flash of light blinded Isco and he stepped back along the hall. When he blinked away the spots in his eyes, a body fell at his feet, the neck gaping where the throat had been hacked through.

Isco skittered back out of the blood pool, preparing to face the attackers that would issue his death.

Instead, a single soldier rounded the corner.

Where the prisoner's eyes had turned black, the man's were molten gold, shifting and curling and undone. His white uniform held the mark of the Shadowed Sun, denoting him as one of the Legatus's elite.

Isco backed away, but he knew there was no point in running. The soldier's cuffs were thick with blood, proof that it was his hands that had ripped through the Cardea's hidden compound. His grip tightened on twinned blades, the handles white beneath the smears of blood, and he charged.

Isco was slammed into the wall, the air leaving his lungs in a gasp.

"Stop."

The prisoner's voice echoed in the hall, and the tip of the man's blade buried itself in the rock next to Isco's ear. He could feel the stickiness of the blood that coated the metal against his skin.

The soldier turned to the voice. "Kanna."

The Cardea's captive had managed to stand at the open door of the cell, but she leaned her shoulder heavily on the jamb. Evidence of her torture was streaked on her shaking body. Beaten and bloodied, barely clinging to whatever strength that remained in her, the single command carried enough authority to halt an army.

Or the equivalent of one.

The soldier abandoned Isco and rushed to the prisoner as her knees loosened, overwhelmed by the strain of weeks of torture and pain, and she fell against him.

"Haru," she whispered as the soldier eased her to the ground.

Once she was safely settled, he shrugged out of his once white jacket and draped it to cover her.

"I knew you'd come," she said.

Far gentler than blood-stained hands should be, he placed a hand to her cheek. His fingers wrapped around her neck and he tilted her head back, dropping his forehead to hers. "I was too late."

She shook her head, a smile ghosting across her lips. "You weren't. I am alive."

Haru shut his eyes. "Why would you do this?"

"We found them, didn't we?"

The soldier's eyes opened. They had settled to a crisp blue and slid over Isco like a winter chill. He unfurled from his crouch.

"No," Kanna said, shaking her head. "Leave him."

Haru turned back to her, met her level gaze. They stayed that way, locked in a silent debate, until Haru relented with a nod.

Haru moved to Isco, stopping just before him. He reached forward and Isco winced. The soldier gripped the hilt of his knife and yanked it from the wall where it had been buried.

He sheathed the blade and returned to Kanna, carefully lifting her in his arms. She leaned into him, mangled hands cradled against her chest.

Isco understood then why the Palamidia dressed in white.

It was the perfect canvas for blood.

# 9

# THE LAST TRIAL OF TENGRI

## HARU

IRKALLA SUNK beneath the pristine halls of the Palamidia's Tower like an ancient, hibernating creature. While there was structure and reason to the twists above, a living maze of dead-ends and false exits lurked below. In the depths of it, Haru counted his breaths.

The layers of Irkalla dampened loa abilities, though the knowledge of how or why had died with the gods. There was little use for guards in this place, but Haru had them. Whether they had earned Velinius's ire or volunteered to gain favor Haru couldn't guess, but they had settled into routine.

Reading intent wasn't something that came to him naturally, but he had trained as the hand of the master. He knew enough to feel when the wariness of the guards faded and was replaced with fatigue and boredom.

Absent all light, he concentrated on his body's movements as he shifted through practiced stances. Time had stopped here, and he wasn't sure if it was days or weeks since he had been imprisoned, but it didn't matter. He knew patience, and he knew the dark. He knew the weight of it, where the edges were, and he knew just how far he could go.

Haru finished his stance with his fingers brushing against the rough wall. He shifted in the black and pressed his back against the stone, his skin scraping as he slid down against it.

Beneath the door, there was a light. He shut his eyes, concentrating on the pain in his skin to focus. All he had left was his mind. They wouldn't take that.

The sound of voices in the hall was unfamiliar and jarring after so much silence.

"Please, Exalted One, it is dangerous. At least leave the light."

"Then how would I see, child?" a woman asked, her voice laced with command.

Haru could hear the guards' boots against stone as the shifted.

The woman sighed. "The others do not have the courage to face him. Since you know who I am, are you implying I am a coward?"

"No," one of the guards answered quickly, "of course not, no."

The voices moved closer until they were outside his door. The glimmer of light beneath it peeled away the dark and Haru's eyes squinted to adjust after so long. There was a fumbling of keys.

Haru relaxed his body and hunched against the stone. He turned to face the back wall and unfocused his eyes, playing the part of a broken man. The door opened and the light entered, bleaching the interior of his stark prison. He could see the dirt streaked on his hands and forearms and the grime buried under his nails, but he could feel the potential, the strength of it.

"Leave," the woman said. Her tone was sharp and brooked no argument.

The door slammed and the locks clicked back in place.

Haru continued to stare at the wall as the guards retreated. His eyes adjusted to the pale lantern the woman had brought with her, and the light clawed at him. It took most of his will not to yank the lamp from her and cradle it against himself.

"This is a terrible spot we have found ourselves in, is it not?"

The woman moved closer to Haru, but there was no fear in her movement, nor was there anything careful about it. If anything, she was more relaxed than he feigned to be. He risked a glance at her, his eyes widening at the resemblance.

Haru shifted from his prone position and pulled his back straight. He pushed the hair from his eyes and rested his hands on his knees as he looked up at her.

She smiled as she set the lantern at his feet before settling across from him on the floor. "That took longer than I thought it would." She adjusted the long robe she wore around her body, then interlaced her fingers in her lap. "You realize who I am, then?"

Her eyes were kohl-lined, so dark they were nearly black, and light wrinkles webbed their corners. An intricate braid of brown hair streaked with grey fell in a cascade over her shoulder.

"You're the Exalted Mother," he said, his voice foggy with disuse.

"That is the title they have given me." She tilted her head, studying him. "You may call me by my name."

He cleared his throat, not wanting it to crack. "She said your name was Aksana."

Aksana smiled, then nodded. He wasn't sure what else to say, or why she had come to him. She shifted to match his posture and he waited, not daring to hope.

"I am going to tell you a story. I need you to remember it. Can you do that?"

Haru didn't trust himself to speak so he nodded instead. Aksana reached forward, pushing the lantern closer to him with the tips of her fingers before leaning back once more.

"In the beforetimes, the world was whole and the gods were limitless.

"It was in this time that Adita ruled. She loved her people, dearly, and did everything to protect them. She blessed them with warmth when they were chilled, light when they were scared, stories when they had no hope."

Aksana was a practiced storyteller. Her cadence was smooth, her voice low, and Haru hung on the story as she spoke.

"Forces began to conspire against Adita. Peace, you see, was as unsustainable then as it is now. Others feared her, the way she was able to make and unmake the reality of her people. The other gods seethed with jealousy, and, one day, they amassed at the borders of her land.

"She knew she had to face them, but she could not leave the people undefended. So she called for a champion, and she declared five trials."

"The trials of Tengri," Haru said. He had been entranced by the lantern, forgot to bite back the words. He tore his eyes from it to meet hers.

"Yes," Aksana confirmed. "Tengri volunteered himself, without thought of consequence."

Haru looked back to the ghostlights flickering in the lantern.

"After the trials, when Tengri stood victorious, he swore to lay waste to those that would oppose Adita. However, Adita did not need a stead for battle. She needed someone to protect her people when she went to war."

Aksana paused. Haru, transfixed by the lantern, did not look away from it. She reached down, pushing it closer to him. Inside, the ghostlights flickered and pressed against the glass. It seemed the light wanted him as much as he needed it.

"At the field where the battle was to meet, Adita challenged the leader of the rebel gods. If she felled him, his followers would leave in peace. If he succeeded, her kingdom, and her self, would be his.

"The gods clashed, and the battle raged. Adita emerged the victor, and she ordered the others away from the killing field.

"However, she had sent them away so they could not see. Adita had been dealt a mortal blow. No one saw her leave that place, and those who waited to welcome her back were left with empty arms."

Haru brushed his fingers along the glass of the lantern and the ghostlights gathered beneath them.

"None felt the emptiness as keenly as Tengri," Aksana continued. "The warmth Adita gave her people was replaced with something else, and they shivered."

The lights followed Haru's fingertips as he traced them over the glass.

"Tengri knew he had to find Adita. He knew she was not lost because at night, he would dream of her. He saw her in a place that wasn't a place, a land that was neither for the dead or the living. It was a place between, and Tengri knew he must guide her home."

Aksana stopped. Haru shifted back on his heels, pulling himself away from the lantern. The lights within flickered and buzzed in a disturbed swarm before settling into a slow, shifting dance.

Something in Aksana had changed. Her brows knit in disapproval as she looked around the room, truly seeing it for the first time. Haru had heard of the way she shifted, moving from lucid to incomprehensible in the space of a breath.

He cleared his throat. "Aksana?"

Her eyes snapped to him, focusing.

"The story?"

"Yes," she said. "The story."

Aksana patted her sides, then the flowing robes near her feet. "I will admit, I'm not sure how it will end," she said. "But you will need these."

Aksana rose, leaving a black cloth-wrapped package where she had been sitting. Haru saw the glint of metal and curled his hands into fists. With a sandaled foot, she slid the collection of knives closer to him as she stepped forward.

He looked up at her, unable to speak, not sure what to say if he could.

She leaned down, brushing a kiss on the top of his head. "Find my daughter," she whispered, "she will end this. She was always meant to end this."

With that, Aksana picked up the lamp and knocked on the door of the cell. Haru hunched his body over the knives, turning to the corner as the guards let her out.

Haru was left with the darkness, but he had something else. When the hallway silenced, he uncurled his fist. The single ghostlight flickered in his hand then steadied, clear and brilliant.

# 10

## AN INVITATION

### KANNA

KANNA WAS ANGRY, every moment. The anger was part of her, and it made her, even more than the aches in her hand or the scars on her skin. Sometimes, she wondered if she always had been, or if the anger had moved in when everything else was lost. But she didn't allow herself to think about that. She couldn't allow herself to wonder what was before. She had to keep her anger tight, carry it calmly. When she first arrived at the Theatre, she could use it. Now, even that had stopped being a relief.

After their bout, Kanna waited outside the door of the Keepers' station while Yassen collected their winnings. She leaned against the wall opposite the door in the dim, enjoying the respite of the cool shade after the bright heat of the day. The governor had created a decent spectacle, but it hadn't been enough. Her anger rode high in her chest, sticking under her throat.

Yassen ducked out of the office, a few coins richer than before he had entered. Kanna leaned away from the wall and set her weight back on her feet, leading them to the exits.

"So," Yassen said to her back. "What was that back there?"

Kanna's steps almost faltered, her hand covering her side. In the midst of the chaos of the bout, a sharp pain had brought her to her knees. It was as if something inside of her was being pried out.

"I thought you were going down," Yassen continued.

She dropped her hand. The pain was gone. Whatever happened was finished, and it left only a lingering trace that it had been. "I didn't."

As they exited the passage into the heat of the streets, Kanna stopped short. Ahead, Keepers flanked Astar, her father, and someone new. He wasn't Gegenii, that was certain. His skin was lighter than their deeper tones, and his dark brown hair had begun to rebel, falling from its half-back twist. However, the fear curled deep in him was his most notable feature. It came from an old place, like the cold ache of a phantom injury on a damp day.

Kanna recognized the expectant gleam in the Governor's eyes, but he would wait. She tilted her head to Yassen, not taking her gaze from the trio that stood out of earshot. "Who is that?"

Yassen looked to the gathering that waited, then to her. "That's the Governor."

"I know the Governor," she said. "The other one."

He leaned forward and squinted against the sun, then straightened from his bent position. "Don't know," Yassen said. "But he's dressed like an Adurian. A fancy one."

Kanna looked to him finally, cocking her brow. "What do you know of Adur?"

Yassen smiled and held his hand against his chest. "I'm from Adur."

Kanna was growing tired of the surprises this day was bringing. She shifted, waving a hand from Yassen's head to his feet, then crossed her arms in front of her to await his explanation.

"I'm adopted," he said. "You never hear of war orphans?"

Kanna considered, then sighed out. "I made an assumption."

"Well," Yassen said, straightening to his full height and casting a shade over her. "You know what they say about making assumptions."

"No." Kanna tipped her head to the side. "What do they say?"

Yassen scratched the back of his neck. "I'm not sure. It's just something people say."

Having grown tired of waiting, Hautman moved to them, his companions dragging behind. Astar fell in step, the spark in her features dulled into her role. The other man looked everywhere but at Kanna.

"Harbinger," Governor Hautman crowed, his arms held wide.

When Hautman stopped before her, Kanna took a step back. His attempt to make her feel small by crowding her space with his size was feeble at best. She tilted her chin to meet his eyes. "Governor."

"Congratulations on another beautiful show." Hautman let his hands fall, then clasped them behind his back.

The gesture caused something the dark in her to snap. She curled her toes in her boots and kept her place. "What do you want?"

The Keepers at his side tightened their grips on their weapons, but he held up a hand to stop them. He laughed, exaggerated and boastful, and his guards relaxed. They accompanied him with uncertain chuckles, unaware of the joke but wanting to be included.

"Such impudence," Hautman said. "Makes one wonder how you can put on such airs."

Kanna ticked her head to the side. She considered the number of Keepers and their weapons, then tilted to consider the sun. It was heavy in the sky, and she was tired. Her shoulder dropped as she turned away.

"Peace, Harbinger," the Governor said, holding out his hands in surrender.

She stopped. The sand shifted beneath her boots and settled beneath her weight.

"I'm sure you've noticed my guest." Hautman waved his hand at the Adurian behind him. "This is Isco Madeiros. He's an accomplished medicus who came to view the Theatre's plays. He is staying in my home, and I came to invite you to join us."

When Hautman's lips pulled back into another too-wide smile, Kanna narrowed her eyes. There was a flake of pepper caught in his canine. She slid her gaze to Isco, who turned to study the passing crowd, then back to Hautman's teeth.

"No, thank you," she said.

"Dinner, then," he said, his teeth not moving. "I insist."

Kanna took a moment to consider. The Governor's sudden interest in making nice with her, the timing of the Gala, and the appearance of the medicus were too well aligned to be coincidence.

"You can bring your," he waved his hand toward Yassen, "friend."

Even at rest, Yassen's expression was soft and open, his lips hinting at an upturn as if he was always on the verge of a smile. The last thing she needed was him getting tangled in the Governor's blatant schemes.

"He isn't hungry."

"The dinner will be tomorrow," Hautman said, his smile dropping with a commanding finality. "Astar will fetch you."

Kanna dropped her chin in an affirmation and Hautman's smile split his lips again. The pepper flake was still caught against his enamel. He turned his back, cutting off any objections. Astar smiled over her shoulder from her place at the back of the group, but it didn't reach her eyes.

Yassen let out a deep sigh. "Dinner at the Governor's house," he said, then grinned down at her. "I wonder what they'll serve? I bet it'll be fancy."

"Maybe," she said. "You aren't coming."

His smile fell. "But I am hungry. And I can be hungry tomorrow."

"No." She softened her tone, turning up. "We'll get you food from that street vendor you like." The Governor and his entourage wove into the bodies on the street. "But I don't trust him."

# 11

## PREPARATIONS

### ASTAR

IT WAS late afternoon when Astar deposited Isco in one of the guest suites on the second floor of the Governor's home. Her home, she had to remind herself, though it never felt quite right.

After her mother left, when Astar was old enough to remember her existence but too young to retain the details of it, Declan Hautman had thrown himself into his career. Without someone to stand between her and the rest of the world, Astar was thrust into the spotlight and expected to become a paradigm for Gegenii noblewomen.

Astar was taught how to weave, how to paint, how to dance, how to properly drape traditional fashions and what accessories were enough and what was too much. She learned to drive a chariot and shoot a bow. She could read ledgers, run numbers, and calculate interests without aid.

What she couldn't do was gain her father's respect.

While that was the kind of thing that bothered a child, Astar was no longer one, and she no longer wanted it. She had given her respect to her father as was expected of children, and he had done nothing to keep it.

Astar was awarded, accomplished, and when that hadn't gained her father's attention, she had tried other tactics.

Hautman failed to notice any difference. He simply could not be bothered to care, too busy with his schemes. Even when she'd stumble home intoxicated, smashing his antiques, he'd send a servant to tell her to keep the noise down.

Astar started fights, came home late, and when that didn't work, she tried running off without warning to another region altogether.

That didn't go well, but Astar met Kanna. However, all Hautman noticed when Astar returned was Kanna. The first time Kanna fought, his eyes lit with a wild greed so intense that Astar had to take a step back.

Astar placed a loose hand on the curving wood banister, taking each of the steps to the first floor with care. At the foot of the stairs Manni waited, his hands twined together in front of him. The setting sun cast his white-blonde hair in a warm light, bringing back some of the once golden glow that the years in her father's service had faded. Manni was Hautman's personal assistant, and when Astar saw him it was because he had been sent to fetch her.

"Again?" she asked.

Manni nodded. This was the second time that Manni had come for Astar in less than a week. It was a new record.

Manni held out a hand so Astar could walk before him. She cut through the open foyer, the bright murals that flooded the walls so familiar now that their artistry was lost on her, and Manni trailed behind. Her feet slid over the plush rugs, mussing the parallel vacuum marks, and stopped before entering the hall that led to Hautman's wing.

Astar turned on her heel then waved her hands at Manni to shoo him away. He frowned but backed up with only the quickest of bows, disappearing into one of the hidden doors that concealed the servants' paths.

Hautman kept every light in his wing lit, the electricity buzzing in the otherwise quiet air. A sconce bedecked the hall every few feet, and doors to the sitting rooms, each with its own collection, were left ajar. The lights from the rooms cut slashes across the deep navy runner, the golden threads woven into patterns in the deep pile glinting in the artificial glare. At the end of the hall, Astar paused. She held up a clenched fist to knock, but changed her mind and entered her father's study.

The study was one of the larger rooms in the home, save for the dining hall. There were sets of furniture in three different seating positions and still room enough for the overly large, solid wood desk. It would dwarf a smaller man, but Hautman was Gegenii. He was proud of his heritage, and at least that was something that Astar could relate to.

There was nothing else alike about them, and the rift between them had become more obvious to Astar since Kanna's arrival. Sometimes, she wondered how she had never noticed the wrongness in his smile or the emptiness of his every gesture.

He looked up with a smile, but it didn't reach his eyes. Behind them, Astar could see his mind working. When he recognized that it was just her, the practiced smile slipped ever so slightly but didn't fall.

"Daughter." Hautman placed his hands on his desk, using them to leverage himself to standing.

Astar stayed in her place, her hands at her sides. "You wished to see me?"

Hautman nodded, stopping at the small bar in his office. It was a dainty thing, in comparison to him. He righted two glasses, then removed the stopper from a crystal decanter. "I wanted to be sure that we were clear on some things regarding tomorrow's dinner."

He tilted the decanter, pouring one portion of honeyed brandy smaller than the other. He replaced the stopper on the decanter before waving to one of the sitting areas.

Astar could have stayed standing. She told herself she didn't need to move, that there was no reason for her to sit, but she followed his gesture. Still, she did not sink into the plush armchair so much as perch upon it.

Hautman brought the glasses over, offering the smaller portion to her, and Astar was aware of how bare her feet were. She crossed one over the other and pulled them tight against the chair as Hautman settled across from her.

Astar lifted the drink and inhaled. It was smokey, with a hint of cedar and elderberry. "Did you want something formal?"

"Yes," Hautman answered. He lifted his own drink in the same manner, then sipped from it before relaxing his hand on the chair's arm. "I will need you to make the Harbinger presentable."

Without taking a drink, Astar leaned over and placed her glass on the low table between them. "What about her isn't presentable?"

Hautman laughed, the corners of his eyes wrinkling together. "You've seen her. She is like a wild thing."

Astar moved back, sitting upright once more. "I thought that was her appeal."

"In the Theatre, certainly." Hautman shook his head, amused by Astar's simplicity. "Not in the company of the Cardea."

Astar tried not to let her surprise show. She had not heard of the Camarilla group that Isco supposedly represented, but she did know of the Cardea. They were well known, if only because they were an unknown. They had money and means, but their purpose remained hidden to outsiders.

Hautman's eyes drifted to Astar's abandoned glass, and he brought his own to his lips. She followed his gaze and retrieved the crystal from the table, this time relaxing her shoulders.

"Of course, Father." Astar brought the brandy to her lips. It was thick, sweet, but burned in her throat. She swallowed to clear it. "Is your intention to join them?"

Hautman laughed, and Astar drank. "No," he said, "but they will be an important ally in the times to come."

Astar kept her eyes on the liquid in her glass, cradling it in her lap with both hands. "Is there something happening that I should know?"

Hautman was quiet for a moment. When Astar looked up, he was watching her, his brow furrowed. He finally broke his trance with a sigh and leaned back. He shifted his weight, crossing one leg over his knee, before uncrossing it and settling both of his feet back on the ground.

"I suppose it is time." He leaned forward, though there was no one else near them to overhear. "There is a rumor that the Palamidia has a new Legatus. Shipments have slowed in the borderlands, and there is an... unease. There haven't been any reports of troop movements yet, but we may find ourselves in need of powerful allies sooner rather than later."

Astar raised a brow. "You think this Isco can gain you the favor of the Cardea?"

Hautman's smile returned with a gleam that would have made Astar's stomach turn even without the sickening brandy. "I know he can."

Astar tried to find her way through the fog of information. She knew she had all the pieces, but they wouldn't quite connect. "What does Kanna have to do with this?"

"The Harbinger is an asset."

Astar's fingers tightened around her glass and she felt the liquid shift inside of it. Hautman had never used Kanna's name, but something about his correcting tone made her defensive.

"She's not a weapon," Astar said with as much force as she could manage with Hautman, which wasn't much.

Frowning, Hautman placed his glass on the table between them and it settled audibly. "She's as human as the rest of us," he conceded. "I simply wish to show her the respect she deserves."

Something about the way he said it made Astar want to become smaller than she was. Astar cleared her throat, but before she could ask anything else, Hautman waved her off.

"That is all, daughter," he said, leaning back into his seat. "I am tired, and would like to rest for tomorrow."

The dismissal was abrupt but final. Astar closed her mouth around her questions and stood, abandoning her glass at the table.

"One last thing," Hautman said, stopping Astar when she reached the door.

She turned to look over her shoulder.

"Make sure the Harbinger isn't armed. It would be rude, don't you think?"

# LIGHT THE WAY

## HARU

HARU SET the ghostlight in the dark, pulling his hand away from the small lifeline. Its glow flickered and he held his breath, ready to reach for it again, but it returned to its dull equilibrium.

"Good," he whispered to it. "That's good."

The fleck of ghostlight brightened a shade. On instinct he pressed his finger to his lips to quiet it, and the light dimmed. Keeping his body between the light and the door, Haru checked the weapons that Aksana left. She'd wrapped the six knives in the same fabric of her cloak to conceal them, and the metal glinted in the dim glow of the single flicker of borrowed light.

Vahn's paired set had pale natural wood handles that were darkened from the oils in his hands, while Osawa's were inlaid with a viridian chrysocolla composite. The last set was his.

The first of his knives was made for him. The handle was set with a white turquoise webbed in a subtle gold, the gemstone of his family's house. The second was black, from the grip to its end, the back spine of the blade mottled. He ran his fingers over the small gouges in the handle, charting the scuffs on the dark gem handle to assure himself it was the same. Under the ghostlight he tilted it. Under the right light, it revealed a prism of color. Long veins of indigo and deep violet twisted in the black. Shards of gold inclusions in the handle caught, winked, and disappeared again before his eyes. He tilted it away from the light, and it became a solid, unassuming black once more.

Satisfied that Aksana hadn't pulled a switch, he wrapped Vahn and Osawa's back in the material and slung it around his back, knotting the ends together so it was tight against his skin.

He stood, and the flicker of light followed his movement. At the door, he pressed his palm against the lock before considering the ghostlight. It wouldn't work, not the way he wanted it to. Ghostlights couldn't be molded, their shapes couldn't be controlled or bent. He could ask, but it didn't mean they would comply. They were shards of light, broken pieces disconnected from any conceivable source.

His dipped in the air as if it read his thoughts.

"Don't worry, I have another idea," he said, not sure why he felt the need to comfort something with as much sentience as a roadside pebble. "I will need your help in a moment, though."

Haru adjusted his grip on his knives, then felt the rough cut of the wall with his fingertips. The guards outside were already stirring, his movements and voice drawing their attention, so he would have to be quick.

He pressed the flat of the white-handled blade against the stone and yanked it across. It hissed against the rock and threw sparks. Which was all he needed.

He caught the sparks of light and threaded them through the lock on the door, shoving the pins up and yanking the tumblr free. The door unlatched with a heavy clack.

Two guards had made it to the door, with another pair further down the hall. Haru had an advantage, though. The dark would hinder their sight, making them slow and unbalanced. The dark didn't bother him.

Haru slammed open the door, running the first guard through before he could react. Haru shoved his weight back into the open door, shoving it into the guard at the other side and knocking him off-balance. A thrust of Haru's second blade cut off the warning shout, but not soon enough.

The ghostlight buzzed past Haru's shoulder and down the hall, darting past the second pair of guards that rounded the corner.

Glass shattered ahead, and Haru smiled at the fresh guards. They hesitated, then turned at the buzzing static sound.

Haru called and they came. Dozens of ghostlights tore through the guards' bodies. The second pair fell forward as the lights pulled through their skin, speckling the halls in a thin spray of blood.

The ghostlights swarmed excitedly around him. One hovered in his eye line and he waved his hand, bidding it to join the others.

Haru rummaged through the guards' pockets. The first pair had nothing. No keys, no maps, nothing that would help. He moved to the second set. On the first guard he found a comlink and pocketed it. When he moved to the second, he was stopped by the man's grip on his wrist.

It was weak, his strength failing. He glared at Haru, his mouth working around the blood and curses that rose in his throat, still believing his twisted purpose was the true one. Life fled his eyes and they unfocused, settling on something beyond the living.

Haru shrugged off the limp grip at his wrist and continued his search. In the soldier's pocket, his fingertips touched metal. Withdrawing it, he eyed the silver rectangle. He flicked the lid of it open, then pressed his thumb along the wheel. He was rewarded with the sound of flint on metal and a flickering flame.

Pocketing the lighter, he stretched back to his height. The lights had calmed their erratic whirls but kept close as he continued through the narrow hall of the prison. It opened up to a guard station littered with pierced bodies, their movements arrested in mid flight. At the center was a circular table with a shattered lantern and a cascade of blood spattered cards. A canteen was tipped over, its contents spilling over the wooden table.

Haru moved to the table and righted the container, replacing the lid before shaking it. There was still a portion of water left, though not much. He set it back onto the table and placed the knives he carried besides it.

Haru continued his search, but didn't find anything else of use amongst the bodies. He unbuckled the sheaths from three of them then returned to the table and fit the knives he carried into them. He strapped his own to his back, then belted the others at his waist.

He shut his eyes and reached for the lighter he had pocketed. He turned and leaned back on the table, his thumb toying with the lid. It opened and closed with a sharp snap of metal as he tried to calm himself enough to think.

Then he felt it: a small tug of memory, a dim glow in a dark place.

# 13

## A SAINT, A SINNER

### VAHN

Vahn shivered in his cell. The cold had long seeped past his skin and into his bones, and if he moved too quickly it felt as if his cartilage would crack. Whoever had built the Tower's prison was a creative sadist, and Vahn took comfort in the fact that they were long dead, gone to the gods and rotting with them.

The thought did little to warm him, though.

He curled his legs against his chest and wedged his arms between them. Shutting his eyes, he leaned his forehead onto his knees and thought of the east gardens. It wasn't the landscape that gave him comfort, as picturesque as the area was. The trees were dense, and the sun slanted through the leaves in long dappled lines. The ground underfoot was rocky and scattered with branches that dug into the soles of his feet, and it was nothing like the soft grasslands and open skies of his Atarrabi homeland.

But he was grateful to that area of the Palamidia's compound. It was one of Kanna's haunts, and where she had found him. She had been the first person he met who had been kind to him. After the trading ring that held him was broken apart by the Palamidia, he was taken to Lugos and shoved with a few others into the newest group of Prospects due to his abilities.

The former slaves didn't do well in training. Vahn and those like him had spent their lives barely flirting with survival while the other Prospects prepared to enter the Palamidia. In a way, they had all been raised to understand that kindness was weakness and brutality led to greatness. For the Empire's own, that meant destroying the competition, as feeble as it was. For Vahn, bruised knuckles and broken noses meant he may get a chance to eat or an hour of uninterrupted sleep.

Vahn hadn't been a good fighter. He was tall, but too lean and gangly. His skin wrapped tight against his bones and there was little weight behind his strikes. At least he was hard to pin down, the joints jutting from his skin giving him sharp edges to jab into muscle and exposed curves. He often found himself cornered outside of training areas by the others, the ones who enjoyed inflicting pain, those that saw him as a dark spot on a shining canvas and set themselves to the task of ripping him from it.

He had run to the trees hoping the area would give him a place to hide from another attack, when Kanna dropped from the sky in a hail of cracked branches and crushed leaves between him and his pursuers.

Vahn had been young, but Kanna was a child. The top of her head was chest level with the others that surrounded her, but it made little difference to her. While his pursuers paused in their shock, she'd taken him in. Cold steel eyes studied the white of his hair, the violet of his eyes, and paused at the slave bands tattooed on his wrists. When she reached out he flinched away, but her fingertips were soft against the black lines on his skin. He couldn't remember the last time a touch wasn't meant to bruise or take.

Vahn had never seen anything move like she did. She looked small, seemed almost fragile even before him, but when she attacked there was no quarter and no mercy. She was smooth, sharp and honed from her short life of violence.

Sometimes he wondered how things would be different if she hadn't dropped from the sky like his own personal feral saviour. More than likely, he would have ended up in a grave, just another tally in another book.

Not that freezing in Irkalla was a better option.

Vahn lifted his head and shook it. He shrugged his shoulders and stretched them out and back before uncurling his legs. Thinking about Kanna wasn't going to get her back if she didn't want to be. While Haru had insisted she was alive, he was unmoored without her. His limitless drive and devotion had become directionless, and all he had been good for was slamming himself into walls at every opportunity. Which left Osawa to make sure he didn't knock something loose that couldn't be put back.

Vahn had kept his head down and his eyes open. Every missive that came through he scanned, looking for evidence of Haru's hunch. Any trace of things tilting sideways and he'd look a little closer. After all, Kanna had never been subtle.

Most of the trails he followed staggered into dead ends until recently. But he had to be sure. He'd needed more time before he was willing to open his mouth. They had both been captives to cruel masters, in their own ways. He understood more than anyone the vicious need to escape a leash.

He paced in the frigid cell to keep his blood moving, hoping the feeling in his feet would return at some point. He cupped his hands around his mouth and blew out, but even the heat from his breath had been stolen.

What a stupid way to go this was.

Vahn tightened his hand to a fist and pulled back to slam it into the blank door of his cell. He wondered if he would feel it, or anything, ever again. Before he stuck, though, he heard something. The walls of the cell were insulated and freezing. He pressed his ear against the door anyway and was rewarded with the muffled clash on the other side.

Then, the click of metal and the brush of flint. Then heat. Not just heat, but pure flame. Everything in his body screamed for it and it ignited on the other side of the wall, devouring its source fuel and then expanding, burning hotter and angrier until it filled the hall.

The guards' cries were short lived. From inside his cell, Vahn fed the flames his rage, his hunger. It devoured the guards, spread to the stone walls, and Vahn pressed his body against the metal door, needing to feel the heat again. It crawled against the walls, melting the hinges of his cage.

He stepped back before it scorched his skin. Finished with his work, he shut his eyes and pressed the anger down, locked it deep within him where it belonged. He calmed the inferno in the hall, left only a single flame to flicker against the stone.

When he opened his eyes again, the door of the cell shuddered once. Then again, and the melted hinges loosened. The third time the door fell open, wrenched and hanging from the lock on the opposite side.

Haru stood on the other side of the door, dusting ash from the shoulder he had used as a battering ram. He rolled it back and forth, and his piercing blue eyes narrowed on Vahn.

"You didn't have to melt the keys," he said.

"Maybe." Vahn stepped into the soot-filled hall, admiring the black scorches on the pale grey walls. "But then you wouldn't have the chance to burst through my door like a storied prince."

Vahn stopped next to the single flame that he had left in the hall and unfurled his hand. The fire snaked to him and he cradled it between his hands, admiring the dance at the heart of it, before pulling the heat inside of himself. Warmth seeped through his veins, the color returning the tips of his fingers.

Behind him, Haru unbuckled one of the sheaths strapped to him and held it out to Vahn. Vahn didn't ask how Haru had acquired his knives. The wood was warm against his palms as he flexed his hands around them, his sense of touch coming back with a thousand pricks of needles against his skin.

"Weird that Os isn't with you," Vahn said, his eyes on the slim curve of his blades. "I'd think he'd have to convince you to come for me."

"You were easier to find," Haru said. "You were thinking about her."

Vahn felt his body tighten before he could stop it. He shrugged off the momentary lapse. "Doesn't seem like something I'd do."

"Of course not," Haru replied, his voice flat. Then, he stared at Vahn.

"What?"

"Your turn."

Vahn sighed, dramatically he hoped, before shutting his eyes. It had taken a sadistic mind to think up ways to keep the loas in check, and Vahn knew the type. It wasn't hard to think like one. Didn't take much trying, either. To keep a water loa from using their powers, all they needed to do was dry them out.

Deprivation worked in his favor. Having been ripped from the fire, all it wanted was to have him back. The borrowed heat from the flames in the hall weren't enough to assuage the hunger. His body tuned in to any hint of warmth, any promise of fire.

Drying things out took heat. Heat meant fire. And keeping a loa like Osawa in check would take an inferno.

# 14

## HOLDING STEADY

### OSAWA

WHILE VAHN and Haru were forced into the Palamidia by virtue of circumstance, Osawa joined the moment he realized his abilities were more than just an uncanny affinity for sailing and the skill to hold his breath under water for extended periods. He didn't have the rigorous training Haru had been gifted with throughout his youth, nor did he have anything similar to the life experience that Vahn or Kanna had been subjected to. Osawa had simply stepped off and signed up in hopes of finding a place to set his feet that didn't heave beneath them.

He hadn't thought he'd miss the Icaunian seas of his birth, with its open water and vast skies and all the blue nothing that went with it. Not once had he thought back to the floating cities of his childhood with anything more than a vague neutrality. His cell in Irkalla, however, made him nearly nostalgic. Hot, dry air had pumped through the vents, and he understood how sailors sometimes went mad on the seas and gorged themselves on saltwater. If a body had nothing, anything was a relief.

When Vahn had opened his door, leaning on the jam with a wink and a smirk, the fire that danced behind him felt cool against Osawa's skin.

Osawa trailed behind Haru and Vahn as they raced through the twisting labyrinth beneath the Tower. The water that Haru had managed to scrounge up barely made a dent in his thirst. His muscles felt like sludge and his side was a splitting ache. They took a turn in the maze, only to run into the bloody bodies of the last group that had been sent in after them.

Haru practically growled. He ran his hand through his hair as if he was going to tear it from the roots and began pacing the confined hallway.

"This is fantastic," Vahn said. "What now, your highness?"

"I need a moment to think," Haru replied.

"Sure, take your time. We're not trying to escape a death trap or anything."

In the silence that followed, Osawa bent over, one hand on his knee and the other on his stomach. He held back a retch, but his stomach had nothing to give up anyway.

"Why don't you ask your new friends?" Vahn asked.

Osawa straightened up in time to catch Haru's eyes narrowing at Vahn. Ghostlights hovered around Haru, even more having been gathered from the twisting mze. Haru turned to them, considering.

"I wasn't serious."

"Then stop wasting our time," Haru replied through gritted teeth.

Osawa sighed and shut his eyes as the argument continued. He breathed deep. There was a faint hint of fresh air, and it carried the scent of water. Osawa opened his eyes and began to follow it.

Haru and Vahn had been attempting to fight back to the entrance that they were originally taken through, but Osawa's trail led them deeper. As he moved forward, the ground inclined upward and the cells stopped appearing. The path narrowed to the point that they walked in single file. Osawa's shoulders scraped against jagged rock, and he could hear Haru grunt and shift as he sidled sideways through the narrow path.

Haru's ghostlights buzzed past Osawa, their white luster lighting the deep dark of the tunnel. They flitted back and forth over the group, sometimes wandering further ahead before returning to them. Eventually, the walls became slick with moisture and the path ended.

"I don't know about anyone else," Vahn said behind him, "but to me, this seems worse."

Osawa pressed his hands to the blank wall. He could feel the water on the other side, how the currents turned down in a rush and broke below, calming and eventually settling. "The waterfall that cuts into the river, it's here."

Haru's voice had a muffle to it when it reached him. "It isn't far from the stables."

Osawa turned back to the wall. "Perfect."

Every loa had a connection to their element, and it went both ways. The elements laid claim to a loa just as much as they used them, and Osawa was dry as desert bone. He reached past the wall to the fall on the other side and it reached back, slamming into the rock hard enough that it shivered beneath his hands. The water wove through the cracks of the rock and Osawa willed it to ice and expand.

Vahn wrapped his arm around Osawa's waist and pulled him back before a chunk of rock fell on him, stepping onto Haru's foot. The wall cracked, the solid stone turning to rubble and leaving enough room for them to pass through.

The light from the outside was bright and blinding after the dark of Irkalla and Osawa stumbled into the small cave hidden behind the waterfall with his arm over his eyes. His lungs took deep, gasping breaths of fresh, water drenched air.

The cave was shallow, but it was enough space that the three had some distance between each other once again. Through the cascade of water, the Tower rose through the verdant green backdrop of the Lugosian forests. The path had taken them away from it, but not far enough for comfort.

Osawa stretched out his hands beneath the waterfall. The force of it pounding against his skin was painful, but the cooling sensation in his body as the water moved into his parched skin was a relief. He pulled his hands back and scrubbed the dirt from them before reaching out again to gather a sip.

Haru approached next to him, leaning over the lee of the cave opening to gauge the distance. It was a decent drop, but Osawa could use his abilities to get them down easily enough. Before he could offer, Haru took a few steps back, then took a running leap from the lip of the cave.

Osawa's heart shot into his throat. He and Vahn leaned as far as they dared, following Haru's trajectory to his impact. Tense moments later he rose to the surface, then began to swim to the shore.

Not to be outdone, Vahn tightened the holsters for his knives then dove after Haru once he'd cleared from below.

"Well," Osawa said to himself. "That is one way to do it."

---

AFTER HARU and Vahn's individual leaps from the waterfall, Osawa used the currents to carry himself down at a more sedate pace. Despite that, they were all still soaked when they cut through the overgrown barrier forest of the east gardens, using the cover of the trees to make their way to the stables.

Occasionally Vahn would dart off the path, only to return with a leather travel bag. He had tossed the first to Osawa, the second to Haru. At the stables, he pried up a few floorboards from the tackroom and retrieved another bag, which he kept for himself.

Inside Osawa's was several changes of grey sweats, as well as a spare uniform, jacket and all, and every article of clothing was his own. The jacket was somewhat outdated, reminding Osawa of the time that his hadn't returned from the launderer and he had to have a new one fashioned. There were also tightly wrapped rations and crisp bills tucked in with a thin all-weather blanket and empty canteen.

Neither Osawa nor Haru asked Vahn why he had them, and as usual Vahn didn't offer any explanation for it. It wasn't a matter worth pressing. They peeled the ragged clothing they had worn in Irkalla from their bodies just as the comm that Haru had taken from the guards began to issue an alert.

Gathering their horses was the work of a moment and they'd set out.

Under the cover of the trees, the heavy underbrush slowed the horses. Still, Haru pushed Amon faster than wise. It would have almost been difficult to keep up with him if it weren't for the fact that Kanna's horse was hard to miss, even in the tree cover. Amon was huge, black as night with a blanket of small white spots that became more prominent along his hindquarters.

At the edge of the woods, Haru pulled his mount up until Vahn and Osawa were even with him.

"What now?" Osawa asked. Julius shifted beneath him and he

wobbled, still weak from his time in the prison. He threaded his fingers into the horse's dark mane to keep himself steady.

"We need to stay ahead of the civilian alerts." Vahn said. He reached forward, patting Mud's red-toned neck.

Haru nodded, his gaze trained on the city at the edge of the garden.

They needed to move. Through the streets wasn't an option, and back through the Tower was an even worse idea than leaping from a cliff. He turned Julius and nudged the mount along the outskirts of the trees. They could ford the river they had dove into and follow the banks on the opposite side of the city.

"We get out of Lugos," Osawa said. "What then?"

"I have a connection in Atarrabi," Vahn replied, nudging Mud to pull alongside Osawa. "She should be able to get us to Gegenes."

"Gegenes?"

Vahn and Osawa turned in their saddles when Haru spoke. He'd said little since they managed to escape Irkalla, and the exhaustion from his captivity and subsequent escape was starting to show. Since their punishments had been custom tailored to their powers, Osawa didn't want to think about what Haru had been subjected to.

Osawa noted that one of the ghostlights had remained with Haru, hovering near his shoulder, though Haru himself seemed unaware of its presence.

"I've kept an eye on things," Vahn said, turning so he wouldn't face either of them. "There were some disturbances in Adur a while back, but nothing notable recently."

Amon's hooves hit against the ground as Haru pushed him to catch up with the other two, then skittered when he was pulled back. The horse was ornery on his best days, and while it adored Kanna, it tolerated the rest of them. It made Osawa somewhat uncomfortable to have it at his back. Thankfully, Vahn reigned Mud in enough that they travelled in a scattered line.

"Gegenes has this place they call the Theatre," Vahn said. "They throw fighters against each other as entertainment."

"That's barbaric," Haru said.

"That's funny coming from the guy that took out his anger on Prospects every chance he got," Vahn said with a shrug. "Anyway, as I was saying, a new fighter showed up following some riot in an Adur town. Could be Kanna."

"What makes you think that?" Osawa ventured to ask.

"From the reports the fighter is about ten pounds of murder in a two pound bag."

Osawa turned enough to try and gauge Haru's reaction. His hands tightened on Amon's reins and the light at his shoulder flickered erratically. He turned to the woods, looking back to the Tower.

"Does anyone else think this was too easy?" Haru asked.

Vahn shrugged. "I wouldn't call the torture and fall from a cliff easy."

Osawa decided it best not to point out that the leap from the cliff was unnecessary. "The hard part will come later," he said instead.

"And what's the hard part, in your wise opinion?" Vahn quipped at his back.

It was Haru that answered. "Getting back in."

The sound of water reached Osawa's ears. Tages, the city near the Palamidia's compound, was built on the banks of a curving river, but it was mostly built on one side. If the trio travelled along the opposite bank, they could avoid the heavily trafficked areas of commerce by skirting through and around the scattered residences without having to move too far away from the faster paths out of the region.

At the bank of the river, Osawa dismounted, taking an extra moment to free his foot from the stirrup. Vahn came around Julius, taking the horse's reins.

Osawa took off his boots, slinging them over the saddle. He rolled his pants up the best he could and signalled for the others to do the same before stepping forward.

Ankle deep in the river, he shook out his hands and placed his palms on the surface, feeling the currents as they moved below. Water wasn't as stubborn as earth or as unpredictable as fire, but it came with its own set of guidelines. Water liked to move, but it wanted to go where it had always been. Convincing it to move in a different way was the trick to Osawa's abilities. It wasn't a battle of will so much as a negotiation.

He shut his eyes, reaching out through the water. He turned the currents, moving the flow in opposite directions. Slowly, the water began to recede. He didn't want to push it too far—he would have to hold it while they crossed.

Osawa began to move, Vahn following behind and leading their mounts. Haru came last, Amon prancing nervously.

Osawa kept his attention on the water until they arrived at the opposite bank. He let out his breath and the water careened back to its original path as Osawa fell, exhausted.

Amon shot past him, and he heard a yelp from behind. Haru hadn't made it out of the water fast enough and the waves had crashed around him, drenching him from his chest down.

Vahn burst into laughter while a sodden Haru glared.

"Well, it needed to happen sooner or later," Vahn choked out. "You smelled like a sewer."

Haru glared back at them. "Speak for yourselves."

"Excuse you?" Vahn said, aghast. "I smell like something went bad in a refrigerator."

Osawa righted himself, sitting on the dry bank. He grinned and flicked his wrist. The water rose up, dousing Haru again.

Vahn doubled over with laughter when Haru came back to the surface, sputtering for air. When Vahn straightened, he moved to Osawa and offered his hand.

"And Osawa smells like dried shrimp, which is kind of weird."

Haru pushed his hair out of his eyes, wading the rest of the way up the bank of the river. He peeled off the soaked shirt and wrung it out before retrieving a pair of the sweats that Vahn had packed.

Osawa took Vahn's offered hand. "Thank you so much for including me."

"Anytime," Vahn said with a wink, and pulled Osawa to standing. After, Vahn knelt down next to Osawa's horse, cupping his hands for Osawa to use as a boost to mount.

Osawa accepted the help. There wasn't any other way he would be able to get back into the saddle on his own. He had always been the weakest of the group. He was decent at hand-to-hand fighting, but using his abilities tired him out faster than the others. Vahn could make flames burst from nothing when he needed them, and Haru and Kanna were on a different level entirely. The scope of their abilities were a mystery to everyone. Sometimes, Osawa wondered if even they were aware of their capabilities.

A shrill whistle from Haru, and Amon crashing back through the underbrush. Haru mounted and they set off again, this time with the river between them and the bulk of the city.

Osawa kept his eyes ahead, but he could hear Haru behind him. Vahn had taken the lead, increasing their pace as the sun moved across the horizon. They moved into a full gallop for a short distance, but Vahn slowed the pace when the sun dipped low and threatened to set. Haru overshot them, though, and they had to catch up to him.

Osawa clung to Julius's neck. His legs had gone numb and his jaw ached from keeping it clenched. Vahn spurred Mud forward and cut off Amon, stopping in front of Haru. Osawa pulled Julius up several paces behind.

"Enough," Vahn said when their mounts settled. "We still have a full day ahead of us. We need the horses to make it to Atarrabi, unless you plan on walking through the plains."

Osawa walked his mount up, looking back. He could see the lights of the city in the distance, a haze against the night sky. Vahn dismounted and held Osawa's horse so he could follow suit. Osawa stumbled, his legs weak from moving the river and holding on to the horse. He leaned against the saddle, propping himself up.

"I'll take care of the horses," Vahn said. "Why don't you go cool off somewhere."

Haru dismounted, grabbed his pack, and stalked away, not sparing a word or a glance for either Vahn or Osawa.

"Don't go too far," Osawa managed to call, belatedly.

Under the cover of the trees, Osawa collapsed. He watched Vahn as he worked, removing the horse's saddles and bridles before tethering them into place. Out of one of his bags, Vahn took out a comb and began to brush them down.

Osawa was calm. He shouldn't be. He had committed treason. He deserted the Palamidia, the Tower. He'd worked hard for his position, followed orders he would have rather not, because the Palamidia had promised him solid ground.

As Vahn moved, Osaw could see the sharp angles of bones beneath the white of his shirt, and the way his shoulder hunched when he didn't think anyone was looking. Osawa could feel the currents in the near river, how they curved around Haru and his broken, sharp-edged anger.

And Osawa didn't feel like he'd betrayed anything.

# 15

## THE SHADOW'S CALL

### HARU

HARU'S MIND WAS BURNING. His nerves had been coiled taut since he'd lost Kanna, and the idea of having to be still a moment longer when there was finally a direction that would lead him to her angered him beyond reason. He knew enough to keep it in check, and take himself away from Vahn and Osawa.

At the bank of the river, he sorted through the pack that Vahn had given him. The single ghostlight he had retrieved from the lantern in his cell remained with him, and it lit the contents of the bag. Inside were Haru's own uniforms and sweats, his jacket neatly folded on the top of the pile. He pulled it out and shook it loose, finding it wasn't the one he had been wearing the last year. It was an older one that Vahn had apparently snuck out of his quarters, the longer jacket of the Second that he'd hung up when Kanna didn't return from her last mission.

He refolded it, careful not to crease the adornments, his fingers lingering on the shadowed sun that had become Kanna's emblem.

Turning away from the pack, Haru waded into the cold waters of the river until it was at his waist. He held his breath and ducked beneath the surface. Below, the current pulled against his body, trying to drag him away. He opened his mouth and screamed into the undertow, the air escaping his lungs, the water threatening to fill them.

When he couldn't stay beneath any longer he rose to the surface, gasping for air. His breath came out jagged, the sound disturbing the quiet of the night. When it stilled and settled, he set to work. Haru brushed his skin clean and rubbed his nails through his hair to remove the caked dust and blood. He ignored the chill, gritting his teeth against the cold.

It was well into the night when Haru climbed out of the river. He pulled the rough blanket from the pack to dry off before slipping into a new uniform set. He didn't don the jacket. There was a cool breeze in the air, but the night against his skin was a comfort.

He shifted his weight and bent his knees, his hands rising slowly. He had been practicing his forms in the dark, but he still felt stiff from being locked away. The technique required concentration, but after so many times it was as if his body knew the movements before he did. The light inside of him flowed as he shifted the power, bright against the edges of the night.

He felt the lingering tug, the leftover glimmer that anchored him to her.

The darkness was a reminder. It always called her forth. He had been in a prison since they'd met, the idea of her keeping him captive.

Haru had transferred to the Palamidia's Tower in Tages after passing the initial trials in his ancillary school. The Palamidia was sewing up the remaining pockets of resistance in Atarrabi at the time, and he and Osawa had arrived while many of the officers fought on the front.

With nothing else to do, he and his fellow transfers set to sparring among themselves. The rules of the Tower were brutal. It was the Prospects' responsibilities to keep the blood in their bodies, and the overseers left behind rarely interfered.

It didn't take long for Haru to stand out. He had been taught from childhood the methods of war, and he had been a natural even then. He was born built for combat, then honed and trained to move. He would watch his opponents, seeking out their weaknesses and exploiting them to his advantage.

There was nothing extraordinary about the match he had that day. He had long grown bored of the same opponents, and often took them out in mere moments just to have the fight finished. His peers would watch greedily, discussing his technique among themselves as they attempted to discover the weakness in him.

There wasn't one. Not until she arrived.

He hadn't noticed when the whispered conversations around the sparring amphitheatre silenced. When he finished his bout and turned back to the seats that surrounded the arena, no one was watching him.

Instead, everyone had turned, their eyes locked on the east entrance at the top of the stairs. Two officers had arrived, fresh from the front, their uniforms darkened with soot and blood. One was tall, his white hair and violet eyes a stark contrast against bronze skin, though Haru barely registered him.

The other stood a step ahead of him, the top of her head not even reaching the other officer's shoulder, her gaze locked on Haru.

The waiting Prospects held their silence. No one knew who the officers were, but the sight of the blood spattered against the white of their uniforms was arresting. Vahn wasn't yet the Saint, the buttons at his jacket loose to show the bloodied armor beneath. Over his shoulder he had looped the collar of another jacket around his finger.

Kanna inclined her head to Vahn, who leaned down to her. A whisper passed between them and he straightened and nodded, his knowing smirk fading to confusion before correcting itself.

Kanna shoved her hands in her pockets, her shoulders somehow both back and slouched at the same time as she made her way down, one calculated step at a time, to the sparring arena.

Her eyes were the sky promising a storm. The light gathered around her, curling like a halo around her body as she moved. The time it took to reach him was both eternal and an instant, and when she stood before him he was already done.

Haru couldn't look away.

Before him, she tilted her head, the endless grey of her eyes studying him. She was so close he could see the scattered freckles over the bridge of her nose and the scar bisecting her right eyebrow. The ring of black around her irises that pulsed with the beat of her heart, and in them he could sense the anger inside of her, the smothered depths of it, and it called to his own.

She paced around him, the same smooth skulk from before. He stood still, unable to breathe, turning his head in an attempt to follow her. After circling him she stopped, then looked over to Vahn. He had followed her to the edge of the sparring area, the toes of his boots grazing the mats. Vahn met her gaze and shrugged.

Haru felt a flare of resentment for the man that had taken her attention away from him, but it was short lived. Kanna turned back to Haru, flicking her eyes over him.

"What are you?" she asked.

The words hit him like a kick in the teeth, bringing him crashing back to reality. Before he could find an answer, the side door of the arena opened behind Kanna.

The Legatus's guards entered first, fanning out and stepping to the side as Velinius appeared. From the corner of his eye Haru saw a shift in Vahn, as if he was bracing for an attack.

Haru knew he should have stepped back. He didn't move.

"Ananke," Velinius said. "I was waiting for your report."

Kanna's eyes slid to the side, her body belatedly following the movement as she turned. The line between her shoulders straightened, her spine grew rigid, but she didn't remove her hands from her pockets.

"Veil," she said, a false brightness in her tone that bordered on mockery. "I was on my way to see you."

"You found interrupting the Prospects' practice more important?" Velinius asked, her voice laced with reprimand and cold condescension. Vahn stepped onto the mats, moving back to Kanna's side. He slid the jacket from his shoulder and shook it out, holding it up. Kanna slipped her arms into the sleeves and shrugged it on.

Haru held his breath and his ground. The Second's jacket reached past her knees, heavy with the embroidered weight of victories. A shockwave moved through him with the realization. The Legatus's Second was a legend, spoken about in hushed whispers across the Empire. She was the only loa of her kind, a deathless creature thrust upon the world. They said you could find her by her eyes, that she didn't have a soul to color them.

Kanna pulled the hair out of her collar and let it fall down her back before shoving her hands back into her pockets. She glanced over her shoulder at Haru, her scarred brow quirked.

They were right about one thing. It was in her eyes.

"Maybe," she said.

The legend slunk after Velinius, her steps hissing as she dragged her heels across the mats. Vahn followed, his long legs eating up the distance. When she disappeared behind the guards, she took a part of Haru with her.

Haru opened his eyes, taking a shuddering breath and grounding himself. To his back were the forests of Lugos, and ahead were the grasslands of Atarrabi. She was somewhere beyond them, just out of reach. As always, she was wherever the light went when the shadows came to call.

# 16

## DENIAL

### KANNA

IN THE DEEP calm of the night, Kanna paced the roof of the barracks. She slid her feet over the debris, kicking aside small stones and listening as they clattered in the quiet. The slight night breeze caught in the wind-tower that rose from the center of the flat roof, and she turned and shut her eyes, listening as it whistled softly through the vents and was carried into the building below.

A tuft of grass had managed to lodge itself into the dirt on the roof and grow in spite of the conditions, and she squatted near it. A long stalk grew from the center of the array, its end bristling with soft seeds that the wind was meant to carry. She kneeled on the rough ground and tipped a broken tile nearby up and over, but there wasn't anything beneath it.

Kanna shifted back to her heels and looked around her. She crawled to the short barrier walls at the outsides of the roof and squinted. She drew one of her knives and ran the tip of it down a long crack that had formed in the wall, then tried to peer closer into it. With a breath she attempted to clear the dust but it blew back into her face.

The seeking was nothing more than habit at this point, but one that she couldn't shake. She didn't know what she was looking for, didn't know if she wanted to find it, but she couldn't stop even if she tried.

Kanna sat back, rubbing her eyes to clear the grit from her lashes.

She was both relieved and disappointed that she hadn't found anything, and she wasn't sure how those things existed inside of her at the same time but they did.

After blinking the last of the sand from her eyes, she looked up. The dark of night was never pure. It was littered with lights, burning somewhere so far away that she couldn't wrap her mind around the distance. For all she knew, the hearts of them could have long gone out. The light was still a constant, a reminder that something is always left behind.

Kanna sighed, then leveraged herself up from the ground. She dusted off the palms of her hands and paced the roof until she found a clear space. Here, she set her feet. She shut her eyes, and let out her breath before inhaling again, deep, feeling the air in her lungs and the night in her veins. Properly settled, she began.

Her body moved through the motions of the routine, knew each step to take. She reached out her hand and her weight shifted forward then back as she withdrew and turned.

The Governor's invitation was the first thought to return to her mind. It nagged at her, even as she tried to clear herself from the distraction. There was too much pull to him, too much champing for acknowledgement from the world. Hautman's greed was simple, which made it dangerous. He wanted power, wealth, things to fill his home and wear on his neck and wrists to show everyone that he was someone important, someone who should be revered. Kanna was a prize he could stand before proudly, an anomaly of the universe that he could parade for favor. The heavy familiarity of it soured in the back of her throat.

People were always taking from others. Always desperate to fill some yawning ache inside of them. She'd seen it over and over again, and what she had learned from the world she had woken to was that everyone was rotting for the want of something.

She wasn't so different from them in that way.

Her foot lifted from the heel. She stepped and set it forward, shifting her weight to her toes and then back. Her muscles burned with the slow restraint. They wanted to move faster, to strike hard and true. Even in the quiet, her body wanted to fight. It wanted to attack. It was as greedy as Hautman, but it knew what it wanted, and it terrified her. The scars on her body weren't from a life well lived, she knew. There had to be a reason why her instinct was to hurt, why the single moment she had that was anything like a memory was of violence.

She didn't want to know the reason.

Her hands swept through the air and she felt the breeze traveling between her fingers, sensed the shadows as they curled and bent around her form.

Kanna didn't know what she wanted except everything, anything, something her hands could grasp and hold and not break. Since she couldn't have that, she would take peace. But she couldn't have that, either.

Her hands cut through the air, her feet turned, and her thoughts slowly cleared. There was nothing left but her, in this place, in this body that moved confidently, precisely, knew without knowing where each step she took would lead, how her hands would follow, when her lungs should breathe.

When her first routine ended, her body found another. It moved quicker, turned sharper. Her heels dug into the ground and the debris scraped against the roof.

She finished breathless, her muscles burning. She listened to the rasp of her lungs in the dark, felt the slight tremor of her fingers and her heart beating and knew she was alive.

She opened her eyes to the world again and turned them skyward.

The stars clustered in long sweeps. Those branching arms of galaxies reached across infinity, but in the vastness of the sky there was a gaping distance between all of them. They were beautiful, and they were alone. She wondered if they knew the light of each other, or if they, too, were lost in the black.

# 17

# FATE'S PATIENCE

## ISCO

THE ROOM ASTAR deposited Isco in had felt large at first, but as time ticked by the walls shrunk around him. After having paraded him in the Theatre and the streets then leaving him here, Isco had yet to receive a visit or an invitation. Meals were delivered to him, but otherwise he had only himself for company.

Isco walked the halls of the second floor where he was staying, noting the sitting rooms, a small library, and other spare bedrooms, but didn't wish to intrude further into the Governor's home.

In the bath attached to his room, he took another shower in an attempt to further wash away the grit of Gegenes and the sweat of panic that soured on his skin. It left him refreshed, at least physically, but after he had nothing else to bide his time with before the Governor's planned dinner.

Digging through the night stand in the room, Isco found the now familiar box of matches and deck of cards. He sat on the bed and shuffled, the cards bending at the corners and dropping from his hands to mock his awkward attempts to keep them under control.

Isco never spent time on card games. The decks had been used by the ancients to divine futures and though the gods were dead and gone and those old practices were buried with them, he didn't need to draw the ire of any remnants of a vengeful fate. As it stood, he had his hands full with coincidence.

That didn't mean he didn't know how to play. Games of Palamedes were ubiquitous and inescapable, popular for passing time with friends or gambling the night away in bars. It was a game of strategy and trick, and his fellow students at the university had often played to unwind while covertly testing what they viewed as their competition.

There was also a version that could be played alone, for those that weren't exactly welcome in group settings. Isco flipped the Legatus card between his fingers. The ultimate trump. He considered it for a moment, the suns in the center overlapping and shifting direction until they appeared as an eye, then tucked it into the stack.

After attempting another shuffle, Isco set a board in front of him and kept the deck in hand, his fingers worrying over the creases along the sides where the cards met. For hours, he worked on the game, hoping it would either distract him from his thoughts or give his mind the chance to sort through events that had led him here, to this moment, playing a fool's game in the home of a brutal Governor, while somewhere else in these same walls an omen was preparing to sit at a dinner table with him.

If this was a new ploy by the Palamidia, it didn't make sense as to why now, why here, deep within the territory of Gegenes. After the decimation of Cardea in Adur, a tentative peace had settled in Lifrasir. The Palamidia turned its focus inward, uniting and building up their already claimed territories. They had even pulled back the front lines, with Atarrabi serving as an unspoken neutral buffer between the Solarian Empire and the three remaining independent regions.

Governor Hautman didn't seem concerned about an encroaching attack. There was no real milita from what Isco had seen, the once proud Gegenii fighters reduced to mercenaries and entertainers.

Perhaps the woman had deserted. She was a loa, he was certain of that, and the hardest lesson had learned was that a Palamidia loa was never alone. The Cardea had believed her to be helpless, only to be struck down by the terrifying force that arrived in her wake.

She had commanded him with a single word.

She had saved Isco's life.

It was a stalemate. Isco didn't know where to move, couldn't even if he tried. He swept his hands over the cards, scattering them across the room. He covered his face with his hands and sighed, flopping back onto the pile of pillows at the head of the bed.

A knock sounded on the door. He removed his hands from his eyes, registering the fading light of day. He stood and stretched, trying to ease the tension in his limbs, before opening the door.

Instead of a servant as expected, he found himself facing Astar again. She was wearing what he was coming to know as her usual mischievous grin, this time accompanied by a deeper blue wrap. Gold threads snaked over the fabric, curling into intricate leaf patterns. Her eyes flickered over him.

"You're wearing that?"

"It isn't like I have anything else." Isco pulled down the hem of his waistcoat to smooth any perceived wrinkles. "And not everyone has the chromas for fancy dresses."

"I didn't take you for someone who spent money on fancy dresses," Astar quipped.

She looked past him at the room and the scattered cards, her brow rising. Her eyes traveled to the few that had scattered near the doorway and she bent to retrieve one. Her easy grin returned.

"Looks like I win," she said, turning the card to reveal the Legatus.

Isco whipped the card from her hand and bent to frantically gather the rest. Finally retrieving the mess from the room, he straightened the deck as best he could and set it back in the nightstand.

"Oh," Astar exclaimed behind him, and he jumped. "You look wonderful," she said, leaving the threshold in a flurry of silk.

Isco crept to the doorway.

"I mean," Astar said, "I know I do good work, but not this good."

Standing in the hall was the Harbinger. Kanna was clothed in a nude fabric that was only a few shades deeper than the unusual porcelain of her skin. The shoulder of the gown was stitched with beads of varying sizes and shades of red that caught the light. Despite the fact that she was cleaned of dirt and blood, the dress lent itself to the illusion of it, turning violence into a strange beauty.

It was no wonder the Gegenii were so enthralled with her. The cut of the dress did little to mask the long healed scar between the curve of her neck and shoulder or the crudely stitched gash on her upper arm, but she stood with a practiced ease and simple confidence. Her deep red hair was braided back, which brought attention to the striking grey of her eyes.

"I knew that would suit you," Astar said.

Kanna trained her inscrutable gaze on Astar. "I will have to take your word for it."

Astar clapped her hands, then linked her arm with Kanna's. She pulled them around, turning away. The back of Kanna's dress was open, coming together at her waist. The scar on her shoulder reappeared along her back, ending abruptly just before reaching her spine.

"That's Isco, the guy father invited," Astar said as an afterthought, waving in his general direction.

Kanna turned her head just enough that she could see Isco over her shoulder.

"Kanna, right?" Isco asked, struggling to keep his voice from betraying the fact that his heart was leaping at the bottom of his throat.

Her eyes flicked from his toes to his face, but Isco there was no recognition in them. His pulse stilled, bracing itself for an attack.

"Why are you here?" she asked.

Isco swallowed as his heart hammered back to life in warning.

"He came to meet you," Astar said, unknowingly saving Isco from himself.

Kanna's brow arched and she turned her gaze away from him and back to Astar.

"The Theatre," Isco hurried to correct, grasping for the easiest lie. "I came to see the Theatre."

"Which is pretty much just Kanna at this point," Astar said without missing a beat.

Kanna didn't respond as Astar pulled her along. Isco followed them as they took the stairs, watching Kanna. She shifted her gaze around her surroundings, the slightest tilt of her head the only indication. Although she appeared relaxed, bored even, it was a practiced. She was on high alert, scoping out her environment without giving herself away.

As they passed through the foyer at the bottom of the stairs Kanna stopped. Astar was tugged back, not having realized that Kanna had halted so abruptly.

The room's walls were bursting with murals, one bleeding into the next. Older paint had faded with an aged warmth, but newer ones bordered on garish. Isco recognized some of the scenes. There were the stories of creation and the fall of the gods, some obscured and reinvented into newer work.

Tengri's trials morphed into a battlefield. Astar followed Kanna's gaze. "It's the battle of Ganglere," she offered. A few soldiers in white stood on earthen walls, facing what should have been insurmountable waves of fighters. "The last time the Independents faced the Palamidia on a large scale."

"But we lost," Isco said. He clamped his mouth shut. It was a stupid thing to say. Everyone knew that.

Astar nodded. "Spectacularly."

Kanna's gaze was steady, her body still.

"Then why is there a painting of it?" Isco asked, partially to fill the tense silence and partially out of true curiosity.

Astar shrugged. "Beats me why he does the things he does."

They stood that way long enough that Astar's offhand disinterest shifted to concern. When Kanna didn't move on her own, Astar tugged her arm and broke her trance.

"Come on," Astar said, almost gently. "Father will be waiting."

# 18

# THE CARDEA'S GIFT

## KANNA

THE GOVERNOR'S murals continued into the hall, their shifting colors calling to Kanna. As they trekked to the dining room the unfinished paintings became rough outlines and slashes of charcoal, empty suggestions of stories that were threateningly close to familiar. Astar's steady hand in the crook of her elbow kept Kanna moving forward through the incessant pull of the images.

At the threshold of the dining hall, they finally ceased. This hall was washed in a solid, imposing merlot, though subtle fissures in the walls hinted at hidden entrances. The cavernous room boasted a barrel vaulted ceiling, and a dark wood table stretched through its center.

A servant detached himself from the wall to pull out Astar's seat at the left of the head of the table. Before the man could scurry around the side, Kanna dragged the chair opposite Astar out and slouched into it gracelessly.

The man fumbled, attempted to recover and aid in adjusting the seat, but Kanna cast a glare at him and he jumped back.

The entire place set Kanna's nerves alight. The Governor's manse was dripping with color and sound. Even the walls screamed at her, causing her head to pound and her side to ache. Her fingers itched for her knives but Astar had taken them, citing etiquette.

Isco settled next to Astar just as the wall opposite of where they had entered slid open.

"Welcome!" The Governor's voice boomed in the near empty hall. Astar looked over her shoulder and back at Kanna, rolling her eyes in a kind of apology.

It didn't bother Kanna. She didn't mind loud people. Either it was because they were hiding something, or because they couldn't. Everything about Hautman was false, from the white of his teeth to the frozen grin that pulled at the corners of his lips, contorting his face but never quite reaching his eyes. After settling into his seat, Hautman placed his hands on the table.

Kanna glared at the paw that had invaded her space and shifted her weight, dragging her chair against the floor with a long screech.

Hautman cleared his throat, which served as an unvoiced command for the servants to begin their tasks.

The longer Kanna sat in the dining hall, the more uncomfortable she became. She didn't like the way the dark walls shifted as the servants entered and disappeared, shuffling through hidden pathways, and the constant movement and interchanging of staff made it hard to discern their locations or intentions.

She also found it difficult to tell them apart from one another. They were dressed in matching outfits, dark skinned and mostly grey-haired. She tried to track them by their eyes but they were either green or deep brown, all worn in the same way, and their faces shifted and interchanged into an unbroken obscurity.

A woman circled the table, setting down silver mugs at each seat, followed by a man who poured dark wine. Kanna reached for the heavy cup, the thick hammered metal cool to the touch. She watched Hautman take a deep pull from his before lifting her own for a drink.

"So, Isco," Hautman said, his voice booming. "I am curious to know how my dear friends in Adur are faring now."

Isco choked on his drink, gulping air to clear his throat. "Yes," he croaked out, "our friends."

Astar kept her eyes on her drink. "Your friends in the Cardea?" she asked lightly, not moving her gaze.

The name stuck in Kanna's ears, clanged around empty spaces and lit on broken pathways.

Isco said, "They are... fine?"

Astar set her cup down, the silver hitting the wood with a solid thud. She leaned her elbow on the table, turning her head to face him. "I thought you were from the Camarilla Group."

"I, yes, them, too, as well," Isco fumbled, "are fine."

Astar leaned back. "You came to see the Theatre, right?"

"He came because I invited him, daughter," Hautman interrupted. "I wanted to meet the One Who Lived."

Kanna turned her eyes back to the table. She still hadn't figured out her place in this beyond being a trophy to display, and she had no desire to join a conversation that could continue easily without her.

"That's a pretty ominous title," Astar said. Her tone was suspicious, but Astar was nothing if not curious. Astar saw people as mysteries waiting to be solved. Kanna was Astar's favorite project and, so far, her greatest failure.

Isco shifted. "So is 'the Harbinger,'" he deflected.

Kanna traced a finger along the gold embroidery that bordered the cloth over the table. She could feel the attention in the room on her. "I did not give it to myself."

"That's right," Astar said, reclaiming the conversation and drawing attention away from Kanna once more. "I did. Neat, don't you think?"

"It has been great for the Theatre, daughter," Hautman said, "but I was speaking."

Astar crossed her arms at her chest and leaned back heavily in her chair.

Plates were laid in front of the group, each one portioned and set. Kanna frowned and lifted her fork. She pushed the meal around, the metal tines scraping against the plate. The rich smells curdled in her stomach.

"As I was saying," Hautman said after waving away the servants. "Years ago, I had a bit of a rapport with a group in Adur, the Cardea. They did great things, really helped the people. Of course, most of their research was about loas."

Isco lifted his fork and busied himself with his plate.

"I guess the Palamidia didn't like that, though," Hautman continued. He sighed, his smile turning into a bereaved grimace. "They wiped out most of the Cardea. An entire faction just gone, slaughtered, isn't that right Isco?"

The silence coming from Isco was palpable. He didn't even seem to be breathing.

Kanna put her fork down. She straightened it, lining the bottom up with the edge of the table. She reached for the cup as Astar did and pressed the metal against her mouth, tilting it back. She kept her lips sealed, not allowing the liquid to pass.

Astar set the cup down, and Kanna followed the movement. Astar propped her elbows on the table and twined her fingers. She rested her chin on them but stared into her cup. "Yes, Father, please continue," she said, disdain dripping from her words.

Astar's boldness brought a small smile to Kanna's features, but she was distracted by the designs on the tablecloth. She continued to trace the gold threads. She knew they didn't mean anything, but she thought that they should.

"Isco here was the lone survivor of the Palamidia's attack," Hautman said.

The gold whirls on the cloth blurred at the seams. Kanna slid her eyes to the side when new servants appeared. They didn't carry themselves like the others. These were alert, aware. They stepped to the side after entering and kept their backs against the wall.

"Lucky for me, they sent a gift many years ago."

Isco's attention snapped to Hautman. "What are you talking about?"

"What do you mean, medicus?" Hautman responded, though it wasn't a question. "I believe it was of your design."

Kanna's lips tingled, then burned. She pressed her fingers against them.

It was familiar.

Hautman leaned over, his voice unnervingly close. "How was your drink, Harbinger? I added a little something, just for you. Of course, I didn't trust that you would drink. But a loa only needs to touch it. We, what do you call us? Ungifted? Aren't so susceptible."

The walls around her pulsed. Somewhere deep in her shattered mind, a memory shuddered and knocked.

Isco shot to his feet. "What have you done?"

Kanna shut her eyes tight, covering her mouth with her hand. Her fingers didn't want to move. A phantom of pain shot through her hands, and she could almost hear the sound of bones snapping. She stood, her hands tangling in the silk of the gown and coming up empty. The nude fabric was a skin she couldn't move in. The heavy chair she had sat in fell back as the new servants rushed forward.

Keepers, not broken cogs like the others. She should have known, should have been better.

Kanna's instinct had always been to fight. She ducked under the first guard's arm and tried to roll away, but he stepped on the folds of her dress. Her legs tangled in it, her joints becoming looser every second.

"Did you really think me such a fool?" Hautman said, his voice rising as he stood. "As if I wouldn't recognize one of your kind?"

Astar screamed, leaping from her chair and rushing to Kanna, but another guard grabbed her from behind, pinning her arms and dragging her away as she kicked the air.

"All these stories passed around Lifrasir are meant to keep us in line," Hautman continued.

Kanna yanked the fabric of the dress and it ripped, tripping the guard that had held it in place. She made it to her feet.

"You are nothing, Harbinger," Hautman was screaming now, his fists slamming against the wood. "You are human, like the rest of us."

Arms wrapped around Kanna's waist and pulled her down into a tackle. Two others grabbed her arms. She bucked against them but their weight kept her pinned. She couldn't get her limbs to align, couldn't get them to do the only thing they had ever been good for and fight.

"Stop!" Isco leaped across the table, the plates scattering and drinks spilling. "You'll bring him down on us all!"

He tried to pull at one of the guards that had Kanna pinned, but another shoved him back into the heavy table.

"You don't understand," Isco said, his voice panicked and pleading. "He'll come for her."

There was a sharp sting in her neck.

Kanna's body stopped listening first.

Then her mind stopped.

The darkness moved across her vision, then closed in, and there was nothing.

# 19

# NEITHER HERE NOR THERE

KANNA KEPT HER BODY STILL, listening for anything that would give her a warning as to what she had woken to but there was only silence. A remarkable silence. There was no shuffle of feet, no sound of breath, and no low thrum of intention rattling against her bones.

Wherever she was, it shouldn't exist.

The chill on her skin registered, colder where her back lay against rough stone. She opened her eyes, slowly at first, then snapped them open. Above her was once a dome, the supporting metalwork criss-crossing against an ink black sky glutted with pinpricks of light. Whatever roof had once been was mostly gone. Panels were missing, and the rest was cracked glass, the fractures running between the stars like an ill-conceived constellation map. Kanna had often turned to the sky, spent entire nights watching and waiting, but there was not a single beacon above that she could recognize.

Tearing her eyes away, she rose and attempted to get her bearings. The windows of the place were long gone, their arched frames open to the vast nothingness of the barren landscape. She took in the grey walls of the cavernous room, how they glinted in the star light as only Ilazkin stone could.

They reminded her of the temple she had sheltered in when she first woke, alone and empty. With her only thought on survival, she'd hunched against the tearing storm winds that drove the cold deep into her bones until she reached the once sacred ruin.

It was that temple, but it wasn't at the same time. With a start, she realized she was dressed in white. She ran her hand along the sleeve of the long jacket, upwards to the shoulders, her fingers skimming over the intricate embroidery.

The weight of it was unbearable. She yanked at the cloying jacket, struggling to free herself. It tangled against her body, clinging to her like another skin. When she finally ripped herself from it she tripped, her knees scraping against the hard stone.

Kanna shut her eyes, curling her fingers against the rough ground as the echoes of her struggle subsided. She could feel the pain in her knees, the cold of the stones, but something was wrong.

She breathed deep, filling her lungs. The air was cold and crisp, but her breath fogged in the cold only because it should, because it once had. She pressed her hand to her chest and her lungs expanded, but she couldn't feel the air.

Deeper inside of her, there was a hollow where the darkness lived. The clawed thing inside of her was gone, leaving behind an empty chamber. It wasn't inside of her. It was everywhere. Before she could figure out what that could mean, the lilting echo of a laugh reached her ears.

"Hello?" she called, tentative at first, as she rose to her feet.

The laugh rang out again, sharp and bitter and close. Kanna turned, trying to trace the source of the sound. It was both familiar and foreign. Like the rest of this place, it was a part of something she remembered, but not the whole of it.

The skitter of rock outside set her feet in motion. She ran toward the sound, not wanting to be alone in this place again. As she crossed the threshold of the temple she found herself in an open field and she slipped, spinning her arms to keep her balance. Beneath the thick sheet where she stood, plumes of white were frozen under the clear surface, like gasps of air suspended in time. The wind picked up, blowing shards of ice against her skin.

She needed to retreat.

Kanna turned around, but the temple was gone.

WHEN HARU WOKE, there was light. He could feel it against his body but it was different, distant and somewhat alive. The sound of birdsong reached his ears but it was muffled and discordant, like a recording of someone's impression of birds. Blades of grass brushed between his fingers, his sleeping mat absent. With a surge he rolled to his feet and reached for the knives at his side.

He stood ready, but alone. Haru relaxed his grip on his knives as he turned, taking in the smattering of trees within the grove and the smooth white path that wound between them. He recognized it, or something like it. It was a facsimile of the gardens near the Tower, but blurred and off-kilter. The sound was wrong, for one. There were no birds near the Tower, and the spindly grey tree that had fallen across the path before he'd ever arrived was rooted, its blossoms blood red.

He was off the main path, down what should have been the cobbled offshoots of the garden. Further along it should become wild, the walkway disappearing as the garden twisted east.

He sheathed his knives. He was in the Neither. Which meant she was here. It was Kanna's place, after all. It had not opened to him since she'd gone, but now it was proof that his hope had not been misplaced.

Just before he took a step onto the path to head east, the ghostlight that had followed him from the Tower zipped past his shoulder and ahead. It stopped before disappearing from his sight and hovered, waiting.

As he moved further along, the area became more familiar, shifting closer to its known counterpart. Time passed with every step and the path began showing the wear of neglect. Grass grew and died in the cracks that formed in the white walkway, and the light began to dim, the overcast grey of the sky sliding into a fogged haze.

A cold wind blew across his skin from somewhere else, calling him. He shut his eyes, breathing it in and hoping it would bring him closer to where he needed to be.

When he opened his eyes, the sky was dark. The ghostlight was still with him, now circling a statue in the center of the path. It wasn't anything he had seen before. It was partially ruined, the arm broken off, the base fractured. The face of it was lit by the glimmering ghostlight, which illuminated the crack that ran from the temple, the fissures in the stone splintering down the body.

The face was Kanna's. He moved closer, reaching out to it. As his fingers brushed the cold statue it crumbled beneath his touch, and the pieces fell in a cascade at his feet. He clenched his fist, his thumb running over the scar between his thumb and forefinger in an attempt to resist the urge to gather the pieces and try to force it back together. He could neither scream nor fight, not here, not like this. He could only move and witness.

There was nothing else anymore. Just an endless grey nothingness stretching out around him, illuminated only by the single glimmering light.

He shut his eyes again, taking a steadying breath to calm himself and focus. He needed to think of something that would resonate with her, a moment that would scar.

He let out his breath, trying not to let it shake, and stepped blind into the void.

# WELL TRAVELED

## OSAWA

OSAWA HADN'T SEEN many other cities in peacetime besides the one that housed his ancillary academy and Tages, the capital where the Tower resided. There were the floating Icaunian villages of his childhood, but those weren't even cities, really, just flat-bottomed rafts moored haphazardly together.

Where Lugos was clean and brisk, Atarrabi was hot and loud. After the Palamidia had forced the surrender of the Atarrabi sultans, the population that remained settled into a handful of smaller cities. They were quick built of wood and sun-hardened clay, not quite square and so leaning against each other at jutting angles. Atarrabi had always taken advantage of the narrow plot that it ran through the center of Lifrasir to move trade, and battered signs advertised local and import goods.

Their Palamidia uniforms were a beacon in the mess of primary colors the Atarrabians favored. Atarrabi was the last region to fall, and the people still distinctly remembered a time before. The Empire's hold on the area was tenuous, especially after Kanna recalled the soldiers from the area.

"We should find a place to stay," Vahn said, pulling Mud up next to Osawa.

Between them, Haru slumped, corpse like, over Amon's neck. The morning after they'd escaped the Tower, Haru wouldn't wake. Something inside of him has slipped away in the night. It had happened before. Not long after Kanna left for Ilazki, Haru had collapsed. The medicus had no explanation for it. He didn't wake for days, but he did wake, eventually.

"Do you have any suggestions?" Osawa asked.

Vahn had taken Haru's slumber in stride, as he did with most things, and Osawa had agreed that it was better to try and move forward than to have to tell Haru they had lost days of travel. They had decided it would be best to get Haru onto the horse and tie him down, but the idea was better in theory than in practice.

"No," Vahn answered. "Why would I?"

On the first attempt, the pair had lifted Haru's boneless body onto Amon, only to have him slide off the other side of the horse and hit the ground with a weighted thud. The second attempt spooked Amon, and the horse took off into the trees. It took Vahn several hours to coax Kanna's cranky beast back.

Eventually, they figured out a system. Both of them would lift Haru's body up, and Osawa would run around Amon, avoiding the horse's gnashing teeth, to make sure Haru didn't tip from the other side while Vahn shoved him into place.

"You are from here," Osawa said.

"I was, once," Vahn said, decidedly not looking at Osawa. "But I don't think you'd like the beds I could direct you to."

As usual, Vahn had found a way to lash out. Osawa was well acquainted with his double-edged quips. Osawa focused instead on a rusted sign with two birds, their necks entwined. It swung from chains that whined with each slight breeze that passed. "That place looks decent."

Vahn's brow wrinkled. "Two Swan Inn," he said. "The pun could use some work."

Vahn nudged the horses toward the entrance of the building and dismounted, taking hold of both Mud and Amon's leads. "There's a stable attached. I'll put the horses up and bring the baggage around back."

"Do you mean Haru?"

"We can't drag an unconscious Palamidia officer through the front door," Vahn replied. "I mean, we could. But we probably shouldn't."

Osawa decided it was better to not argue with Vahn this time. He was tired, and the promise of an actual bed was calling him. He dismounted, handing over Julius's reins.

Walking was harder than Osawa remembered. His body wanted to move in time with something else, and his legs were wobbly from the ride. Still, he managed to make it through the door of the boarding house with most of his dignity intact.

The room he entered was gloomy at best. Spots flashed at the corners of his eyes as things came into focus. The architecture was simple and worn, nothing like the clean elegance he was used to in Lugos. The interior was a rough unfinished wood and there were few windows to let in the natural light. The scattered furniture was mismatched, and a fine layer of dust settled on every surface.

Osawa shoved his hands deep in the pockets of his coat, pulling it closer to his body in the same motion. He stepped lightly across the room to the check-in desk, which appeared as abandoned as the front room. He tapped the bell on the counter with one finger before yanking his hand back.

There was a cough from around a corner, accompanied by an older gentleman. His skin was dark and wrinkled, and Osawa was relieved that the man didn't tower over him like Vahn did.

The man's amber eyes narrowed, taking in the cut of Osawa's jacket. "Help you?"

Osawa cleared his throat. "We would like lodgings for the night, sir," he said, keeping his voice even. He didn't want to speak down to the man, but he wasn't going to cow, either.

The man looked over Osawa's shoulder at the empty lounge. "We? Just see you, son."

"My partner will be joining me."

"Ah." The man reached below the counter, pulling out a cardboard box and dropping it. Its contents jangled, and he began sorting through the tangle of keys. "Thirty a night," the man said, mostly to the box.

"That seems a bit high."

"It's the price," the man grunted, pulling out one of the keys and sliding it across the counter.

Osawa reached out to take it, but the man slammed his hand over the key, holding the other out. Osawa handed the man his payment in crisp bills from Vahn's stash and pocketed the key.

The hall to the rooms was dark, the lamps lining the wall dormant in the daytime. Osawa followed it to a rickety door at the back of the building. He unlatched it, checking over his shoulder when the disused catch grated against itself.

When Osawa opened the door, he had to blink once more as the bright day seared his vision. Vahn had Haru's body half-leaning against the building, one of the unconscious man's arms around his shoulder. There was dirt on one side of Haru's uniform, evidence that Vahn had likely shoved him off Amon and let his body fall wherever it landed.

Together they managed to drag Haru up the flight of stairs to the room that Osawa had acquired, dumping him onto the bed of the first one they managed to open.

Vahn stepped back, stretching his back and frowning down at Haru's still form.

"Now what?" Osawa asked.

Vahn stretched his back then let his arms fall at his sides. "Watch him. There's someone I need to meet."

"Right," Osawa said, flattening his voice despite his concern. "Who?"

Vahn nodded. "Hopefully someone that can cut our travel time, I just have to convince her it's a smart move on her part."

"And if she isn't convinced?"

Vahn smirked, though it didn't quite reach his eyes. "She will be."

# 21

# NO LAUGHING MATTER

## ISCO

THIS WAS the last place that Isco wanted to be. The wings of the Theatre were built to hold the fighters that waited for their bouts, whether or not they stepped onto the sands willingly. After trying to stop the Governor's guards at the dinner, he was forced into chains himself, locked in a cell next to Kanna, the only thing between them rusted bars.

She was still dressed for a banquet, the silk dress torn and stained with dirt from when the Keepers dragged her through the tunnels. They could have easily carried her, but Isco had a feeling the dragging was meant as a humiliation.

Not that it mattered. Kanna still slept, her breath slow and cold. Isco couldn't figure out why she hadn't woken up yet. Even when the Keepers dropped her in a heap and dragged the shackles around her wrists and ankles, she remained boneless. He again reached through the bars to check her pulse. It was there, faint but even.

At first Isco assumed it was a ruse, but she hadn't stirred by morning, or the night. Isco shifted her shackles, sliding them into new positions so they wouldn't wear sores into her skin.

There was nothing else he could do. He crouched onto his heels, resting his hands on his knees as familiar footsteps sounded. Astar visited multiple times a day. Every moment trapped with his nightmare was an eternity, so at least her arrivals meant that time was passing.

"She still sleeping?"

Isco nodded, rocking back and sitting on the floor. "As your father requested."

The glare that Astar shot at him could have cut diamonds, but Isco had seen worse. Worse was breathing in the cell next to him. Worse could wake up at any moment. And still worse would rain down if she didn't.

Isco turned away from Astar. "Why do you keep coming here?"

"Why did you try to stop the guards?"

Isco started, glancing at Astar before turning away. "I have my reasons."

"So do I."

Isco scooted away from the bars as Astar lowered herself to the ground. She couldn't reach Kanna from her position, so she just watched her.

"This is my fault," Astar said. "She wouldn't be here if it wasn't for me."

Isco straightened, pulling his legs in toward himself. "What do you mean?"

"I met Kanna in Adur," Astar said. "Sometimes I just need to get away from all this."

Isco scoffed. "You mean all the food, and tapestries, and money and power, and the complete lack of want for anything?"

Astar turned over her shoulder but this time, she didn't glare. Her eyes were sad, distant. "There was this bar I went to," she said, turning away. "I have to give it to your people and their alcohol. Powerful stuff."

"It has been the downfall of many," Isco said when the silence became drawn.

Astar changed her position, pulling her knees up to her chest. "It was a pretty shady area, but I guess I just didn't think about those things. There was this group and..." she stopped, her voice cracking.

Astar let her legs fall and rolled her shoulders to straighten them. "I don't know what would've happened to me if she hadn't been there."

She took a breath, letting it out in a long heave. She turned to look over her shoulder at Kanna in the cell, the barren walls and the chains holding Kanna captive. "I told her about this place," Astar said. "I brought her here. I guess I figured I could protect her, being who I was. I could help her keep her secrets."

Isco jerked, his spine snapping straight. "So you know who she is, then? You've known all this time?"

Astar's eyes widened on him, then narrowed. "Not exactly. But she doesn't remember, either."

"What do you mean?"

"I mean just that. She doesn't remember who she was before. She won't way it, but I get the sense that she doesn't want to." Astar rubbed her hands against her eyes. When she turned to Isco, her eyes were dry. "But she saved me. That's all I need to know."

The earnestness of the statement caught Isco off guard. He didn't know how to react, and before he knew it, he was laughing. It started as something small, and he covered his mouth to try and keep it in, but it built inside of him all the same. His sides ached with trying to stifle it and he wrapped his arms around himself, bending over as the sound of his own laughter hit his ears.

It didn't sound like him. He had never made a sound like that before. Isco didn't know why he was laughing. The one who commanded his nightmare didn't even know the power she had, and that wasn't funny in any way. It should be a comfort that she wouldn't recognize him, didn't know him, but he was terrified.

Isco knew the light loa would come for her. He had hoped that he would be able to reason with her, to try and help her escape and perhaps prevent another tragedy. But she didn't know who she was, and the one she controlled was untethered.

He had been on edge since he was told about his mission to Gegenes, and after seeing the soldier there his stomach had turned into a knotted pit. They had no idea what was coming, but he did. And he was locked in these bars, chained to this place.

He had survived the first time due to sheer luck. Because, like Astar, Kanna had deigned to save him. He was not nearly lucky enough to survive a second time.

So what could he do but laugh?

# 22

## NEITHER HERE NOR THERE

KANNA TRIED to gain her bearings but there were no landmarks, only the blank expanse of frozen ground and the fog of her breath. The cold buried under her skin, so she wrapped her arms around herself in an attempt to keep it at bay. Then she began to walk, her body hunched against the silent wind.

The last thing she remembered was Hautman's dinner. When she awoke before she'd had nothing, not even her name. She thought of the faces she knew, forced their memories into her mind. Astar, with her teasing green eyes and her rounded cheeks. Yassen, smiling soft and guileless.

Others flitted into her consciousness, in glimpses given up by the dark: a man with glasses and an unamused line of a mouth; another, with shorn brown hair and haunted gold eyes. There was another, a woman, pretty, dark hair in a long tail and the kindest smile.

There were others, before. A man with black hair and blue eyes, flecks of gold that made her heart warm then stutter and shy away, only to slam into the vision of a man with white hair and hollow cheeks, burning a guilty hole in her stomach.

There had always been others, and it ached in her like an old wound.

She couldn't know how far she'd traveled when she stumbled, falling to the snow covered ground. Pressing her palms into the ground she pushed herself up, looking back to see what she'd stumbled over.

It was a body. A young man in a Palamidia uniform, his hand outstretched to her and his mouth open and screaming soundlessly. Dead eyes leveraged accusations at her. She shuffled back, her hand landing in a sticky puddle.

Behind her there was another, a woman, her body slashed and crumpled like a discarded doll.

Kanna's feet tangled on themselves as she scrambled up to run.

Bodies appeared with her every step. Men, women, even children, mangled into things almost unrecognizable but distinctly human and she knew it was her fault. It was because of her that they were in the dark. She slid in the carnage, but she kept running.

She had to escape, find some place safe.

In the distance, a platform took shape. She raced towards it, her feet pounding and her blood throbbing in her ears. The structure became clearer as she neared. It was a bed, its four posters rising up and disappearing into the fog above. She slowed enough to drop to the ground and pull herself beneath it to safety.

Her breath came ragged and rasping in the enclosed space. She swallowed, gulping air to help slow her racing heart. As it slowed, her body began to warm, the ground beneath her softening. She stretched her fingers at her sides to feel the plush surface beneath her.

When she opened her eyes, there was a dim glow beyond the shade of the bed. The walls beyond the narrow space between the floor and the bed were a deep jewel green, and she could see the spindly wooden legs of multiple pieces of furniture lined up. Crates of glassware were shoved into a corner of the room, their blue, green, and yellows reflecting the sunlight. A layer of dust settled on it all, the motes floating softly in the gloaming light.

The bed was bigger than when she first saw it, the bottom shifting further away from her body and allowing her more room to move. It was almost comfortable. She turned to look up, the underside of the far enough that she could see the wooden support slats beneath it.

Something hid between them. Kanna maneuvered her arms and elbows enough to fit her fingers between the slats. It was harder than she thought it would be to move but she persisted, gritting her teeth together as she concentrated. The wood tore into the sides of her nails as she pried her fingers between the slats until they shifted. She bit down harder when the wood scraped in the silence, her back teeth aching under the pressure.

Reaching into the space, she pulled out a mask. She spun it between her hands until it faced her. The closed eyes of a young boy were set in the mask. Not a toddler, but not much more than one. She brushed her fingers along the boy's lax brow, down his shut eyes, and over the soft planes of his face. Beneath the clutch of youth, there was something familiar about it, and something forbiddin in its secrets.

"What are you doing here, kidling?"

Despite the calm in the voice, Kanna jerked the mask out of sight, knowing she had been caught with something she shouldn't have.

A woman knelt next to the bed, her wild deep brown curls spilling over her shoulders and brushing against the carpet as she bent to peak into Kanna's place. There was something loose in her dark eyes, as if the world had rattled her just a bit too much. "Child," she coaxed, "will you come out now? I was so worried when I could not find you."

The woman held out her hand and Kanna stared at the thin, shaking fingers.

"We have all been trying to find you."

Drawn to the comfort the hand offered, Kanna reached out. She paused, her eyes searching the woman's face. She couldn't feel the woman, didn't know what she intended, and her gaze shifted to anger and desperation. A thrill of fear shot down Kanna's spine, and the woman's hand grasped to close the distance between them.

Kanna jerked back before their fingers touched, and the vision was gone. The woman, the room, even the mask in her hands dissolved into the grey.

She was alone again in the cold.

---

WHEN HARU OPENED HIS EYES, he was deep in the Neither.

The ghostlight at his shoulder darted away unbidden. It zipped through the black and then stuck, joining the rest of the stars in the unsettling sky. Haru clutched his jacket tighter as the wind picked up and the cold tore into him. The Neither was fighting his intrusion. It kept flickering and shifting, the landscape remodeling itself with his every step.

Before him was a tower. It was black and square, its windowless facade rising until it became one with the sky. It shuddered when he moved, but it didn't fade. As he approached, there was something resembling a doorway. It was cut out of the wall of the tower, a deeper black that opened to more darkness beyond. His breath fogged in the cold as he waited, but the tower stayed. He stepped inside.

The echo as his boots hit marble was familiar. After another step, a room formed around him. It was illuminated by floor to ceiling windows along one wall, the night sky the same one that appeared before him each night. The spires of Lugos were lit below, but the scene was wrong. Everything was frozen, time stilled to a moment. The beacon lights weren't flashing and no trains moved along the rails. The scene was flat, a painting captured by an amateur hand.

Haru was backing away from the window when he felt a shift around him. He turned.

Kanna was leaning against the wall opposite him as if her legs could no longer support her weight. Her shoulders were hunched beneath her battle regalia, and she watched him.

She didn't know what to do with her hands. She took them from her pockets, ran them through loose ends of her hair, then shoved them further into her jacket pocket. Her elbows stretched out, then relaxed again.

It wasn't her, though. The edges of her were blurred, a fuzzy halo circling her. When he moved to the vision, her eyes didn't follow. She wasn't looking at him as he was now, but as he had been then. This was a moment. She was an echo.

Kanna yanked free of the Legatus jacket, heavy with the symbols of a life passed in service to the Palamidia, and let it fall. She sighed, her shoulders straightening once she was free of it.

The mirror in his room hadn't shattered yet. The bed was still made.

It was the night before she left for Ilazki.

When she looked up, he tried to place his body where it had been before so he could see her eyes once more.

"Haru, I just..." she stopped, searching for words.

Her voice wasn't the same. It was hollow and the pitch flickered. She brushed away a tear that fell from her eyes and glanced at the back of her hand where it streaked, confusion casting itself across her features. He tried to catch the next, but his hand passed through her and he felt nothing.

Haru knew what she was going to say. He'd remembered it so many times he was sure it was branded on the inside of his skin.

"All I do is strangle things," she said. "Destroy things. But then you look at me like I am more than that, and I can almost believe it."

She shook her head, and he was helpless to do anything but witness. "This is all I know how to be, and I'm sorry. I couldn't stay away. I tried to let you go but I couldn't." Her voice caught, crackling like static in the air. "I can't."

When she looked up, she met his eyes even in this place. "I'm sorry, Haru, but I love you."

Haru reached out, unable to stop himself from trying to pull her to him as he had done then. He wanted to feel her skin against his again, watch as the walls she built around herself collapsed.

His hands passed through her and he was left holding nothing, standing once again in the wasteland. Haru shut his eyes, his empty hands open before him.

"There is nothing to forgive," he said. This time, it was to the wind as it howled.

# 23

## HOMECOMING

### VAHN

VAHN LEFT Osawa to watch over Haru, stopping on the other side of the door. He buttoned his shirt up and adjusted the collar, though it didn't quite hide the slave bands tattooed on his neck. On the streets, he shoved his hands deep in his pockets to further conceal his wrists and kept his shoulders back, his eyes trained in front of him. While he could hide the marks on his skin with the respectable pressed Palamidia white they still burned, a constant reminder that this place was not safe.

No place was safe.

He ducked into one of the abandoned warehouses strewn along a side thoroughfare and took the stairs to the roof, avoiding the missing and broken treads. On the roof, he made out the first of the suspension bridges. While legitimate business was dealt on the Trade Street, the smugglers lurked above. Rickety wooden bridges suspended between roofs, and they took advantage of the twisted landscape to keep their dealings out of sight.

The bridges swung beneath his feet, threatening him with splintering cracks and the creak of ropes. He wound his way over the rope suspensions and beams that connected the roofs until he arrived above the grocer.

He hopped off the final beam, his boots crunching against the asphalt shingles scattered on the flat roof that had fallen from a higher vantage. A service entrance stood at the back of the roof, the rusted grey door painted with a stylized rose.

Edin had done well for herself.

He knocked. Behind the door a chair scraped as it was dragged across the floor. The peep hole on the door slid away momentarily before dropping back into place. Footsteps led away from the door, and the creak of the chair followed soon after.

He knocked again, louder, hammering the side of his fist against the metal.

"Go 'way."

"I'm here for Edin," Vahn said, not bothering to raise his voice.

"So's everyone else," the voice replied, muffled through the layers of steel, "doesn't mean you get 'er."

Vahn pressed his palm against the door, just above the handle. "You get Edin, or we go with option two."

"Oh yeah?" the voice said behind the door. "What's that?"

Vahn pressed harder against the door. He shut his eyes, feeling the heat on his skin, the rage inside of him, and he forced it into his palm. It was easier here, in the warm afternoon, than locked away in a freezer. The metal of the door began to heat, turning red under his touch. The fire licked at his skin, warm and waiting. "Option two is I burn this place to ash, and you won't even have your bones left to mourn you by."

The metal crackled, hissing as it melted. It slid beneath his hand, the liquid creeping down and cooling in rivulets. Vahn stepped back and slammed his heel into the door. It broke open, hitting the wall in the room beyond.

The guard stared at him, his mouth agape. Vahn didn't move from his place in the threshold as the guard leapt to his feet and scampered back, upending the chair he had been sitting in and sending his card game flying.

Vahn waited until the guard's retreating footsteps faded before letting himself into the room. People generally went with option one, he'd found. He righted the chair and settled into it, crossing his ankle over his knee. He drew one of his knives and ran the tip of it under his nails, removing the dust that had caked beneath them from his jaunt through the smugglers' territory.

He didn't have to wait long. The sound of arguing issued down the corridor that lit the guard's room, followed by an assortment of foot-steps. He glanced up when the interior light was blocked, squinting at the door frame and the new guard filling it.

"Not looking for you," he said, returning to his nails.

A quiet moment passed.

"Move," a voice from the back grumbled. The bodies in the corridor attempted to press into the side of the wall, unwilling to venture into the room with Vahn.

From the mass of tangled limbs, a woman emerged. She stepped into the room, hands on her hips. Her hair was cut shorter than he remembered, and the slave tattoos on her neck had been traced over, turning into curving flowers that wrapped around her throat.

"Hey," he said, waving with the knife. He straightened his leg to sheath it.

Edin met Vahn's gaze with a glare. They had both belonged to the same bagnio in Adur, a while ago. Edin caught the eye of a merchant with a penchant for violence, so Vahn stole his attention from her. Vahn figured he could take it, and he could. For a while. Until he couldn't, and burned the merchant and the house along with it. Edin disappeared in the fallout, but Vahn was scooped up and sold to other hands.

She stalked forward, bending to meet Vahn's eyes. He met her violet gaze with his own. "Will you be paying for my door?"

Vahn glanced over his shoulder where the metal door hung useless on its hinges. "No, I don't think I will."

Edin crossed her arms at her chest, her eyes narrowing. The bands on her wrists had been turned into snakes, their open mouths devouring roses. "You want to tell me what a Palamidia officer wants with me?"

He had looked for her after he'd become an officer, but by that time, Edin had turned her skills to smuggling. She commanded a small fleet of engines and she was careful, creative. Her people always found a new and better way to get around the patrols. It was this creativity that Vahn was relying on now.

"Calling in a favor." He uncrossed his leg and pushed the chair opposite of him out in invitation.

Edin gripped the back of it with one hand, the other waving off the men gathered at the door. After their audience dispersed, Edin collapsed into the chair, her elbows on the table. "You look well."

"I am."

"A bit thin."

Vahn reached up with one hand, unhooking the top button of his collar and loosening it. "Always have been."

Edin relaxed her elbows and knitted her fingers together, resting her hands on the scattered cards still present. "It's been years."

Vahn nodded. He didn't have anything to add to that.

"I looked for you," Edin continued, "but by the time I was anything, you were already more."

Vahn smirked. "Slave to Saint. I'm a poster boy."

"Yeah, and that poster has a bounty on it now."

"Already?"

Edin leaned back in her seat. "Your family would've been proud."

"She is, even if she's not great at showing it. Though it brings us back."

Edin crossed her arms at her chest. "I'm listening."

Vahn twined his fingers together and leaned forward. He placed his hands on the table, then pressed them down. "I am getting my friend back, and you are taking us to her."

"If I don't?"

Vahn froze his smirk, not allowing it to flicker. He leaned back, crossing his arms to match Edin's stance. "No one likes option two."

# 24

## THE LOCALS

### YASSEN

YASSEN STARED into the mug in front of him. It wasn't his first draft of the evening by a long shot, and its empty companions clustered on the small table in the corner of the Dirty Trick.

Kanna had stopped by his room before the Governor's dinner. She'd given him all the coins she'd earned and told him to leave town. But something told him that he shouldn't. He knew something was wrong, and he wanted to help her if he could. She had helped him, and it was only fair.

That same night, Yassen was attacked in his room. He wasn't sure if they were mercenaries or officials, but he managed to fight his way out by crashing through the wall of his room. It had made such a mess.

Since then he'd kept his head down, but he didn't leave. He'd managed to get another room above the Dirty Trick, and the next morning he had a message from Astar. It was short and to the point, urging him to meet her here. That was it.

Yassen didn't know what to make of any of it, but he hoped Astar could help. He hadn't heard anything from Kanna, and even the Theatre had gone quiet, the stage standing empty for days.

Yassen had sat at their usual table. Kanna always chose the table in the corner, and he from there, his back was to the wall and he could see the entire tavern. He'd been sipping mug after mug of the hoppy brew the bartender had recommended. It wasn't a pleasant taste, but it was fine, and he needed an excuse to be here.

Halfway through his fourth draft, the door to the tavern swung open. The midday light pierced through the dark interior, bathing every sad soul in the room in a harsh cast. Astar slunk to his table, the other patrons returning to their drinks in the dim. Reaching him, she dropped a wrapped package on the table. It hit the wood with a solid *thunk* as she slid into the seat across from him with a rustle of silk.

She nodded to Yassen, then signalled to the barkeeper.

They sat in silence, waiting until Astar had her own mug to bend over. She brought the drink to her lips, cringing when she sipped. "Not a good year." She put the mug back on the table, sliding it across to Yassen.

"You sent me a message," he said, replacing his newly emptied drink with the one that Astar offered.

"Yes." Astar leaned back in her chair and crossed her arms over her chest. She cast a glance over her shoulder before turning to Yassen. "They've drugged her."

Yassen choked. He coughed, pounding a fist on his chest to clear his airway.

Astar rolled her eyes and snatched the drink from him. "No one drugged you."

"Who did they drug?"

"The dinner was a set up. That guy, Isco? He's from this... cult, in Adur. They sent my father some kind of special drug or something. They got Kanna with it."

"Why would he do that?"

"Father thinks she's a spy. I told him he was being ridiculous, but he won't listen to me."

"Is it really so ridiculous?" Yassen found himself asking. "She seems to know a lot about loas, and I've never seen anyone fight like she does."

Astar sat back in her chair. "Even if she was one of them, how does poking the Palamidia help anyone?"

Yassen shrugged. "A lot of people lost people. They might want revenge."

"All right," Astar said. She shoved back her chair. "I just wanted to see where you stood on this."

Yassen grabbed Astar's wrist before she could stand. "I didn't say I was one of those people."

She stopped, settling back into her seat. "I don't know the whole story, but neither does anyone else. All I know is this doesn't feel right."

Yassen studied his assortment of mugs. He had to agree with Astar. Something about the entire situation was off, like there was something important that was missing.

"He's going to put her in the Theatre again, but this time, he doesn't plan to let her leave alive."

Yassen scoffed. "Kanna won't fall on the stage. I mean, you've seen her. She's so strong."

Astar leaned in, her hands on the table. "The drug they gave her, it's supposed to block a loa's abilities."

Yassen tried to remember what Kanna had told him about loas. "That's ridiculous. You can't block a person from a part of themselves. Even then, how do we even know she has them?"

Astar breathed out a frustrated breath. "I don't know. But she passed out at dinner, and they threw Isco in the cells with her. If they keep her drugged, she won't be able to defend herself."

"That ain't right at all," Yassen said, rubbing the back of his head and leaning an elbow on the table. "Wait, why did they throw Isco in?"

"He tried to stop them. He kept yelling about something coming for her."

Yassen's other elbow joined the first on the table. "This is a real mess."

Astar nodded. "That's not all."

"How can there be more?" Yassen asked, his head already swimming.

"Father is advertising a once in a lifetime event for the Theatre."

"Why's it so special?"

"He means to expose Kanna. It's an execution."

"He can't do that," Yassen said, his voice rising. "He doesn't even know if she's really one of them."

"Do you think it will actually matter, once he says so?"

Yassen crossed his arms, slamming back into his chair with a creak. "What do you need from me?"

"For one, you need to get these to her."

Astar pushed a thin, hastily wrapped package across the table. Yassen pulled off the top layer of brown cloth to reveal mismatched hilts. He dropped the fabric, shoving it back across to Astar. "No way, no. Give these back to her."

"I can't give them back." Astar grit her teeth and lowered her voice as she shoved them back to Yassen. "And if I keep them, my father may find them."

Yassen met Astar's glare with his own. He gave in first. With a sigh, he slid the knives beneath the table. Kanna was never without them. Just the idea of her not having them made him queasy, as if he was clutching a severed limb. "For two?"

"Need you to get a message out. There's a depot at the rail yard, they should be able to send a signal."

"Sounds easy enough...."

"I need you to send a message to my friend, Edin. She'll be able to get us out of here."

Yassen's grip shifted around the wrapped blades. "Is she special, too?"

Astar's features locked into a frown. "Just do it, Yassen."

He nodded and she rose from her seat. "Give it a minute before you leave. I don't want anyone getting suspicious if they see us together."

With that, Astar left Yassen alone once more. He reached to the half-filled cup on the table and drained it, slamming it back down. The other cups rattled.

He ran his hands along the knives, not daring to remove the fabric that covered them. They seemed small in his hands, but he'd seen them part many lives from this world. The chair scraped across the floor as he shoved it back. He tucked the blades into his pack and slung it on his back before moving unsteadily into the bustle of the city streets.

## 25

### NEITHER HERE NOT THERE

KANNA PULLED her knees to her chest and wrapped her arms around them, bending over to rest her forehead against the ground. The strange place was achingly familiar. It was a void, and it was everything.

She didn't want to be here. There was so much waiting for her in the dark, and she didn't want to understand. It hurt, all of it. It was a weight on her shoulders, a phantom that followed her and was always wanting. She shut her eyes, willing them to open back to the dusky orange sky of Gegenes.

"Why are you on the ground?"

Kanna jerked her head up at the sound of the voice, but shock kept her rooted. She'd stared at the face enough in mirrors, trying to discern its secrets, that it was impossible not to recognize it looking back at her.

It wasn't exactly the same as her own. There was a surety to her gaze that she hadn't felt before. The other her stood calmly, in control, her hands in the pockets of her white trousers and her shoulders slack.

"Better," she said, nodding her approval.

Kanna took in the other, clad head to toe in polished white. Her echo slouched, but there was a predatory self-assuredness in it. This one never worried about a knife in her ribs or what the darkness held. She was a vision with nothing to lose, and the power to take what she wanted. Kanna's spine bristled at the implications of it. Kanna's eyes narrowed on the mirrored image of herself.

"What are you?"

It smiled, slow and sharp. "I would think you would recognize yourself."

Her reflection's voice came with an echo, as if spoken across some great divide. It was clipped and calculated. It was unnerving.

"Why are you talking like that?"

The figure stood straighter, taller. "This is how we speak."

Kanna straightened her shoulders in response. "I do not speak that way."

The other chuckled, the sound empty and mirthless. She relaxed her shoulders once more. "There are more important things to discuss."

Kanna's body sank and she shook her head. It was like she was a prisoner in a construct that both was and wasn't hers at the same time. "What is this place?"

Her echo shrugged. "It is neither here nor there, so we called it the Neither."

"You and me?"

"No," her other self replied. "What is more important is what is here, or what should be." The echo paced the ice, the heels of her boots sounding like strikes against marble with each step. "I would pick the end of the world as a starting point. No one looks here, do they? Not even the gods." She looked up to the dappled sky, smiled and shut her eyes. "But he will find me, always. He will tear apart the universe if he must."

Kanna knew she was right. She'd felt it. There was an ache in her chest that sung of loss. She had fed it the only way she knew, with blood and violence, but it still screamed.

The echo pivoted, turning her smile to Kanna. It was fearless and knowing.

A sound in the distance caught Kanna's attention and she turned towards it. Cursing herself, she turned back, but she already knew the woman would be gone.

She choked on her frustration as it curdled into fear.

The bodies were back.

HARU OPENED his eyes and flexed his empty hands, the cold creaking in the joints of his fingers and tightening the skin around the scar on his palm. The tower was gone, and so was the ghost. He couldn't shake the emptiness, the heavy need to feel her near him once more.

He had never been able to shake it.

Then, she was there again. Kanna stood in front of him, her hands in her pockets and her shoulders set back. But she was still blurred at the edges, and this one had a dangerous confidence. It was how she stood before him when they first met, except it lacked the subtle questioning that always hid in her gaze.

"Kanna?"

The vision smiled, and her shoulders shrugged. It was not a no, but it was not a yes either. He wasn't sure how many more visions he could stand. He pressed his palms into his eyes, pushing until he felt pain, willing the ghost to leave him to the wreckage. He didn't want these aspects, these visions, these pieces of her. Haru wanted Kanna. He wanted all of her.

The figure turned, looking out into the distance. Haru followed her line of sight.

A flash of white appeared, stepping out of a rip in the landscape, running at full speed.

Another Kanna. The smirking ghost flitted out of sight.

The other was still running. She didn't flicker at the edges, and she stumbled through this world as if it was foreign to her. He could hear the crack of her boots against ice, feel her fear over the distance.

He felt the thread that bound them pull taut. The echoes had all been empty, void of Kanna's innate gravity.

This wasn't a ghost. She was right there.

He started after her, trying to intercept her as she raced ahead. She was stumbling, sliding, tripping over nothing that he could see.

Haru pushed himself faster, closing the distance between them.

As suddenly as she appeared, she fell. Her arms flailed as the ground dropped from beneath her and she slipped down and out of sight.

He didn't stop running. Even if he told himself to, he wouldn't be able. He would never stop. Not until he found her.

# 2 6

## A SISTER'S LOVE

### VELINIUS

THE RENOVATIONS to the temple were taking longer than Velinius would have liked.

She didn't see the need for new benches, so the ones that remained were rearranged. The intricate chandeliers were exchanged for clean-lined pendants, which wouldn't attract so much dust, and the smaller shattered windows were replaced with clear glass instead of the gaudy mosaics from before.

A thick layer of paint was being applied to the mural beneath the rose window, which had been untouched in the scuffle. Velinius smiled as the worker rolled the white layer over the image of elements melding and consuming each other. Ananke had been fascinated with it. She hadn't visited the temple often, but Velinius always caught her gaze drifting to that space. She would disconnect, her head tilting as if it whispered some unknowable secret only to her. Velinius should have known, even then, that Ananke could not be saved.

Velinius had spent hours here, contemplating the legends that blanketed the walls. Nothing whispered to her. The tales of the old gods were pressed into plaster and glorified, but there were no secrets in the flat images. No truths in the stories. Those were spoken throughout Lifrasir, a remnant of a shared past when the land was whole.

The people loved their stories, though the power wasn't in the story so much as the telling of it. A story could divide people just as well as it could connect them. A story could conquer.

"Legatus?"

Velinius flattened her smile, dug into her long-suffered sorrow before turning on her heel to face the voice. The girl was young, fresh from the Prospect culls. Her uniform was pressed clean, her dark hair shaved close to her head. "Nissa. You know I am not truly the Legatus."

Nissa crossed her arm over her chest and bowed in deference. "You have always been the true Legatus."

Velinius allowed herself a smile, but kept it humbled. She was meant to be concerned about the state of the Palamidia, about her attempted assasination, not pleased. She placed a light hand on the girl's shoulder before pulling away. "It gladdens me to hear that, but it is not fair."

"It has nothing to do with fair. It is about what is right. The Consel failed us when they did not return your control sooner."

Velinius clasped her hands behind her back and turned to the front of the temple. "It is true they were hesitant, but they had their reasons. This empire is built on our honor. There are traditions, though none for this particular situation."

"Apologies, Legatus. I forgot your sorrows."

"Never mind that." Velinius straightened her shoulders then cleared her throat. Grief had its place. "What news of the traitors?"

"They were last seen following the river south. Few of the outposts in Atarrabi are manned, so they may have slipped across the border."

"You are saying they cannot be found?"

"No, Legatus," Nissa's voice rose in her rush to respond. "We will find them. There are scouts in the area, and the Eyes have been deployed as you ordered."

Good," Velinius said. The Eyes were meant to be everywhere, always. The fact that their borders were not being properly observed was more evidence of Ananke's failures. "Have they brought any useful information?"

The young officer cleared her throat. "There is news coming from Gegenes about an event in their Theatre. Though the information regarding it is nebulous at best, it is luring many."

Velinius's fingers tightened. The Theatre would call Ananke. She would not be able to stay out of a brawl. It was how Velinius had kept her, ready to snap at any moment. Barely tethered, but tethered all the same to the spare morsels of approval that Velinius would offer.

"Is that all we know?"

"Eyes have reached the city," Nissa offered. "We are awaiting their reports."

Velinius could not wait. Not now, not with Ananke's loyal collective loose. She turned to face Nissa. "You are from Chromandae, correct?"

The girl beamed her teeth shining against her ebony skin. "Yes, I am of the fire."

"Do you know Salinae?"

"The Saint of Water," Nissa replied, with no shortage of awe in her tone. "He is readying a detachment to aid in securing the Atarrabian borders."

"He will be meeting me here in a moment. I have something to share with him, and you as well if you would stay."

"If that is your command, Legatus."

Velinius turned back to the altar. Salinae was undeniably loyal, and Nissa was primed to bloom. Still, the matter would be delicate.

The people loved stories, and she needed to tell the right one. It was why she'd kept a watch on the Prince. After Ananke, Velinius had to find a fitting ending for him. Once, she'd held hope that he could be a great asset. The man's single-mindedness would have been a weapon that could bring nations to their knees. But he had become distracted by Ananke and slipped from Velinius's influence.

Velinius had intended to send the Prince to the front, where he would die in battle like so many other soldiers. He would be mourned but a moment, then forgotten like all those before him. His attack on her was unexpected, but she could bend it to her favor. After riling him to action, she could have executed him for treason. His escape was a wrinkle in her plans, but wrinkles were easily ironed out.

There was the larger issue. Ananke was still alive. Velinius had been certain that she had succeeded, but when she had found the Prince's connection to the light, it had been split. It branched to something else. Someone else.

A shift in the air announced the opening of the Temple door. Velinius glanced over her shoulder to Salinae. His blonde hair fell to his shoulders, the ends cut blunt and straight, clean and well tamed. It somewhat distraced from the unattractive scar that cut over his face, the unfortunate evidence of an inappropriate overreach. But he was loyal to her alone, and that loyalty was useful.

"Have you readied your troops?" Velinius asked him.

"Yes," he replied, stepping past Nissa before stopping. "There are two hundred ungifted soldiers, and twelve officers ready to lead at your command."

Velinius nodded. "See them doubled. Claim them from the other detachments, if needed. You will need those strong of both mind and body. Take Nissa, as well."

Salinae's eyes widened only slightly in response to the increase.

"I have a new assignment for you, but it is of a sensitive nature." Velinius pivoted, revealing her profile to the two officers. She bent her head, pressing her fingers between her eyes as if the thoughts strained her. After a beat, she let her hand drop. "I need you to travel to the Gegenes capitol. To their so-called 'Theatre.'"

Salinae opened his mouth, but snapped it closed.

"I know," she said, "that it will be seen as an advancement, but it is what we must do." She paused, took a visible breath, and turned to sit at the bench closest to the altar. "I believe that the former Legatus will be there."

Nissa's sharp inhale was just short of a gasp.

"Ananke?" Salinae asked, careful to keep his tone level. "Legatus, you reported that she died in Ilazki."

This was the part that Velinius would have to play correctly. She kept herself turned away, her shoulders curled in. "I believed she did, and in a way it was truth. I always feared that Ananke had too much of our mother in her, and with Aksana's refusal to reveal her paternity there was no one to provide balance for Ananke. It was why I was granted as her guardianship, and she was raised here, within the Tower. Unfortunately, long held suspicions proved true. The long dark of Ilazki caused something in her to break."

Velinius clasped her hands in her lap, lowering her head. "She went mad. She slaughtered the detachment. By my own hand, I tried to stop her. When I fled those bloodied grounds, I did not look back."

Velinius raised her eyes to the altar. "When her body was not found, I hoped it was a mistake. That something had perhaps taken her. But I have begun to fear the worst: that she is still out there, wreaking havoc on the land.

"You understand," she looked over her shoulder, pleading, "that I wanted to keep her memory pure. I did my best to raise her, to make her a light, and I could not bear my own failure. I thought she was gone, that we were safe. However, it seems that I may be wrong."

The mural gave out its last gasp as the painters finished the final coat of white. A calm came over her as it disappeared. "If Ananke is out there, she will not be able to resist the Theatre. I need you to find her. If she has lost her sense, there is no telling what she may unleash upon our world."

"Yes, Legatus," Salinae replied. "If that is your order."

Velinius sighed, long and slow. "It must be so."

"Then it will be."

"You may go." As the steps of the officers began to recede, she lifted her head and jerked to face them. "May the gods not greet you."

Salinae nodded. "They will wait for me longer."

When she was sure they were gone, Velinius rose from her seat. She straightened her back and looked up to the rose window.

The world didn't need the chaos of the old gods.

It was time for order.

# 27

# NEITHER HERE NOR THERE

KANNA RAN until she thought her heart would stop. Her shins ached from pounding against the unforgiving ice, and a sharp pain stabbed into her knee from when a slip wrenched it. The surface of the wasteland was coated in blood and bodies that she dodged and leapt over, but they paraded endlessly in the cold grey.

She had begun to recognize them.

Kanna stepped around a body that barred her way, and her ankle folded beneath her. The ground dropped and she slid, scratching at the surface and tearing off her nails as she tried to gain purchase on the slick incline that had appeared where the land had been solid moments before. The world spun, her shoulders and hips bruising against the unforgiving rock. At the bottom she landed in a heap.

Her breath came in jagged gasps, her lungs unable to be relieved by the thin nothing of the air. Her blood rushed in her ears like an echo, and beneath it she could hear the waters Ilazki's Iss river, the floating ice cracking and popping like bird bones breaking. The pain from the fall reverberated through her body, and she shut her eyes against the throbbing hurt.

"No," she begged, pleading with whatever force controlled this place. "Not here."

In the dark behind her eyes, she searched for the door in her mind.

She needed to pull it shut, but it wasn't there. Kanna opened her eyes to the pointed tips of white boots. They were clean, unmarred, and shone like mirrors in the dark. She tried to pull herself up, but only managed to push herself onto all fours.

"You were never graceful, sister." A hand reached down, grasping her by the arm and yanking her to standing.

Kanna followed the woman's short-cropped nails to her face. Her hair was pulled back into a tight braid at the base of her neck. It looked flat brown in the dim light, but Kanna knew it gleamed with copper in the sun. The woman's eyes had a familiar tilt to her own, but they were a dark tarnished gold.

Kanna tried to jerk her arm away but the woman's grip tightened and held. The hand on her arm was a vice, and no matter how hard she struggled she couldn't break free. Defeat settled on her, it's weight familiar.

"Why are you calling me sister?" she asked, stilling her struggles.

"Because that is what you are. My dearest sister," the woman said. She leaned in, her lips unnervingly close to Kanna's ear. "The dark stain on my name."

The flash of metal caught Kanna's attention. Instinct gave her a burst of strength, and she twisted hard, wrenching her body out of the woman's grasp.

Kanna backed away as the woman stepped forward. Her foot slid. Another pool of blood was at her feet, but this one wasn't old or tacky. It was slick and freshly spilled, still steaming against the icy ground.

"Look at what you have done this time," the woman said, her sibilant voice carrying an air of disappointment.

Kanna shook her head. "I didn't." The defense was hollow even in her own ears. "I wouldn't."

The woman smiled. "It is not hard to believe. You have murdered so many before, and you will continue. It is all you are good for, Ananke. You are a weapon, nothing more."

Kanna covered her ears, trying to calm the pounding of her heart that had begun anew. The dark thing inside of her fluttered to life, as if confirming the woman's words.

With a single finger, the woman lifted Kanna's chin to meet her eyes. "It's all right, sister. I will fix this."

Kanna looked into the woman's eyes and knew what she said was true. She could make things right again. Even as the shell of a person, Kanna had not touched anything without leaving claw marks in it. The temptation to give in, to let the woman take the responsibility and the burden of keeping her contained was almost too great to deny.

"Kanna!"

The sound of a new voice interrupted her thoughts and she turned to it. It rang clear, cutting over the ice and through the stillness. It was different from the others. It did not echo, it did not slide or sift through the air. It sliced through, solid and true and warm.

A man appeared at the rise of the incline. His hair was dark as the night, but his eyes shone bright against it. Crisp and blue, they were interlaced with a gold that was pure and alive. There was a clarity in them that shocked her. She didn't want to be what the woman said, couldn't be. There had to be something more.

The dark thing scratched and screamed a name.

"Haru?"

The man's eyes widened, looking past her. "Kanna, run!"

She tried to turn but the woman's arm circled her neck and trapped her against her body.

"A shame," the woman with snakes in her voice said.

A blinding pain tore into Kanna's side. She felt the skin break, the muscles rip as the metal entered her body. It found its way in through the loose ties at the side of her armor, angling up, seeking her heart.

Kanna watched as the blade withdrew. Her traitor heart pumped harder and the blood spread over the white of her uniform.

Her blood.

Kanna felt another kind of pain and locked eyes with the man across the waste. Haru, the dark whispered. His eyes had darkened, his hands reaching out as he ran to her.

The woman lowered her lips to Kanna's ear. "You should have stayed in your place."

Kanna knew she had to keep her eyes open. If she kept them open, she could stay here. Haru was so close, and she reached for him.

She realized her eyes were open, but it didn't matter anymore.

HARU SLID to a halt where Kanna had dropped from view, stopping short just before tumbling down the incline. He scanned the ground below until he spotted her.

She wasn't alone. A vision of Velinius held Kanna by the arm, stopping her from pulling away. Haru could hear Kanna's voice drifting over the expanse between them. She was arguing with the vision, but he could only hear Kanna's words.

"Kanna!"

She stopped speaking to the echo of Velinius, her head snapping at the sound of his voice. Haru slid down the incline, racing to her. The tether between them pulled him forward as everything else faded away.

Velinius flickered into view behind Kanna, her dark eyes glimmering with old gold.

"Kanna, run!" he called, forcing the words through his lungs.

It was too late. Haru saw the flash of steel as the knife sunk deep into Kanna's side, watched as the pain broke over her and the red blossomed over her white uniform.

Kanna met his eyes over the distance. They were alive, sparkling grey, a sky that promised storms. She kept her eyes open, forcing herself to stay on her feet as the glint in them dimmed.

Haru reached her as she fell, his arms out to break her fall.

The world cracked, and he was cast away.

# 28

# LINGER

## HARU

HARU JERKED AWAKE, his screams in the Neither echoing in his ears. There was a vacancy in his hands where she should be, his fingers tangling in empty sheets on a soft bed. The room came into focus around him as the last of the Neither slipped away. It was night, the semi-sheer curtains drawn in front of the windows. A warm breeze moved in, causing the hem of the fabric to sway. There was enough ambient light that he could make out Osawa and Vahn sleeping on the floor. Vahn faced the door, his back to Haru. Osawa slept at Vahn's back, closest to Haru. He had one arm on his chest, his glasses resting beneath his hand there.

Haru shifted his weight, careful of the unknown mattress, and swung his legs over the side of the bed. The wood of the frame let out a quiet creak when it released his weight. He took a moment to straighten the pants on his hips and reorient himself into his body.

Moving was like wading through mud. His body was aching and heavy, both unused and worn out. It screamed at him to rest, to be still, but he refused. He crept past his sleeping companions, easing the door of the room open just enough to slide through. It clicked shut behind him, ringing bright and clear in the vacant hall.

He found his way to a stairwell at the back of the hall and followed it up, seeking an aerial view. At the top of the stairs he found a service entrance. It stuck at first, but he leaned his shoulder into it and shoved it open. The night air greeted him with its faded warmth. A subdued hum carried over the city, as if it purred in sleep.

At the edge of the roof he stopped and leaned his elbows on the thick guard wall. The buildings around him butted up against each other, the flat roofs staggered at different heights. Narrow lines connected them, silhouetted against safety lights. A smog nestled around him, blocking out a more distant view.

"You're back."

He looked over his shoulder to Osawa, then back to the cityscape. "I didn't mean to wake you."

The loose stones on the roof skittered under Osawa's boots as he approached. "Vahn woke me. We both know he doesn't sleep. Not really."

"Neither did Kanna."

Osawa approached the guard wall then turned back to the building, leaning back against it. He rested his hands on the lip of the wall.

"We made it to Atarrabi," Haru said. He turned and leaned next to Osawa, but shoved his hands into his pockets.

Osawa nodded. "Vahn found us transportation. We can leave from here in the morning, and it should be a short trip to Gegenes."

"Do I want to know how the two of you managed to get me across the plains?"

A smile snuck onto Osawa's lips. "Some things are probably better left unsaid."

Haru straightened and stretched, wincing with the movement. "I'm assuming the somewhat bruised ribs are Vahn's work."

Osawa's smile dropped. "He did his best, considering."

"Considering what?"

Osawa's expression narrowed on Haru, before he looked away. He cleared his throat. "Not everyone mourns the same, Haroun."

Haru tilted his head back. He had dug into his own darkness, his own anger and loss. He spent his time struggling to breathe around it, but Kanna's light had never only been his. Her absence left a hole greater than any empire.

The smog above the city made a mess of the sky, though the stars still managed to valiantly shine through. But it was the dark that was beautiful to him. Here he could see hints of the violet and indigo twisting in the inky black, but the breadth of it was lost.

Osawa pushed himself away from the wall, his boots crackling against the uneven roof. He put his hands in his pockets and made to leave but stopped short. "I know you don't want to tell me about what happened, but I'm glad you're back with the living." He glanced over his shoulder at Haru, checking on him one last time. "Try to stay here this time."

Osawa disappeared into the open doorway at the head of the stairs, the white glow of his shirt fading into the black. Haru sighed heavily, leaning back onto the roof wall. He wished he could tell them what had happened, but it wasn't something he could fit into words.

The Neither was a place that wasn't a place, somewhere between here and everything else. And, somehow, Kanna was there. Parts of her, at least. Despite the visions in the Neither, he still didn't know what happened the day she disappeared. The Neither could twist things, make them more or less than they actually were.

Kanna had died that day. But only for a moment.

A breeze picked up, carrying the scent of the grasslands through the smell of the city industry. He breathed deep, remembering another roof, another time.

Kanna had spoken about her brother once, and only once. She told Haru about the death mask that her mother kept hidden in the upper floors of their estate, and how it would call to her. She hid it under the bed in a guest room, the same bed that sat atop the rug with the blood-stain from Salim's fall down the stairs.

When she felt alone, she'd said, she would hide beneath the bed and stare at the mask. Resting on the ghost of his blood, she would try and figure out what her brother was trying to say. For Kanna, death had never been something to run from, but something to dare.

She told Haru she always wondered what had happened to Salim, that she thought he would be able to tell her the truth, somehow. She believed that when death was a surprise, the soul must linger for a moment. Just a moment, to wonder what had happened.

That moment was all they needed.

## 29

# WAKING THE GHOST

## KANNA

KANNA HIT THE GROUND, her palms scraping on the cold stone of the temple floor. She gasped for breath, her body shaking. The pain was gone, a memory once more. She checked her hands, but they were pale and clean in the starlit night.

They were also empty. She clenched her fists and screamed. The loss she had always carried had a shape now, a form and a name, but she could feel it being pulled away once more. It left a void and the ache filled her, scratched at the places inside of her that she once thought abandoned.

She screamed until her throat was raw and she couldn't anymore. She wrapped her hands around herself and hunched over, trying to keep the shattered pieces of herself from falling apart.

Footsteps approached. The sound of boots against marble was now familiar. She leaned back, resigning herself to whatever was to come, and looked into the grey of her own eyes.

"Is that enough?" her echo asked.

Kanna shut her eyes and nodded wordlessly.

"Good. It is time to stop hiding."

Her echo reached out, pressed a finger lightly between Kanna's eyes. A door opened, and Kanna fell through, through the long dark and into a light.

KANNA'S HEART was a hollow echo in her chest. It stuttered to a start once more and her mouth opened, gasping in stale air. Her body jerked up, and her head spun. The visions flashed back to her and she reached for her side. Her hand came back clean, but the ghost of the pain lingered.

The skin on her wrists was red and raw. She flexed her fingers as they warmed in the dank air, her nerves prickling back to life. While her dreams were often erratic, what she had awakened from was far from a dream. She had been somewhere else, at some other time. The Neither, she called it. And someone else. She shut her eyes, trying to cling to the memory but it slipped behind something.

She shook her head, but the movement didn't align the pieces inside. The fog in her head stayed stuck, muting her surroundings. The light was soft and hazy, an orange glow casting long shadows of cell bars. There was an oil lamp in the hall on the other side, somewhere further down than she could see. The walls of the room were solid, carved out of bedrock. She tried to breathe deep to catch the scent of the area and was met with the musty odor of straw and unkempt bodies.

Her own body was stiff, her mouth parched and her throat raw and burning. She rolled her shoulders, concentrated on the joints as they shifted. On her right, the pull of her skin was uneven as it warped around the scar on her back.

"Hey."

The whispered hiss came from behind her and she scrambled away, dragging herself across the dusty floor.

"You're all right."

The practiced voice soothed her jarred nerves. She felt her body calm, her legs shifting away from her chest. On the other side of the bars, a man crouched. His clothes were rumpled and stained, the dust clinging to the spots where he had sweated through his shirt. His brown hair was disheveled, dirty and sticking out at odd angles. "Isco?"

Isco groped the bars between their cells and she could see orange dirt caked under his jagged nails. A few of them were chewed to the quick, red lines at the end of the tips where the beds had bled. The soft light made his dark eyes owl-ish, and his gaze kept darting from her to the empty hall. She felt like she should know him, but save for having met him in the Governor's house, he remained vaguely familiar at best.

The events of the dinner came back to her. He had tried to stop them. It was a wasted effort, but it was brave. She followed his darting eyes to door at the end of the hall, but she couldn't see anything beyond it. When she tried to sense the guards, the effort made her dizzy and she tipped to the side.

Her body was weak, and that weakness felt like a betrayal. She crawled closer to him. The short distance winded her and she stopped, leaning her back against the bars between them.

"Stay quiet," he said, his tone velvet smooth, "or they'll dose you again."

Kanna closed her dry mouth and opened it. "Dosed?" She croaked.

She heard him shift behind her, landing with a thud onto the ground. "They have a drug that suppresses loa abilities."

She choked on a bitter laugh, her throat too dry to make the sound. "That's impossible."

"I know. They don't need to, though," he said, "but it'll make it hard for you to move or concentrate."

Kanna opened her eyes and looked down at herself. The white shirt she was wearing glared in the dark and she yanked on it, pulling it away from her body. It was plain cotton but woven with something rougher, cheap and loose. Her legs were wrapped in tattered denim a size too large that had seen better days.

"The guards changed you a while ago," Isco offered.

"Oh." She reached up, her fingers brushing the scar at her shoulder. It was old, whiter than her skin and smooth. "Did you see?"

He didn't say anything. She tilted her head to try and look at Isco, but he wouldn't meet her eyes.

"I didn't mean to," he said, "but it's hard not to."

Her body was a maze of scars, with some more prominent than others. There were even a few on the back of her right hand, thin and straight, clean, purposeful cuts that were then mended. Those explained the stiff aches in her fingers on rainy days, the bumps of metal she could feel beneath her skin.

Then there were the veins of gold that wrapped below her ribs. They radiated against the scar tissue, the light pulsing against her skin.

She couldn't fathom the map of any of it, didn't know where they came from or where they led. "Right," she said, lacking any other words.

"Do you," Isco started to speak but his voice caught. He cleared his throat. "Do you know who I am?"

"No," she replied, glad that he wasn't asking questions she didn't have answers to. "Do you know who I am?"

"No," he said, something like sorrow in his voice. "Not really."

Kanna always knew when people were lying. He wasn't, not fully, but she didn't want to dig further. She squeezed her eyes shut as the new memories found paths in her mind. Everything was chopped apart and tossed together. She knew her name. She knew what they called her. But there was something vital missing, something important.

Kanna knew who she was, and she didn't. She had facts, statistics, but nothing more. Even that much felt like too much. It was too heavy.

"You should rest," Isco said. "They're putting you in the Theatre."

"Hmm," she said, her body growing heavy. "When?"

"Tomorrow."

Kanna couldn't help the smile that curled her lips. She knew this moment would come. She had felt the tug calling her to the empire's lands, but at the same time she couldn't help but yank away. There were answers there, and she didn't want them. But it didn't matter how hard she pulled away, she knew her past would come for her. The world was dangerous and broken, the hatred sown so deep it was a wonder anything had lasted this long.

She remembered the man in the wastes, tried to remember what she had called him and why he was important. But the more she tried to concentrate on it, the hazier it became until she couldn't even remember why she was trying to remember anymore.

She would have to find him to know, and she wasn't sure she wanted to. But first, she would have to survive whatever it was that Hautman was planning. Sleep pulled at her limbs, and whatever drug they had given her drifted in her veins like an oil. Morning would come too soon and with it, she would take the stage.

Her hands were empty, her mind was a cloud, but she would survive.

She was good at surviving.

## 30

## THE STAGE IS SET

### ASTAR

THE MORNING of the Gala dawned hot and vicious. Astar felt the
sweat hit her back before the sun broke, red then white and sharp.
Despite the heat, people had been packing into the Theatre, wanting to
get the best view of the promised action.

Attending the Theatre's plays had always been something that was
expected of Astar as the Governor's daughter, and while this was not the
first time she had to watch her friend upon the sands, it was the first that
she felt watched in turn. Their personal Keepers loomed behind them,
but she was uncertain if they were there to protect her or guard her as a
prisoner. The whirring fans inside the Pulvinus created an artificial
breeze, shimmying the burgundy silks that shaded the private box, but
she was still suffocating.

She was surrounded as usual by prominent Belisarians, the ones that
had offered fighters for the day's events. Their clothes glinted with inlaid
jewels and threads, catching the bright glare of the sun. Despite her
angle, the flashes of light gleamed directly into Astar's eyes.

Hautman had also offered an invitation to some wealthy Adurians,
who Astar had not been introduced to. Their clothing wasn't nearly as
decorative as the Gegenii's. Adurians weren't a showy people, but the
rich earth tones of the fabrics were finely cut. He was hoping this show

would lure them into supporting him against his political rivals, both with money and force.

The crowd beyond was heavily Gegenii, though she could still spot Adurians and Atarrabians. Some could have been from Kirin, she guessed, but the people of Kirin were insulated and isolated, by both choice and circumstance.

At least Yassen had shown up. He kept his head down, his hood pulled over his face, as he jostled his was through the general assembly. If he was close enough, perhaps he'd be able to do something to help. Astar bit her lip, the tang of the pain reminding her where she was. This was the Theatre. While it was used for entertainment now, it had a history as a central fortification, a construct that the people and fighters of Ganglere could retreat to and hold during an invasion. The only way up to the stands were narrow, enclosed stairwells, and the only way to the stage below was through a series of twisting catacombs. The walls were made of solid stone, risen from the bedrock and formed by loas in their prime, when their blood wasn't so thinned from the constant threat of the Empire.

Among the antsy crowds, another caught Astar's eye. It wasn't that the woman stood out, but more that she blended too well. She'd found a place between two groups much the same way as Yassen had, but there was space around her. The clothing she wore was Adurian, but it was ill-fitting, and Adurians were all about fit when it came to style. The woman's features were soft, amber eyes set into a rounded face. Her skin was a bit off to Astar, and when she reached up to adjust the hood of her cloak, it didn't quite match the shade of her hands.

Hautman turned and gave a nod through the curtains around the Pulvinus, and a deafening horn blast rippled over the audience and quieted the rowdy conversations.

In front of her, Hautman rose to begin his address. "Welcome, my fellow Gegenii, and our esteemed guests."

Hautman paused, waiting until the scattering of conversations and the muffled shifting of bodies went still. Yassen had turned but kept his head angled low, attempting to blend his bulk with the rest.

"You have gathered from the free territories to be with us here today, and I am glad to welcome you. This will be a glorious day for us, as I have promised, but first, I must make a confession." Hautman clenched his hands together, wringing them in an exaggerated apology that would carry the distance. "I may have misled you, but I meant no ill will."

The crowd shifted, a chorus of murmurs rising.

"Peace," Hautman held his palms down to signal for quiet. "My people, I had to keep quiet about the true nature of this great day, for you see, I have uncovered a traitor among us."

The gates opened. Two keepers flanked Kanna, half dragging her by the elbows and dropping her onto the sands.

"Some of you may know this creature."

From where Astar sat Kanna seemed so small, hunched over on her hands and knees in the dirt. They'd dressed her in white, the contrast against the orange sands drawing all eyes to her.

"We welcomed her, and we named her Harbinger. But I have come to learn that she is not one of us. She is a Palamidia soldier, sent here to whittle us down and sway your loyalties."

The crowd's voice turned sour, boos and hisses taking over the people in a wave. The strange woman from earlier stiffened, rousing Astar's suspicions further.

Kanna shifted her weight, sitting back on her heels. Her eyes were closed, but she turned her face up to the sun. Her stillness was unsettling.

"It has been declared that the Harbinger, this traitor, is to be sentenced to death on the stage."

## 31

# FIRST BLOOD

## KANNA

THE SUN WAS warm against her face. It had been too long since she'd felt it. The heat of the day soaked into Kanna's skin, the pain in her side dulling and the lead in her limbs melting. Her body was heavy, but she knew what it could do. She knew it would listen, and she trusted it would get her through this.

There was still so much missing, but she could feel the edges. She could move right up to the memories, but she couldn't reach them. She knew she had survived worse, though. She didn't need the memories to know that.

Kanna braced her hands in the shifting sand, focusing on the feel ofe the heat in her bare palms, dull and distant against the calluses that marked her. She pushed herself to standing as the gates opened on a single fighter. She cocked her head to the side, trying to study him. He wasn't Gegenii. He was light and lean, more likely an Adurian hoping to earn a name here.

She took a step, staggering when the world spun. Isco had warned her about the drug's side effects, but her entire center was missing.

Her opponent charged, his feet kicking up dust behind him.

Before, the fighters in the arena didn't know her. Her anonymity and size had lulled them a false sense of security, but that was gone now. Her opponent bore down on her with the full weight of his hatred.

Kanna set her feet, willing the world to stop spinning just long enough.

The fighter's sword slashed down and she slid to the side. She hooked his foot with her own and yanked.

The fighter lost his footing and stumbled into the outstretched heel of her hand. She jabbed his throat with the other and twisted under his arm. She grabbed his wrist, her arm locking around his elbow and crooking it forward. She stabbed the fighter's own knife down into the meat of his thigh.

He howled, the mixture of anger and pain amplifying in her ears and slamming into her skull. The sound drove her back, her feet sliding in the loose sand, and she clutched her head and willed the ringing to stop.

A flash of light and fluttering of fabric caught her attention. It flew through the air, unfurling, her knives landing and scattering. Kanna's body screamed to hold them. It needed them. Her opponent forgotten, she dove.

The man followed close behind, limping from the wound in his leg.

Her left hand found the white hilt first, and it felt like home. She rolled with it as her opponent's sword came down. Metal met metal as she blocked the strike and twisted out from under it, grasping the second knife.

She jumped to her feet at ready, the world still spinning as her opponent's sword swinging wide. She matched it with her own blades and stepped into his reach. She back gripped the black knife and stabbed from the side. She felt the resistance from the blade as it found its mark in his neck. It carved its way through the flesh and muscle and stuck at the hilt.

His limbs loosened, his mouth opening as blood leaked from the corner of his lips. His sword hit the sand as his fingers let go, his body going limp. There was shock in his eyes, the life in them lingering. He was trapped in that moment.

She knew that moment. The last glimmer in his eyes faded, and she felt the ghost of him as it flickered through the Neither, disappearing beyond.

Kanna yanked her knife free and stepped back as the body fell. He was staring sightless into the morning sky, and he would be the first of many. She crouched next to him and drew his eyelids shut as a chime rang, and a gate opened.

The white shirt was already spattered with blood. The governor had dressed her this way to anger the crowds, to show her as an enemy. But they thought she was just a soldier.

She would show them a monster.

# 32

## FATED

### ISCO

ISCO COULDN'T LOOK AWAY from the spectacle even if he'd wanted to. The Keepers had chained him to the wall behind the gate before dragging Kanna out. When they were finished with her, he was next. Through the grates another opponent rushed her. She stumbled back, the momentum of the heavyset fighter throwing her off her balance and causing her to trip over one of the fallen bodies.

Isco had never seen someone move the way that Kanna did. He wasn't sure if the others were even trying. Kanna had entered into the flow of the fights without remorse, without mercy. It was as if every instinct she possessed was attuned to slaughter.

She rolled through the carnage, tangling in the corpses that littered the stage. The fighter charged again in the same way, learning nothing from his first attempt. Kanna stepped aside when he was a breath away from her, swinging her knife up and across the man's chest. He staggered, losing his footing. She leapt on him, her knee in his stomach and her knife plunging into his chest as he fell.

The chime that announced fighters had stopped its incessant sounding around midday, and Hautman's wide toothed grin had pressed into a thin line. He had advertised a legendary event and he was delivering, but not in the way he had hoped. After Kanna dispatched her latest opponent, she sat down and buried her knives in the ground at her sides as she waited. The crowd threw things from the stands, cups and discarded food and stones, but they didn't reach her amid the corpses.

Isco almost missed the sounds behind him as the Keepers approached. One grabbed his arm, yanking him to standing. She began to unlatch the shackles around his wrist while two others removed the heavy bar that blocked the grate.

"What—"

He dug his heels in as they dragged him to the open maw of the gate, the sun on the other side hot on the sands. He was no match for the guards, who shoved him onto the stage. Isco stumbled and fell, blinking in the bright glare.

The inevitability of the situation had not prepared him for the moment that it presented itself. He had known his death was coming, and he'd doubted each breath he had since the moment he'd laid eyes on Kanna once again.

Anger flared in her eyes, her lips set into a thin line, and she pushed herself to standing. But the chime didn't ring for him. It rang after.

Three new fighters entered the stage across from him, drawing her attention. They moved in a loose formation, two swordsmen flanking a spear wielder. Kanna closed the distance between them, an urgency in her movements. She met the first swordsman with a ringing of metal.

The spear wielder went for the opening, but Kanna kicked the swordsman back, launching herself out of the spear's reach and throwing the first swordsman off balance.

The three attacked together, Kanna twisting away in a dance of survival. The swords came for her, while the spear reached through them, forcing Kanna to dodge the bladed tip.

The spearman overreached and Kanna struck. She knocked the spear tip down and it dug into the sand. She leapt onto the wooden shaft of the spear, the snap of the weapon as good as a killing blow.

The spearman fell forward, stumbling into one of his allies. Kanna lashed out at the swordsman that was pushed off-balance and he went down in a spray of blood, his hands clutching his chest as if to hold his life inside of it.

With his weapon decimated, the spearman was left defenseless against Kanna. She opened his throat, and he sunk to the sands.

Her last opponent charged with a scream, his movements hastened by desperation. Kanna met his attack and stepped to the side, slashing down the inside of his arm as she slid from reach. He dropped his sword with a scream, cradling his arm and gasping. Kanna drove her blade down into the back of his neck, cutting off his struggle.

Without any others on the sand, she turned to face Isco. He wanted to run, but his legs wouldn't move. A slash on Kanna's arm left a line of blood from her bicep to her elbow. Cuts where she had not dodged quick enough lined both sides of her torso, her own blood thicker and darker against the white shirt than that of her challengers. Her breath was ragged, her eyes weary, and the only thing that seemed to be holding her upright was the will to remain so.

Then, it wasn't the chime. It was something else.

# 33

## COMING STORM

### YASSEN

YASSEN'S NAILS carved half moons into his palms as he watched the challengers fall before Kanna. The day grew longer and the seats grew hotter, setting tempers in the crowd on edge. Even the Governor's special guests had begun to argue. He couldn't make out what was being said, but by the tone they didn't seem pleased with the way the day's events were unfolding. Astar met his eyes, and she acknowledged him with a quick glance and a slight nod before turning away.

In his private box, Hautman crossed his arms at his chest and leaned back. Even he couldn't hide the flare of anger in his eyes when Kanna felled every opponent that he set on her. His smile had changed from the crowd-pleasing grin to something more sinister.

Yassen was still pondering what that look might mean when Isco was tossed out on one end, looking all the world like a student that took a wrong turn into a bad neighborhood. At the same time, three new fighters emerged.

Kanna went on a vicious offense, taking out the three quicker than she had previous opponents. When she was done, there was only a short pause. Then, instead of the expected chime, a heralded blast nearly deafened him.

"Is that Galman?" asked the man next to Yassen.

"Shit, that's Adalbar and Roka, too," his companion said. She hid her mouth behind her hand and leaned into the man.

Yassen had spent several of the past seasons in the Theatre, but they were behind the bars. The names meant nothing to him. "What's the big deal about them?"

The man shot a puzzled look at Yassen, blinking slow and long, before looking back to the stage. There were two men and one woman, but besides the fact that the fighters that entered were Gegenii, Yassen saw nothing about the trio that made them more intimidating than any of Kanna's previous opponents. They did not carry themselves any different than the fighters she had already put down.

Kanna's shoulders heaved with forced breath but she pulled them back, half-heartedly shoving errant locks of hair away from her eyes. She tilted her head to the side, considering the three before her. She spun her knives into a back grip, the metal gleaming between the drying blood that clung to the blades.

The first, Galman, clenched his fist in the air and pulled.

The ground erupted.

These were earth loas. And Kanna had to be exhausted. She dodged at the last moment, her movements sluggish, as the sands rose in a wave. She leapt high, running along the wave of earth until it bottomed out, sending her careening through the air. She hit the ground, stumbling.

The loas ignored Isco, focusing on the bigger threat. Adalbar joined. A rough pillar rose under Kanna's foot, tipping her balance. A wall rose at Kanna's side, slamming into her. The impact loosed the knives from her grip and sent her body skipping over the sand.

Then, Kanna went still.

The earth loas' attacks paused as they enjoyed the satisfaction of having knocked down the most vicious thing that had ever haunted the sands. It didn't feel real, and it didn't feel right. Kanna was unstoppable. She was something more, always more to her than what she seemed, and Yassen didn't like this.

Isco was still on the sands. The loas turned their attention to where he cowered, and the ground around him began cracking apart. He wheeled backwards, scrabbling on his heels in an attempt to get away.

Yassen gripped the rail tighter and leaned over, hoping he could figure out a way down. It was hard to see, and he had to squint in the dying light.

He froze. He turned his gaze skyward. The day had been unrelenting, the sun pulsing a white heat. There had been no clouds, and the sky remained clear. There was nothing to block the sun, yet the world was cast in a darkening gloom.

Yassen wasn't alone in his confusion. The rest of the crowd had also turned skyward to try and discover what was causing the sudden shade.

Kanna shifted in the sand.

Her body rose, unfurling and jerking up like a marionette pulled by strings. She moved, or must have, because she was beside Isco before Yassen could blink, shoving him out of the way before he toppled into the hungry earth.

Kanna stood above the fracture in the ground, hovering over nothing. She advanced on the loas, slow and unhurried.

And the shadows below her feet moved with her.

# 34

## INEVITABLE

### KANNA

THE DARK HAD ALWAYS BEEN WAITING.

It dug its claws inside of her, clenching and retracting the sharp points of it. It bided its time and stewed in its neglect. It wanted her to give in, to let it loose, to become it.

Kanna's echo had given her a name, and it had given her victories. A list of a life bathed in blood and the glory that it hailed. She knew what the darkness could do.

The day was too long, the sun too bright, her limbs too slow. When she hit the ground, her options narrowed to two simple choices: she could lie there, or she could give in to the thing inside of her.

Isco was innocent in this, a pawn played by others. If he hadn't tried to intervene the night they'd taken here he wouldn't be here. She wouldn't let him die because of a foolish mistake. Because of her. *Not again,* the shadows whispered, echoing her own voice. *Never again.*

She let go.

The dark came for her, blotting the sun as she rose. It folded around her, and she shoved Isco out of the way. The dark stayed with her, churning beneath her feet as she stalked across the sands, as they turned black beneath her feet. The earth loas began their assault anew, and a rock wall rumbled in Kanna's direction. She didn't break her stride.

It was insignificant. It was all so small, so pointless.

She swept her arm and a sickle sliced through the wall. She held her hands out to her sides and the remaining pieces rose from the ground, bolstered by the shadows gathered beneath. They moved with each of her fingers, a symphony of darkness, and it was hers to make or break. With a shrug of her wrists, the rocks crashed harmlessly to the side.

The screams of the crowd were different now. Kanna could feel their panic, feel their racing hearts and their fear beneath the blanket of her shade as they fled. They would run, they would scream, and they would hide, as they should. As they had before, and as they always would—fear of the dark was old as time.

The three loas joined together, gathering their tricks. The earth rolled toward Kanna, rising in a serpentine path and gaining speed. But she could see the threads of it, the way they wove their will and urged the earth to move. Kanna held her palms forward and the darkness gathered. When the rock collided with the her dark, she uncoiled their work, unraveling them from the earth and blowing it back.

The loas ducked, shielding themselves from the debris that rained down. They continued to ready attacks, but they were too slow. And they were far too weak.

The shadows shifted with her slightest movements, eagerly racing to follow her command. It was easy, once she freed the dark gathered within her. All the pain she held, the fear and anger she kept deep, became her. The feathered thing unfurled beneath her ribs and stretched into her veins, burning cold through her blood. In the hollows of her bones, in her soul, she knew it could be anything, anything. Anything she needed. Anything she wanted.

Kanna's right hand slid in the air and the first loa's shadow rose around him. She flicked her wrist, and the darkness hurled him into the arena wall. He hit it with a sickening crack and slid to the sands.

The two remaining loas attempted to stop her, but she couldn't be. Pillars of earth jutted up from the ground, so she leapt on the first and caught it, dangling from the side as it rose. She dropped to the next, the darkness at her feet skipping her from pillar to pillar.

When she reached the loas, she commanded the shadows to bring her to the ground. They sharpened to a wedge, driving through the rock and carrying her down in a hail of stone. Kanna landed in a crouch, the contact jarring her and, for a brief bright moment, reawakening the pain of the day.

It reminded her that she was a body, that she had a body and was not only the dark.

A coil of shadow detached from those gathered near her and lashed out, catching one of the two remaining loas around the neck. The loa tried to claw at it but scratched her own throat, unable to grasp the unrelenting darkness.

Kanna twisted her wrist and the loa's neck snapped, the sound clean and clear. Her head lolled to the side, her body hanging suspended until the shadows released.

Kanna gathered her breath, gathered whatever sliver of control she had left, and rose from her crouch.

There was one more. There was something twisted inside of him, and the shadows were hungry for it. He tried to run, but he jerked to a stop. Kanna reached into him, untangling the knot. His wife's bruised green eyes became violet, his son's fists against a locked closet became a dark box.

Her anger alighted, and she wanted him to suffer for it. The shadows knew how to make it so. She found the well of anguish inside of him and ripped it open. She yanked at the dark parts of his soul and pulled them free, dredging up his fears and digging out the memories of his own worst days. She brought it back all at once, a thousand times over, making a prison in his own mind, just for him.

He fell and he shrieked, his soul shredding beneath the onslaught. Her hand stilled at her side, the work complete, but he continued to scream. His cries rose in a mad crescendo, even as she turned away to retrieve her knives. She weighed them in her palms, carefully turning them over in her hands.

Returning to the writhing loa, she tipped him over with her boot. He grasped her ankle. He was weeping, begging in a jumble of sounds that weren't quite words. She lifted the knives high and drove them down into his neck, cutting the sound off into a garble.

His hands released her ankle, falling to his sides. He stiffened, his splayed fingers hovering over the dirt and his legs jerking straight, and she felt him slip through the Neither.

She held onto the last trace of him, examined what was left. He wasn't whole, not anymore, just a shattered bit of light in a fathomless dark.

She stepped back and looked up. The panicked crowd had evacuated, and her body relaxed, her shoulders sagging and her arms falling loose at her sides. The orange of the setting sun cut through her lingering shade, and she closed her eyes.

She was Ananke Strepheim. She was the Harbinger, the Shadowed Sun, the Last Eclipse. She had finalized Solarian rule over Atarrabi, crushed the uprising in Gegenes at the battle of Ganglere, and brought about the downfall of the Cardea in Adur. She was the frontline of an Empire that had reaped thousands, and she was angry, and she was tired of fighting.

The shadows hummed around her, sliding over and through her skin. She had awakened too much, released too much, and it did not want to yield.

Behind her, she heard shouts. Isco was running toward her. Further, Yassen and Astar leapt from the stands, riding the earth down to the stage and falling in a heap. They were so far away, and they moved so slowly. She could see each beat of their feet against the ground, each breath they took. She could see all the parts of them, the hope and the sadness twisting in their bodies.

The weight of the shadows pulled her to her knees. Her chest tightened, and every lung full of air she took was ice. The scar on her side burned, the sharp pain trying to remind her. She braced her hands against the ground, clenching her fists as if it would help her hold back the dark.

It was too late for her, but not for the others. She could hold out, if only for a moment. It would have to be enough.

She gathered the air she could and forced her throat to speak. "Go."

Isco was just steps away. He hesitated, lifting his foot to move again.

"No," she said, "Run."

The dark found its path through her. Like the night, it was inevitable.

## 35

# A GOOD SOLDIER

## HARU

THE WHEELS of the train had barely ground to a halt when Haru leapt from the car, the others on his heels. He knew Kanna was there. The magnetic pull had snapped taut the moment they entered the city's walls. He was close enough now that he could follow it directly to her.

He ignored Edin's protests as she followed behind the trio of soldiers as they raced through the near empty streets of the city. When the Theatre came into view, they paused. The walls loomed over them, nearly blocking out the sun and casting a shadow. The sound of the crowd within reached his ears, their jeers and cries muffled by the thick stone.

He found a side entrance and descended on the guards. Haru shoved the first one behind himself, and he fell into Osawa, who snapped its neck with a clean twist. Haru covered the second's mouth so that he couldn't scream out and slammed him back into the entrance, drawing his knife against the artery in his thigh.

He was getting closer. The dark maze beneath the Theatre was dusky and dank, but the structure was simple to navigate. It was nothing in comparison to the labyrinthian halls of the Tower that he'd endlessly wandered, constantly following Kanna's call before he even knew what it was.

The sound of the crowd grew louder and he stopped, holding up a hand to halt the progress of those behind him. They waited, quiet for once. A thousand voices were crying out, gripped by terror and confusion.

Osawa grabbed Haru's wrist, stopping his charge. "Haru, she's synching."

Haru shook his head, pulling his arm from Osawa's grip. "No."

"Just because you say it doesn't make it true," Vahn growled.

"Then stay here, or run," Haru said, "but I'm getting her back."

Haru pushed himself faster as the temperature dropped, a cold wind licking through the tunnels. He had spent a year agonizing over the worst situations imaginable, but Kanna synching had never been a possibility he was willing to entertain. Of anyone, Kanna had the most control over her abilities. The shadows were her companion and her burden, and she knew how to maintain the line between herself and the dark.

Even underground, the tunnels had darkened and driven the guards from their posts. They met a few who scrambled in retreat, summarily dispatching them in the same manner as the first group they encountered.

The party turned a last corner, the way ahead opening to the air of day. Screams from the sands reached the tunnel, echoing in the closed space.

Haru rushed to the gates that blocked his way. And she was there. Kanna, his Legatus, his Kanna, blood spattered and battle weary. His heart stuttered as she swayed on her feet, the black creeping through her veins and out of her eyes. Three others were on the sands, shouting for her and trying to approach as she dropped to her knees.

He yanked at the grates, but they pulled and stuck in place. Just beyond them, he was running out of time. "On me!"

The others joined Haru, following his gaze out.

"That's Astar!" Edin proclaimed, pointing to the blonde woman on the sand.

"Fuck," Vahn said, the sentiment sharp but accurate.

Together, they lifted the heavy bar blocking the gates and tossed it aside as the shadows began to howl.

"I won't be able to use the light," Haru called over his shoulder as they ran through the opening, "not until I can get close. Get me through, then get the civilians to cover."

The group ran out as the shadows spread, screeching their way through the air. One of the men on the sands created a barrier of rock and Vahn shoved Edin behind it as they passed.

Haru kept his eyes on Kanna. The dark that she contained was flowing out of her, sliding from her skin and pooling around her body. The world split and she disappeared into the place between.

The other man tripped and began to scramble back, but the shadows caught him and held fast. Vahn put on a burst of speed and Haru dropped back for him to clear the way. A wall of fire erupted, a howling violet between them and where Kanna once stood, clearing the shadows that had encroached and stopping more from screeching through, for the moment at least.

Vahn moved to lift the prone stranger from the sands, and Osawa moved to the forward position. He gathered what water he could and broke an opening through the fire. "Haru, go!"

Haru didn't need to be told twice. He spun around Osawa and through the flicker in the fire wall that allowed him to pass, before closing behind him once more, leaving him with nothing but the dark.

He would have to remind the shadows that he wanted her more. Needed her more. If he had to fight the darkness for her, he would.

Haru was a good soldier.

He couldn't see Kanna anymore, could barely feel her now. The world had ripped open where she had stood, the dark widening and moving. The swarming shadows tried to seize him, tried to take hold of his weaknesses and turn them against him. He could feel them slide over his skin, tempting him to give in.

He'd fought them before. The dark nights at the Tower when he knew Kanna was so close, yet so far out of reach. She ignored him, avoided him, and he convinced himself that he would never be enough.

He accepted that. He accepted them. Even if his name had never passed her lips, he would still follow her. But that wasn't how the story had ended. She turned to him, time and again. He'd held her when the dark became too much. He'd heard her screams, witnessed her pain.

He also witnessed her triumphs. He'd seen her smile. Not the smile of knowing, the dangerous glinting thing that took over her when she was challenged. He knew the slow one, the one that reached her eyes. He'd seen her when she was herself, when she let go of the burdens she forced herself to carry.

She'd looked at him like he was the only bright thing in the world.

*I'm sorry, Haru...*

The echo came to him in the wind, the way she stumbled over her words. The dark had found his weakest moment. He had been too caught in her that he'd forgotten to give his own confession a voice. Then she was gone, and he never had his chance.

Nothing was going to stop him from righting that mistake. He reached the shadowed gash in the world, but he didn't stop. He didn't hesitate. He knew she was there, just as he had always known where she was.

The world shifted around him as he stepped through the barrier and then shadows' screeches no longer reached his ears.

There was only silence, and darkness.

# 36

## ADVANCED THEORY

### VAHN

THE MASS that was evacuating from Kanna was screeching, hissing, the sound caught somewhere between a scream and a cry. The darkness pooled like mercury, like it had a mind of its own. Vahn gritted his teeth against the sound and burned his fires hotter. They shouldn't have worked against shadows, but they were Kanna, and he had been blessed by the dark long ago.

Vahn skidded across the sands, grabbing the man that had fallen to the shadows' grip as Haru and Osawa raced past. "All right champ, time to go," he muttered while, with a grunt, he hefted the man over his shoulder.

"Here!"

Vahn turned to the shout, where the earth loa was holding a barrier. Osawa was already racing to it, and Vahn had shoved Edin behind it before, so he joined them. The small party huddled behind the barrier, but the shadows that made it through his flames were dark, twisted things. They curled and reached, and the earth shuddered.

Vahn turned to Osawa. He always had the better plans. "Now what?"

It took Osawa a fraction of a moment. "We'll get back into the tunnels and block them. It might help."

"Might?" Astar asked, a bite in her voice.

158

"No time," Vahn grunted, the weight of the other man bearing down on him. "Count of three."

The others nodded, and readied.

"One—"

The pillar they hid behind cracked.

"Move!" Vahn shouted, the others running ahead of him.

The shadows chased at their heels but thinned as the group put distance between themselves and the epicenter of it all, which was Kanna. And Vahn wasn't going to think about that right now.

Osawa and Astar made it through the open maw of the tunnels first, Edin right behind them. The Gegenii man braced himself and started to bring the earth to close over the entrance.

Vahn dove through just before the opening shut behind him, and they were sealed in the dark, a different kind of blackness than the one outside. The screeches of the shadows outside the cavern became a muffled wail. They hit the wall but retreated, moving to easier prey. Vahn crouched down, dropping the man from his shoulders as carefully as he could.

With his hands free, he snapped his fingers. A pale glow danced in his palms and he coaxed it higher, enough that the tunnels were illuminated by the soft flames. The Gegenii man's back was pressed to the stone covering the entrance, his breath coming in hard gasps.

Vahn leaned over the man he'd carried, bringing the light closer. He was dirty and bruised, but otherwise in one piece, at least physically. There was a glazed look in his eyes, the trapped one that Vahn knew too well.

"They got him?" Osawa asked.

Vahn nodded. "I don't think it's too bad. I might be able to get him out."

"What do you mean get him out?" Astar asked. "If you can help him, help him."

Osawa put himself between Astar and Vahn. "Why would we do that? We don't know him, or you, for that matter."

Astar pressed her hands to her hips and pulled herself up, meeting Osawa eye-to-eye. "I don't know you, either, so I guess we're even. But all things considered, we might need a doctor, sooner rather than later if you don't back up, pretty boy."

Edin grabbed Astar's arm and pulled her back, shaking her head in warning.

Osawa blinked, his head jerking back in shock. "Pretty boy?"

The raw laugh that shook Vahn's body set him off kilter and he had to put his hand down for balance. "Pretty boy. I'll help just for that. Though one has to wonder what a doctor did that the shadows would get him all twisted up. What's his name?"

"Isco," Astar said, turning her glare away from Osawa.

"All right, Isco," Vahn said, crouching in front of him. "Watch the pretty light."

What Vahn had was not more than a parlour trick, but it worked sometimes. He settled another small flame in his palm again, keeping it calm and steady. He slid it from one side to the other, shifting the heat so the color changed. The light flickered on the planes of Isco's face, until his dark eyes began to follow its path.

He slapped his hands together and the fire flashed and crackled, turning blue and white and shooting out and away. Isco snapped out of his trance, throwing up his hands to block the flare and scrambling back against the stone.

The flame returned to a steady glow in Vahn's palm. "You in there?"

Isco studied his hands, turning them over in front of himself. His gaze met Vahn's, still somewhat distant but present in the moment, and he nodded. Vahn smiled, hoping the half-titled smirk would be something like comfort.

"Good," the Gegenii man said, his breathing calmed from his previous exertions. "Now will someone tell me what's going on?"

Vahn rose to standing, stepping away from Isco so that no one was behind him. "How about some introductions first?"

"It doesn't matter who they are," Osawa interjected, "and it's probably better if they don't know us, considering."

Astar jerked to attention, turning her gaze on Vahn. "Considering what, exactly? What are Palamidia soldiers doing here, anyway?"

"Soldiers? What did we do to earn that kind of insult?" Vahn shoved his hands in his pockets and leaned back against the wall. "You'll have to excuse Osawa, he thinks he has manners. I, for one, would like to know who I'm spending what's possibly the last few moments of my existence with."

Osawa glared at him, shoving his glasses up his nose before crossing his arms.

"I'm Vahn," he continued, "I've got Isco's name already. That's Edin," he indicated her with a nod, "and you're Astar. She showed us a picture, part of our deal to get here. I assume our part is done?"

"Nice try," Edin's glare was icey, but not enough for Vahn to shiver. "The deal was you get her out, not trapped in a cave while *Ananke Strepheim* loses her shit. And by the way, it would have been nice if you three had mentioned you were chasing after her of all people."

Vahn smiled at Edin. His tone low in warning, he said, "I don't understand how you think you have the high ground here."

Edin had grown wise in her years as a smuggler, at least enough to not challenge him. She clenched her jaw and turned her attention to Astar instead. "You want to tell me what you were doing on the stage?"

"Something weird happened and everyone started to run out of the Theatre," Astar said by way of explanation. "We were trying to get to Kanna, and then the shadows touched Isco and weirder things started to happen."

"I'm Yassen," the Gegenii man interjected, and raised his hand so everyone turned in his direction, "and I would very much like to get back to that whole 'last moments of existence' thing."

"Kanna appears to be synching," Vahn said. "Haru might be able to stop her but if not..." he shrugged.

"Synching?" Yassen asked.

"You're a loa and you don't know what synching is?" Osawa replied.

Yassen shook his head, and Osawa looked to Vahn.

"Lecturing is more your thing."

Osawa sighed so loud Vahn could swear it echoed in the cavern. He adjusted his glasses, uncrossing his arms and clasping his hands behind his back. "When a loa syncs, they become one with their element, in a sense. The fallout tends to be near cataclysmic, depending on the loa's strength. A fire loa synched in Tages and devastated several city blocks. She wasn't one of ours, so she didn't even have enough power to pass trials.

"Kanna, on the other hand," he continued, "is one of the most powerful loas in known history. And considering her abilities, there's no telling what will happen if she does sync."

"I have a theory," Vahn said, more to the ground than anyone else. "Everything came from the dark. Who's to say it can't return to it."

As if on cue, the light in his hand flickered. He raised it overhead, turning to the entrance they had used. "Yassen, right?"

"Yeah?"

"Get away from there."

Yassen looked up and scrambled to his feet.

The dark was seeping through the wall.

Vahn yanked Isco to standing, shoving him back with the others before recalling the flame. Blessed or not, he wasn't nearly enough to hold back the dark. Vahn wasn't even sure he wanted to, which didn't help. But Kanna would not give up. They may bend but they did not break, and they did not give up, and it would have to be enough.

## 37

# BECOMING

## KANNA

THE FIRST THING that Kanna lost was the feeling of touch. She tried to curl her arms around herself but there was no comfort to be found. She couldn't tell where she began, or where she ended. There was no sound, no cold, no place at all. She was the dark.

There was nothing left to feel and so nothing left to hurt. What was left of her ached at it, howled at being trapped. It wanted to be something. But it was so easy to resist. Outside was where the nightmares lived, where she never had a moment to rest.

The world was safe only if she was here.

Time worked differently. Entire universes bloomed and died in the span of a moment. Everything and nothing existed as one, and she was all of it. At some point between eons and milliseconds the other arrived. She felt a yank, as if everything that made her was being pulled away from the dark.

She scrambled to fight it but she didn't know how. She didn't know where her hands were to grasp it, or where her feet were to dig them into the ground, or where the ground was, or even if there was one.

The call was persistent. The more it drew her together, the more she could feel. There was an up and down, first, and then she stood in the black. She was separate from it, though. She could feel where she ended and where the dark began.

The sensation of touch traveled over her and through her and she looked down at the outline of her hands against the dark. They were such frail things. They had taken so much, but it was no wonder why they had held so little.

*Kanna*, a voice said. It was far away, echoing at the corners.

She looked up and he was there. Whole and brilliant, he reached out to her. He'd been in the Neither, in her half-remembered dreams, always chasing her, always reaching. A light she couldn't fathom. She shook her head, tried to back away. But there was no distance between them, nowhere to go except back into the dark.

She wasn't ready to go back. Not yet. But she didn't want to go forward, either. She was stuck.

*I can't.* She felt the muscles move in her throat, the vibration of her voice as it came through. *It is better if I am here. I am a monster. I should never have been awakened.*

*No*, he replied. His voice was calm, sure. It washed over her, through her, and it was something she knew like her own soul. *You had to exist, because I do.*

She couldn't figure out why she wanted to be near him.

*You were made by monsters,* he continued, *but you aren't one. You never have been.*

The way he looked at her, even now, even here, was something she couldn't understand.

*Everywhere I go, there is death. It follows me. Everyone meets it when I am around.*

*Everyone meets death. People follow you because they believe you. They need to believe in you.*

She forced herself to meet his eyes, the shining blue of them, a cloudless sky on a brilliant day. *Why?*

*You give them hope that there is another way. That not everyone will leave them alone when they need them. Hope is dangerous. You cannot let those who would destroy it win.*

Kanna didn't answer. She couldn't carry the burdens of others, didn't want to take the weight of it.

*Kanna.*

His voice cradled her name like he knew it, like he knew everything it contained and still wanted to speak it.

*Please, come back.*


*Come back, or take me with you.*

---

BECOMING HURT.

Kanna could feel every bit of herself. She could feel her bones where they met, the muscles that ached and burned from exertion, the tears in the fibres of them from being battered and pushed beyond limit.

Her skin was seared from the sun. She could feel where it was ripped open, where her blood flowed out and dried. She could even her body's effort as it desperately tried to knit the wounds closed.

It was too much. She wanted to climb back into the dark.

"Kanna?"

Her lungs awakened with a gasp and she coughed, choking on the grains of sand that cut down her throat. She remembered to exhale, then breathed again.

The smell of dust and old bones, the copper of her own blood, and the lingering scent of panic assaulted her nostrils. The sun against her eyelids was too much and she turned her face, met with the easy rise and fall of another's breath.

There was the beat of another heart outside of herself.

Her focus snapped back with a jolt. She shoved the body that held her and sprang away. The arms around her released reluctantly, resigned to her need to escape.

Kanna blinked against the glare of the light. She covered her eyes with one hand to protect them from the burn while scuttling back on the ground. Her legs wouldn't work, still numb from the dark and quaking with exhaustion, but she needed to put distance between herself and this new threat.

Her hand touched the hilt of her discarded knife and wrapped around the grip, stopping her mad escape. The burning in her eyes subsided and she blinked a few times to regain her sight.

Nothing about this was right. The sand beneath her had changed.

Around her, the world was black. Panic rose in her chest, but the dark thing had returned to its nest, and it fluttered and grounded her.

The man in front of her rose to standing. The specter from her dreams had manifested here, and he was still looking at her in a way she couldn't begin to understand. His uniform gleamed white, her own blood smeared across it. He held his hands at his sides, away from the hilts of his weapons but in a ready ease. The light around him was impossibly brighter, the deep black of his hair set against it in a vicious contrast. Gold burned in the blue of his eyes, moving like molten liquid.

The dark thing inside of her nearly purred at the sight of him, settling back and retracting its claws. Her heart clattered for new reasons. She didn't know him, but she should. Everything screamed that she should know him, that she was somehow found and safe here.

It had to be a trick.

Kanna shook her head, trying to focus on something, anything, but it was impossible. Everything was so slow and so fast in the light. She grit her teeth together, the ache in her jaw a solid thing she could understand, and settled her gaze back on him.

He hadn't moved. He was still there, unwavering and steady, demanding nothing.

She relaxed her jaw, waiting for her breath to still long enough that she could trust it enough to ask, "What are you?"

# 38

## A COMMON THREAT

### OSAWA

THE CREEPING DARK stopped its progression and the shadows ceased their cries. The group exchanged glances, none of them willing to be the first to test their luck until Osawa extricated himself from the pack. He approached the darkened area, half expecting it to come back to life and pull him down. It didn't move, and the sounds didn't return. "I think it's clear."

"All right, let's open it up and see what we got." Yassen placed his hands on the stone blocking their path, but nothing happened. He stepped back, scratched the nape of his neck, before trying again with the same result. "It's... dead?"

"What do you mean it's 'dead'?" Vahn asked, moving to the front. "Here let me—"

When his feet touched the darkened area of the cavern, the flame he held spluttered out. Vahn jumped back, the fire coming to life once again in his palm. He looked from the flame in his hand to the rock, retreating from the blackened area.

Yassen stepped back. He picked up a loose stone and skipped it over the area. It kept going, smacking harmlessly into the covered opening. "Oh. I got this."

Yassen lifted a boulder from the earth outside of the blackened space and hurled it towards the enclosure. The wall shattered under the force, cracking into sharp-edged shards and opening to the outside.

Osawa blocked his eyes as the light pierced the cavern. It wasn't right. The orange sand of the Theatre was a ruined black. It shifted beneath the heels of his boots, sliding slick beneath them. The evidence of the day's battle was frozen in a barren relief. Pillars from the earth loas, half destroyed, jutted up from the ground, and the bodies that had lain there were simply... gone. The ground was cracked open and shattered. The black crept up the walls like clinging ivy, ending in the Theatre seats. He breathed out, his breath fogging in the chill that crept over the area.

Haru stood apart from Kanna on the Theatre's once grand stage, looking at her with a combination of concern and confusion. She glared back a warning, tense and alert.

"K!" Vahn exclaimed, his long legs eating up the distance as he jogged forward. The others followed, calling her name in celebration.

Osawa hung back. Haru moved to intercept Vahn, grabbing him by the arm and stopping his progress while the ragtag rebels moved past them. Vahn tried to wrench from Haru's grip, but he only held tighter.

"Kanna! You're alive, holy hells, what was that?" Yassen exclaimed, practically vibrating with excitement as he drew near.

Kanna scrambled back, her hands clutching her knives like lifelines. She held one up, leveling it at them. "Stay away!"

Her voice was desperate, a near screech. It stopped Osawa in his tracks. Kanna was commanding, smooth. Even when she raised her voice there was a low thrum of dangerous challenge beneath it. The others backed away, drawing even with the soldiers.

Haru had his eyes shut as if it was the only defense he could summon. "She doesn't know me." Haru released his grasp on Vahn, his voice barely over a whisper. "She didn't even recognize me."

Vahn scoffed. "That's ridiculous." He turned toward Kanna, attempting an approach. "K? What's going on?"

She changed her grip on the knife and threw it at Vahn. He cursed, drawing his own blade to deflect its loping arc.

"I said," she growled, "stay back."

"Still Kanna," Vahn muttered, whirling on Haru, "but what did you do to her?"

Kanna struggled to her feet, swaying uneasily as she stood. She'd found Haru's white handled knife in the sand and she leaned to the left as if it weighed more than she could lift.

"Wait here," Haru said, motioning to the others to step behind him.

Vahn bristled next to Osawa, but he stepped back, detaching himself from the others.

Haru held up his hands, taking each step slow, pausing after each while Kanna's eyes roved over him. She'd move to skitter back and he'd stop, waiting until she settled once again.

Haru took another step and Kanna stumbled back, teetering before regaining her balance.

"Kanna, please. I've been looking for you." He gestured behind himself, to Osawa and Vahn. "We've been looking for you."

"Stop." She shook her head. Her hand went to her side as he moved closer and she nearly doubled over. "It hurts. Why does it hurt?"

"I don't know," he said. "We can figure that out, though."

"We?" She looked up, barely focusing once more.

"Yes, we'll figure it out. But you're hurt. You have to let us help you."

"Us..." she looked up past her shoulder, focusing on the group behind him. A smile snuck onto her features, a kind of relief, as if she was seeing them for the first time. Yassen waved, but he was far less jubilant. "They're safe."

"Yes, they're safe. So are you," he said, moving closer.

She turned back to him, swaying on her feet. The knife fell from her hand, settling back into the black sand.

"No," she said, "I'm really not, Haru."

Her knees gave out and Haru rushed forward in a flash of light, catching her before she hit the ground. The flash caused Osawa to jump in his skin—none of the other loas' abilities worked in the waste that Kanna had created, yet Haru didn't seem to even notice its effects.

Haru lifted Kanna in his arms, her knives pinging brightly against the blackened glass sand. Vahn approached, slow, and retrieved them. He tucked them into their holsters, and then, carefully, brushed the hair that had fallen over her face.

A trilling sound broke the spell.

Vahn stepped back and away, turning his back to face Osawa. "Of course you kept a comm."

It rang again, and the misfit gathering turned its attention to him. Osawa glared over his glasses at Vahn and patted his pockets, producing the thin device he had tucked away. "It's the one Haru took. I thought it would be useful if anyone came in range."

"What's that thing?" Yassen asked, looming above Osawa's shoulder.

Osawa unlocked it with a click, squinting. Black text scrolled over the paperlike screen, but it didn't make sense. Not at first. When the message finalized and settled, he froze. He hated always being the one with the bad news.

He looked up to Haru as he approached, cradling the exhausted Kanna in his arms. "What does it say?"

Osawa shook his head, turning the tablet to Haru.

SURRENDER THE LEGATUS

Haru's grip around Kanna tightened, and above them, a single wail set off a cascade of warnings as the city's raid sirens began to howl.

# ACT II

ECHOES OF THE LEGATUS

# 1

## UNDER THE HEEL

### SALINAE

Salinae had pushed his contingent to near breaking, bypassing easy rest. The vastness of Gegenes had always been a quandry for the Palamidia. Gegenii fighters were strong enough, making up for poor skill with bulk and bravery, and they had an abundance of earth loas that the Palamidia lacked. It would be difficult to hold such a region, as they could not draw a line and push through it without the possibility of the threat circling back around.

The distance worked in Salinae's favor in this. Though they were sighted by a handful of smaller settlements, the desert couldn't hide the riders that attempted to carry warnings ahead of them. His contingent arrived like a tsunami breaking, and the city of Gaoler surrendered with nothing more than a skirmish at the walls. He had been suspicious at first, but the looming dread over the city hadn't been his doing. They had a monster within the gates.

In what remained of the Theatre, he grabbed a fistful of the blackened sand and sieved it through his fingers. It was cold and glassy, as if part of Ilazki had somehow skipped over the border and inserted itself into the heart of Lifrasir. Ananke always destroyed, but this was too far. He held no soft feelings for the rebellious regions, but they would be part of the Empire, eventually. All that was living would bend the knee, and there was no reason to destroy land when so little remained.

Ananke needed to be stopped, before the world was nothing but glass and shadows.

He rose to standing as two of his officers brought out the Governor. He had been found cowering in a meager bunker, but his home was easy enough to locate. He hadn't been shy about flaunting the wealth he leached from his people for his own pleasures, and his compound dripped with unearned treasures.

The man stood a head taller than the Palamidia soldiers, but when they shoved him forward he stumbled over his pageantry and hit the ground with a thud. He attempted to stand, but the officers at his back held him down by his shoulders. He tried to shake them off and Salinae waved a hand to dismiss their efforts. This time, the man stayed in the dirt.

Salinae grasped his hands behind his back, looking down at the man. "It is strange. Your people were once brave, feared even. Yet here I stand, unaccosted and curious. What happened here?"

The man glared, his jaw visibly clenching to keep his mouth shut.

Salinae paced. "Your resistance was so paltry it was practically a welcome, so something terrible must have occurred. Quite recently, if the pall in the air and the bodies outside of this thing you call a Theatre are to be considered evidence. Which only means you fear something else more than us."

Salinae bent and, with the back of his gloved hand, he brushed stray granules of black sand from the Governor's shoulder. "This is a good fear. An intelligent one. We have come to deliver you from it, but you must tell me: where is the Legatus?"

The Governor scoffed. "In that ivory tower of yours, I'd guess."

Salinae stood, shaking his head. "I should have been more specific. I meant the once Legatus. About this tall," he held out his hand beneath his chin, then frowned and lowered it closer to his chest, "pale of skin, eyes like wet limestone? Surely, she would've stood out amongst you."

The Governor's eyes widened before he could stop himself.

"That is what I thought," Salinae said. "Who aided her escape?"

The Governor shook his head. "I don't know," he gritted, near spitting with rage. A lie, swimming in half-truths. "And I wouldn't tell you if I did, but you can have that gods rotted monster back when you find her."

Salinae chuckled. "I do not need your permission to take what is already ours. You have nothing else for me then, besides vile words and false bravado?"

The man clamped his jaw shut once more, jutting his chin out and up toward Salinae.

"Very well." Salinae stepped forward, patting the man on the shoulder once more. "I thank you for the city, Governor. I am sorry that you will not see the jewel that it becomes within the Empire."

He drew his knife and set it at the back of the Governor's neck, driving it down through his spine. The Governor fell forward with a thud, though not even dust rose from the dead ground. His blood pooled on the glassy surface, forcing Salinae to step back to avoid getting it on his boots. He wiped his blade on the man's corpse before sheathing it.

Nissa stood just behind the Governor, unmoving and unflinching. When she looked to Salinae there was neither doubt nor question in her dark eyes, only anticipation for new orders. Velinius always had a way of discovering the perfect soldiers, culling them from the trash that flowed in from the Empire's boundaries.

"Block all egress from the city," he ordered. "Lock and guard the gates, shut down the stations. Do not let them free from these walls."

"Yes, Saint," she replied, saluting neatly before turning to the task.

"And the body?" Masao asked.

Salinae frowned, and stepped away from the slow growing pool of blood. "Get rid of it."

Masao crouched next to the Governor's corpse, propping his chin in his elbow in thought. Salinae did not care to know where those thoughts wandered, but it was no matter. Masao would do what was needful.

Salinae turned to the woman behind him. The young Eye, Kenzi, had stood by in silence, one of the two that he had for this assignment. He did not hold this one in high esteem, but the other was favored by Velinius and had requested this companion. "You were telling me about the ones who helped her."

She removed her hood and her pale blonde hair gleamed. "There was one they set onto the stage with her, a woman that was in the Governor's private area, and a third who handed over her weapons."

"That was all you gleaned?"

Kenzi crossed her arms. "The dark was seeking me. Would you prefer I had fallen and offered you nothing?"

"No," he said, after considering. He didn't appreciate the girl's tone, but the Eyes were a different type of soldier. The nature of their work meant they could only function with some spark of independence. "I suppose you made the wiser choice."

"The city is a maze," she continued. "There are tunnels beneath this Theatre, though I can't be sure how far they go. My time was limited before your arrival."

"I trust you can find more?"

"Of course." Kenzi replaced her hood and tucked her blonde hair behind it. "The Eyes of the Empire see all."

# 2

## WHAT LIES BELOW

### ISCO

Beneath the city, the newly formed cadre of misfits and traitors huddled in a rock-covered alcove of Yassen's design. When the white boots hit the city streets, they dug into their newly formed shelter, hiding from the army that flooded the streets. Kanna had awakened from her exhaustion swinging, but enough of her sense had returned that she was able to recognize her companions. Some of them, at least.

Isco set himself to the task of assessing Kanna's injuries. Being able to focus on something he knew how to do burned away the last vestiges of the shadows that lurked in the corners of his mind. Besides the obvious dehydration and exhaustion, most of Kanna's injuries were, to his near astonishment, already half-healed.

Kanna hadn't stopped glaring at Haru, who leaned on the wall opposite of her, his arms crossed at his chest. He returned her stare, and Isco was at least grateful that he was too distracted to notice him.

Yassen raised his hand. "I have a question." The many glares turning on him didn't deter him from asking it. "What did they mean by 'Surrender the Legatus?' We don't have a Legatus."

"I'm the Legatus," Kanna said, her voice plain and even. The declaration was met with silence as the information seeped into the gathering.

Astar stuck her hands to her hips. "I've known you for a year,

Kanna. You could barely remember your name when we met. How are you the Legatus?"

Kanna shrugged. "I am."

"Why didn't you tell me?"

"I didn't know."

"But you do now?"

"Yes."

Astar rubbed her hands against her face, running them through her hair and yanking at the ends. "How?"

"I don't know," Kanna said, then turned her stare back on Haru. She shook her head as if clearing it and refocused. "Who are we up against?"

Osawa cleared his throat. Standing next to the other two men, he seemed out of place. The other two radiated danger, so there was something about the calmer man that made Isco worry more. "The message was signed by Salinae."

"Oh, wonderful," Vahn muttered.

"Is that supposed to mean something?" Yassen asked.

"Salinae is the Saint of Water, and one of Velinius's most loyal soldiers," Osawa said. "And Vahn's ex."

Vahn shot a glare at Osawa. "Did you really need to add the last part?"

"Hold on." Astar held her hands out in front of her, shaking her head. "You break up with the guy, and he brings an army after you and wrecks my city?"

"In my defense, I don't think the two are related. Besides, he's probably more pissed at Kanna. She's the one who rearranged his face. Violently, and permanently."

Kanna's brow furrowed. "Why would I do that?"

Vahn's grin slipped away, and the teasing lilt in his voice grew cold. "Who knows? Doesn't matter. But of all the people that bitch could send." Vahn sighed, his head lolling back behind his shoulders. "Sorry, K, didn't mean to call your sister a bitch."

"My what now?"

"Her *what now*?" Astar asked, her voice a near shriek. She whirled on Kanna. "You have a *sister*?"

Kanna's expression remained blank. "Maybe?"

"Yeah," Yassen said, "I'm still not sure what's happening."

"Join the club," Edin joined, breaking her previous silence.

"There's a club?"

Astar covered her face with her hands and groaned. "What the fuck."

"Stop." Vahn's voice echoed in the cavern, rising only enough to be heard over the convoluted din. "Everyone stop, for a minute, let me think."

Isco turned to Vahn. The man was lean and sharp, but he appeared to Isco like a wild thing at rest. Osawa was buttoned down and crease-less, and while Haru wore a simple tee beneath his open jacket, there was something impeccable about him that still screamed uniform. Vahn was loose, his collared shirt untucked and half-buttoned, and yet there was something about it that made him all the more dangerous. He turned to Kanna. "Ananke?"

"Yes?" she answered.

"So, we've got that much." He gestured to include Isco, Astar, and Yassen, who were standing on Kanna's side of the expanse. "Who are they?"

Kanna looked to them in turn, her eyes locking on Isco for a moment. "My friends."

"Now, what about us?"

Kanna looked at the others in turn, carefully considering. "I don't know her," she indicated Edin, "but that is Osawa Tando, a water loa. You are Vahn Noson, the Saint of Fire. He is... Haroun?"

"Sure, when he's in trouble." Vahn turned to Haru, who raised a hand and shook his head to stop Vahn's questioning. Vahn turned back to Kanna. "Anything else?"

Kanna paused, her thoughts flickering behind her eyes as she searched for the right expression. "You are my friends?" she said, a half-question more than something known.

"Fantastic," Vahn said, sarcasm biting at the word. "Now that we've established some common ground, can we all stop growling at each other? We have to get out of this current mess, then we can figure out the rest of it. Objections?"

No one raised any.

"How is she?" Haru asked.

Isco flinched. Haru had stayed silent during the chaos that had followed their route following Kanna's fallout. The sound of Haru's voice was enough to trigger a near panic, memories from the night the Cardea fell threatened to curdle Isco's precarious calm. Instead, he chose to focus on the arm he was assessing. "Her injuries are mostly mild, or as mild as sword wounds can be, but the amount of them is concerning."

Kanna looked from her arm up to Isco, but he couldn't meet her gaze, either. "Why are you so nervous?"

Isco was always nervous, but that didn't seem worth mentioning. He cleared his throat and sat back on his heels, taking his hands from her skin. He wasn't sure how by her abilities worked, but some distance between them couldn't hurt. "I need supplies. Something to clean the wounds and bandage them. You also could use a transfusion, though I don't think that is something readily available."

Her eyes narrowed on him, and he had a feeling this wasn't the end of her questioning. She left it alone, though, and turned to Astar. "Does your father have medical supplies at his compound?"

"Basic things, sure. Nothing for transfusions, though, for that you'd need a Medicium."

"That's fine. The needles seem unnecessary, anyway."

Kanna patted the side of Yassen's knee to get his attention, holding out her hand when he looked down. He took it, lifting her to her feet easily. Once upright she swayed, and Haru stood up as if to move to her. She steadied herself on the wall, and he leaned back to his previous position.

"Maybe unnecessary," Isco said, "but it would help you regain your strength faster."

"We'll discuss it later," she said, but in a way that Isco knew they would not. "Astar, I assume your father has tunnels connected under his home?"

Astar nodded. "Of course he does, but it's like you're forgetting we're occupied. That's the first place any force would go, right?"

"Why?" Osawa asked, "It's just your house."

"Astar is the Governor's daughter," Kanna said.

The soldiers turned to her in near unison, their expressions a mix of concern and pity.

"So, that's where they'd go?" Yassen asked before the implications could be weighed.

"Yeah," Edin adjoined, seeming to catch on to Kanna's trail of thought. "They would, which means they would have already checked the place and left. No reason to check the same place twice."

"Besides," Kanna said, "my horse is there. I go nowhere without her."

"Your horse?" Vahn's sarcastic tone was heavy with bitterness. "We just hauled your bastard horse halfway across the continent."

Haru pushed away from the wall. "Leave it, Vahn."

Vahn turned on him. "Fuck you, Haru."

"All right." Yassen clapped his hands together and stepped into the center of their makeshift cavern, interrupting whatever was happening. "Which way?"

"There are tunnels that go west between the Theatre and the compound," Astar said.

"And I'll be going east, to the railyard and away from here and you lot," Edin said. "Astar, you coming?"

Astar looked between Edin and Kanna and back. "No. I don't think I am."

Haru looked up, his eyes sparking momentarily. "Loose the horses before you go."

Edin snorted. "Gladly. Now can you open this thing up?"

Yassen turned to study the walls.

"East is that way," Osawa offered, pointing to the wall behind Haru. "West is the other one."

Haru moved next to Kanna, but kept a spare distance between them. He was clearly agitated, but holding back with a practiced detachment.

The earth shifted, opening under Yassen's guidance as Astar led them into the tunnels, Edin taking her own path in the opposite direction. Osawa was the first of the soldiers to follow behind Astar. Vahn looked back, his gaze flitting over Isco then landing on Haru.

Isco stayed close to Kanna. He knew the others would leave him alone as long as he was useful to her because, despite her current unsteady gait, she was still commanding. Her memory was a patchwork of facts, and she didn't seem to remember the time she spent on Adur. At least, not yet.

He had no illusions with regards to his ultimate safety. Once Kanna remembered him, that would be the end. All he had to do was look behind him to the blue-eyed soldier to know his fate had been sealed long ago.

# 3

## BACKLIGHT

### VAHN

WITH ASTAR AS THEIR GUIDE, their group navigated the tunnels, slipping safely past the danger above. Eventually they arrived at the Governor's manor, emerging into a humid basement stocked with myriad dark bottles. Vahn pulled one of the bottles from the shelf in passing and tucked it under his arm before catching up with the others.

They ascended the stairs to gloaming light spilling through the windows, casting long shadows in vast rooms. Even in the dim, Vahn could still make out the excess in the home. Never had he seen opulence like this, even if it was tossed and scattered from the soldiers that had come through. The wood gleamed, the hangings were the finest of weaves, and the murals were nothing like he had seen before. It was too much of everything all at once.

"Wait," he stopped, pointing at one of the murals in a long hallway. "Is that Ganglere?"

Osawa paused, squinting at the broad strokes of the work in progress. "I think it is?"

Haru came up behind the two. "Why?"

"I asked the same thing," Isco said. Isco was outright supporting Kanna at this point. Haru had stayed behind her, reaching out a barely-there touch to steady her when she'd falter. But the tunnels were uneven and winding, and she had soon lost whatever was remaining from the adrenaline that had surged through her.

She'd leaned on Isco, of all people. His touch was clinical, even confident, as he took part of her weight on the short journey. Astar led him and Kanna, and they breezed past the trio that had gathered at the murals.

Haru detached himself from the group admiring the walls and followed behind Kanna, far enough to not set off her internal warnings but close enough that he could step in if needed. Vahn shook his head and looked away. The sight was familiar.

Yassen approached the remaining soldiers and squinted at the mural over their heads. Vahn was often the tallest in a room, but Yassen dwarfed even him. "What's the big deal about this picture?"

"You've not heard of Ganglere?" Osawa asked.

Yassen shook his head. "Seems familiar but..." he trailed off, shrugging.

Vahn grinned up at Yassen. "Where did she even find someone like you?"

"I got stabbed in the leg."

"Sounds about right," Vahn said. "Osawa?"

"Ganglere was the last battle fought between the Palamidia and the people of Gegenes," Osawa started. "At the start of the siege, the odds seemed even. The Palamidia forces were outnumbered, but we had strong positioning. We built walls of earth around the city to ensnare the people, but the citizens had plenty of stores. The independent militias outside were being reinforced, while we...."

"We worked with what he had," Vahn finished where Osawa paused.

Osawa cleared his throat. "Eventually, the Legatus said that the progress was too slow. In the night, a water loa entered the city and synced. She sacrificed herself, and the city drowned in the waters that she summoned. Then there wasn't anything left to fight over."

"Wait a gods rotting minute," Yassen said, his brows knitting in concentration. "Kanna ordered that?"

"No," Vahn said. "Not Kanna." He turned away from the mural. There wasn't any point in looking at something he'd lived.

"Hey Yassen, glasses, hot guy," Astar called. She stood in the open archway, arms crossed. "This way."

Yassen practically skipped to follow Astar, his head easily clearing the arched passage. Osawa followed at a more sedate pace. Movement caught Vahn's attention and he turned in time to see Isco pass behind them.

"I'll catch up."

Vahn went back the way they had come originally, pausing to watch Isco as he half-sprinted across the foyer and darted up the stairs. He followed behind, his hand on the cool wood of the banister as he took the stairs with light steps to avoid any creaks of protest.

At the landing, he listened for indications of where the other man had gone. Rummaging movements came from one of the rooms and the artificial light from within slanted out in a narrow streak.

Through the crack in the door, Vahn watched Isco as he flitted about the room. He unbuttoned the wrists of his shirt and rolled his sleeves up to his elbows. Crouching on his hands and knees, he shoved half his body beneath the bed and crawled out, dragging with him a soft leather bag. It was worn from use, but care had been taken to keep it maintained.

One of Isco's sleeves fell, and he paused to roll it back up. He stepped back, brushing his hands over his torn waistcoat. Vahn had watched Osawa make this same movement, unconsciously trying to remove nonexistent wrinkles, but on Isco the gesture was nervous and uneasy. And the wrinkles were real.

Isco brushed his hair back from his forehead then froze. His shoulders tensed, nearly climbing to his ears, before he turned. He leapt in place when he spotted Vahn, his hand going to his chest as though he was trying to stop his heart from escaping his ribcage.

Since it was pointless to continue hiding, Vahn pushed open the door of the room and it creaked on tired hinges. He stepped into the doorway, leaning against the jamb and blocking Isco's escape. When he crossed his arms he glanced down, checking that the black bands on his wrists were exposed in full. Isco's eyes were wide, his lips slightly parted in shock.

"I have some questions," Vahn said. "Hope you won't mind answering them."

Vahn stepped into the room, and the medic stepped back until his calves banged against the wood frame of the bed and stopped him short.

Vahn held his empty hands up to show he was unarmed. Sort of. The thought must've occurred to the medic, because he kept his guard up.

In Vahn's experience, someone as attractive as Isco was either arrogant or cruel. He needed to know which the medic was. Vahn moved to a bookshelf set into the wall, and Isco pivoted to watch him. Vahn didn't have to see the medic to know he was there, just as he didn't have to see Kanna to feel the heat of her on the main floor.

The books were apparently there to be there, not because anyone had ever read them. He traced along the top of them and hooked his finger around one. He pulled it out with his fingertip, allowing the spine to slam into the wood shelf. Behind him, Isco jolted. A quick flare, like kindle snapping in a flame.

Vahn didn't turn. "What were you doing in that place?"

"I—"

Vahn pulled out another book and let it drop. The man's nerves scattered again, which was the point. It was harder to lie that way.

Isco coughed to cover his throat clearing. "The Governor held a dinner and invited Kanna. It was a trap for her. When I found out, I tried to stop them, but I couldn't."

"How did you find out?"

Isco forced a laugh. "It was obvious when they drugged her."

Vahn studied the dust between his fingers. "How was it obvious?"

"She tripped over her own feet. She doesn't seem the type."

Vahn smiled. At least they were getting somewhere. "And you, what? Jumped to the defense of a stranger? Against the wishes of your Governor?"

"I'm not from here."

"Where are you from, then?"

"Is that what you really wanted to ask me?"

Vahn turned to him, his smirk falling and his eyebrow rising. It wasn't anger in Isco, but something else. "Why did the shadows want you so badly?"

"I don't know what you're talking about." It wasn't a lie, but it didn't feel like the entire truth, either. "I'm tired, and I am hungry. I need to eat, so if you're done, I'll excuse myself."

When he attempted to leave, Vahn held his arm out to block the passage. Isco had to stop himself short so as not to collide him, but Vahn wasn't finished. "You didn't answer my question."

Isco shut his eyes and stepped back. He went defensively cold. "Does it matter?"

"Of course it does," Vahn replied. "Everything matters."

"Not this."

Isco stepped forward again, but Vahn didn't move. Isco wasn't a small man. He was broader than Vahn, but Vahn was taller, and Vahn had faced worst than a nervous medicus that was hiding something. Everyone was allowed their secrets, but not this man. He was too close to Kanna, in a position that allowed him the access to harm her. Haru was keeping watch, but that wasn't good enough. Not to Vahn, not when he'd just gotten her back.

Vahn leaned down the fraction to close the distance between them, his face a bare gasp from Isco's. "Just because you're gorgeous doesn't mean we won't kill you."

Isco breathed in, and then out. Then, he wrapped a hand around Vahn's wrist. He didn't twist, or shove, only moved Vahn's arm and met his eyes while he said, "I'm well aware."

Vahn rubbed his wrist with the other hand, the burn in his skin subsiding as Isco stepped past him. Vahn shook it off. He gripped the top of the doorframe and leaned against it. When Isco was at the edge of the stairs, he asked, "Of what part?"

Again, that sharp flare of tinder heating and snapping, and Isco looked back. Vahn smirked, and when Isco righted himself forward, he tripped down the first two stairs in his haste. Vahn watched, and he smiled, because it was amusing. Just because it was amusing, and for no other reason.

4

# A NEW NORMAL

## ASTAR

ASTAR HADN'T REALIZED the pure size of the kitchen until it was emptied of servants. Double stoves, triple sinks, and an overly large refrigerator gleamed despite the night outside the windows that looked into the back gardens. She hurried to close the curtains and block the view of the room from outside, but that didn't make them safe.

They were at war. It was the first time the thought had a chance to stick and land, and it sent a chill into her bones. With the Palimidia invading Gegenes, the dying embers of conflict sparked anew. The city itself had been spared, before. Gaoler was more central and southern, nestled deep in the region's territory. Its location was strategic in that it was tucked in, but at the same time, it wasn't the kind of stronghold that kept the Palamidia out. Her father had been flirting with the attentions of the Adurians, who thrived due to having the natural resources the deserts lacked, but they focused their support on cities closer to their borders, those that stood between them and the Empire, not far-flung ones like Gaoler.

She remembered the years before, the dwindling resources, the haggard faces of those returning from the front as they ambled about the city or drunkenly slept in doorways. In the lull, when the Palamidia folded in on itself, those people had nothing to do. Peace had given rise

190

to the Theatre, and the Theatre had then tempted the enemy to their city.

The enemy was making a sandwich in her kitchen.

Astar turned on the mellow accent lighting that hovered over the long counter in the center of the kitchen and invited them to help themselves. Yassen nearly yanked the refrigerator's doors from their hinges in his haste, then grabbed an entire foil pan of sliced roast. Astar managed to hand him a fork, at least.

Osawa removed his jacket and draped it over the back of a counter stool before tightly folding up his sleeves. The man was quiet, his gaze distant, but hunger was a common need no one could deny. He eyed the contents of the refrigerator and removed another pan and set it aside. Somehow he managed to find a cutting block and the rest of his ingredients, asking after the things he couldn't locate with short, polite questions.

Astar didn't want to like the soldiers. She knew she should hate everything about them. When Yassen half-choked on a chunk of meat, Osawa stopped his own work and waited until the larger man managed to clear his throat before continuing again. When he finished the first sandwich he was putting together, he cut it in half diagonally and slid it wordlessly to Astar.

Then he started again, his focus on his task. Astar looked from the sandwich to the soldier and back again. She lifted the sandwich to her lips and bit into it, and her stomach demanded more. She polished off the first half of the sandwich just as he finished putting together the next.

Isco wandered in, his eyes darting over the gathering. Vahn swept into the room after, grabbing one of the halves of Osawa's meal with a wink and shoving the corner into his mouth before collapsing into the stool next to Yassen. Osawa didn't miss a beat, though. He plated the rest of the sandwich and slid it across the slick counter to Vahn, who stopped the plate from falling.

Vahn scooped the plate up with his free hand and shoved it at Isco. When Isco hesitated, Vahn let the plate go, forcing Isco to catch it before it crashed onto the floor. Astar met Isco's gaze and nodded to the empty seat on her far side, which he gratefully sunk into.

Osawa turned and retrieved two more plates from an upper cabinet. He put one between Vahn's elbows to catch crumbs while he ate.

"Where did you go?" Osawa asked, his eyes on the cutting board in front of him.

"Just wanted to have a chat with the healer," Vahn said between mouthfuls.

"Did you learn anything?"

"Mm," Vahn hummed, "Maybe. You?"

Osawa shrugged. "The big one is powerful, but he seems harmless enough. The woman doesn't trust us, but she also doesn't want us caught."

Astar coughed around the bite she was chewing, forcing herself to swallow. "I have a name. And we are right here."

"We know," Osawa said, finally seating himself next to Astar and across from the other two. When he slid beside her, Astar's eyes caught a flash of viridian grips on the knives at his hips. Somehow, she'd forgotten for a moment that the soldiers were armed. She swallowed the last bite of her small meal while Osawa began his.

Astar dusted crumbs from her hands over her plate. "I have no reason to trust you."

Vahn grinned across the counter. "And we're supposed to trust the daughter of a Gegenii governor?"

"Kanna trusts us," Astar replied, including Yassen and Isco.

Vahn snorted. "I've known K since she was eleven... ish. She doesn't even trust herself. On a good day, maybe she trusts Haru," he dropped the half-eaten sandwich on his plate. "Pretty sure this isn't a good day by anyone's definition."

"I thought it was a good day," Yassen said between swallows. "I almost died, but then I didn't. That's a good day."

Vahn propped his chin on his palm and turned to the man. "That's a bit of a low bar."

Osawa looked up from his plate and adjusted his glasses, as if that would make things clearer. "He isn't wrong."

Astar shoved her stool away from the counter and grabbed her dish. She turned, but couldn't decide which sink she was supposed to put it in. She went for the one further from the window and dropped it in, the porcelain rattling against the steel tub. She twisted the water on and began scrubbing at crumbs.

"This is insane," she said, more to the sink than anyone present. Finishing, she dropped the dish in the rack and turned to lean back, her hands still damp. "There is a war outside, my city has fallen, and I have two Empire soldiers in my house. Eating sandwiches."

"I think there are four in the house," Yassen said. "Is Kanna a soldier? Does the Legatus count as a soldier?"

Astar felt the twinge of a headache forming. "Yassen, please don't remind me of that part of this madness."

"Once Kanna gets put back together, we'll be on our way and out of your hair," Vahn said, leaning back in his seat.

"You will not," Astar responded. "You start a war and then you what? Walk away? Leave me and my people here to pay for your mistakes? I don't think so." She marched over and yanked Vahn's plate from him before slamming it into the sink. It broke, so at least she didn't have to wash it. "No."

Vahn chuckled. "What's the other option? We hang out here and play house?" he stretched, but didn't move from his seat. "Not really my thing."

Astar moved back to the group, swiping the fork from Yassen's hand.

"Hey!" he protested.

"You're gonna make yourself sick," she scolded.

Osawa rose unbidden and began to stow away the food items, rewrapping the unused portions and putting them back in their respective places. He grabbed the cutting board, the dull knife he'd used, and his own plate and walked them to the sink, where he scooped out the shattered pieces of plate and began to wash the remaining prepware.

Behind him, Astar paced. She knew they had to get out of the city, but she didn't want to give it over, either. It wasn't like the militia would follow her, and from how the soldiers were acting, this Salinae person wasn't one to underestimate. Still, they had Kanna, and that had to count for something.

A flash of white caught her attention and she jumped. It was Osawa's abandoned coat, and the man himself quirked an eyebrow at her as he dried his hands with a dishtowel he'd located. She looked him up and down, from the tips of his white boots to the starched collar of his white shirt. Palamidia uniforms were unmistakable, designed to be noticed by anyone with eyes.

"All right," she said. "We'll need supplies to travel. And ya'll need to get out of those uniforms."

Vahn raised his brow. "Did that sandwich count as you buying me dinner?"

"Since when do you consider dinner a prerequisite?" Osawa removed his glasses and held them up in the dim light to check for smears and frowned before setting them back on the bridge of his nose. "She has a point. We will have to at least blend in until we are out of the city."

"So happy you agree with me, really needed you to support the obvious."

"How do we know that you won't run to the nearest sympathetic ear you can find and turn us in?" Vahn asked.

Astar rolled her eyes. Vahn's delivery was petty, but the argument was logical, and fair enough. Her gaze landed on Osawa, who folded the dishtowel in half and hung it to dry. Between the soldiers in her kitchen, she'd rather not take a chance on the whims of a supposed Saint. "I'll take him."

"That seems to defeat the purpose," Osawa said. "I don't have other clothes."

Astar waved a hand at the lush compound around them. "I might have something."

# 5

## RAZOR'S EDGE

### HARU

KANNA HAD BEEN as brilliant and bloody as the day he'd first seen her.

Ever since they'd entered the tunnels, the steel of her gaze had held him fast. He did little to escape it. It made it easier for him to look back. There had been a thick red strike on her cheek, and it would have been hard to tell if the flecks on the bridge of her nose were dried blood or freckles if he hadn't known each one by heart.

The Governor's daughter had shown them to a large suite in the lower floors and left them with the medicus. Haru stood by as the purported healer struggled to get Kanna clean and tended. He hid his smirk behind his hand when she hissed at the man, kicking him in the shin at one point. Isco remained unfazed. He grit his teeth and continued his work with more care and determination than Haru had seen from Kanna's previous attendants.

Still, there was something about Isco that Haru didn't like. Once he finished his work he left them, and then there were more important things to focus on. Kanna balanced on the settee at the end of the bed, her hands hovering protectively over the knives she'd set there. Though exhaustion threatened to take her, she struggled against it. It showed in the flare of her nostrils, the rigidity with which she held his stare.

He sat back in the armchair he had claimed, hiding his clenched hands in his crossed arms, well aware that his every move was being tracked and reviewed. It took everything he had to keep them still, to not reach out and shake her until the splintered moments of their shared past realigned.

Haru cleared his throat. "You can rest. I will watch over you."

Her head ticked to the side, that achingly familiar motion when she was considering, wondering, trying to make sense of things that didn't fit her understanding. "You didn't answer my question."

He shifted under her gaze. He could feel every part of him being measured under her steel gaze. It was enough to take his breath if he hadn't grown used to the weight of it. He stretched his legs, feeling the burn at the back of his calves before pulling them back, crossing his left ankle over his knee. "It is a difficult question to answer."

Her eyes narrowed on him, a knife blade's edge. The tilt in her head became more evident as thoughts flew behind her eyes, shifting the black in her irises. A glimmer of gold sparked in them for a moment before being consumed. He didn't have the opportunity to wonder at what that meant.

"How?"

Haru smiled. It was something that he couldn't help even if he wanted. At least some things didn't change, but he had to be careful. Kanna had been shattered, cast off into the Neither. Instead of weakening, her jagged edges had multiplied, making her deadlier than before. He'd always known to hold on to her with care, never too tight, but he'd never minded coming away with bloody hands if that was what it would take.

She huffed, petulant and proud, then straightened to standing. The movement was too quick, though, and she swayed. He was at her side within the moment, his arm around her waist to catch her before she toppled.

The brush of her body against his sent a magnetic pulse through him. Beneath his hand he could feel lingering gold in her skin as it leapt at his touch.

She didn't pull away. He didn't let go.

When she looked up at him, his pulse ricocheted in his veins.

"You should sit down," he said, "and rest."

Kanna's eyes narrowed. "You should not tell me what to do."

"Fine." He retracted his steadying hand, ignoring the way his body screamed in resistance.

She tilted and fell back to sitting, safe but so far away from him he wasn't sure he would be able to reach her. Upon recovering, he was relieved that she had the energy to glare at him.

Haru turned and settled on the floor, his back against the upholstered bench and his shoulder nearly but not quite touching her. He pulled up one knee, resting his arm over it. In front of him, the white of his boots had become scuffed and worn in their travel, but it was still a harsh contrast against the gleaming dark wood and jewel tones of the home's decor.

Next to him Kanna had shifted back onto the settee, her heels not quite brushing the floor. An indigo bruise graced the top of one where someone had stepped on her foot. Her gaze was distant, staring beyond the walls. In the quiet of the room, she was coming back to the present, descending back into herself. Her hands on her knees shook almost imperceptibly. He reached out, a single touch barely tracing the scar on the back of her right ring finger. The shock of it stilled her hands and he dropped his own with a sigh.

"You asked me that before."

She blinked into focus and looked down on him, but she was still not quite there. "What?"

"Your question, 'What are you?'" he said. "You asked me before."

"I did?"

"The first time we met." He smiled, turning to face the wall once more. He leaned back further against the sofa until the wood frame of it pressed against his shoulder blades. "I didn't know how to answer then. How was I supposed to? I hadn't yet figured it out myself."

"But you know now?"

"Yes. I do."

The quiet lived between them. He wasn't sure how to continue, or what he would be able to tell her with words that she would be ready to hear. But she was watching him, waiting, expecting him to have an answer that would make sense to her.

It wouldn't make sense to her. Not the her that was there now.

There was only one way that he could make it make sense, but he wasn't sure if it would be worth it to her.

The least he could do was try. Haru lifted his hand between them, an offering to the altar where he'd placed his soul. "Will you let me show you?"

# 6

## MOMENTS LOST

### KANNA

KANNA EYED the hand offered to her, unsure as to what it would mean to take it. She was tired, but something about the man seated at her feet imbued her with another kind of strength. One she didn't quite have the name for. When she placed her hand in his she felt a familiar connection. The shadows inside of her cooled their lashing wrath, soothed by the warm glow that passed between them.

Nothing happened, at first. Then—

She was in the grey.

Kanna jerked her hand out of Haru's grasp, tearing herself away from his touch. Around her, the horizon stretched flat and empty. It seemed lighter than when she was there before, a shade brighter that magnified the lonely stretch that went on as far as she could imagine. When she looked down, she was dressed in all white, but it wasn't the same as his. Her clothing was blank, blurred and rough at the edges.

"What is this?" she demanded.

Haru turned to look out onto the space. He seemed to be expecting something to happen. His brow furrowed when nothing did. "It's the Neither."

"I know that. What did you do?"

"It wasn't me. I learned the way here, but I cannot walk this path without you."

Haru stepped forward, and she backed away.

He shouldn't be there. She should not be there. She could feel things waiting in the dark, the creaks of hundreds of hinges straining in her mind. She pressed her hands against her ears, but it didn't block out the sound. The scraping was inside of her.

The brilliant blue of his eyes was amplified in the empty landscape. "I learned to navigate this place, but it is yours."

She wrapped her arms around herself as a chill ran up her spine. "I said—"

"Yes, Legatus," he responded, his tone even and flat. Still, something about the way his voice wrapped around the title gave her the impression that it meant more. "I'm not sure how this works, all I know is that this is where you are."

"What is that supposed to mean, Haru?"

He raised a brow as she lifted a hand to her lips. There was something about the way his name felt that was comforting, and there was an instant where she felt as if she knew him. As if she'd said the same thing before. There was something more, something she couldn't quite reach.

Around them, the grey began to lighten. Walls of marble pressed out of the blank canvas and cut him off from her. She tried to get to him but she couldn't. She was trapped in the pull of the white around her, and her limbs were both hers and not her own at the same time.

The world slammed into focus.

---

KANNA TRIED TO LISTEN. She was trying to stay away from the Prince, as Velinius had warned, but he made it difficult. He was everywhere she turned, and when he wasn't she felt his absence like a physical loss, as if all the air had been taken from the room and there was nothing left to breathe.

Kanna turned to anger. Anger she understands. The flash, the danger, the hard edge of it. The feeling when he would look at her was similar though it didn't quite fit, but it was close enough.

The sound of bodies struggling and the occasional shout of encouragement in the amphitheater were muffled white noise to her ears. No one dared get close as she circled with Vahn, shifting her weight over her feet in anticipation.

She clapped her bastons together as Vahn stretched and readied himself for the assault. The clash of the sticks against each other—the hard staccato clack of it—she knew this rhythm. This she understood. An exchange of blows, of reason, of instinct and understanding without knowing.

Vahn lunged and she captured his arms, used the momentum to climb to his back and ground him.

"Enough," he wheezed out, despite her knee pressing against his ribs. He flung his own pair of sticks away.

Kanna stepped back, swinging the bastons in a simple formation and revelling in the whistle of the air. It wasn't the clear singing of metal, but it was enough. "Again?"

"Fuck no." Vahn rolled over onto his back, his arms splayed out at his sides. He wriggled enough to squint at those waiting in the closer seats. "Use him, he's salivating over getting a chance."

Kanna followed his direction even though she knew what she would find. The Prince, leaning his elbows on his knees and watching, his eyes burning into her every move. She shifted the practice bastons beneath her arms and held them there, shoving her hands in her pockets.

"What's his name again?" Kanna asked, as if she didn't know.

"Haroun," Vahn answered from his prone position on the mats.

"Haru."

"No."

"Okay."

She stepped over Vahn, leaving him to sulk. The Prince was still a Prospect, yet to be challenged by an officer to prove himself worthy of the white. Velinius was waiting, for some reason, but it was only a matter of time before she would have him. She met Haru's eyes and inclined her head, bidding him to approach.

His form was precise, honed from obvious training. She let her bastons hang at her sides, loose in her grasp as she circled.

Kanna moved first, testing the limits of his training, and each practiced stance he met with grace and ease. She shifted tactics, pulling in mid strike and changing direction, only to again meet resistance. She fell back to consider, waiting for his offense.

Haru took his time, watching her slow circle. When he jumped in to strike she locked his arms with her own, using his momentum to swing and toss him away.

He approached again, and she danced back and out of his reach. There was a calm calculation in him when he readied. He seemed to be trying to figure her out, and she smirked. With a flick of her wrists she tossed her wooden weapons aside.

He moved to strike and she stepped around him, twisting his wrist back and behind him.

She felt a jolt when she touched his skin. A force passed where she made contact, a warmth flowing through her fingers and up to her elbow. She staggered and released him.

Perhaps Velinius had been right to warn her to stay away from him. He was dangerous in a way she hadn't anticipated. "What did you do?"

He stood away from her, his own form slack. "Nothing."

He was lying. The shadows didn't detect it, but she knew.

Kanna attacked.

He dropped the second baston as she forced him into an ill-balanced defense. He met her strikes, but only barely, and it was only a matter of moments before her blows began to land.

It wasn't fair.

It wasn't right.

She didn't care.

He lived in the light, shining like Velinius. Like Velinius, he didn't know what the dark would do. Kanna could do nothing against her sister, but he was nothing.

He was nothing.

She knocked him back, a knee in his chest and her arm at his throat.

It happened again. She could feel a connection between them, her anger seething and trying to take over. But he wasn't afraid. Despite everything, there was a calm in him. He didn't meet her anger with his own, and he certainly didn't fault her for it.

It didn't make sense.

She loosened her grip to withdraw before she felt the burn. It wrapped around her throat and yanked her from him, pulling her away before she could understand the soothing unknown of him.

The light was blinding and she screeched, just for a moment before she clamped down her teeth and swallowed the pain. It dove past her skin, poisoning the black of her. Moments of her life were sorted and counted and she was found wanting. She was a dark thing. She was not meant to know kindness.

Kanna put her hand where the light coiled but knew better than to fight it. Every struggling breath was a reminder that she took it only because it was allowed.

Though her vision skewed and blurred, she could see Velinius's boots as she approached. Each step was another twist of the coil around her neck until her breath was a reedy whistle.

Velinius stopped in front of her, but she didn't deign to lower herself. Instead, the light coiled taut and pulled, forcing Kanna's head back until she glared up into Velinius's honey brown eyes.

"I warned you, Ananke."

The light burrowed deep, clawing through the dark behind her ribs and eviscerating the comfort she had barely grasped.

Kanna screamed.

# 7

# THE EYES

## KENZI

THE TAVERN that Kenzi found herself in was packed, but she wasn't surprised. With plenty of tourists trapped in the occupied city, there was little else for people to do but sit and wonder about their fates, and Gegenes's earthy brews were a decent accompaniment to a general malaise. They would grumble and question among each other, share in hushed whispers rumors and strange sightings. It was the kind of environment that Kenzi would have thrived in, blending and prodding until she wrung out each and every truth from the tales, but someone else was already at work here.

She skirted around the throng, spotting her target in a side table. Ira had done little to mask his appearance, but considering the variety of people in the city it was somehow less suspicious than her own guise. His light brown hair was shorn close, highlighting citrine eyes that squinted in concentration. Like her, he was dressed in Adurian clothing. Unlike her, it looked as if it fit him, as if he belonged in it.

Kenzi flopped into the seat across from her older brother and propped her chin in her palm. The disturbance didn't register on him. He ran his nail along a final fold before handing over a tidy paper crane. She took the proffered gift and turned it over in her hands before setting it down amongst the swarm of napkin animals on the table.

"You've been busy," she said, her fingers tapping each of the folded creatures in turn.

"Idleness leads to ruin." Ira tilted back in his chair and grabbed the mug in front of him. He tilted it to his lips, looking over the rim at Kenzi. "You're in a mood."

Kenzi let out a long exhale, her eyes darting to the side. "Ol' Salty didn't seem pleased with my work."

"He'll have you on a pike if he hears you refer to him that way," Ira said, though a smile softened the small reprimand.

She surpressed a shudder. "That seemed so unnecessarily gruesome."

"It is war." Ira leaned forward and slid the mug across the table, narrowly avoiding his forest of paper creatures.

Kenzi took a gulp of the drink, coughing when it burbled uncomfortably in her throat. "It was Masao's idea. He volunteered to put the body up. Can you imagine volunteering for that sort of thing?"

"I can imagine Masao doing so. Quite easily."

Kenzi raised her brow as he leaned back, steepling his fingers in front of him. The press of his brow meant he was going to launch into a lecture, but it eased when he decided against it.

Following her brother's footsteps through the ranks of the Palamidia was as natural to Kenzi as hop-scotching in his footfalls when they were children. The soggy Panotii ground would leave imprints where he passed, and they would dwarf her own smaller steps. Even now, she didn't measure up. She hadn't expected to, though, and sometimes she was glad for it.

She put the mug back on the table and considered the paper frog on the table. With a flick of her finger, she sent it hopping toward him. "What are you thinking about?"

"It is nothing to concern yourself with."

"I'm not a child anymore, Ira. I am an Eye, same as you. Tell me."

He sighed heavily, leaning onto the table. "Something is not right. What Velinius says happened to Ananke, it doesn't make sense."

"Why not? Velinius has never done anything to make us not believe her."

Ira leaned back. "Velinius is too clean. At least Ananke was honest. A cold, vicious mess, but honest about it."

It was odd, to hear Ira speak this way of the former Legatus. He tended to keep things to his chest, though sometimes, like now, his gaze would go somewhere else. "I wouldn't know," Kezi said, half-prodding when he began to close up. "I didn't know her."

"No one did. Not really," he replied. "There's something about serving with Ananke in the field that is hard to explain in words. It is just a feeling. As if you were invincible. She was always in front, we just cleaned up."

"We?"

"Hmm," he said. "The ones that deserted. The Lugosian Prince, the Saint of Fire, and the last guard."

Kenzi propped her chin on her palm. "I wonder what it would be like to fight with Velinius."

Ira scoffed. "Velinius doesn't fight. Not anymore. Why would she, when there are those like Salinae to bloody their hands while she stays clean?"

Kenzi snapped her fingers together, eyeing her brother. "See, that doesn't make sense. First Velinius was the Legatus, then Ananke, and now Velinius again? Isn't the Legatus the Legatus until they die?"

"It is the most basic and unshakeable tenet of the Palamidia," Ira said. "Anyone can issue a challenge, and the Legatus must hold their position through force. Whoever lives gets the title."

"What happened, then?"

Some remembrance darkened his features, the glow in his eyes dimming. He cleared his throat and reached over, reclaiming his brew. "Another time."

"But—"

"Another time."

She shut her teeth with a clack. "Fine, don't tell me. I'll find out."

"Good," he said, his smile returning. "That is your duty, is it not?"

Kenzi rolled her eyes and shoved her chair back. It scraped against the floor, but the sound didn't rise above the din of the tavern. "Speaking of which, I should get back to it."

Ira nodded, his eyes once again sparking to life. "You're better than me."

"You know that's not true," she said, leaning over to brush a kiss on his shorn hair. "Take care of yourself."

"Don't I always?"

"Still feels good to say it."

With a final wave, she left the tavern and its noise behind. The harsh light of the day was a shock to her attuned senses, but it didn't fully dissolve the remaining questions she had. But there was work to be done, and time enough later for answers.

# 8

# THE LAST

## ISCO

THE NEXT MORNING, the house was quiet. Isco had slept fitfully, and his eyes were crusted with exhaustion. The night had brought back what the shadows had pulled from him—

His mother in the clinic, nodding as the doctor gave her life a time-line. Her hands gripping the cane she needed to maintain her balance as her body revolted against her.

Shaking hands with Cardea leaders who would fund his research, their nods of understanding and approval and the glittering glass vials lining the shelves of his lab. The blood turning in the centrifuge, pressing between slides, splitting under his watch. Sleepless nights and endless days, hitting wall after wall, not asking questions, only wanting answers and demanding more. More specimens, more time.

Then a wrong turn one night. Emaciated bodies, their veins bloated and bruised, hooked up to machines that drained them, the needles piercing the black slave bands on their necks. A woman's eyes snapping open, looking into him as she lunged against her restraints and the machines beeped and clicked and pushed more sedatives so she slipped back into nothing.

Kanna in the cell, silent and broken. He wasn't the one who shoved the drug into her blood but he might as well have been. If it weren't for him, they wouldn't even have it. He tried to set her bones, clean her wounds, but it didn't erase the others, the ones that were methodically picked apart and drained. For his research, for his cure. For his cure that never even came close to working, that only led to something that was used to harm others instead of help them.

He'd tried to cheat death and failed spectacularly. He'd wished it would be wiped away, scrubbed from the face of the world and maybe then he could forget.

And then it was. Or, at least, they were. In one fell swoop, in one bloody night, they were destroyed but he wasn't free of it. He would never be free.

The memories had been so raw it was like he was living them again, a thousand times over. He couldn't breathe around the loss, couldn't make sense of it.

Then—

Isco splashed water on his face and ran his damp hands through his hair. Kanna's power had been overwhelming, pulling him down, suffocating him beneath the weight of his worst moments. He didn't know how it worked, if she had felt it, too, or seen it, before it was burned away by the soldier with fire in his eyes. If she had, he was sure he wouldn't still be here, and his breath was already threatening to stick in his chest, so if he didn't leave the room, didn't find a purpose, he would be trapped there, in that moment, unable to move or breathe. Dressing quickly, he grabbed his bag and exited the room in hopes that he was the first to rise.

He was mistaken. Vahn waited in the hall outside his door. They didn't exchange words, but something made Isco think that Vahn had not been satisfied with the way he'd dodged the man's questions. Perhaps it was the fact that Vahn continued to follow him down the narrow hall, down the bright wood stairs, and through the parlor.

Isco didn't allow himself to turn. The Palamidia's soldiers had a way of looking that made it so that he could feel their stares, and Vahn's was an intense burn between his shoulder blades. Vahn slid behind him, quiet as an alley cat, and didn't peel away until Isco turned to the room where he'd left Kanna.

Isco took a breath before turning the knob of the door, but the room offered even less relief. While Kanna slept, Haru sat in a chair beside her, his thumb quietly tracing the back of her knuckles.

The click of the closing door was a cymbal crash in Isco's ears.

Haru didn't look up.

Isco swallowed, bracing himself. "It is good she is asleep. She needs rest."

Haru still didn't look up.

Isco placed his medical bag on a small table in the room and turned his back to the couple. The sound of the zip on the bag rattled in the still air, and he almost flinched for breaking the quiet.

"I, uh," he said, not trusting himself. "I need to get there."

Without acknowledging him, Haru slowly relinquished his position and stood behind Isco.

Isco could work better now, but he had another soldier at his back again. While most of Kanna's injuries from her day in the Theatre had healed, the gash on her arm had been older, deeper. He found the wound salve he kept with him and unscrewed the metal lid from the green glass container. The grassy smell of the tincture wafted into the room. It was a mixture of his own design, and sometimes he wished he had found a way to make it less pungent, but it was the best thing to sanitize and expedite healing.

"She still has trouble with her hand some days."

Haru's voice rolled down Isco's spine. It was calm and even, but it was dark. "Especially buttons. She didn't say anything, of course, just stopped wearing things with buttons."

Isco turned to face Haru, only to be met with a hand at his throat.

Haru wrapped his hand around Isco's neck and shoved him across the room. Isco fell back, the glass container dropping from his hand and crashing on the floor.

Isco scurried across the floor, his heart hammering in his chest and his vision blurring from the panic. But he couldn't get away. Not this time. His back hit the wall.

Haru yanked Isco to his feet by the front of his shirt, slamming him back against the wall. Something near his ears clattered and fell from a nearby shelf, landing with a solid thunk against the floor.

Isco tried to pull Haru's arms off, but it was pointless. They were of similar builds, but Haru was a trained soldier, and fueled by a rage that burned so bright Isco could feel it coming off of him. Haru grabbed Isco by the wrist and twisted him around, shoving his face against the wall and pinning him.

"I'd bet you need your hands for your work, wouldn't you, medic?"

Isco felt his finger being twisted back and he whimpered as the pain ran up his arm.

"What the—let him go!"

The grip around Isco's wrist released when Haru was yanked back. The fear that buckled his knees sent him crashing to the floor. Isco cradled his hand to his chest, assuring himself that it was still in one piece.

Haru lunged for Isco again but Vahn caught him and shoved him back. Haru paced in short bursts, a caged predator being denied by another.

"What are you doing?" Vahn demanded.

"I knew I recognized him. I couldn't place where, then I smelled that. It was all over her when we found her," Haru growled. "He was with the ones in Adur. He's Cardea." His voice dripped with hate as he spat the word.

"We killed them all." Vahn's spoke matter of factly, but his voice carried a barely contained smolder of anger.

Haru stopped his pacing, levelling his gaze on Isco. "Except one."

Vahn stiffened, his back straightening into a rod. When he spoke, his voice came out cold and strangled. "What?"

Haru began moving again, his rage seething. "Kanna told me to leave *that one* alive."

Vahn shifted. He knealt, following the trail of green to the tincture. Vahn recovered it and lifted it, his eyes closed. Then, they snapped open. He replaced the cap and turned, his gaze cold as it raked over Isco. Isco flinched away from the stare, curling his shoulders in an attempt to become invisible.

Kanna screamed. The raw ragged jolt of it set Haru in motion, but this time not at Isco. Kanna was flailing, scratching her nails into her neck, tearing at her own skin. Haru threw his arm over her, pinning her hands so they would stop trying to rip into herself.

"Get him out!"

Her eyes were shut. She lashed out at Haru but he caught her wrist before she could dig into his skin.

"Haru—" Vahn yelled over the din of Kanna's screams.

"Out!"

Isco tried to get to Kanna to help but he was stopped by Vahn's hand around his arm. Vahn turned him to the door, shoving Isco ahead.

Isco looked back over Vahn's shoulder. Haru had positioned himself behind Kanna and locked his arms around her. He hummed something low and unfamiliar.

The door closed.

# 9

## THE GOVERNOR'S DAUGHTER

### ASTAR

ASTAR LED the way through the crowded streets of Gaoler, dodging bodies as she went. With the tourists trapped in the city with little else to do, they milled in the streets, pretending that it was a day like any other.

It wasn't a day like any other. Following close behind her was Yassen, who was possibly wanted by her father's men, and just behind him slunk Osawa. She'd found a set of clothes one of the servants left behind to fit him into but he wouldn't stop scratching at the fabric, as if he wriggled in it enough it would somehow manage to turn back into his uniform. Out of the white, Osawa looked... normal. Or, as normal as an Icaunian in Gegenes could look.

And she'd taken him shopping. Paper bags wrinkled under the curve of Yassen's elbow, filled with a variety of clothing from the atelier and equipment from the general store. Astar wasn't sure exactly what they were going to do, or where they were going, so she'd tried to get things that would prepare them for a variety of climates.

All of them. Because, sure, a bunch of Palamidia soldiers had showed up to take her city. And, yes, they claimed that her friend was one of their own. But the point was that Kanna was Astar's friend. She hadn't had one of those before. Her father's title built a wall between herself and others, people wanting to be near her because of it, or wanting to stay away for the same reason. Kanna had never cared.

They rounded a corner and Astar jumped back against a store facing as a loose horse barrelled past them in a mottled streak of black, chased by a squadron of Palamidia officers. Osawa ducked his head, hiding most of his body behind Yassen.

The horse turned on the soldiers, rearing back and striking out with its hooves when any came near. They jumped back into a semicircle, trying to corral the beast. Instead of backing away, it charged through them. One of the soldiers fell into a group of his companions and they became tangled in a mass of white and curses. When they recovered, they once again gave chase.

"What was that?" Yassen asked when the dust settled.

"Kanna's horse," Osawa replied, as if that explained the entire situation.

It did not. Kanna had always been particular about her horse, and even before Astar brought her to Gaoler, she'd made a promise to take care of it. "Then what's with the big grey mare in my stable?"

"Bia," Osawa answered without inflection. "She's Haru's."

Astar gaped at him. "I have a stolen horse on my property?"

"Of course not. Bia is Haru's, so it doesn't count. It wouldn't, even if it was another. Kanna is the Legatus. Anything that belongs to the Empire belongs to her."

Right. That. Astar was trying to forget about the Legatus part of things. She still wasn't sure she believed it. "Must be nice."

Osawa's shuttered expression didn't even flicker. "You live in a haveli that cools with a touch, yet your people are stacked on top of each other, baking in the heat. And you judge us? Kanna?" Osawa shook his head. "It is a burden she never asked for."

Astar frowned. Though Kanna had made Astar promise to care for the horse, she had made no plea for herself. It was only later, after a night when she'd broken her father's curfew, that she'd found Kanna sleeping in an alley. Kanna refused to stay in Astar's father's house, so Astar brought her to the old barracks, instead.

"I'm sure she had a choice," Astar said. "People don't just get handed an Empire."

Osawa's lips thinned. "What about the people that wear this

uniform?" He waved a hand at the servant's set that he was wearing. "Is their choice between begging in the streets, or putting this on?" He turned his gaze to Yassen. "Was your choice between letting your family starve, or fighting in that Theatre? Are those truly choices?"

"We weren't judging," Yassen said, quiet and soft. He shifted his weight from one foot to the other, the bags wrinkling in his grip. "She's our friend."

Osawa stepped back, his gaze moving between them. The other soldiers' looks made Astar go cold, as if they were trying to decide if and when to get rid of them. Osawa, at least, looked at them like he was actually seeing them. It reminded Astar of Kanna, in a way.

Osawa breathed out, his nostrils flaring. Astar thought for a moment that he had more to say, but instead he pulled the hood from the servant's jacket over his eyes. "Excuse me," he said, then, "Please wait here."

Turning in the direction the horse had barrelled from, Osawa slipped into a side alley. They were near the old barracks where Yassen and Kanna had taken residence. The buildings were tightly packed, the alleys a maze. Astar would have worried, except that the alleys here all let out near the Theatre. Besides, she needed a break from him.

Even if it meant she was waiting in the heat for him to return.

"I don't think he meant anything by it," Yassen said, after Osawa had been gone a minute. "I always knew you were fancy, being the Governor's daughter and everything, but you were still you, and you were nice to me. That counts for something."

Astar squinted up at him. "Why would anyone not be nice to you?"

"I've always been bigger than others, and different. Different is scary to some people." Yassen shrugged. "But Osawa seems nice."

Astar glanced across the boardwalk. A couple strode by, one woman glancing her way. The other tugged her forward, moving them quicker, and whispering something in her ear. "People can be nice to you, but that doesn't always mean anything."

Another one-shouldered shrug, another wrinkle of the shopping bags. "He's good people. I can feel it."

"How?"

"Just do."

A burst of screeches, and a group of barefooted children ran by.

"You've gotta see it!" the leader crowed, waving a stick as a guide. "This way!"

There was a burst of nervous laughter as others followed him, dirt streaked and thin. One at the back slowed her race, looking up to Astar. Many of the street children recognized her—when her father was out, she'd often give them access to food, baths, and shelter—but the girl didn't stop for a favor. Her eyes went wide and she stumbled, before turning to catch up with the rest of her pack.

They were drawing more attention standing there than they would on the move. If Osawa had gotten lost, their best bet was to retrieve him from the Theatre. "Come on," she told Yassen, moving to the alley that Osawa had disappeared into.

Yassen took a few skipping steps to catch up with her. "He told us to wait."

Astar snorted.

The alley Osawa had chosen was a wider one. Not broad enough for a cart, but enough to make for an easy footpath. Doorways opened at the sides of it, some with pots of welcoming succulents near. The shade grew thinner as the path opened up to the Theatre grounds.

Osawa met them as they stepped out of the alley, two horses obediently in tow. They had no leads, yet they followed placidly behind him. Astar eyed the horses that waited on the soldier. They were a bit dusty, and one had caked mud on its side, but otherwise they were inconspicuous. At least, on first glance.

"Let's get back," Osawa said.

Ignoring him, Astar dug through one of the bags Yassen carried and pulled out a rope and a camp knife. She cut two lengths and tied them on the horses' halters. Even if they seemed content to follow, a couple of horses tagging along would attract attention. She tried to hand Osawa the new leads, but he hesitated in taking them.

With a sigh, she passed them to Yassen, who accepted their newfound companions. "I don't follow you're orders," she said, meeting Osawa with a glare.

"We should get back," Osawa said again, with slightly more insistence. He reached for Astar's arm, attempting to turn her. "The longer we're out, the more likely we'll be seen."

Astar squinted, taking in the people around them as they stopped their daily routines to look up into the shadow of the Theatre. There had been a pall over most of the city, but the air here was thick with it. She ripped out of his grip, stumbling back a step. "Yeah, like I really needed you to state the—"

Then she saw it. The piteous looks made sense, now.

Above the entry gates of the Theatre, Declan Hautman was on display.

A dark bird used the bloodied end of the wooden pike as a landing. Its beak stuck into the side of flesh and the head bobbed and jerked as the bird yanked back, ripping away the lip from the decaying mass. It smiled wide, teeth flashing. Another carrion swooped in and the two fought over the prize, their squawks muffled by the distance.

Astar felt everything.

Astar felt nothing.

Astar was going to be sick.

# DIRTY TRICK

## OSAWA

OSAWA WATCHED Astar as she leaned over the slick bar of The Dirty Trick, refilling her glass from the tap. The white foam gurgled over the top and she tipped it off before falling back into her seat. After Astar witnessed her father on display, she'd headed away from the square with a purpose. Osawa wished he had surmised that her purpose was to get inebriated.

The bar was crowded, but at least it was filled with locals and tourists. The soldiers wouldn't be seen in such a place, as it would go against the image of the Palamidia. With Salinae at the head of the invasion force, every effort would be taken to maintain that image. That didn't mean the danger wasn't here. He didn't doubt that Velinius would have allowed Salinae at least one pair of Eyes, if not more.

Osawa ran his fingers along the condensation outside of his own glass. He'd sat on Yassen's far side, away from the door and Astar, so at least Yassen's bulk could hide him while he pretended to not know the people sitting next to him.

Which wasn't hard. He didn't really know them. That didn't mean he couldn't feel sympathy for Astar. After the display in the square, he wouldn't blame anyone for needing something to get rid of the image. When he witnessed the body of the Governor, split through above the

Theatre, he'd known it was Masao's work. His cousin had a fondness for violence.

"You wanna know something?" Astar asked, more to the room than anyone in particular.

"Sure," Yassen answered.

"Didn't really like my father," Astar said, her woods clipped. "But he was still my father."

"I don't really remember my birth parents that much."

"Oh right." Astar's glass sloshed as she leaned. "How'd you grow up in Adur anyway?"

"My parents were killed in battle. My dad's friend took me in."

Osawa's fingers clenched around his glass.

"That sucks," Astar offered. "Sucks a lot."

Yassen shrugged. "My parents were really good. I got to have a big family."

"When?" Osawa asked. He regretted it almost immediately, as the two turned to him. He shouldn't have asked. There were countless battles it could have been, but he didn't believe in coincidence. He couldn't take the question back, so he clarified, "When did they die?"

"I was just a kid." Yassen's eyes squinted in concentration. "I was four? So I guess it was something like eighteen years ago."

A sickness settled in the pit of Osawa's stomach. "Do you remember what the battle was called?"

Yassen's brow furrowed, and he shrugged.

"Why you want to know?" Astar said, a bit of a fight in her tone. "You would've been what, twelve? Even the white coats can't send babies to fight."

Osawa kept his silence, his gaze turned to the bottles behind the bar. The door opened and the afternoon light caught on the curves of the glass, casting colored spots in the room.

"Wait," Astar prodded. "You fought when you were a kid?"

Through the crowd, a new figure took an empty chair a few seats down from Osawa.

"No," Osawa answered, an unease moving between his shoulder blades. "Not me."

The man at the end of the bar pulled a napkin from the holder. He bent the square into a triangle, then turned it and creased it once more.

"Then what are you talking about, you weenie?" Astar demanded.

Osawa couldn't be bothered by the insult, if it could be considered one. A girl near Yassen's age dropped quickly into an available seat. "Yassen, get Astar out of here."

Yassen's back straightened and his head swiveled. "What for?"

"I don't want to go, this is getting interesting. Why won't you answer my question?"

First, Salinae. Then, Masao.

Now... Ira.

This wasn't the best place for a confrontation. The Eyes would use the crowd to their advantage, but he could at least block Astar and Yassen's escape. "Don't tell Haru how you found the Governor, and tell him I said to get out."

Osawa brought his other hand around the water glass in front of him, just as Ira finished folding the origami beetle and set it on the bar. The woman on the other side rose from her seat.

The Eyes thrived in subtlety and did their best work in anonymity. Osawa stood, the barstool scraping as he pushed it back.

He smashed his glass, catching the fragments with the water and propelling them at the girl. Osawa counted on surprise and her lack of experience. She leapt to the side, tripping over the leg of one of the bar's chairs and clearing the exit.

Yassen didn't hesitate. He wrapped an arm around Astar's waist and yanked her from the stool, bowling through the crowd and carrying her out in a tangle of curses and silk.

"He's one of them loas!" the woman shouted.

Some of the patrons in the tavern took the opportunity to flee, covering Yassen and Astar's escape in their rush for the door and throwing the girl off balance. Others chose to fight. He couldn't blame them. The Palamidia had taken their city with barely a whisper, murdered their leader, and kept them locked in like animals. Even without the white of a uniform, Osawa was a soldier throughout. That wasn't something he could hide.

With a sweep of his hand, Osawa called the water from the bottles behind the bar. They shattered in a ringing cacophony, and the stinging mix of alcohol and glass moved to meet him. He circled it around himself, keeping the civilians at bay.

But not the Eyes. Ira charged him from behind, not daring to use his powers after the girl's play. Before he fell, Osawa let loose the gathered liquid and it pelted the crowd. The glass cut into skin, the alcohol burning behind it.

Osawa fell under Ira's weight. He went for his knives but Ira locked his elbows and blocked his reach. Osawa swung his head back, colliding with Ira's jaw with a clack.

Ira lost his grip and Osawa extricated himself from the tangle, but not soon enough. The girl's boot dug into his side and his breath left him for an instant.

His breathe didn't come back. He gasped, his eyes widening as she bent over him, her finger over her lips as she pulled the air from his lungs.

The world flashed in spots.

Then it went black.

# 11

# CASCADE

## VAHN

VAHN HADN'T HEARD Kanna's screams in a while. He hadn't missed them, either. There was something bone chilling about the sound, the way it sapped the structure from under his feet.

Kanna carried things. Sometimes they were heavy.

Isco's eyes were stuck open, all dark pupil. He clutched his hand to his chest, and he was shaking and frozen at the same time.

"Come on," Vahn said, passing the man and expecting him to follow.

"She needs help."

Vahn turned on his heel. Isco hadn't moved from his place. "That's nothing new. Let's go."

"But—"

Vahn didn't want to hear it. Not now, not here, not with the echoes of years ringing in his ears. He leaned over Isco. "I will let him have you if you don't move."

There was nothing that Vahn could do, and there was certainly nothing that Isco could do. It still took another moment before Isco's feet unstuck. Vahn took a few wrong turns, but eventually passed through the kitchen and to the mudroom at the back of the house.

"Where are the others?" Isco asked.

At the door, Vahn sat on a short bench to re-tie the laces of his boots. "Out."

"Where are we going?"

"A different out."

Isco fell quiet, which was for the best. Vahn needed to think. Astar had informed him that Kanna's horse was in the stables, which he found odd, considering Amon was currently terrorizing the denizens of the city.

The dry crackle of Gegenes heat hit his skin. He was used to more humid climes, the way the air throbbed with the thick of it. The heat of Gegenes was thinner, purer, and he could practically taste it in the back of his throat.

Vahn declined to take the delineated paths, instead aiming for a diagonal approach to the stable. Isco followed. Vahn slid to the side, slowing his pace so that Isco wasn't at his back. Vahn wouldn't let the medic surprise him again.

Their steps hushed together against the transplanted and manicured green of the Governor's lawn, distracting Vahn from his whirling concern for Kanna. Haru was with her. She was not in immediate danger.

That didn't mean she was safe. Not with one of the Cardea in their midst. And, Vahn wouldn't be able to simply get rid of him. Kanna had shown an attachment to the man, and she was ferociously protective of things she was attached to. He could lie, but Kanna knew lies. Since Osawa had gone out with Yassen and Astar, Vahn would have to handle this.

Stepping into the stable, Vahn let out a low whistle. The ground in the middle breezeway was packed hard and clean, and there was no over-whelming smell of manure, mostly the scent of horse hair and dust. At the first stall, a large roan horse poked its head over the door. It flicked its ears, curious at the new arrival.

"Oh hello," Vahn murmured, moving to pet the creature. Vahn liked horses. It snuffled, leaning into his hand. A scuff from behind caused him to turn, but his small peace wasn't broken.

Isco bit his bottom lip, as if trying to eat another question. At least he'd realized his hand was still attached to his body. For now.

A familiar face appeared over Isco's shoulder.

"Hey, beautiful," Vahn said.

Isco stiffened as Vahn stepped around him. Vahn slid a hand up the pale grey muzzle that peaked over the stall, scratching beneath Bia's dark forelock. "I was worried about you." Bia knickered and leaned into his touch, so he let himself into the stall. "No, not too worried. I knew you'd take care of our girl."

Bia was an impeccable creature. Her body was a mid toned grey mottled with lighter spots, and the color darker on her legs. Her mane, a mix of silver and dark hues, was scattered with random braids. "Though I'm not sure if I like this bougie look on you." Vahn began untwisting the course hairs and untangling them. Bia leaned against him, and he almost let himself get distracted by the creature's comfort.

"I didn't know," Isco blurted.

Vahn stopped his work. He turned, propping an elbow on the stall door and leaning his chin into it. "What didn't you know?"

"What they were doing. I didn't know."

"What were you unaware of, Isco? The trading of people, or the torturing of them?"

"Neither." Isco sighed, the breath coming out hard, before he swallowed. "Both?"

Vahn raised his brow. He had learned patience from one of the best.

Isco searched around himself, but whatever he was looking for wasn't there. He finally leaned back on the stall opposite of Bia's and slid to the ground. Unable to look at Vahn, he rested his elbows on his knees and cradled his head in his hands.

"I loved my mom." His voice was muffled by his hands, but it wasn't difficult to make out the words. "I don't say that because she was somehow unusual, or beautiful, or talented."

Isco let his hands drop, and his head fell back to bang against the wood of the stall. "She was my mom, though, and she was good."

Vahn couldn't remember his real mother. He was certain he'd had one, and that she smelled like the rustling of dry green leaves and honey. That was all.

"She got sick," Isco continued. "She and my father had worked hard to support me while I studied medicine, and then she got sick. There should have been something I could do, some way to help."

Isco cleared his throat. He put his hands down at his sides to move his weight. When he lifted them, he began to rub away the orange dirt that clung to his palms. Isco still wouldn't look at him. He looked at everything but Vahn. "The Cardea offered me unlimited funding for my research. They provided me with a lab and all the equipment I could want or need. I didn't know where the money came from at first, or the samples for my research. I didn't care. I knew I could find a way to make her better, to fix her."

Vahn was aware of the Cardea's sample gathering. They'd taken his blood, stuck needles in his back and drained his spine, and cracked open his skull and told him to think of home. They branded him, then dumped him in the bagnio when he wasn't interesting enough.

"At first," Vahn lead.

Isco started, his eyes finally settling on Vahn. He nodded. "At first."

"Then you found out." Isco met his eyes, and he nodded. He didn't turn away, didn't try to hide or deny the implications of his admission. Vahn lingered in that moment of knowing. He let it settle, let it suffocate, before he asked, "Then?"

"Eventually... well, I think you know what happened."

Vahn remembered how Kanna looked when Haru brought her out of the Cardea's compound, blood covered and barely human. Her hands were mangled, her body torn apart and put back together. "I was there."

Vahn slid on a smirk. It was easy. Far easier than remembering how Kanna's blood streaked against his skin, how at one point in their race back to the Tower even Haru's comforts failed. How all Vahn could do was steal away the edges of her fever while she argued with shadows in an ancient tongue. *Ir saviit,* she'd said, over and over. *I promised.*

Isco shrunk. "I didn't see you."

"Would you have noticed?"

"I would."

At least he wasn't shaking anymore. And it wasn't Isco's fault that Kanna had fallen to their hands. That was on Vahn. It was a line of events that started when she fell from the trees to rescue him.

It hadn't ended with the Cardea. After, the Legatus disappeared from view for months. There was the physical damage to be repaired, but even when that was done Kanna wasn't quite healed. She hadn't lived an easy life by any standards, and the powerlessness of being caught manifested in sleepless nights, restless days, and overzealous nerves that made her jump with any sudden movements in her vicinity.

The whispers started, but they only grew louder as her physical condition improved. Kanna forced herself out at every opportunity, allowed herself to be seen, but only if she had one of them. Which only gave more weight to the rumors. All anyone could see was Haru shining next to the black hole that the Legatus had become. So she left them behind. To prove to others, or maybe just to herself, that she could.

But she didn't come back.

"Let's skip ahead," Vahn offered. "How did you end up in Gegenes?"

"Right. That." Isco brushed back his hair, but it fell back into his eyes. He shifted his legs again, wrapping his arms around his knees. "The Cardea isn't gone, and it isn't really the kind of organization that you can leave. I tried, but I was valuable," he spat it. "Adur is keen on its debts, and the Cardea owned mine. If I brought them 'The Harbinger,' they would release them. It seemed like it would be easy, and I would be out."

It wasn't the full story. Vahn could feel the emptiness in the skipped spaces. "Why you?"

"Because who would suspect me?" Isco snorted and waved a hand around himself, encompassing his mussed hair and torn waistcoat. "I mean, look at me."

Vahn tilted his head to the side. He was looking. "Seems like it would be too easy."

"Should've known." Isco laughed. It was bitter, and it wracked and wrecked him. "And now here I am."

Isco stayed on the ground, a single card in a cascade that started to fall before he'd been placed. "Yeah." Vahn let himself out of Bia's stall, giving her one final pat after the latch shut behind him. "There you are."

Vahn reached down, testing a theory. Isco hesitated, but took the offering hand, and there it was. Vahn clenched Isco's hand in his own, pulling him close. It was the same warmth that had wrapped Vahn's wrist when Isco touched him before. Vahn knew how bad men burned, and this wasn't that. "And now what am I supposed to do with you?"

There was something that the man was hiding. Vahn could feel it like a trapped ember, and he was deciding whether or not it changed anything, or if he even gave a shit, when a clatter in the yard alerted him to a new threat. "Always something."

Vahn released Isco and left the horses behind. On the manicured lawn, Astar and Yassen dismounted from Mud and Julius. As happy as he was to see the horses back and safe, there was something distinctly wrong.

"Where's Osawa?"

Astar and Yassen began speaking at once, but their words jumbled and Vahn couldn't discern them. They gestured wildly at each other while Yassen kept the unsteady Astar on her feet. Vahn unsheathed one of his knives and flung it behind him. It flipped end over end and buried itself in the side of the stable.

The two quieted, and Vahn pivoted back. "It was a simple question."

Yassen looked over his shoulder. "I thought he was behind me, but then he wasn't."

"We got jumped at the Dirty Trick," Astar said, her tone shifting in volume with nearly every word. "So I guess your guy is with your other guys."

"One of them was a girl."

"Was it, Yassen? Was it a girl?" Astar whirled on him. "Sorry I didn't notice, I was too busy trying to get the image of my father's bloated corpse being eaten by fucking birds like some kind of festival shiskabob out of my brain!"

All Vahn's fire turned to ice.

"He said not to tell him about that," Yassen attempted to whisper, but he was bad at it.

"I'm gonna be sick." Astar put her hands over her face. She swayed, then sunk to the grass. "I mean, he was a dick. He was really just the worst, but... he was my father."

Isco knelt in front of her and placed a hand on her shoulder. "People don't have to be perfect for us to care about them."

Astar let out a choked sob then threw her arms around Isco. He returned her embrace, a reassuring hand at her back as she leaned into his shoulder.

Vahn stood an awkward witness to the woman's anguish. Grief was a locked room he didn't want access to. He focused his attention on Yassen, instead. "What else did he say?"

Yassen squinted his eyes, as if it would somehow push the thoughts closer to the surface. "He said not to tell Haru—that's not you, that's the other one—about how we found the Governor." The boy paused, then asked, "Why didn't he want us to say how we found the Governor?"

Astar's zealous description was enough for Vahn to muddle through. Piked. It was excessive, and most couldn't stomach it. "Because we'd know it was Masao."

"What's a Masao?"

Vahn turned his face to the sky. "Who, big guy."

"Who is a Masao?"

Salinae was ruthless, but he wasn't one for spectacle. Salinae didn't parade things he found shameful, he hid them away. Which Osawa would have known. And Osawa knew Masao's cruelty better than anyone, but he also knew the only thing that would keep him distracted.

"That self-sacrificing fuck," Vahn muttered. They weren't leaving him behind. What was left of them was together once more. When they lost Kanna, the world nearly fell apart. They couldn't lose Osawa. They wouldn't.

"What're you going to do?" Yassen asked.

Vahn sighed, rubbing his face with his hands. He was not looking forward to telling Haru. He stalked to the barn to retrieve his knife, prying it from the side of the building. "We're getting him back."

"He said for us to leave."

"Lucky for him, I don't listen well."

Isco looked up from comforting Astar. "You are aware they have a whole army out there, right?"

"Not a whole army," Vahn said. "Just a part of one."

"We don't have an army," Yassen offered.

Vahn turned back to the house. "We have better."

## 12

## BEFORE / AFTER

KANNA WAS a collection of broken moments, a list of befores and afters.

THERE WAS before she was taken from her mother—

HER MOTHER WOULD TELL STORIES, her fingers braiding and unbraiding her hair. Aksana's voice was soft, her heart adored Kanna, but there was something dark inside of it. Kanna asked about her father, and Aksana told her another story. A story of the night sky, a story of things that existed before time. It didn't answer Kanna's questions, but her mother would focus and soften. Until Kanna became too loose, let herself relax in her mother's hold, a twist would be too tight, a braid became a knot.

ARE YOU LISTENING? It is important that you remember.

—AND THERE WAS AFTER.

. . .

RUNNING BAREFOOT over the cold marble of the Tower, a thing too small to wear so much white. Kanna was eye level with legs that would dance out of the way when she passed. She wandered not because she wasn't seen, but because no one wanted to acknowledge that they did. She imagined herself a spirit, an animal, a wild feathered thing set loose. It became a game. She would count how many of them she made skitter away between lessons with Velinius.

Lessons with Velinius, where pain was her teacher.

She learned quickly.


THERE WAS before her first battle—


BEFORE THE HEAT OF GEGENES, the dust that bit her lungs and the sun that burned her skin. There was blood and pain and she couldn't shut her ears or her eyes and she wasn't allowed a voice, didn't know how to scream. She could only hold on behind Velinius as she cut through the lines of the enemy. Until Velinius dropped her from her steed and left her at the heart of it all.

The shadows came for her, because the shadows always came for her. She saw the dark of it, the dark of all of them, felt them as they passed through the world and became nothing.


—AND THERE WAS AFTER.


SHE WAS A SPIRIT, she was an animal, she was the dark and the dark couldn't be hurt or stopped. She was a thing too dark to wear so much white. They decorated her, praised her, and she gave them reasons to fear with every enemy slaughtered. Against the harshest odds, the greatest challenges, she would walk to death and come out every time.

. . .

THEN—

THERE WAS HARU.

LIKE HE HAD ALWAYS BEEN WAITING. A brilliant thing that was everything she was not. She felt herself teetering on the verge of another before, but at the same time that didn't seem right. He had always been. He was a comforting light that she didn't know could exist. He saw it all, somehow, and still followed her with no expectations, no demands.

KANNA HAD ALWAYS BEEN WANTING.
He followed her to follow her, and nothing more.
She had never wanted anything so much.

*Kanna.*

She didn't want to acknowledge that there was a before.
Because for every before there had ever been—

*Come back to me.*

THERE WAS AN AFTER.

# 13

## THE LEAST OF THEM

### OSAWA

OSAWA MUDDLED his way back to consciousness, but at least he had the sense to remain still. His hands were bound at his back and he slumped off-kilter in a seated position that irritated the pain in his ribs from the boot that had kicked them in. The sounds of voices passed through a thick barrier and became nonsense, growing higher and then fading as their owners moved along.

The most uncomfortable bit of the situation was that he was still in the itchy servant uniform that Astar had provided. For a people that enjoyed their luxury silks, he'd swear this fabric was made of sandpaper.

Salinae's voice slithered over his skin. "I know you are awake."

Osawa preferred the feel of the sandpaper.

Osawa took his time to upright himself, rolling his neck to loosen the muscles strained from hanging at an awkward angle before facing his captor.

The tent was white, but blurry. He squinted involuntarily. What he assumed was Salinae from the broad stature and the wash of blonde hair sat across from him, with four other figures scattered about.

"Pardon us. Kenzi?"

One of the figures detached from the wall and settled his glasses back in their place. In focus now, he recognized her as the other Eye from the tavern. With the paints on her skin gone, she held a familiarity that he could place. Osawa leaned around her, raising a brow to Ira. Ira shrugged as Kenzi backed away to join him.

Besides the now obvious pair of siblings, there was a Chromandaen girl that Osawa recognized as one of Velinius's prize pupils, Nissa. The last one was a face he wished he didn't have to see again. Masao's hair hung in his eyes, but it didn't hide the sadistic delight in them. It was a gleam Osawa knew from childhood, when Masao would hold him under water just a bit longer than could be considered a playful dunking.

"Good to see you again, cousin," Masao said.

"I would say the same," Osawa replied, "but I'm not fond of lying."

Masao closed the distance between them and pulled his arm back. His fist collided with Osawa's cheek, whipping him to the side. The skin of his lip split against his teeth. The chair threatened to tip, but returned to its position.

"Enough," Salinae ordered.

Osawa sat back up, using his shoulder to straighten his glasses. Masao returned to hovering behind Salinae's shoulder.

Nissa was as implacable as usual. Kenzi held her fingers over her lips, her eyes wide. Ira lifted a hand to lower hers, a subtle shake of his head a warning.

Salinae leaned back, crossing his arms at his chest. "You've done well," he said, his eyes not leaving Osawa as he addressed the gathered officers. "Leave us."

Nissa was the first to leave, followed by Ira and Kenzi. Their departure opened the tent long enough for Osawa to note it was late in the day, and the sun was beginning to set. Masao grudgingly followed, likely annoyed that the prospect of torture had been removed from the equation.

For now.

After the others left, Salinae continued to watch Osawa. Osawa met his stare with a bored dispassion. Once, when Osawa first glimpsed him, Salinae had appeared mythic. He was broad, hard and strong, the planes of his features carved as if from the marble of the Tower itself. He appeared the very image of a Saint. But Osawa had learned the truth of Saints, and the truth of Salinae. When Kanna cut to the bone of him, she did the world a disservice. Salinae looked far too human now. His Sainthood could be mistaken for having been earned.

Osawa licked the blood from the cut in his lip then swallowed it, the metallic tang ringing down his throat. Salinae could barely hide his cringe, and Osawa hid his satisfaction behind a mask.

When Salinae recovered from his slip, he stood. At Osawa's back, he untied the ropes that kept Osawa in place. The feeling returned to his hands in a wash of needles, but he refused to rub away the niggling burn.

"I believe we have some things to discuss," Salinae said as he resumed his seat across from Osawa.

Osawa had not interacted with Salinae as often as Kanna or Vahn, and he had seen no need to. Despite the fact that Salinae was his own supposed Saint, there was little about the man that Osawa found worthy of attention. Osawa rolled his shoulders, stretching out the stiffened joints.

"I must say, I'm disappointed," Salinae said, not giving away that the silence made him uncomfortable. "You had so much potential when you came to us, Osawa. You were the first Prospect plucked from your culling group, yet you throw in your lot with those that will only make you smaller than you are."

Salinae had studied closely under Velinius, but far too closely. They sought weakness were there was none, or tried to create it and take advantage. Salinae's attempts fell short. It was not Salinae who had chosen him, nor was it Velinius. It had been Kanna.

"This is simple," Salinae continued. "You give the Palamidia the information it needs, and you come back to us. I can raise you to something higher. I know you can shine. We will give you that chance."

Osawa rolled his shoulders, stretching out the stiffened joints. "How?" He leaned back in his seat, crossing his ankle over his knee. "There is nothing higher than the guard, save for the Saints and the Legatus. Are you intending to die, and grant me a Sainthood? Besides that, there is nothing greater than what I am."

"A guard for a false Legatus," Salinae said through grinding teeth. "You could serve a true one."

"Perhaps to you," Osawa replied. "I already serve the true one. You serve nothing but your own ego. What are you, even, besides a lesser version of Velinius?"

Salinae may have studied closely under Velinius, but Velinius knew peoples' weaknesses, nothing more. People were also made of passion and strength, and those things were far more important. Those things were what truly made a person what they were.

Salinae was all pride, and he placed that on the idea that serving Velinius was his calling and his right. As a Saint, he was a disgrace. A Saint's true master should be their element, and nothing more. Vahn was evidence of it, the fire in his eyes and beneath his skin, how he burned for nothing and everything all at once, all the time. Salinae's jaw clenched, a movement so fine it wouldn't be noticed unless one was looking for it.

Osawa crossed his arms over his chest. "You aren't wrong about me being the smallest among them. But the least of the gods was still a god. It makes me wonder: what will you do when you face a great one?"

Anger curled Salinae's scarred lip over his teeth. "The gods are dead, Osawa."

Over Salinae's shoulder, a thread of the twilight showed the first bright stars of afternoon through the tent's seem. "True. But first, they rose."

Salinae's frown deepend, the blue of his eyes darkening like storm water. He rose from his seat and moved to the exit. He pushed aside the tent's opening, and nodded. Masao slunk in, a broad smile on his face.

"Find out where they are hiding." Salinae handed the bindings he'd removed over. "Do not make a mess."

Masao grasped the back of the chair that Salinae had abandoned and turned it, sitting down on it in a straddle. He propped his elbow on the back of his chair, his chin in his palm, and grinned. "Alone at last, cousin. Did you miss me?"

# 14

## A LIFE PASSED

### HARU

HARU WATCHED Kanna's back in front of him, her spine straight and guarded. She'd come back from the Neither in a slow crawl, sliding back into her skin and waking as if from an easy sleep. He wasn't sure how much of her returned. Too much had happened too quickly, and Kanna always focused on the danger outside of herself. There was always something, some reason for her not to face him.

The city of Gaoler was quiet, the residents shuttered in their homes due to the Palamidia's curfew. They'd passed a few guard details, but it was quick work to silence them, tucking their bodies in the myriad side streets and coves that ran through the squat city.

Behind him, Bia's hoof falls were muffled against the packed earth streets. Amon pranced at Kanna's side, ecstatic to have his true keeper back. They'd found him in an alley they had ducked into, and with neither a lead nor any coaxing he fell in step at Kanna's side.

Kanna didn't pay her stead much head, though she had greeted him with a familiarity that gave Haru some comfort. She was still lost in her own thoughts, wandering these strange streets as if they belonged to her.

Closer to the city center, the buildings were smashed together. Residential lights burned above shuttered shops and the occasional strain of conversations drifted from open windows, riding through the air and jumbling before reaching their ears.

They arrived at a squat building, its façade blank and unyielding. Kanna did not approach it from the front, however, but turned instead down a side alley. Haru would have missed her approach if he had been but a few more steps behind. Taking a running start, Kanna darted to the wall and jumped against it, pushing away and launching herself to the hanging fire escape ladder. She hoisted herself up and waited for Haru to follow.

Haru jumped, grabbing the bottom of the ladder and pulling it down to ground level, then climbed up. Kanna eyed him, her head cocking to the side when he made it to the top.

Kanna tended to make things more difficult than they needed to be.

She climbed the stairs of the fire escape, making her way to the top floor. There she stopped and pressed her hands against the glass of a window. It opened easily, and she disappeared inside. Haru followed, folding to fit through.

The room was dark, but by the ambient light he could make out the shapes of the interior as Kanna moved in the enclosed space. While he waited in the Tower, Kanna had evidently holed up here, in Gegenes. A cracked mirror of an empty basin reflected a soft glare, a single bed was shoved against the wall with the window, and a thin-legged chair on the verge of collapse waited in the corner. A layer of dust settled on the surface of everything. Life here had been passed, not lived.

A scraping sound interrupted his thoughts and he turned to see Kanna pulling a chest from beneath the bed. It was once navy, but the color had faded and mottled with time. The top was dented in and the brass trimmings rusted. She settled back on her heels and opened the latch with a rasp of metal.

*"Inara..."*

She didn't look at him. Her hands stilled at the edge of the chest, unwilling to go further. He moved next to her to open it. The lid was lighter than he had been expecting and it tilted back, stopped at an angle by the frame of the bed. Inside, an assortment of clothing was tossed haphazardly, wrinkled and piled in heaps of red and green and black.

Kanna began to shift the items, removing them from the chest and tossing them aside until she reached the bottom. A dark grey blanket, tattered and thick, lay smooth along the bottom. Her fingers flexed again, but the last step was hers.

She peeled away the corner of the blanket. "I don't have all of it."

The Legatus jacket rested at the bottom, the arms folded at the chest. Kanna pulled it out and passed it to Haru before reaching for the armored vest beneath. Dark red stained the white ties on the right side. Her blood had seeped into the soft leather and refused to be removed or forgotten. Kanna tossed the armor onto the thin bed and began to change. Before Haru could look away, she peeled off the dark red shirt that Astar had given her and dropped it to the ground.

His breath stopped. He knew she carried a part of him, but he had never thought that was literal. Along her right side, gold veining pulsed near the scar where Velinius's blade had pierced her skin. The gold was alive, shifting on her skin in a lazy rhythm.

"Kanna."

She turned to him this time, but she wasn't there. His fingers hovered over the gold along her skin, felt it reach for his touch, but she'd shut down, shut out everything but the task at hand. She pulled one of the black cotton shirts over her head and let it fall to cover the scar.

Next came the armor. She fumbled with the ties but her patience grew thin and she left them loose. Haru draped the jacket she had handed him over his shoulder and pulled her close, tightening the stays at her sides. On her right, he forced himself to ignore the blood stains as he knit the leather around her.

It was something so natural to him that he hadn't thought before doing it. His fingers lingered as her eyes met his, unmoving save for the shadows that ghosted through her irises.

He took the jacket from his shoulder and held it open and out for her. Kanna hesitated, as she always had, but gave in to the call. First one arm, then the other, and he settled the jacket over her shoulders.

Kanna pulled her hair from her collar and stepped forward. "They wanted a Legatus." She stretched her arms in front of her and brushed her hands down the embroidery details that curled along the sleeves, tracing the fine details that recounted her forgotten triumphs. "I will show them one."

# 15

# THE PRETENDER

## VELINIUS

VELINIUS DIDN'T SPEND much time in the lower tiers of the Tower. She didn't see the need to mingle among the Prospects and lower officers, though she did like to make the occasional appearance. After her scheduled round, she checked her watch. There was still time before the meeting with the Icaunian council to discuss their trade dealings. Time enough to pay her mother a visit.

After Aksana's involvement in Haroun's escape was uncovered, Velinius had her placed under watch in the outer rings of Irkalla. She had provided accommodations that suited her mother's status, assuring Aksana's favorite trappings were provided. She wasn't completely heartless.

Ilma walked behind her, stiff and silent, though Velinius knew she didn't approve of the way the "Exalted One" was being kept. Many pitied the woman, assuming her madness had driven her strange behaviour. Velinius knew better. It was Velinius who had sowed that tale, and Aksana was only mad when it gave her an advantage.

At the top of the steps that led to the Tower's underbelly, Velinius turned to Ilma. The Saint of Air was the eldest of the Saints, someone that Velinius had inherited rather than placed. "You may go."

The light dimmed as Velinius descended the stairs to Irkalla. It was a psychological trick, one that was meant to create fear. It reminded others that this was but a hole in the ground beneath the feet of greatness.

It was quiet in the guard room. Velinius had relieved the contingent from their duties, especially after their last showing. Besides, there were no others being held here, and it was better to keep people away from Aksana. She had a way of swaying sympathies to her side.

Velinius unlocked the large cell that held her mother. Inside, plush Gegenii rugs covered the stone ground and a collection of ghostlight lamps lit up the corners. Aksana had hung her silks along the blank walls, choosing deep blues and violets that reflected the lights and glittered like a night sky.

Her mother sat at the vanity Velinius had brought to the cell, brushing out her hair. Loose from her braid, the dark brown waves shot with grey cascaded to her waist. Aksana paused momentarily, her eyes meeting Velinius's in her mirror, before sliding away and back to her task.

Velinius shut the door behind her and it latched with a heavy thud. "Are you comfortable, mother?"

Aksana began to hum, then set the brush on the vanity. She pivoted on the bench to face Velinius, her brow wrinkling in disapproval. "What have you done to yourself, child?" Lifting a thin hand, she motioned for Velinius to move forward.

It was harmless to appease Aksana, at least in this, so Velinius moved within her reach. Aksana grasped her wrist and pulled Velinius to take her place in front of the miror. Aksana began undoing the braids and twists in Velinius's hair, inserting a few pins between her lips before tossing the remainder to the vanity. They bounced when they hit the wood and rotated around the heavy heads, a few falling to disappear into the carpeting.

"Mother," Velinius warned.

Aksana waved her hand, dismissing the cool tone. "Give me this, at least."

Velinius frowned, but she didn't move. Aksana reached for the brush on the vanity and began to pull it through her hair. Unlike her mother, Velinius's hair was straight as silk and trimmed to a manageable and presentable length. The brush slid through it, the bristles reaching her scalp. "You are being pleasant today."

"I am always pleasant to my child."

Velinius noted that she did not specify which one. "I have matters to attend to."

"Not with your hair like this."

There it was. The manipulative twist that Velinius had learned at her mother's knee. Velinius's eyes narrowed on her mother's reflection.

"I want to tell you a story."

"Aksana…"

"I gave you a voice to speak my name, you will now loan me your ears."

Aksana had taken away her choice. Velinius couldn't leave with her hair unbound, and it would take time for Aksana to finish plaiting it. She waved a hand for her mother to continue.

"In the beforetimes, when the nights were long and the gods were limitless," she began, as all the old stories began, "the warrior Kosein roamed the land, completing the trials that would name him as a champion. He had completed the first of them, and the news of his victories had travelled throughout all of Lifrasir, so everyone whispered his name in hushed adoration.

"He was in search, this time, of the Abyssal Mirror. You remember what that is?"

"It is the artifact that reflects a person's true self," Velinius answered, as dutiful as she had as a child, as bored as she was now.

"A person's true soul," Aksana corrected.

"There is no difference, mother."

"You never listened, child."

Velinius turned her wrist to check her watch. The meeting was soon, and she had no time to argue Aksana's interpretations.

"When Kosein came upon the village that kept the mirror, he heard strange news—he was already there. A stranger had taken his deeds and claimed them for his own." Aksana twisted a lock of Velinius's hair. She wove a pin through and Velinius felt as it caught and held in place. "This did not bother Kosein. After all, Danu would know the truth of things, and that was all that mattered to him."

Another pause, another pin. "He went to the hall of the Council dressed as a stranger to request a viewing with the mirror. However, when he arrived, the hall was full. It was the day that people made all of their requests to the leaders of the village. This time, with The Pretender in place, there were more people than ever.

"One of the prostrators had come from a neighbouring village. His city was being assaulted by bandits, and he requested The Pretender's help. The Pretender refused them."

Aksana turned Velinius's head with an almost caring touch to study her work before continuing again. "Kosein himself stepped forward, urging The Pretender to listen and help, yet he was also refused.

"It seemed though, The Pretender was not happy with Kosein speaking up. In the night, assassins came to slit his throat in his sleep. Kosein subdued these interlopers and left to challenge The Pretender.

"Once again in the hall, Kosein brought his accusations of The Pretender. Of course, the man claiming to be the great warrior denied any wrongdoing. At this, Kosein issued a challenge: they would both face the Abyssal Mirror to find the liar among them.

"The Pretender, once again, refused."

Aksana took a moment to finish the braid she had woven and set it in place. The pin once again touched Velinius's scalp before dancing away without scratching her. "Kosein decided it was not worth his time, and he would leave to help the neighbouring village. But first, he still wished to face the mirror. He found the temple, and the two Watchers therein brought him to the artifact.

"He had thought the mirror would be ornate, massive and carved and encrusted with jewels. Instead, it was a marvel in its simplicity. It was much smaller than he had imagined, a simple oval held in an unadorned gold frame that was worn with age. It did shine, though, in such a lovely way.

"In front of that simple mirror, everything that he was and everything that he could be was reflected back upon him. He knew his task, he knew his purpose, and he was filled with a quiet peace. With the knowledge of his soul, Kosein left to defeat the bandits in the neighbouring village. However, the story does not end there."

Aksana switched brushes, choosing a thin, fine comb to tackle the stray strands that had escaped her touch. "The Watchers brought news of what they had seen to the villagers, and they rose up to unseat The Pretender on their own."

Finished, Aksana placed the last comb back to the vanity. She met

Velinius's eyes in the mirror and smiled, satisfaction and approval in her gaze. Velinius had always wished for Aksana to look at her that way, the way she looked at Ananke. Even now, though, she knew it was not herself that Aksana saw.

Velinius rose from the vanity and Aksana resumed her place. She picked up her brush and once again passed it over her own hair, humming a soft lullaby under her breath. Before she left, Velinius turned back. "I thank you for the warning, mother, but it is hollow. I know my purpose."

Aksana stopped her work and turned to Velinius. Her smile was innocent, her gaze distant. "I don't know what you mean, daughter. It is just a story."

# 16

## RETURN OF THE LEGATUS

### HARU

IN THE DARK, the waning crescent moon hung like an ax ready to fall on the gathered white tents below. Haru and Kanna had approached on horseback from the east, arriving at a narrow point in the elongated semicircle encampment that hugged the walls north of Gaoler. A boundary of floodlights strived to keep the dark of night at bay, and within the glare, the camp was lit with the cold flicker of ghostlights.

Kanna dismounted from Amon, though she didn't make a sound when her feet hit the ground. Haru followed, standing behind her and awaiting orders. The lights from the camp reflected in the steel of her eyes, turning the cool grey into a starry silver. Black and a gold that had not been there before mingled within the expanse, a galaxy trapped under a bell jar, a touch of divinity that surveyed the camp, steady and knowing.

Kanna was measured and cold. The last time Kanna had been so detached was when he'd first met her, when she was the Second and hiding in her own skin while bending a stubborn knee to Velinius. He'd found her, beneath it all. He would find her again.

"Kanna?"

She blinked and focused, her eyes sliding under red-tinged lashes and up at him. Her head followed belatedly at a tilt. "There are more loas than usual," she said, but her voice wasn't hers. It lacked any spark of emotion, every hint of feeling sapped from it. "A few dozen. Water, mostly."

Haru tried to ignore how empty it was, how it made him ache to hear it. "I expected as much."

Kanna's head tilted to the opposite side, her gaze returning to the camp. "She sent as many as possible without rousing suspicions."

Haru followed her gaze to the sprawl of tents, through the ring of light and into a world that was once theirs. A realm that Kanna had commanded, a life that they could all know and understand, a place where they had been safe, together, even if everything else about it was rotting and violent.

"Is it time?"

Kanna's gaze slid to the line of trees between the camp and the rest of Gegenes. "Keep casualties to a minimum."

His eyes narrowed, something hard and vicious shivering inside of him. "They are going to try to kill you," he reminded her as the feeling slipped over his spine. "They are only here to kill you."

Kanna shook her head.

Haru grit his teeth together, resisting the urge to argue until she saw the danger she put herself in, or until she cared enough about herself for that danger to matter. If he spoke, if he argued or pushed, it was likely she'd seal up whatever had shifted to allow the narrow hint of care.

"Yes, Legatus," he said instead, his voice brushing against the title with care, allowing it to mean more than it possibly could.

Kanna's fists clenched then released, catching the softness but scared to hold it. She turned to Amon and threaded his reins in his mane. She looked at him as if she could puzzle him through, a thing that belonged to her, intricately and inexplicably, a piece that had been lost and found without realizing it had been missing.

Cool anger moved through Haru, scraped against the back of his neck with its callous scales. Kanna had been taken from him, but everything had been taken from her. He wouldn't let it happen again.

He couldn't let it happen again.

Kanna's hands slipped from Amon's neck, and she turned over her shoulder at him. "Haru?"

The chill of command was gone, her voice small and alone, concern nipping at it. He breathed deep, tempering his anger until it was a low hum, until the monster inside of him settled in its place.

Kanna turned fully, her eyes darting from the camp to the ground, her hands shoved deep into the pockets of her jacket. Either she didn't know what to say, or she didn't know that it was allowed. As if there was anything that she could say that Haru would not want to hear.

Haru let go of the tension he held, the small threads of anger wrapped in fear. She couldn't trust him if he was afraid, even if it was for her. Kanna didn't flinch when he reached for her, and he took it as a welcome. His fingers grazed her cheek and threaded into her hair, and he wanted to tangle them in the silky mess of it. She relaxed into his touch, only barely, a gesture that could be mistaken if he knew her less, her head tilting into his palm as if she had to chase something that was already hers.

Kanna's hand rose slowly, the way a wary prey animal would approach a stranger with an offering, and wrapped around his wrist. Her thumb brushed against his pulse, light and testing, before pressing into it. His heart beat harder, his body humming alive as it always did for her.

Haru felt the breath pass over his thumb when she sighed. She stepped away, her fingers uncurling from around his wrist and letting go. At the boundary of the light, the white of her uniform created a halo around her silhouette. On her back, her own eclipsed sun was stitched over the many twists of her past victories, her shoulders bearing the interconnecting circles that counted the dead in a code.

Kanna flexed her fingers at her sides, pulled each in with her thumb to stretch it before curling them to fists and shoving them into her pockets. As Haru watched she sorted what was necessary of her self, locked away what she believed wasn't, and as she did her shoulders rose and set into a bold line. When she turned over her shoulder, the black had clouded the shining brightness in her eyes. They slid from Haru to Amon.

A nod to the camp, and a simple command was all the horse needed. "Go."

Amon crashed through the light barricade, a massive shade barreling through the sentry tents at the perimeter of the encampment. Kanna stalked after, and Haru took his place a step behind her.

The Palamidia had come for the Legatus. Unfortunately, she was coming for them.

Haru's heart raced, his blood pounding. Before them, the dark coalesced in long strokes like spilled ink dragged through the light with a battered brush. The shadows at Kanna's command were thicker than natural shade, a dark that almost hurt to perceive.

The shouts of alarm started low, crescendoing on the wave of their approach. A brave handful attempted to breach the boundary, but the merest flex of Kanna's fingers had the deep shadows curling up, grabbing their ankles and dragging them back.

The shadows began to shiver when they grew closer, Kanna's physical grip loosening as they dug for something deeper, something more primal. By the time they reached the edge of the camp, the soldiers within were already on their knees, wracked by their own nightmares. Haru kept his senses on alert, his hands ready for the first that would make it out of Kanna's miasma.

Amon's route had roused the first wave, and their screams brought more. Kanna's hands flattened at her side, her fingers splayed, and the shadows were set loose.

The sound of creaking wood turned into splintered crashes. The soldiers were not unprepared. Water barrels had been placed throughout the camp, their contents freed at the sign of attack as the loas within gathered their defenses against the invading force of two.

Kanna braced herself when the loas sent waves of water toward her, threatening to grab her ankles and trying to pull her down. But they weren't nearly as strong as she, not even close to having the same control. While she fought to keep her feet, Haru rushed past her to keep the approaching soldiers at bay.

The lights in the camp whispered to Haru in ringing, desperate voices, so he called them. The ghostlights in their caged lanterns buzzed and brightened, whirling together maddeningly until they built the force to crack through their glass containments.

The camp plunged into darkness. The darkness had always been Kanna's.

Kanna clenched her fists and shadow wrapped from her knees to her ankles, forcing itself between her and the water and creating a barrier that the waves couldn't breach. Free of the watery chains, she continued through the center of the camp. Kanna kept her blades sheathed, instead bringing the force of her abilities to bear, a reminder of who she was.

Haru guarded her, a barrier of flashing steel and blunt attack while Kanna managed the dark. The ghostlights buzzed above, darting throughout the camp and casting eerie, moving shadows that disguised Kanna's attacks. Some dipped low, tearing through an attacking soldier of their own choosing.

One buzzed down, felling a soldier that had neared Kanna, and a water loa attempted to take an advantage when she skipped aside to avoid the falling body. Sandy lashes of water rose above her protected knees and shot towards her.

Kanna balanced on a single foot and brought the shadows up, angling the attack away and using the opposing force to right herself. Her other hand tightened a whip of shadows to knock her attacker back. The snap of his ribs rang out from the impact as he was lifted from his feet and slammed into one of the tents, which folded in on itself and trapped him in a cocoon of white canvas.

Another came, but before she could attack the shadows grasped her by the waist and flung her into the soldiers behind her, toppling them into a heap.

Haru turned to meet one of the foot soldiers. Haru dodged the spear's point and grabbed it by the shaft. He yanked forward to loosen the man's grip then shoved the blunt end into his stomach.

The air around Haru shifted, pulling his attention back to Kanna. The shadows churned, reacting to her panic as she clutched her throat with one hand. Her eyes were wide, the shadows flickering in them as she struggled to breathe. Haru found the air loa forming the attack behind a defense grouping and readied the spear, but Kanna spotted him at the same time.

So did the shadows. They shot past the defense line and wrapped around the air loa, spiralling around his body and trapping his hands against his sides. The dark yanked him from his feet and dragged him across the ground and into an upturned water barrel. His head cracked and split, and the shadows pulled back his twitching body and slammed him into the barrel again before twisting around the corpse, his bones snapping within their grip.

Haru changed his aim and launched the spear at one of the loas in the defense line before they could recover from the shock of the attack. He hit her in the chest, the sound heavy and wet and solid.

Kanna rose from the ground. Her eyes had eclipsed in the moments when Haru looked away, their entirety black as a starless night, lines of it spilling out at the corners and moving in the veins under her skin. Haru could feel her anger taking over, the rage like the promise of lightning before a storm.

She drew her blades.

The soldiers moved in an attempt to fence them in and Haru pulled closer to Kanna, turning his back against hers. This close, the rage in her burned across their shared connection. Anger was easy. Anger was pure. And they had enough of it to bring the world to its knees.

The ghostlights buzzed and gathered, then dropped down into the massing soldiers. They shot through them and kept going through the next, their trajectories unpredictable and neither slowing nor stopping.

Kanna launched herself into the soldiers, no longer waiting for them to approach.

Haru cut through, tore through white uniforms and insignias, spilled blood on intricately embroidered lines that meant everything, that meant nothing, lines that stood on rotted faith and broken loyalties.

Haru raised his knives to block an attack, the impact ringing into his wrists. He shifted his blades and his weight, catching it between them and twisting the wielder off balance. He kicked out to knock the man back. His attacker lost his grip, and Haru moved in for the killing blow.

As Haru fought off the next, a ghostlight buzzed a warning past his ear. After taking out the soldier, he took a breath to gain his bearings. They had made it through most of the camp, drawing the soldiers where they needed them. They were close to their exit point at the north of the camp.

At least, he was close to their exit point. Kanna had not followed.

The night was dark, the chaos and screams mingling into a heavy web.

The night was dark, and Kanna was angry.

# 17

## A WITNESS

### KENZI

KENZI WAS RETURNING from retrieving her and Ira's uniforms at the far side of the camp when she realized that, despite the intense training she'd endured in the Tower, nothing could actually prepare her for the chaos of battle.

Especially against the former Legatus and her Second.

Especially against a power that couldn't be studied or understood.

She was running her fingers over a particular pattern on Ira's jacket that had caught her eye when she heard the first scream. It brought her attention up, and she searched for the source of it. Then there were more, looping over and under one another. The first shouts were warning, the following ones anguished as they ripped through the night.

Nothing human should make those kinds of sounds.

The known elements could be sensed. They could be understood in their relationships to one another, how they worked and what they could achieve, but shadow and light were a visceral unknown. The only way to stop them was to stop those that bent them to their will.

Kenzi abandoned the bundles of cloth in her arms and ran to the source. Around her other soldiers did the same, shouting orders and attempting to pass information to rally, but it was hard to pick them out from the screams.

The closer Kenzi came to the invaders, the more she could feel the

Legatus's reach. The ghostlights that lit the camp flickered, brightened, then shattered from their cages. Kenzi ducked when one burst near her ear, covering her head with her hands as splintered pieces of glass blew out, shards falling into her collar and slipping behind her neck. She kept her head down as a buzzing cut just over her head, looking up in time to witness one of the ghostlights break away from its pack. It doubled back.

Kenzi had loved the ghostlight lanterns in the Tower. She hadn't seen anything like them before, the gathered specks of light drifting lazily, languidly in their closed confines.

Zipping low, the freed light rounded another soldier then paused, bobbing in the air. The woman lifted a hand and attempted to swat it.

It shot through her.

Red blossomed on the chest of the woman's white uniform and she stopped in her track, her mouth gaping in shock. She spread her hands wide and stared down, and in that instant her mind hadn't caught up with the fact that she was dead.

It had only been an instant, a blink between alive and no longer. There was nothing Kenzi could do, nothing that could be done. She ran past the woman when her knees buckled, finally, and she fell.

Kenzi couldn't quite tell the difference between the shadows of the night and those that Ananke controlled. The ghostlights darted around the camp, flaring in unpredictable patterns. The walls of the white tents waved in the night breeze, the dark dancing into shapes with feathers, shapes with teeth, while the running limbs of soldiers tangled on the ground, on the walls, in front of and behind them.

Kenzi tried to avoid the shadows she had seen in the Theatre, the ones that were something more than a shade. Those around her tripped over nothing, fell to the ground in heaps that tangled anyone too close. Kenzi jumped away from any shadow that moved on its own, tried not to watch the others fall around her, but she couldn't avoid it all.

The flickering lights were diving down as if they were picking and choosing individual victims, their paths through the bodies spritzing blood onto the white walls of the tents. The buzz sounded near Kenzi and she jerked her head up, missing a step. Her foot crossed into shadow and her blood ran cold.

*Not enough*, a voice whispered, coming from somewhere inside of her. *Not enough*, it hissed, repeated, a mix of sibilance and nails against chalkboards, a sound that whispered the secrets that only she held, the things that kept her awake at night, in a voice she didn't know.

The soldier in front of her dropped to his knees, his hands over her ears. His scream broke through the voice and rattled Kenzi enough that she leapt out of the dark trap. He curled into himself, pressing his hands harder over his ears and sobbing into the ground, caught in his own nightmares.

Kenzi hadn't even managed to lay eyes on Ananke or her Second, and already they were laying waste to everything around her. It was chaos and madness and it was infectious, the panic growing the closer she came to them.

*Not enough.*

A tendril of shadow wrapped around Kenzi's ankle, brushing gently against her skin as if it was the most tender of lovers.

"Fuck off," she hissed at it, shaking her ankle free.

Its laugh was an echo inside of her as it let go, the shadow withdrawing to seek other prey.

It was too easy. She didn't know how, but she knew that it shouldn't have been that easy to shake it. The shadows in the Theatre had latched into the people there, refusing to let go, driving in until they were driven mad.

Kenzi raked in her breath, squeezing her eyes shut and standing still amidst the frantic rush of bodies around her, standing still against the screams and the cries and let them pass through her.

They had studied Ananke in the Tower, dissected her battles. She was a force, a devastating frontal attack in a singular mortal body with no mercy and no quarter. The ferocity of her onslaughts should be unsustainable yet, somehow, her forces prevailed. They lasted days at the same intensity, weeks even, until something in their enemy's lines faltered and broke.

Something wasn't right. They were missing something. Kenzi's nostrils flared, bringing in the clean night air. There was a heavy scent of water, of sand dusted air, the dry smell of the earth beneath her feet.

There was no ash. There was no burning.

A singular force would break against any wall, eventually, and the former Legatus wasn't even using her full arsenal. She was holding back a Saint.

Kenzi turned on her heel and began to force herself back against the tides of bodies that wanted to pull her into the attack. Another rammed into her shoulder, nearly sending her to the ground. She dug in her heels and continued to fight her way back to the center of the camp, keeping her head down when the ghostlights whistled their deadly warnings overhead.

This was a blitz strike, and the intensity of the attack only needed to be maintained until something specific was achieved.

Or someone was retrieved.

# 18

## THE SEA'S FAVORITE

### ISCO

MOST OF GEGENES was open desert, but there were still sporadic remnants of what had been before. Isco hid with Astar and Vahn in a copse of oncetree, woods petrified in an instant in an age past. There were thicker forests similar to this closer to the Ilazki border, some brushing against the southern spur of Adur where Isco had once studied.

Yassen had separated from the group, taking the horses to the west end of the treeline. The rest of them were to cross the open divode, grab Osawa, and angle back to reach Yassen. At best the plan was half-formed, at worst it would get them all killed. Their part relied heavily on Vahn's ability to keep everyone alive, and while Isco didn't doubt Vahn's combat skill, he wasn't sure that Vahn had a good enough reason to keep him breathing.

Vahn was taking the entire situation with the same air of feral boredom that he seemed to have for everything. He was leaning against one of the trees, running the tip of his blade under his nails.

Isco jumped when the silence was broken by Astar's voice. "How will we know when it's time?"

Vahn looked up from his nails enough to smirk, then his eyes slid past Isco to the opening between the trees. "That's as good of a signal as any."

From their vantage, Isco turned in time to see a black horse streak across the open space on the eastern border of the camp, the sound of snapping tent poles and scattered shouts of surprise ringing out in the night.

Kanna followed, stepping into the light around the camp. She was dressed in Palamidia white, her jacket nearly brushing the ground. Even across the distance, Isco could see the details that snaked over it. The thick ornamentations cast shadows over the white, victories and titles layered upon each other when there was no free space left to stitch them.

"She always knew how to make an entrance," Vahn said, admiration and amusement mingling in his tone.

The light around Kanna dimmed as the shadows gathered around her despite the artificial glare. The camp came alive with warnings and calls to arm, the canvas tents shuddering with the activity. When Kanna and Haru disappeared into the camp, the first screams reached across the night, carrying fear through the dark.

Isco's stomach clenched and twisted, but he didn't have time to hesitate. Vahn took the lead, drawing his knives and rushing across the clearing. Isco followed behind Astar and they approached the camp from the north, as close as they could get to the center command tent.

When they entered, the soldiers were already too preoccupied to notice new faces. Everyone was running in the same direction, and Isco and their small group blended into the rush to meet the attackers.

When the lights in the camp flared and shattered, it caught Isco unaware. The shards were cast out forcefully, a few cutting across his face and temporarily blinding him. In the dark the world flashed in white and steel and he was caught by the current of bodies and the spike of his own hammering heart.

A hand wrapped around his arm and pulled him from the undertow, dredging him from the sea of panic. Another clamped over his mouth as if to cover a scream, as if it wouldn't have been confused with the rest of them.

"You're all right, medic." Vahn's voice was shockingly cold and even. "They don't want you."

Isco didn't trust himself to speak. He was certain that if he opened his mouth either nothing would come out or he would howl until he no longer had the breath with which to do so. He nodded instead.

Vahn and Astar had stopped behind one of the tents, slipping out of the main avenue the soldiers rushed down. There were entirely too many shadows snaking over the ground, moving independent of anything to cast them.

A strange light whizzed past them, while others milled overhead.

"What are they?" Astar asked, her voice a low hush.

"Who knows." Vahn's grip on Isco eased and Vahn retreated, leaving Isco cold and shaking once again. He stalked to the end of the tent then turned, pressing a finger of his lips and signaling to them something Isco interpreted as a command to stay.

Vahn held one of his knives in front of him, turning it at an angle, before ducking around the back corner of the tent they hid behind. The sound of fighting in the distance muffled the scuffle. It was the work of moments before Vahn reappeared, fresh blood on his uniform, and waved for them to follow.

Astar took the lead, stepping over the bodies that Vahn had felled.

There was an acrid metallic twinge in the air that Isco could taste in the back of his throat. A spray of blood dashed across the outside of the tent they had hidden behind, dark against the white canvas. Isco didn't allow his eyes to follow where the trail would end.

The sound of Isco's heart hammering in his ears almost drowned out the cacophony around him. Vahn had taken them behind the main thoroughfare in the camp, but Isco could still hear the soldiers calling warnings. He could hear their strangled cries, their sobs, their pleas of innocence when the shadows ensnared them.

They stopped before a wider opening in the tents. Beyond it was one at least three times the size of the ones they had passed before. Vahn had woven them expertly through the encampment, reading signs in the layout that Isco couldn't begin to understand.

Again, Vahn signaled for them to stay back. He sprinted across the empty alley, his lean figure bent low, and rolled under the edge of the tent, disappearing from view.

Isco held his breath as seconds turned into moments, the screams moving closer, before Vahn's hand finally appeared under the tent and waved them over. Astar darted ahead. Isco followed, careful not to bump into her as his eyes darted around, wary of any seeking shadows or buzzing lights. Somehow, though, Kanna and Haru's attacks left this one place untouched.

The large tent was quiet, the disaster outside muffled by the thick canvas that surrounded them. An open flame danced playfully on a table covered in maps, but it didn't so much as singe the paper around it.

In the center was Osawa. His head hung loose on his neck, rolling forward. He canted to the side, and the only thing keeping him in place on the spindly wood chair were the ropes that bound his hands at his back, his feet to the legs of the chair.

Astar had begun working on the knots while Vahn pulled back the side of the tent's entrance to peer outside. Isco joined Astar, kneeling in the thick rug that covered the Gegenii dirt. Isco balked when dampness seeped into his knees and rocked back on his heels to find that at least it appeared to be just water.

When Isco reached for the ropes, he realized why Astar was having trouble. The ropes were water logged and bloated, making it difficult if not impossible to loosen them.

"Why is everything wet?" Astar muttered.

"Why are you here?"

Isco jumped when Osawa spoke. Osawa's head hung low, his damp hair falling over his eyes but not dripping. His breath came in rasps as he blinked, slow and careful, his entire body protesting the movement as he tried to right himself.

Osawa's eyes were bloodshot, his capillaries blown. Isco's stomach dropped.

"You don't get to be my hero, I don't even know you," Astar scolded, though the worry in her voice took the edge out of it. She continued to struggle, growling in frustration. "Can't get these damn ropes off."

"Here."

Isco turned in time to dodge out of the way of the knife that Vahn casually tossed.

"Nice catch," Osawa rasped.

Isco leaned over to retrieve Vahn's knife. The moment the natural wood hand settled into his grasp, he could feel the danger that the blade held. Isco couldn't fathom how many lives this thing had taken and he would have imagined it to be cold, but there was a lingering warmth in the handle. It was like holding something sacred, something he shouldn't have.

Isco adjusted his grip on the knife and attempted to saw through the sodden fibres, but they wouldn't give. A scream sounded outside the tent, reminding Isco of where exactly he was.

"Can we at least pretend we are in a hurry?" Vahn hissed.

Osawa sighed, and it rattled in his lungs. "Get back."

Isco thought he heard the sea. The ropes lightened in color as the was leached from them. The rivulets that formed began to spin, and the now dry ropes crackled as they tore. The ropes fell in pieces, the water falling with them and darkening the rug. Osawa coughed, a hacking, wet cough, and Astar had to move quickly to keep him from falling off the chair.

"You couldn't have done that sooner?" Vahn asked.

"No," Osawa managed to choke out, before the coughs interrupted him again.

Vahn was holding out his empty hand. Isco gladly relinquished the knife and Vahn's fingers wrapped around it, fitting into every worn groove of the handle.

Isco joined Astar, hunching and ducking under Osawa's arm so that they could balance Osawa between them. Vahn cut through the canvas at the back of the tent to create a better opening, but before they made it out, the front of the tent opened.

A young woman burst in, blonde curls flying behind her. She held knives at ready, but her hands shook. In less time than Isco could blink, Vahn was across the room, twisting her around and pressing a blade at her throat.

"Vahn, wait," Osawa croaked.

All of Vahn's momentum, his quick and careful reflexes, stopped at once, his body coiling with the energy. Vahn twisted enough, taking the girl with him, and cocked a raised brow at Osawa.

"That's Kenzi."

Vahn's brow furrowed and he pressed his knife tighter against the girl's throat as he leaned in. Her hands tightened around her knives as she tilted her head back to avoid the sharp edge of Vahn's blade.

"Oh, yeah," he said, an unnerving lightness in his voice. "I can see the resemblance. Air, right?"

Osawa nodded.

Vahn leaned closer to the girl's ear. "I feel so much as a breeze I don't like, and my hand might slip. Understood?"

The girl swallowed against the blade and nodded as much as Vahn would allow.

The tent's entrance was pulled open again and Vahn stepped back, keeping the girl between them and the new arrival. The man stopped in his tracks, his hands held up and his eyes widening.

"Hey, Ira," Vahn said, his voice a threatening purr. "Cute sister."

# 19

## THE SAINT OF FIRE

### KENZI

KENZI TRIED TO SHOUT A WARNING, but when her throat tried to find the sound it pushed into the sharp edge of The Saint of Fire's knife, turning her warning into a whimper.

Ira froze in place, his palms open and pleading. His eyes were wide, wider than Kenzi had ever seen them. That was the worst part, and Kenzi had felt her death coming the moment metal touched her skin.

When Vahn hesitated, she dared to think that she may find a way out of this. But the way Ira looked at her, the terror he fought to hide in his citrine eyes made her less sure. Ira attempted to step forward.

The knife around Kenzi's neck pressed against her skin, forcing her back against Vahn's heat. The Saint of Fire burned hotter than any fever could, his body all wiry strength coiled in matchstick bones ready to strike.

"So much as twitch another finger, and you'll be sobbing in her blood," Vahn said, his tone even, spoken almost like he was passing off an account of the weather. It was too close to Kenzi's ear and her eyes shut. There was nowhere for her to go. She was trapped between a bonfire and a blade.

"So," Vahn continued, "how've you been?"

He wasn't talking to her, and there was a familiarity in his tone she didn't like.

"Better before this moment," Ira replied, his voice tight.

Vahn made a humming sound, and Kenzi felt it reverberate in his chest. "I can see that being the case." He shifted his weight from one foot to the other, settling into a more comfortable stance. Kenzi resisted his hold, and the knife's edge bit into her skin. It broke under the pressure, a trickle of blood sliding down her neck and into the collar of her uniform.

Ira's nostrils flared, then his eyes narrowed as he forced himself to look over her shoulder. "What do you want, Vahn?"

In that instant, Kenzi knew. The only reason she was alive was to be a part of the Saint's show, to be dangled in front of Ira.

"Oh," Vahn purred in response, "this and that."

Specifically Ira. Ira, who let his hands fall from the air, who kept his eyes on Vahn as he straightened the cuffs of his sleeves before crossing his arms. Kenzi's grip tightened around her remaining knife, and Vahn tilted the cold blade that sat against her neck until her head bent back and away from it, until she rose from her heels to avoid it cutting any deeper.

"Drop them," he hissed.

Everything in her told her not to let go, but she forced her hands to uncurl her grip.

The moment her fingers let loose of the blades, Ira spoke. "I see you're working with the Governor's daughter. Astar, right?"

Vahn's attention moved away from the falling knives, his head jerking away from Kenzi to his companions before settling back on Ira.

"There was a big guy, too. I'll assume he's guarding the retreat." Ira squinted to study the last one. "Not sure I know him, though."

"That's Isco," Vahn said, his tone light. But pressed so close to him that Kenzi could feel his every breath, she caught the strain in his voice. "Say hi, Isco."

Giving a name to Ira was as good as handing over a life. Even if she was Ira's weakness, Ira knew Vahn's, and he was working it at a slant. The grip around Kenzi loosened enough that she at least dropped back to her heels, able to breathe once more.

"Hi?" a man answered, uncertain and more than a little anxious.

"Now say bye, Isco."

"What?"

"He means we should go," a woman's voice prompted.

"Vahn..." Isco said, caught between protest and plea.

Vahn's grip relaxed for an instant as his head tilted away from Kenzi's. "Go."

The sharp angle that her arm was twisted enough gave ever so slightly and Kenzi attempted to pull away, but he was too quick. His biting grip returned, cranking her off balance once again.

Before Vahn's head turned back, Ira spoke. "The fight is close. They don't look like they have any training. Do you think they will survive on their own?"

Vahn's grip loosened, but not enough. "You shouldn't have left us, Ira," Vahn said, and there was something in his voice that was no longer a game. There was something buried, something sharp.

Ira's eyes flickered, and Kenzi had to catch her breath. "It isn't that simple."

Vahn scoffed. "Because of her?" He tightened his grip on Kenzi. She lifted off of her toes, bent back against the Saint's lean body as his blade pinched into her skin. Vahn let out a short laugh, cut off at the end. "Precious little Kenzi, following you to her grave. Letting her sign herself away to the Palamidia. To *Velinius*. You think she's safe here, just because you're around?" The knife against Kenzi's throat tightened on his point, and she leaned back until it ached, until she was forced to hold her breath to keep her throat from moving. "Does she even know the things you've done?"

When Ira said nothing, Vahn leaned close to Kenzi. His lips turned into a smirk against her skin. "Guess not."

He smelled like a distant forest fire and a nearby storm, like rain after pine burned. He turned his face so his lips whispered against her ear. "You should ask big brother about Ganglere," he said, loud enough that Ira could hear. "Ask him what it sounds like when a city screams."

Vahn gave her enough room that Kenzi could try to meet Ira's eyes, but he refused to look at her. There was anger in them, and it twisted him into someone she almost didn't recognize. "They were orders, Vahn."

"Exactly," Vahn hissed, and Kenzi breathed, "but not Kanna's." He leaned against her again, as if he needed her attention, and she held the air in her lungs. "That part is important," he said, then turned back to Ira. "And no one told you to leave the walls up."

Ira's eyes cooled. "You could have ordered them down. You were the only one that could." He shifted, his shoulders falling and his head tilting at an odd angle, a mannerism that Kenzi had never seen on him. "Why didn't you?"

Vahn's grip loosened, but not enough that Kenzi could attempt an escape. It was enough that she could slip her fingers up the palm of her free hand and slide one of the thin throwing blades strapped to her wrist from its sheath.

Vahn sighed, and after, Kenzi felt his entire body flex back into a hard fighting stance. "I'll give you the chance they didn't have."

Kenzi didn't even have the chance to wonder what he meant before his blade bit into her throat and slid over her skin.

It didn't hurt, until it did. She lashed out with the blade in her hand, digging into flesh and tearing away as Vahn shoved her into Ira's waiting arms.

"It's all right, Kenzi," Ira said, but Kenzi didn't know how it could be all right. She was breathing her blood, and that was where air was supposed to be. Air belonged in the lungs, air was meant to bring life, and she couldn't get enough. She couldn't get any.

She smiled, holding the blade she'd used against the Saint up to Ira. He had given her the signal, told her what to do, and she'd done it.

"Oh, Kenz, you were perfect," he said, taking it from her weak, slick hands.

And there was fire. There was fire everywhere, bright and burning and full of secrets. Ira held the knife to a nearby flame and the blood on it erupted, turning the knife red with heat.

That was strange. She wanted to say it was strange, but her mouth moved and no sound came out.

Ira leaned over her with the heated knife.

"You'll tell me later," he said, and when he pressed the knife against her neck she could smell her own skin burning. The pain turned into a monster that wanted to clamp her in its jaws, but it shocked her lungs enough that they breathed.

"You'll tell me later," Ira said, a comfort, and she believed him.

And she found her voice enough to scream.

# 20

# THE PRINCE OF LIGHT

## HARU

THE SMELL of burning cotton was the last signal Haru had that time was running out. While they had the advantage of surprise when they entered the camp, they were relying on getting out before it wore off. These were their soldiers, trained as they were, and many by them. A Palamidia soldier knew to gain their bearings in a matter of moments, and that moment had extended too long.

The soldiers surrounded Haru, attempting to cut him away from Kanna. Their attacks were reckless but suffocating, and he barely had a moment to think between each strike.

He had to get to Kanna. As skilled as she was, as predictable as their attacks would be, she had already unleashed a massive amount of power. She'd spent an entire day battling for her survival, followed by her own undoing. He knew that Kanna would fight to the bitterest of ends, that she would tear apart an enemy with her bare hands if that was what it took, but he couldn't let her end be here.

Haru pushed his newest attacker away and called for the light. In a blink, a bolt crackled up from the ground, an explosion cutting the night. The bodies near it scattered, blown away by the force.

In the aftermath his ears were ringing, and he shook them clear before pressing his fingers to his lips and letting out a high, shrill whistle. Before the remaining soldiers rallied, Bia wove through them, pausing near Haru so he could mount. Amon followed at a full gallop, circling through the stunned soldiers, knocking those that had remained upright from their feet.

Haru turned the horses back into the chaos and nudged Bia into a gallop, following the thread that would lead him to Kanna, the dissonant note in the sameness of them.

The air hung thick with smoke, the fires Vahn set moving rapidly through the camp, drawing the water loas who attempted to quell the flames. Those loas were no match for Vahn, though. His fire had always been relentless, a fury made manifest in the world.

Those that weren't attempting to save the camp from being ash had gathered around the traitor Legatus. Kanna was nearly surrounded, but she was a vision of grace in battle. Her every movement was simple and brutal, careful and calculated to deliver the most efficient blows and recover for the next, to never give up her guard.

If battle was an art, Kanna was a master. She was a devastating force, weaving through the flash of metal. They attacked three or four at a time, but Kanna slashed down arms so they couldn't hold their weapons, slid her blades across tender joints that buckled entire bodies, found the weak points that no one thought to block when their hearts and necks were on the line.

Haru bent over Bia's neck and neck to urge her faster. Amon streaked across their path through the flickering dark in the camp, a shadow made of muscle and teeth, and those that were too slow to dive from his reach were bitten or trampled.

Kanna's eyes slid to Haru when he approached, as they always did. Even when the chaos was thickest, she would always watch for him. They could always find each other.

Haru flattened his palm, and the ground beneath Kanna shimmered. Her eyes widened and for an instant, as if she didn't recognize it. At the very last moment, the shadows wrapped around her.

The light flashed, bright and blindingly white, washing the camp in it. Then the shadows unfurled from Kanna, darker against the hazy light that lingered in the camp. They cut through the middle of the soldiers and Haru knew it had to be a trick of his mind that they looked like feathers, a trick of his eyes that they were tinged in gold. They dropped to the ground, melting into a fluid ink where they fell.

They spread beneath the feet of her stunned attackers and pulled them down, yanking them until they were ankle deep, knee deep into the sand and screaming.

Kanna sheathed her knife in her left hand as Haru approached and he slowed Bia without stopping, leaning over and offering Kanna his arm.

He trusted she would take it.

She always did.

Haru braced himself as Kanna grabbed hold. He gripped her forearm and turned Bia with his legs, and Kanna used their momentum to mount behind him. She sheathed her second knife as Haru circled Bia around, pointing back to the forest that marked their escape.

Not all of the soldiers had rushed to stop the immediate threats, however. Others had rallied and mounted to block an escape. Kanna's touch was light on his waist as she turned to check their tail. With her free hand, she called the dark.

The shadows pulled from beneath them, sliding across the ground and granting them passage. Cries of alarm rang out as hooves and feet tangled with the grasping black. It caught the riders' ankles, yanking them from their mounts and crushing them beneath the cavalry that followed.

Kanna shifted, her leg sliding up behind him until both were on one side of Bia. She held her hand out and Amon came at her beckoning, his wild stride shifting to match Bia's.

Haru kept Bia steady. Kanna's reaching hand twisted in Amon's mane as she launched herself from one horse to the other. Haru's breath stopped as it always did, but Kanna's foot caught her stirrup and she swung her other leg over Amon, settling back onto her own mount as if it was the most natural thing in the world, as if she hadn't just dared a thousand different fates.

Smoke and ash wrapped around them, and the heat of the nearby fires scorched the thin Gegenes air. Kanna crossed in front of Haru then pointed Amon back, circling to take up the guard position as they neared the inferno at the perimeter of the camp.

The blistering flames shifted colors, the oranges and yellows turning to blue and violet where Vahn emerged, wearing the self-satisfied smirk on his lips that didn't reach his eyes. The cuffs of his uniform were stained in blood, another trail leading down his side. He stopped to brush a bit of ash from his shoulder before meeting Haru's gaze, his brow raised.

Haru pulled Bia to a stop. "I don't remember that being part of the plan."

Vahn tsked then mounted behind Haru, though his movements weren't nearly as effortless as Kanna's. "You really didn't think I'd miss the opportunity to set a fire, did you?"

"Are you all right?" Haru asked when Vahn settled unevenly behind him. "You're covered in blood."

"And you aren't?"

Haru shook his head. "I've got him," he called to Kanna.

She looked back over her shoulder at them. She had disconnected, her expression holding neither heat nor cold. The fire reflected the glass of her eyes and the dark rose behind her, a cloak that was always reaching.

She turned Amon and leaned over his neck, racing across the barrier to join Haru and Vahn.

The Palamidia followed.

# 21

# THE EARTH'S SON

## YASSEN

YASSEN PACED in the outskirts of the petrified forests with three horses for company. He wasn't complaining. There were the two that Osawa had found in the alley as well as one from Astar's stables that Vahn had picked out, and they were very good company.

The forests reminded him of his first home. Not the crowded city in Adur where he and his siblings lived on top of each other, but his home from a time before when he lived in the trees. There was something about the soft clacking of the stone leaves that reminded him of an old lullaby, and he could have drifted to sleep to the sound if it had been another time.

He straightened his back and shook his head. It was not time to sleep. It was time to be ready. He wasn't sure what for, but he was going to be ready. The crack of a thin branch caused him to whirl around, and his forehead smacked a low hanging branch when he turned.

Astar and Isco had Osawa hanging between them.

"Oh, it is so good to see ya'll I was so worried," Yassen said in one breath. Then he sucked it in. "Osawa, you look bad."

Osawa straightened his knees, attempting to take his weight back, but he started coughing. "I can't say I feel great," he said when it stopped.

"Shh," Astar hissed at them, "We are hiding, remember?"

"I really don't think anyone can hear us over all that."

The sound of battle had risen while he waited, the smell of smoke curling through the night and reaching him all the way at the periphery of it all.

Astar rolled her eyes. "Help us get him on... one of these horses, I guess."

Osawa pulled his arms from Astar and Isco's shoulders and righted his glasses, swaying when he let go. "I can manage fine." He stumbled to one of the horses, catching the side of it. Osawa struggled to fit his foot into his stirrup.

Astar held out her hand, catching Yassen in the chest when he moved to help. "No, he's managing just fine, remember?"

Yassen looked to Osawa, then Astar, and said, "I don't think he is."

Osawa pulled himself up halfway, but then didn't have the strength to get the rest of himself over the horse. Astar stepped forward, shoving him up. Osawa winced, but settled in his saddle. Osawa didn't have a chance to argue before she had her foot in the stirrup and her leg over the back of the horse.

"What–"

"What?" she interrupted his protest. "I want the front row seat when you fall off." She turned to face Yassen and Isco. "What are you two waiting for? Get a horse."

Isco backed away.

"What's wrong?" Yassen asked. "They're good horses, Isco."

"I'm sure they are. I just...."

"Do you know how to ride a horse?" Yassen asked.

"Not like that, no."

"Take Mud," Osawa said, gesturing to the other Palamidia warhorse. "At least she'll know what she's doing."

Isco shifted in place but didn't move. Yassen put a hand on his back and he sunk beneath it, so he lifted his hand up a bit higher. He hadn't meant to squash the man.

"I'll help," Yassen said. He guided Isco to the horse who was Mud and bent down, lacing his fingers together to make a step for Isco.

"The horse's name is Mud?" Astar said behind them.

Isco grudgingly placed his foot in Yassen's hand, and Yassen boosted him onto the horse. He overshot a bit, though, and had to catch Isco before he fell off the other side.

"I didn't name it," Osawa said. "That's Vahn's."

Isco froze the horse huffed, stamping in agitation.

"I know it's scary at first being so high," Yassen said to comfort him, "but it isn't that hard when you get used to it."

The sound of an explosion sounded from the camp, a blinding light coming from the camp. Moments later, another, and this time the sound was accompanied by a crackle and a chorus of screams.

Yassen swallowed the lump of worry in his throat. None of that sounded good, even if Kanna and his new friends weren't the ones caught in it.

The fires along the camp's perimeter parted and Yassen could make out two figures racing across the distance to where they lay in wait. The further they moved, the more the fires fell, and more white uniforms followed behind them.

"Please tell me one of you has my knives," Osawa said, his voice strained with exhaustion and pain.

Yassen shook his head. He looked back to Osawa and gave him a thumbs up. "I got you this time. Wait here."

Yassen grabbed the as yet unnamed horse and mounted, spurring it out of the shadows of the stone trees. This was the land of his birth, the place where he had become, and he knew what to do. As the distance grew shorter between them, he could make out all three of the others racing at him and he understood why people would run the other direction. Their white uniforms were coated in soot and blood, the mess standing out against the blank canvas.

Yassen dismounted as they grew near and crouched, his hands on the earth and his eyes on the ground. He judged the distance, the timing, and when the moment was right, he asked a question.

The earth responded. It began to open between his friends and the army, groaning and creaking. His companions thundered past, and he asked the earth for a favor.

"Yassen, what are you doing?" Vahn shouted when they stopped behind him.

The earth moved. It rearranged, it split, it dove down and pushed up and out. It opened for him, splitting so deeply he had to tell it to be a bit more careful. Behind him he could hear the stamp of hooves as his companions stopped, refusing to leave him there. He had to give them distance, give them space and time to get away from the army that wanted his friends dead for no reason he could understand. There was enough death. He didn't want anymore.

It was like Kanna had told him, the earth wanted to help. All he did was ask, and it answered a hundred fold. The earth didn't get tired, it was solid and it was strong and it was reliable and true. When he opened his eyes, he knew it had done enough, so he let it know and gave his thanks. He asked it to stay, at least long enough that it would matter.

The ground stopped shifting and he stood.

Between them was a canyon so vast it reached the horizon. The white of the army was a blur in the dark, a swirl of insects caught on the other side of a trap.

Kanna and the others dismounted, stepping forward to see what he had done. Kanna went to the ledge of the canyon and looked down. When she turned to Yassen, she was smiling. It was an almost delicate thing, like the small glimpses of approval when he'd manage to dodge her strikes. It made him proud.

Vahn whistled, long and low. "That, big guy, is the kind of thing people name.

## 22

# A LITTLE BIT RUINED

## KANNA

THE NIGHT of Gegenes was decidedly cooler than the day, the sand easily giving up its heat. The quiet of the desert was disturbed only by hoofbeats against soft ground, muffled but steady. Kanna pushed Amon at the head of the group, the sound of the others at her back a constant.

Until she stopped. It was enough. She had enough.

The sound of hooves stopped in a broken staccato behind her, and she dismounted.

She couldn't breathe. She needed to breathe, but the dead were still shifting through the black and rattling in the dark. A part of her knew it wasn't inside of her, but she could feel them beneath her ribs, all that despair taking up residence in her bones.

She pulled at the neck of the white jacket she wore, tearing it away from her skin. It was heavy. It was wrong. She yanked the sleeves, but the thick fabric tightened around her shoulders and resisted the bend of her elbows. Her fingers slipped over the cuffs, nails running roughshod over delicate chain-stitched threads, each made with a skilled hand, each one a breath, a purpose, a history she didn't know blending and folding into a tableau of death that she carried.

She needed the sky. She needed the raw nothing of the night, the cold on her skin and the insulating embrace of it all. When she could no longer hear those that followed her and the shadows wrapped her limbs, when she finally kicked herself free of the heavy fabric, she looked up.

The stars were vast, and while their stories were long lost, Kanna could almost hear them whisper their names. The sharp light against the black of the night, the way it broke the darkness.

She couldn't stop looking. Couldn't stop wanting.

She knew Haru was there before he arrived. He was a warmth on the back of her neck, a calm that muted the neverending wails. It even softened her own, the insistent hiss inside of her that reminded her what she was.

She was Ananke Strepheim, named only by her mother. She was the wrath of the Palamidia, a shadow over the sun. Before she cut her teeth she slaughtered hundreds, then used the sharp of them against thousands more.

The air stuck against her lungs, viscous and clinging at her throat.

She was nameless, calling herself by an echo of sounds she felt in a dream. In the Theatre, they called her the Harbinger, a specter that heralded death. When everything had been new, the feel of blood on her hands was familiar.

"Kanna."

Haru reached her when she began struggling with the stays at the sides of her armor. The blood was dry, but shouldn't have been there. It was hers, and it was others, and there was too much of it everywhere.

His arm wrapped around her waist and over her elbows, pinning her hands to her side and anchoring her. His other hand covered her eyes and her mind fell into a sudden, blessed silence. The only sound was her own ragged breathing and the hum of his pulse.

Kanna swallowed. "How are you doing that?"

"I'm not doing anything."

"You are." Kanna wrapped her hand around his wrist, pressed her fingers into his humming pulse. She knew it was wrong. She knew it was the only right thing that had ever been.

Too soft for something so sharp, she said: "I don't understand it."

"Maybe you will remember."

"It's not remembering."

He didn't say anything. She didn't know the right words. "I

remember it now," she said. "But in the Neither, it isn't a memory. It isn't a show, or a story, or a thing behind my eyes. It is... again."

Kanna felt his words in his chest before they were formed, the thrum of them in his body and the breath against her neck when he spoke. "Again?"

She wanted to lean into him but she knew she should pull away. Her legs shook with the indecision and his grip tightened, only enough to keep her balanced without demanding that she choose.

"Again." Identical words echoed between now and some half-remembered thing. "I didn't ask for this."

She wouldn't have known how to ask. Didn't know this was something that could exist. She still wasn't sure what it was.

"What didn't you ask for, *inara*?"

The word was foreign to her, and precious to him. It was a soft word in a brutal place. He cradled it, hummed it in his throat, and it came from something deeper than speech. When she found her voice again it was a whisper. "I cannot be this. I am not enough."

Haru's grip tightened on the curve of her hip and he turned her to face him with deft hands. She could see the stars again, the desert, the nothing that surrounded them. The back of his knuckles brushed along her cheek and moved to follow him. When his fingers tangled in her knotted hair, she tilted her head back because she wanted to. She had to.

"You are everything," he said when she met his eyes. Haru said it like he lived it, as if it was the truth of the universe.

But she was barely human. There was nothing good in her. The Neither had shown her that much. It had given her the horror of battle, the pain wrought against her, and what she herself had done to ease it. She was a force in a body that wanted nothing more than to be near him. Even when the stars burned out, she'd still want him.

That made her even more cruel. She would destroy him as she had so many others, and she couldn't stop herself from doing so. It was her nature.

There was still time she didn't know, a gaping expanse of her life that was missing. All she could imagine there was the same unending violence, the same vicious hurt. Haru had a calling before. Before her. He was tutored and trained, molded to rise and lead. Just by being, she had taken that from him.

Kanna pressed her hand between them, felt the beat of his heart under her palm and knew he wasn't safe with her. She traced a path over his throat, the warmth jolting through her, her hand shaking at the discovery.

His hand tightened in her hair and he leaned into her touch until she could feel the thrum of blood under his skin. A sigh rattled through him when her thumb passed over the corner of his lips, her fingers brushing his hair back before attempting to retreat.

His fingers untangled and caught her wrist before she could pull away. The arm around her waist tightened, and he didn't break his gaze from hers. He turned her hand back and pressed his lips against the soft skin of her inner wrist.

Haru looked at her as if she was something worthy. He chased the ghost of a creature that was trapped between.

"I've ruined you," she said.

Haru's lips curved up into a smile, his eyes softening. They were a cloudless sky, the sun rising in the corners of them like a revelation. He bent his head lower, moved his eyes closer so that he was all she could see.

"If it is a choice between some concept of grace and you," he said, his grip tightening, his fingers pressing into the fragile bones of her wrist that cradled her heartbeat. "Then ruin me."

Somewhere, somehow, she'd crossed a line that she couldn't take back. And he had followed, or led, and she didn't think it mattered now which of those it was.

Kanna wasn't built for surrender, but she was tired. Tired of resisting the pull of him, tired of only knowing vicious hands. It was only a moment, a breath between them. She tilted her head and kissed him, a quiet attempt to reclaim something that was lost.

Haru met her, his longing felt in a held breath, a tension, a restraint he set upon himself. His desire was barely held in grasped hands, closed against themselves.

Kanna had no armor against him. Her body shuddered, but she couldn't pull away. Not anymore. She wrapped her arms behind his neck, pulling herself up against him. He took her invitation. With his lips pressed against her, she was at his mercy.

His arms tightened and she was nearly pulled from her feet, pulled together, so much greater than the sum of her scattered parts. His lips parted and she claimed the bravery she was attributed, meeting his hunger with her own.

Whatever give she had, he would take. Haru kissed her like he would lose her, like it was the first and last time. His hands opened, fingers uncurling along her spine, his palm on the small of her back fitting her against him like she belonged.

She didn't know how or when, but Haru's embrace had become the structure of her world. Her hands opened, dared to unfurl, attempted to hold on to something she shouldn't have. They wrapped in the fabric of his jacket and she felt every linked stitch beneath her fingers.

She couldn't breathe. She didn't care. In his arms she was weightless, standing at the edge of an unknown and alive.

The kiss broke and the night invaded her lungs where he once was. The cold stung, the warmth of her body shivering against it. She held onto him, a solid truth cut from the unknown.

Haru's grip relaxed, his lips traveling up her neck, to her jaw, to her temple, and she slid along his body until her heels met the ground once more. The cold sand shifted beneath her, each grain named by something long ago, each piece of the world holding onto its purpose.

He pressed his forehead against hers, his eyes shut, his breath harsh. Her hand splayed against his chest, feeling the staccato beat of his heart within the cage of it.

Everything was still. Everything moved as it should, a single thread untangled and understood. The universe narrowed, and she knew the reason the sky held on to the stars. Even if they were gone, even if their stories were lost the sky would always know their light. It would always remember what they were.

## 23

# AN UNDERSTANDING

## VAHN

VAHN NEVER SLEPT MORE than a few hours at a time. One here, then waking, another after. Even with everyone where they belonged, with Kanna's uneven breathing against his back and Osawa's steady rhythm at his other side, about three hours at a time was all that he could manage.

This time it was the sharp, throbbing pain in his side that woke him, so at least he had an excuse. A slow slip and he freed his leg from beneath Osawa, then he just had to rise straight up to extricate himself from their formation. Though he tried to carefully tip Kanna's weight off of him, she still shifted, which woke Haru.

Haru was immediately alert and clear but, seeing it was Vahn, he assisted in taking Kanna's weight. After Vahn stood, Haru adjusted their covering over Kanna to make up for the loss of heat before drifting off once more.

Not wanting to step on anyone, Vahn waited until his eyes adjusted to the dim glow of the cavern. Yassen, who was sprawled nearby with Astar, had led them straight to it. A few steps were formed to lead down and the group had a shelter for the night.

On feet trained to silence, Vahn crept past the lone sleeping medic and through the back of the cavern. Turning a corner, he was met with the underground pool that they had used to wash in earlier. The surface glittered, reflecting the shining minerals that hung from the cave ceiling.

Vahn crouched at the edge of the hidden pool and dipped his fingers into the cold, clear water. It rippled at his touch, something once peaceful now disturbed, circles in circles drifting through the dark water. They grew wider, only stopping when they buffeted against the walls of their confines.

Lowering himself to the cool stone, Vahn shrugged out of his outer jacket. It had been uncomfortable to sleep in it, but he'd needed the extra coverage to hide the gash in his side.

He should have known better than to let Ira get a word in. He was too good at getting under peoples' skin, always had been, and he'd trained his sister well.

The water was frigid in Vahn's hands, but he didn't bother to warm it. The chill eased the infectious heat in his side and loosened the white cotton that clung to the wound, which had reopened and bled around his covert bandaging attempts.

"You're injured."

Vahn's hands froze. The surprise hit his spine and soured along his nerves and through his body. It wasn't in his nature to allow himself to be startled. When he was sure the shock had fled, he turned over his shoulder to face Isco. Isco was barely a shape in the dim, his hair skewed to one side.

"Nothing to see here, medic." Vahn turned back to the pool. "Go back to sleep."

Instead of leaving, Isco took his words as an invitation to move closer and drop his bag. "I understand that you are all shockingly comfortable with bleeding, but your body needs that on the inside or you die. It's a simple concept."

Isco crouched, squinting to assess Vahn's injury with only the light refracting from the pool. Van held his palm near Isco's shoulder and called the fire. It sparked into being, the air crackling around it.

Isco's composure dropped and he fell of his heels. He caught himself with his palms and scrambled away, his eyes narrowing on the flame that Vahn held.

"Easy, doc." Vahn set the flame next to himself and it jittered in place before calming to an easy glow. "Just wanted to give you a better look."

Isco returned to his side, his prodding forcing Vahn's smirk to drop as he hissed. Isco shook his head and sat back on his heels. "Lift your shirt."

Isco pulled the lopsided tie out of his hair and it fell almost to his shoulders. He ran his fingers through it and smoothed it back, then re-tied it.

Vahn hooked his thumbs in the hem of his shirt and twisted it up only enough to reveal a sliver of his skin. "What, no please?"

Isco met his teasing gaze with a clinical detachment before he rummaged through the bag at his side. "Please."

Vahn's grin fell. Isco's default was skittishness, all jitters wrapped in human skin, but when he set himself to the task of tending the myriad injuries the group had sustained, he was competent and controlled. Even Kanna hadn't been able to break his calm, and she was a notoriously bad patient.

Vahn's shirt stuck to the wound but he pulled it away despite that, the pull of stuck cotton on damaged skin reigniting the sharp pain in his side he had been dutifully ignoring.

Isco's eyebrows knit in concern, but his jaw clenched to hold in the comment.

Vahn leaned his weight on his other hand and untangled his legs, stretching them while Isco worked. Isco's fingertips against his skin were uneven, the pads of a few smoother than others, and Vahn shut his eyes to enjoy the softness of them against his feverish skin. But Isco was quick, and had the gash covered before Vahn realized he finished.

"You can put your shirt back," Isco said, returning his supplies to his bag.

Vahn let go of the white hem, the stained shirt falling back in place. The wound didn't burn as it had before. He leaned back on the palms of both hands, tilting his face towards Isco. "You had a chance to run."

Isco stopped sorting the supplies. He shifted back on his heels and zipped the bag. "Where would I go?"

"You're a medic. Well trained, by the feel of it. Go anywhere, Isco. Everyone needs healers."

Isco scoffed and shifted his weight, sitting heavily on the ground next to Vahn. His knees were pulled up, his hands hanging over them. "As much work as I've been doing, seems like I'm needed here."

Isco fidgeted, his index finger scraping and catching against the rough skin on his thumb. Then, he pressed his palms together and squeezed his hands between his knees.

Vahn looked to the pool. "Anywhere would be safer than with us." He pulled one of his knees to his chest and wrapped his hands around it. "I'd think the injuries were evidence of that."

Isco shrugged. "Nowhere is safe. At least here I can see where the danger is."

Turning away from the waters, Vahn considered Isco. His eyes were trained on the ripples in the pool, as if they held some great secret only Isco was privy to.

"The only reason you are alive is because Kanna wills it," Vahn warned. "When she decides you aren't worth it, when she remembers Adur, no will stop Haru from tearing you apart."

Isco didn't shift, didn't fidget. "I know."

There was no defeat in Isco's expression, no horror or illusion or even resignation. Isco continued to watch the pool, even as the ripples turned to nothing, with something akin to serenity. Vahn thought, in that brief moment, that he could almost understand why Kanna was drawn to him.

Almost.

# 24

# SMALL THINGS

## ISCO

"WE CAN'T CALL IT MIKE," Vahn said, his tone firm.

Isco was tired. He wasn't used to riding like the others, and for some reason he had been allotted to traveling with Vahn, who seemed to delight in setting Isco's nerves on edge. However, considering Vahn was the main buffer between him and death by Haru, Isco didn't have room to complain.

"Why not?" Yassen asked. "It's a good name."

The group ambled about the open deserts of Gegenes, following Kanna's northwest lead. The plan, as far as Isco could tell, was to cross Atarrabi in one of the narrower stretches, then they'd be in Lugos. Isco hoped the soldiers didn't intend to bring all of them into the Empire's territory. Isco had never been, and he wasn't sure he wanted to go.

"It's a girl horse, Yassen," Astar said. Sitting behind Osawa, Astar was much more comfortable in her position as a second rider than Isco. She balanced on her own for the most part, but as Osawa healed, she'd wrap her arms around his waist and rest her chin cheekily against his shoulder.

Osawa had yet to tell anyone what had happened in the camp. Isco had an idea, but it wasn't his place to share it.

"Girls can be Mike," Yassen said.

As the nights had passed, the group had contracted their sleeping arrangements.

When Osawa's deep exhaustion was sated and he began to sleep lighter, his experiences caught up with him. Isco would wake to alert soldiers, each bending with concern. Vahn would throw his arm around Osawa when he thrashed, press his forehead against his and whisper something that Isco couldn't make out, and Osawa would settle.

Things didn't get better, though. After the third night, Kanna reached past Vahn and pressed her fingertips to Osawa's heart. She recoiled from the touch and, without a word, gestured for Osawa to move. Osawa shifted to the side of Haru that Kanna didn't occupy.

Across from them, Isco watched. Vahn ran his hands through his chopped hair, felt the tips that brushed the back of his neck, and his other hand clenched to a fist. Eventually he settled back down, his back turned against Kanna's.

Isco had always been an early riser, but not as early as Vahn. One morning, Vahn caught Isco out, and he'd told Isco that the sleeping arrangements were a defense tactic.

Kanna had nightmares, Vahn told him. Before Haru, Vahn would stay close to her when they were on missions. That way, he said, he could stop the screams before the enemy could be alerted. Later, they discovered Haru had a latent ability that kept the horrors at bay. It didn't always help but, and Vahn said this with a notable smirk, it helped more than Vahn could.

It made as much sense as anything, but Isco hadn't asked.

Vahn didn't really stop talking. It was as if Vahn believed that explaining things before someone wondered about them meant that they wouldn't actually think too hard about it. But Isco was thinking about it. He was thinking about Vahn's sheared edges, and his empty fist.

After that, Astar made her bed on the other side of Osawa, and Yassen curled next to her. The cool of the night dug into Isco's lone bones until his shivering alerted Vahn. Vahn peeled himself away from Kanna and, without a word, drug Isco and his sleeping mat next to him. It didn't make sleep come easier to Isco, far from it, but at least he wasn't cold near Vahn's heat.

"That's not the point," Vahn said, and Isco jumped when his attention snapped back. "You don't name horses Mike."

"Isn't your horse's name Mud?" Astar asked.

"We aren't talking about her right now." Vahn leaned forward and whispered to Mud. "Don't listen to the mean lady, you're perfect."

Isco found it difficult to align the different aspects of Vahn he'd witnessed, and everything about him kept Isco on the verge of flirting with panic. One moment he was sarcastically offhand, the next he was slitting a throat without blinking. And others, when he didn't think anyone was watching, the look in his eyes was the softest and loneliest thing that Isco had ever seen.

"You going to weigh in here, K?"

Kanna turned from her place in the lead, shifting enough to eye Vahn and Isco, then the horse in question from beneath the silver and gold keffiyeh she'd draped around her shoulders and head to protect herself from the unforgivable desert sun.

The other soldiers had followed her lead and shed their uniforms. The men had mostly opted, like Kanna, for simple jeans and light cotton shirts. Vahn's clothing was more fitted, while Haru and Osawa were eased. Osawa was in a burgundy more common in Gegenii wear and Haru had gone for a dark grey, mimicking Kanna's choice.

Vahn was still in Solarian white. He wasn't a fan of subtlety. He wore his past and dared people to look away.

While they had chosen different colors, different patterned scarves, they dressed similarly enough that they'd effectively exchanged one uniform for another. However, when the dust swirled and stung, they wrapped their coverings to protect their noses and mouths and pressed on without a pause. They had been here before, traveled these lands, knew the world for what it was and, more importantly, how to survive in a place that wasn't even theirs.

Kanna tilted her head to Haru. "What was that poet you liked?"

"Aelis?" Haru asked after a moment of shocked surprise.

"No," Kanna shook her head. "Not that one."

"Saturnina?"

She looked back at the horse and waved back at Yassen when he waved at her. "Mike works better."

"Wait a minute." Vahn kicked Mud into a lope to catch up with

Kanna, and the change of gait caught Isco off guard and forced him to cling to the only solid thing near, which was Vahn. When they reached Kanna and slowed, Isco released his grip, but he didn't know what to do with his hands.

"You remember some dusty poets Haru reads?" Vahn asked once they caught up. "And you didn't bother to tell me?"

Kanna shrugged, her eyes shifting away from Vahn and back to the horizon. "It is a small thing."

"What else?" When she didn't answer, Vahn pressed on. "Anything else?"

Haru guided Bia between them. "Leave it, Vahn."

Isco shrunk behind Vahn when Haru moved closer. Isco had yet to share a spare word with Haru, and considering the last conversation they'd had nearly ended with his arm being broken, Isco wasn't in a hurry to brook their shared silence.

Vahn sat back, meeting Haru's gaze with a glare. He shook his head as he moved Mud's reins to point them back. "Good talk, K."

Isco barely had time to prepare before Vahn dug his heels into Mud and they shot past the group. He slowed their pace and circled around to take up the far rear.

Vahn's shoulders were a tense line.

Isco leaned out as far as he dared, attempting to meet Vahn's eyes. "Are you okay?"

Vahn turned, and when Isco realized how close they were his mouth went dry. But there was no flirting tease in Vahn's eyes, no armored smirk on his lips. Vahn stared at Kanna's back. "Why wouldn't I be?"

And Vahn didn't say anything else for a while.

The sun moved over the desert, and Isco's head threatened to tip on his shoulders as the heat sapped his energy. So when a wail cut through the silence, Isco thought he imagined it.

The group stopped in place, and another scream joined the first.

Kanna leaned over Amon's neck and they shot off toward the sound, Haru at her back.

"Hold on," Vahn said.

"To what?"

Vahn answered by kicking Mud into a gallop, joining the chase.

## 25

# A DISTRACTION

## HARU

IN THE VAST expanse of the desert, the direction of sound can be deceiving. A distant scream can come from anywhere, but Haru followed Kanna, knowing she tracked more than what she could hear. Shapes formed in the horizon, silhouetted against the sun and waving in the heat. A caravan was stopped, one of the wagons tipped on its side. A small group huddled beneath the watch of three guarding figures, while others checked through the wagons.

Chests of colored cloth cracked open and spilled onto the ground, apparently not of any worth to the plunderers. Musical instruments were piled separately, to be taken only if the marauders didn't find anything of greater value for their horde.

Kanna put on an extra burst of speed, heading for the guards around the travelers, so Haru broke away to take care of the ones rifling through the wagons.

Dismounting while Amon was still in motion, Kanna rolled with the momentum and swept the first guard from her feet before she was able to attack. Still on the ground, Kanna rocked on her back and dropped her heel onto the woman's chest, knocking out her breath before regaining her own footing.

Kanna didn't draw her knives, taking on her next opponent hand to hand as well. Haru wanted Kanna safe, wanted the idiot bandits on the ground before they could consider making a move, but he took Kanna's lead.

He slowed Bia on his approach, dismounting at a more sedate pace in front of the four pillaging the wagons. They stopped their work to regard the pair that had come from nowhere before drawing weapons that were nothing more than a variety of cheap, dull swords and chipped knives. Haru held out his arms, his hands bare, welcoming the attack. The first charged headlong, throwing himself into the fight with weight opposed to skill. Haru shifted and kicked him unconscious as he hurled past. The man fell into the dirt, stunned and unmoving.

After the first, the remaining three moved together. But they didn't know how to fight as a team, their joined attack only serving to trip them up.

Haru caught the first one's swing. He twisted his arm and the man buckled to his knees, screaming. Haru kicked out at the second that attempted an attack. She stumbled back into the third attacker and they fell in a tangle of limbs and curses.

Haru twisted the arm in his hold until the man's shoulder dislocated with a pop. Haru let him go to crawl across the sand as the other two recovered their footing to attack.

The woman was faster than her male counterparts, but not by much. Not like Kanna. Haru dodged her sword strike and ducked into her reach. A hard jab into already bruised ribs sent the breath from her lungs and she fell, too winded to even cry out.

Kanna downed her last opponent at the same time in a clack of teeth, his head flying back as Kanna slammed an elbow under his jaw.

The last of Haru's made a desperate run at him. Haru grasped his outstretched arm and spun, sending the man stumbling towards Kanna. She grasped him by the arm and twisted, flipping him to the ground. A well-placed kick after he was downed, and he stopped moving.

Kanna met Haru's gaze and smiled, soft and half-lit. Haru closed the distance between them in a slow lope as Vahn began to slowly clap from Mud's back.

"Nice work, team," Vahn called.

Kanna rolled her eyes and turned to the others. "Tie them up. Their people can decide what to do." She then waved to the travelers. "Isco, Astar, help them."

The group dismounted and set to task, with Osawa and Vahn binding the failed thieves while Isco and Astar checked the travelers for injury. Haru could feel the burn in his chest, the weight of purpose, watching Kanna command. But the feeling soured. Something was missing in the way she moved, something missing beneath the surface of her actions.

Kanna waved to Yassen and he ran over, stopping directly in front of her. She pivoted and pointed to the upturned wagon. "Need to tilt it back."

Yassen squinted at her.

"You know." Kanna cut one hand in the air and angled it under the other before turning them together. "Tilt it."

Still somewhat perplexed, Yassen faced the wagon. "Like this?"

There was a low thrum of the earth shifting before it heaved up. Haru jumped back as the wagon creaked angrily in protest, the wood threatening to crack under the sudden assault.

"Wait." Kanna held her hands out, and the sound ceased. "Carefully."

At least there were some things that remained constant, such as Kanna's refusal to use more words than she deemed necessary.

Yassen tried again, and this time the earth rose slower, angling beneath the wangon until it settled back onto four wheels.

Kanna nodded. "Good." She raised a hand to pat Yassen's upper arm. "You need control."

Yassen grinned and nodded vigorously then, without being bidden, began to refill the wagons. Kanna watched Yassen work, but then her head tilted, her eyes sliding to the discarded instruments. Her feet followed, and Haru trailed behind her.

In the rebel lands, music was a part of life. There was none to be found in the Palamidia's halls. The drifting rhythms that snuck into camps in the borderlands had entranced Kanna, often lulling her into danger. Even now, her fingers drifted to the polished neck of a rebec.

"Do you remember when we danced?" Haru asked.

She yanked her hand away from the stringed instrument and shoved both in her pockets, but her gaze stuck to the shine of the wood. "Why does everyone keep asking me the same question in different ways?"

Haru threaded his arm through Kanna's bent elbow and her body tensed, readying for an attack. Between breaths she relaxed, and Haru settled his hand in the curve above her hip. "That was in Gegenes, too. Not far from here. You'd left the camp in the night, and we found you near the town."

Kanna tilted her chin to look up at him, her brow furrowing. "You were worried."

"Of course we were. You were practically in the enemy's hands."

Kanna's eyes slid to the recently freed travelers. Some appeared bruised or dirty, but there were no great injuries. "Why are they the enemy?"

Haru followed her gaze to the gathered locals, ranging from children to the elderly. "They aren't."

"Velinius." Kanna shook her head and pulled away from him. "I know you came because you need me to fight her." She crossed her arms in front of her. It was another moment before she turned around. "I just don't know why."

Haru clenched his hands into fists, resisting the urge to feed her the reasons, to detail every horror he'd witnessed. They'd witnessed. "I can't tell you that."

"Why not?" Kanna's voice rose, and she took another step away from him. Her hands shook loose, and she pressed her fingers around one of the injured joints of her left hand. Haru held back a wince. "Why won't you just tell me and I can get this over with? It isn't like it matters."

And there it was, the reason he couldn't tell her. The thing that was missing. Kanna once again only saw herself as a weapon, a thing aimed by others. She would move to a task, but she would only command as she was allowed. It was as she was when they'd first met, when she bent a stubborn knee to Velinius. Haru moved forward, wanted to at least stop her from twisting the hurt in her hands.

She pulled away. "Do not distract me."

Haru dropped his hands to his sides, then met them behind his back. "I would not dare to, Legatus," he said with every bit of control he could manage.

The shadows in her eyes grow, the gold sparking through like stars falling in the night. She turned away from him and started back towards the others.

Haru followed.

Osawa broke away, crossing the short distance to meet them. He glanced between Kanna and Haru, noting the tension between them but deciding not to comment. "The troupe invited us back to town to show their gratitude," Osawa said, his mouth a perturbed line. "Astar accepted before I was able to intervene."

Kanna looked past him at the rest of their group. Isco assisted the elderly back into the wagons, and Astar hitched Mike to replace the travelers' missing horse. With Yassen's help, Vahn roused the bandits and tied their hands into a line, attaching them to the back of another of the wagons.

"They aren't used to traveling like this," Kanna said. "It might be good for them to rest and resupply in town."

Osawa nodded. "If you think that's wise."

"I don't," Kanna replied, "but it is the best option now."

# COMBAT WOUNDS

## KENZI

EVEN THOUGH IRA kept telling Kenzi to let the wound heal, she couldn't help but rub the heel of her hand into the bandage. The glue that the combat surgeons had used to stick her neck back together made her itch, and it was more irritating than being stabbed in the first place.

The heat and sand of the desert didn't help. At least the heat of Panotii was sticky, and the air didn't carry grains of sand that wiggled their way into the nooks of her clothing and under her bandages until she wanted to scratch her skin off.

"Kenz."

She jerked her hand away, but not fast enough. Ira had a way of always knowing when she wasn't listening to him. Kenzi tried to distance herself from him as they travelled, but he'd manage to weave his way back to her side.

"Is it still bothering you?" he asked.

She shook her head in answer, keeping her eyes on the others.

After the decimation of the camp, the Palamidia's grip on the city was questionable at best. The camp had been too easy of a target for the former Legatus and her band of traitors. While there was strength in numbers, there was also weakness. Being an Eye was knowing where to find them, and even Kenzi could spot the flaws in their previous defenses.

Though she did not know much about Ananke, she knew that she was a master strategist when it came to the field of battle. Her tactics were unexpected, inventive, and no two battles were the same. Every officer candidate's first tactics assignment was to choose one of Ananke's battles, study the strategy, pick it apart and try to understand the mind that created them. Each was different, and there was no inherent logic that connected one to the next. It was an impossible task.

"I'm fine, Ira," she said, though her voice still had a niggling husk to it.

After Salinae moved the remainder of the military into the city proper, he'd divvied out a detachment of soldiers for their task and hand selected their current group to lead.

The fact that Nissa was there was no surprise to anyone. While her abilities weren't a match for the former Saint of Fire, it was no secret that she was being groomed to replace him when his time came. Masao was an interesting choice. A fierce fighter, certainly, but since they had Salinae with them another water loa didn't seem necessary. Still, that wasn't for Kenzi to question.

Ira fought with the traitors before and he was an earth loa, a rare ability for a Solarian soldier. The only reason they'd brought Kenzi was to appease him, and she knew it. Air loas were prized, but there had been others available in the camp. After Kenzi's bumbling mistake during Ananke's attack, she should be dead. There was no reason for her to be alive at all, except as some twisted favor to Ira. It would have been better to be killed than to live with the shame of it.

Since then, she'd been trying to put some distance between herself and her brother. It wasn't that she didn't care for him, but she needed to find her own way.

But, there was also what Vahn said before he slit her throat. Kenzi couldn't figure out what he meant about a city screaming. Ira had told her story upon story of victories and battles. While she knew that Vahn was just trying to get under Ira's skin, the fact that he was able to ruffle her stoic brother was disconcerting.

She turned to Ira, opening her mouth to ask.

She shut it again. Instead, she clicked her tongue to the roof of her mouth and urged her mount forward, pulling alongside Nissa.

While Ira and Kenzi wore their traveler garb, the others had kept their uniforms. "Aren't you hot in that?" Kenzi asked.

The sun slanted against the dark, sharp cant of Nissa's cheeks. "No."

Kenzi waited, hoping that the other woman would make more effort for conversation, but her wait was in vain. She cleared her throat. "So, chasing high-profile traitors. A once in a lifetime mission, huh?"

"Yes," Nissa replied, her voice flatter than the desert they slumped across. "I am proud to serve the true Legatus and bring these heretics to justice."

"Wow," Kenzi started, taken aback by the harsh fervor that rose in Nissa's tone. "That's a strange thing to call them."

"Is it?" Nissa asked, her brow rising. "They threaten our way. What else would you call someone that does that?"

"Hey, pretty thing."

Kenzi startled and turned in her saddle. Masao had moved in while she was speaking with Nissa. He sidled his mount next to Kenzi, close enough that their knees nearly brushed. "Why not chat with me? I'm a much better conversationalist than that ice queen. I even know big boy words that others haven't shoved in my mouth."

"No one has put anything in my mouth," Nissa snapped at him.

"I bet they haven't," Masao leered, then leaned over so far that Kenzi had to sit back to avoid him. "Not for lack of trying on your part, though."

Nissa glared before she caught herself, her expression locking back into rigid impassivity. She pulled her horse's lead and dug her heels, driving it forward toward Salinae.

"Yeah," Masao said, tilting back into his saddle. "Go run and tell daddy."

Masao turned to Kenzi, brushed the hair from his eyes, and leaned back toward her. "Now that we're alone...."

"Gross."

Kenzi guided her mount around, turning it to face the back of the group. But she paused when she caught sight of Ira taking up the rear.

"Going to hide behind big brother again?"

Kenzi ate the reply she wanted to roar back. Instead she circled, taking a second point at the back of the group. With Nissa and Salinae in the lead, Masao in the center, and Ira on her far left, the distance between them seemed greater than the desert itself.

# 27

## GOOD INTENTIONS

### ASTAR

AFTER THE DAYS of harsh travel, Astar was looking forward to a bed and a proper meal. While she had seen her fair share of the free lands, it was typically from the comfort of a train coach with a welcoming lodge at the end of the line, not riding as an awkward second to a bruised Palamidia officer.

Though the city could barely be called such, being back in civilization brought a wave of energy to Astar. She wasn't meant for the open plains, and thrived on the buzz of life that hummed along city streets. After she and Yassen delivered their fresh captives to the local constables, they found the rest of the group that had lingered behind. They weren't overly difficult to spot.

Haru and Osawa stood as straight-backed sentinels at the mouth of a shaded alley between a grocer and a carpenter. Within it, Kanna sat in the dirt, twisting the tip of her white-handled blade in the sand. She was pressed close to Isco, who had also plopped onto the ground. He kept a wary watch on Vahn, who slouched against the wall across from them, his head tilted back and his eyes closed.

Astar sighed at the sight and crossed her arms in front of her. "I thought I told ya'll not to be suspicious."

Haru's watchful gaze turned to her. "What about us is suspicious?"

A group of young townsfolk passed on the sidewalk. Haru's attention shifted to them like a guard dog on alert. Their eyes darted away from him and they stumbled to quicken their pace, but they glanced back to the alley and its occupants.

"Nothing at all," Astar replied as his hackles released. "I'm sure people see a bunch of obnoxiously attractive out-of-towners in near matching outfits playing with knives in alleys every day. That is a completely normal thing that happens."

Vahn tilted his head forward, his eyes opening bright and alert. "Admit you like it, because at least we're not boring."

He was right, but she didn't have to admit it. Astar rolled her eyes in response.

Beside her, Osawa cleared his throat. "The troupe agreed to keep the horses with theirs, but that leaves us without shelter."

"That's not a problem here." Astar held a hand out to the city streets. "We're in Bomazi. Plenty of places to stay in this trap. Just act like tourists and you'll be fine."

Haru's surveying gaze sharpened, his entire body jerking around. "Wait."

He moved out of the alley, scanning the streets. It was the same as most Gegenii cities, with stone buildings and clusters of businesses cramped together along wide avenues scattered with hitching posts. Pedestrian pathways lined the dirt packed streets, but people walked on foot wherever they pleased, skipping aside to avoid chariots, wagons, or single riders.

Haru planted himself in the middle of the pedestrian walkway, forcing other passersby to go around him. "This is Bomazi?"

If Astar wasn't mistaken, the man was downright giddy. She lifted her brow and turned to the others, pointing to Haru. "Act just like that."

"This is Bomazi." Haru rushed back to Osawa, and Astar would describe his pace as a skip. He grasped the shorter man by the shoulders and shook him. "We're in Bomazi."

Osawa righted his glasses on the bridge of his nose. "I heard."

"We all heard," Vahn added from the alley.

Haru released Osawa and turned on Astar. She took a step back when he approached her, shocked by the wild intensity sparking in his eyes. "Where is the Shadestone?"

Astar eyed the city's layout. They had come from the outer areas, and the streets were becoming more congested as they walked. "In the square, I think," she said, pointing where the streets were beginning to widen. "That way, probably."

Without another word spared, Haru set off in the direction that Astar pointed at a barely contained jog.

Astar turned back to the others. "He's not acting, is he?"

"Not even a little bit," Osawa said.

In the alley, Kanna held her hands in front of her. Vahn moved as if he was going to offer assistance, but she awkwardly rocked to standing, and in the same movement Vahn pocketed his hand.

Isco scrambled to his feet behind them and dusted off the seat of his pants.

"Let's go," Kanna said, taking the lead and following Haru's trail.

Unlike Haru, though, they took their time weaving through the people that gathered along the streets. Astar bit her lip, eyeing the stiff draw of Kanna's shoulders. She reached out, grabbing Kanna by the arm to stop her progress.

The men stopped as well, Osawa raising his brow in question.

"You boys go ahead," Astar said, shooing them away. "We'll catch up."

Vahn and Osawa looked to Kanna, a gesture that Astar had understood to be a check in between the soldiers, but Kanna didn't react. Vahn had the nerve to roll his eyes before turning away, his boots scuffing in the dirt, and the others followed him.

Around them, decorations were being strung up. Paper lanterns were run from the cover of one storefront to the other, the wires snarling together as they criss-crossed above them.

When the others were out of earshot, Astar crossed her arms and turned to Kanna. "So, you going to tell me what's going on with you?"

Kanna raised her brow, the scar at the corner of her eye pulling with it and making the gesture almost threatening. Astar pressed on. "You have your memories back?"

Kanna shook her head, then shrugged. "Some of them. Not all."

"Why not?"

Kanna's returning glare was definitely meant as a warning.

Astar chose to ignore it. "I get that you probably have a lot of shit things in your past, but it can't all be bad. And apparently tall, hot, and heroic over there knows how to get them back but now you're pissed off at him for some reason."

"I am not 'pissed off'," Kanna said, though the phrase sounded strange coming from her.

"So, you agree he's hot?"

Kanna crossed her arms at her chest. "I have eyes."

Their conversation was interrupted when they shifted out of the way of a young girl with a ladder. She set it in the street and climbed up to the newly raised light strings and lit the candle wicks inside. The girl climbed back down and nodded to them before moving to the next unlit string and beginning again.

Kanna made as if she was going to walk away to meet the others, but Astar caught her once again. "Wait."

"What if knowing makes me something else," Kanna said when she turned. "You might find out that you do not like what that is."

"Why are you talking like you're some kind of object?" Astar asked, but she didn't expect an answer. Astar reached out to take Kanna's hand. She swung it a few times to make sure she had her attention. "Remember when we first met and you handed those guys their own asses? For me?"

Kanna shrugged, but nodded.

"You didn't have to stop, or do anything, You could have walked by and ignored what was happening, just like everyone else. But you didn't." Astar squeezed Kanna's hand and cleared her throat as the memory tried to collapse it. "You saw someone in trouble and came to help. You barely knew your own name then, but you knew what the right thing to do was."

"Was it really the right thing to do?" Kanna said, though the question seemed to be more to herself before turning her eyes to meet Astar's. "I didn't have to go that far."

Astar sighed and bent her head down, pressing her forehead against Kanna's. It wasn't something she'd done before, but she'd watched the soldiers' similar exchange. Kanna relaxed against her. "You did whatever it was that you couldn't not do."

Kanna squinted, pulling back to eye Astar. "That is a confusing way to say that."

"Well, it's true. And the thing is, it isn't just me. You've been saving Yassen's ass since you met him, same with Isco, and I'd bet the gorgeous pieces that raced to find you have stories just like ours."

"Gorgeous pieces?" Kanna asked.

"Yeah," Astar said, looking into the middle distance and sighing purposefully. "Especially Osawa. I just want to put him in my pocket and watch him frown about it, y'know?"

Kanna thought for a minute, her brow furrowing, before she relented with a nod. "But I don't know about 'raced. It has been over a year."

"I'm sure there's a reason for that. Probably not a very good one, though." She linked her arm with Kanna's and turned them to follow the others.

"My point is," Astar said, nudging Kanna and causing the shorter woman to miss a step. "We're on your side, and we need you. We're not going anywhere. So, you do what you have to in order to figure out your shit, and know that when you come out the other side, we'll still be here for you."

Kanna smiled down to the ground to hide it.

"I do have one more question, though, and I need you to be honest."

Kanna looked up to her, her expression serious, and nodded for Astar to continue.

Astar leaned down. "Just how good of a kisser is Haru? I bet he's real good."

Kanna's eyes flew wide, red rising in her cheeks that couldn't be explained by the burn of the sun. She opened her mouth as if to reply, clamping it shut once more.

Astar tilted her head back and laughed. "So good he leaves you speechless? That tracks."

Kanna shook her head and smiled as Astar laughed, and they meandered arm in arm under the flickering glow of the paper lanterns as the light of day faded.

# THE SHADESTONE

## HARU

THE SQUARE WAS A CENTRAL, park-like hub where Bomazi's roads ultimately met. Cobbled pavers covered the area and planters spilled over with arid loving desert plants, their leaves swollen and heavy. Single, bright flowers bloomed among the succulents, despite the cool late autumn nights. Here, the lights that were being strung around the city converged, flickering brazenly against the darkening sky. As beautiful as the square was, it was nothing in comparison to the monument at its center.

Haru was transfixed by the stone, and he moved toward it to get a better look. There was little remarkable about its shape. It was a near solid block of black stone, nothing more, nothing less. There were no plaques, no engravings, just a soaring rectangular rock that nearly blotted out the setting sun.

"Neat rock," Yassen said, alerting Haru to the belated arrival of the others. "What is it?"

"It's the Shadestone." Haru didn't look away. "At least, that's how it's commonly referred to. It's actually the seat of Nehebkau."

"No head cow," Yassen said. "Got it."

"No, that's not—" Haru started, but he lost the thought when he turned. "Where's Kanna?"

"She and Astar are on the way," Vahn said. "They stopped to have a chat."

"About what?"

"I don't know," Vahn replied with a shrug, his usual smirk creeping in. "You worried its about you?"

"Of course not," Haru said, though the thought did cause some unease to curl in the pit of him.

"What's the seat of Nehebkau?" Osawa asked.

Haru was aware that he said it to distract him, but he couldn't resist the draw of the artifact. Besides, he could feel her near, her steady approach. Haru tucked his hands in his pockets and leaned back to take in the full height of the monument. "During Kosein's trials, he was tasked with traveling to the lands of the godking Nehebkau. Nehebkau was a friend of Danu, but they hadn't heard from him in some time. It was Nehebkau who provided sustenance for the people, and the stores were becoming low. When Kosein arrived in the godking's land, however—"

"The fields were fallow."

Kanna had arrived at his side. She stared intently at the Shadestone, as if she could see all the way through it to the center.

"You remember this one?"

She turned to him, then back to the monolith. "I think I learned it from my mother."

Before, it was Kanna that would share tales with them. She often accompanied hers with dancing shadows while they huddled together on the fields of battle, in the aftermath of victory or defeat, trying to hold on to their small circle of safety. She wove them gracefully, her fingers finely tuning their curves as fire reflected in her eyes.

He must have paused too long in his remembrance because Kanna looked away from the stone, tilting her head at him. "Are you going to continue?"

This was something he could give her back, at least a part of it. "As Kosein made his way through the godking's lands, he learned from the people that Nehebkau had not been the same. They could not place what was wrong, but Nehebkau's advisors had been dismissed and his children imprisoned.

"Hearing this, Kosein snuck into the prison in the cover of night.

He moved stealthily past the soul-eating chimeras to where the children were kept. Astonished by his arrival, they revealed to him the fate that had befallen the land: that Nehebkau had been slain, and in his seat was The Pretender.

"Kosein was furious. He had not thought The Pretender a threat, just a trickster with no true goal, but it seemed that they were determined to bring chaos in the land. Kosein marched to the seat of Nehebkau to do battle with The Pretender there.

"The fight was hard going, with neither able to gain an upper hand in the struggle. Until Kosein was able to land a blow across the face of The Pretender, and their guise fell away."

Here, Haru paused for effect. "However, beneath the mask, The Pretender's face was that of Danu."

"Gasp!"

Haru turned at the interruption. Yassen had his hand clamped over his mouth, his eyes wide.

"Did you just say 'gasp'?" Isco asked.

"It was surprising," Yassen insisted, before turning to Haru. "Well, don't stop there. What happened?"

Vahn groaned, his head lolling back on his neck. Osawa elbowed Vahn and he flinched, his hand covering the spot. He cast a betrayed look at Osawa.

Haru smiled, then faced the stone. The sky was entering twilight now, streaks of violet merging with the thick oranges and reds of the old sunset.

"Kosein was stunned by the revelation. He could not move, could not strike, and in his hesitation, The Pretender fled."

Haru let the last moment stay in the air before moving into the tale's end.

"With The Pretender gone, the godking's children could reclaim their birthright. When the rightful rulers were seated on Nehebkau's throne, the land flourished once again."

As Haru finished the story, Kanna had drawn closer to the stone. She pressed her fingers against its face only to yank her hand back. Haru felt a surge of energy, the line between them thrumming. Haru grabbed her wrist, turning her hand over in his palm to check for injury as their connection faded back to its usual hum.

"Strange," she said, staring at her unmarred skin.

"Yes," he agreed, his nerves settling.

Haru wasn't sure if it was a trick of his eyes or the fading light, but he could have sworn the dark around the Shadestone grew and it pulsed, just once, like the last thud of a dying heart.

# 29

## UNSPOKEN TRUTHS

### VAHN

WHILE HARU WENT on about the rock, Vahn had the time to take in their surroundings. As Haru's words gelled into a mess of syllables in Vahn's ears, the square filled with people.

"Hey, Astar," Vahn nudged the woman to get her attention.

"What's up, sexy?" she asked, turning away from Haru's lecture.

Vahn nodded at the crowd gathering in the twilight. "What's going on?"

Merchants pulling wagons behind them filled with goods were setting up tents on the outskirts of the cobbles, and the smell of cooking began to overtake the arid night.

"They're setting up for the festival."

The word was familiar, but what he knew of festivals didn't align with this.

"Is it Remembrance Day?" Yassen interrupted.

"I knew it was close," Isco said. He turned his wrist over reflexively as if checking a watch, but he didn't have one. He swung his arms and clamped his hands behind his back to hide the motion. "Hadn't realized it was already here."

Vahn turned to his fellow soldiers. Osawa shrugged, and Vahn took comfort in the fact that the others were as confused as he was.

Kanna looked up expectantly to Haru.

"It's a day that those in the independent regions celebrate. They gather to give thanks for their fortune and remember those who passed," Haru recited by rote.

"Right," Astar said flatly. "More importantly, though," her voice lifted, "there's food and lots of drinks, stuff to buy and gifts and music and dancing, and did I mention drinks?"

"Music?" Kanna asked.

"Yeah, music," Yassen said. "People make a bunch of sounds together. It's nice."

"We know what music is," Osawa said.

"Oh," Yassen said. Then, his brow wrinkled in concern. "You sure?"

Before the soldiers had a chance to respond, a new voice interrupted. "That's him."

Vahn turned at the sound, his fingers reaching instinctively for the handles of his knives. An Atarrabi man had stopped at the outer fringe of their gathering near Vahn and Kanna. One of his hands was linked with that of a long haired Gegenii woman cradling a baby at her hip while the other pointed through the group. Vahn followed the gesture past the man's black-ringed wrists, almost a match for his own, to Isco.

Vahn shifted to place himself between the new arrivals and Isco, preparing for an attack. His eyes roved the square, looking for the clearest route of escape.

The woman eyed them warily. "He seems a bit pale, honey."

Vahn felt Kanna moving behind him, the others shifting in tandem with her. What he didn't expect was the hand at the back of his elbow.

"You think everyone is pale, sugar, but that's him," the man insisted.

Kanna took a step in front of Vahn and shook her head. Whatever was happening, she didn't sense danger in it. Vahn tried to relax, but his nerves refused to let go of the inexplicable urge to fight.

In the moment that Vahn was distracted the woman rushed forward, shoving her child into Kanna's hands in passing.

"Nope." Vahn moved to take the infant from Kanna as she held it at arms length from her body. Unfortunately, once he had it he was unsure what to do with the small human. "Oh, no," Vahn muttered, meeting the child's eyes. It reached out with sticky hands and Vahn held it further away so it wouldn't touch him.

Osawa stepped in, removing the child from Vahn's hands and balancing it in his arms with ease. "Really, you two?"

Vahn was grateful that at least Kanna seemed as locked in place as he was. It took another instant before his senses returned and he was able to track the woman. She'd thrown herself at Isco, wrapping him in her arms. Her husband managed to breeze past while they were distracted and joined her embrace.

Yassen, the closest to the now trio, had also joined the hug for no reason that Vahn could determine.

"Yassen." Kanna approached the huddle. "What are you doing?"

"Kanna, you won't believe it. This is Tanno, and Isco saved him."

Kanna slid her gaze to Vahn and Haru. "Tell us more."

"So, what happened was, Tanno was a slave a long time ago in Adur, and these people were using him as some kind of lab experiment, but Isco got him out of there. And this is Silvie," he added, squeezing the woman tighter. "They met after that, and they're a family now."

Tanno extricated himself from the group embrace, rubbing the back of his hands against his eyes. This gave Vahn a clearer view of Isco, who steadily avoided his gaze.

"Sorry," Tanno said, "we didn't mean to barge in on your friends. I didn't have a chance to thank you before, didn't think I ever would."

Tanno surveyed the group, his gaze catching on Vahn. "You too?"

Vahn tucked his hands in the back pockets of his jeans to hide the tattoos on his wrists. "No."

He must have still been glaring, because Tanno took a step back before Vahn had the chance to set his features. Taking the chance to do that now, he relaxed his eyes and turned up the corners of his lips.

Silvie released Isco, stepping back but keeping her hands on his shoulders. "You are coming to the festival, right?"

"Of course he is." Astar sidled up to Isco, throwing her arm over his shoulder and causing him to hunch. "We wouldn't miss it."

"We have to tell the others, muffin," Silvie said to Tanno. "They'll be so excited."

"Others?" Vahn asked, the word escaping before he had a chance to hold it fast.

Tanno grinned at Vahn. "A lot of us ended up here. It's close to the rail lines, but far enough away that it was safer."

Vahn narrowed his eyes at Isco. "How many are there?"

"A few dozen, maybe?" Tanno said. "What do you think, chickpea?"

"At least," Silvie agreed.

"Before you go," Osawa interjected, "don't forget this."

Vahn turned in time to watch Osawa wrest his glasses from the infant's hands, only to have it grasp them once more and set them at an odd angle. Osawa removed them from the child's hand and righted them again, and it grabbed his hair. He bent his head as the child pulled, but didn't show any frustration with the toddler's grasping.

"Oh, my baby salad." Silvie shuffled to Osawa. She paused in front of him, her finger on her chin in thought. "Hold on a tick."

Silvie loosed the pack on her back from one of her shoulders and unzipped it, pulling out a knit cap. She placed it on Osawa's head, pulling it down over his hair before reclaiming her child. "There, now don't you look smart."

"Silvie knits." Tanno wrapped his arm around her waist. "Mostly hats, but she's getting better by the day. Her socks almost match."

His hands free now, Osawa adjusted the placement of the knit beanie. "Thanks?"

The family turned back out of the square, waving as they left. Isco raised his hand, a semblance of a farewell, dropping it when Vahn turned on him.

Vahn didn't like surprises. Surprises were usually a knife in the back, an elbow in the face, or any number of things that never led to anything good. He drew close enough to Isco that the other couldn't pretend to be occupied by anything else in his space.

"A few dozen?" Vahn asked.

"I didn't count," Isco said.

"You left that part out."

Isco shifted in place until something steeled inside of him. He shoved his hands in his front pockets and tilted his head back to meet Vahn's eyes and Vahn was mercilessly, irrevocably trapped in his own game.

"Would it have mattered?"

# 30

## TAKE MY HAND

### KANNA

KANNA KNEW music as a distant thing, a lilt carried on a breeze. In the thick of it, it was more alive than she could have imagined. It filled the night and slipped beneath her skin, and it was as if she was living inside of it.

The square was lined on three sides with rows of booths along the outskirts offering novelties, fortunes, and refreshments, with an open area in the center where revelers danced. People crowded on the pavers beneath criss-crossing lights strung from one side to the other, the colored papers around the flames casting the celebration in a warm glow.

She sat cross-legged on a bench in the dim outskirts of the festival, beyond the halo of the light. In the square, her friends whirled, shifting and laughing in time. Vahn and Astar spun together until he released her to Yassen. Osawa's grace extended to dance, and he wasn't short of willing partners who jostled through the crowd to take their turns.

Kanna rested her elbow on her knees and pressed her hand over her lips when Vahn made his way through the milling bodies to Isco, who was still surrounded by those he had helped. They attempted to press gifts into his hands, but he steadily refused them.

Vahn slowed at the outskirts of the crowded bodies near Isco before veering away. Kanna sighed, her smile fleeing. The things he could do with even a small measure of Isco's courage. At the thought, something in her creaked. She shut her eyes, wincing as something warm whistled through her mind.

"What's wrong, *inara*?"

Haru returned to her side with a drink in each hand. She shook away the sensation, turning back to the festivities.

"Here." He settled next to her and offered one of the drinks he had acquired.

The drink was foggy, and small bubbles rose to the surface and clung to the sides of the thick glass. When she shifted it, the bubbles swirled away from the cubes of ice that floated in it. "What is it?"

"It's a local drink. They make it with a native fruit and add carbonated water—"

She brought it to her lips and gulped, coughing when it burned in her throat.

"—and a clear grain alcohol," he finished.

After the shock of the initial taste wore off, she sipped it to clear her throat. "Maybe mention that part first."

Haru grinned, bringing his glass to his lips to hide it. "I'll try to remember that."

Kanna looked up from her drink and glared. He winked, and a thrill raced through her when he smiled.

The memories of the amphitheater came back to her unbidden. Seeing him for the first time, knowing the world had shifted but not why. Then later, when she tried to set it back to before the only way she knew how.

She wrapped her hands around the cool glass, tracing her fingers through the condensation that had gathered against the dying heat of the night. She watched the pinprick bubbles rise and break the surface of the liquid. "I'm sorry I hurt you."

"What are you talking about?"

She couldn't look at him. She saw the bruises on her knuckles, his blood on her hands. She uncurled them from her drink and they came away slick with it. She dropped the glass, the puddle splashing and red. The night flashed with lightning and she felt rain, saw the drops hit her palms and cut trails through the red. It ran down her arms and slid into the curve of her elbows.

"Kanna!"

The vision snapped away at the sound of his voice but the feel of it lingered. She was breathing through sludge, drowning in the dark of it, and she couldn't find her place. Haru was kneeling in front of her, his hands on her knees. She blinked but she couldn't focus, couldn't see him. She flinched when he reached for her but he held steady, grasping her face between his hands. "You're in Gegenes."

Gegenes was a region of Lifrasir, a small, insignificant sliver of the universe. "Gegenes."

The sky flashed and she jumped, trying to find the source of it.

"No, don't look away," he said. "Look at me."

Kanna clenched her eyes shut to clear them and then focused. The gold in his eyes shot through the blue, molten and alive and transfixing her in the moment. Her breath began to even and she wrapped her hand around his wrist, pressing her thumb into the steady beat of his pulse.

"I have you now," Haru said. "You're with me."

The tension released from her body and she sighed, the dark thing releasing her lungs. "You're with me," she repeated. The rush in her ears calmed and the sound of music returned. The glare of light became a warm glow. Laughter and movement carried on the breeze with the smell of simmering meats, fried sugar, and the heady mix of flowers that decorated the festival.

He took her hand in his own and pressed a kiss into her palm before linking them together. It was his turn to not meet her eyes. "Are those the only things you remember?"

She shook her head. "It's all twisted together. One moment leads to another, and then back, then forward again." She pressed her hands against her temples, shutting her eyes. "I can feel the parts that are missing. It's like I can walk right up to it but I can't see or know it." She sighed, a rough ragged thing. "Then there's what I was then, and who I am now, and I don't know which I'm supposed to be."

"*Inara*," Haru said, his voice soft and coaxing. "It doesn't matter what you're supposed to be, that's not who you are."

She couldn't help but take her hands away to look at him. "That doesn't make sense."

"It will." He rose to his feet, dusting the sand from his knee and stretching to his height. "In the meantime, this is a celebration. We should join them."

Kanna crooked her brow at him. "Are you going to tell me again why they are celebrating?"

"No. That's not important right now." He smiled, and held out his hand.

As always, she couldn't resist it. Kanna was never sure what was coming, or where he would lead, but she wanted to know. She wanted to understand him. He offered her the chance, and she took it each time.

Haru pulled her to her feet, leading her into the light of the square as the music slowed. He made an exaggerated sweeping bow before taking her wrist and placing her loose hand on his shoulder.

"I don't know how to dance," she reminded him.

"You do," he said, settling his hand beneath her shoulder blade. "Trust me."

Haru stepped on the beat and her body dragged behind.

"Don't think," he said. "Just be here."

Kanna followed, and the world fell away. There was nothing but that moment, their bodies as they flowed through the current of sound. She was surrounded by music and she could feel it in her blood, under her skin, in all of her. She lived in this moment, breathed it and felt all of it. The warmth of his hand, the strength in their shared connection.

When his weight shifted she moved with the momentum, turning beneath his arm before he drew her back with nothing more than a curl of his fingers.

Haru pulled her in, wrapping both his arms at her waist and closing the distance between them. They swayed together and she felt his breath against her temple, the smile that brushed his lips against her skin. "See? I told you that you could dance."

As they swayed together the song faded to an end, rising back to a high-tempo dance beat. Kanna lingered in his arms, holding on to the moment.

"K!"

She jerked her head round at the sound of Vahn's voice. He'd cut through the dancing crowd and stood with his arms open. He threw his head back in mock disgust, his hands falling to his sides. "Why are you two always like that? It is *exhausting*."

Vahn took her hand, then winked. "Let's dance."

They wove deep into the crowd, ducking and turning between the twisting bodies. Haru followed behind, his fingertips at the small of her back in order to stay with them.

"Look who I found," Vahn announced ahead of her.

Astar raised her glass in cheers, but didn't stop dancing. Yassen's neck was draped with several necklaces that were too tight, most likely Astar's purchases. He cheered when Kanna arrived and wrapped his arms around her waist, lifting her from her feet and spinning her before putting her back down.

She laughed when she rejoined the ground, the world taking a moment to stop spinning.

Even Isco had joined them, nodding to the beat of the music as he sipped his drink, the smallest of smiles reaching his eyes.

Osawa broke away from his selection of dance partners to grab Haru, drawing him in back to through the mill of dancing bodies. Kanna met his eyes, and he smiled and shrugged, allowing himself to be swept away as Vahn reclaimed Kanna's hand and dragged her into the rhythm.

Kanna knew how to move. Even when she didn't know anything else, her body did. There was peace in letting go, letting it guide the way. So she danced.

It wasn't like fighting, where every movement was meant to attack and where pain was inevitable. There was no anger in this, but the barest stirring of something else.

She closed her eyes and let the music guide her, felt the lightness in her friends and understood it to be joy.

# 31

## EYES IN BOMAZI

### KENZI

THE CITY of Bomazi was warm and welcoming, reminding Kenzi of a dryer version of her hometown in Panotii. The architecture was a far cry from the stilt-legged wooden constructs she was used to, but there was a connection between the people here that was near palpable, even though the Remembrance holiday had passed the week prior.

She leaned in an alley catacorner to a small residence, crunching on a local pastry of fried dough twisted and dusted with sugar and cinnamon. While the sugar melted on her tongue, she watched a long-haired Gegenii woman step out of the home, a toddler balanced on her hip.

In the dark doorway an Atarrabi man appeared, dusky brown hair catching the light. The woman turned to place a kiss on his cheek and he bent and dropped one on the toddler's crown. He stood in the doorway waving even as she turned around the corner and out of sight.

Kenzi crumpled the paper pastry bag and tossed it in a nearby bin. She wiped her mouth with the back of her hand then dusted them off on the thighs of her simple brown trousers.

She ran her fingers through her hair to muss it, then shook her hands out and cleared her throat. With a skip to start, she angled across the street in a rush.

"Excuse me," she called, waving her hand over her head to catch the man's attention. "Excuse me!"

He turned to look up the road and down, then pointed to himself in confusion.

Kenzi stopped in front of him and bent over, her hands on her knees as she puffed the breath in and out of her lungs. "I'm sorry," she said, slowing the fake breathlessness and standing. "Thank you for waiting."

"Is there something I can help you with, miss?"

"I've been looking for my sister. She was traveling with her friends, but she's been gone for a while now and—" Kenzi choked up, her eyes bristling with unshed tears. "Our father died while she was away. I need to find her, she's all I have left in the whole world now."

"Oh," the man said, reaching an awkward hand out. His hand hovered, unsure if comforting her would be appropriate. "There, don't worry, why don't you come in? You can tell me about your sister."

Kenzi sniffed loud and rubbed her nose on the cuff of her shirt. "Okay."

Kenzi blinked as her vision adjusted to the dim, cramped living space. She had entered the sitting room, with a single dusky couch shoved against one wall and a wood carved rocking chair next to it. A low table in front of that was strewn with lengths of unfurled yarn, and a blanket with child's blocks and stacking cups sat nearby.

The kitchen was attached and open, a small table with two regular chairs and one for children shoved against another wall. Behind it was a curtain-covered door that Kenzi assumed to be a bedroom.

"Please, sit," the man said, pulling out the chair at the table that backed the curtain.

Kenzi dropped herself into the one nearer to the door she had just entered, letting the weight of her body slink down. The man stepped away from the table and retrieved a blue glass from a cabinet, its construct foggy and flawed. When he reached the cuffs of his sleeves fell away, revealing slave brandings at his wrist.

From a pitcher on the counter, he poured a glass of water and placed it in front of her before sitting himself. "I'm Tanno. You are?"

"Kahla." Kenzi tilted the water glass to her lips. She slid her eyes to the paints on her hands, noting a smear near one of the fingers. She pulled it into her lap.

"You said you were looking for your sister?"

Kenzi nodded. "Astar." The old Governor's daughter was the least suspicious to be seeking, being Gegenii. "She was with some of her friends, a big group of them. They wanted to visit different landmarks, but I haven't heard from her in forever."

"Oh, Astar," he said, a smile cracking over his features. "She was with Isco. I'm sorry to say, though, but you've missed them by several days."

Kenzi looked down at her lap, twisting her hands together. "Do you know which way they went?"

He shook his head. "They left after the festival." He looked down, sighing at the wood table. "Didn't even say good-bye."

"She never does," Kenzi said, not trying to hide her disappointment. "Did anyone see them leave?"

Tanno shook his head again. "Sorry again, miss."

"It's fine. Apologies for bothering you."

She pushed the glass back with the tips of her fingers and stood, Tanno following suit. She cast her eyes once more over the home. Watercolor illustrations, tapestries, and family photos hung on the walls, leaving empty space a rarity. Knit blankets were folded in every corner and draped on every chair, with a few unfinished projects stashed in a basket near the rocking chair.

As much training as they had to become Eyes, she'd only realized while working that finding the smallest strand of honesty was the easiest way to play a character.

"You have a lovely home," she said.

Tanno smiled, nestled in comfort among the things that made his life. "Thank you."

Back on the streets of Bomazi, Kenzi let the air from her lungs in an angry exhale. The light of the sun was fading to orange, which meant she was about out of time before her meeting with Ira. Kenzi followed the streets to the town square, the smell of flowers making a sudden assault on her senses.

At the center of the square was the town's looming monument, and seated with his back to her was Ira. His shorn hair was growing in their travels, and the sun caught on the blonde that shot through the brown of it.

Picking her way across the cobbles, she dropped onto the bench next to him. It shifted on the uneven stones, but that didn't disturb the neat crease he was making in the fold between his nails. "They were here. Long gone, though. You?"

Ira made another crease. "They saved a group of musicians from thieves on their way into town. The Gegenii man from the Theatre, Yassen, is an earth loa. They witnessed him use his abilities."

"The man I found mentioned that Isco guy again," Kenzi offered, a pale comparison to Ira's information.

Ira nodded. "A doctor. Apparently, he helped run some underground operation to smuggle slaves out of Adur."

"Great," Kenzi snorted, crossing her arms and hunching. "So they're regular folk heroes now."

"That isn't new." Ira spun the paper in his hands and inverted his last fold.

"Any clues which way they went?"

He shook his head. "They kept their horses with the caravan, but the caravan left yesterday."

"So, we have nothing."

"Not nothing," Ira replied.

Kenzi turned to Ira, her brow raised. He finished the last fold on the storm petrel he was working, unfolding its wings in triumph. He lifted the bird, pinching it between his thumb and forefinger, and released it.

It sailed in an easy arc, catching a slim breeze and drifting until it landed at the base of the black stone in the center of the square.

# 3 2

## BLANK VERSE

### YASSEN

Yassen held Mike's reins in the same hand as his notebook, squinting at the scrawl of words. After their travels together, he trusted her to follow the others while he worked.

Currently, he was trying to record their visit to Bomazi. Rounding up the bandits that had attacked the caravan was easy, and Osawa had helped him fill in the parts of Kosein's trial that he'd forgotten.

He managed to trip through what he knew of how Isco smuggled out the slaves from some cult, but Isco wouldn't talk about it enough for him to get details. When Yassen tried to ask him about it, Vahn would ease Mud away until Yassen had to yell.

He had a few scratch notes to fill in for after that, about how Kanna had woken them before the sun the following day and insisted they sneak out of town before anyone noticed. Yassen did his best to record it after but the moment itself was a bit of a blur. His head had been splitting and his mouth was fuzzy which made it hard to concentrate, so he'd followed Kanna's guidance. She hadn't led him wrong yet.

Yassen sighed and Mike huffed in agreement.

After he recorded the story of Kosein's battle with the Pretender, he still wanted to write an ekphrastic poem about the big rock itself in the town square. The problem was that there weren't really any true rules that he could follow for that sort of thing, so he was stuck trying to muddle through it. He'd tried several of the styles he knew, once in a villanelle and another time in a sonnet. He'd tried limericks and haikus and sestets, but nothing fit the mood he was trying to convey.

"Yassen."

He pulled the gnawed pencil out from between his teeth and turned to Astar. She was smirking, and there was the dangerous glint in her eye that meant she was bored and about to start trouble.

"What are you doing?"

"Nothing." Yassen tried to close the book and tuck it back into his pocket but she reached across the distance and snatched it from his hands. She leaned back behind Osawa far enough that she could fit it between their bodies and began flipping through the pages. She thumped Osawa's back to get his attention. "Hey, check this out."

"What is it this time?"

She reached in front of him with the open book, shoving it in front of his nose. He grabbed the book from her and handed her Julius's reins to hold. Adjusting his glasses, Osawa held the book a proper length away so that he could make out Yassens scrawl.

Yassen fidgeted with his pencil. "Don't make fun of me. It's just a thing I like to do."

Osawa flipped through the pages, slow and steady, his expression never shifting from its usual neutral set, before snapping it shut. "Haru, look at this."

At the head of their group, Haru slowed Bia and turned back. He pulled Bia to a stop and waited for them to amble near. Osawa tossed the notebook to Haru when they were close. Yassen bit back a whimper as the battered green clothbound journal sailed through the air before landing neatly in Haru's hands.

Haru held Bia's reins and the notebook with one hand, wiping the other off on his jeans before carefully shifting through the pages, taking his time as he turned each one.

"What are we looking at?"

Yassen jumped in his skin as Vahn's voice issued on his other side. He hadn't noticed the arrival of the others. Even after the weeks passed, Isco still only had small moments where he actually seemed comfortable to be there. But with Kanna now riding closer to Vahn, Isco relaxed more.

"Yassen's poetry," Haru said, his eyes not leaving the pages.

Kanna nudged Amon closer to Haru, leaning toward him. He angled the book so that she could view it.

"Not another one of you," Vahn said.

"That's wonderful, Yassen," Isco said at the same time.

Vahn turned in his seat to look back at him.

"Not enough people appreciate the arts, and..."

Isco stopped in mid sentence, looking past Yassen to Haru. Haru had paused in his turning of the pages, the sharp blue of his eyes cutting into Isco.

"...and who cares what I think."

"I agree with him," Osawa said.

Haru's jaw clenched and his attention was momentarily drawn from Isco, but his glare remained.

"Just when I was starting to think you were cool," Astar said.

"I am cool," Osawa replied flatly.

Haru pointedly flipped another page before turning his attention back to the notebook.

Yassen twisted Mike's reins in his hands. "It's not good. I just sometimes have trouble understanding things. It helps if I think about it longer."

"It is good." Haru closed the book and passed it back to Yassen. "Try using blank verse for the piece you're working on. You're forcing a rhyme, but more contemporary takes on the form lean on meter and rhythm instead of structured schemes."

Yassen reached over, taking the book from Haru's hands.

"There's a natural flow to your work. Stick with your strengths when in doubt," he added.

"Thanks?" Yassen was a bit confused on how they had gotten to this point.

Haru made a clicking sound and Bia started ahead once more. Kanna flashed Yassen a smile before following him, pushing Amon to a trot until she caught up.

Yassen was grateful when they began moving again. He wasn't fond of having so much attention on himself. He fell back. Ahead of him, Astar wrapped her arms around Osawa's waist and leaned her chin on his shoulder. When Osawa turned to her she beamed at him. He shook his head and faced forward.

Vahn had pulled to the back of the group once more. His eyes turned away from the others, watching something that no one else could see. Isco hovered behind him, keeping as much distance between them as possible.

Yassen opened his notebook and started on a new page.

# 33

## ACT OF WAR

### KENZI

KENZI FOLLOWED behind Ira as they made their way to the outskirts of the town. She had entered the town first, so she wasn't sure where the others waited. Ira stopped near a stand-alone residence that faced out of the town and into the open desert. He entered without knocking, and Kenzi found herself in a home similarly built to the one she had been in prior. Larger than Tanno's family apartment, the residents of this dwelling had more space, and though the items inside were worn, they didn't have the same homespun quality and ragged edges.

Two sofas were in the living area, and Masao lounged on one with his boots on the cushions. He didn't look up from the hand mirror he held overhead. The back of it was polished silver with roses and vines inset around a swirling inscription, more an ornamental item rather than a practical one. He brought his reflection close, screwed up his face, then pulled it further away again and checked his profile.

The kitchen table had a proper set of matching chairs, and Salinae sat at the head of it. The handle of a delicate porcelain teacup with pastoral blue design was pinched between his fingers. Nissa sat further down at the table, sipping at her own cup, the saucer raised beneath it to catch any stray drops. The image was unsettling, as if she was looking through a fish's eye.

Ira slid into a seat next to Salinae. "They aren't here, but they were."

Salinae shifted in his chair, yanking his jacket out from behind him so it wouldn't hinder his movement. "Anything else?"

While Ira relayed the information they had gathered, Kenzi kept herself out of the way and studied the dwelling. She leaned on the counter, pulling her hands back when she touched something wet.

The sink had been recently used. Drops of water clung to the stainless surface in one of the bowls, while the other contained dirty dishes. There were five glasses on the drying rack, two large and three small, and three dinner plates. Two more plates remained dirty in the sink, along with an assortment of cutlery and two large serving dishes, their sides scraped clean save for grains of rice that clung doggedly to the surface.

"Tell me about this monument," Salinae said, dragging Kenzi's attention back to the conversation.

Ira's fingers traced a water ring on the table's top.

"It's a black stone," Kenzi said when Ira hesitated almost a moment too long. "Taller than you, but not by much. It's in the town square."

"They call it the Shadestone," Ira added after a beat.

Saline's brow arched and he put his elbows on the table, lifting his entwined hands in front of his lips. "Is it just a stone?"

Kenzi ran her fingers along the counter, past the chilled icebox, and passed behind Salinae to the open doorway next to the kitchen.

"Maybe," Ira offered. "It could be more."

She turned away from the darkened opening. "Some of the tourists were calling it the Seat of Nehebkau, if that helps anything."

Ira's lips flattened into a line, a light sparking and dying in his citrine eyes as Salinae turned to her.

"Did they?"

"Yeah," she said with a nod. "Just looked like a rock to me, though."

Salinae turned away from her and reset himself, his index finger absently tracing the back of his hand as he thought. "Ira?"

The sound of a teacup settling against its saucer rang in the quiet when Nissa set her drink down.

"It could be," Ira said, "but you know how the Independents are with their legends."

"The Others," Salinae corrected.

"Apologies. The Others."

Salinae nodded his forgiveness before looking away, his brow knitting in concentration.

While she waited for Salinae to mull, Kenzi turned back to the darkened hall. She blinked as her eyes adjusted to the dim light. Two doors were to her left, slightly ajar, and a third was on her right.

She stepped into the hall and her foot slipped from under her. She reached out, her hand grasping the frame of the door to regain her balance.

In the dark she hadn't noticed the heavy lines on the tile floors. From the middle room, a thick trail of red curved out of the door and down the hall, a wider swathe coming from the one further away. They met at the final door.

Kenzi stepped through the drag marks, following them to the last room. She pushed back the door with shaking fingers and it creaked on its hinges, opening almost reluctantly. It was enough to see.

She yanked her hand away, backing down the hall, slipping in the tracks of blood. Retreating back to the kitchen, she tried to quiet her breath and set her features. She slid out of the hall, pressing her back against the wall and facing the kitchen.

Five dishes. Five cups, two large, three small. Five bodies. Two large, three small.

Masao watched her from the couch, having twisted his head enough to look behind himself. He grinned at her, winked, then turned back to his mirror.

Salinae dropped his elbows from the table, placing his hands flat on its surface as he finalized his decision. "Take their monument, send it back to Lugos."

"What if..." Kenzi started, swallowing when he leveled his gaze on her. "What if they don't let us?"

Salinae arched his brow. "Let us? This town harbored fugitives. Traitors to the Empire." He lifted the small cup to his lips, then set it back in place. "That is an act of war."

# 34

# REMNANT

## HARU

THE DAYS BECAME COOLER as they travelled along a northerly route. When they first started, their travel time was limited to the less intense parts of the day and into the night, but as they moved closer to the Atarrabi borderlands the air began to carry the cool smell of greenery. Tufts of flowering weeds invaded the sands, and eventually they found themselves in fields of wild tobosa grass that rustled in the occasional breeze.

In the distance, the specter of Ganglere loomed. First it was a blot on the horizon, but as they moved closer and the sun dipped behind it the rough circumvallation came into focus. The walls had been formed by a single earth loa, and his haste was evident in the erratic line of its precipice. Haru knew, though, that when one stood on the flat crown of it the rise and fall was unnoticeable. Distracted by the dread it settled in his stomach, Haru almost didn't notice when Kanna pulled ahead. He kicked Bia into a dash, grabbing Amon's reins just before Kanna drove into her own trap.

Amon tossed his head, snorting to get free. Kanna raised a brow at Haru in question before checking the ground in front of her. Her eyes widened and she eased Amon back.

Even after all these years, the trenches were evident in the slope of the ground. That was, if one knew they were there. Haru dismounted Bia and slid past the dry grasses that covered the trench, careful of his descent. At the bottom, he yanked up the sharpened spikes that protruded from the ground, testing the loamy soil with his feet and kicking aside the ones that had rotted and fallen over with time.

Finished, he climbed out the other side and signaled for the others that the way was clear. Haru waited to help pull them from the trench. Vahn was first, helping Haru to coax the horses from the ditch, followed by Kanna, then Astar. Vahn helped Osawa, then pulled Isco up. Yassen had the least trouble hoisting himself out.

On the other side of the trench the land flattened into a plain, the walls outside the town faceless and blank. The grass had taken over, covering the once trampled ground but failing to hide the detritus of battle. Even Vahn failed to find a remark to break the tension that had descended.

"How long?" Kanna asked.

"The Ganglere battle was five years ago," Astar answered, her tone muted.

Kanna waved at the dead city. "Why is it like this?"

Astar laughed, but it was bitter. "Gegenes has more land than people. None of them want to live in a graveyard, especially a haunted one."

"A graveyard?"

All eyes turned to Kanna, but no one said anything.

Vahn was the first to look away.

"Let's go," Osawa said. "We can sleep between the walls for shelter tonight."

His statement drew Isco's attention. "Walls?"

"There are two." Osawa pulled Julius's reins forward. "What you see is the outer ring. There is another within it."

Vahn caught Haru's eye. Haru called to the straight line of Osawa's shoulders, "Are you sure?"

"Yeah," Yassen amended, "did we forget the haunted part?"

"It'll be fine." Osawa didn't stop walking, didn't turn. "We know what haunts it."

Vahn was the first of the others to follow, picking his way across the waste between the trenches and the walls, through broken weapons, cast off arrows, and blackened, rotting siege towers. Save for Haru and Kanna, who stood rooted to her spot, the others fell in step behind him. Isco was at the rear leading Mud. He was the only one that glanced back.

Amon snorted, shaking his head when Kanna didn't move. After they were out of ear shot, she turned to Haru. "What happened here?"

Haru knew that this time would come, but now that it had arrived, he was unsure if he wanted to proceed. After Kanna's revelation that she had to relive her memories as they returned, this was one that he would give anything to protect her from.

It was important, but so was she. The Kanna that lived and breathed in front of him was a kind of echo, but she wasn't a ghost in the Neither, wandering the desolate landscape of shattered memories. She had made new memories when the old were lost, found a way to survive with the skills she had. Though things were missing, she had not lost the spark that made her.

The proof of it was in the strangers that were with them now. The three odd civilians that trusted her, followed her, and believed she would get them through the mess they'd found themselves in.

Kanna shut her eyes, tilting her head to the side as if hearing a distant call. "I was here," she said, opening her eyes. "I can feel it."

If he told her, it would be easier. He could have Osawa relay the battle strategy, the plan of action she had made, a near stroke of genius that had kept most of them alive. But Osawa was pressing a hand against the inner wall, listening to a current that should have long eroded.

Vahn could give her the details of the close combat, describe for her the way she had fought with everything she had.

Haru focused on Kanna when she dropped Amon's reins. She stalked toward him, her head tilted, her eyes questioning. "Why are you afraid?"

He didn't have the answer.

She reached for him, her fingertips pressing into the tension of his brow. She pushed aside the hair that had strayed into his eyes, and traced a path to his jaw. Her thumb grazed the skin of his lips and he bent his head, pressing his forehead against hers.

He rested his hands on the curve of her hip, swallowed against the clenching in his throat, and steadied the shake of his nerves.

"Haru?" she said, her breath passing over his skin.

"Yes, *inara*?"
"Will you show me?"

# 35

# THE PRICE OF RECKLESSNESS

## KANNA

IN THE BLACK, the night flashed.

The sky opened over Ganglere, the rain falling in thick sheets and turning the trodden land to a sticky-slick quagmire. The white of her boots was buried in caked mud and blood and the ground slipped beneath them, the soil washing from the top of the circumvallation and threatening to take her with it.

Kanna was soaked in rain, and the gusts of wind in the cold night stiffened her already tired muscles. She threw everything she had left into defending their location, cutting through the attackers that mounted the walls in an endless parade.

Her people were still falling. The Gegeniis had used nature's aid to attack the Palamidia's lines in a last desperate gasp. The few loa officers she had were contending with disparate natures, but the dark and the pummeling storm only served to heighten their precarious positions.

The Gegenii had amassed an impressive force to meet the Palamidia, and the numbers and landscape had been against them from the start. It didn't help that the Gegenii were being reinforced by neighboring militias while her own troops hadn't received additional aid since the onset of the campaign.

Velinius had once again set her up to fail.

But Kanna hadn't yet. And she wouldn't now.

At the start, Kanna ordered the circumvallation built to block supplies going in or out of the besieged city. When news reached them that the arrival of reinforcements from other Gegenii cities was imminent, trenches lined with traps were dug into the open plain and another ring was built to defend the siege wall.

Kanna's forces were on these walls, split while they were attacked on both sides.

Kanna faced the fresh reinforcements that charged the outer wall. On her left, Vahn cut down the enemies before him. In the pause between, he'd call the fire to crawl upon the siege towers that rolled near the walls through the bodies below. The water extinguished the flames when his concentration broke on the next insurgent, but it slowed their attack.

Further away, Haru caught the lightning that flashed from the sky and redirected it at the soldiers before him. At his back was Osawa, one of the few water loas with the detachment, deep in his element and dominating.

Despite all this, Kanna could feel them dying. All of them, running their lives into the points of blades for a patch of land that didn't mean anything to the Empire. But if not here, it would be somewhere else. Some other unholy place that would open its maw and issue them into the dark.

Everyone was angry. Everyone was terrified and screaming and she could feel it vibrating in her bones as her blades cut through flesh, as their lives spilled into the muck, when she wasn't sure if her feet were in water or blood anymore and it rolled down the sides of the walls in waves.

They passed through, they moved out and into nothing, and the nothing was peace if only for the fact that it wasn't here any longer.

The pull of a trebuchet's triggered release followed by the dropping counterweight was muted by the singing of blades. Kanna recognized it almost too late, saw the boulder hurtling towards them at the last moment.

"Down!"

She yanked one of the slower Prospects out of the way with her as the heavy volley hit. The ground beneath her shook as it smashed through their defenses, cutting her off from her soldiers on the other side.

Cutting her off from Haru.

"Vahn!" Kanna scrambled up, untangling herself from the shaking limbs of the young soldier.

"Kinda busy, K." Vahn grasped the ends of an escalade that the Gegenii were attempting to breach with. The flames rose at his bidding, the sodden wood sending up thick clouds of smoke that further obscured their sightlines.

Kanna rushed to cover him as he went for another of the siege ladders. "Get Ira to reinforce these walls before they fall with us on them."

"Can't." More fire, more choking smoke. "He verged, we took him off the line."

Kanna slammed her foot into the face of a woman attempting to breach, bent to slash the hands of another. They fell from the wall, flailing limbs topping others on their way down, the bodies hitting the ground with a wet thunk.

"What about Farro?"

Vahn met her eyes, and he shook his head. Kanna growled, running her blade through the heart of another that tried to breach and stepped back for Vahn to work on the next escalade. "Someone," she bit through the desperation. "Get me *someone*."

"That's all the earth loas we had."

The ominous crank of the trebuchet readying itself began again.

Kanna's gaze caught on Osawa and Haru, stuck on the other side of the chasm the last volley had created. Haru was covering Osawa while he used the rain to his advantage, creating ice flows and currents to knock back the advance on their flank.

"Water."

The mayhem was too loud, too frenetic, she wouldn't be able to get orders across the divide that separated them.

"It's a pain in the ass," Vahn said, withdrawing his blade, fresh blood sliding from the metal, "but what of it?"

Her attention snapped back to Vahn. "Get Yua, have her freeze the walls. It should harden them beneath us, and ice will make it harder for the siege ladders to gain purchase, at least."

Vahn's gaze went over her shoulder, and she slid to the side so he could meet her attacker. In the moments that he was busy, she took in the lay of the battle.

The trebuchet loosed its volley, aiming for another section of the wall and she shouted a warning. The boulder smashed at her other side. Bodies of the slow and unlucky catapulted from the wall, their limbs bent or flailing as they toppled.

"They'll shatter if that thing hits them," Vahn said behind her.

"I'll take care of that." When he didn't move immediately, she narrowed her gaze on him. "Go."

Vahn backed away, turning at the last moment to seek out Yua.

Steadying her breath, Kanna sheathed her knives. She could feel the exhaustion in every cell of her body, the burn of every muscle beneath the steady hit of the rain.

Kanna called the dark. The shadows came, each one fighting over the next, a single entity that churned and split and cycled. They swarmed at the bottom of the escalade in front of her, the screams of those below beginning as a warning. They pulled the bottom out at an angle. The ladder and the bodies on it tipped into the next, creating a cascade and buying her time.

It was dark, everything was so dark. The shadows were in her lungs and she breathed them. Her body shook, too tired to do this much but she demanded it anyway. The shadows would listen, if only it meant that this may be the time they could take her.

She saw with them, felt herself within them, and raced with them across the plain, reaching beyond the trenches to the trebuchets behind their attackers as the pulleys tightened and lifted the counterweights.

The dark swarmed and Kanna shut her eyes, gave the shadows what strength she had left, and they leveraged the trebuchets. The machines tilted, toppled, and broke against the ground.

Kanna fell to her knees, gasping through the black. She tried to untangle herself from it but it was everywhere all at once. It was under her skin, behind her ribs, sinking into the marrow of her bones. The confusion and desperation was a part of her, and it was suffocating.

She thought of daylight, of the sun cascading through the rose window in the temple. Tried to remember warmth and time as the ground crackled and froze beneath her.

Something else cut through, something outside of her. A clear and calm intent thrummed. She sat back on her heels and pushed the hair from her eyes but it was so hard to see. The sky rumbled a warning and the night flashed alive, the light in the dark a strobe that wouldn't let her eyes settle.

She found him only because she always did. She had never needed sight to find him. Haru's attention was sharp, focused on the enemies that came at their front. He met her eyes, even across the distance, falling back to give the lead to Osawa.

Between the enemies before them and her own gaze, he missed the true threat. Kanna wouldn't have been able to dissect it from the rest if she had not known, had not felt it before. It was intent and belief once pure turned into something it was not meant to be. It was eating itself alive and it believed it was the right thing to do.

She followed it through the amassed bodies to a soldier at Haru's back, one of their own dressed in muddied white. Haru followed her, turning into the flash of metal.

Something ripped from her throat and she tried to get to him. All she knew was that she was here and had to be there.

She was the dark. Distance was irrelevant.

Planes splintered and she was with him.

She arrived to see the metal breaking his skin and drawing a brilliant crimson line across his chest and she had to stop it.

She dove in front of him and felt the blade hit her neck, digging into her shoulder. Surprise loosened the hand that wielded it as it tore down her back and opened her skin to the harsh pelt of the rain.

Haru pulled her against him and with him as he leaned away from the attack, his other hand lashing out to slash the throat of the traitor.

Kanna's knees buckled and she could feel the tip of the world on its axis, the way it spun in the universe, consistent and inevitable. Haru staggered with her in his arms, falling to his knees in the thick mud, his hands shaking against her.

She pressed her hand against his chest but it was so weak, it didn't feel like hers, but maybe it would be enough. It could be enough to keep him out of the one dark she couldn't feel or know. Beneath her palm his heart beat, his breath moved in his lungs.

"You're bleeding," she said, tears stinging the corners of her eyes.

Kanna wasn't sure if the cold in her bones had always been there or arrived with the shadows that claimed her.

---

KANNA WOKE to pain so harsh it was all that she was.

Thousands of screams, piled on one another, hit her in an instant. She felt their souls rush through, bottling up the path and getting caught in the Neither. They slammed into each other in that purgatory, terrified and confused, looking and searching, holding onto existence and hope and screaming again when they found mothers, fathers, children, all in that infinite black.

They were suffocating her, living and dying all at once, somewhere inside of her that she couldn't reach, couldn't scrape away. She struggled to breathe, to understand, but she was torn open out and in and it was blinding. Slick bloodied hands tried to hold her down but she slipped in their grasp until it was too much.

It was all too much.

She let the dark have her again.

---

THE NEXT TIME SHE WOKE, there was still pain.

She could hear it thrumming in her ears and it settled in her jaw, her teeth aching from clenching them to keep her own screams in.

It was quiet. Everything was quiet and clear and at least the pain had settled in her body and wasn't deeper, in that space in her soul. The sound of gulls cut through, their cries sharp with delight. The air carried the smell of ash and the sea. She was on her stomach and when she tried to turn she hissed, involuntary and immediate.

She opened her eyes to the inside of an unfamiliar tent, the heavy canvas swaying in a soft breeze.

The day was bright and she was alone.

A panic tightened her body, seizing up in her marrow and driving her from where she lay despite the burning in her back, her shoulder, her arm, her body that screamed with her every breath.

She rolled from the cot that cradled her and tried to rise but her legs refused to hold her weight. She gripped the rugs that covered the dirt, wondering at the sense of having rugs on the ground but grateful for them anyway, and tried to pull herself forward.

"What the fuck, K?"

Vahn's startled concern stopped her momentarily, but she didn't feel like reason was important at the moment. She needed to find him, needed to know that he still breathed. So many had gone through the black she couldn't track them, couldn't pull out the individuals from the exodus.

"Wait, fuck, you're going to rip open your stitches and start bleeding everywhere again."

Kanna paused and rolled on her side to catch her breath. Vahn sank next to her on the ground. He went so far as to lie down, tucking his hand beneath his head so he could meet her eyes as she gasped for breath.

"That was some pretty reckless shit," he said when her breathing steadied. "It's a good thing you're hard to kill."

She had enough energy to glare.

"I need you to breathe."

"I am breathing," she said, and it hurt. It scraped against a raw throat like glass.

Vahn was quiet. Vahn was only quiet when there weren't any jokes to be made. Considering the things Vahn could make amusing, she felt the fever in her body chill to a cold sweat. She tilted her head, trying to listen. After the cacophony of battle, the cries, the constant clash of work and danger and fear since they had arrived at Ganglere, the silence was suffocating. She shut her eyes and tried to feel anything, but she was met with a deep, numbing dread and awe.

When she opened them to meet Vahn's, he was staring into her, waiting.

"He would be good for you," Vahn said.

"You're good for me."

"I know," he grinned, "But he would be better. If you let him."

Kanna had the breath to scoff, at least. "I don't know what you're talking about."

Vahn rolled his eyes. "You should. So, let's agree you do, and I just want you to know it seems like a good thing."

She didn't say anything, at first. Then, "Is he okay?"

Vahn smiled, and it was a beautiful thing. When it was real, there was something so pure about it that it made Kanna ache. It made her want to destroy the things that had hurt him so much to make this smile so rare, instead giving him nothing but smirks and casual shrugs.

"I think he's fine. They sent him back with the other wounded. You weren't in a condition to be moved."

Kanna tried to shift her weight from her hip and lay back, but the attempt sent an unbridled pain through her body that stole her breath. She rolled forward instead, tucking her head into her arms to catch it.

She hated this. She needed to know. She hated that she needed to know, needed to feel his heart beating, needed to watch his lashes open around his eyes and have him look at her, see her. She had to know he was, he was still and would always be.

"Vahn," she said, her voice muffled against the ground.

"Hmm?"

"Why is it so quiet?"

He didn't answer. He considered too long for it to be a search for something witty.

"What did she do?"

When he still didn't answer, Kanna lifted her head from her arms. She pushed herself onto her elbows even though her shoulder screamed, her skin stretching at an artificial limit that kept it from ripping apart.

Vahn rolled over and tried to stop her, but his hands were too scared. He didn't know where to grasp her without causing more pain and she was counting on his care to distance himself if need be. "Will you stop, please. You are going to make me age prematurely."

"Your hair is already white," she said, and continued to claw, to crawl.

"That is not okay. Low blow." He moved enough to crouch in front of her so she would be forced to stop. "Fine. We will do this. But I am going to help you, and you are going to accept it."

Kanna stopped her progress and glared.

Vahn took it as acceptance. He moved to her uninjured side and helped her to shift so that her arm was around his shoulders, his hand around her waist. "On three," he said, then counted them out.

Kanna took a breath, as deep as she could, and grit her teeth as he helped her to rise. Upright her vision spotted, her head throbbing when her blood plummeted to her feet momentarily. Vahn waited long enough for the world to stop spinning and shift back to right before taking a step.

Kanna dragged behind him, only moving what was absolutely necessary. When Vahn pulled away the heavy canvas that kept the tent enclosed, the bright white of day blinded her. Kanna shut her eyes and tilted, biting back a groan as the heat hit her skin.

Finally blinking away the glare, Kanna had to shut her eyes once more as light prismed off the surface of a lake.

That wasn't right.

She forced her eyes open.

She lost the strength in her legs and fell, Vahn barely managing to soften the jarring blow.

"This is Gegenes?" she asked.

She had to be sure, because sometimes she wasn't sure, and she wanted to be wrong. She wanted this to be a fever dream, and she was on the coast, waiting for the next ship to arrive and take her back to Lugos where she couldn't damage anything else.

"We're still here."

Kanna nodded. "That's the city."

Vahn said nothing. She didn't need him to.

Below her feet was the highest, outermost ring the earth loas had built, but there was no longer a trench and a lower siege ring. There was a short drop to water, clear as glass. She could see all the way to the bottom of it—discarded weapons flashing in the sun, a splintered wood wagon that was carried by a deluge and smashed against the walls she had built.

There was nothing else.

When the troops had first arrived, when Kanna ordered the siege wall built, she would stand upon it and watch the city. She told herself it was to get a better understanding of who they faced and to keep a watchful eye for any sorties that attempted to breach the wall.

Ganglere was smaller than the Lugosian cities she'd known. She wasn't even sure if it constituted a city. It was rougher and dirtier, but it had been alive. From her vantage above she watched people pull wagons loaded with goods, children in tow being herded when they wandered too far. Neighbors distributed what they had, some adding, some subtracting to the loads. Nothing went in, but no one went hungry.

Even as the siege wore, even with the city locked in, she could still hear laughter carry. At night, sometimes, there was even music. Lights, voices, and melodies that were warm and full of hope and power and longing. The thin desert air carried it out of the city and to the wall where she listened, hanging on each curving note.

They hadn't sung when they died. Their mouths opened and water filled the air where music once lived.

Velinius had never wanted the city. She didn't care about this rough patch of land or the people that cut a living from it. If Velinius couldn't have it, then no one should.

Kanna should have known. Things did not exist that didn't belong to Velinius. She reached out, her fingertips dipping into the water. It was familiar, as a friend would be.

"Yua." In the distancce, something moved in the water and rippled the surface. "It's my fault," Kanna whispered. To no one, to the ground, to the dead.

Kanna shut her eyes and she could feel every muscle of her body shaking. Pain, exhaustion, anger, grief, there was so much and she couldn't contain it. She pressed the heels of her palms into her eyes and bent over, her face to the ground as a sob fought its way through, and she wanted out.

It had to end. There was no other choice but to end this.

---

KANNA WAS TORN from one body and shoved into another, but the pain carried with her. She rolled onto her stomach over the damp ground, lights flashing behind her eyes, clenching her jaw to bite back the screams.

Hands reached for her and her memories short-circuited: they were blood-slick and she was ripped open. The sounds escaped from behind her teeth and she curled her knees to her chest, reached for her shoulder as if she could hold herself together.

Insistent hands returned, wrapped around her waist and pulled her from the ground and she tried to fight them.

"Ananke."

She hated that name. It was something forced on her and it had so much weight.

"Kanna!"

That one made more sense, was easier to breathe around. It was backwards and shifted, and it took what she was given and made it her own.

Hands pressed against the side of her face, held her still. Warmth cradled her, reached into her body, and she hadn't realized she was shivering. It crept under her skin, pushed back the dark until it was in its place again.

"My heart, open your eyes."

She turned her fight to the pain, the sharp edge of it receding enough so she could hear him, know he was there, and opened her eyes. Blue as sky promising freedom. Molten gold moving, living, burning pure without scalding to black.

Haru. Steel against skin. The tear of it, crimson on white against rain and mud and lightning.

"You're bleeding," she said, her voice catching on the past. She pressed her hands against his chest, strong enough now they may be able to do something. She scrambled against his skin as grey and dusty flickered to white and blood covered and back again and she tried to hold him there, keep him.

He grasped the back of her neck, angling her up and pulling her in.

Haru kissed her. It was a hard grounding thing at first, lips pressed tight against teeth, a reminder of what existence was.

The fracture in her mind calmed, the misfiring shocks fading. She relaxed against him, her hands trapped and stilled. She allowed herself to surrender a battle that was long won and he pulled back, feather soft.

His heart beat beneath her hands, rapid and strong.

Her mouth parted and he breathed into her, alive and here. She met him and exhaled. She fit against him, with him, as if creation had somehow bent to her will for once and gave instead of took.

She clung to him, her grip tangling in the fabric at his back and the tremors in her hands stilled. His hands found her skin, his fingers pressing along the scar on her shoulder, following it until it broke away at her spine and she was knit back together.

The night was just that then, a night. One filled with stars, a thing outside herself.

"I'm with you," he said, breathless for greater reasons.

When she couldn't find the words, he gave them to her: "You're with me."

Kanna lived in mantras, found solid ground in their repetition.

"You're with me," she said, and she didn't just know it. She understood. Word by word, countless times repeated, he had found a way for her to understand what it meant.

# 36

# MAKE ME A LION

## KENZI

KENZI STARED out of the window of the train car as the landscape passed. The deserts had become grasslands, but she couldn't remember when they had entered Atarrabi, and she couldn't think of a reason for why it should matter. Beneath her feet, the train's wheels hit against the rails, thunking over each juncture.

As many times as she scrubbed her skin, ran water through her hair and scraped her scalp until it nearly bled, she couldn't get the smell of thick smoke and burning flesh out of her nose. She'd tried to pull it out like air and nearly suffocated herself, and Ira found her gasping for breath and hacking.

After that he didn't let her sleep alone anymore. He'd given her space, but he drew the line at her almost accidentally killing herself.

When they'd left the camp in Gaoler, she wanted to distance herself from him. Not through any sense of anger or jealousy, but because she needed to prove herself to the others as a valuable member of their team, a good and loyal soldier.

A good and loyal soldier wasn't supposed to dry heave after a battle, but she didn't think she'd call what had happened in Bomazi a battle. Those who were able to escape the flames fled into the desert. Salinae wasn't pleased that they had gotten away, but he said that either the desert would take them or they would serve as a proper warning to those who would harbor Ananke.

After, Salinae had studied his maps, his gaze roving the open empty deserts of Gegenes, drawing lines between where they had begun and where they were now. After a while, he smiled again to himself, and called up a messenger from among those who had arrived to take the monument.

The scout raced ahead to Lugos, and a small honor guard followed behind with the Shadestone.

They left that razed ground, no longer a town, cutting a sharp path to the nearest train depot.

At least Salinae had taken a private car. Kenzi didn't have to worry that she would accidentally meet his eyes, remember the red glow that reflected in the icey blue while flesh crackled and he smiled.

The sound threatened to rise in her ears and she shut her eyes, focusing on the grind of wheels against the track.

In the front of the car she currently occupied, Masao chatted ceaselessly with Nissa. The conversation was one-sided, but he didn't seem to notice or care. He had been near giddy since they'd left Bomazi in ash.

"Kenz?"

She tore her concentration away from the window and met Ira's gaze. His brow knit, his eyes shadowed in concern. She smiled, though she didn't feel it, and returned to watching the blur outside.

He took her acknowledgement as permission and settled in the seat between her and the aisle.

"I guess I know now," she said.

"What do you know?" he asked, as if his words trod on broken glass. Ira tried to keep his voice controlled, but she could sense his relief that she'd spoken.

It had been some time since she could. She heaved a breath, felt it rattle in her lungs. The air moved through her, a force of life, a constant. "What the Saint of Fire meant. About a city screaming."

It was his turn to look away. "It happened in Ganglere, just another way."

"You didn't tell me," she said, unable to keep the accusation from her voice. "You knew, but you didn't say anything."

Ira shook his head looking forward once more. "I didn't think I had to tell you. It wasn't supposed to be this way. Not anymore."

Kenzi didn't reply. She couldn't. There was too much, so she tried to focus again on the movement of her breath, the steady cadence of time.

"Things were different after Kanna became Legatus, and that's when you said you wanted to join."

Kenzi narrowed her eyes. "Why do you do that?"

Ira blinked, as much as a startle as he was capable of. "What do I do?"

"Every now and then, it slips. You call her Kanna."

"Only those that never met her called her Ananke," he said, a faint smile on his lips before it fell again. "Or Velinius, and those loyal to her."

"Are you saying that doesn't include you?" Kenzi asked, and then, there was something else. She sat forward in her seat, turning to Ira. He still wouldn't look at her. She forced her voice low, wary of the other passengers in the car. "You didn't just watch them, did you? You knew them. You knew her."

Ira's gaze flickered to the front of the car, then to the paper between his fingers. "It isn't secret."

Kenzi took a steadying breath and fell back against the bench. Her hand went to her throat, to the tender skin healing there. Vahn had been ready to slit her throat, would have, if Osawa hadn't intervened. Kenzi thought it was because they knew of her brother. An earth loas was a rare talent in the Palamidia, and Ira was a powerful one. That wasn't it, though, not at all. "He asked why you left them."

Ira's hands stilled.

"What happened?"

Ira folded his square, one end meeting the other. "I lost someone important to me." He took a steadying breath. "I transferred to the Eyes after Ganglere, after Kanna became Legatus. They weren't looking for weaknesses or openings then. We weren't sabotaging food stores or stirring up discontent against the leaders of the Independents."

"The Others," she corrected, but only barely.

He shrugged it off. "Many of us actually ended up back at the Tower, waiting for assignments that didn't come."

"So that's it?" Bitterness crept up her throat. "You thought I'd just safely twiddle my thumbs in some fancy tower all my life?"

"I hoped."

"Well," she said, but stopped. She wanted to be angry, but she couldn't find it in herself. Not anymore. "That isn't what happened."

"I know."

Kenzi breathed out, hard, and shut her eyes. "What do we do now?"

He didn't answer. He reached over instead, putting his hand over hers and squeezing. She turned her palm up, threading her fingers with his, then leaned onto his shoulder.

"Ira?" Her voice was small, like when she was a child, when she pleaded for him to not join the Palamidia, to not leave her. She looked down to the paper in his opposite hand.

"Hm?"

"Will you make me a lion?"

Ira smiled against her hair. "I can't." He turned the paper he had started over in his hand, then offered it to her. Kenzi traced the beginning folds that crossed each other on opposing sides. "Only you can."

# 3 7

## THE COLLECTORS

### VELINIUS

IT HAD BEEN QUITE some time since Velinius had been to Aksana's villa, and longer still since she had been welcome. After Salim's death, Velinius kept to the Tower. It was better for her, anyway. Officers were not meant to live outside the Tower's reach.

The crumbling villa was high in the mountains, tucked into the deep woods north of Tages. She urged her steads on, the wheels of the chariot clattering over the uneven footing and dipping into the cracks that had grown between the paving.

It was years before Velinius saw her mother again, and only to give her the news that she had ascended to Second. When she arrived, she had not been greeted by Aksana, but by a strange creature with soulless eyes who demanded in an ancient tongue to know her business there.

Velinius stopped her horses and stepped down from the chariot, leaving them at the base of the wide steps that lead up to the door of the villa. From a distance the climbing vines along its face could be mistaken for appeal, but closer one could see the roots had begun to crack the stucco, parts of it sloughing off the front of the building and lying in algae covered heaps at its base.

When Velinius reached the door, she twisted the levered handles and it opened without resistance. Despite the remote location of Aksana's villa, she had not feared the outside world. It was others that had feared her.

Velinius stepped into the vestibule and dust settled against her skin. The house hummed when she turned on the light switch and the generators warmed, vibrating the floors. The harsh electric lighting grew in intensity after the slightest of delays, settling at its peak.

Before her, the wide staircase that led to the next floor opened in welcome beneath the glittering chandelier above, bedecked in once-clear crystals now yellowed with time and neglect. At the base of it, rugs had been cast one over the other at unmatched angles, the color and pattern of each clashing with the next.

The years had not softened the bulbs that Aksana had placed, and the white light cast shadows over the mounds of collections inside that hid the villa's ornate woodwork. Assorted glasswares piled on any surface that could hold them, small side tables were stacked in precarious towers, and bolts of silks were tossed in corners, in baskets, or even into the empty mouth of the cold hearth.

Velinius did not seek the stairs. The way up led to tangled rooms that served only as storage for Aksana's distractions. The true purpose of the home was below.

Velinius picked her way through the villa's living and entertaining areas, careful not to touch anything. If anything upset the piles there would be a cascade, and she had no desire to stir up whatever might lie in the depths of the collections.

As she traversed one room after the next, Velinius paused. She had seen the same rug six times before, the same bottle more times than she bothered to count. The same silk pattern in the dining area and the hearth and the corner.

Of all the ways for Aksana to sell her madness to others, she'd chosen to buy it.

The library predominantly had books in it. Velinius repressed the urge to recoil from the faint traces of mold that had begun to form on the spines. On the third shelf from the top, the second from the window on the left, Velinius grasped a stack and pried them loose. They had bloated in the humidity, and the swelling pages made it difficult to free them from the loaded shelves. When the weight of them released, the pressure latch beneath clacked and the shelf slid open.

Velinius was greeted with a light even brighter than that in the foyer, and stairs that descended beneath the villa's main floor. She tried the basement door, but it was locked fast. A rapid beeping warned that it was also alarmed.

Velinius flexed her fingers and opened her palm, before clenching her hand to a fist to capture the cool light. She pulled it between her fists and hardened it between her hands, then used the bar to pry open the basement door.

Aksana didn't care for the villa above. It was an old property, one that had been passed through generations of her family, a sign and symbol of her privileged lineage and nothing more, so she'd filled it with things and left them to rot.

The basement, however, was her sanctuary. After the deaths of Aksana's husband and second child, Velinius had kept an eye on her mother for any signs of a threat. Amid the procurement orders for the various collections strewn above, Aksana had placed orders for medical and diagnostic equipment. Enough to equip an entire medicium, as well as research facilities.

Beneath her collections, she had outfitted the basement into a clean room. The room was sterile, and the various cabinets were hermetically sealed and climate controlled. Save for a simple working desk, the room also boasted a steel pediatric examining table.

When the alarms sounded, she shifted her grip on the light and formed it to a point, launching it into the control center on the wall. The wails cracked and distorted, winding down into helpless chirps.

Before the alarm silenced, there was the sound of a latch falling, and the faint tinkle of thin glass as it shattered.

Velinius followed the sound to a black box at the end of one of the display cases. A weight had fallen inside of it, crushing whatever had been beneath. On the front of the display case was a label written in her mother's precise hand:

ABRAXAS

Velinius frowned, turning away from it. It wasn't what she had come for.

In Aksana's work as an anthropologist with the Palamidia, she amassed a collection of Ilazkin texts that she was meant to translate. Unlike the books in the library, these were encased and protected.

Velinius only needed one. She paced the perimeter of the lab, noting the varied texts. Handwritten diaries butted up against communal reports and shipping manifests, which sat next to full copies of what was suspected to be mass produced volumes that had been found in pieces and stitched back together.

They were sorted by age and paper type, with variables in each containment unit set to preserve the works inside. At the end of the line, in one of the cases meant for later works, Velinius found it.

It was not a book like the others. Accounts from witnesses, articles from engineers and scientists, and poems and pieces from great thinkers of the time had been collected and loosely bound into a rough codex that chronicled the fall of the gods.

The latch on the container hissed when Velinius cracked the seal to retrieve the manuscript. She held it in her hands, running her fingers over the debossed Ilazkin script on the cover.

She left the glass door to the chamber open.

The rumored seat of Nehebkau had arrived, and Velinius had tested it. It fed from her ability and looped it back a hundredfold, a perfect conduit of loa energy and proof that Velinius was right. That the fabled godsworks weren't fables at all.

Velinius smiled and brought the codex close to her chest.

Aksana was not the only one that could collect things.

## 38

## WELCOME TO PYRGOLIS

### ISCO

Isco had only been to Atarrabi once. When he was younger and it was still an independent region, his father brought him to gather supplies from a trading station near the Adur border. He remembered that the land felt much hotter then than it did now. However, after the scorching heat of the Gegenes desert, anything was a relief.

Though their sightlines weren't as clear as in the desert, Isco welcomed the small bit of cover the hills provided as the stunted town of Pyrgolis appeared before them. Isco's feet grazed the tips of the long yellow plain grasses, the occasional burr catching on his hem.

The small junction towns of Atarrabi they had passed through after leaving Gegenes held an oddly similar layout, as if someone had decided this was how the towns should be, which was a strange notion considering the loose tribal structure of Atarrabi. Each had a wide main thoroughfare and an assortment of buildings lining it, with no real rhyme or reason to their locations or sizes.

"Let me get this straight," Astar was saying. "You dated that Salinitty person that's after Kanna?"

"I wouldn't call it dating," Vahn replied.

"And Osawa?"

Vahn shrugged.

Osawa shrugged.

This town boasted a stable at the left and an open corral across from it, with a cluster of residences near what appeared to be a large temple, complete with a bell tower that would ring to announce births and deaths of Pyrgolis's residents.

"All right," Astar announced. "Show of hands: who here *hasn't* slept with Vahn?"

Ahead of them, Yassen raised his hand straight into the air. Haru also raised his, though more conservatively. Running point at the head of the group was Kanna, who kept her head forward and her free hand resting at her side.

"I get Haru, but *Kanna*?" Astar gasped, covering her grin with her hand.

Kanna glanced back, shrugged one shoulder, then looked ahead once more.

"She's taking it literally. But also, why do you 'get' Haru? You think his majesty is too good for me?"

A windmill circled overhead, the metal screeching as it caught the wind gusts that ushered in the soft drizzle of rain that had long been threatening. The rains would be a relief from the heat, at least, but Isco would prefer to stay dry.

"I thought I was the princess," Astar said with a pout.

Osawa patted Astar's hand. "You are, but Haru is an actual Prince, and Vahn likes to remind him constantly of that fact."

"Seriously?"

The first drops of rain hit Isco on the nose, and he wrinkled it against the chill. The rain shouldn't be this cold, not in Atarrabi. It was a fair sign that the storm season was approaching, and another reminder that time slipped by despite how disconnected he was from what he once knew.

"He has the tiara and everything," Vahn said, the low rumble in his chest warming Isco.

Isco wanted nothing more than to press his head between Vahn's shoulder blades to hide from the storm that approached.

He didn't.

Haru turned back in his saddle to face them. "It is a circlet," he said, in a way that let Isco know this was not the first time they'd had this discussion.

"Yeah, sure. That makes it better."

Across from the temple was an inn, which Isco was grateful for, and a general store, which was the closest thing to civilization that the junction town seemed to boast. Behind and between those rose a water tower.

Kanna slowed Amon, and Haru brought Bia next to her. They didn't exchange words, but she was distracted by something. Isco followed her gaze and squinted at the windows of the general store. The orange glow of oil lamps flickered between rows of short aisles, but no one moved behind the heavy glass panes.

Beneath the light touch of his hands, he felt Vahn tense as the horses slowed and the conversation ceased.

With a sudden jerk, Kanna pulled Amon around. His head reared back angrily and Bia pranced to the side to avoid a collision. "Ambush!"

Vahn turned Mud and Isco had to cling to him in order to not slide off the back of their mount.

The rumble in the sky became something both like and unlike thunder. There was a mournful creak and the sound of splintering wood as the water tower cracked, its contents rushing in front of them and blocking their escape back the way they had come.

Kanna's voice projected clear through the din. "Shield for volley!"

Everything spun and Isco was ripped from his seat. Above, the silver of arrows flashed against the twilight grey sky before Vahn landed on top of Isco, nearly knocking the wind from his chest. Vahn caught himself on his elbows, one on each side of Isco, and ducked his head.

There was the sound of waves in the tide, of arrows hitting water and falling in a clatter around them. One brushed against Isco's arm, another near his thigh, but it was harmless. It was nothing in comparison to the heat pressed against his body.

Vahn's face was so close to Isco's that they breathed the same air. But when Vahn's eyes opened and met his, he didn't wink, didn't smirk. He unthreaded his fingers and rolled off of Isco before dragging him from the ground.

Around them, a dome of water whirled, mingling with dark threads of shadow. Osawa kept one hand up, the other back, as he held their cover in place. Kanna's hand rested on his shoulder, lending her shadows to fill the spaces between the water's currents. The sporadic arrows that breached the wall lost their velocity and fell harmlessly to the ground at their feet.

The group had dismounted in the flurry of activity, the horses scattered somewhere beyond the barrier. Vahn dragged Isco behind him, keeping his own body between Isco and the attack as he approached Kanna. Isco caught sight of Yassen attempting to do the same to cover Astar.

"We have noncombatants," Vahn hissed.

Kanna didn't look at him. "I know."

The doors of the general store burst open and a wave of white surged forward.

A second wave came from the temple on their other side.

Vahn stepped forward, his hands open at his sides and lifting. Flames caught on the store, but they weren't as bright as they had been in Gegenes. Still, the heat was enough to cause the glass to crack and burst out, which only gave more room for the soldiers that had hidden inside to escape.

Kanna's gaze shot up on the opposite side of the street, the predatory glint alighting on the belltower. "We're taking the temple," she announced, unsheathing her blades and finding the center of the group. "Yassen, wall off the store to buy us time. Osawa, you're on rearguard."

Kanna faced the wave that descended from the temple steps while her soldiers fell in behind her. Vahn left Isco at the center of the group before joining Kanna, with Haru at her other side. Osawa guarded their backs.

Isco didn't think his heart could hold the terror that was gripping it, but it stayed true. A hand brushing caused him to jump, but he turned to meet Astar. She bit her lip, twined her fingers with his and held on, the shake in her hand stilling when it met Isco's steady grip.

It eased the lock in Isco's knees and he breathed. At least, for a moment, before Kanna broke the simple spell.

"On me."

# 39

## HIGHER GROUND

### KANNA

THE STORM STROBED, the flash of lightning outside the leaded glass windows the only thing lighting the stone interior of the Temple, locking them into this dark place.

There was nothing but this. The shadows came at Kanna's bidding, and joined by Haru's scattering light, they tore through the first wave of the Palamidia's soldiers that attempted to block them from gaining the Temple.

Once inside, though, they were trapped with the soldiers that had yet to descend. The quarters were too tight for wide attacks, and there was no guarantee that one of their own wouldn't be caught in them, which left Kanna, Haru, and Vahn to cut through.

The clash of the melee reverberated against the stone walls, and the clamor caught and echoed in the unornamented vault of the ceiling. Kanna took the lead, breaking whatever formations the enemy soldiers attempted. She focused on the few that pulsed with power, the elements tethering themselves to mortal forms.

On her left, Vahn kicked over one of the long benches that lined the Temple to trap an attacker. The benches dominoed, and Kanna used the flattened surface to launch. She passed behind Haru and came down, all knees and blades, on the soldier at his back. Her knife buried in the body, hitting the floor beneath and shifting enough to stick.

She left it and turned to meet a new attack. Haru tossed one of his blades and she caught it, shifting to the side to avoid a thrust. Haru knelt behind her to retrieve the knife she had left behind, and she plunged the one he had handed off into the wrist of her attacker. She twisted it on the withdrawal and turned to the next body that offered itself to her.

There was chaos and blood and this, only this. Her body moved, honed in on allies and enemies alike. Without needing to see, she still knew where they stood. Osawa guarded Isco and Astar in a back corner, the tether of the water as thick and blue as it had always been. She couldn't see it but she could feel it there, stronger than others, grasping for acknowledgement. Yassen fought with him, heavy and slow but accenting Osawa's light maneuverings.

Kanna flung her knife at an attacker at Vahn's back.

Vahn turned, tossing one of his own set her way, then retrieved the knife that had buried itself near him.

Haru was blunt and brutal, doing as much damage with bare limbs as with knives. Vahn moved similar to Kanna, vicious and cutting, quick and always lethal. Having them with her was like an extension of herself.

The enemy was thinning, but they wouldn't have much time before Yassen's walls were breached. His ability was uncanny, but the earth would eventually yield.

Kanna kicked out, her foot landing in the chest of an assailant. He stumbled back into Haru, who yanked back his head and slid his knife over the man's throat. .

She turned as Vahn finished the last of the combatants and the man gasped, the blood gurgling in his lungs before the light faded from them.

In the quiet that followed, the rain played a muffled rhythm against the shingled roof of the temple. It hit the leaded glass windows in an accompanying melody. Haru, Vahn, and Osawa were calm, their eyes locked on her. They seemed more sure that she would get them out of this than she was. The same look was reflected on Yassen.

Isco was pale, and Astar's hands shook around a bloodied knife. She looked down at her hand and released it, letting it clatter to the stone floor.

Kanna glanced at the knives in her own hands. In her right was a smooth, natural wood handle, the wood darkened over time by the oils from Vahn's hands. In her left was a black blade.

Vahn offered her her own black handled knife, and they switched weapons.

"Vahn, Haru," Kanna said, pausing a moment to swallow her dread. "And Yassen. Take Isco and Astar. There are shorter buildings along this road—go through them, behind them, I don't care, but get them to that yellow one on the corner."

Haru switched the natural wood blade he held with Vahn for his own white one, then sluiced the blood from the blades off on his jeans.

"The saloon?" Isco offered.

"I could use a drink," Astar said.

Kanna frowned at her hands, turned the twinned black blades over in her palms. "You can have a drink when people aren't trying to kill us."

From the corner of her eye, a white handled blade was offered. Kanna followed it to Haru. Her fingers brushed his as they swapped blades, a shock extending through her fingertips. When she held the white blade in her left once again, there was balance in the uneven weight of them.

"I'm taking Osawa," she said, unlocking her eyes from Haru's and turning to the group. "We're going up the bell tower."

"Kanna," Haru attempted to interject.

"We'll draw their attention."

"It should be me," Haru said when she finished. "I should be with you."

Kanna clenched her jaw, shaking her head. She wasn't the one who needed him right now. "None of you are as agile as Osawa, and I need someone that can keep up. Besides," she waved her hand toward the storm battered windows. "He is the best of us."

Haru's gaze was cold but determined. He would do as she asked. He was a good soldier. Kanna sheathed her blades, but her feet wouldn't walk away. She turned back, crossing the distance between them.

Kanna twisted her fingers in the front of Haru's shirt, felt the splatters of blood that was hidden by the black cloth, and pulled. Haru gave no resistance, his body bending to her. Their lips met, and his fingers tangled at the back of her hair and brought her closer. The contact lasted only long enough, and not nearly long enough.

Kanna backed up a step, taking one last look at those that stood with her, each one of them stronger than she could ever be but, for some reason, relying on her to find a way through this.

While not all temples were the same, Kanna knew enough about them. At the front of the nave, she felt along the side wall of the dark temple until she found the handle for the door. She cracked it open, allowing in a sliver of grey light. Sheets of rain fell into the alley, misting into the temple and darkening the stone at the threshold. With part of Salinae's troops spent on the attack on the temple and the rest being held momentarily behind Yassen's construct, the way was clear.

Haru eased out first, pressing his back against the outside wall. Yassen followed, moving past him, with Astar and then Isco.

At the door, Vahn stopped. He kept his hands at his side, but when he met her eyes, he spoke in an ancient language that was as familiar as her blood. "*Do not let the gods greet you, K.*"

Kanna reached up, pulling down the back of his neck and rising on her toes until his forehead met hers. "*They will wait for us much longer.*" Kanna stepped back, pushing Vahn towards the door. "Take care of each other."

Vahn slipped out, rain steaming off his shoulders, and Kanna shut the door behind him.

Finding the access to the belltower took a bit more work. She and Osawa set to searching the chancel of the temple. Osawa found a switch beneath the low set altar that, when triggered, caused the inset sepulcher to creak forward.

At least the dank hall behind it wasn't riddled with webs, unlike the halls leading to the bells of the Tower. Its bells had long grown silent, and caretakers tended to shuffle the keeping of the halls further down their lists of duties. However, the town of Pyrgolis maintained their old traditions. For an instant, she wondered what had happened to the residents.

She didn't allow herself more than an instant to dwell on it.

Following the grey slant of light at the end of the hall, they came into a square channel that went straight up. At the center, the bell's chain wavered in the storm.

Osawa sighed. "I was hoping for stairs."

"I assumed there wouldn't be." Kanna pressed her palms against the walls, testing the surface for purchase.

"You know what they say about assuming things."

Kanna stopped her prodding and tilted her head. "I don't. Am I supposed to?"

Osawa adjusted his glasses to better study their path. "Nevermind."

Kanna followed his gaze through the gloaming light, the bell looming above them in shadow. "You first. I can call the shadows to catch you if needed."

Osawa pushed up the long cotton sleeves of the tightly woven shirt he'd opted for when the weather shifted and secured his knit hat down further over his ears. "That's a good incentive to not fall."

He rubbed his hands together before stepping back to get a running lead. He started on one wall, leaping across the narrow channel, launching across it to move back and up with each subsequent jump.

Kanna waited below, ready for if he would slip. But Osawa's movements were sure, and he took the last leap and caught himself on the ledge, then pulled himself over. When his head peered back over the square at the top of the channel, Kanna began her own ascent.

The rough walls gave her feet purchase, her hands pressing against them as she braced herself with each jump. Her mind cleared and she focused on the back and forth, the way the muscles in her calves and thighs tightened and pushed off the stone, burning ever more with each jump.

She fell short on the last leap, and her nails skidded off the top of the ledge. Osawa caught her, grasping above her elbows and leveraging her to the belltower floor. They fell into a tangled heap, and Kanna rolled onto her back while they caught their breath.

The weathered copper bell hung almost even with the floor they sprawled on, its face green and foggy. The clapper swung with the wind of the storm and their disturbance, but not enough to issue a warning.

Rolling onto her stomach, Kanna pulled herself over the bell tower floor. It was thick with years of dust turned to dirt, and the rain that slanted through the open arches of the tower turned it into a thin mud beneath them. While Kanna had a view of the town from the road, the myriad heights of the buildings had blocked her sightlines. Careful to keep herself low, she peeked through the arches surrounding the bell.

The storm didn't help. The weather had been dry, and the cold rain created a haze in the air, kicking up dust and mustering a thick fog. She could see past the intersection, though. An office building was past the yellow saloon, a clinic on the other side, and the road dead-ended at a train station. There wasn't much room for cover, but an escape could be made if they managed to get clear of the town.

She pulled her head down, leaning back against the stone. "Salinae is commanding from the general store roof, staying clear."

"The others?"

Kanna shut her eyes and sought the lines of power. She could pick out Haru and Vahn as they moved along the south side of the street. They were familiar and distinct, like a favorite line of poetry moving in the dark. The rest were individual but unrecognizable. "Strong grouping of water loas near him. Some fire gathered further away, probably near the train depot." She opened her eyes. "One air. One earth, besides Yassen. Moving toward the side street."

"Probably Ira, and his sister, Kenzi."

Kanna raised a brow at Osawa. "Why is Ira here?" Osawa hesitated, and didn't answer. The odds that Ira would be here accidentally were slim. "Doesn't change what we have to do," she said, a small comfort to herself. "Most are concentrated here, but there are archers near the train station."

Osawa snorted. "He hasn't learned anything new."

"Nope." It was Salinae's way: to throw as many people onto blades and traps as possible, seeking to overwhelm the enemy in the first strike. "Ready?"

Beside her, Osawa unsheathed his blades, his hands flexing over the smooth viridian grips. "Am I ever?"

Kanna smiled, slow and half-lit. "Always."

Kanna stepped onto the slick open ledge of the bell tower and leaned out into the storm. The rain lashed against her face, instantly chilling her skin. The sky above crackled with lighting, and for an instant her heart thudded in her chest as another moment, another time flashed and overlaid itself onto the present.

Below, Yassen's walls had crumbled under the onslaught of the water loas. The soldiers squeezed through the opening, crowding at the other side. They were once at her back, under her command. Once, she had used their numbers to crush others beneath an empire, and now the weight was turned on her. There were the expected shouts when she was spotted, forces redirecting their focus.

Kanna leapt onto the slanted roof of the temple, her heels digging into the asphalt shingles to help slow her descent as they crumbled and cascaded around her. When she reached the ledge, the shadows met her and slowed her fall. They released her reluctantly when her boots settled into the mud road. Settling around her ankles, the shadows waited her command.

If Kanna could not find a way through, she would make one.

# 40

# REPRIEVE

## HARU

AFTER PARTING with Kanna and Osawa, Haru led his group behind a long line of squat storefronts. After darting across an open alley, he waited at the other side for the others to pass, swapping positions with Vahn in an attempt to get a view of the street.

Peering through the narrow opening between the temple and the store fronts, he watched as the wall that Yassen constructed crumbled. He brushed back his hair as it attempted to tangle in his face, using the rain to slick it back and keep it out of his eyes. He was still distracted by his search for Kanna when he heard the cracking of a door frame. Turning to the sound, he caught sight of Yassen slipping behind the others into a back door of one of the stores.

Haru rushed to follow across the second alley and into the building. Inside, the room was stifling with heat. Half finished blades sat on a workbench, some with their handles clamped in vises. In another area, a covered drum sat in front of a wall of bows in various stages of completion.

Shouts arose from outside, and Haru tripped across the cluttered workroom to the front windows. Through a haze of grime, he made out Kanna and Osawa's arrival in the street. The rain offered Osawa endless support, and with Kanna taking the lead, they were a powerhouse of destruction. They were quick and unpredictable, using surprise to break Salinae's heavy assault tactics.

They had their mission, and Haru had his. Tearing himself away from watching the brawl in the street, Haru eyed the other direction. They were closer to the junction, but there was still open ground to cover in order to cross.

"Do we have an opening?"

Haru whirled to face Vahn, irritated that he had managed to sneak up on him. The man was like a wild cat, surefooted and stealthy. While Kanna and Vahn both reminded him of predators, Vahn was a different kind of animal all together. Of them all, he was the only one that insisted on continuing to wear white. Now he was soaked in both rain and blood, the cloth sticking to the lines of his ribs and jut of his shoulders.

Not all the blood on him was the enemies'. Haru's eyes caught on Vahn's side where a swathe of red was forming on the wrong side of the fabric.

Vahn lifted a brow, but before he could smirk he followed Haru's line of sight. "Right... figured that's where the stinging was coming from."

Isco ducked under Vahn's arm, prodding the spot. Vahn winced, but lifted his arm to give the medic access in a practiced motion.

Too practiced. Haru grit his teeth. "When?"

"Must've pulled it open just now," Vahn said with a shrug to Haru, then glanced down at Isco. "How are your hands warm?"

"I told you to be careful," Isco said, his annoyance palpable.

"That isn't what I was asking, Vahn." Haru turned his glare to the medic. "You knew?"

Isco had the gall to turn his attention from his patient long enough to glare at Haru before returning to his observations.

"I'm sure there's some confidentiality thing," Vahn said.

"Look what I found!" Astar crowed from across the room. Her exclamation pulled Haru's attention to the other two in their group. Astar held a complete composite bow aloft in triumph.

"I found a knife," Yassen added, revealing his own prize. "Now I have two things. I'm like a Pally boy now."

Yassen swung his blades together, but the weight of his khopesh made the movement awkward. Astar snatched the knife from his hand and tucked it into the loop of his belt for him.

"I'll put a quick pressure bandage on this for now." Isco reached for his shoulder, but his palm flattened against it. Isco then looked around himself, then patted his hands against his pockets, before looking up, eyes wide and voice numb. "I don't have my bag."

"Where did you have it last?" Vahn asked, with a notable lack of teasing in his voice as he attempted to focus the medic.

"It was on Mud," Isco continued, his words beginning to lose their confidence and return to his typical nervous shake. "My supplies are soaked through by now. They'll be near useless."

Haru pressed his fingers into his temples. "What good is a medic without supplies?"

Isco's back straightened. "I'll find something here. Give me a moment."

"I can probably scorch it closed," Vahn said, his hand moving to cover the wound.

Isco grabbed Vahn's wrist and pulled his hand away. "No," he said, a different panic in his tone. "You're not doing that. I can fix this."

Vahn's eyes narrowed on Isco. "Find something, then."

"Be quick about it," Haru snapped, but Isco had already turned his back and set himself to rummaging through the room's contents.

Haru turned his anger to Vahn. "Did you really think you could hide that from Kanna? You thought she wouldn't know?"

Vahn let his shirt fall back, shrugging. "She seemed preoccupied with you. Didn't seem to really care about much else."

Haru shook his head. "You like to think you know her more than anyone else, yet you can't be bothered to consider anything outside of yourself, can you? Why do you think she didn't take you or I with her?"

"She said it herself," Vahn replied through clenched teeth. "The elements are in Osawa's favor, not ours right now."

Haru stepped back. "Keep lying to yourself, Vahn. That's worked out so well for you thus far."

Vahn's eyes narrowed, but before he could put together a misdirecting retort they were interrupted by the sound of metal screeching as Isco wrest a battered metal first-aid kit from the wall.

Isco opened it while still in motion, pulling out the things he could use and dropping the rest with a clatter onto a nearby workbench. Without a word, he returned to Vahn's side with his procured supplies, motioning for Vahn to move his shirt.

There was a tense silence, which Vahn broke. "No, really. This rain is freezing. How are your hands warm?"

Isco sighed, and for once Haru was in agreement with the medic.

"The forge is still going," Isco said, not looking away from his work. "My hands were cold, so I warmed them while you two were arguing and those two were shopping."

Haru walked over to the corner that Isco had indicated. The blacksmith's coal forge smoldered, left to burn out on its own when the residents of the town fled.

Vahn joined him, and he held his hand out over it. The flames leapt back to life, rising to caress his fingertips. He turned to Haru, his smirk returning. "That'll work."

# 41

# THE COST OF TIME

## KANNA

THERE WAS an ease to the shadows. Kanna hadn't noticed the difference before, but with her memories returning, she was able to recognize it. Before it was like moving a thick oil, a viscous clinging thing. Now they were slick and whispery, feather light and almost delicate.

They danced at her fingertips, marionettes tied to unfathomable strings. She wove them through the soldiers that attacked, past the forward charge that Osawa hammered with vicious slicing waves, to the ones further back. She left the shadows to slow their feet and their hearts, disrupting their plans to overwhelm.

Osawa battered the line, holding them back from attacking at once. It allowed Kanna to weave through those that broke through, tearing through them one by one. She didn't bother to try and go through the Palamidia's light armor, going around it instead. Kanna ducked under a soldier's curving slash, and drove a knife up. She slipped beneath the white armor where it failed to hug against the curve of their waist, and yanked back.

The mud beneath her feet thickened with blood, and she felt the rain flutter against her skin. Kanna ducked down again, and Osawa unleashed a volley above her that pierced through another grouping that had gathered too close.

Kanna braced her feet in the mud against the current that Osawa pulled. She sprung up, and drove her blade through the underside of an attacker's jaw.

A jubilant voice broke through, drowning out her opponent's last breath. "Cousin!"

Masao held his arms wide and, despite the rain, was dry as bone. The water streamed around his body, warping around him.

Kanna regrouped with Osawa as the remaining Palamidia soldiers moved back, parting around Masao and another. Kanna's eyes slid from him to the woman at his side. Masao reeked of darkness, but there was nothing about the woman that Kanna could twist or untwist. She was a believer, her faith true and unrelenting.

At her side, Osawa shifted his weight. "Masao."

Kanna shoved her sodden hair from her eyes and ground her teeth together. Osawa hadn't shared with them whatever had happened in the camp, but he didn't have to. Kanna knew pain, knew fear, knew how it felt when it slept next to her. He carried a darkness at the surface, and it would take time to set that right again.

Kanna reached out with the shadows, but not the ones that seethed in the air. The ones inside, the ones that hid in the dark reaches of the soul. She wanted to awaken the well of pain inside of Masao, turn the suffering he caused back on him.

Masao staggered, clutching at his heart, and bent over. The woman stepped back, her black eyes narrowing as Masao braced his hand on his knee to steady himself.

Then, he laughed.

Kanna stumbled back, stopping only when she nearly collided with Osawa.

Nothing. There had been nothing there. Despite the darkness that surrounded him, Masao remained unbothered. She couldn't turn horror onto someone that couldn't know it.

Masao righted and rolled his shoulders. He shook himself off then stretched his neck until the bones cracked. "Tickles. Nice try, though."

The woman at Masao's side relaxed, her piercing stare returning to Kanna.

"Oh, not sure you two have met." Masao indicated the woman at his side. "This is Nissa. Nissa, this is Legatus Ananke Strepheim." Nissa didn't react, so Masao continued. "The Shadowed Sun? The Last Eclipse?"

She narrowed her gaze on Kanna. "Heretics deserve no names."

Masao stopped his forward approach, and glanced down. With the tip of his boot, he turned over one of the bodies that had fallen face first into the street. "What about her?"

Osawa's light touch at Kanna's elbow settled her. "Let him talk. It'll buy time."

Nissa's gaze flickered to the body, and back to Kanna. "Her name was Tarin."

"Aw, poor Tarin." Masao crouched by the body and brushed back the long brown hair that stuck to her face. "Wasn't she the one with the secret boyfriend in Ilma's regiment? She was a pretty girl, but this? This is art." He whistled, as if impressed. "Up the underside of the jaw, through the soft palate and then *tch*"—he clicked his tongue—"into the brain."

Kanna was trying to sort the emptiness, locate it, but she couldn't. Her efforts ricocheted off screams and the warmth of blood on her hands.

Masao stood from the ground, making a show of looking in each direction. "Where are your buddies? Can't wait to meet the fresh ones after we're done here."

Kanna's grip tightened on her knives. The rain was cold, the ground was slick, and she turned to Osawa. "That is enough time."

Osawa folded his sleeves back over his elbows. "Masao is mine."

# 42

# A FRIEND OF THE DARK

## VAHN

VAHN HADN'T BEEN able to slip the low fever that had settled in him after Ira's sister injured him in the raid against the Palamidia camp. They had traveled quickly, the motion not allowing his body to settle and rest. Vahn ran hot normally, his body always burning, but the spike was annoying. With his internal temperature fluctuating, it made it more difficult to focus his control.

"I'll keep the flames lower so they last in the storm, but we have to stay down." Having the forge meant he could put his effort into directing the energy where it was needed, burning low and hot like chemical fire so it would resist being put out by the rain. He looked behind himself where the others were lining up. "Especially you, big guy."

Yassen gave a thumbs-up for acknowledgement, which Vahn returned, and he hunched over. Vahn nodded to Haru, who kicked open the door of the smith before leaping out of the way.

Vahn's body heated as it channeled the fire, his head going light. But he tempered the flame and focused. It licked under his skin, a cleansing burn against the frigid shell and the dirt of him. The line of fire drug across the floor of the blacksmith's and through the door, growing high when it reached the outside. It sizzled in the rain but he tended it well, coaxing the heart of it to burn.

The fire served as cover, but it also alerted the soldiers lying in wait. Haru took the lead as they raced across the line, staying down to avoid the hail of arrows from the saloon's roof.

On the other side of the flames, Kanna and Osawa faced Masao and another in a pile of the dead. Vahn hoped Kanna's rabble collection had the sense to find safety and stay there. Except for Yassen, they mostly served as dead weight and distraction in a fight.

He and Haru moved first, cutting a path through the soldiers to get to the back of the saloon. Vahn didn't know how Kanna planned to make it there with Osawa, but he trusted she had an idea. They'd always trusted each other, and more than their abilities or skill, it was what had kept them alive.

This close to the saloon's front, the archers could no longer get an angle on them. The archers attempted to shoot down, but the arrows caught on the building's rough shingled sides or pinged off of protruding window frames and balconies.

Vahn slashed at one of his attackers, but he jumped back. Vahn grabbed him by the arm and twisted under it, burying his knife into the man's side before moving to the next.

A yelp behind him caught his attention and he turned as Isco came under attack. Isco was stumbling, weaving between the white of the soldier's uniforms and the flash of blades.

Vahn turned his attack in Isco's direction, grabbing the woman that had him cornered from behind and sliding his knife against her throat before letting the body drop.

Vahn sheathed one of his blades and grabbed Isco by the front of his shirt, dragging him behind him. He slammed Isco against the side of the saloon beneath one of the protected balconies. "Stay."

Isco nodded. His pupils were blown wide with panic, but they shot over Vahn's shoulder. Vahn turned to follow his gaze, and an arrow buried itself in the neck of the soldier that was attempting to attack him from behind.

Vahn followed the track of it to Astar, who nodded to him before grabbing another handful of castoff arrows and turning to aim up at the archers leaning over the roof. She fired in quick succession, and the bodies of the archers above fell to the ground, a single arrow in each.

At least they didn't have to worry about her so much.

With Vahn's attention turned away from the flames, they had begun to wane. Through them, he caught sight of Kanna and Osawa in the center of the main street. Osawa was holding off Masao, sending waves of water and scattershot in one breath, turning Masao's attacks back at him in another.

Vahn didn't recognize the woman that Kanna fought. She was nimble and controlled, but predictable. Yet, Kanna's movements were heavy, each one ever so slightly off, a breath late. There was a haze around her, blunting the instinctual sharpness Vahn had come to know as if it was his own. Never questioning, always knowing. The only other soul they could trust on this gods-forsaken plane.

Before, they had known each other better than they knew themselves, two feral lost things against the world.

Kanna was too slow. Kanna was looking for something, missing her opponent's tells.

After they found Kanna again, Vahn wasn't sure who she was. She was both an old self and a new one, and neither had the time for him. Vahn wanted to reach her, but he wasn't who she needed. He never had been. Vahn's gaze found Haru as he tossed another assailant over the railing in front of the saloon with brutal efficiency.

Vahn turned back to Kanna. There was a panic in her eyes and she was lost, trapped in the battle and nothing else. Not even this battle, but somewhere else. Some other place and time was pulling her down.

Kanna had always been cold to the touch. The shadow's kept her chilled, shivering, especially when she hadn't yet learned to keep them off her back.

Vahn had. Vahn stoked the flames and they snapped to attention. For the briefest of moments, Kanna met his gaze and her eyes cleared, and he smiled across the distance for her. A reminder that he was still here, and would always be.

Kanna knocked her attacker back and returned his smile, her eyes focused, her guard falling for him. But then they hardened, and she jerked her attention to something else, something no one else could sense.

Vahn followed her eyes as an arrow came from the roof of the general store, whizzing over his shoulder and cutting into the side of his neck. A second followed, burying itself in his thigh. His leg buckled beneath him from the hit, from the pain that exploded from that steel point, and his knee sunk into the ground.

The attack was not finished. It wouldn't stop, he knew. He raised his arm in an attempt to block, and a third arrow split through his forearm and lodged between the bones.

Vahn fell forward. He felt the mud beneath his hand when he tried to catch himself, and he slipped across it. The heat drained from his body, the fire leaving him as the flames he had tempered and tended were extinguished by the sheets of rain.

Vahn felt only the cold, the chill of the fabric that clung to his skin. He dug the heel of his good leg into the muck to roll himself over as another arrow sunk in the ground where his chest had just been, biting back the howl as his punctured arm tangled under his body and the arrow shaft snapped under the force.

His vision spotted as he tried to push himself up from the ground with his good arm. It wouldn't do, being like this. Not when she could see. Not while she watched. She'd replay it, over and over, add it to her tally of burdens. His elbow shook, and he fell back to the mud.

Vahn had imagined better deaths than this, but it seemed appropriate in its own kind of way. He was born from the mud of Atarrabi, it was right that he should die in it.

If only she weren't a witness.

Vahn saw every bead of rain fall, watched it hit the ground and break apart on the rebound, the dying orange of the fire's light reflecting in the scattering drops.

The ground beneath him shook and the earth leapt where the fires once danced. It was solid, barely a scorch left to mark that it had ever burned. Large hands wrapped around Vahn's arms and dragged him from the mud, but it didn't matter much anymore. He shut his eyes against the rain and the world faded into an echo, something far away that couldn't wreck him anymore.

It was dark, but that was all right.

The dark was a friend of his.

# 43

## A SHORT DISTANCE, A LONG WAY

### KANNA

LIGHTNING FLASHED, and Kanna flickered between memory and present with each strobe of it. They were in Gegenes, then Atarrabi, and back again. She was on the walls, she was on the ground, and the rain was cold and the world was thick with bodies and blood.

Osawa kept Masao at bay, focusing on his cousin as the rain pummeled the street. He gave as much as he got, if not better. Masao was chaos, but Osawa was a controlled and daring current.

Kanna tried to focus on that steady point, that simple connection, but she couldn't find an anchor. The dead still clattered, and she could feel their names as they carved their way through the Neither, grabbing at the corners of the dark in a plea to stay.

A warmth at her back pushed away the shadows, shaking her from remembrance long enough to regain the upper hand. She kicked out, knocking Nissa out of range.

Kanna looked back to the flames and caught Vahn's eye. The burning violet glinted, the practiced smirk turning to something real and she couldn't help but smile back. Even in the madness, in the mess of it all, he stood steady with her, and that was something that felt right in all this wrongness.

But then, she felt a dark intent. It wasn't the same as in Ganglere, not some kind of corrupted belief. This was twisted passion, anger and disgust. She tried to follow it, but it was too late.

Arrows struck Vahn, her heart thudding and sinking deeper with each hit. As he struggled to rise the fires that had burned so fiercely, that kindling that had kept them both alive, extinguished.

There were shouts of voices she recognized and the earth heaved, blocking her view. Her breath came rapid and quick, her feet sticking in the mud as the world narrowed and blurred.

Osawa cried out at her back and she turned in time to see him take a blow from Masao, tumbling off a wave that he had been riding and rolling over the ground. His body hit, and skidded.

They had to get out of this place.

The sky flashed with light and the landscape lost its color. The rain turned to shards and fell, thousands of cuts that tore bodies asunder and all she could do was watch and bleed and fade.

She had to get them out of this place, or there was no point in any of it.

As Masao readied another blow, Kanna moved.

Or, the ground moved beneath her.

The shadows came in droves, gathering in a thick miasma as they responded to her desperation. She fell over Osawa, and they fell together, toppling through the ground and into the black of the Neither.

There was a lifetime in a moment. Shades of things passed and yet to come, the world folding and unfolding in a way that wasn't meant to be understood.

Kanna realized, too late, that Osawa shouldn't be there.

But she was the dark, and it would do as she willed.

The ineffable silence broke, the world ripped, and she dragged him with her through and out.

# 44

## OLD WORDS

### HARU

WHEN VAHN FELL, the group moved in. Yassen pulled Vahn from the mud, leaving Astar to cover their retreat while Haru cut through the rest of those that stood between them and their resting point. Behind the saloon, Haru pressed his fingers to his lips and whistled, a two-toned shrill that brought the horses to them. Yassen raised walls, creating a makeshift cover and casting the party into the dark.

Haru called the light. It came out of the dark, glittering and shifting like motes of ghostlight. He bound it together above them, lighting the cavern. Amon tossed his head, agitated by the confinement, but the other horses only shifted with the sudden light.

When Yassen lowered Vahn to the ground, the jarring movement brought him back to consciousness with a pained groan.

Haru sensed Kanna's arrival before it happened. He jumped back and turned as Osawa and Kanna tumbled into their makeshift cavern, falling sideways from nothing. Kanna didn't pause, racing to Vahn and dropping on her knees in front of him. Osawa teetered upon reentering the world, and Haru caught him as he tripped forward.

Kanna's grip twisted in Vahn's shirt, her lips forming his name though no sound escaped.

"Hey there, K." Vahn lifted a bloody hand, brushing his thumb over her cheek. "What's with that face? You're not the only one that's hard to kill."

She wrapped her hand around his wrist, her fingertips overlapping around the bone.

"What was that place?" Osawa asked, looking up to Haru. "Is that where you go?"

Haru glanced away from Kanna to Osawa and back, only to do a double-take. Kanna's panic pulled at his spine, but he recognized his own as it rose. He dug his fingers into Osawa's shoulders, trying to anchor him to the earth, the land, anything.

Osawa's eyes were brown. Haru had known them since they were children. "You're verging," Haru said, because it was the only explanation he could think of.

Osawa turned his hands over, studying them. "No. I'm not."

"Your eyes are *blue*."

"I'll have to take your word for it." He was steady as he looked past Haru's shoulder with eyes like ocean depths. "Vahn—"

Astar lunged across the small cavern, wrapping her arms around Osawa's waist and burying her head in his neck. "At least you're all right."

Osawa's arms were out at his sides but he slowly relaxed, patting Astar awkwardly. "I am, but what happened to Vahn?"

Isco fumbled with the clasp of his belt before pulling it free and, without a word, he leaned over and wrapped it above the arrow in Vahn's thigh.

"Still no dinner?" Vahn asked, but the pain in his voice thinned the joke. Further comment was cut short when Isco tightened the belt. Vahn yelped in the back of his throat but clenched his jaw to keep the sound in.

Yassen wrapped his arms around Kanna's waist and pulled her away as her teeth snapped at the medic.

Isco didn't even flinch at the attack. He pulled the gauze from the blacksmith's kit from his pocket and, with shaking hands, he began to unwind it. "Maybe when you aren't bleeding."

Vahn grinned, but it was strained. He leaned his head back against the rough exterior of the saloon, his eyes drifting shut. "Never, then."

Kanna managed to wriggle out of Yassen's grip and drop back to the ground, swearing in Ilazkin and scrambling over to Vahn. She held his face between her hands, then pulled back and slapped him.

The sting of it woke him from his stupor. "Ow," he grumbled, blinking back to consciousness.

"*You stay,*" she commanded.

Haru knew the language, could understand it, but forming the words to sentences had been something he struggled with.

Kanna crouched low, turning Vahn to meet her eyes. "*That dark is not yours.*"

Vahn smiled weakly, lifting his good arm to grasp her elbow while Isco tightened a tourniquet on his injured one. "*My dark is not finished with me.*"

Osawa disentangled himself from Astar and retrieved Isco's bag, handing it over to the medic. Isco rummaged through it, his frustration growing with every sodden bandage his hands came across. The rain had ruined the supplies, even if he had anything to treat drastic wounds.

"What do you need?" Haru asked.

"Gauze," Isco said, throwing up his hands before diving back into his bag as he tried to dig for more as if there was another bottom to it, one that would open and reveal an outfitted medicium. "Antibiotics. A bovie, an imaging machine, everything." He shoved the bag away. "Anything."

Kanna's focus remained on Vahn. She clutched his wrist with one hand, pressing it to her chest, the other supporting his face. She spoke to him quietly, in that ancient language. Vahn's lips were turned into a soft smile, a thing lacking arrogance and harsh lines. She kept him there though his eyes threatened to drift shut, and Haru was reminded once again why he followed her. Why he would always follow her.

Haru turned to Isco. "There's a veterinary clinic across the street from here."

"I'm not a pet," Vahn managed to utter.

"*<Nir vhak>.*" The hissing cadence of the language transformed into something quick and precise. There was no venom in Kanna's tone, but Vahn quieted.

Isco shook his head. "They would have something, at least."

Haru nodded. "Let's go, then."

## 45

---

# TRUCE

## HARU

IN THE OPEN alley near the saloon, nature's primordial quiet had taken hold. The Palamidia's soldiers were regrouping, struggling to find their exact position. Bodies rushed and moved in the town, but the clamor and chaos of the ambush had reached a stalemate.

The rain and dark helped them maintain cover, but at the same time it made it difficult to determine what they would be up against to cross the narrow side street. Haru wasn't able to make out much of anything. He leaned back in, shutting his eyes and slamming his head against the saloon's exterior wall. "Can't see."

Behind him, the medic shivered occasionally. Haru wasn't sure if it was from the cold of the rain or fear, and he wasn't going to ask.

Osawa bent around the corner. His now blue eyes turned toward the train station, then back to the intersection before retreating. "The train station is guarded. There are people moving in the windows there but nothing in the smaller buildings. No one is in the open, but there are still archers pacing the roof of the saloon."

Haru raised a brow at Osawa, who shrugged.

Haru cleared his throat. "They'll know once we move the general location of the others, so we have to be quick. Are you sure they have what you need?"

"They'll have it." Isco's jaw was clenched to stop the chattering, his eyes were wild, but there was a determination in it born from needing to believe.

"Fine," Haru relented. "But do not get in my way."

"I'll take Astar out far enough to take out their archers then get back to cover the others," Osawa offered.

Haru nodded. "On your mark, then."

Osawa stretched out his fingers, and the water that pooled on the Atarrabi ground heeded his call. In a subtle pull, it began to gather, until he had enough to work. He turned to Astar and motioned for her to move behind him.

They darted into the open area. Osawa called the water to shield Astar, opening it as she turned and fired at the roof.

The arrow clattered against the stone.

"Higher," he coached, "and to the left."

She drew once more, and her next shot hit true.

Haru led Isco behind the barrier, keeping them safe while in the archer's range. Shouts went up as soldiers from the train station began to muster, but they reached the door of the clinic before the soldiers descended.

Haru slammed his heel into the door and it blew back and open. He grabbed Isco and shoved him ahead into the dark clinic before following, shutting the door behind them and leaning against it.

In the veterinary office, lightning flashes glinted off of shelves of bottles, each labeled and aligned in neat rows. Isco squinted and ran his fingers over the labels as he scoured the bottles, filling his hands and dumping his selections onto the open counter. He was pulling out a drawer along the back wall of the clinic when the door next to him opened.

A female soldier entered, blonde curls tangled and clinging to her neck. There was something familiar in the citrine eyes that met Haru's in surprise, but he couldn't place it. Behind her, a handful of others crowded into the space. The man on her right recovered in a flash and dove for the closest target.

Haru knew that he wouldn't make it in time. He could see every action falling, cascading into the next, everything failing in this one moment.

Without Isco, he wasn't sure that Vahn would survive.

If Vahn didn't survive, they would lose Kanna to the dark.

Haru moved, but the woman was faster.

Her arm wrapped around the neck of the soldier that struck out at Isco, her knife burying to the hilt in the soldier's side.

The soldier gasped, anger and betrayal in his eyes as he met a mix of horror and near disbelief in hers. Her expression hardened and she twisted the knife.

Haru was already across the room when one of the soldiers at her back went for the woman. His hand overlapped the attacker's face and he pushed him back into the corner of the clinic's workbench, his skull cracking against the steel table.

Isco didn't waste the opening. When his immediate threat was cleared, he once again began pillaging the clinic and piling his finds together.

With his unexpected ally, Haru and the woman made fast work of the remaining soldiers. The woman turned against her own people, and though her movements were not untrained they were stiff. Her body wasn't used to combat, the memory of it not yet etched into her. The basic skill was enough, though, to handle the quick skirmish.

The cramped clinic wasn't the best place for a fight. Isco ducked between the soldiers, weaving through the action and grabbing supplies. His hand darted out to grasp a stack of something on the counter and he yanked back with his prize just before Haru slammed another soldier against the wall.

The last of the errant soldiers handled, Haru turned and leveled his knives on the woman.

She was doing the same.

The woman's fingers loosened then tightened on her blades as she shifted, and Haru followed her stance as she circled away from Isco. She kept her blades out, but she backed away slowly before dropping her guard and darting out the back door, disappearing into the storm.

Isco wrapped his supplies, tying them together inside of a plastic sheet before sweeping them into his bag.

Haru should have gone after the woman, but there wasn't time for it. Instead he relaxed his stance and sheathed his knives. "You have what you need?"

Isco threw his bag back over his shoulder and nodded.

Haru stepped across the clinic, glass from shattered bottles crunching beneath his boots. He checked the medic over his shoulder before preparing to open the door. "Stay close this time."

# 46

## LUCKY BREAK

### HARU

When Haru and Isco crossed the street, there were no more archers remaining to pin them down. Haru's every breath was charged, but the obstacles had cleared enough to give them a safe path back.

They met the others in the alley between the saloon and the office next to it. Yassen and Kanna flanked Vahn, holding him in place at the front of Mud's saddle. Vahn's injured arm hung at his side, while his free one twisted in Mud's mane, his knuckles white with the effort of holding to consciousness. The wound in Vahn's thigh had bled through Isco's quick bandaging and ran down the horse's coat, tinting it in red.

"Isco—" Haru turned to tell the man to hold on to Vahn but he was already mounting, taking over his support.

"A train is coming," Kanna said, her eyes focusing past the mayhem and at something beyond that they couldn't see.

They were rounding the side of the office, nearly to the open ground between the town and the tracks, when a figure emerged from the dark. Haru pulled Bia to a stop, angling her to block the others.

Ira had one hand on the side door, his body half out of the building. He scanned over the group, and Haru realized what he had recognized in the woman from the clinic. Ira turned behind him. "No one this way. Check the other side."

Ira met Haru's gaze and nodded. The door shut behind him, the metal lock clicking in place. Not wanting to wait for another encounter, Haru kicked Bia into a gallop. The others followed as they angled away from the town and toward the tracks. Behind them, the soldiers stationed at the train depot mounted and followed.

As Kanna predicted, the single light of a steam engine cut through the dark, the train barrelling along the tracks. Haru felt the rush of wind as it approached their backs. Kanna and Osawa veered closest to the tracks as they caught the downdraft and it pushed them back.

Kanna shifted her feet from Amon's stirrups and crouched on his back, one hand on the reins as she moved him into place. When she was close, she launched from his back and grabbed the service ladder on the side of the train. She climbed up the side of it, giving Osawa room to make the leap across and leave Astar on Julius.

As Kanna crawled to the top of the train and over, Haru strained to keep his eyes on her. He dropped back, even now with the others. The whistle of the train sounded, the brakes of the train screeching as its momentum slowed.

Osawa found handholds in the side of the train and inched himself closer to the back of it, and Kanna appeared on the other side. She hung from the top of the train, her hands on the lip of it and one foot braced on the side. With the other, she kicked at the latch that kept the loading dock of the train closed.

The first kick shifted the bolt, but it stuck. Kanna's body recoiled with the unused force, and Haru's breath caught before she managed to shift her hold and recover.

Osawa held on with one hand, one foot on the ladder and the other hanging into the air as he reached for the latch on his side and pulled it free.

Kanna's second kick loosened the bolt on her side.

The back of the train released, falling from the top and crashing down. Sparks shot up from the tracks as Haru yelled for those behind him. Astar made it into the train first, Julius's hooves hitting the angled door and launching them into the back of the car. Isco followed with Vahn and Mud, then Yassen.

Amon ran in next, and Haru pushed Bia forward. He ducked his head and Bia jumped twice, once to hit the angled metal of the train and a second time to get into the car.

Yassen had already dismounted, and Haru was out of his own saddle the moment Bia entered the car.

Yassen grabbed Osawa's arm and hauled him around the side of the train.

Kanna hung down from the top of the train, and Haru caught her by the waist as she dropped. He turned her body around and covered it with his own as the pursuing army fired a volley of arrows at the back of the train. But they were too far away, the storm too strong.

The chains attached to the metal dock rattled as the train picked up speed. Yassen gripped one side and braced himself against the floor. Haru grabbed the other and, with the help of Osawa, the three heaved on the chains together.

The last soldiers were distant white blots in the night. Beyond them, Pygolis's disheveled vista faded away as the metal door clanged into place.

# PRESSURE

## ISCO

ISCO HAD BEEN TRAINED in the best of institutes, stood out as a prodigy among his peers. This, however, was not something he had prepared for.

Vahn slumped in his arms, the final escape draining whatever had kept him conscious in these last moments. Before Isco could register the dark, there was a static crackling and the train lit. Above, a sphere of light hovered and pulsed, turning with white and gold light and casting the interior of the car in a day-like glow.

Haru reached up to Vahn, grasping him under his shoulders and dragging him from Mud's back while Yassen caught his legs so they wouldn't fall.

"Wait." Isco dismounted clumsily, his foot catching in Mud's stirrup. He struggled to free it. "We need to put him on something clean."

It probably didn't matter in the grand scheme of things, but it was Isco's only chance at normalcy. Wordlessly, Kanna yanked her pack from Amon and dug into it, pulling out the thick white Legatus jacket. She snapped it open and spread it over the train's wood floor.

Haru and Yassen lowered Vahn onto it and Kanna knelt beside him, taking his face between her palms. Isco dropped his supplies as Kanna lowered her forehead to Vahn's, whispering something in the language they had spoken, the one that Isco had heard only once before.

Isco sorted the things in his reach. He would start with the arrow in Vahn's leg, get it out and hope that he could stop the bleeding with what he had.

What he had was some stolen supplies from a veterinary office and the most powerful loas in existence watching him as one of theirs bled out under his hands.

If Vahn didn't make it through this, Haru would kill him.

It was a bad time for Isco to realize that if Vahn didn't make it through this, he wouldn't mind if Haru killed him.

Isco tightened the tourniquet above the wound on Vahn's leg before unwrapping the makeshift bandage, unwinding it around the broken shaft that stuck from his thigh. With steady hands, he pressed to find the location of the arrowhead.

A body was a body. He could fix a body.

He shifted and swallowed, going over contingencies as fast as his mind would work, visualizing the path and where his hands would travel as he doused the wound to clean it.

Vahn was already weak. He was too thin, his body too malnourished to handle the blood loss.

"Light," Isco said to himself. Haru moved the hovering sphere closer, but Isco shook his head before turning to him. "Can it make heat?"

"If I ask it."

Isco turned back to Vahn, the pale stretch of skin over bone.

"He said he could cauterize his wound earlier. Could you do the same? But as a... fixed point. Focused."

Haru paused in thought, then crouched next to Isco. "Yes. Probably."

Before Isco could find a way to argue himself out of the decision, he pulled the arrow free, pressing his hand against it. Isco followed the wound. It was the one thing that he could do. He found the bleed with one hand and grabbed Haru's wrist with the other, guiding him to the spot.

The smell of burning flesh filled the silence in the car, sickly sweet and smokey. Isco tensed at the familiarity of it, tightening his mind on the task at hand and refusing to follow where it wanted to lead.

Haru's work done, he pulled back. Isco rinsed the wound again to check the bleeding. He folded gauze, pressing it against the wound with one hand and binding it down with the other.

He nodded to Osawa to join them. "When I move my fingers, put yours here. Press hard, don't worry about hurting him. If the blood comes through, use another of those gauze pads, but don't remove this one."

Isco switched places with Osawa, who followed his instructions to an exacting degree. But Vahn's blood began to pool out under Osawa's touch, and Isco shoved him back and took over, stemming the flow once again. He turned to glare at Osawa, who stared at his hands.

"It wanted to be with me," Osawa said, his voice awestruck. "The water in it."

"Tell it to stay where it belongs, then."

Osawa's now-navy eyes narrowed. "I don't tell it what to do."

"You do now," Kanna said, her voice flat. Her gaze didn't leave Vahn's face, and her fingers continued brushing the hair at his temples.

Osawa looked up from studying his hands, and nodded. They switched again, but this time Vahn's blood stayed.

Isco moved to the next point, the next thing he could fix, though he kept a running list of possible disasters in his mind. Now at Vahn's arm, there was less of a chance for catastrophe. The arrow had gone through completely, the damage mostly done. Again, Isco unbandaged the field dressing and cleaned the surface.

He breathed, not sure when he had stopped, before continuing.

The arrow shaft removed cleanly and, to Isco's surprise, the bleeding stayed contained. Whatever Osawa was doing had affected not just Vahn's thigh, but the rest of him. Isco wasn't taking chances. He placed a pressure gauze on each side of the wound and taped them in place before nodding to Haru, who pressed his hands where Isco's had been.

The wound on the side of Vahn's neck was superficial, at least. Still, Isco tended it. He needed to keep as much of Vahn's blood in his body as possible. Finished, he pressed his fingers to check Vahn's pulse. It was weak, his heart struggling to keep what little remained in Vahn's body moving.

"It couldn't have been a human hospital with human blood, could it," he said out loud. "Nothing can be that easy."

"Take mine," Kanna said. She released Vahn's face and reached out both of her arms, turning them back like an offering.

Isco shook his head. "That's not how it works." Isco ran his hands through his hair, felt that if he could rip it out then maybe things would be clear. "That isn't how any of this works. There's typing and cross-typing, he could die if you don't match."

"I match."

"You can't know that," Isco snapped. "People develop immunities, they don't just stay the same always. Even if it worked once, doesn't mean it will work now."

"It's Vahn," she insisted. She kept her arms out. "I match."

Isco looked to Vahn. The violet eyes that burned him were shut, dark lashes standing out against skin that had lost its luster.

"It isn't done," he said, grasping for an argument. "It's dangerous. It is unsanctioned."

Kanna lowered her hands to her knees and leaned in. This close, Isco could swear he saw black move in her eyes. "What is more important, your rules, or his life?"

"Just do it," Haru said. When Isco turned to him, he looked away. Haru's jaw was set, concern and determination bridging his eyebrows together.

If Isco did this, Vahn could die.

If he didn't do this, it was more certain that Vahn would die.

Isco dug through the supplies, finding the largest bore needles he had grabbed. He had tubing in his own bag, and thankfully the rain wouldn't have made it useless. He upturned an empty crate, and pointed to it. "Sit."

Kanna reluctantly left her position crouched next to Vahn and settled onto the crate. Isco applied a tourniquet at the top of her arm, pulling it tight against lean muscle before checking the veins on the inside of her elbow.

"Kanna," Haru hissed from his place next to Vahn.

She turned to Haru. "Stay there." She met Isco's eyes as he brought a needle next to her skin. "I'll be fine."

Despite her tone, Kanna's hands shook when the metal contacted her skin. She jumped, then tensed her body to keep it in place. Beneath his hands, Isco could feel her body trying to run, but she refused to let it.

"Hey," Isco said, hoping to distract her while his own heart slammed against his ribs. "How'd you meet Vahn?"

Kanna's body relaxed, if only slightly, her eyes going distant as her head tilted. "I fell from the trees."

"That seems odd," Isco said, keeping his concentration on his work. Kanna was tense beneath his hands, willing to give but unwanting to trust. "Breathe."

The rest of Kanna's body flinched, but she kept her arm still as Isco slid the needle into her vein. Kanna let out the breath she was holding, her hands still shaking. "It does, doesn't it?"

"Seems right, though, considering you two," he said, removing the tourniquet on her arm. "Clench and unclench your fist."

The blood from Kanna's arm moved down the tubing and Isco followed it, waiting until it made it to the end before placing the line in Vahn.

After a moment, nothing happened.

Nothing continued to happen.

"Good," he said. He fell back with a sigh, his legs losing their tension. "Good."

As the moments ticked by, Kanna's arm drooped slightly, and he used his fingertips to prop her up again. He kept his eyes on the line of red connecting the two loas.

Isco looked up from Vahn to the others. Haru's eyes weren't sparking with controlled violence, but there was an edge of danger. He slid them to Kanna and kept them there, his glance softening.

Osawa kept his concentration on Vahn, on keeping the blood where it belonged. The white jacket beneath Vahn's body was soaked in what Isco couldn't save, the red bright against the unforgiving canvas. Vahn's chest rose and fell, each of his ribs moving as his breath stretched beneath them, scattered but present.

Yassen cleared his throat in the corner, breaking the trance they had fallen into. "Sorry," Yassen said when they turned to him. "But, uh, whose train is this?"

The inner door of the car slid open and a woman stood in the doorway, her hand over her eyes to block the light. On her neck, a blackwork mix of florals overlayed tattooed slave bands. "Mine."

## 48

## THE WAY THROUGH

### KANNA

KANNA FOUND peace in the dark.

After Edin discovered them in the back of her train, they had shifted to more comfortable quarters, leaving behind the storage car. But the horses were still there, and it was a quiet place now. She pressed her face into Amon's neck, her eyes shut as the images that had flashed in her mind during the battle resurfaced. Some of them she recognized, but some she didn't, and they moved too fast for her to focus on any.

They lingered on Osawa, hunched over after they retrieved him from the camp.

On Vahn as he fell into the mud.

Haru, the knife coming down against his heart.

She grit her teeth, clenched her fist around her wrist until her nails dug into skin until it broke. The blood welled, the small pain distracting enough to calm the racing thoughts.

The train vibrated beneath her feet, the rough knock over uneven tracks threatening to shake her loose as she made her way through the cars, moving through thick southerly air and stifling confinement. She paused outside the fifth car, the wind whipping around her as she balanced on the junctions, before she slid the door open.

Inside, oil lamps were set at a low glow. The sleeping car was mostly empty space, with wide benches along the sides that could serve as elevated bunks.

Sleep had taken Osawa first. At the back, he was cradled between Yassen and Astar. Astar slept on his arm, her head tucked into his shoulder. Yassen was on his other side, his arms curled around the both of them.

Haru sat on one of the benches, his ankle crossed at his knee and his hands relaxed over it. His eyelids drooped, his eyes soft and unfocused. Instead of looking to her when she entered, it took the closing of the door to jar him back to the present. His head left his palm, his body turning to her though he didn't stand. There were questions, worry, the words unspoken from fear of having her turn away.

Kanna dropped her hand to his shoulder and she felt his body ease under the touch. He took her hand in his, his fingers running over the scars on her knuckles before his brow knit and he turned her hand to the side.

The half-moon slits in the side of her wrist had stopped bleeding, the surface abrasions already knitting back together. He shut his eyes but decided once again to stay silent before opening them. He brought her wrist to his lips, then sat back and covered her hand with his own.

When she pulled away he released her, but she carried with her the comfort.

Closer to the front of the car, Isco slumped on the opposite bench in an exhausted daze, his chin propped in one hand and his elbow on the arm at the bench's end. His arms were clean from his fingers to his elbows, but the rest of him was dotted with spatter of dirt and old blood. There was even a smear across one of his cheeks from wiping the back of his hand against it while he had worked.

Not his blood.

Vahn's head was resting in Isco's lap, his bronze skin sallow as an unlit candle.

Kanna sunk to her knees in front of him. The hand Isco had draped over Vahn's waist tightened before releasing. The familiarity of the motion sunk inside of her. She knew what it was like to want something that she shouldn't have.

She reached out, brushing back the stray silver hairs that had fallen over Vahn's brow and stuck in the fever sweat that broke upon it. His hair had grown out, almost long enough to braid again.

The breath from his lips hit her palm, and it was feathery and static.

Kanna sighed and leaned her head on his chest, her ear against his heart. It was too faint for someone who had always been filled with so much life, but it was there. She shut her eyes and concentrated, hoping that if she willed it enough it would harden and strengthen once more.

"He lost a lot of blood," Isco said, though there was a tremor in his usual stoic delivery. "But he will be all right."

Kanna didn't open her eyes. If she hadn't pushed them to race to Lugos, this wouldn't have happened. But that's what she thought they wanted, that's what she was supposed to do. She'd leapt headfirst without looking, assuming she'd land safely, and forgotten to consider those who would follow. "Are you saying that because I want to hear it, or because you need it to be true?"

Isco's voice caught on something previously unspoken. "Both."

It took a long moment before she was able to tear herself away from listening to Vahn's heartbeat. She sank back on her heels and shifted, pulling her knees to her chest and half burying her face in them. She held onto Vahn's wrist, pressing her fingers as hard as she dared into his pulse.

"Isco?"

He shifted, but her question was acknowledged.

"How do you always know how to do the right thing?"

Isco barked out a laugh, quieting when he realized she had been serious. He picked his chin up and let his hand fall before clearing his throat. "I really don't know what you're talking about."

There was longing in his voice, as if he wanted it to be true that he did, but the idea of it was foreign to him.

"I don't think I've ever done the right thing," Kanna said, the words tiring her. "At least you help. All I do is break. You can fix things."

"Small things, maybe," he said. "A bone, a tear, even a heart is simple if you know how it works. But the world, life. It isn't a simple thing, and sometimes there isn't any way to fix something you broke." Isco sighed, his head falling back and his eyes closing. "But I think you can still try. To be better, at least."

Kanna leaned over, resting her head once again on Vahn's chest, unable to resist the primal comfort of its beating.

She was on a train. She was on a train in Atarrabi, or maybe somewhere else now, but that didn't matter. She was moving south and away from the Empire's borders.

The train was on Lifrasir, which turned under the star of Danu, which was a speck in the universe.

She counted the beats of Vahn's heart. When she lost count, she started over. They were a speck to the universe, yet they held one.

"What am I supposed to do now?" she asked Isco.

His eyes were still shut, his fingers tightening again on Vahn though she wasn't sure if he even knew it happened. "Whatever you can."

# ACT III

## OF MONSTERS & GODS

# 1

# END OF THE KNOWN

## KANNA

AT THE EDGE of the known world, the air carried a warning of storms. From her lookout on the rocky bluffs, Kanna watched the Icaunian sea as the orange haze of the horizon burned away the black shadow of night. The waves held a lingering darkness, though their crests whitened and reflected the sky. Heavy storm clouds were lit from behind, but above them the azure sky was clear and untouched. Kanna stared into the brilliance until her eyes hurt, until the prism of the morning faded and the sky was just a sky, was just a sky like any other.

This far away from the farmhouse, the thoughts and feelings of others were devoured in the crash of salt waves. All that remained was the faint, ever present tangle around her lowest rib, the trace of divinity that led to Haru. The first time, and the last time, she had known a quiet almost like this was when she had woken in Ilazki, but that time she didn't even have her own thoughts for company. She would have preferred that aching silence to what crowded her head now.

After Kanna failed to protect the group in Pyrgolis, Edin delivered them to one of the few outposts in Kirin and gave them directions to a smuggler safehouse. They'd weathered most of the storm season in these narrow wilds, nestled between the sea and the unknown. But wherever she went, she was. After her trips to the Neither, her memories were slipping back unbidden. Old connections from one thing to the next short-circuited and fired off whenever she least expected it. At night, in the day, in silence or in company, there was no difference any more. Where the trail of her memories once led to empty spaces, echoes now lingered.

Beneath her Amon stamped the dirt, shaking his mane to loose the night from it. With the day settled, she needed to return. If she stayed too long, Haru would seek her. He would look at her in that way of his, as if she was something sacred, and she would forget how to breathe, forget what she was supposed to be.

Kanna shifted her weight to turn Amon inland and let him go. If she slipped at these speeds, if she fell, something could break. If Amon managed to throw her she would be trampled, and her last view of this world would be the dusky purple sky. She clung to his mane until her knuckles turned white, urging him faster. The heads of dandelions burst and the morning dew that lingered on in the field kicked up beneath Amon's hooves, wetting the hems of her jeans as the fields blurred by in a haze of greying violet and new green grass.

When the back of the two-story farmhouse came into view, Kanna shifted back to slow Amon. He complied, though grudgingly, attempting to sprint every few paces. Kanna tightened the reins, pulling his head down until he settled.

The house appeared small on the horizon, but she could already feel the lives inside. The conflicting emotions reverberated inside of her until they were all she could feel. She pressed it down until it was a low hum, then further until it was nothing.

Dismounting, she took Amon's reins in hand and opened the gate at the far end of the property. The wood creaked on rusted hinges but she led them through, tying the gate with a frayed rope. After it was secure, she unhooked the leather buckle of Amon's bridle and released him. Free of the bond, he set off at a run to seek the other horses that roamed the property.

Kanna watched as he flashed across the field, darker than shade either in spite or because of the patterns of white that splashed over his hide. She looped the sweat-slick leather reins over her sunwarmed shoulder and shoved her hands into the pockets of her jeans.

Though it was overcast, the sun continued its relentless beat. The moisture in the air warmed and stagnated. The sky rumbled a threat, but it refused to mercifully break the cloying morning heat.

As Kanna dragged her heels through the field, the farmhouse took shape. It wasn't the best of shapes, but it was solid. Grey stone walls rose up two stories but meandered wide, making it almost squat. Mismatched curved tiles covered the roof, which jutted at one angle then another as if it could not decide which direction to take.

Along the side of the house, two figures stood in the small training corral. Kanna stopped her approach and squinted into the sun. Osawa held his hands up in front of him at sharp angles, his elbows bent. Isco mimicked the stance, but kept his hands too close.

"Hold your arms further away from your body," Osawa instructed. He reached out to pull Isco's elbows forward and adjusted his arms to shoulder width. "It will give you more time to respond."

Isco nodded, his attention fixed on Osawa's hands now.

"If I strike here..." Osawa continued, moving his arm in a slow hook.

Isco turned his arm, blocking with the outside.

"That's how people instinctively block. But if I go here—" Osawa went forward with the strike, and Isco blocked with the inside of his other arm. Osawa pulled his hands back, smiling at his new trainee. The smile faded when he turned his attention to Kanna.

His eyes were as blue as sea depths. Her fault, she knew. It could have been worse, she knew. She hadn't been thinking when she pulled him through the Neither, hadn't even considered that it could destroy him until it almost did. He lived due to sheer luck and nothing else. And he was changed. Not for the worst, not for the better, but changed.

She hadn't given him a choice in that.

Isco followed Osawa's gaze. He didn't move when he met her eyes, but tentatively lifted a hand in greeting. He held it there, and Kanna turned away.

Osawa cleared his throat. "Let's see if you are any better today, Isco."

A wood porch ran the length of the back of the house, its black paint chipped away to show layers of green and blue and even the bare aged wood beneath. The three steps leading up sunk into the wet earth. Kanna took them carefully, telling herself it was so she wouldn't go through the wood as her feet grew heavier with each step.

The light screen door was the only thing blocking the entry. It opened with little effort beneath her pull, and Kanna winced when the hinges screeched.

In the kitchen at her left, conversation ceased. Astar's elbows rested on the table, her light expression creasing into a false mask. Yassen leaned against the counter, smiling with unrestrained delight that was unearned on Kanna's part.

"Mornin', Kanna," Yassen said. "You want breakfast? I can make you something. I made Astar pancakes."

"They were delicious, even for pancakes." Astar said, a tension in her usual easy tone. "Who knew it would be Yassen with all the hidden talents?"

"No." Kanna tried to soften her eyes, attempted to turn up the sides of her lips without baring teeth. "But thank you." She turned away before she could see the disappointment slump his shoulders, using the excuse of hanging the bridle near the door, only to catch sight of Haru.

He sat in the living room in a slant of light, one of the abandoned journals left behind by previous settlers over his knee. After he'd read one, he'd moved to another, then another. Late one night when the others were sleeping, Kanna had attempted to study them. They contained page after handwritten page of dry accounts on herd health and perceived hierarchies in nearby wild horse bands, interspersed with the occasional familial anecdotes. She didn't understand what he saw in them, but she didn't understand what he saw in most things.

Haru had his reading glasses in hand, having removed them when she entered. It wasn't that she didn't know he was there. She had felt his eyes on her since she walked through the door and had avoided looking at him because she knew she'd be trapped, like she was now, her hand lingering on the leather reins. He was never subtle about his glances, and never tried to hide his attention. He was an empty shelter, unlocked and waiting for her.

Looking at him was like staring too long at sunlight over water. Eventually, it hurt.

She stepped back, turned her body because her head would have to follow, and made for the stairs that led to the second floor. She needed distance. She couldn't breathe. The air was too thick, but there were no gods to pray to for storms, no great and knowing power that could fix this. No way to fix any of it.

When she was almost at the top of the stairs, Vahn appeared on the rise. One hand on the banister, the heel of the other rubbing into his waking eyes. A small play. Vahn never slept deep enough for it to stick to him.

The marks left behind by the arrow in his forearm, the gash in his side, still held the color of blood. They would fade, joining the other white scars that moved along his skin, but unlike them, Kanna had caused these. They both bore small marks dealt to one another from practice slips, but none of those had brought either of them so near to death. Kanna had felt when the life in his skin began to fail, though the lingering clutch of death had faded over the past weeks.

He opened his eyes. They were nothing like the dusky purple of the sky and everything like cut stained glass. Bright, clear, always alert, always as sharp as the man who bore them.

"Hey, K." Vahn didn't wait for her to finish her ascent, instead making his way down the stairs. He was still thin and Kanna was still infinitesimally small. At least they could pass on the narrow stairwell so she didn't have to retreat back to the main hall.

Vahn didn't say anything else. She watched his back for a moment, taking comfort in the healthy sheen that had returned to his skin. Then, she cleared her throat. The small noise halted his progress and he pivoted, looking up at her.

There was so much to say, but no place to start.

"Yassen made breakfast," she said instead. Instead of *it was my fault*, or *I never deserved you*, or *I don't have words for this*.

His smile hardened. "Have you eaten?"

Kanna looked to the side, up the stairs, to the wall at her side again to avoid the answer.

"That's what I thought." He began to take the next step down and away.

"I'll join you," she said before she could think about it. It was a bit loud in her ears, a bit more desperate than she had meant to sound.

Vahn stopped and turned over his shoulder. He didn't smirk, not this time. His lips were soft, his eyes gentle and, if she dared to think it, hopeful. "Promise?"

Kanna looked back to the top of the dim stairs and thought of the empty rooms, dusty and collecting the heat but quiet. It was above the others, high enough that she could pretend the waves of emotion emanating from them was some trick, that it wasn't real, that all that heavy weight had nothing to do with her.

If she didn't join him, Vahn wouldn't eat. It was probably why he was so thin now, after she had been gone so long. She would forget to eat. He would remind her. She would insist that they share, that there was enough, that just because he had something didn't mean the rest of the world would starve for the want of it.

She didn't know how to fix anything else. She could try to fix this one small thing.

"I need to change," she said, because she needed a moment. Just another moment, first. "Then I'll join you."

He raised a brow, crossed his arms, and stared at her.

She rolled her eyes, but still said: "I promise."

"Good." Vahn rubbed the back of his neck, hopping down the last of the steps. "Hope it isn't pancakes again. The boy needs to branch out."

# 2

# UNDERTOW

## HARU

HARU WAITED. Haru knew how to wait, how to bide time, but there was no right moment when every moment was the same, day after day. Even in the year that he tortured himself over whether or not Kanna was alive he could at least feel her, knew without knowing that she had been out there. Now he could see her, watched her leave for her morning rides and return but there was an emptiness he couldn't breach.

He could hardly feel her. It wasn't like the first time, after Adur, when she'd severed the tie between them. Then he could find the end of it, reach into the limit and know she was on the others side. This was like the string of a violin at rest, encased then jettisoned into a watery chasm, caressed on occasion by the undertow.

Haru closed the journal he had finished and rose to return it to its place. His body protested the movement. It had been at rest too long. Haru had fallen out of his routines, knew he should have stayed in practice, but as long as Kanna haunted the second floor he would keep it safe.

On the other side of the open study was the kitchen, which had become a gathering point. The others were deep in another game of Palamedes, Osawa sitting at one end of the rectangular table with Astar on his right, her back to Haru. At the other end was Yassen, and Vahn straddled the chair next to him to share the hand of cards. Yassen hadn't won a game, even with Vahn's help, but he stayed in them longer. The two of them together could possibly succeed if Vahn wasn't constantly distracted.

Vahn's distraction set down the mug he cradled and rose from the table. Isco began to search through the crooked cabinets along the far wall. Vahn's gaze turned from the cards in Yassen's hand to Isco's back, watching the other man only while he was turned away.

Haru shook his head and turned his attention back to the shelves in the corner of the study. When they first arrived the shelves were near bare, but he found the journals piled in the shut cabinets below the bookcase. There was no order to them, as if their author had simply finished one and tossed it with the others without rhyme or reason before beginning again. Haru brushed the dust from them and managed to dig some kind of chronology from the ones he had read, and he studied the spines to find the place where the one he had finished belonged.

Haru didn't want to think about the way Vahn watched Isco, didn't want to consider what it meant when the hard, vicious spark in Vahn's eyes turned into something else. Unfortunately, he had to consider it. To care for Kanna meant to care for Vahn in some way. Their bond was formed before he knew her, and it wasn't something that would break. Their joy was each others'. Their pain was shared.

And Haru didn't trust Isco. Isco was a man with something to hide, something important, and Haru knew there was more to him than he was telling. While Isco had tended to both Kanna and Vahn with care and skill, Haru couldn't shake the first time he laid eyes on him in Kanna's cell, in that dank prison where she was beaten and nearly broken. Isco's face was the only one that Haru had needed to remember from the Cardea's bunker, and it was a constant reminder of the pain of that day and everything that followed.

The thin volume he was holding slid into place, between the birth of the farmer's son and the time he became ill as a toddler. Before he bent to retrieve a new volume from the cabinet, movement caught his eye.

Isco was moving to the stairs, a cup in each hand.

Haru was across the room before the idea even triggered in his mind, his body blocking the stairs. "Where are you going?" he demanded, probably louder than he had intended.

Vahn's gaze no longer pretended to look away and snapped to Haru, the line of his shoulders tensing like a predator preparing to strike.

Isco stumbled back, and his heel caught the leg of Yassen's chair. One of the mugs dropped from his hand and shattered on the stone floor, sending a cascade of tea at Vahn's ankles.

Haru reached forward in an attempt to catch Isco before he fell, but his grip upset the second mug. It tilted back, the hot tea spilling onto Isco's chest.

The panic that jolted in Isco's eyes had nothing to do with pain. His hands scrambled at his shirt, trying to pull the scalding patch away from his body as he skittered back, his eyes staring at something far away and nothing at all. He slammed into the kitchen counter but refused to let go of the wet cloth twisted in his grip.

Vahn sprang from his chair and moved in on Haru, putting himself between him and the rest of the group as they got to their feet.

Osawa made it to Isco first. With a wave of his hand, he pulled the scalding water from Isco's shirt and guided it to the sink. But Isco couldn't let go of the cloth, his eyes still rattling in that familiar way, between now and remembrance.

Yassen set a heavy hand on Isco's shoulder. The weight set Isco at a lean, but he unwrapped his fingers from the now dry shirt. "You all right?"

Isco refocused and he smiled, strained, though his hand still shook. "I am, thank you."

Haru looked away from the group to meet Vahn's anger.

"Getting real tired of your shit, Haru."

"It was an accident, Vahn."

"An accident?" Vahn's fist clinched, and he forced himself not to look back. "Like when you *accidentally* beat those Prospects' faces in? Or how about when you accidentally started a fight. With *Velinius*. In the *Temple*. Which then got us all *accidentally* thrown into an inescapable death hole in the ground?"

"I got us out," Haru said through his teeth, fighting to keep his voice level.

"And you did that all by yourself, did you?" Vahn shot back "But not before we all got some of that good Palamidia torturing. Mostly us. Poor little prince, you didn't have a flashlight." Vahn swung his hand to gesture behind himself. "They literally hung Osawa out to dry."

"Don't bring me into this," Osawa said, glaring in their direction.

Yassen smiled at them, now that they were both looking his way. "Isco's okay, guys."

Vahn growled in frustration. "Who asked you?"

Astar's eyes sparked. "Don't snap at him!" She grasped the metal tea tin that Isco had been using and hurled it at Vahn. But Vahn's reflexes were as quick as they had ever been, and he ducked out of the way. The tin hit Haru in the chest before falling to the ground with a clang.

Osawa stepped between the group at the counter and Haru and Vahn, throwing his hands out between them.

"Enough!"

His voice was joined by another.

At the stairs, Kanna had one hand on the banister as she looked over the gathering. A single braid, half finished and abandoned, tangled in her loose hair. The echo of her command faded as she stalked down the final steps. As she drew closer, Haru felt her. A muted note, ghostly and dangerous.

Haru moved to meet her. "I'm sorry, were you resting?"

"It is the middle of the afternoon, man," Vahn said. "What is wrong with you?"

The empty grey of Kanna's eyes turned to Vahn. "I said that was enough."

Stepping past them, Kanna crouched near the table and retrieved the fractured pieces of the ceramic mug. She cradled them in her palms as she stood and slowly released the shattered bits onto the table before backing away.

The pieces hadn't even made a sound.

Kanna's gaze roamed over the now quiet group. She studied each in turn, her expression unchanging even as she looked from Isco's wrinkled shirt to his eyes. She cocked her head to the side, her brows narrowing, then turned to the door. The note Haru felt took on a pitch of anger.

"Outside," Kanna said.

Vahn and Osawa said nothing. They didn't even exchange glances before moving to the door.

"Kanna," Haru started, but she turned her cold gaze to him.

"Everyone," she said, then turned to the others that still remained. "Now."

Yassen and Astar moved first, but Kanna stopped Isco.

"Get your kit," she told him.

"My kit?" he asked, his scattered gaze bouncing between Haru, Kanna, and the door. "Why?"

Kanna didn't answer. She turned to Haru once more, her glare a pointed command, before exiting.

Haru sighed. Then he followed her.

# 3

# VICIOUS SEASONS

## KENZI

WHEN THE STORMS ARRIVED, it was the first time that Kenzi was grateful for the vicious storm season. Growing up in Panotii, her childhood had been wracked with them. After each, the soldiers would appear. They'd begin the day in a spotless white and despite it, or in spite of it, they would work. United under a single cause, the Palamidia's soldiers restored what they could from what was lost. Water loas coaxed back tides. Fire loas burned detritus. Earth loas rebuilt fortifications.

It was the duty of the air loas to find the people in the wreckage. Kenzi stood on damp banks and searched for weak breath in lungs crushed by debris. When she found no more survivors, she followed the currents of the air. They thrummed against closed larynxes, recoiled from the water where they were meant to be. Not everything could be saved after a storm.

At the end of every day she was weak with exhaustion, the heat and effort causing the world to spin around her so that she didn't have time to think. Didn't have to weigh her conscience. The Palamidia's relief efforts served as a welcome distraction to their pursuit of the Legatus. Former Legatus, Kenzi corrected herself, but then corrected back. As long as Kanna lived, until there was proof of her death, Velinius could never truly claim the title.

Ananke.

Shit.

Kenzi picked her way down from the rise she had been using as her perch throughout the day. She promptly tripped over a sodden beam, stumbling when her knees were too slow to react in time and colliding with another body. Arms wrapped around her, keeping her from falling.

"No need to throw yourself at me, sugar."

Kenzi looked up into Masao's leer as his thumb brushed along her arm. Although tired, she had enough strength to shrug him off. It was pointless to waste breath on Masao, so she turned away. Masao's gaze lingered, and she could feel the slick press of it against her spine. He was the one that she'd hoped wouldn't survive Pyrgolis. But he had, with barely a scratch. Kenzi had never thought she would be the kind of person to be disappointed to find out that someone hadn't died, but there were so many that had, and she would have traded Masao for any of them.

Even those she had slayed with her own hands.

Especially those.

The Palamidia had made camp at the edge of the former town, where what passed for roads turned into dirt tracks. She reached the large relief tents first, one on each side to house those who no longer had homes. After that were the smaller tents for the soldiers, which had increased by the day as reinforcements arrived to refill the ranks that had been depleted after their failed entrapment.

Kenzi wove through the sea of white, the canvas sides rippling the bare breeze, until she found Ira sitting on a crate outside of their tent. He hadn't changed into his uniform, instead opting for the loose denim and heavy work boots common in Panotii. No one questioned it. As usual, his fingers worked scrap papers into new forms. His eyes slid when she approached and he held a lotus out to her.

With the tips of her fingers, she took it and placed it into her dirty palm before sitting on the crate next to him.

After she'd fled the veterinary office in Pyrgolis, the rain washed away the blood from her hands. Not all of it, though. When Ira found her, he pressed her hands together, used the sky's torrent to get rid of the rest of it before placing his hands on her shoulders.

"You were overwhelmed," he'd coached her. The rain had been so cold, her fingers as numb as her heart. "They caught you by surprise."

Kenzi focused on the lotus cupped in her palms, the paper cast in the orange of the sunset. She tilted her hands and the fragile paper flower tilted with them, rolling against the mud on her palms. There was writing on one side, but it was folded in and over itself so she couldn't make out what it had been before. "Is Nissa back?"

"Not yet." Ira stretched his legs and reached to the pile next to himself, pulling out another slip of paper. He folded one side of the rectangle over itself a few times before tearing it off to form a square.

He didn't say anything else. Ira often had an air about him that kept others away, but it wasn't directed to Kenzi. At least it hadn't been before. Since he'd found her, shaken and covered in her companions' blood, he had withdrawn. Kenzi garnered little respect from the other officers, but with Ira now keeping her out of the loop, she was lost.

"Where have they been going?" Kenzi asked. Both Nissa and Masao had been taking small detachments from the camp in the last week, returning a few days later.

"Not sure."

"Do you not know," Kenzi asked, the lotus shifting once again in her hands, "or do you not want to tell me?"

Ira's sure hands paused in their work long enough for Kenzi to notice.

"Ira..."

"You should rest."

"Ira—"

"They will need you again tomorrow."

"Ira!" Kenzi grit her teeth as she shot to her feet. The lotus fell, half-trampled under her boot. She shifted her foot off of it, instantly regretting her movement, but she kept her fists clenched. "I'm not a traitor. I don't know what you think happened—"

"What happened?"

Kenzi clenched her jaw shut, then loosened it enough to speak. "I told you."

"I know what you told me."

Kenzi released her palms, forced air through her lungs. She crossed her arms at her chest, turning her back on him. Within the camp, the soldiers moved in a slow exchange as they changed shifts. The exhausted and filthy were replaced by those just waking, their uniforms clean and ready for the day.

"Why won't anyone tell me anything?" she sighed.

"No one should have to." Kenzi turned over her shoulder. His brow raised and he tilted his chin up only enough to look at her. "If there is something you want to know, discover it yourself."

Kenzi wanted to argue, but Ira was right, just as Ira was always right, but he had never been so cold about it. Perhaps, she told herself, she had simply not noticed it before. She told herself this was how things had always been, that it was her paranoia keeping her on edge. "I think you're right," she said, "and I should rest. Aren't you on duty now?"

Ira squinted up to the dying sun, then nodded. He dropped the half-finished piece he had started onto the scrap pile next to him and, without another word, headed toward the town. He waved a loose hand over his shoulder in farewell before shoving his hands into his pockets.

As he grew smaller against the distance, Kenzi looked to the perimeter of the camp. The pair of sentries bent together over a comm, and the rest of the soldiers were thinning as they finished the exchange of their shifts.

She ducked into the tent she shared with Ira. It was hotter inside of it than out, which explained why he was sitting idle outside, but at least there was shelter. Peeling off her sweat and dirt caked uniform jacket, she dropped it into the waiting basket and shoved it through the back of the canvas where it would be retrieved, cleaned, and replaced by unseen hands.

She meant to visit the utility tents, but she made the mistake of sitting on the end of her cot. The dusty hems of her trousers rose up, and she bent over and ran her thumb through the grime that ringed her ankles where her socks ended. She rested her elbows on her knees, and stared.

Across from her, Ira's neatly folded blankets rested at the end of his cot, and an origami horse perched on top of his travel pack at the head of it. He'd had the same piece keeping vigil over him since they had first met up at the beginning of this baseless campaign.

There had to be something else. After losing the traitors' trail and nearly half of their forces, Kenzi expected that they would need to return to report to the Tower. Instead, they lingered on the border of

Atarrabi. As much as Kenzi wanted to believe the relief work was just that, after Bomazi she was beginning to understand that nothing was only one thing. Salinae claimed the razing of the city was due to their harboring fugitives of the Palamidia, but that didn't explain why he sent their monument back to the Tower. And it didn't explain why their ranks were steadily being replenished to the point that they swelled past their original number.

Kenzi tasted sand and blood and spat, realizing belatedly she had been chewing the corner of her thumb. She wiped her hand on the side of her trousers before standing.

Ira said she should find her own answers. She was going to do just that.

4

## AN OLD WAY

### ISCO

OUTSIDE, the air stuck to Isco like a film. More people had left Kirin than had ever belonged to it, which left grand sweeps of grasslands and storm-ravaged cliffs with little in between. At least those who made attempts to build there knew to build with stone, so the homes survived their abandonment, which had been a grace for their troupe.

Next to the farmhouse was the corral, the wood tilted and some of the slats missing or half-fallen. When Isco had asked Osawa for a few lessons in defense, Isco had discovered that the ground in the corral would mercilessly bruise the hard way—by being dropped onto it multiple times a day. After Vahn had mostly healed from his injuries, Isco would wake in the early morning to Vahn practicing alone. From the second-floor window, he watched as Vahn's body healed, his strength returning over the weeks until the frail image of him so near death was nothing more than a dream.

Or a nightmare.

The sky growled a warning, but the soldiers below had no use for idle threats from dead gods. Kanna paced to the center of the corral followed by Haru. Yassen, Osawa, and Astar went next, with Vahn last. Isco stopped before stepping in. Vahn looked over his shoulder, then shifted around to wave a hand in front of him, motioning for Isco to join the others before falling behind him.

At the center, the group spread out around Kanna. Her gaze studied each of them, stopping on Astar. With a nod of her head, she dismissed Astar. Astar's brows knit together, but she backed out of the corral. She didn't go far, standing instead on the other side of the fence.

Kanna turned to those that were left. "First blood," she said. "Osawa, you're up first."

The other soldiers backed away. Isco generally relied on Yassen to ask questions he didn't want to, but for once he didn't seem to have any. Kanna surveyed the rest of thm, her gaze landing on Isco. "And you."

"What's happening?" Isco asked.

No one answered him. The others left Isco and Osawa at the center of the ring, taking up positions along the perimeter. Kanna hoisted herself up to sit on the top rail of the fence. Haru found a place beside her while Vahn stayed near the open gate. Yassen circled around to stand near Astar, who was at Kanna's other side.

"When you're ready," Kanna called.

"Ready for what?" Isco asked. "What did she mean by 'first blood'?"

"I'm sorry about this," Osawa answered.

Before Isco could ask what Osawa was sorry for, he was interrupted by a fist hitting his jaw. The skin on his lip split against his teeth and Isco instinctively pressed his hand against it, his other tightening on the strap of the medical kit that was still slung over his shoulder.

Knowing it was enough, Osawa stepped back after delivering the blow.

"Isco."

He blinked through the water in his eyes, looking for Kanna. She straightened her arms, bringing her shoulders near her ears before relaxing again. "Get out of there."

"Gladly," he muttered, retreating from the corral and the glare of attention.

"Yassen," Kanna said. "You're up."

Yassen grinned. He slapped Isco's back as he passed him, the heavy weight causing Isco to stumble. Safely on the other side of the fence, Isco pulled his hand from his lip. The sting was sharp, the red on his hands different when it was his own.

"Here," Vahn's voice startled Isco. "Let me see."

Before Isco could answer, Vahn tilted Isco's chin back. Isco tried to look at anything except the burn of Vahn's eyes, but it was impossible. The flex of Vahn's finger turned Isco's face to study the damage, though there wasn't much to see. Vahn's eyes lifted to Isco's, his fingers lingering. A flare of heat from Vahn's skin touched Isco's jaw, like the warning heat of the sun.

Vahn's hand dropped away, and he took a step back. "You'll heal."

Isco cleared his throat, relaxed the hand that gripped his bag and shifted it back up his shoulder from where it had slipped. "I could have told you that."

Vahn's lips tilted into a guarded smile. "I'd hope so, or else I'd question your skills, medicus."

Isco fought against clearing his throat again. He hadn't realized how parched he was, but the heat of Kirin was staggering. He didn't want to break the strange spell, didn't want Vahn to stop looking at him, but he had to ask. "What is the point of this?"

As Isco had predicted, Vahn's expression hardened, his smile sliding back into a smirk. He shifted away from Isco, resting his hands on the top of the fence. Within the enclosure, Osawa was squaring off with Yassen.

"Can't get me with that move," Yassen said to Osawa. "Kanna already introduced me to it."

Yassen rushed forward, his head bent down in an intended tackle. Osawa side-stepped the charge, ducking low and catching Yassen's leg in passing. Yassen hit the ground and rolled out of the way, reclaiming his fooding with an agility Isco wouldn't expect from his bulk.

From her place at the fence Astar whooped joyously, though Isco couldn't be sure who she was cheering for.

"Why didn't she have to get punched?" Isco asked.

"Most of us like her," Vahn told him, not looking away from the ring.

Isco's gaze traveled involuntarily to Haru. As if sensing it, Haru jerked around to meet Isco's eyes. Isco turned away as quickly as he could, focusing on the fight that was still underway.

Osawa and Yassen looked for openings to strike. Why Kanna would match the two, Isco couldn't fathom, as Yassen was easily twice Osawa's size. Yassen charged again. Osawa ducked under the swing, but this time he moved in close. Springing up, he slammed his fist into Yassen's solar plexus. The larger man stumbled back, the breath knocked out of him in a rush.

Osawa kicked high, his boot connecting with Yassen's jaw. Yassen's head snapped back and he fell to the dirt. His hands went up, and Osawa stepped back his advance.

Yassen spat, a stream of blood speckling the thrashed grass.

Kanna braced herself on the fence post and leaned back. "Next."

Vahn stepped back from the fence and moved to enter the corral.

"I don't understand," Isco said, as if Vahn could change anything that was happening. "He wasn't trying to hurt me."

"But we did," Vahn said, still not looking at Isco, "and isn't that what matters?"

Isco swallowed past the constriction in his throat. "No?"

Vahn half-turned over his shoulder and pointed at him with one hand, his thumb up. His wink sent heat into Isco's cheeks that he couldn't blame on the weather, which he hoped that Vahn missed when he turned back to the corral. When Isco yanked his attention away, though, he met the ever-knowing grey of Kanna's gaze.

Haru followed her line of sight, meeting Isco again. Kanna turned back to her makeshift fighting ring, but Haru lingered until Yassen crossed in front of Isco to join Astar.

At the center of the enclosure, Vahn swung one arm in front of him and stretched it with the other. Osawa removed his glasses while he waited, rubbing the lenses on the hem of his shirt.

"Kanna," Haru said, gaining her attention. He stepped up onto the bottom ring of the fence. "This isn't fair."

Kanna turned to him, her brow raised, then back to Vahn and Osawa in the ring. "Osawa?"

Osawa raised his glasses up to check if they were clean. He squinted in Kanna's direction, then shrugged.

"Vahn?"

Vahn glared at Haru, then turned to Osawa.

Osawa set his glasses back in place.

"Fine," Vahn obliged, grudgingly.

With the wave of her hand, Kanna permitted Haru's entrance into the ring. He didn't need any more for an invitation, swinging his leg over the fence to join the others.

Kanna propped her elbows on her knees, her body leaning forward as if it wanted to join them but was held back by will alone. "Begin."

While Isco had witnessed the soldiers in action both in Ganglere and later in Pyrgolis, it couldn't prepare him for when they faced each other. Strikes moved in and away, feints and jabs and counters one after another. With the speed they moved, it took him a moment to realize that Haru and Vahn were working together against Osawa.

Osawa moved between his larger opponents with ease, turning their momentum against them and disrupting their footwork so that they tangled together. Vahn and Haru's seething animosity didn't help. They could not find a proper rhythm to work together, and Osawa used it against them.

When the three stumbled away from each other, regrouping and resetting their positions, Haru and Vahn would glare daggers at one another before beginning another unbalanced, ill-timed assault. Isco wasn't the only one that noticed. As the soldiers began their attack anew, Kanna turned away from the ring and dropped onto the back side of the fence.

Osawa managed to land a hit on Haru, his heel connecting with Haru's brow. It split, and Haru stepped back momentarily, wiping the blood with the back of his hand.

They didn't stop. They pressed on, something else on the line, something they had to prove. The bout had turned away from being a team match, with Vahn and Haru beginning to actively work against each other, even outright.

Kanna's nostrils flared, though her eyes remained flat and unmoved as she paced along the outside of the fence.

Yassen looked away from the fight, his head tilting in concern. "Whatcha doing, Kanna?"

She stepped around Isco, ignoring Yassen's question.

"Aren't you going to stop them?" Isco asked her as she passed.

Kanna halted further along the fence. Bending slightly at the waist, she peered into the old wood watering trough before straightening and propping her foot at the lip of it. "Why would I do that?" she asked, her gaze honing in on the soldiers in the ring. "It is about to get interesting."

Kanna kicked her foot out and the trough tilted. The half-rotted wood legs holding it cracked, and rainwater from the storm poured into the corral.

# 5

## BURIED HOPE

### ISCO

Isco DIDN'T KNOW if he could heal burns with the supplies he had on hand, and he had never learned how to treat lightning strikes beyond theory. Not that either of those things would matter, with the way things were going.

Haru readied a strike, but Osawa twisted a controlled whirlpool, only large enough to catch Haru's foot and send him to the ground.

Vahn's flames did somewhat better against Osawa's tactics, but only somewhat. The heat of the flames caused the water to sizzle, steam rising each time Osawa suffocated the fires until thin clouds lingered around the corral.

While the men exchanged blows, Kanna paced. She stepped into the corral for a better view, leaning back against the fence.

Meanwhile, Astar and Yassen had taken steps back.

The loas shifted from specialized attacks to rapid hand-to-hand. Their elements followed their bodies, chasing along their limbs. The way the soldiers moved wasn't like the earth loas of the Theatre, and it certainly wasn't like the traveling performers Isco had seen as a child. He had attended a show with his parents, once, where a fire loa dressed in crimson and silver made grand gestures, a sweat breaking on her brow as she concentrated on a single moment, a simple flickering flame.

After that performance, Isco berated his parents with questions. He wanted to know why they were different, what made them different, how it was that people could do those things and others couldn't. His father laughed, told him that they were just people. That everyone had a gift, and that was theirs.

A cynic even then, Isco couldn't accept that answer. There had to be a reason, something in them that made them able to do those things. He became a medicus, so drawn to the idea of tearing apart what made a person that he was awarded for it and it still wasn't enough. He identified minute differences in the makeup of their blood, but the results couldn't be repeated. It was as if every one one of them was different, was made of something else despite their shared affinities.

He still didn't know anything more than when he started, and the loas that battled before him were evidence. Isco should have been terrified. He was scared of most things, but watching the loas ignited in him a sense of wonder he thought long forgotten.

Vahn scorched the ground to glass with a flick of his wrist, contorted fires that burned so hot they were violet, blue, crimson. Osawa lifted puddles, split them to rain, and created devastating vortexes the size of a tea cup. Haru stretched light itself, using it as shields, as spears, and charged it until it crackled and became something else entirely.

There was no struggle, and the sweat on their brows came from the heat of the day, from the sheer physical movement. Everything that Isco had witnessed before meeting these loas was nothing more than parlor tricks.

Haru sent an arc of light at Osawa, but in an instant he drew a clear circle. The light passed through and veered off, what was once white splitting into a spectrum of color as it was refracted by the bend of water.

The twisting maneuver caused Osawa to lose his footing, and the multi-hued light fired over the heads of the watching group.

Isco ducked to avoid the light and he felt the crackle of the air. It whistled as it passed overhead, the light giving out above the farmhouse with a boom akin to thunder.

The force of the eruption disturbed the sky. When the artificial echo stopped, it was joined by the primal rumble of nature in response. The suffocating humidity lifted from the ground, and a drizzle of rain began to fall.

In the enclosure, Osawa's stunned gaze traveled between his hands and where the light had disappeared. He didn't even attempt to get up from the ground. Haru and Vahn also kept their silence for a moment, staring.

Until Kanna stepped forward. That shift caught everyone's attention.

The first time Isco had seen Kanna's abilities in the Theatre seemed like a lifetime ago, and he still couldn't understand the dark that writhed at Kanna's feet. He didn't think he was supposed to. There was something too uncanny, too unreal and otherly about them that his mind rejected what his eyes saw. It could have been the way it shifted, or it could be that they weren't really shadows.

A shadow was cast by something. A shadow passed over things, darkening what was beneath. What rose to Kanna's bidding was the pitch of night itself. There was nothing to cast it and no seeing through it, no other side.

Guilt rose in Isco, a darkness thick enough to choke. Sensing the rot in him, the writhing dark at Kanna's feet stretched. Osawa scrambled up from the ground and joined Haru and Vahn, but none of them readied a stance. If anything, they backed away.

Kanna's hand at her side shifted, two of her fingers an unseen leash curling into her palm, and the power that had expanded over the grass condensed at her feet. She stopped her skulk, and the shadows shuddered. "My turn."

Vahn's jaw tightened. Haru stepped forward, but Kanna twisted her wrist and the shadows leapt at the mens' feet.

All three backed out of their reach.

Haru held out his empty palms, the lightest smear of his own blood on one, and put himself between Kanna and the others. "Kanna." His voice was smooth, non-threatening. It reminded Isco of the time when he'd once attempted to coax an injured street cat, attempting to soothe while knowing it could lash out. "What are you doing?"

As deftly as she had turned the dark, she yanked it back with the twitch of a finger. "I could ask you all the same thing." Kanna's voice was even, commanding. There was not even a hint of her usual slouch, and the person Isco was looking at wouldn't even know what a slouch was.

Vahn crossed his arms. Even in the face of Kanna's wrath, he appeared to be leaning on something.

"Vahn," Osawa hissed, an attempted warning. "Don't."

Vahn rolled his eyes anyway. "We're just having a little fun, K."

"Fun?" Kanna shook her head. "None of you were ready. None of us. What is fun about another hopeless war?"

"It isn't hopeless," Haru said. "We have you, and we have each other."

Kanna's eyes narrowed. "And what good are we? You"—she turned on Vahn first—"too busy creating tragedies and hiding behind them to take anything seriously. You refuse to see the things that are weighing you down, yet use it as an excuse to ignore everything in front of you.

"And you," she continued, gesturing to Osawa now, "spend more effort getting in your own way than allowing yourself to be what you can. To be what you are." She shook her head, pulled her shoulders back to look down her nose at Osawa. "It is a waste of yourself."

Astar stepped around the fence and into the corral. "Hey," she said, as if she could help by taking Kanna's attention away from the men.

Kanna's lips twisted at the corner, so far away from a smile it was frightening. Her head tilted on her neck. "What?" Kanna's body followed slowly behind the tilt of her neck and aligned. "I am not talking to your friends. I am addressing soldiers. How am I supposed to win a war with soldiers who ignored a simple command? Who are afraid of themselves?"

Astar shrank. Isco had never seen Astar shrink from anything save her father, but Kanna didn't stop.

"That is what you want, isn't it? The only reason you three are still here." She waved a hand to include Isco and Yassen at the fence. "You want your empty land back, your broken cities. Never mind the bodies I will have to pile at your feet for you to have it. Bodies that I trained. Bodies I swore I would protect by breaking those of your people."

Kanna laughed, though it was more like a clawing bark than anything human. It stopped, eyes like steel, eyes like weapons leveling on them. "And I was very good at breaking them. I have stood ankle deep in the blood of your people more times than I can count. I am the monster all of your warnings are about. I sometimes doubt there are numbers that can hold those I've butchered. The Battle of Ganglere," she said, passing her eyes focusing on each of them as she named their terrors. "The Cardea's slaughter." Her gaze landed on Yassen. "And Rough's Peak."

"You couldn't have been at Rough's Peak," Astar said, trying to garner her conviction. "That was twenty years ago."

"Eighteen," Kanna corrected, though it choked in her throat. She shut her eyes, tilted her face back to the sky to welcome the rain. "It was eighteen years ago."

"No," Astar said, her voice too quiet. "That can't be. Osawa said... Osawa?"

Kanna opened her eyes to slits that pinned on Osawa.

"You said they didn't send children to fight," Astar continued.

Osawa's gaze flitted between Kanna and Vahn, who looked away from them all, before he faced Astar. "I said they didn't send me."

"*Inara.*"

Kanna's shoulders tensed at the quiet call, and even Isco flinched at the softness that brushed against the raw pain that the light drizzle failed to dampen.

"That was different," Haru said. "You couldn't do anything about it then."

"What makes now different?" Kanna asked, but it wasn't as if she expected an answer. The anger that had carried her voice to that point split and faded, leaving an exhausted sorrow. "You are so blinded by a lost cause that you cannot see the damage it creates." Kanna hung her head, her eyes closing. "There is no point to this. A weapon is always a weapon, and all I am is another to lead by."

The shadows at Kanna's feet compressed to a single point before sliding along the landscape. Behind her shoulders, the point stopped. From that, like a slow shattering of glass, the lines of black radiated out, expanded, and peeled back the world.

"You should have let me die."

The next step Kanna took back was into the black, and she was gone.

# 6

# THE STORYTELLER

## KENZI

KENZI USED the activity during the shift change to position herself closer to Salinae's tents, but with the loss of foot traffic she had no reason to appear to be lingering there. Thankfully, she didn't have to wait long. When the sun began to redden, dipping below the horizon, Nissa returned. The angle of the sunset's glare provided some cover, as Kenzi positioned herself exactly where people would look away to avoid it.

Nissa dismounted at the head of her scouting group, though the other soldiers remained ringed around the low wagon they had brought back with them. The tracks it left weren't overly deep, and the bundles within were rounded and curved as opposed to the typical angles of supply boxes. Nissa approached Salinae, who waited with his hands clasped at his back. He bent his head to receive her report, nodding as she spoke.

Kenzi was too far to hear anything. Cursing her lack of foresight, she slipped along the sides of the tents, using the white maze of canvas and disruptive lighting to blend her movements until she was close enough that she could catch the strains of the conversation.

"... past the Kirin borders," Nissa stated, then waited.

Kenzi had missed the entire thing.

Salinae nodded. "Did he say anything when you questioned him?"

Nissa shook her head. "He wouldn't speak to me."

"Bring him."

Nissa turned over her shoulder, nodding to her soldiers. Two dismounted and moved to the back of the wagon. They yanked one of the bundles from it, letting it fall to the ground.

It groaned, and then it moved.

Each of the soldiers found the crook of an arm and pulled the bundle up. Whoever was inside couldn't move, their feet bound and bagged, so they dragged them until they faced Salinae.

With a sweep of his hand, Salinae unleashed the tie around the prisoner's neck before removing the cowl. Kenzi could not place the man's origin from his features. His skin was too light for a Gegenii, too dark for Adurians. Coal black eyes were clouded with age, and his grey hair was matted with dirt from rough handling.

Salinae bent at the waist, bringing himself closer to the cowed man. "What good is a storyteller that will not speak?" Salinae asked, though it was more of a musing than anything else.

The man's rheumy eyes narrowed, and his jaw tightened.

Salinae turned to Nissa.

"We brought the family," she informed him.

Salinae nodded. "Good." He looked over Nissa's shoulder to the other soldiers that had gathered. "Take them all to the detention area," he ordered, before turning to Nissa, "and bring me Masao."

Salinae turned his back to Kenzi. Having found as much as she could, she began to retreat. But Salinae's shoulders stiffened, and he turned over his shoulder. The dark sun against the snarled scar that marred Salinae's face was all Kenzi caught before a hand fell over her mouth and she was yanked through the flap of the tent she had been using for cover.

Kenzi bit her teeth together on instinct to compress the shocked gasp that attempted to work its way through her throat as the camp spun around her. She reached for her knives, blinking her eyes hard to adjust to the change in lighting.

Ira spun her around, his finger over his lips.

Kenzi relaxed with a sigh, and he removed his hand. "What was that?" she hissed at him when the hammering of her heart stilled. "You could have given me away."

"You were doing a fine job of that yourself," he whispered back. "Why are you here? You are supposed to be resting."

Kenzi forced her jaw to relax. "And you're supposed to be on duty."

The knit of Ira's brows didn't relax. "Get back to our space, and don't let anyone see you."

"You're the one who told me to find out what I wanted to know."

"And you were almost caught," Ira retorted. "What do you think they'd do if they found you sneaking around? After Pyrgolis, you've been under watch, if you hadn't noticed that much."

A chill overtook Kenzi in an instant. "That's why you're here?" she asked, stepping back. "You're watching me, for them? That's why you keep asking me...."

"No," Ira interrupted, "Kenz, that's not it."

Kenzi couldn't listen to any more. She backed away from Ira and ducked through the tent. A thousand eyes could see her now, and it wouldn't matter. The risk she had taken to find answers only led to questions she hadn't thought to ever ask. Questions she never wanted to ask. Halfway back to her tent, a sharp pain stitched along Kenzi's side. She stopped her reckless flight and bent over, her hands on her knees, heaving great breaths that only made the pain keener.

When her breath finally eased enough, she straightened to standing. Her nostrils flared as she struggled to force air into her starved lungs. Mouth dry, knees shaking, Kenzi began to walk. Her feet carried her back to the shelter she shared with Ira.

She knew less than she had when she started. Kenzi stripped from her sweat heavy uniform, dropping it to the ground. The day was too heavy, and her mind had gone blank as the last of her energy fled. She slid to the side on her cot, her eyes on Ira's empty bed and the origami horse that stood sentinel next to it.

It was strange.

Ira didn't even like horses.

7

# A MISTAKE

## HARU

WHEN THE SHADOWS rent the plane behind Kanna and she stepped back into the nothing behind her, Haru did the only thing he could.

He followed her.

The dark wasn't the same as when Kanna had verged. What was infinite now felt folded, compressed into a thin barrier. Haru tore through the other side, like falling through a parchment wall. His shoulder took the brunt of his fall, and the impact forced the air from his lungs. He rolled onto his back and heaved a breath in, his eyes opening to a too bright, too starry sky.

Haru sat up and his head spun. He pressed his fingers to his temple and they came back tacky with the blood from Osawa's hit. The sand stuck to the sweat on his shirt, which rapidly cooled in the chill, thin air.

Around him was the Neither, the contrast within the greyscale sharper, more defined when viewed through his own eyes. He grasped a handful of the sandy ground and shifted it through his fingers. Each grain was a different shade of grey, white and black and all between.

Kanna wasn't near him. Haru shot to his feet, the sand cascading from his fingers. It hit the icy ground, each grain chiming its own note. "Kanna!"

His voice echoed back and he spun in place, but there was nothing but drifts of grey dunes. The ground beneath him shifted to the right, what was once down became something else and Haru's balance tilted, the sudden vertigo sending him falling sideways and into rough-hewn stone. Haru braced himself for the impact, but ended up pushing himself away from the wall and stumbling back.

The room smelled of pain.

When he reclaimed his footing, he saw her. The relief turned into something cold. Hunched in the corner of the damp cell, Kanna was bare and smeared in blood both new and old. Her arms wrapped around her body, her knees tucked against them. Haru started for her, but a voice froze him in place.

"That one can't hear you."

Haru turned, slow. Kanna, another Kanna, the Kanna he had followed through a rift was in the opposite corner. She sat with her back against the wall, one knee up and her other leg tucked beneath it, the fabric on her shoulders damp from the rain. A trace of red from the heat of the day graced her cheeks, the freckles across her nose darkened from the exposure. Her arm rested on her upright leg and she leaned into it, her eyes on her own ghost in the corner.

Haru knelt in front of her. In the Neither, she had always been ghost like, and this was no different. It should have been. He could feel the thread connecting them as it hummed but he reached out, his fingers brushing over the scars between the knuckles of her right hand, the ones that this place had left her with. She flinched and drew her hand away, but not before he felt her, solid and alive.

"Why did you follow me?" she asked.

"How could I not?" Haru shifted his weight, settling on the ground between Kanna and the memory of her. Neither of them moved, so he kept his focus on the one he could reach, tried not to remember how, some time after this moment, she screamed until the lights shattered, until her voice broke, and all he could do was hold her until it stopped. And it stopped, but it never seemed to be over.

"*Inara.*" He tried to ignore the way her shoulders flinched and waited for her to turn to him. She always did, but the waiting was like being caught between eternities. "How are we here?"

"I don't know." Kanna rubbed the back of her fingers, traced the scars on her hands before curling them back to her chest. "When I passed through with Osawa, I felt it here. I thought that...."

Kanna swallowed, shifted enough to curl her knees closer to her chest, wrapping her arms around them as if she could become smaller. She wouldn't look at Haru, but he waited. Haru could have asked questions, had more than he could form words for, but this was a moment when she just needed time. "I thought that if I came here, it wouldn't disturb everyone else."

Haru remembered how empty the nights had felt in the last weeks, the strange distance he felt between them. "You've been coming here at night, haven't you?"

Kanna nodded. "It was this, or sever the tie between us again."

Haru's head jerked around, the panic hammering in his ribs. "Kanna, please don't," he said, a whisper, a plea. "You can't," he begged as though it would matter.

She shook her head. "You're right, I can't. I'm not sure what you did, but I can't undo it."

The first thing that Haru felt was the tension leave his shoulders, his heart calm back to a manageable rhythm. The second was confusion. "What do you mean, what I did?"

Kanna met his eyes like a challenge. They sparked gold, as if she was proving a point. Haru rose, put his palms on her knees and lowered his eyes so she would have to look at him. So she could see him. "That wasn't me. I felt you reach for me, but I couldn't reach back until you did."

Her eyes darkened, her head tilting as it did when she was trying to understand.

"I felt you die," he continued. "You were gone, but then you weren't. Do you think I have that kind of power? Do you think anyone does, except you?"

Kanna shut her eyes, covered them with her hands. As gently as he could, as forcefully as he dared, Haru wrapped his fingers around her wrists and pulled them away. He had to bring her back before they were both lost in a place that hadn't existed before she made it.

"Kanna," he pleaded. "Why are we here? Why this time?"

"I told the dark to bring me where I belonged," she said, her gaze drifting back to the shattered vision of herself. "But it made a mistake."

A drop of moisture pinged from the roof to the stone floor, the sound filling the space like a bomb.

Haru leaned forward, but before he could ask another question there was a sound outside of the cell. Timid steps sounded in the hall, impossible to hear if one wasn't attuned to everything in that dark space. They didn't hesitate though, not until they stopped outside the cell door.

Haru shifted his body and crouched between Kanna and the door, as if there was anything he could do in this helpless place. Haru never knew what happened here. Kanna wouldn't tell him. He once thought that not knowing made it worse, because it left him to trace the map of her injuries and imagine their source. But the true scars weren't on her body, and no one could heal something Kanna had decided was meant to hurt.

The lock of the cell slid back, the memory of Kanna and the true one both jumping as the bolt scraped. The door opened only enough for a figure to slip through and shut it behind them.

The echo of Kanna didn't stir. The figure stepped forward as if approaching a wounded animal, finally coming into focus.

"Isco." Haru ground his teeth until they hurt.

---

THE MEMORY of Isco knelt next to Kanna, who still didn't move. He reached forward, but in a flash Kanna had his fingers in her grip, his wrist twisted back.

Haru wanted to smile. He would have, if the situation had been different.

Isco's body twisted with his arm, trying to get away from Kanna's grip. "I was going to check your pulse," he managed to hiss, "but you are very alive."

Kanna's eyes narrowed, and she released his hand. Isco fell onto his backside. After he recovered his breath, he dug into the pack he had brought and uncorked a canteen. He offered it to Kanna, who glared at it. "It's just water," he said. "See?"

Isco tilted it back, and Kanna watched him swallow. Her tongue darted out, pressing against cracked lips, and when he offered it again she snatched it from his grip before returning to cowering in the corner.

She continued to glare at him, then drank. Her eyes slid shut after the first sip, and she drank deeper.

"Wait," he said, reaching forward to tilt it away from her. "You need to drink slowly."

Haru thought the echo of Kanna was going to fight him again. But she stopped, her head tilting and looking past Isco.

Footsteps sounded in the hall, heavy and slow. Isco's head darted around, his eyes blowing wide. The echo shoved the canteen at him and pointed to the wall by the door. It took time for Isco to move. He grabbed the bundle he had brought in with him and darted back across the cell, pressing his back against the side of the door.

He didn't appear to be breathing. Haru tried to move closer to him, but Isco was fuzzy and out of focus. His hand clutched the bundle he had brought tight to his chest, his knuckles white.

The view panel on the door scraped open, orange light spilling into the room. Kanna glared at the disembodied guard on the other side, the black of her eyes shifting, and the view window slammed shut. The footsteps moved back up the hall, faster than they'd arrived but not quick enough to count as a retreat.

Isco breathed.

"He was more afraid of them than I was."

Haru turned back to Kanna, who watched her own memories as she spoke.

"And yet."

Isco peeled himself away from the wall and returned to Kanna's side. She didn't shrink so tightly this time, her gaze softening with curiosity. He crouched next to her, dumping the bundle's contents before offering her the thin cover. Kanna leaned back, and he sighed, but unfolded the blanket enough to drape it over her before offering her the canteen once more.

When her hands went out to snatch it, he pulled it back just enough to avoid her quick grasp. "Slowly."

Kanna complied, and Isco shifted to put his back against the wall next to her. He winced. Then he pulled up his knees, rested his arms on them, and leaned back fully.

Kanna's voice behind him made Haru turn, step toward her.

"He did this often," she said. "Sometimes, he would try to bandage my wounds. Others, he would just sit."

Haru slid down the wall, sitting next to his Kanna. Her hands were at her side now, and he reached for them. When she didn't immediately pull away, he dared to thread his fingers with hers.

"Are you all right?" Isco asked the phantom. Then he snorted, choking back a laugh that held the beginnings of hysteria. "Sorry. That's a stupid question."

Isco reached into his pocket and pulled out a thin, foil wrapped bar. He pulled it open and broke off a piece, offering it to the echo. She tilted her head, studying it.

"This again?" He sighed. "I'm sure there are people out there waiting for you. That you need to get back to, right? You need something more than will to get through this."

Kanna's hand in Haru's tightened. "I thought it was part of it, at first. That they were trying to break me by showing kindness. But he never asked me anything. At least, nothing he expected an answer to."

The echo yanked the offered bite from Isco, base need taking over. After she showed restraint by not wolfing it down, he handed her the rest of the nutrient bar.

Isco closed his eyes, tilted his head back and leaned against the wall. "Have you ever been to the circus?"

The echo stopped chewing, raised a scarred eyebrow.

"Mostly," Kanna said beside Haru, "he would just... talk."

"My dad took me when I was a kid. They had these loa performers. I had never seen one before, and after I wouldn't stop asking my parents questions. Where did they come from, how could they do things no one else could, and why." He smiled, but he didn't open his eyes. "I wouldn't even sleep without asking the same questions, over and over. My mother got so sick of it that one night, she told me the craziest thing."

Isco opened his eyes to look at the echo, but she was just watching him. He closed his eyes, leaned back. "She said that, maybe, when the gods were destroyed, there were parts of them that couldn't die. After all, the gods each held a piece of existence inside of them, she said, and if that was lost, then so was the world. She said maybe, perhaps, what was left scattered over what remained of Lifrasir, and from that, the loas came."

Isco's smile faded, turned to something small and melancholy. "What do you think?" he asked the echo.

The echo's eyes drifted across the cell, staring right into Haru. Her head canted to the side, then she looked back to Isco.

"Yeah, it doesn't make sense." He smiled softly, then stood up. "Besides," he said, his voice turning into something hardened and heart-sick, "if there were gods in this world, they would have a lot to answer for."

The memory of Kanna finished chewing the last bit of the nutrient bar then, almost shy, held the wrapper and empty canteen out to Isco.

"That place was full of monsters," Kanna said. "I could feel them everywhere. The hate was so thick I could taste it, but he wasn't the same. I don't know how I knew, or why, but there was something so human about him it hurt."

Isco took the echo's offerings, pocketing the wrapper and holding the canteen to his chest. When she tried to untangle the blanket to return to him, he shook his head and backed away. "Keep it. Everyone deserves comfort, even if it's small."

After Isco let himself out of the cell, the clack of the lock when it set itself back into place jolted the scene. The rough walls softened, losing their focus, though the echo of Kanna appeared in a slight illumination in the far corner. She pulled her knees to herself and leaned her head onto them, then, after a shaking sigh, was quiet.

In the moments that followed, Haru felt the slight tremble in Kanna's hand. When he looked at her he cursed himself for not noticing that the way her body had tensed wasn't due to the memory. She was fighting, exhausting herself. It showed in the way her brows knit, the hard line of her jaw. He moved to kneel before her, taking the hand he held with him and pressing it against his chest. His other hand cupped her cheek, and he tried to turn her to look at him. "What's wrong?"

She shut her eyes, but he wouldn't let her take her hand away to cover them. "It is difficult to keep them like this. The memories always want to take me somewhere else. I can't always control it." She opened her eyes, met his. "Sometimes the pull is too strong, and I can't hold on."

"Then don't," he told her. He knew it was a simple solution, and he knew that it was dangerous. "You said that you asked it to take you where you belonged."

Kanna's eyes narrowed, her head tilting, asking in her way without words that he explain.

"What if it didn't make a mistake, Kanna?"

She tried to look away, but he brought her gaze back to him.

"It is time to stop fighting it."

Kanna bent her head, her lashes shadowing her eyes. "It is too easy to be lost here," she said, her words cradling a soft warning.

"I always find you, *inara*," he said, leaning his forehead to meet hers.

Kanna's fingers curled against his chest. "It won't just be me."

The room around them warped, stretching and fading back like the corner of a fish's eye. The next drop that fell from the ceiling broke against marble, the ring increasing in pitch and sticking in the air like a warning. The sound pierced Haru's ears and tore into his mind until it was the only thing left.

8

# DUST IN THE UNIVERSE

## HARU

KANNA NEEDED THE MEDICUS. She didn't want one, but Haru got one anyway, and while he knew it was needed it didn't mean that he didn't hate it when the woman mercilessly set the bones of Kanna's fingers back in place, when she untwisted the misplaced joints, when she strapped metal splints around Kanna's hands and taped them in place.

Kanna fought every instance, her body thrashing in Haru's arms. She refused to take anything for the pain, and when the medicus suggested that she be sedated Kanna went for the windows that wouldn't open, then tried to get to the door, and Haru had to catch her, lift her by the waist from her feet so she couldn't run.

*No!* She'd screeched, the end of the cry choked by a sob in her throat. So raw, Haru felt it. She tried to scratch at his arms but the pain of moving her fingers caught another scream. Instead she tried to use her palms to push him away, tried to twist, her body finally going limp and breathless.

Haru, please, she'd whispered to him when he carried her back to the bed, her broken hands moving against his chest, unable to grasp. *Haru, <avtandil>, please do not let them put me back in the dark.*

He wondered if she knew she was speaking in Ilazkin instead of Common, that he could only understand some of the words. Some was enough. When the medicus attempted to prepare a sedative, Haru shook his head.

"It will help the pain," she said. "If I don't use anything, it will hurt as much as the first time. Worse, since the injuries are old and setting."

"*Nir*," Kanna muttered against Haru's chest.

"No," he said.

He held her while the healer worked. He trapped her elbows so she couldn't yank her hands away, held her hips against him so she couldn't twist, and when her teeth bit into his arm he didn't let go.

Haru held on to her, because it was all that he could do. He held on to her, because he could do nothing else. He held on even when his skin broke, when he felt the blood flow, because what hurt more was that he could feel the screams vibrating in her throat. He held her against him, felt them in the way her spine tried to retract, in the shaking of her ribs as she held the sound in her lungs. He hoped she'd lose consciousness but she clung to it, bearing the misery on the off-chance that if she closed her eyes, she'd wake up back in the Cardea's prison.

Finished with the worst of it, the medicus wiped her brow and moved for her kit. Haru eased his grip, softened his arms around Kanna when her head lolled against his chest, her eyes shut.

"Make her leave, <avtandil>."

The medicus unpacked simpler items, setting them on the bureau with it's missing mirror.

"She's not done," he said, keeping his voice low.

Kanna attempted to curl her hands beneath her chin, the metal of the splints scraping against each other. "*I am done.*"

He knew he should convince her to let the medic continue, that it was necessary for Kanna to be prodded, bent, ministered by hands that weren't his. He called the medicus because had known many of Kanna's injuries were beyond him, but she had done her work. The rest would be his. "That is enough," Haru said to the medicus. "Go."

The woman turned, a hand on her starched hip, Kanna's blood smearing where it landed. "I am far from finished."

Haru tightened his hold on Kanna as if he could cover her, keep her from the world if only for a moment. The anger that tore through the monsters that had kept Kanna prisoner reared its head, a thing hardened and scaled and cold burning. The medicus must've seen it in him, in the way his body wrapped around Kanna, his shoulders hunching forward.

The hand on the medicus's hip fell and she turned to her bag. "I'll leave after she is on a drop."

The thing cooled, but he could feel its scales slide along his spine. "For what?"

The medicus pulled out a metal tripod, snapping it open and setting it next to the bed. "The Legatus is dehydrated and malnourished. Her body cannot heal without help, unless you want pyrexia to take her."

The medicus stood next to the bed, needle at ready.

Haru eyed the shine of it. "She hates needles."

"But she is not afraid of them," the medicus said, leaning forward as Haru closed himself around Kanna. "I'll leave when it's done."

From the cage of his arms, Kanna offered her hand, though she didn't look. Haru held her wrist up, taking some of the weight of her arm while the medicus inserted the needle and taped it down.

The medicus backed away, but she motioned for Haru. He didn't want to release Kanna, hated the idea of letting go, but he did. Grudgingly, he unfolded his arms and slipped from her.

"She needs surgery," the woman told him, casting her eyes to Kanna then away. "If she wants to use her hand again. We should send her to the medicium."

The scaled thing slid into the back of his neck, pulling his spine up and tilting his head forward.

The medicus didn't back away. "I'll send for a surgeon. You will have to bring her tomorrow."

Kanna stirred behind him.

"*<Avtandil>*?"

Haru held open the door for the medicus. "Tomorrow."

She nodded, then turned her appraisal to Haru's arm where the blood ran fresh red over the already spattered white of his shirt. "Take care of that, as well."

Haru shut the door at her back, slammed the lock in place.

"Haru?" Kanna called, her voice small and alone. "*Ver shtu, <avtandil>?*"

*Ver shtu*, she asked. Ilazkin questions shifted in context, so she could be asking where are you, or why, and he didn't know how to answer either of those right now. He didn't know *avtandil*.

Haru sat next to her, ran the tips of his fingers through her hair but they tangled in the matted knots and would go no further. "Hold on, inara. We will get you clean, at least."

"Hold on," she repeated, and laughed through a raw throat. "How, *avtandil*? These hands do not work."

Haru shut his eyes because he couldn't answer, leaned forward so she couldn't see the burn of tears that threatened him, and pressed a kiss into her hair. It smelled of fear and rot and his throat clenched. "I'll just be a moment," he managed to say, and he pulled away.

In Kanna's attached bath, the lights came on with a warming buzz before brightening to a harsh glare. Haru half-closed the door and turned the light down until it was a glow. The handles to the deep porcelain bath squeaked when turned, and the water growled in the pipes, sputtering to start before running smooth. He passed his hand under the water, used it to cleanse the drying blood from Kanna's teeth in his arm while he waited for the temperature to even, then set the bath's stopper in place.

At the sink, in front of the mirror that ran the length of the wall, he leaned his hands against the porcelain countertop. It was cool to the touch, and he hadn't realized how hot Kanna's skin had been until then. His hand clenched, his knuckles turning white, the scaled thing settling like dread at his back.

Haru had to keep it together. It wasn't the time. He squeezed his eyes shut, pressed his palm against them but the heat of tears escaped. He turned the back of his hand against his mouth and breathed jagged around it, pressed his skin to his teeth to stop from making a sound while his other hand held tight to the counter, willed it to stop.

He had been too late. He should have kept her safe. He should have known something was wrong immediately, should have been able to find her, but he was tripped up by bureaucracy and belief and he failed.

He caught the jag in his breath, held it, and breathed around it. Then he pressed both hands into the counter, and his next breath was easier.

He opened his eyes and met them in the mirror.

It wasn't the time. It wasn't time for him to fall apart. He ran cool water in the sink, splashed it over his face and rubbed it into his eyes.

He couldn't lose his grip, not now, not when she still needed him. He couldn't change what had happened, couldn't go back and find her faster, wouldn't have been able to change her mind if he had known what she'd planned, but he could be here now.

Haru turned off the water from the bath, the knobs' squeak echoing against the clean, hard surfaces of the bathroom. He pushed the cuffs of his shirt back over his elbows, and reentered the bedroom.

Kanna was so still he thought that she may have fallen asleep. But her eyes were open, flat and unfocused, the night sky that lived in them absent. She stared at the empty ceiling above her, her lips moving soundlessly. He kneeled next to the bed, dared to wrap his fingers lightly around her bruised wrist.

"Kanna?"

She didn't look at him, though her lips paused. She breathed in, heavy like waking, then released a ragged exhale.

"I am in the Tower," she said.

"Yes," he told her. "We're in your rooms."

She paused for the time between three beats of his heart, then continued her silent recitation.

"I drew you a bath," he said.

Her eyelids fluttered, but nothing sparked in the overcast grey as the corners of her lips curved into an unlived smile. "*What is dust to the universe?*"

Haru traced the freckles on her flushed cheek with the back of his knuckle before brushing away a damp lock of hair that clung to her heated brow.

"What is the universe to dust?" he asked.

The empty smile fell from her lips and she shut her eyes, her head tilting to listen for an ancient sound that would teach her how to understand.

Haru wanted to let her rest, wanted to hold her how she was, and he wanted to take the suffering from her breath into his own.

He couldn't do that. "Will you let me wash you?" he asked, because that was something he could do. It was something that needed to be done.

She let out a sigh that staggered over jolts of pain. "If it is you, *<avtandil>*."

Taking Kanna into his arms was easy. He knew the weight of her before, but after such a short time in someone else's hands she'd faded. The difficult part was balance, how to hold without hurting while having to drag the clear line that fed into her veins to bring her back.

Kanna didn't say anything else. Kanna's lips didn't move, and she didn't make a sound. Not when he lowered her into the water, and not when he began the careful work of digging her out from under the horror that clung to her skin.

Kanna was awake. Kanna was awake, but she wasn't. Kanna was there, but she was somewhere else.

Haru knelt next to the tub, his knees on the unforgiving marble floor, and started at the bottom of her hair. He unknotted it with his fingers, careful not to yank at any snarls. The water changed from clear to pale pink, with flecks of light stone and dried blood swirling over the surface.

He could feel the fever of her skin, watch the water that carried the filth from her hair down her back as it curved along the scar that saved him, but he couldn't reach her.

His knees ached until they were numb and the water turned to a colourless muck. He couldn't stand the thought of her sitting in it so he drained it, started over.

In the clean water, every color of bruise revealed itself on her pale skin. He sorted the layers of them, could estimate how long ago each was made and counted back the days, the weeks.

He turned his mind away from what he couldn't help, and remembered her strength. He thought of how her body moved like nature, how it felt like home when his name was on her tongue, and he knew she would return there.

She shifted. Her neck rolled over her shoulders until her gaze honed in on the needle in the back of her hand.

The shadows had come alive in her eyes, holding all colors, pressed into and against each other. They were deep violet, and navy, and every color of every temperature of star in the sky all at once.

A spark of gold flashed across them.

"Kanna?"

She moved faster than he thought she had the strength for. Her crippled right hand batted at the needle in the left, slid over the skin, so she tried to twist the tube to yank it free.

"Kanna, stop!"

She was going to hurt herself. She was going to rip her veins, she was going to upset the precarious balance of the bones of her hands, and he couldn't let her. He couldn't let anything else hurt her, even if it was herself. He grabbed her elbow and was shocked by how easy it was, how little resistance she could give.

She bent her neck, going for the metal with her teeth. The water's current pulled her body over the slick porcelain and she slid.

Haru leaned over the tall sides of the tub to catch her, his arm wrapping under her shoulders and pulling her up. He climbed into the bath behind her because he didn't want to think anymore, knew there was something he was supposed to remember, and he needed to hold her.

"I'll get it out, okay?" he said, because he would say anything if it would stop her from causing herself more pain. "I'll get it out."

Kanna restrained her own struggle, though it vibrated over her skin, her body trembling from the tension.

Haru peeled away the tape on the back of her hand and slid the needle from her vein. It fell to the floor.

The ping of such a small slip of metal falling on stone was too loud. It echoed.

Kanna settled, her heartbeat slowing, and she breathed.

Then she rasped out something like a laugh, if the sound of fracture could be considered a laugh.

Haru wrapped an arm around her waist, another over chest, and leaned his forehead into her back so she couldn't see the burn in his eyes.

She tried to wrap her hands around him, because she knew, because she always knew, but the metal of the splints brushed against his forearm. When her fingers refused to bend, the rasp turned into a sob. Her teeth snapped around it and the sound turned into a broken hum in her throat.

"I'm here," he said, because he was. "I'm not going anywhere," he said, because he never would, because he could never go where she was not. He could not exist if she did not, and would follow her into whatever hell she made for herself. He would offer a hand to pull her out, or he would build a temple there for her if that was where she wished to stay, because he knew no other way to be. "Let it go."

When she screamed, he remembered the sound. He remembered the sound of it then, and the sound of it now wasn't the same.

The ghost of the scream hit the walls of the bath, ricocheted against something newer. There was pain, raw and overwhelming, and there was more.

There was loss. There was guilt and anger, broken faith and betrayal. Grief both buried and found, old and new, overlaying and tangled until the beginning was the end and everything in between.

Haru tightened his hold around her because it was the only thing he could do. He tried to keep his own hands from shaking as the vibration of her pain coursed through bruised and healed ribs, her skin pressed against the hammering staccato in his chest.

She was a fever. She was cool to the touch.

The lights flickered and buzzed, grew in intensity until the filaments popped and the glass casings shattered.

The hands that couldn't hold healed, wrapped around his wrists when the strength of them returned. Each joint mended, moved, tested itself, tightened before she thought to let go.

Kanna screamed until the howls ran out, until the air that passed through her throat was a harsh whistle.

Haru unfurled his grip when she no longer fought, slid his arm around her waist to fit her against him. His fingers laced into her untangled hair, his thumb brushing against her temple.

Her body relaxed, not from exhaustion but from a kind of peace, and she sighed into the curve of his neck.

They were in the cool embrace of the porcelain bath, and he held her.

He would hold her at the edge of time, at the end of the known, because without her he was nothing. He was only a part of something when he was with her.

They were in the embrace of the dark and he held her, all of her, as she had been and as she was.

Then he heard thunder, and he felt the rain.

· · ·

THEY RETURNED in the greying twilight, the grass of Kirin crushed and blackened beneath them.

Kanna's hands shook as if she couldn't trust them, but she reached up, her fingertips grazing his cheek.

"*Avtandil?*"

Haru bent to her shoulder, brushed a kiss over the scar that caught the crook of her neck, and she shuddered beneath his touch.

"I am with you, *inara*," he said. "Always."

# 9

# HEARTH IN WINTER

## VAHN

VAHN STARED at the closed door of the bedroom where they'd left Kanna and Haru hours earlier. He wasn't expecting it to open. When Kanna ripped open the world all Vahn could do was watch as she fell back into nothing, as Haru followed her to a place that Vahn could never go because she had been right. He was a coward, and there were things not meant for him that he had no business chasing.

The void hadn't been the same as in the Theatre, the black didn't expand or leap out of control. It retracted, spilled ink returning to the bottle and when it was gone, Kanna and Haru were back. It had been seconds, if that long, but they were battle frayed. Eyes blank, bodies bent from the ache, and an exhaustion that went beyond any physical strain, deeper than anything. The proof of it was in the animalistic hunch of Haru's shoulders, then the slow blink when he recognized Vahn, and the way Haru allowed Vahn to lift Kanna from his arms. Yassen and Osawa propped Haru up between them and dragged him inside, and they deposited the both of them together.

Isco arrived with his medical kit, but Vahn shook his head and he backed away, leaving with the others.

Vahn took the time to unlace Kanna's boots and slide them off her feet before leaving himself. Even in a sleep deeper than death, Kanna rolled to Haru, her fingers wrapping in the front of his shirt and pulling closer. Haru's body shifted like a sigh, curling around her. That was how Vahn left them. Together, where they belonged, how they should always have been.

And that left Vahn on the floor across the hall, alone, staring at a closed door.

He shut his eyes and leaned his head back against the wall. In the last hours the house's occupants had moved past their stunned hush to tense companionship. Vahn had smelled dinner, heard the muffled sounds of Isco's instruction and the deep bass of Yassen's reply. Astar's tinkling laugh accompanied something Osawa said. Vahn wasn't hungry, and no one came for him, anyway.

Time passed. Chairs slid across the floor. Glasses touched wood. The screen door creaked on its hinges, then closed, and the house fell into a relative silence. The door opened again, and shut. Then another time. The third time prompted Vahn that something wasn't right. He stood, his feet prickling from having sat so long in the same position, but he forced them down the stairs.

Astar was at the table draining a glass of something amber. "Did you know," she said the moment Vahn's feet hit the landing, "that your friend can't hold his liquor."

Vahn looked where she pointed to Osawa, who had fallen asleep on the couch. "Yeah. Everyone knows that." Vahn could see Yassen's back through the door, and the kid was staring at something in the dark. "What're you doing out there, buddy?"

Yassen turned, his eyes still shielded by his hand despite the fact that the night was so inky dark there was nothing to cause a glare. "Lookin' for Isco."

Something crawled up Vahn's spine, curled around the nape of his neck. "What?" Vahn turned to Astar. "Explain."

Astar shrugged. "His anxiety was giving me anxiety. He needed to loosen up. How was I supposed to know he'd take the bottle and bolt?"

A feeling sunk in Vahn's gut, a cold coal that made him ill. "You didn't stop him?"

Astar raised her brow at him. "It's fine," she said, then reached beside her chair and lifted a bottle by the neck. "I had a spare."

Vahn didn't have the words to respond, but mostly because he didn't trust himself with the ones that came to mind. With a growl, he pulled open the screen door. "Get inside," he said to Yassen, then took the three steps off the porch without looking back.

The rain had stopped, but the dampness clung to the air. There was a breeze now, enough to cause a chill. This late at night, this far from any type of civilization or town, there were a thousand things hiding in the dark. Isco could have fallen off a cliff, or into a crevasse, or have gotten lost in the wilds.

There were, of course, other options. Isco could have seen the opportunity to get away, to slip from their reach and find his way back to his life. Vahn paused halfway through the yard.

Isco could have just left. He could be on his way now to get a respectable job at a respectable medicium and find a respectable someone who didn't make him jump out of his skin at every opportunity. They could settle down and have an entire passel of little Iscos. They'd have Isco's soft eyes, his long lashes and careful hands. It would be better that way.

That way, the war that was breathing on their necks wouldn't have a chance to take him.

While Vahn could almost but not quite imagine the names that Isco would call them, he knelt to the damp ground and placed his vicious hands against it. Vahn could feel a volcano preparing to erupt in Chromandae, knew a forest fire ravaged the Lugosian border. People, though, had different fires, different degrees by which they burned. Even though she slept, he still knew Kanna's molten presence behind him when he felt it, an oddly cold simmer for someone so furious.

Isco was quieter. Isco was a hearth in winter, he was the warmth of another's body caught under blankets on a cold night. He yanked his hand away when he felt it. Vahn went in that direction, though he was only going to make sure Isco hadn't fallen from a cliff.

The night was black, the clouds blotting out the stars, but Vahn picked his way through the fence, over the smooth grasslands, until he saw a light in the distance.

He found Isco beneath an abandoned rail overpass, tucked within the harsh concrete slabs and illuminated by the orange haze of solar signal lights that someone had forgotten to take down. It wasn't far from the farmhouse, but it wasn't exactly close, either. Isco was leaning back, a bottle propped on his knee, smiling softly at nothing Vahn could see. The hard curve of his neck caught the glow, his practiced hand gracing the green glass of the bottle he held with a soft but steady touch.

Vahn didn't want to interrupt him. He looked peaceful, for once. Vahn kicked the ground, dragged it beneath his feet as he approached, announcing his arrival in an effort not to startle Isco. For once, Isco didn't jump. He opened his eyes and turned them to Vahn, his dark lashes brushing against golden skin when he blinked, and smiled.

"There you are," Isco said, a soft purr in his voice.

Vahn stopped. He didn't know what to do with his hands as he resisted the urge to look behind him. He knew he was alone, but it didn't seem right that Isco was looking at him that way. It was strange, too strange, to be observed so softly. Vahn was used to the hard edge of desire, the burning lust that hit at the corners of peoples' eyes. Isco smiled, warm and content.

"Do you want me?" Isco asked.

Vahn felt a thousand embers spark along his every nerve, his mouth going dry and dumb.

"Wait... that's not all the words." He shook his head, pressed his fingers between his eyes and squinted in concentration before opening them again. "Do you want *to drink with* me?"

Isco lifted the bottle he cradled, shaking the dregs of it at Vahn, smiling wide and proud to have gotten his words out right this time.

Vahn swallowed, attempted to relax the tension in his shoulders, and took the bottle from Isco. His fingers lingered where they brushed together before he freed the remnant of the drink from Isco's hand. He turned it, searching for a label and a distraction. "What is this stuff?"

"Don't know. Got it from Ashner. Ashler... I'll get it. Asssssss—"

"Yep, understood," Vahn cut him off.

Isco nodded in satisfaction, then leaned back against the overpass.

Careful not to lose his footing, Vahn lowered himself to sit beside Isco. The concrete was rough, giving him good purchase on the steep angle. Once settled, he almost brought the bottle to his lips before thinking better of it. There was no way of knowing what it was, and at least one of them needed to be sober. Instead, he set it next to him.

Isco sat up, leaned over Vahn to try and reach it, but his unfocused grip tipped the bottle and it rolled down the incline, smashing at the bottom. "Woo!" Isco proclaimed, pulling himself out of Vahn's lap and raising his fists in celebration.

When the sharp tinkle of glass faded in the air, Isco sighed and leaned against Vahn, his head resting heavily on Vahn's shoulder.

Vahn told himself to breathe. Unfortunately, that meant Vahn caught the scent of him, honey lingering under sharp alcohol. Vahn cut off that thought and buried it.

"You know," Isco said. "You're good."

Vahn cleared his throat, pushed the confidence back into his voice. "I've heard that before."

"No, no," Isco said, shaking his head. His brushed faintly against Vahn's neck when he moved. "Not like that and your whole... thing," Isco waved offhandedly to encompass Vahn, then shifted tighter against him. "I mean you're good."

Isco fit against him, soft against his sharp angles.

"What's wrong with my thing?" Vahn teased.

"That's not—I'm sure your thing is fine, but you're good."

Vahn scoffed. "Usually I have to do a bit more than just sit down to earn that kind of praise."

"Shhh," Isco shushed him, pressing a finger against Vahn's lips.

Vahn's mind went blank. He had no idea how to react to that, didn't like the knowing burn in Isco's eyes as he looked into Vahn instead of at him.

"Why do you do that? Throw things off. Just—pssht—toss it." Isco waved his hands, and Vahn had to lean back to avoid being slapped. "You don't let it mean what it's supposed to."

Vahn laughed. It croaked out of him, strained and harsher than he meant it to be. But he was nothing but hard edges, elbows and knees, and he couldn't help that. Vahn was bone against bone, pain for pain. Isco was wounded, but Isco didn't bite back. He wasn't broken.

"Fine," Vahn said, acid in his throat. "What is it supposed to mean, Isco?"

Isco pulled away from him, curled his knees to his chest. His absence was immediate. Despite the cloying heat of the night, Vahn felt a chill.

"Sorry," Isco muttered. "I don't know what I'm saying." Isco put his face in his hands, pushing his palms in his eyes. He pressed hard, his hands curling around his head. "I'm sorry," Isco said, his voice catching. "I always say the wrong thing. The wrong thing."

Vahn's heart stopped. His body was bloodless but heavy. "Hey," Vahn leaned in, trying to reel Isco back as he spiralled.

"Sorry," Isco repeated, flinching away from Vahn. His hands pulled at his hair. "So sorry."

Vahn knew how to miss things without wanting them back, but he wanted Isco back. Even if all Isco did was sit next to him, loose and honest, and tell him strange things that seemed like the truth, that seemed like they mattered. But Vahn wasn't good at comfort, didn't know what it was like or how it worked.

"Isco."

He shifted to face Isco, pulled himself up onto his knees and tangled his hand in the back of Isco's hair. He tightened his grip and Isco leaned back into his palm, his face turning upward.

Isco didn't open his eyes, but he leaned into Vahn's touch. Vahn bent, pressing his forehead into Isco's. He breathed deep. Isco smelled of alcohol and dust, honey and salt and skin. He could get lost in it, so before he did, he pulled away.

Vahn opened his eyes and brushed his thumb beneath Isco's. They were hot and damp from tears that refused to actually spill. "Look at me."

Vahn hadn't expected to forget what breathing was when Isco opened his eyes. Vahn was certainly not expecting to not care. He no longer needed lungs, he only needed Isco to keep looking at him like he was the world. "You're kind, Isco," Vahn said when he was able. "This world tends to break kindness, but not yours."

Isco shut his eyes, shook his head. "But I—"

"You helped Kanna when I couldn't," Vahn said. "When we couldn't," he corrected himself. "And you even managed to keep me alive for some reason."

Isco looked at him, looked into him like Vahn could hold some kind of answer.

Vahn unlaced his fingers from Isco's hair and let him go. "Whatever it is you think needs to be forgiven, I'll forgive the part I can." Vahn smiled, knew it was bitter. "It can't be much, but I can forgive you that much."

Isco didn't say anything. His eyes dipped lower, to Vahn's neck, and his fingers reached out. They brushed against the black lines that wrapped Vahn's throat and it reminded him that there were things he wasn't meant to have.

Vahn cleared his throat and stood, pulling away from Isco's touch. "Come on. Unless you were waiting for a train."

Isco squinted at him, his fingers still lingering in the air that Vahn no longer occupied.

"Train's broke," Isco said, like it was the most obvious thing. Isco was still staring at him from the ground, and he didn't look like he was going to move. Vahn reached out a hand, and Isco still stared.

"Kanna will be worried if you aren't there when she gets up."

Vahn bent, and Isco's arms were around his neck, and when he stood Isco wobbled uneasily then leaned heavily against him. Vahn almost thought he felt Isco sigh.

Almost.

"She's good," Isco said, his voice muffled against Vahn's shoulder.

"Yeah?" Vahn shifted, wrapped his arm around Isco's waist so he wouldn't fall.

"Yeah," Isco said, nodding and leaning against him.

Vahn sighed. "I have some words for Astar, though."

"She's good, too."

Vahn turned to him, his nerves firing. Isco's tears had dried, and his eyes gleamed, relaxed and honest.

"I thought I was good," Vahn said, trying to remember what direction he'd come from.

"You are."

"You have low standards."

Isco grinned hazily. "Top of my class."

Vahn stared. Then he laughed. And it wasn't a forced thing, it wasn't something that he faked because it was expected and there was no sarcasm in it and he wasn't exactly sure how he was making the sound.

Isco smiled, soft and loose, and he tapped his fingertip against Vahn's nose. "Boop."

# 10

# BE A LION

## KENZI

THE SOUND of the alarm woke Kenzi from sleep. She kicked out against her bed roll, her legs tangling in the slick fabric as the off-kilter wail cut through the night.

The world came back slow even as her senses sought an attack: the smell of fire, the rush of water, the screaming cry of light or shadow as it defied itself. There was none of that, just the frantic pound of feet, the sharp draw of metal against holsters, and the bark of commands that her half-asleep mind couldn't sort.

Kenzi whirled, knives ready, when the back of the tent was torn through. Ira stopped long enough for her to drop her guard, his eyes flitting over her to take in her state. The instant relief of seeing him was replaced in the exact same second that it arrived with a deeper panic.

He paused for the moment their eyes met before he grabbed her travel bag and began shoving whatever his hands touched into it. "Get dressed. Hurry." There was no rhyme or reason to the things he flung together. "We have to run."

It wasn't a command, a demand, or a warning. The simple statement, told in the clearest of tones, gave Kenzi all of the information she needed in that moment. Kenzi grabbed the uniform she had discarded, yanking the still-filthy trousers over her hips and shrugging into the button down. Her shaking fingers would only allow her the time to button three of the loops. She fit her knives into their sheath in time for Ira to shove the pack into her chest.

While Kenzi looped it over her shoulders, Ira snatched up the origami horse. He guarded it against his chest, then peeled away the back of the tent.

Kenzi wanted to ask why there was only one bag.

Kenzi wanted to ask why there was blood on his sleeves.

Ira signaled that the way was clear, and she followed behind his quick clip. They moved away from the route Kenzi had taken earlier, weaving through the tents, checking each bend before scuttling across the wide, open pathways. As they rounded another turn, Kenzi skidded to a stop. "Enough. What is going on?"

Ira stopped, turned over his shoulder. Kenzi's feet were planted, and she refused to move. He walked back to her, his eyes darting around them. "The Storyteller you saw?"

Kenzi nodded.

"They had his family. Grandchildren, even. Masao worked them in front of him so that he would talk, but he refused."

Kenzi covered her mouth with her hand, the scene entirely too easy to imagine. "What information could a Storyteller know that they wanted?"

"He knew all of the stories," Ira said. "All of them."

Kenzi tried to remember the tales that had been spun by their village's own Storytellers, but she had never been interested in dusty legends. Something between a sigh and a growl ripped through Kenzi. "What is so important about old stories?"

Ira's yellow eyes gleamed in the starlight. "Everything, Kenz. And I couldn't let them figure it out."

Kenzi's throat clenched. "What did you do?"

A shout nearby halted their conversation. Ira's eyes met hers in question. Kenzi grit her teeth, and followed him. The tents were becoming sparser, making it harder to hide their escape as they moved closer to the horses. Unfortunately, eventually, the tents ended. The outlines of the tethered mounts could be seen from anywhere, and so would they.

With a last burst of speed, they raced across the open expanse.

The shouts went up immediately from the camp when they were spotted. The uproar upset the horses, and they began to stamp, their hooves digging into the sodden ground as they shifted and snorted as Ira wove the pair through them.

Ira turned, and Kenzi almost bumped into him. "They'll be in Kirin. Smugglers keep safe houses out there."

"Ira, what?"

"There's a map in the side pocket of the bag, I marked a few of the places they may go. Memorize it, then destroy it."

Kenzi shook her head. The soldiers from the camp were closing in, and she could feel the water pulling from the earth as they prepared to attack.

"Find where the tracks end, move south. Don't go into any of the villages, avoid them, they won't take kindly to the uniform."

Ira was certain, sure. Kenzi didn't like what that meant.

"You're coming with me."

Ira pressed the origami horse into her hand, closed her fingers around it. "Get this to Kanna."

Kenzi's head still shook, her fingers trembling even as she clutched the figure close to her chest.

He grasped her by the shoulders, met her eyes. "It is important, Kenz. It is the most important thing."

"You'll get it to her," Kenzi choked out. The ground dried beneath her feet, cracked where it was once bloated. "We'll bring it together."

Ira's knowing smile sunk every hope she tenuously held. He bent his forehead to hers briefly, before handing her the horse's reins. "Be a lion."

Kenzi mounted as Ira backed away.

She didn't want to remember him like that, with a smile like a goodbye.

She didn't have a choice.

Kenzi turned the horse away, dug her heels into its sides, and it bolted.

He stepped back, between her and the encroaching army. Fire and water, the whistle of a tearing wind, every element converged on Ira's silhouette.

The ground shifted, and the earth rose around him.

And then Kenzi couldn't see him anymore.

# 11

# SPECIAL LITTLE MONSTERS

## ASTAR

ASTAR MADE a lot of bad decisions. She had made a decent number of good ones, she would admit, but the bad ones always had the most direct and immediate consequences. For instance, when she found the sealed bottles in the farmhouse basement and decided that everyone needed to relax a bit. Now, her mouth was filled with cotton and her hair hurt. Whatever the people that had been here before claimed passed for a good time was apparently enough to knock a horse off its feet.

She would have preferred staying in bed, but her body rebelled at that idea, as well, so now she was sitting at the kitchen table and unable to do anything else.

Yassen had his face pressed into the table across from her. He wasn't moving. Astar slouched enough to kick out her foot, whacking against his legs to make sure he was still alive. Yassen groaned in response.

"Breakfast," she demanded.

"When did we get on a boat?" Yassen asked, his voice muffled by the table. "Did I miss the fight?"

Astar squinted at him from behind the shaded glasses she'd put on that morning, but he didn't lift his head. "What?"

His shoulders shrugged. "We get in a lot of fights."

It was apparent to Astar in that moment that she was not getting breakfast unless she made it. Before she could will herself to get out of her chair, Isco descended the stairs. Unlike the two at the table, or Osawa who hadn't moved from his position on the couch, there was an almost spring in Isco's step.

"Good morning," he announced.

"Is it, Isco?" Astar asked. "Is it, really?"

Behind Isco, Osawa stirred. Osawa sat up but hunched over, propping his elbows on his knees and putting his head in his hands. "Why?"

"You had one drink," Astar shot back at him.

"Please lower your voice."

Isco's brow knit in concern, and he went to work. Astar wished he wasn't so loud about it, and she wasn't exactly sure what he was doing beyond dedicating himself to slamming cupboards and attempting to turn on the kitchen sink's squawking taps, which didn't work. The near antique refrigerator at least opened with only a muffled sigh.

Astar opened her eyes when Isco set a glass in front of her, and one in front of Yassen, filling them from the pitcher of the water in the fridge. He brought another to Osawa. Osawa squinted at him, then missed when he reached for it. Isco found Osawa's glasses on the coffee table and offered those instead. Osawa put his glasses on, then managed to take the water.

Isco returned to clattering around the kitchen, this time pulling out a rattling plastic pill bottle and cracking it open. He dumped the contents into his palm before distributing them, starting with Osawa.

Next, he tapped the back of Yassen's hand. Yassen turned his hand palm up on the table, but didn't pick up his head. Isco dropped the pills in his palm then pulled at his shoulder so Yassen had to sit up to take them. Another two were deposited in front of Astar.

Isco returned to the counter and knocked back a few of the white tablets himself, following them with a swig of water, before setting to work again.

While Osawa rummaged in the couch to retrieve his knit cap and pull it over his ears, Isco worked. The oven clicked on, and the scrape of metal against cast iron soon rewarded Astar with the smell of melting cheese.

Osawa pushed himself up from the couch. "Too loud," he muttered, then left the farmhouse through the open screen door.

Isco turned to place a plate piled high with grilled sandwiches onto the table, and Astar swiped one immediately.

The slam of the screen door announced Osawa's return. "Too bright."

Isco managed to shove another glass of water and a napkin wrapped sandwich into Osawa's hands before Osawa disappeared past the stairs and headed for the farmhouse's cellar.

Back at the counter, Isco put a kettle of water onto the stove and prepared a mug for tea before turning around with the remaining water in the pitcher.

Astar stared at the glass in front of her as Isco refilled it. "How?" she asked around a mouthful of bread and cheese.

Isco had the audacity to look from the small pills on the table to Astar. "Medical school?"

Astar scooped up the pills and swallowed them after she finished her bite of sandwich. "No," she said after her mouth cleared. "How are you upright?"

Isco shrugged. The tea kettle whistled on the stove and he removed it, pouring the heated water into a chipped mug. "It's the same answer."

Isco set the kettle back on the stove, but as he did his gaze caught on something in the window over the sink. He was transfixed for a moment, before a realization lit in his eyes. He backed away from the counter and bolted up the stairs, abandoning both his tea and the remaining duo at the table.

Feeling somewhat more human thanks to the medic's sandwiches, Astar sat up enough to grab another from the pile before sliding the plate across the table to Yassen. Yassen let his head loll forward from his neck and stared at the food.

"Eat," Astar said. "It helps."

Resting both elbows on the table, one on each side of the plate, Yassen retrieved a sandwich half and bit into one corner. He chewed tentatively, but after the first swallow finished the half in two bites before starting on another.

After finishing much of what Isco had made, Yassen was more alive. He stood from his place and retrieved a jug of water from the counter, bringing it back to the table. He refilled his glass before setting it in the center.

When he sat again, he hunched over on his elbows. The glass between his fingers began to spin over the table wood, slowly, as he worked his hands against it. Occasionally, he'd glance from the glass, to Astar, and back again.

"What is it?" she asked when the sliding sound started to grate her nerves.

Yassen cupped his hands around the glass, his fingers covering each other. "Do you think it's true what Kanna said?"

"Kanna doesn't lie. I don't even think she'd know how to." Astar sat up and refilled her own half-empty glass, but left it untouched after. "You thinking about what she said about being at Rough's Peak?"

"Sort of," Yassen replied, "but not really."

"Yassen, sweetie," Astar said, rubbing her temple. "Isco may be a miracle worker, but I'm still coming around. You're going to have to talk plain to me."

"She had to have been a kid, right?" Yassen said. "And Vahn, too?"

Astar pushed the shaded lenses she was wearing up, balancing them in her hair. "No one tried to scare you with stories of the Hollow Children?"

Yassen shook his head, his eyes wide. "Why would people want to scare kids?"

Astar bit off her laugh. "You really are something else, you know that?"

Yassen shrugged and leaned forward, his brilliant green eyes wide and open as they always were when he listened to anyone speak.

"It was one of those stories that was too silly to be true, you know?" she said. "When I wouldn't listen right, or when I skipped my lessons, my father would tell me that I needed to behave or the Hollow Children would get me. Special little monsters, he said they were."

She lifted the glass of water to her lips and wished she had something stronger. The thought of her father caused a pang in her chest, even when she wasn't fond of the memories. "They were Palamidia, but they were shaped like kids. Hollow Children were more vicious than any soldier, more powerful than regular loas, and," she grinned and rolled her eyes, "he said they took souls. Especially those of children that didn't listen to their betters."

When she was finished, Yassen blinked. His brow crunched in

thought and his arms crossed as he leaned back in the chair. After sifting through the information, he shook his head. His eyes met Astar's again. "Kanna ain't a monster. Neither is Vahn."

"I know that," Astar said, but she didn't snap around the words. "But you have to admit, there are things we've seen Kanna do that should be impossible, even for a loa."

"Maybe," Yassen said, "but everything is impossible until it isn't."

Astar sat back, another small laugh finding its way through her haze. Yassen had a way of saying things, of being, that was a wonder. They sat together in a comfortable quiet while Yassen continued to stare at the table, his thoughts turning over behind his eyes.

"I wonder what they called them," Yassen mused.

Astar raised a brow. "Who?"

"The Palamidy," Yassen said, raising his gaze from the woodgrain of the table to meet hers. "Your dad called them Hollow Children, but I wonder what their own called them."

"Soldiers."

Astar turned at the sound of Kanna's voice. She hadn't noticed when she entered, and a soft panic hit her stomach when she wondered how much Kanna had heard.

Kanna's expression remained flat, her voice even. "They called us soldiers."

# 1 2

## BETTER FOR YOU

### KANNA

WHEN ASTAR and Yassen turned to Kanna, eyes wide, she wondered if she'd spoken with too much bite. She still didn't quite fit in her skin. Dragging her feet across the hardwood so she could feel it beneath them, so she could know it didn't move, she made it to the kitchen counter. The butcher block top had lost its shine in places, was gouged in others, but it was solid and didn't shift.

The light streaming through the window above the sink was further proof that she'd crossed back across the planes. Kanna always woke before the dawning, in the moment when the dark burned away with a hollow echo, but that morning had been different. As her consciousness crawled back under her skin, she knew it was day, and she'd known that Haru was with her. She knew it from the breath in his chest, from the silence between each beat of his heart.

Like every time she could recall, she slipped from his arms before he woke.

From her place near the sink, she caught sight of Vahn in the corral. He was moving through a basic routine, slow and grounded. Kanna knew it. It was one of the first ones she taught him, the one he always fell back to when his thoughts refused to be stifled. If they were anywhere else, any time else, it meant he would be searching for a new bed to suffocate them in by nightfall.

Kanna turned her attention to the counter and an abandoned cup of tea. She removed the infuser and placed it in the sink, flinching when the metal scraped in the stainless bowl.

"Are you going to sit down?" Astar's clear voice snapped Kanna's focus back. "You're making me nervous just standing there."

Kanna looked from Astar to Yassen, and both continued to watch her. They weren't judging her, never had, weren't expecting her to be or do anything except make up her mind even after she'd attacked them while standing on empty ground. "You want me to sit with you?"

"Why wouldn't we?" Astar asked, raising her brow. "It's not like you nearly went full pissed-off-god mode yesterday."

Yassen smiled.

Kanna carried the tea with her to the table, sitting in the chair between the two of them with her back to the window. She wrapped her hands around the still warm mug, and the remaining heat drove away what remained of the phantom pain that lingered in the joints of her fingers. Small leaves had escaped their cage and sunk to the bottom of the mug. "I shouldn't have said those things."

"Yeah, you should've." Astar crossed her arms at her chest and tipped her chair onto its back legs. "You probably should've said them earlier, actually."

Even if Kanna's throat wasn't hoarse from her journey to the Neither, she wouldn't have known what to say.

Astar was considering the ceiling. "I don't think any of us thought this would be easy, but I don't think we thought about... whatever it was we were doing much at all." She shrugged. "I know I didn't. I was just along for the ride with my hot friend and her shockingly attractive entourage, trying not to think too much about what was actually going on.

"It wasn't a revenge thing, for me at least, and definitely not for Yassen. I mean, look at him." Kanna turned to Yassen, who waved. "There isn't a vengeful muscle in that boy's big body."

Kanna let Astar's words turn over in her mind. "But... your city?"

"My father's city," Astar said, then she let her chair drop to the floor. "My people, though. All I want is them to be free. Not in the way you might think, though," she added before continuing. "Free from fear. Free from constantly wondering when the war will start again, because there is always the war. Don't know when it started, can't find an end. How are people supposed to live like that? Actually live, not just survive."

Kanna bit her teeth together.

"I don't know what I can do about any of that," Astar continued, her fingers tracing the grain of the table. "I don't know what we can do. There aren't many of us and there are so many of them, but it feels like we can do something. For once, it feels like I can do something." Astar sighed, tilted her head to the ceiling once more. "I mean, we can at least try, right?"

Astar's words reminded Kanna of Isco in the train car, of Vahn's uneven heartbeat and unsteady breath. She shut her eyes and lifted the tea to her lips when words refused to come. It had been steeped too long, but the underlying bitterness felt like what she deserved.

Yassen cleared his throat and she opened her eyes. "How's Haru?"

Kanna couldn't answer that either, not fully. "He's still sleeping."

"He's gonna wake up though, yeah?"

Kanna smiled at Yassen's pure concern. "Yes. He'll wake up."

He sighed in relief. "Good," he said, and nodded. "But, Kanna?"

She tilted her head.

Yassen was almost sheepish when he asked, "What happened? What was that?"

Kanna placed the tea back on the table, loosening her hands. "It was the Neither."

It was Yassen's turn to tilt his head at her.

"It is complicated." The pieces that Kanna had gathered didn't fit together. Something was missing. Maybe if she put it in order, gave it words, it would make sense. She looked at the dredges of leaves at the bottom of her tea. "It's between," she said. "Between here and... something else."

The duo at the table were uncharacteristically silent as she searched for words.

"Something happened in Ilazki, before I woke up." Kanna closed her eyes and she saw light. Light like rain, light like blades. Panic and fear and knowing everything was lost. She opened them before the memory stuck. "I think I died."

"Wait," Astar said. "What?"

Kanna smiled, but it was bitter. "It didn't take."

"Is that why your memories are gone?" Yassen asked.

"They aren't gone. They were... misplaced." She dared to close her eyes again, tried to remember the fleeting instant. "I was in the dark, but I didn't want to be. I knew I wasn't supposed to be there, that there was something else, so I reached for it. When I came back, I didn't have my memories. Something about whatever I did to get back wasn't enough. They were gone, and I woke up in a wasteland."

"So, they're there? In that place?" Yassen asked.

Kanna nodded. "But they're scattered everywhere, and they're broken. I go, and I live them again, but some are hiding. Or hidden."

"Could you find them?" Astar asked, a little too eager.

"The ones I've gotten back"—Kanna tightened her grip on the mug and searched for the right way to describe it—"they hurt. Maybe there's a reason I can't get to the others. I am probably better without them."

"Are you sure?" Yassen asked, with neither judgment nor guile. "When I met you, you were kinda scary. Nice, but scary." He scratched the back of his head, then put his hand back on the table. "Don't get me wrong, you're still both those things, you're *you*. And you are different since you got your memories back, but not in a bad way. It's like the thing Astar said about just surviving, that was you. Sometimes...." Yassen looked down, squeezed his hands in his lap. "Before, when you'd smile, I'd think it was the saddest thing I ever saw. Then you started to smile, and it was real." He looked up and grinned at her. "I think that's better. I like that better for you."

Kanna had felt a lot of things since Governor Hautman kicked over the events that had led her to this place, to this table. She had felt an unending, unyielding rage. She had felt fear and pain, and she had slivers of joy and peace, and then a loss so gaping she couldn't crawl out so she buried herself in nothing because it was the only thing she could think to do. Of all those things, Kanna had yet to be struck dumbfounded and she wasn't sure what to do with the feeling, and it certainly didn't prepare her for Yassen's next question.

She knew it was coming when his grin shifted. Something connected in his mind.

"Hey, Kanna," he said. "Do you think the Neither existed before, or did you make it?"

There was a beat, counted by a hard thud in Kanna's chest, then Astar laughed. "Now that's crazy. That can't happen. Someone can't just make a place. Right?"

Kanna didn't have words.

Astar's laughter petered out, and her expression sobered.

"Right, Kanna?" Astar asked again, desperately needing Kanna to answer.

Kanna couldn't answer.

# 13

## A KIND OF UNDERSTANDING

### HARU

"I DON'T LIKE YOU," Haru said.

Haru didn't know why he stopped, but at the same time he knew exactly why. The way Isco stood at the window had been something he recognized. The taut shoulders and almost imperceptible lean of his chest as it pulled away, towards, as Isco stared through the dormitory window at the end of the hallway.

Isco turned abruptly, and nearly tripped over his feet. He looked to Haru, from his bare feet to the top of his head. Isco's eyes twitched in confusion, before meeting Haru's. "I know?"

Haru could still feel the burn in his eyes from when he woke with empty arms. For a brief instant, it was the same as every heartrending morning between when Kanna had disappeared in Ilazki before he found her again. Every morning, there had been a calm moment before he realized, once again, that she was gone.

Every morning, since he'd met her. Every moment was wrong without her in it.

Isco shifted uncomfortably and tried to move further into the wall, and Haru realized he'd been staring. Haru shut his eyes and rubbed the back of his neck. It ached from the press of the porcelain tub and the strain of keeping himself together.

Everything hurt. Even his skin felt like it had been peeled back and replaced.

"At least, I didn't." Haru opened his eyes and bent his head back. He thought of Isco in Kanna's cell, keeping her company in the dark. The rudimentary splints that were on her hands when he'd found her. Then there was after the Theatre in Gegenes, when she hissed and fought and Isco... tried to help.

In Pyrgolis, Isco fought to keep Vahn alive, to keep him together, and, in turn, it had kept them all together. But then he remembered Kanna's screams, the cascade of events that lead to her leaving for Ilazki, and he remembered Isco's part in tipping the first scale.

"I don't know anymore." Haru moved to the window, and Isco watched Haru with a mixture of nervous confusion and curiosity. The second floor vantage allowed for a wide view of the fields below and, notably, the corral. The ground had been blackened where Kanna had stepped into the Neither, but otherwise it was empty.

Haru leaned on the wall furthest away from Isco and shoved his hands in his loose pockets. The wood scraped against his bare back, and the sensation was so unlike smooth porcelain that he welcomed it as a grounding point. At least it was a point of himself that he could know was real.

Haru fixed his focus outside the window. The sun dipped past its zenith and marked the day as late, but the days in Kirin were so much shorter that it was difficult to know for certain. There were no clouds on the horizon and the brightness of the sky stung his eyes, his skin prickling as if it had never felt daylight before.

For the first time in a long time, it seemed the day would pass without a storm.

"Are you all right?"

Haru jumped when Isco spoke, jerking his attention away from the landscape. He forced his shoulders to relax, his eyes sliding back to the window. "Not something you can fix, medic," he said, the sharp bite in his voice tasting like metal.

Isco nodded. "Right."

The concern didn't leave his keen eyes, and Haru did his best to ignore it. An uncomfortable silence sat between them, then Isco attempted to slide along the wall to escape.

Haru closed his eyes, passed his fingers over the scar on the back of his right hand. "In Adur—"

Isco froze.

"—you were the one that set her left hand." Haru opened his eyes, watched Isco run his hands through his hair. He clasped his hands behind his back, then let them fall to his sides, then shoved them into his pockets.

Isco was preparing. Haru waited.

"She insisted on the left." Isco closed his eyes, cleared his throat so it fell into a monotone. "The right needed more immediate attention, but...." Isco's trained medical detachment failed him. Haru watched as his body rebelled against his attempts to distance, to relax. Isco shifted in place, his body pulling away like it was trying to run, but then he swayed back to an equilibrium. "I didn't get to it."

"We arrived."

Isco couldn't meet Haru's eyes. His lips quirked into a pained half grin and he nodded.

Haru turned to the window. "She's left handed."

He wouldn't apologize. The monsters that had attempted to take Kanna apart deserved everything that he'd rained down on them and more. Despite what Haru had witnessed in Kanna's memories, he wouldn't let it go. He couldn't. Isco, by his very existence, was a danger to Kanna. To all of them.

Haru pulled his hands from his pockets, crossed his arms and leaned back again. Isco didn't try to leave this time. Haru slid his eyes over to him, saw the fear in him while a bastardized version of courage kept him in place.

"What are you going to do about Vahn?" Haru asked.

In an instant, relief passed through Isco before his nervous energy spiked into another kind of the same thing. "I don't know what you mean."

Haru raised his brow.

"There's nothing," Isco stammered, then his voice fell. "It's nothing."

"Nothing?"

Isco opened his mouth to respond, but then shut it and looked away.

"Then you need to leave."

Isco's eyes widened and he focused on Haru.

"I've never seen Vahn look at anyone the way he looks at you. I doubt he even knows. He's always too busy trying to distract people from actually seeing him by making them look at something else." Haru uncrossed his arms and pulled himself away from the wall. "If he is nothing to you, as you say, then leave. He will recover from something that never was. Vahn learned how to lick his own wounds long ago."

Haru stopped in front of Isco, the same thing that stopped him the first time stopping him now, and he met him eye-to-eye. "I don't know if your absolution is here, Isco, but you may find something else."

## 14

# A HILL TO DIE ON

## OSAWA

OSAWA DIDN'T LIKE to drink. He didn't like the flush in his cheeks, or how the ground became off-kilter. But the night before, he wanted to stop thinking, if only for a moment. The drinks that Astar poured did the trick, but now his head was pounding and every thought he had avoided had somehow risen an octave between his ears.

In addition, now he was cursing himself for drinking in the first place.

At least the cellar muffled the sounds from above, and the cool dark was a balm on his overheated skin. Osawa leaned against one of the casks of water that he had purified since they had arrived. They took up most of the space, while the racks of unlabeled mystery drinks that Astar was fond of sampling lined the walls.

The sandwich and water that Isco had provided, along with the medicine capsules, were slowly working to brush away the edge of the physical ails that nagged Osawa when the cellar door opened and shut. Light footsteps followed the sound, the cadence unmistakable.

"Hey, Kanna," he said to acknowledge her arrival.

Hesitant steps brought her across the room, shushing against the packed earth when she drug her heels to turn and sit. Osawa could feel the nervous rush of the blood in her veins as she fidgeted.

Kanna's weight shifted next to him as she attempted to settle. "Are you hiding from me?" she asked, finally.

Osawa opened his eyes and smiled, shook his head. "Not you. Astar," he admitted. "She is quite loud."

Kanna tilted her head to look at him, grinning when she sensed the truth in the statement. It didn't reach her eyes, even as she teased. "How many drinks did you have?"

Osawa closed his eyes and groaned, knocking his head back against the wooden cask he was leaning on. "Don't laugh," he warned, then held up two fingers for her.

She still laughed, though there was something missing from the sound, and she had the decency to clear her throat to cover it. "Alcohol dehydrates," she said when her voice steadied, "and you're water."

Osawa shrugged. It made sense, like most things Kanna said. Having been raised by people who used words as weapons, Kanna always spoke carefully. She did not waste them, choosing as few as possible to say what was needed, even if trying to figure out what she meant was akin to translating another language on occasion.

"You don't usually drink." Her voice was a hum, whatever brief amusement she'd had gone as her voice fell to just above a whisper. "It is because of what I said."

Osawa opened his eyes enough to see her. Kanna was staring at her hands, running her fingers over the scars along her knuckles. "Now who's inventing tragedies?"

Kanna's hands paused their fidgeting, her eyes widening as she turned to him.

Osawa sighed. He shifted his weight, pulling himself up from his uncomfortable slouch to sit up against the cask he leaned on. "Do you remember when we first met?"

Kanna's gaze narrowed in thought, moved to the wall as she concentrated. She hunched forward, trapping her hands between her knees. "You were losing to Haru in the amphitheatre," she said, finding the thread of memory. "On purpose."

"None of you ever realized that sparring shouldn't be about winning or losing," Osawa said with a shake of his head. "It's about learning. Understanding. And I understood that Haru needed to win." He shrugged. "I didn't."

He titled his head towards her, but she wouldn't look at him yet. He turned away so she wouldn't feel watched. Osawa knew he wasn't the same as the others, but meeting them had changed him. He never really had to do anything to stay with them, because they always looked over their shoulders to make sure he was there.

Osawa had never belonged before. But his friends never made him feel like he was trespassing, never made it seem like he was an imposter or unworthy of their companionship. He cleared his throat, his eyes on the knotted wood wall. "When I was growing up, Masao had a game he liked to play with the cousins. He'd dunk our heads under water, hold us there longer than we could stand."

Osawa thought of the camp outside of Gaoler and the sensation of drowning on dry land. He swallowed the memory. "I later learned the same could be used for torture."

Still unable to look at him, but still herself, Kanna slid closer. She leaned her head on his shoulder in shared comfort.

"The sensation of drowning is incomparable. Trying to breathe something too thick to be air, but it enters your lungs anyway. That's its nature, to fill any space." A shudder ran through him, his diaphragm clenching from the memory. He breathed deep, reminding himself that it was past. Then, Osawa let go of his breath, and a secret. "It wasn't that I was afraid of drowning. It was that when I breathed the water, it felt right."

Osawa shut his eyes and saw the open sea, beyond the waves where it was smooth as glass and every shade of blue, every color when the sun struck and split the light against it. "Water everywhere, and all I wanted was to be a part of it."

Osawa stretched his legs in front of him. Ever since Kanna had taken him through the Neither, he hadn't lost the feel of the water. Now, he sensed the blood as it rushed out to his feet, as it returned to his heart. It was waves under his skin.

"Every day it was like fighting against my own death but there was, I think, belonging there." He bent his head, rested his crown against Kanna's. "I didn't understand, and I didn't think anyone else could. How is it that one can be afraid of something that is supposed to be part of them?" Osawa lifted his head slightly, nudging Kanna's before settling back. "Then I met you."

Kanna slouched against him. "And look where that has gotten you."

"I'll admit, this isn't where I imagined I would be," Osawa said with a short laugh. He tilted his head back, looked to the bare rafters above him. If he listened closely, he could hear the footsteps of the people that moved in the house, shifting from one room to the next. Like tides, they had gathered. "But what I had imagined was far worse."

"What's worse than being run to ground at the end of the world?" Kanna asked, the bite in her tone holding her uncertainty.

"Dying on a hill you don't believe in." Osawa answered with plain words, with concise meaning so that Kanna would know what he meant. She was good at that, only needing the right words, just enough words, the words that belonged together in ways that she could understand.

Kanna lifted her head, shifting to curl her knees into her chest. She wrapped her arms around them, making herself small, and ran her thumb over the raised scars on her right hand. As her gaze drifted away, shadows darkened the bright grey.

Osawa nudged her with his elbow. "We may be here because of you, but we're not only here for you. Do you think we don't know how small we are? That everything is broken?"

Kanna dropped her forehead to her knees, her voice muffled. "I can't fix it," she said. "I can't fix anything."

Osawa rested a comforting hand on her bent back. "Not just you. But maybe we can."

Kanna uncurled from her hunch, a spark of gold flashing in her eyes when she met Osawa's. The way she turned to him reminded Osawa of the front lines, when even with the worst odds and everything falling apart, Kanna would find a way.

"Maybe," she said, her voice quiet but steady. "We could try."

# 15

# RUN, RUN, RUN

## KENZI

Kenzi'd ridden for days, through the nights, through the storms that lashed the borderlands along Ilazki. Her mind kept repeating Ira's instructions, kept playing the moment when he shoved the origami trinket into her hands and told her to ride. Even when her hand turned to a claw, even when her breath came shallow, she clutched it against her chest and maintained a pocket of air to protect it from the rain and mud.

After her escape from the camp, she'd ridden west before veering south, cutting through a dense marsh and crossing through creeks in a desperate attempt to hide her passage. She found the major train lines and followed them, as Ira had instructed, until the line cut off at a dead stop. There was no station, no signal or sign of its ending, and Kenzi paused for a moment to catch her breath.

Then she chose a path.

Kenzi had stopped once, to retrieve the map that Ira promised. She squinted at the marks in the dark, branded them into her mind's eye, then held the map between her hands. It was the only thing she had with Ira's handwriting, the last piece of him she had besides the folded horse that she was to deliver to someone else.

With a shaking breath and dry eyes, she conjured a lashing whirl-wind within her palms and shredded it to almost nothing. She released what remained on the wind and it drifted away, dust against the night sky.

She had already found most of the marks on Ira's map, but there had been no signs of the Legatus or her companions. They had raided the veterinarian clinic in Pyrgolis when Kenzi had happened upon them, so it was likely one of them had sustained injuries in the battle. The safehouses that Kenzi had checked were too close to the borders, and yet still too far from any of the minor rail lines that would aid in transporting the wounded. But she didn't want to miss any of them, just on the off-chance that the one she didn't check was the one where they were hiding.

This was too important.

Another storm had fallen on her beyond Kirin's border, and she hunched over in an attempt to protect herself from the rain. It was easy to get turned around in the dark, in the open wilds, when the stars were covered by clouds determined to unseat her.

She almost missed the town until she was nearly upon it. Her mount reared when she pulled up too quickly and Kenzi slid from its back, falling hard against the muddy ground.

Kenzi grit her teeth as she rolled to lessen the impact, still clutching the origami piece to her chest.

A jolt of panic had her on her feet before her body could give into her exhaustion.

If she lost the horse, she'd never make it anywhere.

And Ira had told her this was the most important thing. It was a thing he was willing to kill for, to die for, and Kenzi wouldn't let that be in vain. She whipped up a gust of wind and it picked up the horse's reins, bringing them to her free hand. The horse pulled back, but she dug in her heels, slipping against the muddy ground.

When her mount settled, she checked that the origami's shield was still in place, then squinted through the dark at the town ahead of her.

It wasn't even a town, but a city. Walls surrounded it, and a flash of lightning illuminated a spire within. Lights sparked in the windows, bright against the violent night, too many for Kenzi to count. There was nothing like it on the map that Ira had given her, and as far as most knew, there weren't any cities of any significant size in Kirin. Dread settled in her stomach when she considered that she may have gotten turned around. Instead of using her abilities to test the wind, she had conserved her energy in order to preserve the message she held.

But if she was going the wrong way, there was nothing to preserve. Already exhausted, already feeling the edge of her limit, she shut her eyes and, with a light touch, checked the wind. It blew frigid and tasteless from Ilazki in the west, cool and salty from the Icaunian Sea in the east. She tilted her face, and there was something else.

Something complicated came from the city. It wasn't a wind like any she knew, but something almost... alive. The wind shuddered against it, as if whatever it was sensed her touch and used the wind to guide its reach. It called to her, whispered of power and knowledge and secrets.

With a gasp, she pulled her senses away, but the feeling lingered like a ringing in her ears.

She told herself the purring brush that reached under her skin was a chill from the rain, from the cold, and nothing else.

She told herself it was her exhaustion, the pull of constantly channeling her abilities toying with her mind. She shook her head and forced herself to refocus her attention to her task.

*South*, Ira had told her. *Avoid any towns or gatherings of people.*

She didn't need his warning to avoid this one. Why it was here, how it was here, it didn't matter. The only thing that did was a folded trinket with a blood toll. She remounted her horse and turned back. She pulled away from the outskirts of the city, giving it a wider berth than necessary.

There were three more marks on Ira's map.

# 16

## THE HOLY IN THE HOLLOW

### VAHN

VAHN SPENT the morning in the sun, in the heat, moving through a meditative routine. He had never been as fond of them as Kanna, preferring other types of distraction, but she had taught him anyway. Sometimes, sometimes, when he wanted to think without thinking, or rest without resting, he would fall into the first she'd taught him. The memory of her voice played its instruction for him—it was that hidden voice of hers, the one that was sad and more than a bit lost but trying so very, very hard to give him something, to teach him something, to help. But he could not stay in that corral forever, just as they could not stay that way forever, as the only two who mattered in their world, and, eventually, he retreated to the dim house.

The shower in his room would at least relieve the sweat that slicked his skin, but the unadulterated water was neither cool enough to chill nor hot enough to scald, so he had to settle for the tepid disappointment of it. Stepping from the shower, he pulled on a fresh pair of cotton pants, ignoring the fact that they slid and barely caught on his hips.

In the mirror above the sink, Vahn's eyes stuck for a moment. His ribs were less defined now, and the water from the shower caught on the mess of burn scars at the center of his chest. He lifted his fingers to it, traced the remaining outline of a wing.

The Cardea's brand had been seared into him when they'd realized he would make a fine specimen. Strapped down and powerless to stop them, to stop anyone, they heated iron and pressed it into his skin. The heat was everywhere. Being a fire loa made him somewhat numb to the effects of fire, but that pain lit him from inside. It boiled the marrow of his bones, burned so hot that they warped and threatened to snap. The blue flames that left his body were a halo, and they reached for his captors in a way that he couldn't.

That hadn't been the worst part. The worst part was the smell. They managed to knock him out, but he still remembered that. It wasn't something a person could forget.

After he'd been taken in to the Palamidia, the brand was the first thing he tried to obliterate. The four wings with the center eye shut haunted his dreams more than anything else. He'd found a small cave in what he thought was an abandoned area of the grounds, just beyond the stables. He heated a knife he'd swiped from a sleeping officer and pressed it against the shut eye.

The acrid smell of his own flesh crackling under the heat burned his nostrils, made his hands shake, but he held the knife in place. He wasn't the same weak thing they'd branded. He felt the heat in his bones and he welcomed it instead of fighting, understood it and focused on controlling it, which was probably why he hadn't noticed the footsteps.

Cursing in a language he had never heard, Kanna arrived, nearly tripping over herself. Her hands were stronger than they should have been, her fingers wrapping around his wrist and yanking it back. She grabbed the knife, still red with heat, and flung it out of the mouth of the cave.

Vahn could see what was in front of him, the wreck of him. Anyone could. The next time the fire tried to take him, he'd allowed it in, and it made him a Saint. And he had grown accustomed to the smell of flesh burning.

Back in the attached bedroom, Vahn rifled through the bag he'd set on the bed in search of something light enough he wouldn't sweat through it immediately, but he had few options. All he had was white shirts. White shirts like emptiness, white shirts like bone, hauntingly white shirts.

A rattle from the half open window distracted him. The corner of the screen had ripped away from its frame, and a breeze that announced the coming of night whistled through the tense metal. The edge curled away, sharp against his touch.

The air shifted, the warmth of a body announcing itself before sound did. Vahn straightened to look over his shoulder where Isco occupied the threshold, his hand held to knock on a door that had been left open.

For an instant, Vahn wanted to cross his arms, cover what scars he could. Instead, he braced his arms on the sill behind him, leaned his weight to be effortless, as if he didn't care. As if he could ever not care that Isco looked at him as if there was something worthy in the hollow whistle of his bones, in the empty space that remained after everything else had either been taken or burned away.

Isco held his silence as he stepped into the room, and Vahn was almost grateful for it. Vahn knew that Isco would voice his regret for the night before, the small moments when the burning was a comfort, and he'd be warming his hands on dark coals once again.

Another step, and Isco was closer. With an almost sure hand, he reached, his fingertips daringly close to the black bands that circled Vahn's neck and drew a dividing line between him and the civilized.

If bodies were temples, Vahn's was cinder and smoke, dead ground where nothing should grow, yet the faintest promise of Isco's fingers against his throat threatened to bloom.

Vahn leaned back against his body's demand to move towards.

"Can I—" Isco started.

"Sure," Vahn said. He remembered to smirk. He didn't let the smirk fall, didn't let his body chase when Isco's fingers curled into fists and Isco stepped back.

"You didn't know what I was going to ask."

Vahn's grip tightened on the windowsill, the years of wear and uneven gouges pressing into his palms. "Does it really matter, Isco?"

Isco attempted to run his hand through his hair, but his hand caught in the tie that kept it up. His hand dropped back to his side. "I should go."

Isco was going to leave. Isco was going to leave, and Vahn was going to die in this war, and he'd never see him again, and that was for the best.

Vahn caught Isco's arm when he turned away because Vahn's body was a traitor. "Wait."

He didn't know what he was going to say when he'd stopped Isco, but it had to be something. He couldn't stand the idea that Isco wouldn't look at him. Didn't want to imagine a time in which Isco never would.

Isco stopped, and turned, and Vahn released his grip. Isco's eyes looked up, slow, and met Vahn's.

"What were you going to ask me?"

The distance between them closed, and Isco tilted his back to raise his eyes, breaching the breaths between them. "Can I kiss you?"

Vahn didn't think of himself as a thing that needed permission to take from. He gave, and he gave until there was nothing left to take. He was a hollow-boned ghost where ash and rage lived.

Isco was kind. Isco had more courage than a thousand soldiers, more heart than any of them could imagine, and Isco waited for him to say something.

"Yes," Vahn said, and he didn't know he was answering until he heard the husk of his own voice.

Isco leaned up, just enough. The first soft brush of Isco's lips left Vahn breathless, and when Isco eased back Vahn tried to follow. Isco's hand curled at the back of his neck and invited him closer as he teased Vahn's lips open.

It wasn't as if Vahn had never been kissed before. He had been kissed quite often, in fact. Burying his damage in the body of another was a fleeting oblivion that he'd pursued constantly, mercilessly, until he'd run himself empty.

Vahn waited for it to hurt, but Isco's kiss didn't take. It was like learning to breathe all over again. It was like coming alive. Vahn pressed a shaking hand to the side of Isco's face, slid his fingers back until they caught in his hair and he leaned in, taking what was offered but wanting more.

When the kiss broke, Vahn's shuddering breath matched the shake in his hands. Before he registered the loss, Isco's fingers slid from the back of his neck.

"Okay," Isco said, his voice a whispered quaver. He stepped back and cleared his throat, met Vahn's eyes, and repeated: "Okay."

Vahn couldn't move. He could only stare as Isco backed away. He turned to leave the room and jerked back, barely avoiding the doorframe.

Recovering, Isco pointed at Vahn with both his index fingers, his thumb up.

And then he left.

# 17

---

# GRAVITY

## KANNA

KANNA KNEW HE WAS SAFE. Every time Haru woke, something dormant inside of her stretched and reached. Still, Kanna needed to know he was safe.

There were things, Kanna had learned, that were inevitable. Death was one. Gravity was another. Of all the forces that she could bend and control, there was nothing that Kanna could do against gravity.

Haru was proof. The pull between them was stronger than her denial, stronger than her fear or anger, and she could feel it with every step towards or away. There had always been danger in that. Just as easily as gravity kept, it could crush.

Everything around her felt too bright or too loud, too dark or too cold, as if her body was still remembering which skin it was meant to inhabit. The day was cooling, the sun slanting lower and attempting to burn Kanna's eyes, and in the corral, at the center of the ground that Kanna had ruined, Haru moved. Deliberate, slow, but his timing was a shadowed tableau of grace.

Her bare feet slid across the grass, warm from the day's limited sun, the blades bending under her soles with each step. Haru stopped, his shoulders sinking and his eyes shut. When he lifted them to meet hers, she remembered gravity. And she knew: as lost as she had been, as untethered and dark, as breathtakingly angry as she had felt, he had felt the same.

Kanna had not been able to remember why.

Haru had not been able to forget.

Neither was a mercy.

The softness turned to cold glass when she reached the ruin, and when she reached him, she reached out, her fingertips hovering over the scar that crossed his chest before retracting.

Haru's inhale was sharp.

Kanna slid her feet back enough, just enough, and tilted her chin to meet his eyes. "*Follow me,*" she said, the comfort of old words returning to her tongue.

Haru breathed, jaw clenched, and nodded.

Her fingertips hovered but did not touch, following the line of his shoulder. They followed his arm, his muscles tensing and relaxing as they followed her guide until, elbow bent, his palm faced the sky.

His breathing slowed, matched her own.

She repeated the other side, tracing the lines of a body honed to precision, dedicated to a simple goal. This time, she curved her fingers at his elbow, turning it in until his palm was at his chest.

Kanna mirrored the movement, giving enough room between them, and she shut her eyes.

Arms light, heart open, Kanna breathed, and she moved.

Kanna's body knew how to move.

Though it was trained to break, it was born to know. It knew where it began, knew where it ended, and it felt the world and beyond in ways she couldn't understand. Flows of time, of life, the threads of death and of potential, she could always feel them, always knew how to move through and with them. She knew Haru followed by the shift in the air, the way the universe balanced around them then fell away. They moved, and she could feel the frayed edges of him sooth as he followed her steady lead.

Kanna could feel the last burn of the day as it made way for the night, the cool of the air as shadows came to claim the land. The simplest of nature's laws, the unending balance of the exchange.

For the final stance, Kanna held her palms wide and up, her closed eyes tilting back to feel the last lingering light. Haru's hands tentatively reached, moved around her waist and to her back. When she closed her arms around him he sighed into her neck, his body heavy as it leaned into her.

Kanna had always pushed him away because she understood what she carried. She knew that, one day, the world would tear her apart if she didn't first, and she had been trained to destroy any fear. What she feared most was what she couldn't understand.

But she had never been able to bring herself to destroy him. She had always known that Haru was a kind of salvation that only she could allow herself.

Haru was light piercing through the black into infinity, glorious and unstoppable. She was nothing but frenetic energy that went nowhere, the shadows always snapping and clawing.

And just as he had become her shelter, she had become his rest.

Kanna threaded her fingers through his hair. "You're with me," she said, her voice a whisper. She pressed her hands to the sides of his face and rocked back to her heels, dragging his forehead down to meet hers. "I'm here."

When she opened her eyes, so did he, and they breathed together. Haru's gaze caught and slid away, his eyes widening.

The barren ruin that Kanna had created was no longer. New grass had sprouted, dotted with small white flowers curled before bloom. It was not the same as it had been before, but it was beautiful.

"Kanna, you—"

"That wasn't me."

Haru turned his eyes to her, questions and wonder alive in the blue. She brushed away the fall of hair that obstructed her view of them. "It wasn't me, *avtandil.*"

A cloud lifted from his eyes, his smile as soft as newly uncovered stars. "I don't know what that word means."

"You do." Kanna cupped Haru's cheek in her palm and brought her lips to meet his, her eyes sliding shut. Soft, like new grass, like flowers that had yet to open. And again, her heels rising from the dirt as she rose to meet him.

Though she reached, he kept her balanced. His hands opened, and the press of his palm against her lower back, between the blades of her shoulders, held her as if they were always meant to.

Kanna pressed her forehead against his again and he sighed. She could feel it in his body against hers, the warmth of him always soothing the cold dark that lived beneath her skin. Being there, holding him as he held her, was so natural it could have only ever been inevitable.

"*Inara?*" Haru asked in a bare whisper.

She hummed a wordless response.

"Where are your shoes?"

The slam of the farmhouse's screen door broke Kanna's trance and she jumped in place, turning to find the source.

Vahn clambered down the wooden steps, nearly tripping on the last one. Without bothering to scan the area, he started walking away. Kanna narrowed her eyes as the ripples of his confusion reached her.

"Go."

Kanna turned back to Haru, who's eyes met hers again. She reached out, her fingers tracing the line of his jaw.

He turned and pressed a kiss into her palm. "I'll wait," he said, his lips whispering the promise against her skin.

# 18

## NOT A FLICKER

### VAHN

Vahn wasn't sure where he was going, but anywhere was better than being trapped in the thin walls of the farmhouse after Isco had left him near panting for just another moment, another second to live under the false pretense of being wanted.

Because that's all it was. That's all it ever was.

His legs ate up the open fields of nothing, the overgrown grass leaning into his calves as he walked against the fading sun. So close to Ilazki, the evernight pressing against the border, the light of day lasted a fraction of the time it did elsewhere. The line of trees at the edge of the property grew nearer, the sun slanting behind them casting spindly shadows over the ground.

Vahn was not so distracted that he missed the familiar rapid fall of bare feet on the ground and the rush of grass as his pursuer tore through it. The footfalls slowed, became heavier to stop their momentum, until they were following behind.

Vahn stopped. So did Kanna.

He turned to face her, and found that Kanna looked the way

Her eyes were a bruised purple on her wan skin, and her hair probably hadn't seen a brush in days. She crossed one arm to hold onto the other, her fingers fidgeting against her skin while her mind worked.

Vahn sighed. "I'm not mad at you."

The stress between her brows eased only for her to cock her head to the side. "Why not?"

Vahn shook his head. "When have I ever been mad at you?"

Kanna paused, her eyes skittering away. Vahn had forgotten, for a moment, that Kanna did not remember him anymore. He turned to continue walking, because at least the burn in his legs could distract him from the burn everywhere else.

"What about the time I brought horses into the showers?"

Vahn pivoted back to her. Once, when they were smaller, Vahn had joked that the horses should get to have a warm shower instead of the tepid wash from the hoses, and Kanna had taken him seriously. She'd lead half a dozen of the Palamidia's warhorses into the communal showers. She was working on bringing the seventh in when Vahn ran into her in the halls and they were caught together.

A quick laugh caught in Vahn's throat. "You remember that?"

Kanna had argued that there was no rule stating that the horses weren't allowed inside the Tower, so one was written in, and signs were added at each of the entrances.

Kanna nodded. "We were assigned to assist in the mess hall. You hated the smell."

The smell of discordant foods cooking and mixing made his stomach turn, and he could taste bile burning in the back of his throat the entire time. "I did hate the mess, but I wasn't mad at you."

"Why not?"

On days when Velinius summoned Kanna, she refused to leave Vahn behind. She didn't have to insist, just nodded her head and beckoned for him to follow. Like bringing horses into the showers, Kanna had a way of doing things in a way that people didn't think to question the validity of the action. It was unexpected, but it wasn't clearly defined as not being acceptable. Vahn would wait, under guard, while the sisters met. Afterwards, he and Kanna would slip their duties and wander the gardens.

"C'mon, K. The horses in the showers? That shit was funny, how could I be mad?"

Because Vahn had a friend after that. He hadn't had a friend before, and he certainly hadn't met anyone that didn't want something from him. As years passed and Kanna weathered punishments Vahn didn't want to imagine, they became more than friends. They were everything to each other, for a time.

Kanna's smile was soft but incomplete. Her eyes slid past him to the trees at the edge of the property, and she started walking to them. Vahn followed.

As she reached the tree line, she began gathering fallen limbs and dragging them into the clearing. Ocassionally, she'd jerk her knees up when she stepped on fallen twigs and seeds, gathering the offenders and tossing them into her pile. Once she was satisfied, she folded her legs beneath her and sat in front of it. In the new dark, she looked expectantly at Vahn.

Vahn heaved a sigh, and dropped to the ground next to her. With a wave of his wrist, he lit the pile of limbs. The fire started at the heart of them, a flame meant to grow naturally instead of overwhelm. It caught the kindling, the small twigs and leaves crackling, then grew enough to catch on the thicker limbs. The wood was damp from the storms, and the fire created a thick smoke in the air.

Vahn shifted, laying down on the ground and resting his head in Kanna's lap, his eyes closing. Time passed in silence, the cooling night kept at bay by the fire. Something its size was easy to keep for him, and he didn't need to think about it. It wasn't angry, it didn't hurt, it just existed how it should. Vahn kept his eyes shut, allowed himself to breathe deep and even. While he never slept well, not anymore, the stolen, quiet moments with Kanna watching over him were the closest thing to what he imagined it would be like.

There were no storms. There was no battlefield smoldering nearby. There was the sound of the horses that had wandered over out of curiosity, the trill of the night's creatures, and Kanna's fingers as they attempted to fashion a braid into his hair. She reached the end of his hastily chopped cut, then unknotted the strands and smoothed them before trying a new approach.

She sighed. "You are not a flicker."

Vahn hadn't expected her to speak, but he didn't find it jarring. He didn't open his eyes. Her voice soothed him just as her light fingers against his temple did. "It is beautiful when you burn. I cannot blame him for wanting to watch you forever."

Kanna's words snaked deep into him, found the point of his hurt and cradled it. He wanted to pry her hands away. Kanna had enough to carry. He couldn't bring himself to do it, though.

He shifted his weight and snorted. "All fires burn out."

"No."

He opened his eyes, expecting that she would be looking out into the dark. But her gaze was on him, the flicker of the bonfire filling the grey with shades of flame.

"I think it depends on what you feed it."

Vahn shut his eyes against her knowing stare, turned his face to the heat of the fire. He reached out one hand to wrap around her knee. As if he could hold on to her, to this moment, and not have to face what came next.

"You know," she said in the wake of his silence, "you've always been enough, Vahn."

He smiled into the warmth in front of him, at the small peace they had found among the ruins of themselves long ago. "You, too."

Peace was fragile. Peace was something that had to be fought for, bled for, and then protected. He wasn't sure there was enough left in his veins to make it to the end.

"K," he said. "I really hope you survive what's coming."

Kanna's gentle touch continued, never faltering. "I hope we both do."

Then, her hand stopped. Vahn felt it moments later, a new, faint heat signature. The horses shifted, and Vahn sat up. Kanna was looking to the west, and the faint sound of hoofbeats carried over the distance.

Whoever it was, they were coming fast.

# 19

## A MESSAGE

### KANNA

THE FRANTIC WAVES distracted Kanna before the sound of hoofbeats echoed across the open fields. She didn't know how someone had found them here, but the fact that someone had meant the sliver of peace they had claimed was coming to an end.

"Kanna?" Vahn asked.

She shook her head. "I don't think it's a threat." Kanna leveraged herself to stand and faced what was coming. She closed her eyes and felt for the thread across the sweeping distance. The emotions were ragged-edged and tangled, frantic and fearful but too tired to draw a line between any of them.

"They're exhausted," she said, her eyes opening. "Scared. And coming directly for us."

Vahn couched next to her, his hand on the ground, before standing to dust off his palms. "Feverish, so possibly injured."

The outline of the figure appeared on the horizon, a flash of white against the darkness. As they grew closer, Kanna's eyes slid to the bonfire, then met Vahn's.

He nodded in understanding, and with a wave of his hand, the fire erupted into a beacon. The horses that had surrounded them scattered, and the incoming rider pulled up short when their mount attempted to bolt.

Kanna raced forward, Vahn on her heels, arriving as the rider lost her grip and slid from her mount's back. The woman fell onto Kanna, who staggered under the sudden weight. The woman's skin was hot, and her damp uniform warm against her fevered skin. Vahn arrived, taking some of the weight, but the woman clung to Kanna, her hands twisted in the fabric at her shoulders.

"Important," the woman rasped.

The fire beacon had alerted the others in the farmhouse. Shouts came from the porch as the others ran across the distance.

Kanna reached out to brush the sodden blonde hair out of the woman's eyes. Her amber gaze lolled, blinking as she focused.

"Shit, it's Kenzi," Vahn said.

Kanna's brow knit. "Ira's sister?"

"Get it to you." Kenzi stood up enough to grasp Kanna's hands, pressing something into her palm. The air that surrounded the object broke at Kanna's touch. It took the last of Kenzi's strength. "The most important thing."

Haru's arm wrapped around Kanna's waist, practically pulling her from her feet when he yanked her out of Kenzi's grasp. Kenzi's eyes rolled, and Vahn barely managed to hold her as she slumped forward. Osawa ducked past Kanna and Haru, catching the rest of Kenzi's weight and easing her to the ground.

Haru's hands searched Kanna for injury, but found none. Isco arrived next, making for Kanna first. Haru waved him off and he nodded, bypassing them to kneel on the ground where Kenzi had been settled. Isco grabbed her wrist in one hand, the other moving to open the lid of her eye before jerking back. "It's the soldier from the clinic."

Kanna turned to Haru. "The clinic?"

Haru nodded, but didn't expand. His eyes, instead, moved to Kanna's hands. Bent and slightly crumpled, but otherwise undamaged, an intricate origami horse rested in Kanna's palm. She lifted it with one hand, holding it up to inspect.

Astar arrived, bending over to catch her breath. "That's cute," she huffed. "What is it?"

Kanna turned the horse over, but she couldn't make anything out in the darkness. "A message."

"From who?" Haru asked, his voice low.

Kanna continued to study the horse, softly running her nails along its folds. "Who else would it be?"

"Neat horse," Yassen said when he arrived at the gathering.

Kanna smiled at him, then nodded to Kenzi. "Help them get her inside. And Astar, do you think you can find something for her to wear?"

Astar, still panting, glared and held up her middle finger.

Kanna didn't understand the gesture, so she returned it.

Vahn sidled up next to her and covered her hand pushed it down, shaking his head.

Astar laughed, breaking some of the tension that their new arrival had brought. She turned on her heel, heading back to the farmhouse at a sedate pace. Behind her, Isco and Osawa walked besides Yassen, who carried the unconscious Kenzi.

Vahn turned to Kanna, and the origami piece in her hand. He reached out a finger, running it over the horse's nose, before offering a last smile to Kanna.

As the others moved out of earshot, Kanna looked back to the figure in her hand.

"Can we trust her?" Haru asked, his voice even and low.

Kanna didn't know the soldier that had raced there, but the woman had pushed herself beyond limits to deliver a message. She curled her fingers around the message, pressing her hand against her chest. "Someone important did."

"What do you think it means?" Haru asked, his voice even and low.

It felt old, and heavy, but beyond that she didn't understand. She didn't know if she wanted to understand. Tears burned at the corners of her eyes. Haru pulled her into his arms, and she pressed her face against his chest where his heartbeat thrummed a steady, unstoppable rhythm.

"I don't know," she said, but she knew.

It meant that it was time to stop hiding. It was time to stop running.

It meant that, soon, Kanna would once again put the lives of those she held dear at risk. And there was no way of knowing if any of them would make it out alive.

# 20

## NEWS FROM THE FRONT

### VELINIUS

VELINIUS ENJOYED the ordered numbers of the Palamidia's ledgers. Columns and rows, the process of goods moving in and out, the numbers aligning in a comfortable march of progress. The knob of her office door rattled, and it opened with a creak it hadn't made before.

Aksana let herself into the office, the hem of her long skirt sweeping the floor.

Velinius made a note to have the hinges of her office door oiled.

Between her fingers Aksana held a missive, the seal of the Saint of Water broken. Her thin fingers ran over the crease where it had been folded widthwise. Aksana wanted her to ask. Aksana wanted her to be angry.

Velinius turned back to her numbers.

"You received news from the fronts." Aksana swept into the room, a tinkling of bells following every other step she made. She lowered herself into one of the chairs that Velinius allowed in front of her desk for when she took an audience.

"Aren't you supposed to be in Irkalla?" Velinius asked, with every scrap of patience and control she could muster.

Velinius could muster quite a bit.

Aksana's gaze roved Velinius's office. Velinius kept the same quarters she'd had as Legatus, even when she had been temporarily maligned. It hadn't occurred to Kanna to demand she move, which was another weakness of Kanna's. She had never realized that even the smallest of things could corrupt her power. Velinius wasn't grateful, but it did make her rise back to her proper place as Legatus simpler. To many, she had never fallen, her place in the Tower unmoving.

"I was held without charges," Aksana answered, "and so I had the Consel release me."

Velinius set down the pen she was using to make her marks, aligning it next to the ledger. "Which member of the Consel?"

"I released myself." Aksana turned away from Velinius's office to the woman herself, gave her a look both disapproving and magnanimous. "I assumed you were finished with your fit."

"I do not have fits, mother."

Aksana hummed dismissively, shifting the letter in her hand. Velinius's eyes were drawn to it, in spite of herself. "As I was saying, you have news." Aksana tsked, pausing her caress of the letter. "I don't think you'll like it."

Velinius flicked her eyes up to Aksana, met the same honey-brown eyes that sat in her own face. "It is an offense to read an officer's correspondence."

Aksana rolled her eyes. "You have already tried jailing me, my daughter. It didn't stick." She sat back in the chair, then with one hand, she used the letter to fan herself.

Velinius clenched her teeth together. The only way to win Aksana's games was to not play. She reached for her pen, turned her focus back to the ease of the orderly numbers.

Wax cracked from paper as Aksana opened the missive and unfolded it.

Velinius focused on the lines that noted the bundles that were received from the embroiderers in the nearby city and their subsequent payments.

"Really, Velinius, if you wanted a storyteller, you could have simply asked me." Aksana made a hissing sound. "You may still have to."

Velinius lifted her eyes from her book. Aksana smirked when she caught her gaze and Velinius couldn't hide the scowl that crept to her face.

"Don't make that face, dear," Aksana said. "It is unbecoming."

Velinius slammed down her pen and leaned back in her seat. "What of the storyteller?"

Aksana smiled. "Murdered, by one of the Eyes." Her eyes flicked back to the letter. "Ira Naquin. He and his sister escaped after." Aksana folded the note against her chest, raising a brow that could have been curious if it wasn't knowing. "Wasn't he one of your favorites?"

Velinius felt an ache in her teeth. She breathed through her nose, relaxed her jaw.

"I didn't know he had a sister," Aksana added as an afterthought. "It seems your list of enemies is becoming far longer than your list of allies."

Velinius pushed herself to standing and turned her back on Aksana. She moved to the floor to ceiling window. Her office was at the face of the Tower, at the height of it, higher than Ananke had ever attempted to claim. The front gardens opened to city sidewalks, and Velinius watched the messengers cut through the crowds as they raced in their duties. Some were on foot, while others clattered by on narrow chariots heavy with parcels. They focused on their tasks, never having to wonder about their greater purpose.

It was Velinius's duty to consider that. It was her calling, her reason, to keep order. She straightened her shoulders, grasped her hands at her back. "Is there anything else?"

Again, Aksana's noncommittal hum, but this time it was less amused and carried the lilt of boredom. Bells rang as she stood, and Velinius turned enough to watch over her shoulder.

Aksana folded the note lengthwise, against the crisp crease that was in it before, then dropped it onto Velinius's desk. "They have not found Ananke," she said, tapping the letter and sliding it so that it pushed the other documents out of place. "I cannot say I am surprised, if even your favored spies are against you."

Aksana smiled again to herself, her eyes lighting with a vindictive joy. "I wonder what else he got up to, right under your watch?" She laughed. "This story is filled with delightful twists."

Velinius left the window and plucked the letter from the desk. She unfolded Aksana's messy work, then folded it back correctly. "This isn't one of your stories, mother." She slid her papers back into their stacks, set her pen back into place.

"Isn't it?" Aksana looked away, her focus pulled elsewhere, her eyes now glassy and distant. "It certainly has the makings of one."

Without another word, without waiting for a dismissal, Aksana let herself out of Velinius's office in a soft chime of bells, leaving the door open behind her.

Velinius paced across the room, shutting the door. The hinges made no sound, and neither did the lock as she moved it into place.

# 21

## A KIND ENEMY

### KENZI

KENZI'S SENSES alerted her to rain, but she was slow to realize it wasn't falling on her. Instead, the soft patter of a light shower struck sharp against glass, each drop chiming in the air. With each breath, Kenzi could smell the faint trace of the sea.

Stuck partially in sleep, she stretched her legs. Her calves protested the movement, the muscles tightening and locking. The pain curled her toes and she shot up to sitting. Dragging her knees to her chest, Kenzi bent her forehead to them and grit her teeth. Her hands shook as she shoved her thumbs into the backs of her calves, attempting to massage away the pain.

Her toes released, the largest first, and she braced for the wave of pain when the feeling returned to her legs. It did, with a vengeance. When the shock passed, she released the breath she had been holding. However, once the immediate threat and pain was gone, her heart began to pound out a warning.

She gasped, pulling her head up.

Despite the lazy rain, an overcast sunshine illuminated the room. The walls were once jewel green, though they'd faded with time. Near the top of the wall she faced, the plaster crumbled to reveal the slat wood beneath.

The last needles of pain in her legs faded, and Kenzi let them stretch in front of her. On her lap was a crochet blanket, bold lines of pink, blue, and yellow weighing her down. She moved each of her toes in turn, her legs returning to normal save for the lingering ache in her thighs that was expected after long rides.

Next to the bed, Kenzi's knives were set on the side table. The sheaths were dry, as was the clothing she was wearing, and her blades had been casually pushed aside to make room for a mug.

Kenzi reoriented herself, sitting at the edge of the bed. No steam rose from the mug, and it smelled faintly of ginger. As she leaned over to inspect it further, muffled footsteps in the hall reminded her that she was within the grasp of the enemy.

She reached for her knives, yanking them from their sheaths and standing. The movement upset the mug and it tipped over, rolling to the ground and spilling its contents against the threadbare rug underfoot.

The door knob rattled and turned, and Kenzi tightened her grip, readying to strike as the door swung open. Kenzi lunged, stopping inches shy from her target, because a beautiful Gegenii woman glaring disapprovingly at her blade wasn't what she was expecting.

The woman casually withdrew from the tip of the knife, then pressed her finger against its end and pointed it away from herself. "Really, you people and your knives."

The woman stepped past Kenzi, dropping a bundle she had carried in her free hand onto the bed. In the next movement, she crouched to retrieve the fallen mug and inspected it.

"At least it didn't break, we're running low on these things," she said. Then, she turned from her hip and gestured with the empty cup. "Kenzi, right?" She didn't wait for an answer, instead sitting on the edge of the bed. "Either that or 'Ira's sister,' I've heard it both ways."

Kenzi's throat clenched at the mention of Ira's name. While she struggled to keep a grip on her cascading nerves, the woman crossed one long leg over the other and set the mug back onto the night stand.

The woman's bright green eyes focused on Kenzi, and she raised her hand in the air. "Speak."

Kenzi jolted from her dumbstruck stare. "You're the Governor of Gaoler's daughter," she said, the first thing that came to mind, the first thing that made it past the memory of the peaceful smile that had graced Ira's lips as he turned away from her. "Astar."

"I was," Astar said, her brow rising as her voice turned to flint. "I believe his position was... vacated."

Kenzi looked down. The floorboards of the room were dark wood, gapped and marred from passing years, cold on her feet. Despite the blades in her hands, there was only one other time that she had ever felt this vulnerable, she'd had a knife at her throat.

"You know," Astar said, standing. "The only reason you still have those is because they aren't afraid of you, right? The thought didn't even occur to them to take them away."

Astar's hand paused on the door's handle, and she turned. "You were in the crowd, in the Theatre, weren't you?"

Kenzi stiffened. The one thing she took pride in had been her ability to disguise herself, and it seemed even that was flawed.

"So, the answer to that is yes." Astar tapped her chin with her free hand, the gesture obvious and pointed. "Next question. What was it like for you when the shadows came?"

The moment when the sun blotted out came back to Kenzi, the raw memory overtaking fresh ones. She had told Salinae that she'd left before, but that wasn't the truth of it. When the shadows came, she heard their whispers. That she was not good enough, not enough, never enough, a burden that weighed down everyone that cared for her. She was pointless, ineffective, nothing. Her grip tightened on the knives in her hands, but they were just another reminder of that fact.

"Thought so." Astar's smirk was self-satisfied and knowing. She shifted and waved a hand at the bundle she dropped. "Anyway. Clothes there. I guessed your size, but I've gotten pretty good at it lately. The others are waiting for you downstairs."

Astar opened the door and stepped out, leaning back into the room one last time. "I wouldn't leave them waiting too long."

When the door shut, Kenzi's breath began to come in jagged gasps. She squinted her eyes shut and breathed through her nose, the odd lingering smell of sea calming her. She held the air in her lungs before releasing it as she tried to regain control of herself. She was under the same roof as her enemy, and she had studied them. While things seemed docile at the moment, almost safe, Kanna had proven time and again that she was nothing if not unpredictable.

Kanna.

Shit.

When she trusted that she was in control, Kenzi opened her eyes. She let the blades in her hands drop to the bed. They were useless, anyway.

A bath was attached to the room she was in, so she retrieved the bundle of clothes that Astar had dropped and moved to it. Setting the bundle on the counter, she dared to look into the mirror. Dark circles ringed her eyes, and her hair was a mess, golden frizz flying away from her head like a halo. There was nothing she could do about the exhaustion that colored her skin, but she attempted to smooth her hair, and sighed when it rebelled against her efforts.

She was in white, the simple t-shirt a Palamidia issue. She pulled it away from her skin and buried her nose in it, realizing it was the source of the sea's scent.

She released the shirt and clenched her jaw together, wary of what Astar might have found for her to wear. However, when she reached a hand to the pile, it didn't feel like a punishment. At the top was a golden-hued sweater, oversized and loose but soft, and warm. It smelled clean, but in a way she expected for something in Kirin. It smelled of earth, of petrichor. Beneath it, a kindness. Astar had included a soft bristled brush, a simple hair tie, and a piece of patterned silk that complimented the gold of the sweater. Black denim and medium-weight socks completed the pile.

An unpredictable enemy. An enemy that cared for dignity.

A kind enemy.

She kept the white t-shirt on and dressed. Using the brush, she wrangled a sense of order from her hair and tied it back, then wrapped the patterned silk around it to keep the fly-aways in check.

Now clothed, the chill of Kirin's storm ridden air was kept at bay. Kenzi padded from the bath. She took a moment to consider the knives on the bed, but decided against carrying them.

Astar was right. She wasn't a threat.

And it was time to be brave, in spite of that.

THE DOOR OPENED ALMOST SOUNDLESSLY, and Kenzi stepped out into a hall. Similar doors lined the passageway, which ended at a dormered window on one side and stairs at the other. From the stairs, she heard voices.

"Try not to be entirely yourself," said the first, a warm, even tone, "you did cut her throat."

Kenzi took a moment to place the voice as Osawa.

"What am I supposed to be, then?" came the response, which sent chills over Kenzi. She'd recognize the Saint of Fire's voice anywhere, after having it whispering so close to her ear. "Besides," Vahn continued, his tone unnervingly light, "did you forget she kicked your ass in that bar? I mean, how did she even manage it?"

"The plan was to distract them while you all got out of town. And my point still stands."

Vahn snorted. "Shitty point, shitty plan. How many times are you going to try that self-sacrifice thing before realizing it doesn't work? I'd think once was enough."

Kenzi took a few more stairs down, the floor below coming into view. Halfway in the side room, where the voices were coming from, was a body on the floor. The back half was in front of the stairs. The man was balanced on his toes, his body moving rhythmically.

Astar's voice interjected. "You tried the sacrifice thing before? And here I was, thinking I was special."

"Does anyone want tea?"

The new voice caused Kenzi to back up a step, her head darting to the side. It had come from the other direction, and she couldn't quite place it.

"Sure, I'll take some." Astar passed along the foot of the stairs, her feet stepping around a man that was sprawled on the ground.

After a short interlude, Kenzi dared to take a few more steps until Vahn spoke.

"What're you doing there, buddy?"

The man in the hall paused, his body half-raised. "Push-ups."

"I see that," Vahn answered. "Why?"

"Pick up heavy stuff."

Yassen, Kenzi figured. She had not seen him with the others since the event at the Theatre, but he had been a fixture at Kanna's side in Gaoler.

"All right," Vahn finished.

Cabinets rattled from the right as someone rummaged in the area. "Where's the sugar?" Astar asked.

The kitchen, Kenzi guessed, with a sitting area on the left and the entry in the middle. Which meant if she tried to run, she wouldn't get far. There were five voices so far, and she could only assume the former Legatus and her Second were also below. Which meant seven fighters between her and the door. At their caliber, it would only take one to stop her.

"What do you need sugar for?" the voice Kenzi couldn't quite place asked.

"For the tea," Astar replied, matter-of-fact.

"No," the man said. "At least use honey."

"What's the difference?"

Kenzi swallowed, and continued her slow descent.

"It's ginger tea."

"Fine," Astar relented. "Whatever you say, doc."

Sweeping out of the kitchen, Astar stopped at the foot of the steps and smirked up at Kenzi. "She's up," Astar announced, lifting the mug to her lips as she continued out of view.

Yassen stopped his exercise and shifted, sitting on the floor in the hall and looking up at Kenzi. He lifted his hand, and he waved.

Now discovered, Kenzi lifted her own hand in greeting as she stepped down the last of the stairs, her heart thudding in her ears.

She had been correct about the arrangement of the home. In the sitting room to her left, Vahn sprawled across a garish, floral patterned sofa, one leg stretched out and over the arm and the other dangling to the ground. Osawa was seated in an armchair next to it, a thin book shut in his hands, though his thumb kept his place. His eyes slid to Kenzi's, and the ground spun beneath her. In Gegenes, in the tavern, they had been a quiet, soft brown. Now, they were a deep, merciless navy.

Astar glided between them. She spun, draping herself across Osawa to sit on the arm of his chair. She handed him the mug of tea she was carrying and he abandoned the book to take it, breaking eye contact with Kenzi and turning his attention quizzically to Astar.

Osawa brought the tea to his nose. "Am I supposed to drink this?"

Astar rolled her eyes, and took it from him. "Guess not." She tilted on the arm of the chair, and he wrapped a steadying hand at her waist. "I told you the clothes would look nice on her."

Osawa looked over, then away, his hand falling. "You did."

From the sofa, Vahn simply watched, his eyes flitting from her to the pack of cards he idly shuffled.

Kenzi fidgeted. Suddenly, she was back in lessons, standing before her peers and expected to recite anthems. But, these were not her peers. These were killers, traitors to the Empire.

"Better than your shirt," Astar added.

"My shirt?" Osawa sighed. "I wondered where that one went."

Vahn tilted his head over his shoulder. "You count your shirts?"

"You don't?"

Vahn shook his head, and his gaze returned. Kenzi realized he hadn't been looking at her, but past her. Kenzi knew she shouldn't have left her back open, but she didn't want to face what was behind her. She took a settling breath and turned, following Vahn's focus to the figure that was waiting in front of a kettle for it to boil.

Isco. Vahn had said his name, not long before Vahn's knife slid across her neck.

Isco wasn't alone in the kitchen. Seated at the table were the Legatus and her Second.

The origami horse that had stood sentinel at Ira's bedside balanced on its four fragile legs before Kanna. Kanna stared at it, her fingers tracing a scar on the back of Haru's hand, while his gaze was riveted to her.

It was last thing she had of Ira. The thing he had told her was most important, the thing he held off an army for, and they hadn't even bothered with it. Instead, it was a decoration on a table.

"Would you like some tea?"

Kenzi's attention jerked to Isco. The soft offer on his lips died, and he lowered the kettle.

"No." Something in Kenzi snapped apart. She had held it together, held it in, kept it under control as she was supposed to. As a proper soldier did, as everyone expected of her. Until.

"No." Her voice rose with each word, growling out of something deep in her gut and rising. "I do not want tea from the guy who slit my throat's *boyfriend*." She whirled on Kanna, unable to keep it together anymore. Even as Haru leaned forward, his eyes flashing a warning, she could taste the venom in her voice. "I want her"—she pointed to the Legatus, then to the horse—"to tell me *what that means*."

Kanna's hand squeezed Haru's to get his attention, and he turned. She shook her head and, slowly, he eased back into his seat. In the silence, Kenzi could feel the others at her back, hemming her in. Kanna turned to her, and Kenzi caught her breath. The thing that had risen curled up into the bottom of her throat.

They had told stories of the former Legatus, even after she was supposedly gone to the gods. They said her eyes were soulless, empty, but Kenzi didn't find that true, now, pinned beneath them. Kanna didn't look at her so much as through her, as if she was sorting her into pieces and putting her back together, her head tilting ever-so-slightly to the side.

Behind her, a throat cleared.

"He's not my boyfriend."

Kanna's gaze shifted over Kenzi's shoulder, and the same eyes that had kept her in place rolled at Vahn before returning. With her free hand, Kanna indicated the chair beside her. She didn't ask, didn't say a word. The command was unspoken, yet evident.

A gentle hand fell between her shoulders and she jumped, turning to stare up at Osawa. He nodded to the table. Kenzi approached, and Osawa pulled out the seat that Kanna had indicated. Her energy spent, Kenzi's knees buckled as she collapsed into it.

Kanna met her eyes again. "I was waiting for you."

# 22

## SCHEMATIC

### KANNA

WRITING LOOPED along the outside of origami figure, and dark ink covered parts of its geometry. But it was all tucked away, each symbol cut off and hidden. Besides the feeling of something old, something heavy and ancient that lurked in its folds, Kanna couldn't fathom yet what it meant.

Isco's hand passed in front of her as he dropped a mug at her side, keeping another for himself and settling in the empty chair next to Haru. Osawa took the seat next to Kenzi, and Astar moved to sit opposite Kanna. Yassen stayed on the ground, and Vahn circled to lean against the counter behind her shoulder.

Kanna plucked the horse from the table. "Ira sent this?" Kanna knew the answer, but Kenzi's nod confirmed it. "What did he say to you?"

Kenzi's amber eyes darted around the table like an animal caught. When Vahn shifted behind Kanna, they jerked over her shoulder. Kanna leaned back, then turned enough to eye Vahn. He gave her an innocent shrug and balanced his weight on one hip, crossing his arms and trying to look anywhere else.

"He said it was important. That's all he said, that it was the most important thing. Right before...." She shuddered, then braced. When

Kenzi's eyes lifted, her gaze was soft and complicated as lace. "How did you know it was from him?"

Kanna felt the smile that slid over her lips, softened by her remembrance. She slid the origami figure across the table to Osawa.

Osawa turned the horse over until he found the last fold. "He learned the craft from a friend, but he continued it after her death." Osawa leaned his arms on the table, the horse in hand, as he began to untangle it. "It was a good way to honor her."

Having started the unraveling of the message, Osawa passed it back to Kanna, who finished undoing Ira's work. It felt like mourning when the horse came apart. So long it had lived a life as one thing, and now it was another. It became two sheets of fragile paper. She traced the smudged lines, pausing at a newer signature at the corner of one sheet.

"My mother found this," she said.

Haru leaned forward. "Aksana's work?"

"No." One sheet was too old to be her mother's work, but the other was not. "Yes, and no."

Kenzi leaned forward, so much so that Kanna could feel her breath ruffle the errant strands of her hair. "What does the Exalted One have to do with anything?"

"Before she was considered Exalted," Haru answered, "Aksana was a noted anthropologist. Specifically, she studied pre-cataclysm culture."

Kanna nodded. "Before me."

The older page was rough with age, weak in places that had been blackened with ink. Interwoven circles locked together, over and under each other in a dizzying arrangement. Along the borders, sharp printed writing circled each layer, while a more elaborate hand had added notations where the designs intersected. She could feel the history under her touch, a texture she couldn't quite place. The other page was simpler, nothing but unlabeled curved lines.

Haru leaned forward, angling to get a view of the overwhelming array. "It's in Ilazkin."

Kanna nodded.

"Ira doesn't know Ilazkin," Kenzi offered. "How could he know it was important?"

Kanna leaned her elbow on the table and dropped her chin into her palm. She turned the sheets, but she couldn't make sense of it. She had, once, she knew. She felt the familiarity of it at the tip of her fingers, but she couldn't grasp it. "I gave it to him, I think."

Vahn stepped forward from the counter. He braced his hands on each side of Kanna and leaned over the top of her head. "That doesn't make sense."

"You know Ilazkin?" Astar asked, disbelief coloring her tone.

"It's not my first language, unlike some of us," Vahn replied, pointing his finger at Kanna's face. "But when you keep getting cursed out in a dead language, you pick it up."

Kanna shoved Vahn's hand out of her eye line to continue squinting at the scrawled notes.

"Why doesn't it make sense?" Kenzi grit out.

Kanna lifted her eyes to the girl. Her knuckles were white, her jaw clenched with restraint. It wasn't anger that she restrained, Kanna knew. She turned the paper to face Kenzi. "It is almost a genealogy chart, but not quite." Kanna ran a finger around one of the circles. "Here is the family of Nehebkau, but," she slid to a connected ring, "it is linked with the Gozais."

"Nehebkau's line ended with his children," Haru said, leaning back. "The Gozai dynasty didn't rise until hundreds of years later."

Kanna nodded. "And yet, they are contained together," she said, tracing the circle that wrapped around the interconnected families, "under another name."

"That's not even the weird part." Vahn straightened to standing, then combed his fingers through Kanna's hair. "Tell them the weird part."

As Vahn began to work her hair into a single braid, Kanna sat back so that he could reach it better and slid the paper back to herself. "Each of the families is numbered, and that corresponds with a note elsewhere. For Nehabkau," she tapped the small circle that interrupted the line that encircled them, then drew her hand across the paper. "'A conduit, serves to channel that which cannot be seen but must be present.'"

Kanna thrummed her fingers against the wood, but the rhythmic sound struck something in her. She held the paper up in front of her.

"That means she got it," Vahn stage whispered over her head.

"It's a map," she announced, "but it's also... more."

Isco's voice was calm, soothing in a way that allowed for truths and thought, as he asked, "How can a map be more?"

"Pre-cataclyms texts are... complicated. Nearly all have more than one meaning, or purpose." She turned the paper at another angle. "I think this is also a schematic."

"Like a schematic for buildings?" Isco asked.

Kanna nodded. "More like machines, I think? Old texts often reference works made by the gods, they were... contraptions that were supposedly imbued with the gods' powers." She flipped the paper, reading over the experiment notes. Dread settled heavy in her chest. "And whatever this was, it worked."

Vahn finished tying off the end of the braid, then draped it over Kanna's shoulder. She took her eyes away from the thin writing only long enough to nod her thanks, and he returned to his place at the counter.

"Neat," Yassen said from his place on the floor. "What does it do?"

Kanna sat back, but she knew it didn't matter how long she stared at the paper, she wouldn't be able to figure out the rest. Even knowing what it was, even with the piece of a key, it didn't fit. She placed her palms against the table and pushed her chair back as she stood. "I don't know."

Kenzi leapt to her feet, her chair falling back and nearly onto Yassen, who leaned out of the way. "You have to know!"

Kanna stepped around Yassen, and Haru rose from his seat.

Kenzi's hands clenched into fists at her side. "Where are you going?"

The question held more weight than the girl could know. Kanna shut her eyes, smiling to herself. The last journey into the black had been so recent her body remained raw from it, but it was the only way. She opened her eyes, but could not bring herself to look at the others as she turned for the stairs. It felt too much like a last look.

"To find out."

# 23

# AN ACHE

## OSAWA

WHEN HARU STOOD from the table, Osawa shifted enough that, if it came to it, he could stop him from getting to the others. But Haru didn't spare them a glance, moving silently to the stairs.

Vahn leaned over the schematic. "Haru." Looking up from the convoluted paper, Vahn met Haru's eyes. "Bring her back."

Haru nodded, then took the stairs after Kanna.

Vahn pushed himself away from the table, turning to the counter.

The quiet of the farmhouse ached.

"Kenzi, step back," Osawa whispered, his eyes on the tense lines of Vahn's shoulders.

She hesitated, but she complied and moved back towards the sitting room a step. Vahn wouldn't hurt anyone else in the room, only himself. It had been years since Vahn's grip on the fire had slipped, flames haloing him as the Saint he was. But each time had been something like this, when he looked like someone else.

At the counter, Vahn retrieved one of the abandoned mugs of tea and carried it to the sink. He upended it, the last cold dregs gurgling into the drain, then set the porcelain against the steel sink. Just before Osawa thought it safe to relax, Vahn straightened and turned. He hurled the mug across the kitchen, and it smashed into the far cabinets.

Vahn ran a shaking hand through his hair, then rubbed it over the back of his neck. Without another word, he stalked across the kitchen.

"It's still raining," Osawa called, but the screen door slammed shut behind Vahn.

Osawa let his defense loosen. While Isco picked up the shattered remnants of the mug and deposited it in the sink, Osawa retrieved the toppled chair and set it right, pushing it back into its place. Finished with his first task, Osawa turned to the door.

Isco was already there, grabbing one of the coats from the rack. "I'll get him."

Osawa sighed as the screen door creaked closed behind Isco and the room became uncomfortably silent.

Astar spun the mug she'd kept between her hands, then lifted it to her lips. When she placed it back on the table, the quiet thump of ceramic on wood resounded through the room.

"Yassen," she said to get his attention.

"Yeah?" he asked, soft and curious.

"Get off the floor, honey."

"Oh," Yassen said, as if only now realizing he was still seated on the ground. "Right."

Though Kenzi was nearly Osawa's height, she still backed away when Yassen rose to his, her neck craning to look up. Osawa had to put out a hand to stop her from colliding with him, and she whirled on him at the contact.

Kenzi was jumping at every thing they did, but it was like a trapped deer in an enclosure. At the table, Yassen picked up the schematic and the second sheet. He held them out, then looked around, before pinning them to the metal door of the refrigerator with a magnet shaped like a fried egg. Finished with that task, he sat in the chair across from Astar that Kanna had previously occupied.

In the living room, Osawa searched the sofa near where Vahn had previously lounged, finally locating the discarded playing cards. He set them in front of Astar, who abandoned the mug and began shuffling, before reclaiming his previous seat.

Despite the casual facade of the group, Osawa could feel the tide of Kenzi's off-kilter heartbeat. Her body was stuck somewhere between fight and flight: confused, angry, and terrified all at once. Osawa listened to the swiftly changing currents too long, and a headache threatened to form in his temples.

"Do you play?" Astar asked, although her gaze didn't fall on Kenzi. She didn't wait for an answer, leaning forward to deal the cards between them and including the empty chair.

Yassen's hand scrambled to catch the cards that Astar flung his way as they slid around the table, threatening to fall off the edge. He rolled them in a pile, then lifted them enough from the table that he could hunch over and peak. "Palamedes," he clarified for Kenzi. "We play cards when we're waiting."

Kenzi didn't move from her position, as if her feet had frozen to the hardwood. "Wait for what?"

Astar paused her dealing and considered Osawa for a moment, before raising a brow at Kenzi. "Not sure what you're doing to Os, but you might need to calm down a bit."

"Astar," Osawa said, a soft warning in his tone. While Kenzi was Ira's sister, she was still an Eye. And she wasn't one of them.

On unsteady feet, Kenzi found her seat. Osawa dared a sideways glance.

Kenzi propped her elbow on the table, her fingers absently tracing the scar at her neck. Her brow furrowed as her breaths attempted to even, as she swallowed them down. Osawa could count the pattern she held in his own mind, but it wasn't easing her.

After he straightened the stack of cards in front of him that Astar had dealt, he sat back in his chair and asked the question that no one else would. "What happened to Ira?"

Kenzi squeezed her eyes shut, her heart quickening. "I don't know. He gave me the message, and told me to get it to Kanna. The others in the camp were too close." Tears threatened to form at the corners of her eyes, but she breathed in again, held it tight in her chest before releasing. "He covered me so that I could escape."

Her blood pulsed with the short recollection, and her anxiety spiked before getting caught in a current of grief. Osawa reached out, placed his hand over hers with a light touch.

Kenzi's hand under his turned, her fingers grasping the sides of his hand like a lifeline. The connection soothed the thrash of currents inside of her. There was no wonder that Ira felt the need to stay behind for her. Despite the training the soldiers endured, Kenzi seemed unable to smother her emotions. There was honesty in her every motion.

There was danger in honesty.

Osawa retracted his hand, used both to slide his cards together and sort them. He leaned back and chose to ignore the knowing, pointed gleam in Astar's eyes.

## 24

## WHAT MATTERS

### ISCO

Standing at the end of the rickety porch, Vahn leaned against the banister and looked out into the corral. The lazy rain that had begun earlier that morning had continued, but the slow fall built up over time. It fell in thick cascades from the corners of the gutterless porch, creating a ditch in the ground deep enough to have its own current. With the sun unable to properly find a release from the clouds, there was a wet chill in the air.

Instead of letting the door free on its hinges, Isco eased it shut. Vahn already knew he was there, anyway. His shoulders had tensed, and he'd refused to turn around.

Isco twisted the jacket he'd retrieved in his hands and approached. Vahn didn't turn, but Isco draped the jacket over his shoulders.

"I'm not cold," Vahn said, but he didn't try to push the jacket away. "I'm never cold."

Isco smoothed the fabric over Vahn's shoulders, his hands pressing against bone that was too close to skin. "Maybe you can't feel it, but you can get sick anyway."

Vahn scoffed. "Wouldn't want to waste all your hard work."

The words were meant to shove him back, but Isco didn't retreat. "That's not it," Isco said, his hands following Vahn's shoulders to the outline of his arms. "You know that isn't it."

Isco's lips brushed faintly against the black lines on Vahn's nape, and he could feel the heat rise in Vahn's skin in response. Isco withdrew before he was tempted to linger.

Vahn's shoulders sagged, and Isco used his grip on Vahn's arm to turn him. Vahn allowed it, leaning back heavily on the railing. Isco curled the sides of the jacket in his fists and pulled it tighter around Vahn's chest. "Why are you worried?"

Vahn scoffed, his defensive smirk falling into place as he refused to look at Isco. "What makes you think I'm worried?"

Isco shifted so that he'd be in Vahn's eye line. "Do I have to kiss you every time I want you to be honest?"

"You could try it out," Vahn said, his voice mockingly light.

"Would it work?"

Vahn opened his mouth, searching for a response that would throw the conversation sideways, but, instead, the tight line of his smirk released, his eyes meeting Isco's before falling away. "You were studying loas, right?"

The question shot through Isco. He'd almost dared to forget that he'd told Vahn about the Cardea's experiments. Isco unclenched his fists from the jacket, but before he withdrew Vahn caught his wrists and jerked him closer.

"Wouldn't want you to catch a chill," Vahn said, his smile slicing.

Isco frowned, but he gave in partially to Vahn's game. He wrapped his arms around Vahn's waist, beneath the jacket, but then held his own wrists to keep his hands from wandering. "Yes," Isco answered Vahn's previous question instead of the last, "I studied loas."

Vahn's eyes unfocused, his hand reaching out. The back of his fingers settled against the side of Isco's neck, his hand resting in the crook. His thumb brushed against Isco's jaw, light and almost absent, if Isco were to believe that any gesture of Vahn's was done absently.

"Do you know what happens to a body when a loa syncs?"

Not wanting to interrupt Vahn's thoughts nor touch, Isco shook his head as gently as he could manage.

"It hurts, until it doesn't," Vahn said, his touch unerringly softly against Isco's skin. "But it's different for all of us. There are countless ways that the elements can consume. All there is to know is that when a loa syncs, they... become something else."

Vahn's thumb stopped its movement, and Isco swallowed. "Have you known someone who synced?"

Instead of pulling away, Vahn's hand turned, now grasping Isco's neck and reaching easier. "Yua. She's the reason your Ganglere is a lake." His thumb moved again, this time close to the corner of Isco's lip. "She is that lake now, and she's also in it. Should put her name on a map."

Isco pulled back, just enough for Vahn's caress to miss. "I know you're trying to make it a joke, but I'm sorry."

"For what?" Vahn smirked, then leaned back to put his arms through the sleeves of the blue utility jacket. "You didn't give the order."

The movement was more than enough that Isco had to untangle his hands and release Vahn, but he didn't step back, even as Vahn made a show of adjusting the collar of the jacket and running his hands over it.

"Why does this thing have so many pockets," Vahn muttered, snapping and unzipping them at random.

Isco shook his head, but he couldn't let Vahn find a way out of this. "There's something you aren't telling me."

"There's a lot that I'm not telling you."

Vahn's hands fumbled on the thicker material as he tried to fold back the cuffs. Isco brushed Vahn's hand away. He folded the fabric around Vahn's wrists, then again to uncover the black bands. He released the first, and held out his hand.

Vahn clenched his fist then, hesitantly, lifted his other arm for Isco to repeat the process. When Isco finished, he wrapped his hand around Vahn's wrist. Then he lifted Vahn's hand, placed it back at his neck.

Vahn wanted Isco to turn away. If Isco turned away, then all that Vahn believed about the world would be true. Isco wouldn't let it be true. Isco stepped forward, the movement pressing Vahn's thumb into his pulse, and placed a hand at the center of Vahn's chest. Isco could feel the brand scars through the thin fabric beneath his palm, and beneath that, the quickening beat of Vahn's heart.

"How do you know that it hurts?"

Vahn took his hand from Isco's neck and pressed Isco's hand closer to his chest. "I verged, once." Vahn's eyes shut, his hand pressing Isco's close, as if he didn't realize Isco didn't need to be forced to touch him. "That's what happens first, before a sync." Then, Vahn's tone became light, his eyes opening with a veneer of amusement. "Not many have come back from them, that I know, and maybe it wasn't even full-out. Maybe it wasn't even close."

Isco shook his head, then splayed his fingers against Vahn's chest. "You did," he said, interrupting Vahn's denials before he could escape. "And it hurt."

Vahn sighed, his eyes falling to where his hand wrapped at Isco's wrist. After another moment he shook his head. "It was more than just hurt. When you get close to something that's too hot, you can feel it on your skin. It's a warning. This was different, it was... inside of me, and I couldn't pull back. There was a moment that I realized if I let go, it would be over, and I'd be something else. There's a moment when you can give in. But I needed the pain. I still wanted to exist, so I held on to it."

"Every time," Vahn continued without prompting. "We thought Kanna was verging, but what I saw in the corral... she's synching." Vahn made a sound that was like a laugh, but wasn't quite it. It was in his chest, at the back of his throat. "I get it. I know, but..."

"But?"

Vahn shook his head. "She comes back. She shouldn't be able to, but she does." Vahn stopped, swallowed. "All that pain, and she keeps coming back for more."

Isco tilted his forehead, pressed it against Vahn and felt him shift toward the movement. "I don't know her like you do, but I think she's probably the most powerful being since the gods themselves. It scares me to think about it, sometimes. But her abilities aren't what make her strong."

When Vahn spoke it was hushed. "She's not as strong as everyone thinks," he said, a long held secret daring its way into the open.

Isco clenched his fist, catching the fabric of Vahn's shirt in his finger-tips. "Neither are you."

Isco said it, even though he knew. He knew before Vahn moved what would happen. Vahn straightened from his slouch and tilted Isco off-balance, and Isco could either step back or fall over. Isco chose what could be considered a noble retreat, moving back enough without falling away entirely.

Vahn shrugged out of the jacket that Isco had brought and tossed it at him. "I believe guard duty is calling me."

Isco fumbled to catch the unwieldy jacket as Vahn stepped past him. He tightened it in his grip, pulled it close, and said, "Something has to matter, Vahn."

Vahn halted his retreat, his back to Isco.

"Eventually..." Isco's voice was quiet when he said, "something will have to matter."

Vahn pulled open the farmhouse door, the hinges of the screen letting out a sharp whine as he eased it shut behind him. Beyond the porch, the soft rain had turned the land into a grey haze, and it was almost easy to imagine that nothing existed outside of this place. Isco twisted the jacket in his hands, then lifted it to his nose and breathed in. Though faint, there was the lingering scent of a distant fire.

# 25

## WHAT IS FAIR

### KANNA

KANNA WATCHED the door of her room, and she waited. No one had been in this room save for her since they'd arrived. Despite that there weren't nearly enough rooms for bodies, the others had floated among the remaining ones, leaving her to her lone shelter. At night, she could feel them moving through the halls, finding places to rest. She could feel their low thrumming fears that tasted of metal, their anxieties that scratched at her spine, and the ache of nightmares scattered throughout.

The silence had been deafening, the feel of them over her skin, the idea that she was the cause. So she'd slipped, night after night, into the Neither, into the Cardea's cells where the stone and the dark insulated her from everything else.

When Haru pushed the door open, there was a momentary surprise when he met her waiting gaze. He kept his eyes locked with hers as he closed the door, the snap of the latch loud in the dark room. However, stepping fully into the room, his eyes shot to the side.

Even the dim interior couldn't mask the black gap in the room's far corner. It was roughly the shape of a door, but the edges were blurred and smudged like ash in the back of a fireplace. Haru walked towards it, strength in his every step, his hands shifting at his sides in a balanced timing.

Kanna could watch him forever. The way Haru moved was a

soothing rhythm that her heart wanted to beat to. He reached out, his hand hovering in the air in front of the black mark on the wall. It radiated a glacial cold, persistent and never ending. He pulled away to meet Kanna's gaze, and when he did she looked away. Every time, when his eyes met hers, it felt as if she had been caught doing something she shouldn't. Wanting something she shouldn't.

"It is better to move through the same spot," she offered, unable to meet his gaze. "The transition is... easier."

"How many times?" he asked, his voice strained, rough.

Kanna dared to look up, meeting the seething fear in his eyes. She turned to the floor. Sometimes, somehow, the way he looked at her made her feel both small and vast.

He took a step towards her.

"Every night," she whispered, taking a half-step back, her weight hovering but not landing on her back foot. "I didn't count."

"Every night?"

She nodded.

"Does that mean you remember more?"

"No," she admitted. "I went to the same place each time."

"Kanna," his voice was sharp and demanding, then, it was a plea. "Why?"

She didn't know the answer, not really. It had seemed right for her to be there, but then she became aware of where she was. And she knew there was something else she couldn't reach. "At first, it was the same as it had been before. Then it changed."

Haru shifted in her silence, but he wouldn't relent. "How did it change?"

Kanna bit her lip, searching for the words to explain, then shrugged. "I learned how to control it, to an extent."

After the first weeks, she was able to remember who she was outside of the memory, and she was able to pull herself away from inhabiting them. After she learned how to do that, she went back time and again, because it offered both a peace and a punishment.

"To an extent," Haru repeated, the question evident in his tone.

"I can distance myself from some of them, but not all of them." The sharper memories, the ones with broken edges that cut, those climbed inside of her. She clenched her fist until it ached, then released it. Tremors shuddered in her damaged joints before settling.

"I know where they are. I could feel them, outside of that one. I found the center, but"—she swallowed, her voice constricting as it did each time she attempted to offer a weakness—"I was afraid."

She didn't want them to take over. She didn't want to feel the pain again, didn't want to know why she couldn't sleep, and she didn't want to remember that every bloody hand, every screaming voice in her head had a name before she took it from them.

But she knew where she put them.

"And I know," she continued, "you are, too." She could feel it coming off of him, radiating like a dissonant hymn. "So I know it isn't fair of me to ask you...."

She stopped. It wasn't fair of her, and it wasn't right.

"Ask me."

He sounded so sure. She looked up, met his eyes finally. Whatever fear had been there was replaced by a steady burn, set and determined. There was power in it, a strength she couldn't understand, and the question tumbled out before she could bite it back: "Will you come with me?"

Kanna had learned to keep herself away from others, to carry her burdens in solitude, but she was tired. She didn't want to be alone in this. She needed his strength, even if it made her a coward.

Haru closed the distance between them, and she was still pinned in place when he brushed the back of his knuckles over her cheek. His eyes slid, following his thumb as it traced her lower lip. Her lips parted in response, and it took everything in her to keep her body from leaning into him. She was a starving thing, always wanting.

"Anywhere, *inara*," he whispered. "I will go with you anywhere."

/

# NOWHERE, EVERYWHEN

## KANNA

THOUGH THE TRANSITION to the Neither was easier through the softened veil, that did not make it painless. It was like being peeled apart, turned inside out, as gently as one could be, and breaking from a cacoon to reform in the other plane. Kanna arrived breathless, her hand clutched in Haru's.

She brushed the hair from his eyes so that she could be sure he was there. His eyes were distant for the first moment, focusing on her in the next. His hand covered her own and he presed his cheek into her palm.

"I'm all right," he said, only the barest hint of lost breath in his voice.

She steeled herself. This was not the time to worry, to question. Her anxieties could pull them away, distract them and trap them in the wrong moments.

Every time she entered the Neither was just as unsettling as the first. It was a constant evernight, the wind unmoving unless she did. The midnight wasteland stretched before them, the cold endless and vast, while above the nauseating gleam of too-many stars spiraled both too slow and too quick, moving in the corners of her perception.

She knew without having ever tried that if she would take a step, and walk, and continue walking, she would never find the end of this. She would never be nearer to the taunting dunes in the distance, and she would never be further than where she started. It was the blank slate, the start and end at the same time. Kanna didn't need to move. She had learned that she didn't need to take a single step, that the Neither would come for her.

Tentatively, she placed a hand on Haru's chest. His heart beat beneath her palm, a live thing, tethered outside of this place. She moved closer, hoping that if she was close enough, the Neither would not flag him as something that did not belong. "Hold on to me."

As if he wasn't sure what she had asked, Haru's arms wrapped around her, one at her waist, the other around her shoulders. She eased closer and his hands tightened, his head lowering to rest nearer to her.

Kanna tilted her head so she could meet his eyes, and she could feel his breath against her skin. There was no questioning in his glance, only a steady patience. "Close your eyes."

When his eyes closed, she did the same. Kanna felt the timing of his heart, waited until his breathing synched with hers, and then held it in her lungs.

In an instant, she followed the lure of memory until she found the center.

Haru's body jerked as it was pulled away from her and she held his waist, buried her face against his chest and pulled as his grip tightened. Even as her body tensed, attempting to lock them in place, she wavered beneath the weight of his steady anchor. Their balance returned and she let out her breath in a shuddering jag, her body shaking with it.

He was still there. He was still safe.

For the moment.

Kanna willed her grip to relax and looked up. There was shadow in Haru's eyes, the dark veining in the gold that moved in the brilliant blue. Where the colors met, however, the gold was brighter, more brilliant, feeding from the shadows instead of being consumed by them.

Haru sighed and nodded at her unasked question, his smile soft and reassuring. Only then did she force her unwilling hands to release him and step back.

Kanna had felt this place, but had not seen it. The landscape was the same washed grey, but it rose as rocky cliffs, isolating itself from the rest of the Neither's wasteland. The stone varied from sharp and cutting to worn smooth. And on the terraced faces of the cliffs, there were doors.

Hundreds of doors, in a myriad of color, and each different from the last. Some were ornate, reliefs carved into the wood and inlaid with iron. Another was flat faced, a deep blue base with accented designs recalling simpler murals, something even childlike in the hand that painted it. Another, bright red, gold lines weaving over its surface, with frayed cloth acting as a door pull that lifted ever so slightly in a haunted breeze that Kanna could not feel.

There were others:

A door inlaid with copper that had begun to take on the blue-green hue of tarnish.

A violet one, with curling ivy and white wildflowers painted on its surface.

Another that was made of hexagonal tiles, some painted and others plain, fitted together at the center.

Some of the passages were locked or barred, and a few were caved in, the mouths covered in rubble.

Every thread of her memory was tied here. It was a heavy, solid place, unlike the open wastelands where fragments of ghosts wandered. It breathed, shuddering with hidden life that called her. Kanna shivered involuntarily in response. The pull of the doors was a physical thing, tendrils of smoke wrapping around her ribs and beckoning, a whisper that was felt.

The ground shifted beneath Haru's feet as he moved to stand at her shoulder. "It's beautiful," he said, awe stealing into his voice.

If Kanna tilted her head, she could almost see it. Beneath the primal fear that hissed in her bones, there was wonder. The colors were made more brilliant against the flat landscape, and every door was finely crafted, rendered with care and inspiration. She focused on that, tried to see it how he did.

"What do you want to do, Kanna?"

What she wanted to do was run. Tremors started at her hands, moved up her arms and to her chest, then radiated over her body in a wave. She wanted to pull him away from this place, and she wanted to forget this existed.

She didn't know what was behind the doors.

She didn't want to know what was behind the doors.

Haru grasped her arm and pulled her around, turning her so that he was all she could see. One arm at her waist brought her back against him. His other hand moved hers to his chest, pressing it against his heart, before falling at her cheek to tilt her head back as he dropped his forehead to hers.

"Breathe with me," he said, commanded.

She breathed in, sharp, and held it until she could match her breath to his, synched again to the rise and fall of his chest. The quick beating of his heart slowed as her own panic eased back into a dulled anxiety.

What she wanted to do was go with him somewhere that no tragedy could ever find them.

"*Inara,*" he soothed, "what do you *need* to do?"

What she needed to do was find the right thread to follow. She took another deep breath in. "I need to find the book," she said when she trusted herself to speak without flying apart.

The sound of bare feet scuffling through the raced past them, then stopped. Kanna flinched, but turned.

A child stared back. An echo of herself, small and unkempt, barefoot with dirt on the knees of her cropped pants. The shirt she wore was smocked in a colorful embroidered flower border at the neck, but it was wrinkled and stained green with grass. Her hair hung in twin braids, falling over her shoulders and past her elbows, the twists loose and uneven.

There was no scar on the brow that quirked curiously, her head tilting askance. Her lips twisted up on one side, and a short giggle issued in the air though her mouth did not move.

Haru's arms around Kanna loosened and she eased away from him. The echo turned, one of her braids flipping over her shoulder, and she ran for the corner of the cliffs. Without looking back, the echo scrambled up the cliff face.

The jagged rocks didn't bother it. Her. She grasped the sharp edges, hoisted herself up on ungainly limbs. She had yet to grow, had yet to tune her body to martial applications, but she made her way up the cliff with the confidence of a child that had yet to feel the pain of a fall.

Standing on one of the thin ledges, she jumped to reach the one above. Her fingertips caught, but she wasn't strong enough to hold on, so she slid back down. Repositioning, she tried again, and this time was able to grasp the edge. Her feet worked up the cliff face, and she rolled over the ledge.

She stood before a copper door, but backed away. She scampered across the second terrace, pausing at a few of the doors, but then doubled back. Finally, she stopped at an emerald green door, a repeating pattern of many-pointed stars carved in relief and stained to a lighter wood tone.

The ghost passed through the door without opening it.

The smell of disinfectant burned Kanna's nostrils. She covered her nose and mouth with her hand, coughing at the smell, but it wouldn't leave. It was inside her lungs and in her throat, so strong she could taste it.

Haru had his hands at her throat, passing over her lungs, his fingers threading through her hair to tilt her head back as her eyes watered, his voice cracking around her name as he tried to call her back, to ground her. He brushed her hair from her eyes and she gasped, breathing deep through the noxious tang as the coughing eased.

Kanna blinked hard to clear her eyes of the tears that had formed in them when the smell attempted to choke her. "That one," she said, her voice scratching over her dry throat. "We have to go in that one."

Haru tilted her face back, waited for her breath to even out. "Are you sure?" he asked. "We can go back. You don't have to do this."

Kanna squeezed her eyes shut, fought the temptation of the offer.

Yassen's words rose unbidden, his soft smile at the kitchen table when he'd offered her his easy wisdom. She thought of Isco, of all the burdens he carried, the guilt and shame that made him fight harder, gave him courage like she had never seen. She remembered Astar's arm twining in her's in Bomazi, under the soft paper lantern lights, letting her know that maybe, just maybe, not every memory was a bad one.

And she wanted to know what they knew, wanted that same confidence of self.

She thought of Osawa in the basement of the farmhouse, the trust he placed in her, the loyalty he held that came from not what she could do for him, but what they could do together.

And she thought of Vahn, of the animalistic protection she felt towards him, of the way he relaxed, let down his guard, only for her.

Then there was Haru, who would follow her anywhere. Who would fight dark itself, for her.

And she wanted to know why.

"I do," she said. "I need to do this."

Haru's hands fell away from her as he considered the door that her ghost had walked through. "How do we get up there?"

Kanna shut her eyes, and when she opened them she turned. A staircase rose at the corner of the cliff, allowing them passage to the second tier of doors. Haru followed her gaze, his eyes widening in surprise.

The stairs were solid when she tested the first, rough enough to give purchase but evenly formed. She glanced over her shoulder, only enough to be sure that Haru followed.

At the second level, the narrow walk brought her to the doors. As she passed they whispered, though she couldn't make out the sounds. She turned to Haru, who gave her a questioning arch of his brow. She was the only one that could hear them, the voices whispering in her mind more than by ear.

Nearer to the green door the sharp, tangy smell of disinfectant grew. It didn't assault her as it had before, and she swallowed past the nervous jittering in her stomach. On closer inspection, the door appeared worn and old, the paint faded in places where the elements had stripped it away. Tentatively, Kanna reached out to trace her fingers along one of the carved stars.

When she touched it the door cracked open, spilling sterile white light into the dark landscape.

Kanna looked back at Haru once more.

He nodded.

Then they stepped through the door.

## 2 7

# NEED & NECESSITY

## KANNA

They stepped into a bright room, and the acrid stink of disinfectant washed over Kanna again. Haru's steadying hand at her hip was a grounding reminder, keeping her in her body as the cloyingly sterile scent faded by degrees. Whitewashed cinderblock walls greeted them, the expanse of them broken up by glass cabinets, framed in a light stained wood, hermetically sealed and softly lit. The room hummed, an unseen generator vibrating through the walls, through the air.

Kanna stood next to Haru, but she also sat on the steel table in her mother's lab. She was an unscarred thing that hadn't yet learned the pain of falling, a slim whisper of what she would become. She was tangled hair and bare feet with dirt black soles that couldn't reach the ground.

Nestled among the cabinets of books and bound research files, Aksana bent over the desk at the side of the room, fresh red vials of blood at her fingertips. A centrifuge whirred, spinning out the next batch.

Kanna's echo swung her feet as the moments ticked and the machines whirred. Every sound was too loud here, the click of glass against glass as Aksana pressed her samples between slides, the scrape of it against metal when she fitted them beneath her microscope, and the clicking of dials as she adjusted the magnification ringing in Kanna's ears.

The echo flexed her fingers, then pressed them above the bandaid in her inner arm.

Kanna winced, hissed, and covered her inner elbow with her hand. *"Mother?"*

*"Why are you still here?"* Aksana asked, but it was more a statement than a question as she waved a hand in dismissal.

Kanna approached Aksana at her desk, and Haru followed behind and peered over her shoulder. The tidy notes on the clean papers were a blur.

"I never saw what she wrote," she said, her frustration clipping her tone. This place would only hold what she knew, what she had witnessed. Which meant this wasn't the book she was looking for.

She turned to her echo, who looked down from the table and gauged the distance between her feet and the ground. Realizing what was about to happen, Kanna reached out, but there was nothing they could do in this space.

It was a memory, she reminded herself. Nothing more.

The echo pushed herself from the table, hitting the slick floor of the lab and stumbling. She caught herself with the heels of her hands, and Kanna clenched her fists when the bruising ache jarred into her wrists.

There were no tears from the echo. She bit her teeth together and sat back, clenching and unclenching her hands. She looked to Aksana, who hadn't turned away from her notes, before pushing herself up from the ground. As the echo moved to the door, Aksana turned her chair, its springs screeching in the room. *"Wait."*

The echo froze, turning, her eyes wide with a small thread of hope.

Aksana stood from her chair, and Kanna jumped back, brushing against Haru who pulled them both out of the way as Aksana moved to the cabinets. The seal hissed when she unlatched one and, from the case, Aksana pulled a manuscript. She balanced it in her hands, running her fingers of the debossed Ilazkin script on the cover. It was loosely bound, the papers within different sizes as evidenced by the ragged edge, some colored with age while others still held the sheen of new white.

Aksana returned to her seat, the book in hand, and began rifling through the pages. Finding the place she sought, she turned it to the echo. "*What do you think of this?*"

The yellowed page curled under the weight of a dark ink drawing. It was a creature, rendered in a near solid black, eight unblinking eyes set into its face. Along its back, countless wings sprouted, and feathers cascaded over the page and blocked out the rest of it. Writing and symbols scattered through the void of the black, the ink filling the spaces around it. Circles in circles, nested triangles, skewed waves with no rhythm that Kanna could reason.

She stared into the eyes of the creature, drawn into its flat expression. Her hand curled out, brushing down the ridge between its eight eyes, pressing at the chest where a pulse should be. Her fingers followed the design, tracing the line of power she felt, the odd thrum, as if she put her hand against its voice box and she could hear it without words.

"*I do not know.*" Kanna pulled her hand away, curling it against her chest. "*What is it?*"

Disappointed turned Aksana's brow and sunk in Kanna's chest, and Aksana closed the book. "*It is nothing.*"

She hadn't given mother the right answer.

Aksana returned the book to its place and sealed the cabinet. "*Go,*" she said, not turning to look at Kanna. "*Leave me.*"

"Kanna?"

She jumped in her skin, whirling to look up at Haru. Then she looked down at her hand, uncurled her fingers from her chest and let it fall at her side.

The echo backed out of the room, slowly, just in case Aksana turned to look at her again.

She didn't.

Half-out of the door, the echo's gaze slid to Kanna, then Haru. Her head ticked to the side. She turned to Aksana, but she was too deep in her study to notice.

The echo slipped out of the room, and the steel door slid shut behind her.

Then, it cracked open. The miasma of disinfectant faded, replaced by the warm scent of dust and old leather. No longer steel, the door was now wood, dark in tone and woven in a herringbone pattern.

Haru followed as Kanna crossed the room. The brass handle on the door was set vertically, and despite the frigid lab, it was warm under her touch.

She pulled open the new door, and they followed the echo.

Into the Palamidia's library.

---

THE PALAMIDIA PRIDED itself on the education of its officers, and nowhere was that more physically evident than in the Tower's library. The marble entry opened to a vast room, soaring countless stories high and anchored by an iron and crystal chandelier set at a low glow. While it was as white as every other room, the mass of books stacked from floor to ceiling blocked the reflecting glare, casting the room in a crepuscular light. Long rows of tables outfitted with low reading lamps marched through the center of the ground level, while shorter tables flanked the sides. Carts were situated at each end of the long tables, ready to receive volumes that the studious had finished.

Curving stairs on each side of the center rotunda lead to the first rise, with a central staircase beginning on the second floor. Each level boasted open terraces bordered with wood railings where white-clad soldiers haunted the selection.

"This is where they keep books," Haru said, his voice respectfully low, as if he was expecting to be hushed even in memory.

He wasn't wrong.

Kanna hooked to the left stairwell, felt the cool banister beneath her touch as she climbed to the second floor. The walls of books gave an illusion of a single row from below, but when they reached the landings, the stacks continued beyond the fronted line. Some of the books' titles were clearly defined, while others were shapeless blurs of writing against varying textured spines. She passed the rows, trying not to let the shifting focus in the corner of her eyes unbalance her.

Four flights up, she paused. The musk of old leather grew stronger, but it now carried a top note of pen ink and copy toner. Winding through the stacks at that level, she followed the scent until she found her echo.

Older but not yet grown, she lay on her stomach on the floor, her elbows propping her above a scattered array of loose copied sheets. Between her fingers, she toyed with an acetate fountain pen, tilting it side to side and watching the ink in the clear barrel shift. Instead of the low, loose braids of her childhood, her hair was pulled back in a single french braid. Strands of it fell loose to tickle her nose.

Next to her, Vahn was lying on his back in the opposite direction, one arm pillowing his head while the other fell across his chest, his eyes shut in a mask of sleep. His long hair drifted over the papers the echo was meant to be studying.

With a resigned sigh, the echo unscrewed the cap of the pen. She brushed aside the silver hair that fell over her notebook and tried to press her hand to the paper. Her joints stiffened around the movement, her fingers fumbling with their placement.

"*Use your other hand,*" Vahn muttered in Ilazkin, not opening his eyes.

The echo grimaced. "*It is not right.*"

"Says who?" he asked in Common. Vahn turned his head, his eyes opening to study her before switching back to Ilazkin. "*If it feels right to use your other hand, then that is the one you should use.*"

Kanna glowered at him, but switched the pen. It was more suited to the task, though her handwriting was still a jilted mess.

Vahn shifted, wriggling his lean body to get comfortable before he shut his eyes again.

The echo looked back to the pages in front of her. Ilazkin texts were felt just as much as read, the words never flowing in a common order but instead following interconnected symbols across the page like maps of constellations. This one, she couldn't quite follow yet.

She sighed, her breath blowing the stray hairs that fell in her eyes.

"*What now?*" Vahn grumbled.

There was an additional piece that she was missing, and she didn't know how to translate it to make sense. "There isn't a word for this in Common, and it is strange in the ancient, too."

Vahn opened his eyes and bent from the waist to sit up. He pivoted while crossing his legs under himself, then propped his elbows on his knees. "Explain it to me."

Behind Kanna, Haru moved closer. Her focus returned, and she smiled over her shoulder at him. "I liked these times," she said, looking back at the two young soldiers, their jackets cropped and not yet heavy with the threads of blood. "We were safe together."

"As opposed to other times?" he asked, his voice still hushed out of respect.

"At least, when we were together, I didn't worry about what Velinius could do to him. Or, what she *would* do to him." She turned to Haru, but she couldn't look at him for very long without the well of anxiety rising, so she looked away. "Velinius knew me better than anyone. She knew my weakness, and how to exploit it."

Kanna swallowed. "Knows," she corrected. "She knows."

The echo looked up at Vahn across from her with a frown. She pushed herself up and matched him, then turned the paper she was studying upside down so he could see it.

"This is about the 'whole'"—she pointed to the larger triangle, containing multiple others—"this area is the body"—one of the open spaces in the triangle—"and then mind." That covered the loose text, but the last space held a twisted ring. "This is soul."

Vahn looked up to meet her eyes, then back down. "I'm following you so far."

Kanna raised her brow. "You don't see the problem?"

Vahn shrugged.

"It has two parts."

Vahn shook his head, pointing to one. "That one is still soul, though."

Kanna bent over to see what he indicated, then shook her head. "No, that's Self." Then, she indicated the second part. "I can only feel what this part is."

"I am feeling a lot of things right now, and none of them are fun."

Kanna stifled a short laugh.

Vahn sat up, stretched his arms over his head and arched his back. "Keep going, I'm listening."

The echo sat back, tapping her fingers on her knee. "It is like a connection, but it is yours." Her fingers brushed against her sternum, below her heart. "It's the feathers."

"Feathers?" Vahn asked, with Haru in tandem.

Kanna, and her echo, nodded.

"*Inside*," the echo said, and closed her eyes. "Like a live thing, like it knows something I don't. It gets angry, or it gets hungry, and if I listen, sometimes, I think I know what it wants to tell me. Sometimes, I can know what it knows."

Vahn thought for a moment, his brow furrowed. "Oh." He sat up straighter. "The quills."

Kanna's echo arched her brow.

"Quills," Vahn repeated. "They're fine if you pet them one way, kind of smooth, but if you pet it the wrong way it'll stab you."

The echo's brow knit in confusion.

"Like a hedgehog," Vahn added to clarify.

"Who's a hedgehog?"

"Not who, what. What is a hedgehog."

"All right," the echo amended, trying out the taste of the new word. "What is a hedgehog?"

Vahn looked at her for a moment, his expression near blank. Then he sighed, and pushed himself to standing.

The echo's fingers traced her collarbone, then she turned back to her notes. "I thought it was just me."

"Nope," Vahn answered.

At her shoulder, Haru's voice whispered, "It's scales, for me. Sometimes they are cold, sometimes warm, it depends."

"What does it depend on?" Kanna asked.

Haru shrugged. "What I feel, I think."

"What's it matter, anyway?" Vahn continued, bringing Kanna's focus back to the memory.

"I still do not know what to call it," the echo answered.

"Call it instinct, or spirit to stick with the 's' theme. Or just pile it all under 'soul.'"

The echo twisted one of the loose strands of hair at her nape, her teeth digging into her lip. "But there isn't only one."

Vahn crouched in front of Kanna, lifted her chin with one finger to meet his eyes. "*You have been at this for hours,*" he said, his voice now soothing, and she could feel the concern hidden in the outside of it. "I'm bored," he added, smothering the softness inside of him as he pulled his hand away and stood. "Just put down whatever, it isn't like Velinius is going to know the difference, anyway."

Vahn turned away from her, disappearing behind the rows. The echo sighed. Vahn was right. If Velinius could tell the difference, she wouldn't need Kanna to translate it. She scribbled out the rest of her notes, then twisted the cap back on the pen. As she was gathering the scattered papers, a heavy book fell, open, on top of them.

"Hedgehog," Vahn said, pointing at the color photograph of the small creature curled in someone's hand.

"Oh," Kanna's echo remarked, leaning closer to stare at the beady black eyes. "*It is cute.*"

"*It is not cute.*" Vahn picked the book up and slammed it shut. "It is mean and pointy." He tucked the book under his elbow, then offered a hand to help Kanna. She finished gathering her papers and bent them against her chest, then let him assist her to her feet. "Let's turn your busywork in and get out of here. I have it on good authority that there is a new shipment of foals coming in, and guess who gets one this time?"

"*Is it you?*" the echo asked.

"*It is me,*" Vahn replied. He reached out with the book, tapping it against the top of her head. "*How did you know?*"

"Instinct?" Kanna replied. "Or maybe spirit."

"Oh, jokes," Vahn said, turning on his heel, his voice mock offended. "I kindly offer my help, and you got jokes."

The two began to leave the quiet corner, and Kanna tried to follow.

"*Who told you?*" the echo asked, but her voice was growing further away.

"Salinae," Vahn answered, "he tells me things sometimes."

Kanna wanted to follow them, to stay in the safety of that moment, but even as she tried, the scenery slipped beneath her feet, keeping her in place as they turned the corner out of view.

"I don't like him."

"You don't like anyone," Vahn replied, and the laughter in his voice echoed, then faded until there was nothing left.

"I have to tell them," Kanna whispered. Her feet found purchase on the ground. She raced after their trail, rounding the corner in chase of the ghosts.

"Wait!" Haru called from behind her, but she almost couldn't hear him.

She had to warn them. She turned, running in the other direction in search of the echoes as the books on the library shelves began to blur and meld. "They don't know what's coming."

She tried another direction, but Haru grabbed her arm to stop her erratic flight. Kanna tried to twist from his grip, but he only held her tighter. "You can't tell them anything," he said, trying to reason with her.

That didn't make it better.

"You can't stop it from happening. It already did. It's *done*."

It took her another moment to stop fighting, and another to let out a jagged breath.

Haru's grip released, and he stepped back and looked away. "Kanna? Do you see this?"

She followed his line of sight to the bottom floor of the library. The lights at the workstations were turning off, row by row. As they switched off the shadows moved in, devouring the library floor by floor.

"This way." Haru took her hand as the black moved in on them from each side, dragging her through the stacks as the shadows chased at their heels.

"A door, Kanna," he called to her. "We need a door."

She shook her head, "I can't."

They didn't know what was coming for them. They didn't know that the world would eat them alive, that there was nothing waiting but blood and fear, death and madness.

Haru stopped and yanked her forward. He kissed her, hard, and the shock released the panicked thoughts that whirled in her mind. He pulled away and met her eyes, again that steady determination, the unending belief. "You can," he said. "You have to."

Haru looked away first, but Kanna didn't want to see it.

"Let's go," he said, dragging her behind him as he raced to the door.

It was white, solid and still as the books shifted around it. There was nothing on its face, a black knob the only protrusion.

The dark licked at her heels and tried to pull her back into its heavy gravity. A thudding echo issued each second, each second becoming longer, as the lights shut off behind them.

Haru yanked the door open and pulled her until she ran ahead, then stepped through. He slammed the door behind them as the last light in the library went out.

---

KANNA HAD NEVER SEEN this room before.

It was white, a room built from the idea of the Tower, but it small and windowless. At the center was a long table with papers scattered across its surface. Some were parchment, others copies, and still more boasted her handwritten notes.

And taking up the white walls was the monster from Aksana's book.

Blacker than ink, it lounged around the room, teeth and claws and feathers—some drifting away as if it had lost them in flight, or in landing. Although two-dimensional, it breathed against the wall. Eight eyes, empty and white, loomed at her. Its stare froze her in place.

She couldn't breathe.

"Kanna."

She jumped, spinning to face Haru. He reached for her, tilting her head back, but she couldn't meet his eyes.

He brushed his thumb against her cheek. "It's all right," he soothed. "I'll look."

Haru dropped a soft kiss on her crown, then pulled himself away. He passed behind her, moving to the table with the scattered papers.

Kanna turned, slowly. He was leaning on the table, shifting through the jumbled schematics and notes as if he could absorb it, as if he could remember it for her.

"You don't have to," she said. He looked up, his back straightening as his eyes burned into her. "I know what's there."

The knowledge had arrived with little fanfare. It whispered in the moment the door shut and filled once empty gaps that she couldn't quite grasp before.

It wasn't everything.

It was like the Ilazkin language, or the schematic of a story. Her memory connected, piece by piece, like following a layline throughout its course.

But a single story never provided all the answers.

And the longer she looked at the beast on the wall, the less the monster was a monster.

Teeth were necessary.

Claws could protect.

And the brush of a feather was a wonder, something so indescribable that there was no other word for it.

The beast's shoulders shifted, as if it was trying to escape from the place that held it. The many wings flexed, and she could hear the rustle of them against each other, taste something volatile on her tongue. Instead of backing away, Kanna moved toward it. Step by excruciating step, until she was eye-to-eye with the beast, and she reached out.

It blinked, the movement cascading from its topmost pair of eyes down, matching the shiver that rattled her spine. The head strained forward, until her fingers brushed it.

The eyes shut, and the beast sighed. It eased back into its place on the wall, and when it did, the wall rippled like a drop in a pool of ink.

The room flashed, and Kanna covered her eyes to not be blinded by the brilliant light.

When she blinked back into focus the beast was gone, replaced by an interconnected weave of writing, symbols, and instruction that crawled over the walls, swept over the ceiling and dipped to the floor beneath her feet.

All the pages Kanna had translated, all those torn apart and scattered remnants from a time long past, a time before the Great Death, merged together in a delicate web. Symbols locked within symbols, lines that fell off single pages connected with another, and so on and forth until it came together in a grand, unified theory that once she knew of it, she knew she had to hide it.

It was beautiful in construct and terrifying in promise.

Kanna stepped away, her back hitting against Haru's. They moved together, taking in the expanse of lines that wove around them. As Haru turned, she turned in his opposite, careful to guard against any new surprises that might creep in.

After a long silence, Haru broke it. "What is it?"

Kanna shook her head. "Something impossible. At least, it should be impossible."

Behind her, Kanna could feel something cold move along Haru's spine.

"If it isn't?" he asked.

A creak broke the quiet of the room, tore Kanna's attention away from the intricate lines that crossed the ceiling.

The green door appeared in the wall, its many-point stars carved in relief and stained a light natural wood. The jamb was cracked open, ever so slightly, and beyond it was a vast sky with too many stars.

# 28

# THE RED DOOR

## KANNA

THEY ARRIVED among the cliffs of doors, stepping out at the second tier where they had originally entered. Kanna breathed in the eerie nothing of the Neither's air. Haru waited beside her, and she could feel the way his eyes burned as they traveled over her, assessing but giving her the time to recover from the overwhelming sensations that pulled at her.

Even if she was outside of it, even when she watched, she could still feel it. Her body knew the memory. Her body remembered the pain.

"Was that enough?" There was concern, even fear in Haru's voice, and Kanna could almost sense the cooling scales that rippled over his spine, curled at the back of his neck.

That, at least, had to be her imagination. She clenched her fingers to fists until pain shot through her knuckles and she could know that it was hers. Finally, she shook her head. "I don't think so. It is just the theory."

Haru stepped forward, but didn't try to touch her. "What theory?"

"The Izanami Gate."

Haru's brow knit in thought, then he shook his head. "I haven't heard of that."

Kanna turned to look around them, but it was the same endless doors and endless quiet. She started back to the steps, making her way back to the lower level.

"What most know of the Great Death isn't everything," she said as he followed. "The stories tend to forget things. From one voice to the next, things are lost along the way." Kanna descended the steps and stood to the side, turning her back to the cliffs to face Haru. "The old gods didn't kill each other in some great war, and that wasn't what destroyed everything."

The cold desert stretched behind Haru, and while it wasn't the exact same, the wasteland of the Neither was a close replica of Ilazki's barren landscape. Once, it had blossomed with fields, forests, rivers, even environs that no longer existed in their consciousness. It had been replaced by the wild, dangerous land that they now knew, with volcanos that never ceased erupting, seas with no currents, and forests of living stone.

"The power the gods had was stolen, but they wanted more. They needed more. So they built a machine that would grant it to them."

"The Izanami Gate."

Kanna nodded. "The scholars that came after, they assumed that something had gone wrong, that the gods had miscalculated somehow and the machine backfired catastrophically."

From the center out, the world had shattered. Ilazki itself was cast in a neverending night, its rivers littered with ice floes, and devastating storms rained glass on fools that ventured too long, too far into the wasteland. The damage even went through the surface, deadening loas' abilities if they moved far enough underground, close enough to the point of origin.

Haru reached out, turning her chin with one finger so she met his eyes. "Why doesn't it sound like you believe that?"

"What if it didn't go wrong?" she said more than asked. "What if it did exactly what it was meant to do?"

It was Haru's turn to shake his head. "You can't believe that they did this on purpose."

No, she didn't believe that. What she believed was worst. "I think they opened a door, and they weren't prepared for what tried to come through it."

Haru's hand fell, but not before he brushed the back of his knuckles over her jaw. "If it succeeded, or even if it failed, that machine is gone. It would have been destroyed with everything else at the epicenter."

She shook her head. "Some things can't be destroyed."

This was where the memories began to fade and, once again, become unreachable. "We still have some of the smaller of the god's works. People can't help but look for things. And some were found. We made stories around them, but..." Kanna trailed off, not knowing how to continue. She shifted in agitation, unable to grasp the idea. "They aren't what they seem."

Haru opened his mouth to speak, but then looked over her shoulder. His eyes widened, the gold whirled in the blue and snapped to attention.

Kanna turned, and faced another echo.

This one waited for her acknowledgement. She stood as a young teen, her hair braided in a low crown behind her neck that pulled it out of her eyes and off her shoulders. Across the white chest of her uniform, her face, there was a thin spray of blood. More soaked the wrists of her short jacket and smeared over her loose hands.

Haru's hand wrapped around the top of Kanna's arm. "We can find another way," he said, once again giving her the chance to leave this place behind.

"There isn't another way." The papers in the library were webs that only she could translate. "I'm the only one that knows all of it."

The echo met Kanna's eyes as she backed away, not even turning around as it drifted through one of the lower doors.

A ringing sound, high pitched but low, rose in frequency. Kanna winced as the pain ripped through her ears, sharp and pointed, and she pressed her hands against them in an attempt to block the sustained note.

The threads of memory yanked at her body, trying to take over and reform it.

But Haru was calling her name.

If she did not go to the memory, it would come to her. She grabbed Haru's wrist, racing to the door that the echo had shifted through.

It was dark red, with layers of other reds painted over it, time and again, each one a shade darker, or a shade lighter, until the wood could not hold it any longer. The door was bloated, rotting at its core, the wood rippling and breaking through the coatings.

Her hand wrapped around the rusted knob, the rough texture changing to the sticky-slick feel of congealing blood in her palm, and she yanked the door open.

# 29

## SLAUGHTER & SACRIFICE

### KANNA

THERE WAS A SAMENESS TO WAR.

The landscapes changed, or the methods, but there was always the white of the Palamidia, the singing of metal and screams, and the rotting miasma of death, adrenaline, and fear.

And they'd been dropped into the middle of it.

Haru turned, pressing his back against hers while the chaos of battle closed them in at all sides. "Which one is this?" Haru asked, his voice raised over the din that surrounded them.

Trampled grass beneath their feet made her think of Atarrabi, but the petrified forests of Gegenes loomed in the distance. The light of the day flickered, from overcast to bright, the breeze around them dying before returning from another direction.

Kanna turned, and Haru turned with her.

"All of them," she called back.

Haru twisted around her, jerking her out of the way as a mounted soldier charged by. "Can it hurt us?"

Kanna's gaze darted around, pulled from one death to another. "I don't know."

In the distance, she heard the snap of a release and the metallic clanking of gears as a trebuchet launched. The load soared from somewhere she couldn't place, landing several yards away. The bodies not quick enough scattered, and the resulting reverberation from the impact hit Kanna hard enough to send her flying into Haru and they toppled together.

Haru hit the ground first, deadening Kanna's fall. The ringing in her ears returned, her vision blurring as she rolled away and came eye-to-eye with a white-clad corpse, his mouth open in a scream against the night sky, blood staining his teeth. She jerked herself up, crawling back away from it as the sky flashed back to day

Behind her, Haru's deep gasp brought her back. She turned to him and he coughed, clearing his lungs as he sat up. Kanna grasped his face in her hands, turning him to check his pupils for signs of concussion. They were even and undilated, and she sighed in relief. "I guess that answers the question."

Haru wheezed an almost laugh that was cut off by another cough as he caught his breath. When his eyes widened and he looked around, Kanna realized that the sound of battle had dissipated. They were not safe, but they were not targeted, at least.

She rose to standing and offered Haru a hand to hoist himself up as she took in the settled landscape. Sparse tabosa grasses rose out of the sandy soil, bending beneath a soft but reluctant breeze.

Kanna squinted when a flash of white appeared on the horizon, then, dozens more as they retreated toward them.

She knew this one.

"Atarrabi," Kanna said, her voice catching on the warning as the white clad soldiers bore down on the pair. She grasped Haru's wrist. "Run."

No sooner than she had named it did the ground begin to tremble.

The other soldiers were around them now, shoving each other when someone moved too close, because they knew. They knew that not all of them would make it.

Kanna stopped, turning toward a flash of long white hair. Vahn tripped, a hail of awkward limbs that had yet to acquire their vicious reflexes.

Behind them, the cause of the retreat made itself known. The ground rippled after the soldiers, the rocks churning and catching those that weren't fast enough, the ones that weren't lucky enough, the ground upending to crush them or changing to a mire to pull them down and drown them in the earth.

Her echo, blood spattered and torn, stopped her route and turned back for Vahn. She covered him as the soldiers' feet attempted to trample them both, pulling him up from the ground as they stumbled back into the flow of the retreat.

Kanna aimed for them, cutting through the stampede until they dropped from view. With Haru in tow, she followed.

Weeks before the library, Vahn had earned his foal at this battle. Near the border between Atarrabi and Adur, the independent regions had managed to amass a contingent of earth loas to stop the Palamidia's advancement. Working together, they had nearly decimated the Palamidia's line.

Then, Velinius had an idea. The Palamidia would rush the independent coalition in hopes of pushing one of their earth loas to sync, therefore taking out their own people, who would be closest to the core of the sync.

It worked.

After the orders were issued, Velinius, along with the remaining ranked officers, rode out of the estimated range of the sync, leaving behind the new, untested soldiers as sacrifices. What was left of the Palamidia's contingent fell back, where trenches had been created as shelters and fortified to the will of their own earth loas, the only things the officers bothered to leave for them.

Kanna slid down the embankment into the trench that her echo had dove for, Haru following behind and ducking low to hide behind the ditch's walls as the land around them continued its furious rebellion. The walls of the trenches were beginning to give, the sides turning to sand and cascading over the soldiers that cowered in the narrow ditch. The stone groaned, cracked, desperately trying to listen to its previous command while a more primal force called to it.

The echo huddled with Vahn, their hands linked and knuckles white as the sand fell in a dry, gritty rain. The earth rumbled around them, a beast snapping its jaws against a cage, and they curled closer to one another.

"Kanna," Haru called, "we have to get out of here."

She shook her head, held her hand out to quiet him.

The echo sat back, her eyes wide. The feathered thing was whispering, as if the animal of the earth had woken it. It knew a secret, and she knew it, too. But she would have to be brave, it warned her. She would have to be the bravest she had ever been, or it would not work. If it did not work, if she was not strong enough, it would take her back.

Vahn's grip tightened on her hand as another tremor shook their meager shelter. His eyes were wild, panicked. He knew as well as her that the earth would not hold. That if they did nothing, this would be their grave.

"I have an idea," she said.

Vahn jumped, then focused on her. "Is it a good idea?"

The echo shook her head.

"*We need a good idea*," he hissed.

Kanna looked up and down the trench. They hadn't been the only young ones on the field, but their numbers had been cut down even further than the adults who, for the most part, were fresh out of training. For some, for most, this had been their first taste of war.

It wasn't Kanna's. And it wasn't Vahn's, either.

She shook her head again. "There aren't any others."

Vahn took a moment to consider, but the moment was interrupted by a scream that cut short. Further along the trench, a portion of the walls had given in. The sand became viscous, streams bursting from the embankment. They wrapped around them like an amphibious tongue and pulled them in to drown in the earth.

He turned to her. "K..."

"I have to get closer," she said. "*I have to be closer to the source.*"

"That is suicide, K."

"So is staying here."

Vahn nodded. "I'm coming with you." Before she could protest, he raised his voice. "You aren't leaving me behind."

Kanna's echo shut her mouth and swallowed her protest. She had not heard him raise his voice before.

"*There is no other reason for me*," he said.

The feathered thing whispered and she knew he could help, maybe. He was strong. Maybe he could help. The echo pulled her feet beneath her in a crouch. "When it starts, run."

"When what starts?" Vahn asked, matching her stance.

"You'll know."

Vahn looked away.

"Promise me," she said through clenched teeth. "*Promise me you will run.*"

"All right," he snapped back. "*I promise.*"

Kanna nodded, then placed her hand against the side of the trench. She shut her eyes and concentrated on the feel of the earth prowling on the other side, seeking the power's source.

She opened her eyes, turned to meet the fiery violet of his gaze. "I hope you survive this," she said, because she did. If nothing else, that was the one thing she dared to hope for.

"I hope you do." He leaned forward and pressed his forehead against hers, then, like it was a secret, he whispered, "*I hope we both do.*"

For the moment, for one brief moment, everything was quiet.

The echo sighed, leaned back, and opened her eyes.

Together, she and Vahn timed the waves of tremors, counting down until, wordlessly, they knew. They rose together, charging out of the trench and into the angry maw of the earth.

Kanna reached for Haru's wrist and dragged him behind as they breached, rising from the ditch and into the rift valleys of Gegenes.


ATARRABI HAD NOT BEEN where Kanna first spilled blood.

This was.

Kanna pressed a hand against her chest as her breath caught and her heart began to pound, every cell in her body charging with fear. The rift valley was deep in eastern Gegenes, and the Palamidia had skirted the borders of Ilazki in a bold surprise attack. They'd lost part of their contingent along the way, but arrived in large numbers.

However, they did not get far into Gegenes before being halted here.

There were few people in the Empire who knew of the rift valley, and fewer that had been there themselves. They had descriptions of it, but nothing could quite capture the jagged terrain. Flat topped plateaus terraced the land, with long, ragged drops at all sides. While attempting to traverse the perplexing maze of the valleys, they'd fallen into an ambush.

And the Gegenii had the high ground. Kanna tilted her neck back, and there it loomed.

"Rough's Peak."

Haru stiffened at her side. He pulled her around, grasped her face between his hands and tilted her back to look at him. "We cannot stay here, Kanna. You cannot be here."

"I have to," she replied, her voice shaking. "This is where it started."

"Veil!"

Kanna didn't have to look for her echo this time. It found her.

She was so small then, armed with nothing more than the equivalent of a castoff pocket knife and her abilities, and she was lost.

On the trip, she hadn't been able to sleep. The nightmares had begun then, once she passed into the evernight of Ilazki, and they hadn't stopped. The things in the dark had moved into her mind, set a hook and never left. Exhausted, she had lost her focus, and when the slaughter began, she lost Veil.

"Veil!" she screamed again, her voice echoing against the walls of the narrow valley.

The bodies were falling, everywhere, and she couldn't see through the ones that remained.

One of the enemy soldiers caught her from behind, dragged her from her collar and she screeched, stumbling back and tripping over her feet as she fell to the ground. Kanna scuttled backwards, but the wild anger in his eyes changed to something like confusion.

She was too small to be there, and she was lost.

And the man was tall enough to cast a shadow, the muscles in his arms rippling beneath bronze skin. He stepped toward her and she crawled back again, covering her face with her arms and screaming.

Then, she heard the clatter as his spear fell, the point landing near her own hand.

When she uncovered her eyes, the man was dangling off his toes. The shadows wrapped around him, squeezing his limbs against his body. His hands flexed as he tried to break free, but the shadows snaked over his neck, around his head, tightening with each wind.

Kanna shook her head. "No."

She turned over onto her knees, tried to reach for him, but it was too late. The shadows clenched, and his body cracked. Bones snapped, shattering in an erratic sequence, like the time she dropped one of Mother's beakers.

The shadows dropped him before her.

Blood pooled from his nose, his mouth, even from the wide-open eyes that bulged from their sockets.

She couldn't even scream.

She didn't even hear the slam of hoofbeats approaching until they were on top of her. A horse circled and an arm reached down, grabbing her by the elbow and pulling her from the ground.

Her shock wore off enough for her to recognize the rider.

"*You lost me,*" she sobbed, but clung to Veil anyway.

Veil spurred the horse away from the outskirts of the fight. "Speak properly, Ananke."

*"Kanna!"*

Kanna clung to Veil's waist, buried her face into her back so that she wouldn't have to see. Veil pointed her mount to the narrow path that led up the ridge. Even with Kanna's grip on her waist, she managed to tear through the enemy combatants that attempted to push her back, and soon she was joined by other officers, more white flashing among the dark earth tones as they pushed the Gegenii back, drove them to retreat to the peak.

One of the enemy soldiers grabbed her leg, tried to pull her down. Kanna clenched her teeth to stop from screaming and disentangled one of her hands enough to grasp the small knife tucked into her waistband. She stabbed down, with everything she had, and the point burrowed through the woman's hand, nicking Kanna's calf, but it forced the woman to let go.

And she took Kanna's knife with her.

Blood welled on Kanna's leg, the red growing out to stain the white of her uniform.

*"It isn't real, Kanna!"*

It was real. The sting in her leg, the screams, the smell of horse sweat and viscera and the close brush of other mounted soldiers, so close that the horses' tails flicked into her eyes.

They breached the top of the ridge, but the mistake belonged to the Palamidia. The bulk of the Gegenii soldiers held Rough's Peak, and the officers that had made it through were few in number.

Veil choked back on her mount's reins as more of their soldiers filed through. "Clear a path," she yelled over the din. "When I give the signal, retreat to the valley."

Their agreements resounded as they rushed past. Veil released their mount, weaving into the middle of the other Palamidia soldiers for protection, until they neared the center of the massing Gegenii.

Veil shifted in her saddle and pried one of Kanna's arms from her waist.

Arms wrapped around her from behind, yanking her out of that small body, that terrified body, that body that didn't yet know how to move, how to break an enemy.

Kanna's head swam, her vision blurring and reorienting as Haru pulled her back, his arms supporting what her legs failed to catch.

Velinius shoved Kanna's echo from the back of the horse. She fell in a heap, her shoulder popping out of place with a bright snap when it took the brunt of her fall.

In Haru's arms, she screeched as the pain reverberated through her shoulder.

On the ground, all Kanna could see was the flash of hooves as Veil turned her horse away.

"Fall back!" Veil commanded, her voice clear over the clash.

Haru kept Kanna in place as she staggered, nearly falling to the ground again. She shook her head to clear it, the pain confusing her while she lived in two places at once.

The Palamidia's soldiers rushed back to the path.

The Gegenii ignored the broken child on the ground. They'd seen her on the horse, known how small she was, and she was no threat to them. But they had identified the leader, and if they could get to her the battle was won.

Kanna covered her head with her one working hand as the soldiers that weren't able to avoid the hazard she'd become stepped on her. A boot landed on her back and pressed her to the ground, and her rib snapped under the force.

Her rib snapped, and the feathered thing hissed. The hiss became a growl as the tears sprung to her eyes, as she struggled to breathe through the wet in her lungs.

"*Inara,*" Haru's voice in her ear. "I'm here. I have you."

The white trail of uniforms was disappearing.

They had left her to die.

*No.*

A sibilant voice whispered, the hissing clear for the first, and the last, time.

*Not yet. You are meant for something.*

"You're with me," Haru pleaded, his voice desperate.

Kanna found the strength in her legs, bit her teeth around the crushing pain.

"Haru," she managed to utter. Kanna turned in his arms, wrapped her own around his neck, pulled him toward her. "Get down."

Kanna asked the dark for help, and made a bargain. She didn't want to die here, like she was nothing, crushed before she could ever be something. If she was supposed to do something, be something, she wouldn't be able to do it if she died here.

The dark answered.

Haru ducked and Kanna leaned over him, pulling him as close as she could and covering him.

The ground beneath her ripped open, and the feathered thing came.

Too-long arms reached up, eight unblinking white irises rising from unknown depths. Wings sprouted from its back, and it covered her.

Teeth were necessary.

Claws could protect.

And the brush of a feather could be described in no other way.

The Gegenii combatants' sure victory turned. They shoved against each other now, their ranks breaking, as they tried to force themselves down the path behind the Palamidia.

It was too late. The creature opened its mouth revealing jagged, unending teeth, and from its chest, it screeched. The sound pitched across scales, a multitude of voices that were not quite in key singing all at once.

It was every nightmare she had before that moment, and every one after. It was every pain, every loss, every drop of blood she never wanted to spill. It emptied her, and it filled her, and it could destroy, and it could create. It was a pure chaos.

More wings sprouted, ripping from the creatures body. They swept out, shoving the Gegenii from the peak. Loose feathers drifted away, falling to the ground and turning into ink-like pools.

Those unlucky enough to not be toppled from the peak were caught by the ever expanding black. The pool around the body moved out, filling with every wrong choice, every time she was not what she was supposed to be, while the smaller ones slid to join it. They caught those on the peak by foot, dragging them to the center. Snaking tendrils sought legs, arms, wrapping around necks and pulling them—body, soul, and all—into the black.

It reached, sharp claws extending, and swept through the mass. There was no smell, no sound, as it tore through them. No blood, because as pieces of their bodies fell, they were raked back and dropped into the inky pools.

When the plateau was clear, eight eyes turned, blinked in succession, as if assuring itself that its work was complete. Then, it settled back.

Kanna looked up as it pulled away, and so did Haru. The pool receded, leaving blackened ground behind.

Before the creature slipped away, it bent its head to Kanna. She met its eyes, then, carefully, her fingers unfurled.

She reached out with her only working hand and placed her palm against its forehead, between its topmost eyes. Each white eye shut and it shuddered, the movement rippling through its wings, rustling the loose feathers. She pulled her hand back, closed it against her chest.

When its eyes opened, it blinked, then lowered its muzzle to her hand. It breathed out, once.

Her shoulder slid back into place, painlessly. Her rib knit, and the bruises and cuts on her skin faded.

The being turned and dove, down, sinking back through the tear from which it had come.

And Kanna's echo sat, alone, staring at the place where the world had torn apart.

She waited.

In the deafening silence, Kanna stood. Haru followed suit, and began to look.

He was looking for a door.

"It isn't over," Kanna said.

From the path, Velinius arrived on foot. She stopped at the edge of the blackened ground and signaled for the others to wait.

Velinius hesitated, placing one foot onto the surface. Satisfied, she began her approach.

Kanna leaned back into Haru. He wrapped an arm across her shoulders, another around her waist, and pulled her against him. He was solid.

He was safe.

Velinius did not bend, did not crouch, but addressed Kanna from her height. "Ananke," she said, in the tone that Kanna knew brooked no argument.

From the ground, Kanna's echo turned, her neck craning back.

Velinius's brow knit together. She raised a single finger, pointing to the hand that Kanna clutched to her chest. "What do you have there?"

The echo looked away from Velinius, down at her hand. She blinked, her lids rasping against dry eyes. "A secret."

Velinius's mouth turned down sharply at the corners, but she corrected it. A smile stretched over her lips, her eyes softening. "Since when do we keep secrets, sister?"

The echo looked down at her hand. It was hers, she knew. It was only hers. But maybe, if she shared it with Veil, then maybe, Veil wouldn't leave her again. She unfurled her fingers, revealing the small black orb in her hand.

It rolled in her palm, smooth and glassy. Within it was black, too deep a black, so black that Kanna could see all of the colors, and none of the colors, all at once, as they moved together. Kanna didn't think that Veil could see it like she could. If Veil couldn't see it, then she wouldn't mind giving it back. She wouldn't mind sharing.

Veil's smile slipped back to a frown, and she reached out to pluck it from Kanna's palm. She held it up to her eyes, between her thumb and forefinger, and turned it, as if she could see it another way, from another angle.

Kanna opened her fingers wider, pushed her palm higher, waiting for Veil to give it back. Wanting Veil to give it back.

Veil looked away from the marble to Kanna's eager, outstretched hand. She rolled the stone between her fingers, then pocketed it and turned away.

Veil took it. Veil took it because she could.

And Kanna knew Veil only took it because Kanna wanted it.

"Have the medic check her," she ordered. "Then we return to the Tower."

Kanna's echo curled her fingers into an empty fist, pulling her hand back to her chest. Tears stung her eyes, because the further Veil walked away with the stone, the more she knew.

It was hers. It was supposed to be hers. It had been trusted to her, and she lost it.

Just like that, that simply, she'd lost the only thing that had ever been hers.

Kanna bowed her head, covering her eyes with her hands as she remembered. It was the first time, but it wouldn't be the last, that something she thought could be hers was taken away.

This time, there weren't tears left to shed for it.

Haru covered her hands with his own, and she let hers slide from her eyes. She leaned back, leaned into him, both of her hands moving to grasp his forearm.

She wouldn't allow it to happen again.

Kanna sighed out, her breath shaking.

Then, a hollow thunk, like a generator turning over.

Haru lifted his hand from her eyes as the air buzzed.

The peak was gone. Everything was gone. They stood in a black emptiness, the ground solid beneath their feet. A single bulb flickered, struggled against the dark, before lighting with a click.

The red door waited.

# 30

# THE WHITE DOOR

## HARU

KANNA SLAMMED the red door behind them. Despite the force she used, it shut soundlessly.

Haru bent over, supported his body by pressing his hands to his knees. He couldn't understand what he had just witnessed in Kanna's memory. It was like seeing an idea, or a concept, or that feeling in the back of his mind when he knew there was something he was forgetting but couldn't pull it out to the surface.

It wasn't something that he had simply seen. He had *felt* it, like an infinite scream. He didn't even know if it was real, if it was somehow alive, or if it was the manifestation of a child's imagination, a thing she'd designed to save herself when no one else would.

Whatever it was, he was grateful for it. If he had prayers he would offer them, but he had only poetry. The shaking in his limbs calmed and he stood, blinking away the flashes of light that spotted his vision.

Kanna's back was to him as she faced the door that held her child-hood memories of war. She pressed her hands against her ears, bent over, and screamed. Frustration and anger, fear and loss, radiated from her until he could taste it, saccharine in the Neither's empty air.

Before Haru could catch her, she launched herself at the door, her bare fists bruising against the wood. He grabbed her by the waist, tried to drag her away, but her hands opened and clawed at it, flakes of paint and splinters of wood coming loose under her nails as she screamed and kicked.

He got her away from it, but she continued to struggle against his hold. Another scream, and Haru could feel feathers against his arms as the air around them bent and rippled, slamming against the red door. The wood splintered and cracked, and the metal hinges screeched as they came loose and the door fell forward, what was left of it breaking on the stone ground.

Behind the door, the cliff's face was grey and empty.

Kanna stopped fighting him, her breath heaving through the tension that locked her muscles. She twisted out of his grip, and he let her go. She paced in front of the doors, one hand still pressed against her ear, her fingers knotting in her hair. She stepped back, spun, looking to the doors along the higher tiers.

The cliffs had grown higher. Haru could barely make out the starry night of Ilazki, blocked as it was by row upon row of bright doorways. All of them memories, all locking away a lifetime of pain.

Kanna's eyes were wild with anger, spiked with fear. "*<Ver shtu?>*" she called, her voice echoing the demand against the stone walls.

He could feel her unraveling, the thread connecting them shuddering as it tried to hold on. "We have to go back."

Kanna stopped her spin, turning to face him.

He'd almost lost her. Again. She was with him one moment and the next, gone, trapped in a lure of memory. He'd called her, tried to reason with her, but she hadn't heard him. That Kanna, the one that Velinius had thrown to be butchered, had not known him.

Kanna shook her head. She took a step back from him. "Not yet."

Haru knew that Rough's Peak was Kanna's first battle. Everyone knew that. But knowing the fact and understanding what it meant were entirely different things. Of course, he had imagined her there, as everyone must have. In his mind's eye, though, he had never imagined how small she had been.

No one wanted to imagine a child in war.

She'd been hailed for that victory, and it had won Velinius her appointment as the Palamidia's Second. The Palamidia's records were simple accounts of fact, that the charge of the plateau was the bold offensive that clenched their victory.

And as ruthless as he knew Velinius to be, he almost couldn't believe it when he realized her plan. Haru had managed to grab Kanna at the same time that Velinius intended to throw her, relying on the hope that some part of her would feel him, remember him, and return.

"We can come back," he tried to reason. "We can try again."

Kanna shut her eyes, shook her head again, the motion loose and uncontrolled. "I can't," she said. "I almost know, but I don't. I can feel it. I can feel it and it is important but I don't *know*."

Kanna yanked her hands through her hair, tilted her head back again. "*Where are you?*" she screamed, now, turning away from him.

"We can try again," Haru repeated. "Kanna–"

"No!" she ran her nails over her bare arms as if she could dig the truth from her skin. "I almost know."

"I almost lost you!"

He hadn't meant to raise his voice, hadn't meant for it to come out that way, so strained with pain that he couldn't hide.

Kanna hands ceased their clawing. She shifted her hip, turned over her shoulder. Her head was canted to the side, confusion writ on her features. She opened her mouth, about to respond, but something caught her attention and pulled it away, and there she was.

The Legatus.

The echo looked down, her features set into a grim determination. Hands tucked almost casually into the pockets of her ornate white jacket, the hem brushing her ankles. Every victory stitched into it, the ones Haru witnessed so old that they had long been covered by other conquests.

At the height of the cliffs, she was a white brand against the black of the Ilazki sky. The stars twisted in her gravity, compressing around her like a halo. White marble steps led to the peak, led to her, cutting through the doors in the grey face of the cliff.

Kanna ran for them.

Haru gave chase, but he couldn't catch up. The world was against him, clinging to his legs so that he couldn't move them fast enough.

The steps began to crack behind her and they slipped apart beneath his feet. At the top, he had to leap to catch the ledge before the stairs collapsed beneath him. He clung to the side, tightening his grip and twisting at the waist to hoist himself over.

The door here was woven white, at least twice his height and four times as wide. It was split through the center, with tall dark wood handles at each side.

Kanna gripped the handles, throwing the doors of the Tower's Temple wide.

Haru had to duck, bracing against a blast of heavy, cold air that tried to knock him from the ledge of the cliff. He leapt for the doors as they began to shut behind her.

Before he could reach them the cliff shook, falling rock collapsing in front of the doors and blocking them as if they had never been there.

Haru's hands smashed against the rock as he threw himself at it, but it wouldn't move. He tried to dig through, but the massive stones wouldn't budge beneath his assault.

He called her name. He screamed it, and it ripped through his throat until it was raw.

## 31

# THE FALL

## KANNA

KANNA PUSHED OPEN the door of the Temple, her nerves firing when the walls of color erupted in her vision. The murals twisted in the corners of her eyes, undulating wildly before settling into their places, the many hues sliding to fit within their bold lines.

It was another moment for her senses to calm. The Temple had always had a strange effect on her, the rich tapestry of it an assault that she was never quite prepared for after the endless parade of white in the Tower. It reminded her of her mothers' home and the rooms of her childhood. There was a reason in the madness, a story that connected one image to the next, just as Aksana's collections had their own inherent order despite the chaos of it.

Halfway to the front of the altar, Velinius sat in one of the pews. She kept her back straight, though her head was bent, and she was as still as the silence that Kanna had broken with her entrance. Each step that Kanna took toward her she hit with purpose, so that the echoing ring of her boots would fill the cavernous room.

Kanna stopped in the aisle just behind Velinius, before easing herself into the bench behind her. "Greetings, sister."

Velinius turned to the side, inclining her head to return the acknowledgement.

Kanna sat back to study the images behind the altar. The elements writhed below the rose window, flowing out of their contained frames and blending from one to the other between. It was a reminder that all things were connected, all things leading to the next and back again.

Kanna crossed her arms at her chest, leaning back to slouch against the hard, wooden back of the bench. "I always thought it strange that you come here. As if you spend enough time in quiet contemplation, the dead will grant you a forgiveness the living are unwilling to offer."

Velinius turned, meeting Kanna's empty gaze, before looking forward again. "You mistake me, sister. I do not ponder forgiveness. I have no need for it. Everything I have done has been for the greater good."

Kanna's lip twisted. "Greater good?" She leaned forward and crossed her arms on the back of Velinius's pew, resting her head on top of them. "Is that what our brother thought, I wonder? As Salim bled out at the bottom of the stairs, did he think that his death was for the greater good?"

Velinius clenched her jaw, her eyes sliding to Kanna. It was a look of warning, but Kanna had long grown tired of her sister's warnings. She had no need for them anymore.

"Mother never got rid of that rug," Kanna continued. "She moved it. Three floors up, hidden under an enormous postered bed."

Velinius looked away from Kanna. "One of the pieces from Gegenes, probably."

Kanna hummed, both an acknowledgement and a dismissal. "I'd crawl under it, hide there, when I was a child. I would lie there on the stain of his blood and wait for him to speak to me." Her eyes slid shut as she remembered the feel of the carpet at her back, the wood slats inches from her nose where she would hide Salim's death mask. "I wanted to know what he thought, when he died in that spot."

"Salim's neck snapped," Velinius responded coolly. "He was not thinking about anything."

Kanna leaned back into her bench. "I am not so sure. I think that, perhaps, when death surprises us, our souls linger. Just long enough to wonder what has happened."

Velinius shook her head. "That is a strange notion. We go to the dark, and the darkness is nothing."

"Maybe, but maybe not." She leaned forward once more, enough that Velinius would feel her breath on her neck. "Perhaps I should ask you."

Velinius turned her tarnished gaze on Kanna, the fire of it too cold to heat anything, like the ghost of promised warmth that only made the one who desired it more chilled. Kanna was small again, a child again, wanting and needing her, or someone, anyone, to see her.

"I did not *think* anything," Velinius said. "I knew in a way I hadn't before. I knew I had been right, and I knew you were every bit the monster that our mother made."

The barb burrowed under Kanna's skin, awakening the feathered thing inside of her with a hiss. It stretched, curling under her ribs. "Mother did not make me a monster," she said through gritted teeth. "You did."

For once, Velinius could not hide the satisfaction that her words had struck Kanna exactly how she meant them to. "No, sister. You were born one," Velinius said, her voice pitying. "I did my best to make you better. And I set you to a purpose greater than our mother's pithy attempt at retribution." Velinius's gaze returned to the front of the temple. "Did you not wonder why she would never speak of your father, or where you came from?

"She hid you from the world, Ananke. You were her plaything, some heinous experiment she divined. There is no knowing what iniquitous acts she committed to give you life, and yet she did. She knew that shadow loas did not live long, and yet she brought you to this world to live numbered days, and kept you a secret out of her own shame and greed."

Velinius turned to meet Kanna's eyes. "I was created from a sordid passion, Salim from some misspent love. You were made from hate, from anger, and out of revenge. You were kept as a secret until I found you. You could not even speak the Common tongue, had never heard another's voice. I brought you into the light, Ananke, and I loved you."

Kanna told herself it was a lie, but there were always half-truths in Velinius's lies. She clenched her hands on the back of the pew, used it to pull herself to standing. "If that is love, Velinius, I do not need it. I do not want it."

"Don't you?"

Kanna's body froze, her fists clenching so tightly her nails cut half-moons into her palms. "It doesn't matter anymore. All you truly care about is power, and you have only what I grant you now."

"I do not need you to grant me anything, Legatus." A smile cut onto Velinius's lips, and her use of Kanna's new title felt like an omen. "You will destroy everything you care for, and yourself. You will do that all on your own, without the help of anyone. It is your nature." Velinius folded her hands in her lap, her eyes moving to the front of the Temple. "I simply have to wait."

Kanna shook her head, backing away. She needed to listen to herself, hold onto her own strengths. Kanna had faced Velinius in an open challenge, and she'd been the victor. It was the first step to making things right. But now, Velinius was trying to get under her skin, she told herself, and she was stronger than Velinius would ever be.

Velinius kept her eyes forward. "I did not break this world," she said, "but you? Oh, the damage you will do."

Velinius was fond of her words, of using them to twist others, and Kanna no longer had to allow it.

Kanna turned her back on Velinius. Kanna reminded herself that Velinius lied. That was what she did, what she had always done. She doled out half-truths, hid everything but exactly what she wanted others to see. And Kanna had learned to see through it.

She had taken Velinius's power for her own, and there was nothing else that she could do to her. Velinius couldn't hurt her.

She couldn't hurt anyone, not anymore.

Kanna had made sure of that.

Velinius chuckled, the sound sharp in the echoing temple as it chased Kanna out. "You always run from the truth, Ananke."

Kanna shook her head, and she shoved open the Temple doors.

*Where are you?*

KANNA HATED ILAZKI. It was too cold, and there was too much hiding in the history of the shadows. Others had gone mad from the nothingness of it, but for Kanna there was too much. The air was filled with secrets, and the dunes of sand were ashes of things that had been.

They'd found the River Iss and kept to its banks, not wanting to stray from a discernible landmark else they could all be lost in this drunken wasteland. At the head of the detachment, Kanna had begun to consider turning back. In fact, she knew she should have by now. But she needed to prove that she wasn't a coward, needed them to see her strength once more. She would not survive the whispers of rumors that echoed in the Tower's walls. If she didn't find a way to stop them, the want of power would soon overcome the fear of her.

She'd been perhaps distracted by her thoughts, which was the only explanation for how she missed the strange outline until they were practically upon it.

Kanna pulled Bia up. She halted easily, unlike Amon's usual flashes of tantrum. Behind her, the detachment stopped. Kanna dismounted, her boots crushing the thin ice that froze the ground's surface. "It's impossible," she whispered, her voice fogging in the air and reminding her that she was awake.

Unlike the repetitious mounds of sand and ice, the building's edges were sharp against the black. A silhouette of turrets, rising to impossible points, was outlined by the brilliant stars of the evernight. It reminded her of something she knew once, something remembered in a dream.

Behind her, the crunch of the ground as the others dismounted, each step they took heralded by the popping of the ice beneath them.

Velinius stepped past Kanna, a gleam of righteousness, of victory, in her tarnished eyes.

"I knew it was real." Velinius's voice was too slick, slid too much over the words. It hissed around her dark joy, twisting in the quiet air.

"What is this?" Kanna demanded. "You said there was activity here, signs of forces gathering. There is no sign of that, only this."

Velinius turned. She smiled.

"What have you done?" Kanna asked, her feet backing into a retreat before stopping, digging into the ice. She remembered who she was. She was the Legatus. "Answer me!"

Behind her, the detachment shifted. A multitude of hands went to their blades and notched them from sheaths, but the confusion of the moment halted any further draw.

Velinius's smile only widened. It was too wide, too... satisfied. Her shoulders pulled back, straightening as they had not done since she'd fallen from her position. In that moment they were returned to what they had always been. Kanna, always trying, trying and failing to stand up under the weight of Velinius's shadow.

"It isn't what I have done, sister," Velinius answered, "but what they will believe you did."

Velinius held up her hand, a black marble tucked into her palm. "Did you forget about this?"

The light gathered. It twisted around Velinius as it grew in volume, and it let out a high-pitched ringing that tore through Kanna's ears. It left her staggering as the sound ripped through her, as it carried the light that tried to take her apart into the depths of her marrow. Her bones were twisting, turning around themselves like they were being wrung clean.

Kanna grit her teeth around the sob, tried to open her eyes against the pain but she couldn't see through it. She tried to call the dark but Velinius pressed her nails into the stone. They bit into the feathered thing inside of her, and it howled.

"No!" she screamed, forcing the words through her teeth. "Veil, stop it!" Kanna sobbed when the light bit down again, and again she was ten, again she was twelve. "Stop, please!" Again she was small and there was no one to help her, no one to listen or care.

*Kanna, I'm coming! I'll find you!*

Velinius eased her assault on Kanna's senses, only enough that she could open her eyes. "Is that a command, Legatus?"

The light around Velinius fractured into countless shards, sharper than diamond. Sharper than a blade. Kanna's guards had drawn weapons, but they were too late. She tried to call the shadows to cover them, but the dark was too thin, too hesitant, choked by the hold that Velinius had placed on her.

Once, before, Kanna had been with a detachment that was caught in the glass rains of Ilazki.

It wasn't like this.

The blades of light rained down on her soldiers, her guards, her allies, and death was not painless, and it was not merciful. The pain drew long as the shards tore through their bodies, pulled off chunks of their arms, of their faces. They tried to press against the wounds, tried to shield themselves, but nothing would stop the raining blades. Velinus had designed them to not hit anything vital in order to prolong suffering, and her designs had always been terrifying in their focus.

Kanna tried to get to them, but Velinius's arm wrapped around her neck, pulling her back until Kanna lifted from her heels and bent back against her. Kanna tried to pull her arm away, both of her hands clawing at it, but she was losing air by the moment and weak from the first onslaught.

"Watch," Velinius hissed in her ear. "Know that you did this. I told you that you would destroy everything."

*Hold on!*

The blade entered Kanna's side, below her ribs. Slow, purposeful, it tore through her skin, through tendon and muscle and scraped bone. She felt every inch of it, even when the tip nicked her rapidly beating heart.

"You never did understand the truth of things, Ananke."

Velinius shifted the blade before yanking it out, ripping a new path through Kanna's body before letting her fall to the ground.

Kanna caught herself before she fell flat, one arm at her side, trying to hold in the slick blood that poured from her wound. The other pushed her back onto her heels.

The dark was coming for her.

She had always lived numbered days, each night one that she might never wake from.

She'd spent every moment of her existence fighting simply to survive it.

She wasn't done. She couldn't be done.

As her vision blurred, the Temple beyond Velinius became clearer, and she understood. She knew what it meant, and what it would mean for the world if Velinius took it.

With her eyes on the Temple, she thought of Haru. She thought of his balance, the heat of his breath, the warm touch of his hands against the wrecked body of her and how he held her like a lost prayer. She thought of the beat of his pulse as her own slowed.

Kanna smiled.

She wasn't done. Her eyes turned up to Velinius as her hand gave out beneath her, and her body fell.

She didn't feel the cold of the ground, didn't feel when her body fell into it.

Because Kanna fell into the black, and she took the Temple with her.

## 32

# IN NUMBERED DAYS

## HARU

HARU SCREAMED HER NAME, but it was the Neither's silence that answered. The boulders blocking the door that Kanna had entered stayed fast, wedged in place and held by their own gravity. He backed away from the cave-in and pressed the heels of his hands to his eyes.

"Get it together," he told himself. "There's always a way."

There were other doors. Haru slid down the rubble of stairs to the lower tier. There were so many, and he didn't know what to choose. It couldn't just be any door, it had to be connected. It would have to connect him to her, somehow.

The first one he tried didn't budge, the knob refusing to turn under his grip.

The second opened to the empty cave face.

"Fuck!"

He slammed it closed, the hinges rattling under the force. Haru closed his eyes, tried to steady his breath. He needed to think.

There had to be a way.

When he opened them, shadows snaked around his ankles. They slid up his legs, threatening to take him away. He stepped out of their grip, pulling himself free of their dark call. "Not without her," he said, though he didn't even know if anything could hear him. "I'm not leaving without her!"

They pulled back, becoming one with the dim environment.

A low chuckle, cut off at the front of it, issued behind him. Haru spun, and he faced an echo of himself.

Haru had never seen himself from the outside. It was like looking at a stranger that he knew everything and nothing about, but at the same time, it filled him with anger. This version of himself wasn't right. It wasn't whole. It didn't care about what he had lost, had never known the ache of missing something that was supposed to be a part of it. It had never failed to protect the person that had saved him.

It turned and began to walk away. When Haru didn't move, it looked over its shoulder, then motioned for him to follow with a simple nod, with a smile that held a secret.

Haru let out a harsh breath, unclenched his fists, and followed.

The echo was sure of his destination, but took his time as he navigated the stairs that formed before his path. It didn't look back again, and Haru stopped tracking their movements as they twisted through the levels of doorways.

It didn't even break stride when it reached its destination. The door was a bright cerulean blue, topped with a half-round moon window. It was laced with gold, the delicate workings twisting over blackened glass and forming the shape of a tree, its branches tangling together along the face of the door. The echo walked through, and it was gone.

Haru reached for the knob, but before he touched it, the door opened before him.

THE WALLS of the Tower were so blindingly white that Haru covered his eyes on instinct. He pulled his hands away when his eyes began to adjust, but the walls didn't get any less glaringly bright. The lines of doorways along the hall melted into the backdrop as if the room itself had become two-dimensional.

Except for Kanna.

She was stumbling through the halls, covered in a layer of dust that had turned to dirt. Her hands rubbed at her wrists, which were red and raw from a binding. She jerked around, facing him. Her head tilted to the side.

Haru moved to her, but he pulled his hands back.

Her pupils were dilated, and she kept slamming her eyes shut, blinking as if it could clear them, but they wouldn't adjust.

"Kanna?"

She shifted a step back, shook her head, then looked again, as if she was trying to see him. She reached out, but Haru's hands clenched at his sides. It was a memory, he reminded himself, and he had not even been here.

Something at the tips of her fingers, something that was between them, shimmered, and bent.

Racing footsteps grew closer, and Kanna turned on her heel to face Vahn as he rounded the corner.

"K!" he called, not stopping his stride until he reached her. Vahn's hands grasped her shoulders and he pulled her against himself. "How long have you been wandering out here?"

Kanna tilted her head again, squinting up at him. "Vahn?"

He smiled, barely, the fear and worry settled deep in the lines. "Yeah, K. It's me."

As if she couldn't believe her own eyes, she pressed her fingers into the pulse at the side of his neck. She sighed in relief, the tension easing from her shoulders. Then, she tilted her head back and brought herself onto the tips of her toes.

The the fear in Vahn's eyes softened, and leaned down to meet his forehead against hers.

"*Are you all right?*" Kanna asked, her voice coming out as a rasp as she lapsed into Ilazkin.

Vahn let out a short laugh. "You're an idiot." He sighed then, and closed his eyes. "I'm fine," he whispered. "And so is the Prince, before you ask."

This was just after Haru and Kanna first sparred, when she lashed out in a panic and Velinius dragged her away. After that, Haru had looked for her, but there was no sign of her. He'd known she was there, somewhere, but he couldn't find her. He had almost begun to think he wouldn't see her again, and the idea of that ached.

Kanna nodded. "*Good.*" She closed her eyes, but her shoulders tensed again and she reopened them. "*That is good.*"

After another moment, Vahn spoke again. "*I'm sorry.*"

565

"Not your fault," Kanna mumbled, in Common now. "Not on you."

"Then you want to tell me what the fuck happened?"

Kanna shook her head. "I don't know. When he touched me, I felt... something. There is a light inside of him, and it was reaching for me."

Vahn pulled back, his jaw clenched as his eyes narrowed. "Did it hurt you?"

Kanna shook her head again. "*No,*" she said. "It didn't, but..." she trailed off, looking to the ground.

Vahn lifted her chin with his finger so she met his eyes. "But what, K?"

"*It could have,*" she answered him. "It was strong. Far stronger than Veil. *I think it could hurt me more than anything else.*"

It wouldn't. Haru would pry it out of himself with his own hands if it dared.

Vahn breathed out after a beat. "Well." He brushed a wild strand of her tangled hair behind her ear before glancing around the empty hall. "We won't figure it out here." He smiled, again a guarded thing, and met her eyes. "Let's get you cleaned up."

Kanna looked down at her hands, turned them over as if she was seeing them for the first time. Vahn wrapped his arm around her, guiding her as they moved away.

Haru started to follow, but a growing whistling sound came from behind him.

He turned around, and the dark was coming for him. It was moving too fast to outrun, eating up the white hall. He covered his head with his arms as if it could protect him and was instantly chilled by the frigid blast that accompanied the dark.

When he dropped his arms, he was in a black so dark he could barely make out his hands in front of him. He turned, but there was nothing.

"Kanna!"

He called her, because it was the only thing he could think to do.

"Where are you?" he called into the dark, but his voice didn't even echo back.

The cold was replaced by a humid balm, and a drop hit water.

Beneath his feet, the black rippled like rings on a pond, and the sound became a soft rumble of water softly hitting against rock. He stepped back from the edge of the ripples, but they continued out and, at the center, the dark peeled away to reveal the thick woods behind the Palamidia's stables.

---

KANNA STOOD at the edge of the stream. The late afternoon sun glinted across her hair, which cascaded down the back of her white shirt. She had stopped to listen to whatever it was that only she could hear. She studied the short waterfall and noticed the dark cavern halfway up the side of the rock.

Haru remembered this.

Kanna approached the rise from the side, gracelessly attacking the climb. She had to stretch almost beyond her reach to find handholds, and Haru held his breath when her feet skidded on the slick rocks. She hoisted herself up the short distance to the jutting mouth of the cave. After managing to summit the thin ledge, she stood and dusted off the streaks of dirt from the front of her shirt.

Haru followed her climb, his hand landing in the wet imprint that he'd left behind that day.

Kanna brushed the damp strands of hair that stuck to her face back over her brow, squinting down at Haru's echo.

And all he wanted to be was what she saw.

When Haru shifted in surprise, the rock wall was rough against his back.

There were storms in Kanna's eyes, the galaxy in the black of them turning as she studied him, and he wanted nothing more than to be lost in them.

Kanna tilted her head to the side. "*<Why are you calling me?>*"

Haru didn't have the best grasp on Ilazkin, having only begun studying it, so he wasn't sure if he'd understood what she asked.

She shifted, looking away from him before meeting his eyes again. "Are you all right?"

Haru still didn't know how to answer.

Kanna held out a finger to point. "What is that?"

Broken from his spell, Haru turned to the crumpled missive he held in his hands. Though drops from the waterfall had smeared the lines of ink, they didn't obliterate the message. He folded it, then set it at his side. "It's just a letter."

Kanna hummed. She glanced around the cave before hesitantly stepping forward. After the first step, she checked Haru for a reaction before moving again.

She crossed in front of him, then crouched at his side next to the note. Her fingers tensed, but she pulled them back and crossed her arms. "It upset you."

Haru tensed, his eyes widening in surprise before narrowing. "How did you know?"

Kanna shrugged, then shifted her stance to sit on the ground next to him. "I do. I don't know how."

She glanced between them, then moved closer. There was a nervousness in her movements, as if she still believed she was unwelcome at his side.

Haru shook his head, lifting the note to hand it to her. She slipped it from his fingers, then unfolded it to study the words written there.

"One of my tutors," Haru said. "From when I was young."

Kanna's brow knit. "What does it mean by 'passed'?"

Haru swallowed before answering. "She died."

"Oh," Kanna said, the word small as a breath. Her fingers traced the lines on the paper. "Branwen Pryderi." She leaned back against the cave wall and was quiet, her eyes closing.

Haru leaned toward her, trying to discern what she was thinking, when she opened her eyes. "She was sick?" Kanna asked, turning to him. "For a while?"

Haru nodded. "Yes. How did you–?"

Kanna folded the letter carefully, setting it aside as she turned away from him. "When people are sick for a long time, some find death a release." Kanna smoothed the paper, then met his eyes. "I don't know if that helps."

Haru looked down at his hands, clenched and unclenched his fists. He didn't know why he believed Kanna's words, but something told him they were true. Branwen had been the one who cared for him as a child, the closest thing he'd had to a mother. His own had sent news of his teacher's death by a letter that she hadn't even bothered to sign, instead having it dictated and stamped with the royal seal.

Beside him Kanna shifted, rising up on one knee. She leaned forward, her fingers reaching gently out to brush back the hair from his brow. Haru wrapped his hand around her wrist before she withdrew and leaned into her palm with a sigh.

Kanna moved closer, wrapping an arm around his shoulders and Haru leaned into her, burying his face against her neck.

He could feel the gentle brush of her fingers through his hair, and he could hear the beat of her heart above the sound of the waterfall and the afternoon calls of the forest's birds.

"I'm sorry," she whispered, "if we're all you have now."

Haru pulled himself away from the curve of her neck. Kanna tried to withdraw, but he tightened his arm around her waist, catching her before she could leave him.

"I'm not," he said. Because as kind as the women who reared him had been, they could not give him a home. It was Kanna who had done that, who gave him a place in her arms and a purpose by her side.

Kanna's eyes widened in surprise, then drifted down as Haru's arm tightened around her. Her body was wary, wanting yet unsure, under his touch, even as he brushed his free hand along her cheekbone, the back of his knuckles tracing her jaw. But when he pulled her down, when he pressed his lips against hers, he could feel her body relax, shifting closer to him.

And when her lips opened for him Haru pulled her tighter, his fingers grasping desperately against her skin because he never wanted to let her go. Kanna slid her knee over him, straddling his hips, and he had to bite back the moan that rose in his throat when she slid against him.

Haru broke the long kiss, pressed another at the corner of her lip, another against her jaw and she bent her face against his palm as his lips slipped across her neck.

Haru felt the pulse of her heart beneath his lips, the soft gasp when he opened his mouth to taste it.

THEN THERE WERE QUIET FOOTSTEPS, stopping just outside his door.

The night was old and quiet, and Kanna was at his door.

·  ·  ·

HE JERKED himself forward and it was like stepping out of a thick pond, something clinging against his skin until he broke the tension of the surface and he stopped.

His echo was standing in the same place he had started, unmoving.

"No," he whispered, demanding that he move. But the echo hesitated.

Haru turned for the door himself and reached for the knob, but it stuck fast. He wrenched his hand around it but it slipped from his grip.

Any night but this one. It could have been any night but this one.

This was the night before Kanna left for Ilazki.

His echo strode to the entry, but paused when he reached for the doorknob. Instead, he slid his hands over the door, leaning his forehead against it, and sighed. He could feel her on the other side, despite their severed connection. Kanna was his gravity. Even the ghost of her touch was enough to move him.

"Haru?"

Her voice whispered, quiet and half-broken. He tensed, and her ragged sigh carried through behind it. Gritting his teeth, the echo twisted the knob and yanked the door open. Kanna had been leaning against the door, and she swayed when the barrier was removed. He'd grabbed her arm and pulled her into the room, her momentum sending her body falling into his as he'd slammed the door behind her.

He'd felt the brush of her armor against his bare skin before she pushed him away, her hands clenched to fists as if she couldn't stand the touch of him. Frustration mounted as he waited for her to say something, to do anything but refuse to look at him.

"Damnit, Kanna." He'd turned away from her, his hands yanking at his hair. "Why are you doing this?" *to me,* he'd added, though his selfishness remaining unvoiced. He had turned back to her when she didn't answer.

Her eyes were locked on him, but his narrowed. He was dressed for sleep, but she had arrived in full regalia. "And why are you dressed for battle?"

Kanna turned to the ground, her right hand rising to cover the eclipsed sun on her armor. As an almost afterthought, she covered the scars on that hand with her other. "It is all I have," she said, her voice smaller than he'd ever heard it.

But he hadn't noticed. He had been too caught in his own frustration, the feeling of being cast off when she ordered him to remain behind. "If all you have is war," he'd said, unable to hold a softness in his voice as the anger, the hurt lace itself into the cracks of it, "then why are you here?"

Kanna flinched. Haru wanted to scream at his echo, warn him, but he had to watch. He had to watch, as his own echo did when Kanna's nails dug into her left hand, her eyes squeezing shut against the pain.

"I'm sorry, Kanna." Although every syllable had carried the ache of his apology, it didn't take away the hurt he had inflicted. "Please, don't leave." He had sworn he would never hurt her, and had done so almost casually. He could not fault her if she had turned around, left him like that.

But she hadn't.

She shook her head as he had neared. "No," she said, and he had stopped his advance. "No," she said again, her eyes still shut, but it came out clearer.

*No!*

Haru jerked around when he heard the echo of a scream.

"I'm sorry," Kanna said. "Before..." she said, then corrected, rerouted the beginning. "I think, or I know, that there's darkness, and that is all I am. All I do is destroy things, and I'm good at it. But that doesn't mean that I ever wanted to be." Kanna shook her head. "I never wanted you to be one of those things, but I wanted you more than anything."

A tear slipped from her eye as her voice cracked, and she scrubbed it away with the back of her hand. Haru's echo crossed the distance between them, but a pain clenched in Haru's chest like a fist tightening.

*Stop it!*

Haru hissed as the invisible hand dug into him, its nails sharp against his heart. It was the same pain from before, the one he'd felt days before Velinius had returned without Kanna.

"I wanted to be what you saw," Kanna said, "I wanted to be worth seeing."

Her voice was fading, but her screams rang in Haru's ears.

"I'm sorry, Haru," she said. "I'm sorry, but I love you."

The echo reached for her. "Kanna–"

"Don't," she stopped him.

*Stop, please!*

"Haru, don't say anything. I don't think I can take it." She opened her eyes, looking up to him. "Will you be with me tonight?"

The pain in Haru's chest burned, and he bent over from the pull of it. "Kanna, I'm coming!" he called through gritted teeth. "I'll find you!"

The memory began to fade like broken static, but not soon enough.

"It doesn't have to be real," the memory of Kanna said, her voice drifting out of focus.

*"It doesn't have to be real, Haru. But I need you."*

He hadn't answered her that night, hadn't given voice to the simple words so that she could know. So that she would know his own heart.

She'd left, and she was gone, and he had never told her the simplest of truths, the only truth that he knew to matter. And now he felt the panic and fear that was suffocating her, her pain twisting with his own.

All he had to do was follow it.

"Kanna," he gasped, then forced himself upright. "Hold on."

When he opened his eyes the memory clicked to black, and the next moment he was weightless.

HARU WAS SUSPENDED in the dark, drifting, painless, through nothing, but then there was a spark in the black. Like a single string of a universal melody had been plucked.

He felt her reach for him, and knew that she gave him a choice.

There was never any choice, no other option. Not to him. Haru would not let her go. He would never live without her.

The choice was made, the pact sealed, and a blinding light cut through the dark. Gravity returned, and Haru fell.

· · ·

HE HIT the ground on his back, the frozen sand cracking beneath him.

Haru groaned, rolling over. He pressed his hands against the frozen sand and pushed himself up. Haru blinked away the flash of light, his eyes adjusting to the simple dark of night.

A night in Ilazki, the twinkle of lights in the sky almost too bright to be real.

And in the near distance was Kanna, her face turned up to the light of the stars.

# A PROMISE KEPT

## KANNA

THE FIRST THING she knew was *cold*.

Then, her heart beat alive, waking with a hard shock and she gasped in frozen air.

Eyes opened, and there were eyes looking at her. Just beyond her fingertips, a young man, his blonde hair matted with bright, frozen blood. Part of his cheek was gone, and his mouth was open but he couldn't scream.

She yanked her hand back and shoved herself away from the ground. Her legs wouldn't catch her so she fell, her hand sliding in a cool sticky pool.

Behind her, another body. Her breath caught and she looked up, and out, and they were everywhere. Among the grey and the dark they were bright white canvases, bodies twisted and torn, the smell of fear locked in the frozen air.

"No. No, no no..."

She knew nothing, except that she had done this.

In the distance, there was the shape of something—a building, spires reaching, its edges fading and blending into the black. She covered her ears and closed her eyes, as tight as she could, and whispered, again, "*No...*"

She opened her eyes, and it was gone. She didn't know what had been there, but it was gone.

When she caught her breath, she saw there was blood on her. It was thick against the pale skin of her hands, caked under her nails and sticky in the grooves of her fingers. She followed it to an ache in her side.

Her hands clawed at the white armor, her joints fighting against the movement. The stays had been sliced through, the ties falling apart under her scrabbling hands. The blood stuck the white undershirt to her skin, and she peeled it up.

Her palms slid over her skin, wiping it away, but there was no wound. Instead, a web of gold pulsed along her skin from a center point, moving in a rhythm that was off the beat of her own heart, a second accompaniment in an ancient melody. And there was one thing more.

*Kanna?*

But she didn't understand it.

She was alone, and the stars were infinite and vast and watching. They glimmered, so bright against the black of the night, and she wanted to watch them forever. She tilted her head back and shut her eyes and she could almost, almost feel the light of them reach for her.

"Kanna."

She opened her eyes.

She had thought the stars beautiful and bright, but she had been wrong. They paled against the man in front of her. He knelt to the ground, and she didn't want him to be cold. He didn't belong in the dirt, didn't belong in the wreckage.

He reached for her, and she flinched. He stopped his advance, but his hand didn't fall.

He didn't say anything, waited until she settled, and reached again. His hand unfurled, his fingers stretching so that the first contact against her skin was barely a brush.

It was warm. It was comfort.

She didn't deserve it.

She shut her eyes and his hand slid over face, the other joining it as he bent, pressed his forehead to hers. A whimper rose in the back of her throat, terrified of the tenderness that was offered but wanting it all the same.

"This isn't real, *inara,*" he said.

His voice held a power, her body bending to it. She grasped his wrists, wanting him closer, trying to understand the words.

This was all she knew, this and nothing else. If it wasn't real, she didn't know what could be.

"You have to stand up," he said, his voice cracking when she didn't move.

He leaned into her, his eyes closing. When his hands tangled in her hair, held her against him, she remembered something. "Haru?"

He nodded. "Yes," he said. "That's right, it's me. I told you I would find you. I asked you to hold on and you did, didn't you? You promised me, you promised me that you would come back, and you always keep your promises." His breath hitched, and he swallowed, then his voice was steady. "Always."

And she remembered the moment in the dark, when she stood at the gateway to an infinity and refused it. But she couldn't turn away alone, there had to be something to bring her back. She had to bind herself to something else.

So she followed the connection she had severed, found the end, and reached.

She didn't know if he would answer, didn't know if he would take the burden but he did.

When she came back, it was like being new again. She didn't want to bring the pain, didn't want him to bear it, so she left it behind. Locked it up, sealed it away in a place that no one could reach.

She hadn't known it would be everything.

Kanna loosened one of her hands from his wrist, traced the bob of his throat as he swallowed and pressed her hand against the pulse on his neck.

"I love you, Kanna," he said. "I'm sorry I didn't tell you. I didn't think to even say the words."

Kanna shivered as the memory of a touch returned. The warmth of him, the way he moved, the way his hands held her like she was the only thing that mattered, like she was a treasure lost to time that only he knew.

"I love you," he repeated, like a mantra. Like a prayer. "That is real. That is the only thing here that is real. I love you," he said, "and I need you to stand up."

Her legs twitched beneath her, and she dragged one of her knees out from behind her. He gave her room but she reached for him, one hand around the back of his neck, the other twisting into the front of his shirt. She leaned into him as she pressed her leg to the ground, wincing as she pushed against it.

"Good," Haru said. "That is perfect, *inara*."

Feeling returned to her body slowly, slower than she moved, and she swayed on her feet. He pressed a guiding hand against her hip to steady her.

Kanna's head spun, memories lighting in a misfiring cascade in her mind as they found their places. They wove together, reconnected, and settled back where they had been before she left them.

"Take a step," he whispered. "My love, remember," he pleaded. "Remember, and take a step."

They were in the Neither, she remembered, a place that hadn't existed before she made it. A place to hold the pain, a pebble she'd lodged in the throat of the universe.

She slid her foot forward, shifted her weight across her body, and it remembered.

He stepped with her, still close, but now too achingly far away. Kanna pulled herself against him and buried her face in his chest, in the sound of his heartbeat.

Haru's hands cradled her face, tilted her head back. "Kanna," he whispered her name, the one she'd chosen when it was the only thing she could choose for herself.

His thumbs brushing along her shut lids and Kanna opened her eyes, met the bright blue of his, bright and full against the stark black sky.

His smile was slow, a hidden thing emerging from the shadows. "There you are."

"You're with me," she said, the words coming without thinking, the words a prayer recited so often they were carved into her, so much more than something simply remembered.

He lowered her forehead to meet hers. "I'm with you," he said, the familiar call and response turned back on her. "Always."

Kanna shut her eyes, tried to hold back the salt that stung her eyes. "Haru, I'm sorry." Her voice felt fragile, new and broken in her throat. "I'm sorry."

Haru shook his head. "I love you, *inara*." His fingers tightened, tangled in her hair. "There is nothing to forgive."

Haru bent, pressed his lips to hers. It was a promise, an offering, and she took it. He held her locked in that moment, kept her safe in the heat of it.

He breathed and her lungs filled. His heart beat and hers ached to match its rhythm.

Their kiss broke, and Kanna tightened her fists in his shirt to steady her shaking hands, pulling her body flush against his.

"Hold on to me," she said, her voice strained with the plea.

Haru's arms tightened, his hands digging under the fabric of her clothes to reach her skin. She closed her eyes when he kissed her, again, and again she found the way back through the dark.

# 34

## HOW TO BE

### KANNA

KANNA KNEW they made it back by the way gravity pulled at the soles of her feet, the empty air of the Neither replaced by the heavy humidity of a storm. The first thing she heard beyond Haru's breathing was the rain falling in sheets on the metal roof of the farmhouse, so loud it would drown out the beat of Haru's heart if she didn't know it, if she didn't always hear it, if it weren't the steady accompaniment to her own pulse that she finally recognized for what it was.

They were back, and she was whole, and she didn't quite know what that meant yet. But his breath was still against her, his face still burrowed in the crook of her neck. It was another moment, a moment for the world to settle back to what it was before, and she felt him lift his head from her shoulder.

Her hands ached. She opened her eyes, saw the whites of her knuckles from the force with which her fingers clenched in his shirt, and she knew it was time to let go. The thought came to her mind, and she sent it to her hands, but they wouldn't listen. She breathed out, felt the air in her lungs and found where she began, where she ended, and forced her fingers to loosen their grip.

"Kanna."

He whispered her name and her hands clenched back to fists, her eyes slamming shut.

Haru's hands left her waist, wrapped around her wrists but they wouldn't move. His hands uncurled, the tips of his fingers tracing her arms, to her shoulders. The advance was slow, and she shuddered beneath it. His touch pressed against her collarbone as his hand fit against her neck

"Will you look at me?" His thumb brushed against her throat.

There was no way that she couldn't. She'd tear apart the world if only he asked her.

When she met his eyes, her breath was stolen, her heart ricocheting against her ribs. Haru's hand slid behind her neck, his fingers tangling in her hair as he leaned over her.

"I love you."

Kanna shut her eyes, shook her head. But before she could form the protest it was interrupted by the brush of his lips against her cheek. His hand at the back of her neck tightened and he shifted closer to her.

"I love you," he said again, his lips damnably light as the words kissed her neck.

She couldn't open her eyes. She couldn't let go of him as his arm wrapped around her waist, his fingers slipping beneath her shirt.

"I'm a monster," she said.

Haru's fingers curled around the curve of her hip, brushed against the gold on her skin and her body shuddered as the touch coursed through her veins.

"If you are a monster," he said, "then I am something much worse."

Kanna's body bent to the promise of his touch, and it hurt. It was in her knuckles, in every starving breath she took.

"Haru–" she said his name and it nearly choked her. She didn't know what was supposed to follow it as her greedy hands curled, scraped, wanted him closer.

"Don't you know how long I've waited to feel you again?" he hissed against her skin, his breath alighting against the shivers that wracked her. His lips ghosted over the heated burn of her neck. "To taste you?" His lips opened, his tongue sliding against her skin and she almost buckled.

His lips met hers and they opened for him, releasing the love she clamped between her teeth to keep it from devouring him. He kissed her hungry, a kiss of worship, as if everything divine was caught inside of her. The heat of it sank through her skin, melted the cold that never seemed to leave her.

He breathed and her lungs filled, his heart beat and hers ached to match its rhythm.

When he shifted his feet, when he turned, she followed their dance. The curve of his fingers, the gentlest shift of his hips and her body knew, her body remembered how to be with him. How to exist, in this moment.

Haru's hands slid up her sides, pulling her shirt up and leaving a trail of heat where they passed. He dropped the shirt as the bed hit the back of her knees and she started to fall. She reached for him, her arms around his neck.

One of his arms wrapped around her waist, held her against him while the other braced them. He bent over, lying her back, then pulled away. But she clung to him, not wanting to let go. Never wanting to let go. Haru's hand tracked from the scar beneath her ribs, moved between her breasts, then splayed over her heart and pushed her back.

Kanna was strong, knew how to fight, had honed every muscle, every tendon of her body to listen when it was called.

Haru knew this. Haru knew her almost as well as she knew herself, almost better, found a single point that her balance couldn't fight. She bent her shoulders, tried to rise up but he held her back until she stopped resisting. But her nerves sparked beneath her skin, her body demanding to be let loose, to feel.

Haru moved slow, his hand sliding back down her body as he stood up, hovering above her. Kanna clenched her fists, pushed herself up with one hand. He reached for the hem of his shirt and she bit her lip, ran her tongue over the taste of him there as he pulled the shirt over his head.

She was staring. Part of her knew she should look away, but another, the greedier part, would not. She tracked the scar carved across his chest. Her eyes flicked up to meet his when she realized he hadn't moved while she'd watched, studied, every line of him, and his eyes burned.

Kanna moved, slow, reaching with her free hand. When her fingers touched his skin, she felt the intake of air in his lungs that he held as she traced the scar on his chest. At the widest, near his shoulder, she could fit two of her fingers, but it narrowed to the width of her nail as it descended, stopping before his heart.

She felt his voice in his chest before he spoke. "Are you going to apologize again?"

Kanna turned up, her fingers abandoning the pulse of his heart to touch his lips before she met his eyes. "No."

Haru's lips tilted into a brief smile, then the gold in his eyes sparked. He leaned down, bracing his arms on each side of her. "Good."

They met again, his tongue licking in to tease, to taste. An arm at her waist shifted her back, and when he settled between her legs she could feel his cock hard between them.

Kanna's hips bucked against him, the whine in the back of her throat caught by his teeth. Her hands flew to the button of her jeans, fumbling with the clasp in her desperate need to free her skin, to feel him.

His lips left hers, his teeth sinking into the side of her neck as he shoved her hands away. Kanna pressed her shoulders back, lifted her hips so he could slide away the coarse fabric between them, sparks lighting on her newly exposed skin as his knuckles brushed against it.

Kanna leaned up on her elbows to watch as his hands moved up her legs, his eyes meeting hers as he turned to kiss her inner thigh.

Then higher.

Kanna shut her eyes and leaned back, and when his tongue licked up her she covered her mouth with her hand to keep in the sound that threatened to escape. Her hips moved against his mouth, his fingers digging into her thighs and keeping them parted. She tried to cover the sounds that wanted to escape her throat, swallowing them into her lungs as his tongue against her built into a brilliant pleasure until she could think of nothing else, feel nothing else until it broke and sparked like a thousand lights in the dark beneath her skin.

The pressure of his tongue was replaced by his fingers, barely sliding over the wet between her legs. Kanna's body jerked as his mouth traveled her body, his lips on the gold scar catching the breath in her lungs with a hiss as the fading sensations moved to her veins and reignited, the dark inside of her wanting more of him even when she wasn't sure if she could stand it.

Haru moved over her, his free hand pulling hers away from her mouth, pinning her wrist above her. "Let me hear you," he said, his lips falling to her neck, his mouth opening and his teeth scraping against her skin. "I want to hear you."

Kanna couldn't think, but she could understand. All she could feel was him and she wanted more, wanted all of him, wanted so much that it hurt. Her head tilted back, her body bending against him, to him. "Haru," she said, her words tangling into something primal. "*Please.*"

"Anything," he said. "You can have all of me, *inara.*"

Haru slid into her, filled her, his breath catching then exhaling into a moan. Kanna's body shuddered as he filled her. He stroked her slow, deep, until her hips demanded more. He answered, giving her all that she asked and more than she could stand.

Her world was Haru, her universe beginning and ending where his fingers dug into the back of her thighs, where he moved inside of her. It was the smell of his skin, the taste of his lips, the feel of his body as it slid beneath her palms and the breath from his lungs as it caught, as he whispered her name, as he gasped his love against her skin.

Her fingers curled, digging into his back, holding onto him when the well inside of her broke. It wrapped around her limbs, her body contracting around him as his own release joined hers and sent her shattering again.

His name was on her lips as his arms tightened around her, nearly pressing the breath from her lungs as they crashed together, a single harmony in the dark of an infinity.

35

# WHAT IS IMPORTANT

## ISCO

Isco made tea. There wasn't much else he could do, and it made him feel at least slightly less useless, so he made tea and, earlier that morning, located a toolbox to fix the screaming hinges on the screen door and tighten the screws on one of the cupboards.

Isco wasn't a soldier, and he didn't quite fit with Astar and Yassen, either. The idle time in Kirin had left him with little to do save for think, and the more he did, the more he understood the distance between them.

Everyone here had made mistakes. Everyone had hurt others, even casually, but Isco didn't see an equivalent for himself. They'd done it to survive. Isco had done it in the pursuit of greatness and out of ego. Even if he told himself he had meant well, that he had the best of intentions, good intentions couldn't comfort the dead.

Through the window in the kitchen, he watched the corral. Yassen leaned against the fence, his arms propped across it, while Vahn and Osawa practiced. They were moving slower, stepping back to mime or discuss actions between quick exchanges. Occasionally Astar, tucked out of Isco's sight, would shout less than helpful advice from the porch. Osawa would roll his eyes or offer a rebuttal while Vahn laughed, his voice through the open yard and sneaking in beneath the sill of the window.

Isco reached out to shut it, but he pulled his hand away before he did.

The tea kettle whistled, jerking his attention back to the task he had set for himself.

Making tea.

He pulled the kettle from the stove and shut off the gas, then allowed the temperature to settle before pouring out two waiting cups. The steam rose, and he thrummed his fingers along the counter while he waited. When the timing felt right, he removed the infusers and carried the tea across the kitchen to the living room.

In the armchair, Kenzi had her knees tucked to her chest, her arms wrapped around them as she stared listlessly at the treeline through the picture window.

Isco set one of the mugs at the side table next to her. "I didn't know how you take it."

She tore her eyes from the window and glanced at the mug. Her eyes tracked from it to Isco, her brow furrowing. "You're kind."

Isco looked away, a single finger tapping on the handle of the mug before he withdrew and shrugged. "It's just tea."

She offered Isco an attempt at a smile. "Maybe to you," she said, then turned back to the horizon.

Footsteps descending the stairs brought Isco's attention around, as well as Kenzi's. She uncurled her legs and braced her feet on the floor, · her hands clutching the arms of the chair to hold her in place.

Haru appeared at the bottom of the stairs, pulling the hem of a dark t-shirt down over his waist. He paused to push back his thick hair, still damp from the shower. His gaze was neutral as it moved from Isco, to Kenzi, then back again, somehow deciding that Isco was the preferred choice. "Where are the others?"

Astar's laughter barking through the screen door announced her position before Isco could, and Haru turned to the sound. Before he exited, though, he inclined his head to Isco in an invitation to follow.

Isco motioned with his hand for Kenzi, and she uncurled jerkily from her position in the chair. He held the front door open for her and she slid through, but she shifted back to stand behind him.

Astar had turned her back on the corral, bracing her palms behind her on the porch railing and leaning into them. "Well, well," she said to Haru, her eyes sliding behind him. "Where's Kanna?"

The others in the corral had noted their arrival, and made their way over to the gathering group. Yassen stood behind Astar on the other side of the rail, while Vahn and Osawa climbed the steps and joined her. Isco and Kenzi stayed in place behind Haru. He didn't bother to acknowledge them at his back, instead focusing on the rest of the troupe.

"She's resting," Haru answered Astar while everyone settled into place. "She's... tired."

Vahn had his hands shoved in his pockets, his eyes downcast and haunted. His weight shifted from one foot to the other, the movement almost undetectable. "What does she remember now?"

"All of it," Haru answered, then added: "Like it was yesterday."

After the silence that followed, Kenzi's voice was small, barely holding itself back from bursting. "That's good, right?" she asked, a low hope glimmering on her tongue. She looked to Isco for support, glancing between the soldiers that kept their uneasy silence.

Vahn scoffed. "Didn't think you hated her that much."

"What?" Kenzi shook her head. "I don't hate her. That's what everyone wanted, isn't it?"

No one answered. Isco doubted anyone knew the answer to that.

"Is she all right?" Osawa asked.

Haru looked down, his eyes lighting briefly as his lips turned up. "Yes," he said, then his expression darkened, his smile falling. "For now. But I lost her in there," he lifted his gaze to Vahn, cutting off his remark, "just for a minute. When she went to Ilazki."

Vahn shook his head. "So we still don't know how that went down."

"Is that when she disappeared?" Astar asked, and Osawa nodded to answer her. "What's so important about knowing that?"

Vahn's eyes slid to Astar, a dangerous glint in them. "It wasn't the first time Veil tried to take Kanna out. I kind of always wondered why."

Haru lifted his head, his brow knitting in confusion.

Vahn smirked, but it was hard won. "You didn't know?" He uncrossed his arms, raising a finger to tap his eyebrow. "How you think she got that one? Veil smashed her over the head and threw her down some stairs. She was slick enough to lie through it, though, even then. Blamed it on Aksana being nutty, and then the Palamidia took K and put her in the Tower." He recrossed his arms. "Point is, Velinius would've wanted to make sure it stuck this time. Something happened there, and I'd guess it's important."

"If it's important, she'll tell us." Everyone turned to Yassen when he spoke. He shrugged. "When she's ready, and when it's important."

At Isco's side, Kenzi chewed her lip, but wasn't able to hold back her question. "But does she know what Ira's message meant?"

Haru turned his gaze on her, and the intense blue would have made Isco shrink weeks before. Not anymore. Isco had grown accustomed to Haru's intensity, and would have been more concerned if it wasn't present.

"She does," Haru answered. "It's a reference to an old godswork they called the Izanami Gate." His gaze turned to the others, but was met with shrugs. He sighed. "I don't know what it is either, but it scares her. It has something to do with how the world got this way, and Velinius is trying to find it."

"What way?" Yassen asked.

Haru shrugged his shoulders. "Broken."

"Shit," Kenzi whispered.

"Fuck," Vahn said in tandem.

"What happens now?" Isco asked, surprising even himself.

Haru lifted his brow at him. "Kanna said that Velinius doesn't have all of it, but she knows where we have to go." He turned to include the others. "We're leaving tomorrow."

# 36

## ANOTHER ANGLE

### KENZI

It was late afternoon, and Kenzi couldn't keep still. The rest had set themselves to tasks without a word spoken, but no one had given her anything to do. She had tried to help Isco, but he kept mumbling to himself lists of things he needed, digging in cabinets and under sinks, and she felt like she was more in the way than being helpful.

Osawa checked everyone's bags, making sure they had enough clean clothes, and Astar hovered about him, adding new garments to different stacks and teasing him about his folding methods, which then led to him unfolding and refolding different things. She hadn't even tried to assist them. Astar wasn't a fighter that Kenzi knew of, but that made her presence even more unsettling. And Osawa wasn't like any other soldier she had met. He was quiet, confident, radiating power without ego or malice.

Yassen would have almost been safe, but he'd left the farmhouse to gather supplies. And something told Kenzi she shouldn't try to leave. She didn't think that would go well for her, despite the fact that they had been inordinatantly lax about her as a captive.

Kenzi was most certainly not going to try and find Kanna or Haru. Avoiding them seemed best.

From the living room, a breeze caught the corner of the once folded schematic. She slid from her place in the sitting chair. She couldn't make sense of any of the lines on the paper, the whirls and dark ink blurring into something so unfamiliar it bordered on the familiar. She slid the fried egg magnet to the side and squinted at it.

She knew she had never seen it before. But, maybe, she had felt it. She slid the magnet back to the center of the paper and shook her head to clear it, knowing the thought didn't make sense. Fresh air would do her good.

Outside, she shut her eyes and tilted her head back. Breathing deep, she let the air fill her lungs, let it whistle a tune in her ears. The soft melody was soothing, and it was enough to lift her spirits ever so slightly, bringing a smile to her face.

The sound of Vahn's voice carried in with the wind. It was curiously soft, lacking in the low keys of sarcasm and scorn that often laced it. Kenzi stepped off the porch, sliding carefully around the side of the house.

Horses clustered around Vahn, who held one's hoof back to inspect it. Behind him, a golden horse nudged his back. He tilted his head, but didn't turn from his work. "Stop it, Mike," he said, his voice warm with affection. "You had your turn. Bia has been waiting."

Another of the horses pawed the ground and he paused his work, leveling the hoof pick he worked with at the black steed. "Don't even start, Amon."

The horse tossed its mane then turned, swishing its tail as it went so Vahn had to lean back to avoid getting whipped with it. He glared at the black horse as it paced, stopping a short distance away with its rear to the others.

When Vahn turned back to his work, it looked back, and Vahn slid his eyes to it and smiled. It looked away, as if embarrassed to be caught. Unfortunately, when Vahn turned back, he caught sight of Kenzi. After a moment of quiet, he focused his attention on Bia's hoof.

Kenzi began to back away, and turn, when his voice surprised her.

"Your horse is gone."

Kenzi shifted nervously. "My horse?"

Vahn didn't look at her, but he nodded. "It ran off not long after you got here."

"Oh," she said, surprised. She hadn't actually thought about the horse, or even how she was going to leave this place. Or where she would go, now that she couldn't go anywhere. "It wasn't mine."

Vahn made a noncommittal sound. "One of the messenger ones?"

"I don't know," Kenzi admitted, "I wasn't really paying attention."

"Lots of wild bands around here." Vahn dropped Bia's hoof, then moved to the next one. "Probably better than having a messenger around, anyway. They rile up the others, and we've got enough trouble with that one." He nodded his head to the black horse, which had at least turned around to watch Vahn from its chosen distance.

Kenzi shifted from one foot to the other. "I'll walk."

Vahn snorted. "Nah." He waved his working hand at the small herd that surrounded him, "We've got plenty of horses."

Kenzi nodded, and Vahn continued to pointedly not look at her. When he finished with the grey horse, he thumped her on the neck and turned to the others remaining. He clicked his tongue, and a bay volunteered.

Before Vahn started his work again, Kenzi cleared her throat. "I don't hate her."

Vahn didn't say anything. He didn't even acknowledge her. But Kenzi could feel the quick spark of anger that lit in him when she mentioned the word, as if the air around him burned.

"Do you..." she stopped, breathed out hard. She knew she shouldn't push her luck, but she had questions, and Vahn held answers. "How did you know Ira? How did she?"

That caught his attention. He turned over his shoulder, a lopsided smirk on his features. "You haven't figured it out?" His hand moved over the horse's back, soothing it absently. "He was one of us."

Kenzi couldn't control her shock, her mouth gaping momentarily before she recovered.

Vahn laughed at her reaction. "What did you think? He didn't exist outside of you?" He shook his head, but his mirth died. "Ganglere changed him. After K challenged Velinius, he left us for the Eyes."

"That doesn't seem like something he would do."

Vahn's smirk was gone, his features a cold mask. He shrugged. Kenzi wasn't sure what to do with this new aspect of her brother, or what to do with her feet. She bit her lip, tried not to think too hard about anything that was happening.

"Hey."

She hadn't realized she was shaking, hadn't realized she was staring at the ground until she jerked her eyes up to meet Vahn's.

He propped his hands at his hips, leaned his head back, and sighed. When his head lolled back, he met her eyes. "Sorry I slit your throat."

Kenzi's mouth gaped, her eyes going wide. She snapped her teeth shut as she tried to find the appropriate response. "Um... sorry about the boyfriend thing?"

Vahn let out a short, light laugh. Something about the way his eyes sparked, how they softened for a flickering moment, made her relax enough to smile with him. "Don't worry about it," he said, the quiet light in his eyes dying out. "Flattered that you'd think someone like me could land someone like that."

"Does he think so?"

Vahn looked up, and for the first time, he looked at her. Kenzi swallowed air, but the words were out. She didn't know if she should apologize, or run, or where she could even go. Then, though, Vahn smiled. It wasn't his smirk. It was slow, lighting him up like a sunrise.

Heat rose in her cheeks. She shifted in place, overwhelmingly self-conscious. "What?"

"Nothing." He shook his head and turned to the heavens, before looking back at her. "You just remind me of someone I once knew."

He bent and began rummaging through a worn bag on the ground. He uncoiled, and Kenzi opened her hands in time to catch the comb that Vahn tossed.

His brilliant smile shifted to a grin. "Nice catch."

# 37

## ECHOES

### VAHN

AFTER YASSEN RETURNED with Julius and Vahn finished preparing the horses for the journey ahead, he wasn't sure what to do. Kenzi lingered with him, and he didn't hate the company. It helped to keep him distracted from thoughts of what they were to face ahead, and what had come before, and it didn't give him a chance to think about how he might miss this rundown farm.

Obviously, it was just the roof over his head that he'd miss, even though it leaked. He wouldn't miss the way it almost, in some twisted way, felt like what people referred to as safe.

Vahn had begun assembling the components for another fire. After battles, when they were weary and nigh broken, they would gather near one. Fire could be comforting, the flames a warmth to the skin even if everything inside was cold and empty. It was always alive, in a way that people sometimes weren't.

Kanna liked them. Kanna used to like them, at least. He wasn't sure, now. He didn't think fire had ever hurt her, but if she had her memories back, well, there was no telling what could set her off. Especially if they were freshly unburied from wherever she shoved them down before. Haru might be a good distraction, a decent nightmare blocking white-noise machine, but there was a lot there.

There was a lot before he'd arrived.

There was a lot before Vahn did.

Vahn could make a fire, though.

Yassen was the first to join them outside, and without prompting began hauling limbs that Vahn couldn't fathom being able to lift and tossing them on the pile. Vahn shoved his hands in his pockets and watched as he and Kenzi worked.

The sound of footsteps on the grass announced the arrival of Osawa and Astar, Isco trailing behind them. He wore the damnable too-many-pockets jacket, and another was draped over his arm.

Vahn shivered. He hadn't realized the cold had moved in with the dying of the sun's light.

Osawa looked past Vahn to the impressive stack that Kenzi and Yassen had made. "Haru said Kanna wanted to get something, then they're coming out."

Astar rolled her eyes. "Finally. I was starting to miss Kanna's grouchy face."

Osawa lifted a brow. "She's not always grouchy."

"She has been lately," Astar countered, then reached under her jacket and pulled out a dark bottle. "I mean, I know why. I don't blame her, but I miss her."

Isco stepped past Osawa and Astar. He didn't say anything, but lifted the jacket from his arm and held it open for Vahn. Vahn should have argued, but he didn't want to. Isco slipped the jacket over Vahn's shoulders then walked around him, pulling it tighter over his chest.

Isco didn't meet Vahn's eyes, his gaze lingering where his hands clasped. "This one doesn't have a lot of pockets. Just the two, for your hands." Isco released the coat and turned.

Vahn slipped his hands into the jacket's pockets and followed Isco's path to the two that were still steadily gathering wood. The pile had grown overly tall, and if Vahn willed it the fire it would bolster could signal the Tower itself. "That's enough. Probably more than enough."

Yassen heaved the last log he was carrying onto the stack and it crashed into the pile, then he straightened his arms over his head to stretch. After, he promptly sat on the ground.

Kenzi collapsed next to him, her legs out in front of her. She leaned forward, grasping her toes and resting her head on her straightened knees.

Isco smiled down on them then. Satisfied that they weren't in any physical danger, he settled between the two groups, his eyes on the rickety pile of limbs.

Astar crossed Vahn's line of sight, toying with the top of the bottle she'd produced, and Osawa followed behind.

"Where do you keep finding that stuff?" Osawa asked her.

Astar stopped attempting to twist off the top of it and waved her free hand. "Here and there."

Osawa sighed. "*Why* do you keep finding that stuff?"

Astar turned, shoving the bottle into Osawa's chest so he was forced to take it. "Makes things interesting."

"Things aren't interesting enough?"

Astar grinned, shrugged. Osawa shook his head at her, but twisted the top of the bottle off with a crack.

"My hero," Astar announced, clapping her hands together before taking the bottle. She tilted it to Osawa, her brow raised.

"No."

Vahn grinned after them, then tilted his head to the side.

Isco was watching him, his expression unreadable. He didn't look away when Vahn met his eyes, and Vahn was trapped in the deep dark of them. Vahn tried not to notice the way the cold chapped Isco's cheeks, the way they flushed red under the wind's bite, tried not to think about how badly he wanted to be the one to warm him, tried not to wonder what it would be like to feel Isco's hands heat against his skin. Isco turned, took a step to Vahn, but then his gaze slid over Vahn's shoulder.

In the dying light of the day, Kanna slunk across the yard. She moved as if she'd had better days. Haru followed, a bag gripped in one hand.

Kanna stopped when Vahn met her eyes, and her chest rose as she took in a breath. Her jaw clenched, and before she released the breath, she raced the final distance between them.

Vahn held his arms out to the side, and Kanna slammed into him. He took a step back to brace them as her arms wrapped around his waist, squeezing him until he almost couldn't breathe.

"You're too thin," she said, her voice muffled against him.

Vahn's lips tilted into a smile, his arms relaxing to wrap around her shoulders. "Always have been."

She shook her head and held him tighter. "I'm sorry," she whispered. "I didn't mean to leave you."

Vahn lowered his head to rest on the top of hers, his hands tightening around her shoulders. "You can't leave me in any way that matters, K." He closed his eyes. "But I did miss you."

She sighed, her arms loosening as she shifted off of her toes and put some room between them. Vahn reached out to tuck an errant lock of hair behind her ear, and her eyes shifted.

Vahn followed them to Isco, who turned to stare at the pile of sticks.

Kanna smiled then, curling her fists in the sides of Vahn's jacket and pulling it closer, almost an exact replica of what Isco had done earlier. "You know," she said, "he could be good for you."

Vahn smirked down at her. "You're good for me."

Kanna let out a short laugh, then tilted her head to meet his eyes. "He could be better, though." There was a mischievous glint there that he hadn't known he missed as she continued to repeat the same thing Vahn had said to her so many years ago. "If you let him."

Vahn's scoff turned into a breath of laughter. "So, you're an expert now?"

Kanna smiled, her hand pressing against the side of Vahn's cheek. Then she pulled it away, giving him a mock slap.

Vahn rubbed at the light stinging in his cheek and watched as she moved to Isco. That same knowing was there as she placed a hand on his shoulder. She looked back to Vahn again before letting her hand fall away and moving on.

Isco looked from Vahn to Kanna, obviously aware that something had been said about him but not knowing what. Vahn smirked, but it fell when Haru stopped at his side, his hand tightening on the bag he carried as he looked past Isco at Kanna.

Yassen had stood from the ground and pulled Kanna into a hug, probably unaware that he'd lifted her several inches off the ground.

"I won't fail again." Haru said, his voice holding a promise.

Vahn turned to Haru, his eyes narrowing as Haru's lifted to meet them.

"It was my fault," Haru said. "I know that."

Vahn shook his head, scoffing. "That wasn't on you." As much as he didn't want to admit it, it was the truth. "You did your best, considering you're trying to protect someone that hasn't ever met a problem she doesn't throw her entire self at." Vahn shoved his hands into the pockets of his jacket, unable to meet Haru's eyes. "You did better than I ever had."

Haru had the audacity to look confused. "You can't believe that."

Vahn couldn't look at him.

"I was in her memories, Vahn," Haru said, his voice even and neutral. "She wouldn't have made it as long as she did without you."

Vahn still didn't want to look at him.

Haru sighed. "I won't let her get lost again. I promise."

Vahn had to look up at that. While Haru's dramatics were often borderline hysterical to him, a promise among them wasn't something taken lightly.

"I promise *you*. So maybe do something for yourself, for once." Haru's eyes slid to Isco. "Even if it's that guy."

Vahn smirked, tilting his head. "You know, the fact that you don't like him makes him more appealing to me."

"Yes, I know." Haru started to walk away, but stopped and turned back over his shoulder. "If he hurts you, I'll kill him."

Vahn felt something in his stomach twist, spikes turning around under his skin. His smirk tasted dangerous. "I would like to see you try."

When Haru smiled, knowing and self-satisfied, Vahn grit his teeth together. Haru always knew the right thing to say, how to lead someone to something they knew but didn't want to admit.

It was fucking annoying.

After Haru turned away fully, Vahn backed up a step and shifted around. He almost collided with Isco, who jumped back.

"Sorry," Isco muttered, his eyes turned on the ground.

Vahn wasn't sure what to say. He didn't know the right words to say, or when to say them, and he certainly didn't know how to say them as if it mattered. While he struggled with the thought, Isco blew it out of his mind when his eyes lifted, his hand reaching for Vahn's.

Isco's chilled knuckles brushed against the back of Vahn's hand. "We don't have matches," Isco said, still staring at the place where his hand touched Vahn's.

"Matches?" Vahn wasn't sure at this moment what the word even meant.

Isco smiled, his eyes sliding to the pile of unlit firewood that had been gathered. "I'm cold."

Vahn turned his hand, subtle offering, just as easily hidden if rejected. Isco's fingers traced the inner curve of his wrist and down his palm before lacing with Vahn's.

"I know a way to get you warm," Vahn said, unable to keep the tease from his voice.

Isco's brow lifted, his eyes turning to meet Vahn's. He smiled, and Vahn was certain that Isco could feel the heat rise under his skin.

"Maybe start with the fire."

## 38

# MOVING THROUGH

## KANNA

THE TINDER CRACKED at the heart of the bonfire, held steady, then caught on the larger limbs above it. Kanna sighed when it shifted the night air back, the warmth creating a haven in the dark that would hold them all.

After Yassen returned her to her feet she bent over, her arms wrapping around Astar's shoulders from behind. Astar lifted the bottle she was drinking from, and Kanna's nose wrinkled against the tangy smell of ferment. Astar rolled her eyes and patted Kanna's arm, tilting the bottle back by the neck and swallowing.

At Astar's side, Osawa fidgeted with the uneven folds in his sleeves, unrolling them and setting them back in place. Kanna put her hands on his shoulders for balance as she leaned down, brushing a kiss on the top of his head. "Thank you for taking care of them," she whispered, low enough that the others couldn't catch it.

Osawa's lips quirked into a half smile, his head ducking to hide it. "You asked me to," he replied, "so I tried."

"You succeeded."

"We ended up in Irkalla."

Kanna tilted her head to the side, considering that, then shook it away. "You all survived it, together. That is what matters."

Osawa nodded, tilting his eyes to meet her. "Then, you're welcome."

Kanna shifted back to crouch, her knees bent. Kenzi sat on the other side of Osawa, and Kanna had felt her stare since she'd arrived. However, the moment Kanna turned to her she looked into the fire, the flames lighting her eyes with preternatural orange glow.

Kanna propped her elbow on her knee, sat her chin onto it, and studied Kenzi. The girl didn't have the same connection to her power as the others, but the air adored her. There were recent shadows that had curled inside of her, but they had yet to lay a claim. "I can see your brother in you."

Kenzi looked away, but this time it was tinged with embarrassment. "He's better than me."

Kanna shook her head. "Just different."

Kenzi met her eyes, and Kanna held her gaze.

Kenzi rolled her eyes and pulled her knees to her chest, propping her chin behind them and staring into the fire. "How would you know?"

Kanna ran her fingers over the scars on the back of her hand as she tried to focus her memories. They still didn't quite fit, as if her new ones and the old belonged to different people, in different spaces. Her head was too heavy and her thoughts too loud, each clamoring over one another. She even wondered if this was how she'd felt before, and if this was how others felt all the time.

She pressed her finger into the joint near her ring finger where the metal pin sat under her skin. Then she curled her hands into themselves.

"Ira didn't want to join the Eyes," she said. "He did it because I asked."

From the corner of her eye, Kanna saw Haru's attention turn even more notably to her, and Osawa also focused.

Vahn leaned away from where he whispered something to Isco. "Wait a minute." He shifted his hip, putting distance between him and the other man. "So, this whole time?"

Kanna's calves began to burn, but she stayed in her crouch rather than sit. "How do you think I found the Cardea?" She wrapped her arms around herself and turned to meet Haru's eyes near the fire. "How do you think you found me?"

Osawa sat up further. "There was a message in your desk." Kanna lifted her brow, and it was enough for him to finish his own trail of reasoning. "And you wouldn't keep that kind of information where it could be found."

Kanna tapped a finger to her temple. "Here. The only place Velinius can not go."

Kenzi pulled her knees closer to her chest. She chewed her lip, then asked, "Why Ira?"

"He was the only one who could. To Velinius, people are simple. She is bored by them, unless there is something about them she can use. She knew that Ira and I... kept each others' company for a time."

Kenzi squinted at Kanna, confusion lining her brow.

Kanna shrugged. "Ira could play the rejected suitor, and that was something that Veil would take an interest in." Kanna straightened the ache that was forming in her back but there was something about it that left her exposed. She curled her arms back against herself and returned to her hunched crouch.

She swallowed, squeezed her eyes shut. The memories had started scraping inside of her skull, dragging themselves out from the dark. "I needed someone to watch Velinius. Someone I could trust. After Ganglere...." She tried to shake her head to free it, but she'd summoned something she couldn't put back.

Kanna brought her elbows to her knees, pressed the back of her hands into her eyes. "They were supposed to be warnings."

There was a loud crack nearby, the sound snapping like a volley release. Kanna's eyes snapped open and her hunched body launched away from the sound, grabbing the nearest person she could protect, and she and Osawa fell in a heap. He tried to grab onto her as her legs kicked back, scrambling away when a clattering sound followed the crash, muffling the ghosts of screams in her bones.

"Kanna!"

Osawa's voice was loud in her ears, solid and so unlike the hollow howls. It was present, it was now, like the arms that wrapped around her and stopped her flight. She gasped, squeezing her eyes shut as she attempted to steady her hammering heart. Osawa released her, his grip replaced by Haru's.

Haru pinned her arms against her body, holding her with the force needed to keep her grounded, to remind her where she was.

Kanna opened her eyes as her breath steadied, as she returned. She unclenched the fist that had twisted in Haru's shirt, relaxing her hold on him. "Sorry," she whispered. She turned her head, cleared her throat despite the tremble in her hands. "Are you all right, Osawa?"

Osawa pulled off his hat and shook the grass from the knit before replacing it. "Of course."

"*Inara.*" The soft touch of Haru's hand against her cheek brought Kanna back to him. He moved her enough that he could meet his eyes.

Her hand tightened in his shirt, twisting as if she could pull her closer, as if she could make him understand. "They're warnings."

He bent over her, pressed his forehead against hers. "I know."

Kanna shut her eyes, breathed in a shaking breath. She swallowed it, then again to unclench her throat. When she opened her eyes again, she knew what was important. "Will you help me up?"

Haru nodded and stood, bringing her with him. Her legs were loose, but when they steadied beneath her she was able to release him. Kanna turned to the bag that Haru had abandoned, and Vahn and Isco shuffled out of her way when she moved past them. She opened the bag, the metal teeth revealing the white beneath.

The old uniforms nestled within. At the Tower, they had been often mended or replaced, but now the layers of fine embroidery and twisted threads stubbornly refused to release the stains of blood and dust of road travel. She gathered the white jackets, the armguards, the light armor, and the stiff pants into her arms. They were heavy, but they had always been.

Kanna stepped to the fire, and she threw them into it.

The flames grew brighter and leapt around the fine cotton. The smoke turned white, smelled of burning paper and leaves. The fire devoured the fabric, licked up the intricate symbols of a vicious past, and turned it into nothing more than soft grey ash.

A light wind moved the smoke, and Isco sneezed. Kanna turned to him as he covered his face with his elbow and coughed.

Vahn placed a hand on Isco's back as he recovered, then met Kanna's gaze. "You know I appreciate a good symbolic burning more than most, K, but what are we going to wear?"

Osawa let out a small laugh, which Haru joined. Kanna covered her lips to contain her own as her friends lit up, relaxed.

Astar grinned, hugging the bottle she had been drinking from to her chest. "My time has come.

When their laughs settled and they turned their eyes to Kanna, she felt the sobering weight that sapped the energy from her smile.

"I need to tell you a story."

# 39

## THE KIND, THE CRUEL

### KENZI

DESPITE THE LARGE circumference of the bonfire, the group settled nearly elbow-to-elbow in a semicircle around the flames, and somehow Kenzi had ended up near the middle of them all. On one side of her was Yassen, with Astar using his lap as a makeshift pillow. At her other side, Osawa was settling his glasses back on the bridge of his nose after polishing them on the hem of his shirt.

Kenzi leaned towards him. "Is someone going to say something?" she hissed, as low as she dared to drop her voice while still knowing he'd hear her. "She is not okay."

Osawa lowered his chin, turning slightly in her direction. There was the faintest hint of an upturn to his lips. "Are you?" he asked as if he already knew the answer. He put his arms behind him and leaned back. "None of us are. How do you think we all ended up here?"

Next to Osawa, Isco curled his knees against his chest. Past him, Vahn stretched his legs in front of him and leaned back on his hands.

Kanna had found a place on the other side of Vahn, with Haru bracketing the end of the group. Haru braced himself against the ground with one arm, and Kanna tucked herself against it. She held her hands open, tracing her fingers over her own palms.

"It has been a long time," she said quietly, her eyes still on her hands.

When Kanna spoke, the group settled like a sigh. It wasn't a hush that had responded to a command, or an authority, so much as it was a breath taken with ease.

Vahn bumped his elbow against Kanna. "That means we're overdue."

The smile the two exchanged was filled with both sadness and comfort, a knowing thing that hid thousands of small understandings.

Kanna nodded. She looked to the fire, her eyes going distant before she closed them. She breathed deep. "I am going to tell you a story." She leaned forward, beyond her crossed knees, and set her palms against the earth. "I need you to remember."

Kanna's eyes opened and her fingers splayed against the ground. Shadows spilled from her palms and moved to circle the fire, shifting in a dark wave. Kenzi's body jerked and she drew her feet closer, but she felt no cold, no strange whispers in her mind that were not her own.

The dark almost at the base of the flames, turning slow, curling and spilling quietly.

"In the beforetimes, when the world was whole..." Kanna began.

*And the gods were limitless,* Kenzi continued in her head, already drifting from the old words.

"... the kind craved more."

Kenzi's back straightened. That wasn't how the stories began. But Kanna was intent on the dark, the flames dancing in the reflection of her eyes. Kenzi wished she weren't so close to the others when her breath became shallow, when she remembered the reasoning that Ira gave her that horrid night in the camp.

*He knew all the stories,* Ira had told her. *All of them.*

*I couldn't let them figure it out.*

Fists clenched, Kenzi folded her legs in front of her. If stories were worth Ira's life, they were the most important thing.

Parts of the gathered shadows detached, moving in and among the fire. The flames parted around the darkness, lining the images with cooler colors.

"The primeval world was yet still raw from its birth. The tides were wild, storms constant, and the earth would quake and tumble anything the kind attempted to build for shelter."

The shadows formed into shapes, twisting to accompany the cadence of Kanna's story. Figures built towers, and the elements toppled them until the masses of people, round heads on rectangular bodies, gathered and bent in mourning.

The tableau swirled into a solid mass, before shivering into a new scene. A long river wound through a blank landscape, and a tiny figure, alone, lay at its bank.

"The kind lived not just by days, but from one moment to the next. They had no strength for legacy, no concept of any time beyond what they could grasp, and no hope to hold."

An unseen wind blew, the figure's hair moving with it.

"We should not judge them for what they did to survive."

Against the dark backdrop, above the child figure, a single star appeared where the shadows fell away. Then another, and they were soon joined by a brilliant sky.

"The kind did not know they were not alone."

Kanna's left hand rose from the ground and her fingers turned, her wrist twisted, and the shadows followed. The scene was swept and gathered into a column, then spun into a creature unlike anything Kenzi had witnessed. Eight bright eyes sat in a triangular face, attached to a body that was both almost-human and serpentine. Too-long arms burst from the torso, and wings began to unfurl around its body, set after set.

"Before the world, before the kind, there were the Numen."

Kanna's second hand rose from the ground as the creature curled, engulfing the abandoned child. "One of the greater Numen took pity on the kind, and it granted them a precious gift."

Both of Kanna's hands gently turned as the setting in the dark cleared. Like a conductor for the quietest, softest symphonies, the pictures shifted with her touch. The child's silhouette stepped from a sea of black and returned to a gathering of its people as they, one by one, formed from the shadows around it, circling the lone figure.

"The Numen gave them a piece of itself."

Then the shadows began to whirl as wind, as fire, as sunshine, and as rain. Storms appeared and the child held them at bay, kept them away from the people.

"No longer suffering under the unforgiving whims of their world, the kind set roots. They built shelters, communities, and could even imagine a time beyond the single moment they occupied."

Now seemingly aged, the silhouette watched over a group of children. They played with simple toys, chased each other in delighted circles and zigzags.

"The kind were safe in the small haven they had carved from the wild, but they began to suffocate in it." The bright scene darkened. "They began to imagine more. More for themselves, more for those that came after, more space and time."

Now there were buildings, houses, towers on top of each other that began to spread until those at the far boundaries rose and were toppled again, pushed back in to the same place when they tried to move.

"The kind learned how to tempt the Numen into releasing their gifts, for they had yet to learn what cruelty meant." The shadows churned to reveal more small bodies, abandoned in broken warehouses and open fields. "So preoccupied with simply surviving"—a figure was thrown from a height by a mob, its hands out and desperately reaching — "they did not understand what it was" —another was crushed under weights, limbs trembling beneath the pressure—"or what it could possibly be."

The shadows lingered, focusing on a figure bound against a rock in a wasteland. Its head hunched forward as their hair cascaded over a bare body. The shadows deepend in some places, split in others. The figure's skin was pressed in by the chains, tore and bled where the red fire burned behind it.

When the flames devoured the last image, Kenzi gratefully blinked her dry eyes.

Haru bent, his lips brushing against Kanna's shoulder. She sighed and pulled her fingers into her palm, stretching them one by one, grimacing ever so slightly with each movement.

Then she began again.

The shadows formed once more and Kenzi's eyes widened. There were intricate cities and rail systems, their fine details carved from the dark. The image panned from overhead, the wonders unfolding as if from the view of a bird in flight.

"The kind prospered, but they were no longer all of one kind. They built cities and then countries, dug out reservoirs and tamed seas, until the world bent. However, it bent not to the many, but to the few, those that had once been deemed acceptable losses."

The intricate cities melted and the now recognizable, blank sacrificial figures formed from the dark.

"Those that had received the Numens' gifts knew cruelty. They understood pain, hate, and fear. They knew it was only a matter of time before those unlike them would recognize the unfamiliar. A matter of time, time that they now had, before they came for them once more, because they were no longer the same as the others.

"Though they were bound to the Numen, the line went in both directions." A single figure became the focus, and the terrible creature from before rose behind it. "They could reach out, reach for more, and the Numen had no choice but to give." Ribbons formed from the silhouette, connecting to new figures that appeared. "Those that were gifted tethered others to themselves, acting as conduits between their Numen and those they bound."

The once simple figures etched away, detailed lines cutting into the sameness of the images. "They fashioned themselves as something greater, and they held power over the people in ways they could not before. They stole the memory of the Numen, and they created their own stories, built their own legacies, so that their control could not be questioned or forgotten."

They were clothed in finery, or armed for war, their hair in braids or shorn short, each one now an individual in a pantheon.

"And they named themselves gods."

# 40

# THE GOOD DARK

## KANNA

MEMORIES WERE HEAVY, exhausting things. What had been misshapen before sharpened, and things that lurked beyond what she could reach now screamed for notice. Kanna wasn't sure yet how to sort the memories that rattled in her mind like broken glass, couldn't pull the right splinter out of the shatter.

She remembered the small slivers of time before she knew war, and the stretch of time and bodies after that saw her rise to Second, to Legatus, and her downfall by the same means in which she had gained her position–death, an endless refrain.

There was more than that, though. There were moments in the sun and laughter shared amongst friends. There were glittering skies after nightfall, and there were sunrises.

Kirin's predawn light filtered soft over the open plain, blue-grey yet warm. Kanna had returned to waking before the sun and had attempted to carefully extricate herself from a shared bed. Even in sleep, Haru reached for her.

She moved through the farmhouse with the shadows, past the doors where her companions and protectors slept. The weight of their expectations, their loyalty, was something that she had once been afraid of, but now, she knew, she would choose to take up it up time and again. She had before. She always would.

Outside, in the heat of the morning, the field birds had begun their fluting. Windy, light calls taught to them by a god of air and song. It had been his first gift to the world, and his only act.

As the sun continued its ascent, the dark ruin of Ilazki curved along the east of the continent, a reminder of some unknowable, incomprehensible tragedy. A reminder that once, long ago, they'd had gods.

And those gods had been mortal, their deaths proof of it. Somehow, somewhere along the way, that had been forgotten, though the evidence of it had always been there. It lived in their stories, in the epics of corruption and the wars for power.

But it was also in the story of an unwanted boy cast out to the world to suffer, who returned and taught birds to sing.

Haru arrived, still bleary eyed from sleep. He said nothing. He only wrapped his arms around her waist and pulled her against him with a contented sigh, his weight leaning into her. She smiled as his breath became calm and even, at rest even on his feet.

Vahn would be the next to wake. Likely, he was already, but waiting long enough that they might believe he had slept. He would help Kanna find the horses, and they would tend them together.

Haru would meet with Osawa, and now, Isco. They would gather the rest of the supplies for their next journey. Kenzi would try to help and then, too self-conscious by far, retreat.

Astar would be last, grumbling about the noise but insisting on checking the bags before having Yassen carry them out.

They would eat breakfast, and then they would continue on.

Kanna couldn't fix everything. She wasn't certain if she could fix anything. But Velinius had something that no one should: a gate to infinity, and a path to immortality. If she was not stopped, then there would be no more glittering night skies, and no more sunrises.

Kanna didn't know if she could stop her.

But Kanna knew this:

She was not alone.

# ACKNOWLEDGMENTS

This has certainly been a long journey. The earliest iteration of *Shadow's Prey* was written in 2011, but it was set aside for other pursuits. I chased the dream of becoming a writer, sacrificed for it, until it ran out. Burned out from a lifetime of running, I gave up. But *Shadow's Prey* didn't. In 2019, I dusted off old drafts and found that the characters beneath still breathed. And now, here we are.

To start, I'd like to thank all of my friends who I met along the way, without whom this book would never have been. Bee, who was there from the beginning, and Juni, whose beautiful illustrations captured not just the characters of *Shadow's Prey,* but the idea of it.

There are also those I have lost: Grim, one of the kindest people I have ever known, and Joanne, whose early support kept me going, and whose art was always an inspiration.

A special and unending thanks goes to my Triple D crew, those that were there to the end: Aca, whose keen insight often helped me see through my own mire; Alex, whose creativity and drive are both enviable and inspirational; and Brills, whose wit and humor can brighten any day.

I'd also like to extend my thanks and appreciation to my family. First my parents, who have supported and believed in me from my wild youth to my careening adulthood. Without them, I'd likely be toothless and lost in the wind. And forever thanks to Ellie—my light, who for some reason thinks I'm cool.

Last but not least, thank you, reader. *Shadow's Prey* was a work of love, and all I can hope is that others might like it, and gain some comfort in it, even if only a little bit. Because this story didn't just demand to be told, it deserved to be told.

# ABOUT THE AUTHOR

**k. d. edge**, née **linaket**, is a fantasy author from the deep southern USA. They fell in love with storytelling as a child and have strived to improve their craft since, earning an MA in English from The University of Louisiana at Lafayette and an MFA in Creative Writing from The New School.

Their works are about about identity and defiance—what we choose to define us, and what we laugh about along the way.

---

## WANT TO STAY IN TOUCH?

Visit me on the web at bylinaket.com, or use the QR code below for links to join my newsletter and follow me on social media.

bsky.app/profile/bylinaket.com
instagram.com/bylinaket

# Tinder Saint

Vahn knows how to survive.

He's spent his entire life doing just that, biding his time in the shadows of others. But when the Saint of Fire falls and a new one is called, Vahn will risk everything to gain a power all his own.

Coming 2026